THE GOVERNESS AND THE ORC

A MONSTER FANTASY ROMANCE

FINLEY FENN

ALSO BY FINLEY FENN

ORC SWORN

The Lady and the Orc

The Heiress and the Orc

The Librarian and the Orc

The Duchess and the Orc

The Midwife and the Orc

The Maid and the Orcs

The Governess and the Orc

Offered by the Orc (Bonus Story)

ORC FORGED

The Sins of the Orc

THE MAGES

The Mage's Maid

The Mage's Match

The Mage's Master

The Mage's Groom (Bonus Story)

Sign up at www.finleyfenn.com for bonus stories and epilogues, delicious orc artwork, complete content guidance, news about upcoming books, and more!

ABOUT THE GOVERNESS AND THE ORC

He'll make all her dreams come true... but only if she can pretend to love him.

In a realm of orcs and powerful men, Geva Okoro is a proud, impoverished governess, trapped in a dismal, dead-end post— until the day the orc breaks in.

He's a huge, insolent, arrogant brute, swaggering with smooth, shameless wickedness. But unlike the orcs from the terrifying tales, he only wants one thing from Geva...

Her employers' gold.

There's no escaping his devious clutches, and soon a furious Geva is reduced to raiding her employers' house with an orc. Compromising her career, and destroying all her dreams... until the orc proposes another shocking scheme.

He'll split the day's plunder with her— *if* she'll pretend to be his mate. For one month. At Orc Mountain.

Sharing his rooms.

Smiling sweetly at his side.

Smelling all over of his deep, decadent scent...

He's offering more wealth than Geva's ever dreamt of, but there's no way she can trust this treacherous thief... can she? Let alone convince all of Orc Mountain that she *loves* him?!

And surely, even her best play-acting would never start to feel real... or win over an orc's cold, broken heart?

*To all my readers who so generously supported me
in bringing Geva to life! Thank you.*

1
___

If Geva Okoro never had to speak to her employer again, it would still be too soon.

"I'm just asking you to consider Cecily's wellbeing," she said to Mrs. Fitzwald, as steadily as she could. "She's a very sensitive child, and I just don't feel that a trip like this one would be in her best—"

She was interrupted by Mrs. Fitzwald's pale, manicured hand, snapping up in front of her face. "This again, Miss Okoro?" Mrs. Fitzwald asked, her voice cold. "You think *you* know better than I what that child needs? You know better than her own *aunt*?"

Geva refrained from pointing out that Mrs. Fitzwald had only met Cecily in person the year before, and drew in a bracing breath. "Of course not," she replied, with effort. "But I've spent a lot of time with Cecily since she came here last year. And I know she's still grieving her mother's death, and this kind of trip—"

"A month enjoying the city?" Mrs. Fitzwald demanded, as she irritably waved for one of her hovering maids to come over to the dressing-table. "With her own *family*? Her own *cousins*?

That girl needs to come out of her shell, and this is exactly the kind of healthy activity she needs."

Geva gritted her teeth, and gazed helplessly down toward where the maid was spreading out a variety of jewels on the dressing-table, so Mrs. Fitzwald could dangle them one by one in the gleaming looking-glass, and evaluate them against her fair skin. "Respectfully, I believe Cecily needs time," Geva replied thinly. "And in my informed opinion as her governess, I believe a few quiet weeks here at the house would do her a world of—"

"*Weeks* here at the house, without her own family?" Mrs. Fitzwald cut in, her voice shrill. "With only *servants* for company?"

Geva's surging retort nearly escaped her mouth, but she bit it back just in time, and clutched her hands to tight fists at her sides. No. *No.* She was *not* rising to Mrs. Fitzwald's usual condescending rubbish. She was here to advocate for her pupil, because this was her damned job, and she was damned good at it.

And... because poor Cecily had wept herself to sleep every night for the past week, dreading this trip. A month trapped in a townhouse in the middle of the realm's bustling capital, sharing a cramped room with her quarrelsome cousins, and being dragged about to any number of stylish engagements, full of strangers and noise and unattainable expectations. It was Cecily's worst nightmare come to life, and Mrs. Fitzwald would know that, if she'd ever bothered to pay any attention whatsoever to her shy, lonely niece.

"I am your employee, Mrs. Fitzwald, *not* your servant," Geva replied now, her voice clipped. "And I assure you, should Cecily stay here with me, I will do my utmost to continue her education to the best of my ability. If you're interested, we could review the curriculum I've—"

"Absolutely not," interrupted Mrs. Fitzwald, as she pulled over her massive locked jewel-box, and signalled for the other maid to hand her the key. "I am not allowing my niece to stay here cooped up with servants, when she could be benefiting from some liveliness, and learning how to properly conduct herself! And besides"—she flicked open the box and plucked out a glittering sapphire pendant—"have you not heard the rumours about the orcs?! Roaming about the village here! Hunting down unprotected females to attack, and seeking out priceless jewels to pilfer!"

Her voice was triumphant, her hand swinging the pendant out toward Geva, as if this were a clinching closing argument, rather than yet another display of infuriating ignorance. Because yes, humans and orcs had been at war for decades, but several years before, the orcs had signed a comprehensive peace-treaty. And since then, to the best of Geva's knowledge, there hadn't been a single verifiable violation on the orcs' part, let alone any blatant attacking or jewel-pilfering. And truly, if the orcs *were* determined to pilfer, one could only hope they would have better taste than Mrs. Fitzwald's garish, gaudy collection—which, to all appearances, served only to remind Mrs. Fitzwald's jealous acquaintances of her husband's obscene wealth, earned upon the backs of the underpaid drudges at his grim, dangerous mill.

"The orcs are bound by a peace-treaty, Mrs. Fitzwald," Geva finally said, into the taut silence. "And I know the house is very secure, and multiple other staff members will be here as well. But if you're that concerned about Cecily's safety, I can make sure to only take her out with an escort, and stay well within the—"

"I said, *no!*" Mrs. Fitzwald broke in, her voice ringing with furious finality. "Cecily *will* join the rest of her family in the city, and enjoy it as the great privilege it is! And if *you* value your position as my *servant*, Miss Okoro, you will respect my authority, and do as you're told. Namely, packing my children's belongings for their trip!"

It took a monumental effort for Geva to keep her expression

neutral, her hands tight at her sides, her breaths heaving thick through her nose. "In that case," she said, through her clenched teeth, "will you at least reconsider allowing me to accompany you? I'm very familiar with the city, and I would be happy to continue our lessons, and take the children out to parks and museums and performances. I'm sure you would welcome the extra supervision while you enjoy—"

"And now you're trying to get a *free vacation*?!" Mrs. Fitzwald demanded, as two red spots appeared on her cheeks. "As if it isn't enough that we're allowing you to stay here, in our house, free of charge, for an entire month, in our absence? Your greed is *shocking*, Miss Okoro, as is your impertinence! And"—she jabbed a pointy finger toward Geva's face—"unless you want to spend the next month out on the streets seeking a new post, you will hold your tongue, and remove yourself from my sight!"

She'd thrown the jewel-box key back at one of the maids, who was twitching a small, smug smile beneath her meekly bowed head. Clearly enjoying the sight of the high-and-mighty governess being so roundly reprimanded, and Geva had no doubt whatsoever that the tale would be all over the servants' quarters by nightfall.

"And make sure to hide the key properly, Mitzy," Mrs. Fitzwald added, with another dark look toward Geva. "We'll need to leave these rooms *very* secure, in our absence."

Damn it. *Damn* it. And there was nothing left but for Geva to spin around and stalk out of the opulent dressing-room, her back very straight, her head held high. But her hands were still clamped in tight fists at her sides, and a cursed rising wetness had begun prickling behind her eyes.

Gods, she hated Mrs. Fitzwald. Hated this huge, ostentatious house. And most of all, she hated these constant, grating reminders that no one here had the slightest regard for her education, her experience, or her expertise. Which she'd gained not only from her rigorous training and tutoring in the city, but also from her unusual upbringing with her well-read, widely travelled parents—both of whom had served as state ambassadors representing Ezira, their faraway home across the sea. A place Geva had never visited herself, but which had always been an important part of her identity—all the way from her brown skin and curly hair to her heartfelt love for tales and art and song.

But the Fitzwalds had never cared about any of it. And after four years of giving her utmost, doing her very best to support and educate the Fitzwalds' three children—plus Cecily—Geva had found that the contempt from the rest of the household had only seemed to deepen. As if her very existence as a well-educated governess was a slight, an affront to the other servants' lower status and salaries, and a critique—or even a challenge—of Mrs. Fitzwald's role as the children's mother.

But competition for governess positions was notoriously cutthroat, and gaining this post had taken months of effort, and had also required Geva to permanently relocate here, two days' journey south from the realm's capital city of Wolfen. Which made seeking out a new post that much more costly and difficult, and it was highly questionable whether a new post would turn out to be any better than this one, and...

"Miss Gee?" broke in a soft voice, and Geva startled in the hallway, whirling around to where—oh. It was none other than Cecily herself, hovering in the doorway of her small bedroom, her little face pinched and pale. "Did you... did you get a chance to speak with my aunt again?"

Geva swallowed hard, and attempted a smile. "I did, sweetheart," she said, as steadily as she could. "But she still feels very strongly that it's best that you go today, as planned."

Cecily's face crumpled, her shoulders slumping, her hands pressing against her eyes. "Oh," she whispered. "Oh. Th-thank you for—trying. I—"

But the words were lost in her great, gulping sobs, and Geva blinked back the wetness in her own eyes as she put an arm around Cecily's shoulders, squeezing as tightly as she dared.

"Oh, sweetheart," she managed. "It'll be all right. It's only a month, and you'll get to see all the sights in the city, too. Everything from fabulously dressed ladies to the most fearless rats in the realm! Speaking of which, have I ever told you the tale of the reckless roaming rat and his troublesome tongue?"

Cecily shook her head, but that was surely a flare of interest in her blinking eyes, so Geva drew her over to sit on the bed, and then launched into the tale. It was one her own mother had often told, full of jokes and mishaps and witty wordplay, and by the end of it, Cecily was giving a small, wan smile, and wiping at her wet eyes.

"Thank you, Miss Gee," she said. "I'll miss you so much. When we come back, we should—"

"There you are!" cut in a grating, painfully familiar voice—and Geva bit back her groan at the sight of Mrs. Fitzwald again, looming in the doorway, her stylish form now bedecked with jewels, her blue eyes flashing with rage. "Lounging about and shirking your duties, *again*, when the children's packing isn't even *close* to being finished yet?!"

Geva shoved down the overwhelming urge to start hurling obscenities into Mrs. Fitzwald's face, and stiffly extracted herself from Cecily, giving one last reassuring squeeze to her shoulder. And then she dragged herself back up the stairs, toward where she could already hear a cacophony of loud, high-pitched voices, emanating from the direction of the schoolroom.

"Miss Gee!" wailed nine-year-old Leticia, catching sight of Geva at the door, and rushing over toward her. "Miss Gee, Cordelia won't stop shouting at me, and she threw Dolly out the window!"

"Because you dumped ice cream on my best dress, on *purpose!*" shouted fifteen-year-old Cordelia. "I was supposed to wear that to a ball next week, and Sebastian's already ruined my new sash!"

"It was a joke!" protested thirteen-year-old Sebastian, recklessly whirling a shining rapier through the air. "Because *you* wouldn't stop whining about how hideous it was!"

Geva's head was already painfully pounding, but she pulled herself to her full height, and threw herself into sorting out the trials at hand. First confiscating Sebastian's rapier, and then sending Leticia after her doll, and escorting Cordelia and her ruined clothes to the laundry. And then turning her attentions to packing the children's belongings, all amidst an ongoing onslaught of questions, complaints, and quarrelling. No, Cordelia couldn't take her entire wardrobe. No, Leticia didn't deserve a new doll because Dolly had gotten dusty outside. And no, Sebastian couldn't leave behind all his dinner coats in favour of his toy army, or his cricket clubs, or his weapons collection.

But finally, what felt like several full days later, the children's trunks were packed and ready, and the children themselves had all been herded out to the waiting carriages. And after a round of goodbyes—including an extra-tight hug for a still-sniffling Cecily, during which Mrs. Fitzwald bitterly glared—the carriages were clattering down the lane, taking all the Fitzwalds away with them.

Geva vigorously waved goodbye along with the other staff, her smile firmly fixed to her face, until the carriages had fully vanished from view. And then, she turned and trudged back up to the empty, echoing schoolroom, which now looked as though a cataclysm had crashed through, and was in dire need of a days-long, top-to-bottom cleaning.

But instead of getting started, doing what needed to be done, Geva only stood there in the middle of the room, gazing blankly around at the mess. And after a long, empty moment, she sank into the nearest chair, and buried her face in her hands.

Gods, this job. This house. And even if she'd been granted a few weeks' reprieve—a few weeks' blessed silence—all too soon the chaos would return, surely even worse than before.

There was no way four weeks trapped together in a townhouse would benefit any of the Fitzwald children, let alone Cecily, and Geva would spend the rest of the year pleading, placating, trying and failing to be heard. Fighting desperately to hold on to a life she loathed with all her being. And then the next year, and the next, until—

Until what? What? Yet another family, another set of miserable children? Until she became too ill, or too elderly, to bear it anymore? And without a steady salary, without any substantial savings, what would happen to her then? Would she die alone and begging on the streets?

And at least her own parents would never, ever know what had become of her. Because what would they think, after all her education, after raising her with the very best they could afford? After they'd given her so many priceless gifts of story and language and song, *this* was what she'd made of her life?

Geva's stomach was bitterly churning, her head hammering, and she lurched for the schoolroom's largest window, thrusting it wide open, gulping down deep breaths of cool air. And then she spun and staggered back to her chair, and again buried her wet face in her hands.

Four weeks. She should be dancing and rejoicing, not sitting here sobbing over all her wasted dreams. She had a job. She had a safe place to live, and food in her belly. She'd *survived*. So many women in her circumstances had fared far worse, and she should be looking forward, she should be grateful, she should be...

"Weeping, already," supplied a low, husky, accented male voice, curling deep into her chest. "Ach, and you have not even *met* me yet."

Geva flinched and flailed upwards, leaping back out of her chair. And oh, good gods above, it was—

It was... an *orc*.

2

———————

There was an orc. Here. In the Fitzwalds' *schoolroom*.

Geva's mouth fell open, her heartbeat roaring in her ears—and she frantically scrabbled backwards, toward the wall behind her. While waves of hot and cold flashed through her trembling body, and her wide eyes swept up and down the orc standing before her.

He was... *massive*. A hulking, broad-shouldered, grey-skinned beast, with long, loose black hair, tall pointed ears, and gleaming black eyes. And his huge body was unnervingly, impeccably dressed, sporting shiny, tightly laced black boots, a spotless white tunic, and a silvery grey fur over a long black cloak, sweeping down wide from his powerful shoulders.

But most terrifying of all was the sword, strapped at his side. Not the slim, decorative rapiers gentlemen often wore, but a deadly, glinting steel broadsword, the kind wielded by armed knights on warhorses. And the orc's big hand—complete with long, curving black *talons*—was hungrily flexing against the sword's hilt, as if fighting the temptation to draw it, and cut Geva to pieces where she stood.

The instinct to shout, to run, was fraying white and wild

through Geva's trembling body—but she somehow, impossibly, managed to hold herself still and silent against the wall behind her, while her thoughts choked and churned. There was no chance in hell of fighting him—of the few orcs she'd seen in her life, he was undoubtedly the largest—and no chance of escaping, either, not with him looming between her and the door like this. And yes, she could try screaming, drawing out the other servants, but what then? Would he retaliate? Attack? Chop them down one by one as they rushed through the door?

"Ach, but no screeching and howling, then?" the orc said, with an approving little nod, as that clawed hand gave his sword-hilt one more slow, reverent-looking caress. "Good. This shows much mettle, my sweet, and bodes well for our day's work."

Their day's work? His *sweet*?! Geva couldn't stop staring at the appalling creature before her, while her heart kept raging and ricocheting against her ribs. And with it, unhelpfully, were all Mrs. Fitzwald's smug, horrible words from earlier that day.

Have you not heard the rumours about the orcs? Roaming about the village, hunting down unprotected females to attack, seeking out priceless jewels to pilfer...

"What," Geva somehow gulped, "do you *want* here, orc."

The orc flashed her a quick, conspiratorial smile, showing off a mouthful of sharp white teeth, not unlike those of a wolf's. And suddenly there were many more voices—all the tales Geva had previously dismissed as fear-mongering rubbish— shouting and clamouring through her skull.

Those orcs are cruel, vulgar monsters. They never birth orc daughters, so they'll do anything to steal away human women instead. And once they trap a woman in their vile mountain, they'll swive with her again and again, feast upon her fresh blood, and whelp their killer sons upon her, until...

The orc had arched a thick black brow toward Geva, and he came a slow step closer, his booted feet alarmingly silent on the schoolroom floor. "Ach, you ken I am here for *you*, poppet?" he murmured, his low, husky voice hitching oddly in Geva's chest. "You ken I am here to charm and cajole you, and lure you onto my powerful prick? To spew my good seed deep into your womb, and spawn my fierce little brats upon you?"

Geva's cheeks felt painfully hot, her shocked gaze fixed to the orc's grey face, to that strange, shimmering glint in his black eyes. To the way those eyes had deliberately dropped all the way down her tall body, holding first on the ample curves of her hips and belly, and then up to her full, heavy breasts. Which, despite being respectably squashed beneath her plain, modest day-dress, now felt far too exposed, bared for his cool, casual perusal. His... *judgement.*

And then, finally, his eyes rose back to her face. Passing briefly over her brown skin and eyes, before lingering, narrowing, on her hair. As if even her hairstyle—a severe bun at the nape of her neck, confining all her thick curls tightly in place— was ripe for his judgement, too.

"Ach, no such joys today, I fear," the orc purred, as he came another step closer, and flashed Geva another wicked, wolfish smile. "As much good as I ken this should do you, angel. No, today..."

Geva could only seem to stare at the bastard, her breath still frozen in her chest, waiting, waiting—until the orc's clawed hand dropped back to his sword-hilt, and slowly, almost reluctantly, drew its impossible shining length from his belt. The movement deft and familiar and deeply calculated, oh gods what was this, what was he doing, what was *happening*—

"Today, sweetling," he continued, his voice still light and cool, as he easily flipped the giant sword in his huge hand. Watching her watch this, wanting her to see it, to *fear* it, and...

And without warning, the sword flashed up to Geva's *neck.* Its polished steel blade gently nudging against her skin, cold and sharp and deadly. Smashing raw sheer terror through her pounding skull, oh gods, oh gods, no, she couldn't die like this, please, not today...

"Today," the orc repeated, with a regretful little smile, "you shall show me each last coin and jewel in this grim, garish house. And if you are very, *very* good, my pretty poppet"—that cold steel bit closer, harder, pain stinging and screaming through her skin—"*mayhap* you shall live to see the morn."

3

Geva gaped at the giant, menacing brute before her, while distant, horrible comprehension cracked through her strange, stilted thoughts.

The orc was... a *thief*. He'd come here to steal from the Fitzwalds, just like Mrs. Fitzwald had feared.

And if Geva didn't cooperate, he would... he would *kill* her.

And he *would*, she realized, as she stared at his cool, glinting eyes. As she felt him tilting his deadly blade against her neck, making sure she could feel its sharpened, unyielding edge. He was threatening her, taunting her, and... *enjoying* it.

"But," Geva gulped, the movement flexing her throat against that cold sharpened steel. "The—the other servants. They'll—"

The orc shot her that wicked smile again, a little colder this time. "The other humans are yet out of the house, and shall know naught of this," he replied softly. "Lest you scream, but then I *shall* kill you, my pretty poppet."

Geva's throat again convulsed against the cold steel, her body still otherwise frozen in place. Other than the trembling, why couldn't she stop trembling, why couldn't she *think*...

"But," she tried again, "you're—the orcs—you're bound by a

peace-treaty. You've kept its terms for *years*. You're not supposed to—to steal, or raid, or *kill* people."

It should have sounded confident, but it came out pleading, pathetic, her voice not even slightly her own. And that was surely anger in the orc's eyes now, flashing just as bright and sharp as his blade, and gods he was going to kill her now, he was—

"*I* have signed no treaty," he replied, his deep voice far more clipped than before. "I do as I wish. And today, I wish to raid this house. And if *you* wish to *die* today, you shall keep babbling of servants and treaties, instead of showing me the plunder that is *mine!*"

His sword pressed even harder against Geva's throat as he spoke, and she gasped as she felt the sharp sting of her skin breaking, smarting with sudden heat and pain. He'd cut her, he'd actually *cut* her *neck*, oh gods, this could not be happening—

But it was, and the orc's eyes had dropped toward her stinging neck, lingering with something like satisfaction as his blade finally, finally eased away. And now—oh *hell*—that was a long, slithering black *tongue*, curling from his mouth, slipping against his parted lips.

As if... as if this bastard truly would kill her, and *enjoy* it. As if he were every terrifying tale about the brutal, ravenous orcs, brought to horrifying life here before her. And amidst the screaming still resounding silently through Geva's thudding skull, there was also exhaustion, and bitterness, and a heavy, hollow defeat.

Of course. Of course this would happen, after such a miserable day, a miserable week, a miserable four years. Of course it would happen just before her month of long-awaited peace. And of course she would be targeted by the one damned renegade orc who didn't care about his treaty, who only cared about her employers' damned coin, and their horrid hideous jewels. Of *course.*

"Ach?" the orc hissed now, his voice pure deadly malice. "What fate shall you choose, my sweet?"

Geva desperately gulped down air, and somehow, somehow, she squared her shoulders, raised her chin. She'd survived this far. She could survive this. Keep moving forward, one step at a time. She had to. She *had* to.

"I—I'll help you, orc," she said, as evenly as she could. "I'll do my best. You'll see."

4

———

Geva's words were followed by a strange, strained silence. By the heavy, prickling truth of the orc's eyes studying her, and then—she couldn't hide her flinch—the distinctive *shirr* of metal, as he slid his massive blade back into his belt.

"Ach, then," he said, with a rather false-sounding lightness. "I am glad we understand one another, my sweet."

Geva twitched another silent nod, a movement that flashed more stinging pain through the fresh cut on her neck. And though she could feel a hot trickle of blood slipping downwards, sliding toward her bodice, she couldn't even seem to lift her shaking hand to wipe it away.

But wait, now the orc was reaching out to *touch* her, his warm finger brushing against that trickle of blood—and as Geva watched, wide-eyed, he brought his red-stained finger to his *mouth.* Slipping it deep inside, while his throat visibly bobbed, and his long lashes fluttered.

As if... as if he *liked* the taste of her pain. As if he was again enjoying this, enjoying her shock and her terror. And *why* was Geva watching him like this, why had her own mouth gone bone-dry, her heart skipping a beat in her chest...

"Ach," the orc muttered, grimacing, as his finger dropped from his mouth, his narrow eyes refocusing on Geva's face. "Then we shall begin at once, poppet. Is there aught of worth in this mess?"

He waved sharply at the chaotic schoolroom around them, and Geva gulped down a shaky breath as she fought to follow his question, to think. To assess the schoolroom's rickety furniture, the faded decorations, the books and papers and toys and clothes strewn all about.

"That—that painting," she made herself say, as she nodded toward a large gilt-framed landscape on the wall. It had surely been hanging there long before the Fitzwalds had purchased the house, and it was one of Geva's favourites, with its vivid colours and strong, striking strokes. "It's a rare piece, by one of the capital's most in-demand artists, and it would likely fetch—"

But she was interrupted by the sound of the orc's laughter, cold and scornful, scraping up her spine. "You seek to mock me, woman?" he demanded, as his taloned hand once again gripped his sword-hilt. "You ken I wish to jaunt about the realm with some great *scribble* strapped upon my back? I said, coin. And jewels!"

Geva's trembling body flattened back against the schoolroom wall behind her, and she nodded, as quickly as she could. "R-right," she stammered. "It's just likely more valuable than— never mind. Jewels are—downstairs. In the Fitzwalds' dressing-rooms."

She was desperately fighting to shove away the memory of speaking to Mrs. Fitzwald, that very afternoon, in that very dressing-room—but before her, the orc was giving a low, guttural grunt, and jerking an imperious wave toward the door. Saying, *Show me.*

Geva nodded, and pushed her shaky body off the wall—but then, curse it, she stumbled over one of the many toys scattered across the floor. Sending her pitching straight toward the solid doorframe, her mouth helplessly crying out, her hands wildly flailing before her—

When something strong and solid caught around her waist from behind, and yanked her back up again. Clutching her against something huge and powerful and... alive.

The... the orc's *chest*.

For a stunned, shivering instant, Geva couldn't move, pinned like that against him, his huge hand spreading wide against her waist. And when she shot a frozen, furtive glance downwards, she found that his long talons had somehow drawn back into his fingers, leaving behind what looked like short, pointed black fingernails. Fingernails that were still gently pricking against the fabric of her day-dress, in a bizarre, confusing contrast to the protective spread of his fingers, their warm capable strength holding her close and safe...

But just as quickly, there was a frantic flurry of movement, and Geva was standing alone again, swaying on her feet. Her own hand slipping down to where the orc's had been, feeling that odd, unexpected warmth, still shimmering beneath her skin...

"Careful, poppet," said the orc from behind her, with a sudden, false-sounding joviality. "Dressing-rooms, you say?"

Geva managed another nod, and again stepped toward the door, far more carefully this time. And though she kept her gaze straight ahead, she could still *feel* the orc following her, his huge body unnervingly close, his footfalls silent on the polished wooden floor. As her own heartbeat just kept thundering louder and louder in her skull, her hands wringing tightly together. Just the next thing, just doing her best...

"These... paintings, then," came the orc's voice behind her, and when Geva startled a look backwards, he was waving his big hand—with its long claws extended again—up at the portraits lining the staircase's walls. "Are these also of worth?"

Geva glanced up toward the nearest portrait—an obsequiously flattering depiction of a simpering Mrs. Fitzwald—

and gave a choked, shrill-sounding laugh. "No, of course not," her shaky voice replied. "Not unless you're the one who wasted obscene amounts of your ill-earned coin on it."

Behind her, the orc made an odd huffing sound, not unlike a chuckle. "Ach, you humans," he said. "Even the vainest orc I know should *wither* at the thought of his own face leering down toward him all day. Much less to pay good *gold* for this."

Geva couldn't bite back her bitter twist of a smile, and despite everything, she felt the furious hammer of her heart-beat fading, just slightly. Enough, at least, to allow her to draw in a deep, shaky breath as she halted before the closed door of Mrs. Fitzwald's bedroom.

"The dressing-room is attached to the bedroom," she made herself say, as she again shoved away the memory of Mrs. Fitzwald sitting there, dangling those jewels in the looking-glass. "Though I'm sure they're both very well secured, and—"

Her voice broke there, because the orc was already nudging her aside, and reaching inside his tunic to pull out a long gold chain, with a variety of slim metal rods attached. And after he jiggled several of them in the lock, the heavy door smoothly swung open, revealing Mrs. Fitzwald's large, opulent bedroom.

Oh. Geva blinked at the orc for an instant, and then back at the waiting bedroom. Which, not unlike the schoolroom, had been left in a state of shocking disarray. The bed unmade, the carpets scuffed and stained, the furniture littered with a haphazard array of shoes, clothing, bedding, and papers.

"Humans," the orc muttered, wrinkling his nose as he stepped inside, his eyes sweeping scornfully over the mess. "Where are the jewels, angel?"

"Over there," Geva said, nodding at the adjoining dressing-room door. And once again, the orc nudged her aside and strode over, jiggling the lock with his chain until that door swung open, too.

"Come, poppet," he said over his shoulder, waving Geva forward. And despite her grimace, she again obeyed, following him into the starkly familiar room. With that huge jewel-box on the dressing-table, as well as a variety of costly fabrics, shoes, hats, and even more jewels, strewn carelessly about the room, and especially across the dressing-table.

"Ach, yes," the orc breathed, as he snatched for a gold locket, and held it to his nose. His breath inhaling deeply, his lashes fluttering, as his long black tongue slithered out to curl against it. Just the way he'd licked Geva's *blood* from his finger, good gods, and her heartbeat again kicked in her chest as she watched. What the hell was she doing, what the hell else *could* she do, there was nothing else to do, but keep moving, forward—

"Here," the orc said, tossing something toward her—and when Geva caught it, she discovered it was a small leather pouch. "Fill it with all you can find, ach?"

Geva blinked down at the pouch, and then around at the room—gods, now she had to participate in the actual *looting*, too?—but the orc's expression was rapidly darkening, his hand again dropping to his sword-hilt. "Quickly," he hissed. "Now, woman!"

Geva flinched, but nodded, and lurched to obey. Snatching up chains, bracelets, earrings, rings, from the dressing-table, the shelves, even the floor, while the orc occupied himself with the large jewel-box on the dressing-table. The very same one Mrs. Fitzwald had opened earlier that day, and Geva could see his frown deepening as he poked at the lock with first his claws, and then with a much smaller pick from his chain.

She watched for a too-long instant, her breath shuddering in her throat—*make sure to hide the key properly, Mitzy*—and without thinking, without following, she stalked over to the wardrobe. To where the maid had reached up inside, perhaps to the back wall, where—

There, hanging on a nail. A silk ribbon, with an elegant little key attached. And Geva swallowed hard as she stared at it, her heart once again thundering, her breath choked in her throat. *Priceless jewels to pilfer. Leave these rooms very secure...*

"Here," Geva croaked at the orc, dangling the key before him. Earning a glance of genuine astonishment in return, followed by a smug, satisfied grin as he snatched the key from her fingers, and deftly unlocked the jewel-box.

"Very good, my sweet," he said approvingly, as he dragged a claw through the box's glittering contents. "Very, *very* good. Although"—he drew out a garish, alarmingly familiar sapphire pendant, his smile fading into visible dismay—"what sort of jeweller forged *this*? Ach. In *very* poor taste."

Geva's mouth helplessly twitched into something dangerously close to a smile, and she lurched away, and returned to collecting the room's remaining visible valuables. Stuffing them one by one into her little pouch until it was full, and then handing that over to the orc, too. He'd likewise finished emptying the jewel-box into another pouch, and he flashed Geva another approving, sharp-toothed grin as he tucked both pouches into his belt.

"A worthy yield, poppet," he said, his voice even warmer. "I should never have *dreamt* of gaining such help from the school-marm, ach?"

But Geva couldn't seem to stop glancing uneasily around the messy room, at that open empty jewel-box. While a dark, sickening awareness plumed up in her gut, surging past the walls she'd been desperately attempting to build around it.

She was really doing this. She was helping an orc plunder her employers' house, just as Mrs. Fitzwald had feared. But then the orc would run off and disappear, never to be seen again. And she would be left behind, and then...

"Now, do not fret, kitten," the orc said, with another satisfied grin, as he turned and snapped the jewel-box closed, locking it with the little key. "They shall find no trace of us here, you ken?"

There was a sudden, wild impulse to laugh—no trace,

perhaps, other than all the missing jewels—but Geva choked it down, and silently hung the key back in the wardrobe. And then she followed the orc back out into the corridor, watching blankly as he locked the door behind them.

"And next, poppet?" the orc asked, raising his thick black brows, and flashing Geva yet another jaunty grin. "That way, mayhap?"

He was inhaling deeply, angling his head down the corridor, indeed in the direction of Mr. Fitzwald's rooms. So Geva nodded, squaring her shoulders, and soon found herself helping the orc plunder yet another set of messy rooms. This time finding a large quantity of loose coin, as well as an excessive assortment of men's jewels, snuff-boxes, and pocket-watches. And then—thanks to a loose-lipped tip from Sebastian this time—Geva pulled out an elegant, jewel-studded dagger, hidden in a secret compartment at the back of Mr. Fitzwald's stocking-drawer.

The orc's eyes widened as Geva handed the dagger over, his breath stilling in his huge chest—and then he snatched the dagger out of her hand, and turned it over with careful, disbelieving reverence. "This is orc-forged," he said under his breath. "My father—he owned one just like this. How did your foul masters gain this?!"

He shot Geva a sharp, accusing look—gods, as if *she'd* somehow acquired the dagger for Mr. Fitzwald—and she raised her hands as she stumbled backwards, shaking her head. "I—I don't know," she gulped. "I just remembered Sebastian—one of my pupils—saying it was there."

The fury kept crackling in the orc's dark eyes, and he leapt to his feet, and ushered Geva out of the room. "Show me the rest," he hissed, as he swiftly locked the door behind them. "All of it."

But Geva was again standing frozen in place, while that cold, clammy dread kept bubbling in her belly, even deeper and darker than before. He *still* wasn't done? After she'd already betrayed so much, risked so much, and now...

We'll need to leave these rooms very secure. Your greed is shocking, Miss Okoro. Unless you want to spend the next month out on the streets...

"All that's left now is the—the children's rooms," Geva stammered. "And the servants'. You surely can't mean to—"

The orc cut her off with a hard, bitter laugh, a menacing grip of his clawed hand to his sword-hilt. "Ach, are these the same children I heard speak to you earlier today?" he asked coldly. "Such soft, *sweet* little ducklings, were they not?"

Geva's words were failing her again—this damned orc had been spying on the house, he'd been *planning* this, of course he had—and he laughed again, even harder this time. "Ach, you are not a fool, woman," he snapped. "These spoilt brats shall be well served by losing a few trinkets. Show me!"

So Geva once again obeyed, numbly guiding the orc through the children's rooms. Not offering any assistance this time, most of all in Cecily's room, which had precious little to steal to begin with. And thankfully, the orc didn't bother demanding Geva's help, and emptied all their drawers and jewel-boxes on his own, before ordering her to take him to the servants' quarters.

But as Geva led him up the narrow back staircase, she only felt that dread deepening, coiling in a hard, nauseating knot in her stomach. Enough that she had to hold her hand over her mouth as she watched the orc ducking in and out of her fellow employees' rooms, moving far more quickly than before. Most of them had hidden their small amounts of coin in painfully obvious places, in drawers or under mattresses, though Cook's was under a floorboard, and several of the junior maids had nothing at all.

And finally, at the very end of the row, was Geva's own room. A fact that the orc clearly understood at once, hesitating as he stepped inside. His eyes sweeping over the neatly made bed, the wardrobe, the little table with her tidy stack of books, before glancing over his shoulder toward her.

"Come, then, poppet," he said, his voice surprisingly gentle. "It shall be done faster if you just show me, ach?"

The bitter fury plunged harder in Geva's belly, so forceful that bile surged high in her throat. And even as she opened her mouth to protest, or perhaps begin begging, her hand twitched reflexively to her neck, and found... pain. The cut the orc's huge blade had made, fresh enough to still be sticky and hot against her finger.

So she bit her lip, blinked back the water pooling in her eyes, and stalked past the orc to her narrow wardrobe. And with shaking, prickling hands, she reached up inside. Groping for the familiar little bag, which currently held fourteen copper coins inside it.

She nearly betrayed a sob as her fingers clutched it, but she somehow spun back around, and thrust it out toward the orc. Keeping her blinking eyes on the floor as she waited, as she felt the little bag's weight lift from her wavering hand.

And surely, this was all this orc could take from her. Surely this part of this nightmare would finally be over, and he would leave her alone to weep and despair, and frantically plan for the hell that would come next. For her total, immutable destruction.

Because it would be destruction, Geva now knew. This vile orc was destroying her. He was destroying *everything*.

It was a certainty that had only grown as she'd watched him move through the servants' rooms, emptying them one by one. Because even if the Fitzwalds' missing possessions went unnoticed until they returned in a month, the servants would surely discover their own lost coin within a day or two, at most. And despite all Mrs. Fitzwald's grand claims of pilfering orcs, the other servants would be well aware of the house, and who had been alone inside it.

Geva.

And earlier that very day, Mrs. Fitzwald had openly repri-manded her. Mrs. Fitzwald had freely insulted her, and threat-ened to fire her, and called her greedy, while flaunting her priceless jewels, and sharing her concerns about thievery. All this, while those two maids had watched and listened to every word—and one of those maids hadn't gone on the trip, either. *Hide the key properly, Mitzy. We'll need to leave these rooms very secure.*

Now you're trying to get a free vacation? As if it isn't enough that we're allowing you to stay here, in our house, free of charge, for an entire month? Your greed is shocking, Miss Okoro, as is your imper-tinence...

No. There was no way Geva would escape this. She had a motive. She had opportunity. And despite her best efforts, she'd never had good relations with the rest of the servants, and the tale of her thorough dressing-down from Mrs. Fitzwald would already have been making the rounds, poisoning them even more against her. And perhaps most damning of all, those cursed orcs *had* kept to that treaty of theirs. There hadn't been any credible orc thefts—or threats—reported in the area in years.

All of which meant Geva had very little time before being accused of this crime. Perhaps until nightfall. And once the full breadth of the theft was realized, she would be—she would be—

"Ach, my sweet," broke in the orc's voice, and when Geva's wet, blinking eyes glanced up, she found the orc carefully watching her. His head tilted, his dark gaze unreadable, as his big hand smoothly tucked her life's savings, her very last hope, into his belt with all the rest. "Do not weep. You are a clever woman, and you have shown a cool head and strong mettle, ach? You shall soon find another way to earn this coin again."

But the dread and the disbelief kept curdling, cracking, breaking Geva apart, and she heard herself bark a loud, painful-sounding laugh. "You're wrong, you cold cheating bastard," she gulped, before she could possibly stop it. "You're so, *so* wrong. You know nothing about me, or my life here. You have no idea what you're doing to me, or how you're ruining me! You're ruining *everything!*"

The orc blinked at her, looking genuinely taken aback, and Geva laughed again, even as hot wetness finally spilled from her eyes, and escaped down her cheeks. "They'll blame me," she gasped. "They'll blame me for all of it. I am *finished* here, orc. And even when I run for the hills the moment you leave, do you think I will ever, *ever* work in education again? Do you think I'm just some nondescript, forgettable governess who will easily find another post under another name, without any references? Do you not realize how impossible that is, even without looking like *this*?!"

She waved frantically at her face and her hair, at the distinctly Eziran features that would stand out in any busy marketplace in the province. While the orc just kept blinking at her, his brow now heavily furrowed, his head tilting further. But not speaking, not even attempting a response, and Geva made a sound that might have been a sob, or a scream.

"Thanks to you, my career is finished," she choked out. "And now, I can look forward to running for my life, and living in poverty for the rest of my days!"

The orc's mouth briefly contorted, his nostrils flaring—but then he squeezed his eyes shut, and turned his face away. "Ach," he said, his voice gruff. "Then mayhap—here. Keep this, woman."

He'd thrust her little bag of coins back toward her, and though Geva's trembling hand instantly snatched it away, clutching it close to her heart, she couldn't seem to stop weeping, or shaking her head. There was no way. This might get her to the next town over, it might keep her fed for a week or two, but then...

"It doesn't matter," she gasped, between sobs. "Nothing matters anymore. You're ruining my entire *life*. And I know it wasn't much, but I've tried so hard, I've survived so long, and now it's *over!*"

There was an instant's thick silence, broken only by the sound of her gulps, the feel of her shaky hand swiping at her tears. Gods, what was she going to do, this foul orc needed to go the hell away, get out of her destroyed life forever, and then...

"Ach, woman," came his low voice, sounding stilted, almost hesitant. "Do not—do not weep thus. Mayhap we—"

But at that very moment, there was a voice. A familiar voice. The voice of the Fitzwalds' *butler*. Calling for her.

"Miss Okoro!" it shouted, as the distinctive sound of footsteps thudded up the stairs. "Miss Okoro, are you up here?"

And it wasn't just one set of footsteps, it was several, and Geva's heart was reeling again, raging through her chest. What if the other servants found her with an *orc* in her bedroom? Oh gods, would he go off and *kill* them?! Or—or even if he didn't kill them, they would see, they would find out everything, she had to do *something—*

But before her, the orc had frozen in place, his hand clutching his sword-hilt, his wide eyes darting desperately around the small room. Searching for escape, for a way to survive this—but there was no other door, no windows, no way out.

They were trapped. *Finished.*

And without thought, without hesitation, Geva rushed forward, grasped the orc's huge arm—and then she dragged him into the half-open wardrobe, and yanked the door shut behind them.

5

———————

Geva was trapped with an orc in a wardrobe.

She couldn't seem to stop trembling as she clutched behind her for the wardrobe's back wall, her ragged breaths far too loud in the cramped darkness. And worst of all, this huge, deadly orc was far, *far* too close, his solid, rigid body pressed tight against hers, enough that she could feel the softness of his belly, could feel his hard chest hollowing as he exhaled.

"Miss Okoro!" the butler's voice called again, even closer now. "Are you up here? The Missus sent word back, young Sir forgot his—"

The footsteps were just outside the room now, and Geva felt her body trembling even harder, shuddering between the solid wall and the orc. Would the servants be able to hear, would they see something wrong with the wardrobe, would they come over and fling the door open? And what then, would the orc retaliate, would he attack them with that deadly sword, it would be grief and misery and death, no, no, not *again*, and—

And then something settled against Geva's *hair*. Something heavy and warm, and moving with careful, gentle strokes.

It was—the orc. The orc was—*petting* her?

Geva should have elbowed him, kneed him in the groin, *something*—she did not need petting, and her hair did *not* like being touched—but instead, she felt herself... sagging. Breathing. The uncontrollable trembling finally fading a little, as that big, warm hand kept stroking her, again and again. Moving with slow, astonishing gentleness, as if it were soothing a particularly skittish cat.

"Could've sworn I heard that high-and-mighty governess screeching up here," said another voice, nasal and waspish. It was one of the Fitzwalds' footmen, and Geva shuddered again as the footfalls came closer, closer...

"Hearing her in your mind, now, are you, boy?" the butler's deeper voice replied, with audible mirth. "Just be glad you're not one of the Master's brats, and stuck in the schoolroom with her scolding you all day."

The footman gave a loud, contemptuous laugh, and they were clearly inside the room now, only a few steps away, oh gods. "Some good it does 'em, too," his nasal voice replied. "Those rotten kids are worse now than they ever were before. She's been a bad influence on them, I think."

The butler muttered some kind of agreement, but Geva couldn't hear it, because the orc—who had leaned even tighter against her in the cramped darkness—had huffed a harsh, angry exhale, alarmingly close in her ear. The sound nearly a growl, almost as if—as if he was *offended* on her behalf.

And gods, Geva could have laughed at the utter absurdity of it, because she'd heard these petty bastards say far worse, multiple times—and that footman, snivelling creep that he was, had even made repeated attempts to grope her in the stairwell. So why was she protecting any of them, why was she still standing here in the damned wardrobe, while this damned infuriating orc just kept pressing into her, breathing against her, his big hand stroking her hair again and again, as a warm, musky scent curled through the too-thick air. And was she inhaling even deeper, or even tilting her head a little into his steady caresses, surely she wasn't, surely...

"Well, she's not here," the butler said, and that was the sound of a drawer opening, and closing again, and then another. And wait, these bastards were looking through her *underclothes*, and Geva's surge of incredulous fury was met by another heavy exhale from the orc, a gentle little shake of that hand still petting her head. A warning. Because gods, what if they came for the wardrobe next, and found her squashed in here with *him*?!

"Did you find her?" called another voice, a new voice, further away. It was the other footman, and Geva's heart thundered in her ears as she waited, straining, listening. Hearing the scrape of the drawer closing... and then footsteps. Movement. Toward the corridor again, please, please...

"Not yet," called the butler, his voice markedly further away. "Did you check the schoolroom?"

And finally, thank the gods, the footsteps were fading, moving back down the corridor. And Geva's breath rushed from her lungs, her body sagging with relief, as the orc's body abruptly relaxed, too. Leaning heavily against her, his head softly thudding against the wardrobe's wall above her, his breath slow and thick in her ear.

But he didn't speak, and his big hand didn't stop petting her, either. Almost as though he hadn't noticed he was doing it, but in this moment, Geva couldn't seem to make herself care. She'd almost been found with an orc in a wardrobe—she might *still* be found with an orc in a wardrobe—and there was no way they could risk moving yet. Not until they were sure those bastards were gone.

The orc hadn't shown any intention of moving yet either, and if anything, his big body had settled even closer, pinning Geva tighter to the wall. His head lowering a little, his hot breath tickling and shivering against her ear, against the damp skin of her neck. And the hand still petting her had even tilted her head slightly sideways, away from his breath, so he could come closer, draw in deeper...

A strange little shudder rippled up Geva's back—surely just more tension, more terror—but her own breaths had deepened, too. Drawing in that rich musky scent, now so absurdly potent in the stuffy air. And her eyes, which had been searching vainly in the darkness this entire time, had fluttered closed, and when the orc's gentle hand nudged her head back against the solid wood behind her, tilting it further sideways, she didn't fight him. Instead, she felt herself relaxing into his closeness, his touch, while a hard swallow convulsed through her now-exposed throat.

The sound had surely been audible, and she could almost feel the weight of the orc's eyes, the taut focus of his attention upon her. The way his breath had stuttered, warmer, closer, until...

Oh. A soft, slick, gentle heat, brushing against the skin of Geva's bared neck. Drawing out her slow, shaky exhale, and then another audible swallow. And in return, there was a low, rumbling hiss from the wet heat on her skin, vibrating deep into her throat as it pressed harder, closer...

And with it, the orc eased even closer, too. His body so big, so solid, enclosing her in such safe heady warmth. His powerful muscles shifting and flexing, his hips slightly rocking, grinding something into her lower belly. Something long and thick and rigid, something that should have been deeply, thoroughly terrifying—but instead, Geva felt her breath catching, her tooth biting her lip, her head arching further against the wall behind her. Almost as if welcoming the provoking press of his big body, that deep shimmering thrill in her belly, that soft slick warmth on her neck.

And in that sweet softness, something slowly, gently sharpened. Something that pricked and scraped in multiple matched points, searching and seeking against her throat. And Geva waited, her eyes fluttering, her heart hammering, as that soft sharpness finally found that fresh stinging slice across the front of her neck, and...

Licked it. Kissed it. *Nibbled* it.

Geva froze in place, while a swarm of sheer, staggering shock shot down the full length of her body. What the hell. She was trapped in a wardrobe with a thieving, deadly orc, who was currently in the process of destroying her *life*—and she was letting him lick her? Pet her? *Bite* her?!

There was a sudden, frantic flurry of flailing, from both Geva and the orc—and then they were spilling out of the wardrobe together, stumbling into the cool, open air of Geva's bedroom. And with the flood of fresh air, there was even more swarming shock, and chagrin, and disbelief. What the *hell* had she been thinking, letting him lick her? *Him*?!

The orc was grimacing too, and even wiping at his mouth with a furious-looking hand. As if he, too, was thoroughly regretting this harrowing, horrifying little incident. Which he damn well should, damn the devious fiend, so why was Geva's stomach plunging, her eyes prickling, as if she somehow *cared*?

"What the hell, orc," she hissed at him, as quietly as she could, despite the frenzied alarm still screeching through her skull. "Were you trying to—to—"

To seduce me, she might well have said, *to bite me and drink my blood, like the orcs in all those horrible tales*—but the orc was still grimacing, and again wiped his clawed hand at his mouth.

"Forget this, woman," he hissed back. "I seek *naught* from you. I have not the slightest wish for a mate, or a son! Most of all—"

He broke off there, grimacing again, but his contemptuous eyes swept up and down Geva's body, all the same. Saying, with dismissive, devastating clarity, that he would never actually *desire* her. Not even after he'd pressed into her like that, petted her like that, and maybe—maybe even *kissed* her like that.

Geva's trembling hand fluttered to her neck, to where the pain left by his sword-blade had entirely vanished, fully replaced by the painful, plunging misery. And gods, what was *happening* to her? She'd long ago learned to keep going, keep looking forward, keep her cool in the face of the worst the world had to offer. So why was this obnoxious thief affecting her like this, why was she nearly weeping like this, *again*?!

And before she could betray anything else, she whirled away from him, back toward the wardrobe. Groping inside for her satchel, which had clearly been trod upon during the proceedings, but was luckily still in one piece. And once she'd also found her precious bag of coins—she'd somehow dropped that, too—she began yanking items from the wardrobe, and packing them into the satchel as neatly as she could. All while desperately fighting to focus her thoughts on travelling, what she would most need, how much she could realistically carry on foot...

"Ach, woman," came the orc's voice from behind her, near enough to make her jump. "What is the meaning of this?"

Geva shook her head and kept packing, not looking, not speaking—but she could feel him shifting behind her, perhaps moving closer. "You do not truly wish to *run away*?" he demanded. "*Now*?"

Geva fought back the all-consuming urge to spin around and scream in his face, and instead kept packing, though her hands were trembling even worse than before. "Yes, I damn well wish it," she gulped. "I'm leaving here. Today."

The orc fell silent, and Geva again fought to focus on her packing, on how the satchel was almost already full. On how— her wet eyes glared back up at all the clothes still left in the closet—she surely couldn't afford to leave a single item behind. She needed every possible advantage if she was going to survive this, and perhaps she could sell some of them, perhaps...

So she shoved up to her feet, and kept her back to the orc as her shaky hands unbuttoned her overdress, and tossed it on the bed. And next she yanked off her underdress, too, and then her stockings and shoes, leaving her only in her thin white shift. And without meeting the orc's eyes, she shoved past him to her small chest of drawers, and then pulled off the shift, too. Meaning that her back and ample arse were fully bared to him, fully exposed for his judgement, and his contempt.

And gods, she could *feel* him watching her, his gaze prickling on her bare skin, but she sought to ignore it as she yanked out more stockings from the drawer, and again began to dress. This time putting on layer after layer, starting with her closest-fitting underthings, and then working her way back up to dresses again. Piling on pieces without any of her usual regard for fit or style, and knowing very well that she looked completely, utterly absurd.

But it didn't matter. Just like being undressed in front of a horrible judgemental orc didn't matter, because it was only running that mattered now. Only the next thing. Only surviving.

But the damned orc was still here, still standing in the middle of the room as Geva bustled around him. Just watching in silence as she repacked her satchel, fitting in nearly everything this time, even the silk scarf she wore over her hair to sleep, and the small bottle of oil she used on her hair and skin. Now leaving only—she couldn't help an unhappy sigh as she glanced toward them—the stack of books beside her bed. The uppermost one was her favourite childhood book of tales, entirely written in Eziran, the language of her family's home across the sea.

She'd drifted closer without quite meaning to, and she picked up the bulky, wood-bound book, turning through the well-worn pages of dense, angular Eziran script. The tale of the reckless roaming rat. The one of the funny fox. The one with the wind and the flies, the angel and his worshipper, the goddess and the demon...

But the book was large and heavy and tattered, of very little monetary value, and Geva knew all the tales line by line, in yet another of her parents' many, many gifts. So she carefully closed the book, and set it back on top of the stack again. Giving it one last, regretful look, one more silent goodbye, before pulling on her boots, grasping her satchel, and turning for the door.

But—the orc. The orc, still standing here, his massive body fully blocking her path. And when Geva made to step around him, he swiftly moved to block her again—and wait, that was the sound of a growl, hissing low and vicious from his throat.

"You cannot run off alone thus, woman," he said, his voice hard. "There is great danger in this."

Geva blinked up at the orc's frowning face, and choked back the sudden, surging impulse to start sobbing, or shouting, or both. "Oh, really, orc?" she demanded, frayed and thin. "Why, that hadn't at all occurred to me. Now get the hell out of my way, and let me go!"

But it wasn't helping, of course it wasn't, because the orc's huge body only seemed to loom even larger, his arms crossing tightly over his chest. "Where do you mean to go," he snapped back. "Who shall house and feed you. Have you family? Friends? A past bedmate? Someone who owes you a debt?"

Geva barked a short, shrill laugh, and once again attempted to shove past the orc—but again, he was far too fast, his big body hovering far too close. "Then where," he growled, "shall you go? How shall you then *live*, if you say you cannot even gain new work?"

That damnable prickling was again accosting Geva's eyes, and she clamped her teeth together, and clenched both hands against her heavy satchel. "I'll try to make my way north to the capital," she gritted out, "where there's less chance of me being found and charged for this theft. And I'll look for other work there."

She couldn't hide her wince at the last bit—that other work was sure to be awful, even if she managed to stay off the streets—and the orc growled again, deep and menacing in his chest.

"You cannot do this, woman," he hissed at her, his eyes flashing. "Is this not also where these humans went? This is not *safe*. You have little coin, and no plan, no help, and no home!"

Another thin, high-pitched laugh escaped Geva's throat, her head whipping back and forth. "And why do *you* care?" she choked at him. "What else did you *expect*, orc? You waltz in here and set me up to take the fall for *your* thievery, and now you expect me to just sit here and wait to be dragged off to the magistrate for sentencing? Do you not *understand* how few options I have left right now?!"

The orc still hadn't moved, that forbidding stubbornness still flaring in his eyes, and Geva heard herself laugh again, clutching the satchel closer. "I have *no other options*, orc," she gulped. "If I stay here, I will be blamed for this. I *will*. And those servants coming up here searching for me—which *you* said you would warn me about, by the way—will only make matters that much worse! No, of course they couldn't find the governess when she was left alone in the house, because she was otherwise occupied downstairs, ransacking her employers' *bedrooms*!"

Gods, she was almost yelling again, risking being discovered again, and she squeezed her eyes shut, shook her head. "I need to go," she whispered. "If I'm going to have any chance of surviving this, I need to run. Today."

There was a hard, hurtling silence from the orc before her, a hitching exhale in his breath. And when Geva darted another furious glance upwards, he was rubbing at his eyes, while an angry, bitter grimace contorted his mouth.

"Ach, woman," he said. "I follow. And thus"—he exhaled again, slow and resigned—"you shall run today. With *me*."

6

She would run today. With *him.*

Geva stared at the orc for a long, appalling moment, as the distant pounding in her skull thudded ever closer. With him? With *him*?!

"Absolutely not," she snapped, as she made to step around him again. "No, orc. *Never.*"

But the great bastard again blocked her path, his big hands upraised, his claws drawn in. "Listen, woman," he growled. "You say no human shall now hire you? Then *I* shall hire you."

He would *hire* her. An orc. Would hire *her.*

"To do *what*?" Geva demanded at him, her voice shrill. "I thought you just said you didn't want children. What, do you already have a secret stash of them hidden away somewhere, just waiting for a governess to teach them?"

The orc's lip sharply curled, his head shaking. "Ach, I have no sons, and I do *not* wish for them," he hissed back. "But there are"—he hesitated, his nose wrinkling—"other services, you might offer me."

His eyes swept purposefully up and down Geva's form, which was now thoroughly padded with well over a half-dozen layers of formless, mismatched clothing. And Geva was again gaping at him, her mouth fallen open, because was this bastard truly saying—was he saying—

He would hire her to share his *bed*?!

Geva's already-warm face was flooding with heat, and with humiliation, and finally, with rage. "You—vile—*parasite*," she choked at him, through clenched teeth. "First of all, how *dare* you ask me to be your harlot, you arrogant *beast*, especially after you threatened me, mocked me, and ruined my career, and my *life*! And secondly, you *just* implied that I was far too hideous for your refined orc tastes! That I'm not slim enough, perhaps, or pale enough! And now—"

But before she could finish, the orc's huge hand had clapped over her mouth, on her *face*, as his narrow eyes darted toward the open door behind them. "Hush, woman," he hissed. "Not once have I called you *hideous*, ach? I called you clever, with a cool head and strong mettle! Ach, this is not what I should seek in a mate, *if* I were to wish for one"—he grimaced, shook his head—"but I do not wish to mate you, I wish to *hire* you!"

Geva gave a bitter laugh behind the orc's hand, and belatedly shoved it downwards, away, fighting to ignore the warm strength of it beneath her fingers. "And what would you seek in a mate, orc," she shot back. "Let me guess, someone small and quiet and obliging? Someone who will bow and simper at your every command?"

The orc's lip curled, and his shoulder jerked a twitchy-looking shrug. "Ach, and what does this mean to *you*?" he snarled back. "Why should I not wish for a soft, sweet, eager woman to share my bed, rather than one who will not even hear me *speak*? One who instead shrieks and wails at me, and calls me a *parasite* and a *beast*?"

Geva felt herself bristling, the retort rising in her throat—she would not even *need* help, if this belligerent bastard hadn't barged in here and ruined her life—but then she squeezed her eyes shut, and dragged in a long, shaky breath.

No. He had a point. There was no use wasting her time antagonizing him, not with so much at stake. She needed to focus on the next step, the next thing. On surviving. And, most importantly, she did *not* care what he did or didn't want in a woman. She *didn't*.

"Very well," she gritted out, as she made herself meet the orc's eyes. "I'm listening. *Why* do you want to hire me."

The orc blinked at her, but then quickly glanced away, and rubbed his hand at his face. "I am... in the midst of a journey southwest," he said, his voice very measured. "To the home of my kin. I have been away from there for some years, and of late, they have asked me to return. But in my time away, I have not yet gained a mate or a son. Because"—his voice hardened—"I have *no wish* for this. But for many orcs, this lack of a woman and sons... this is a weakness. A failure."

Geva made herself consider that, studying the orc's frowning face, the hard furrow between his thick brows. "I have good cause," he continued, even slower, "to show myself *settled* upon my return there. To show that in my absence, I have found only peace, and profit, and pleasure. And thus"—his narrow eyes darted back toward Geva—"I could be well-served by a... pretence. A deception."

Geva kept staring at the orc, as her brain began churning and revolving again, her heartbeat rising in her chest. He wanted to hire her... for a pretence? A deception? As his...

"You have shown yourself quick today, and clever, and clear-sighted," the orc continued, his eyes again distant, almost as if he were speaking more to himself than to her. "You did not buckle or weep under threat, nor betray me to those men. You did not seek to save yourself, at my expense."

Geva couldn't hide a wince, because in retrospect, she should have at least made an attempt—but the orc was still speaking, even slower now. "Instead, you... you aided me. You hid us away. And you unearthed worthy plunder that I would not have found alone."

His hand had absently moved to touch at his belt—or rather, at that jewel-studded, orc-forged dagger Geva had found in Mr. Fitzwald's drawer. "And thus," the orc added, "if you can show such mettle before humans, and before me"—his eyes snapped back to hers, suddenly sharp and watchful again—"surely you can show this same mettle before my kin, ach?"

Geva stared back at him for another stilted, dangling moment, her thoughts still uselessly swirling. He was... praising her? Complimenting her? Truly wanting to hire her, as his...

"And in there," the orc continued, speaking faster, jabbing his claw toward the still-open wardrobe. "You did not cower or flinch from my touch, ach? You did not simper or sob like a silly fearful maiden. And"—he lurched closer, and abruptly ducked his head toward Geva's *neck*, before jerking away again—"my scent even smells pleasing upon you. Strong. Natural. As if we both wished for this."

He began pacing back and forth across the room, his black claws dragging through his long hair, while something almost feral glimmered in his black eyes. "So this is a good scheme for us both, you ken?" he demanded, with rising triumph in his voice. "You shall come with me to the home of my kin, and help flaunt my strength. This shall also keep you well hidden from any humans who seek to cast blame for today's theft upon you. I shall also keep you safe and fed throughout this, and when it is done"—he stopped pacing, whirling around to face her again—"I shall pay you fair wages, and see you safely away from here. Across the sea, mayhap."

Oh. *Oh.* Geva was still staring at him, unblinking, while all those absurd words, those absurd impossible promises, charged deep into her brain, into her soul. Safe. Fed. Fair wages. Across the sea.

And curse her, but it was that last one that clung, clamped, brazen and breathless. She could go across the sea. Back home to Ezira. Back to where she surely still had aunts and uncles, cousins and nieces and nephews. Back to where other people looked and spoke and thought like her.

This was... a good plan. A good step forward.

But wait. No. *No.* That meant trusting an orc, it meant trusting *this* orc, who had already proven himself so thoroughly untrustworthy. Not to mention arrogant, capricious, condescending, and unpredictable. And he was indeed now staring at Geva with expectant, impatient eyes, as if he fully expected her to fall to his feet, and begin frantically anointing him with her tears of worship and gratitude.

"How much coin," Geva made herself say, her voice not at all her own. "Passage across the sea is more than I earn in a year, so—"

She couldn't even finish, her eyes squeezing shut, because it was laughable, ludicrous, *impossible*—but the orc's hand grasped her shoulder, giving it a bracing little shake.

"I shall pay it," he said firmly, and when she blinked her eyes open, he was jostling one of the bags at his belt—one of the bags full of the Fitzwalds' jewels, damn him. "I have yet far more wealth than this, you ken? And the better you play-act before my kin, and the more help and plunder you grant me"—that triumph again flared through his eyes—"the more I shall pay you. Ach?"

Geva was once again struck to silence, staring at this treacherous orc, while that desperation—that hope—kept clawing stronger, closer. This was preposterous. It was outrageous. It was...

"How long," she gulped, swallowing hard. "How many days."

That was most certainly a flinch, curling at the orc's mouth, tightening his hands at his sides. "One moon, mayhap," he said. "I do not seek to stay long. This is only a—"

He broke off there and began pacing again, but Geva was still considering it, her thoughts racing in a dozen directions at once. "And I would only be *pretending* to be your mate," she managed. "I wouldn't actually need to…"

She couldn't help a chagrined glance down toward the orc's trousers, to where there was still a distinctive—though unmistakably softened—bulge. "Ach, no," the orc replied, his voice flat. "There shall be no true mating between us. Only playacting, and only for this one moon. I shall have *no* surprise son from this, you ken? And should this somehow come about"— he jabbed a sharp finger toward Geva, his eyes dangerously narrowing—"we are *done*, woman. And I shall not pay you *one single coin*. Ach?"

Geva blinked, and then felt herself scoffing, glaring straight back toward him. "I assure you, orc, you have no need *whatsoever* for concern," she snapped. "Even if I were fool enough to risk my life reproducing with an orc, you would most certainly be the very last one in the *realm* I would choose!"

The orc's lip instantly curled, his eyes glancing dismissively up and down Geva's ridiculously bundled body. "Neither should I *ever* choose to mate you, woman," he shot back. "So we are well in accord upon this. But…"

But. But? Geva glared at the orc, her suspicion surging against an inexplicable misery, her heartbeat pummelling at her ears—until the orc betrayed a brief, telltale wince, twisting on his mouth.

"But," he continued, far more hesitant than before. "For my kin to believe we are mated, you shall need to… scent of me."

To scent of him. Geva's head tilted, her eyes searching his face, the sudden palpable tension all through his big body. "And what does that mean?" she asked, her voice strained. "You'll need to touch me? Or lick me again?"

The orc winced again, and shook his head. "No, woman," he replied, with the air of one being suddenly marched to his doom. "You shall need to be bared, and bathed all over in my good fresh seed."

7

———

Geva's laugh was loud and disbelieving, escaping her throat in a hoarse, high-pitched yelp.

This orc wanted her to what? To be bathed in his *what*?!

"You—cannot *possibly* mean what I think you mean, orc," she sputtered, between her suddenly shallow breaths. "You want me to bathe in your..."

Gods, she couldn't even say it, but her eyes had again dropped downwards, catching on that too-conspicuous bulge in his trousers. On how—how his big clawed *hand* had dropped here too, adjusting himself with a highly suspect casualness.

"Ach, mayhap *bathe* is not the best word for this," he replied, his mouth thinning, his gaze now firmly fixed to something beyond Geva's head. "Mayhap... *paint*, would be better."

Paint. This orc wanted to *paint* her. With... *that.* Out of *there.* And had he said *fresh*?!

"That is... absurd, orc," she finally said, her voice blank. "That is utterly outrageous. *Obscene.* Why would I—how would I possibly—you cannot possibly—"

The orc was still glaring at the wall behind her, his arms

crossing tightly over his chest. "This is not *obscene*," he countered, clipped. "It is how orcs mark our mates. We have done this from the earliest tales, for this allows us to track you, and guard you, and keep you safe. It is a show of favour and fealty. It is a *gift*."

There was a surprising vehemence in his words, in his flashing eyes, and for a moment Geva was entirely speechless, staring at his set, stubborn face. He truly meant this. He truly wanted her to... to...

"We shall not need to touch one another to gain this," he continued flatly. "You can do this yourself, and then bathe after, or rinse your mouth, as you wish."

Wait. Wait wait *wait*. "Rinse my *mouth*?" Geva demanded, her voice shrill. "You expect me to *bathe* my *mouth* with this, too?!"

The orc's expression remained grim and mulish, and he jerked a sharp, purposeful nod. "Ach," he said. "Once you taste it, you shall see."

Good gods. Strange waves of heat were sweeping up and down Geva's body, swaying her on her feet—and she staggered backwards, until she'd bumped into her bed. And she gratefully sank down upon it, dropping her heavy satchel to the floor, while her hands frantically rubbed at her face. No. No. This was not worth it, passage to Ezira was not worth it, this was utterly preposterous, she would be better off running for her life, and...

The orc was stepping closer toward her, his eyes still narrow and obstinate, his folded arms flexing against his chest. "You shall see," he repeated, deeper than before. "Orcs' taste is pleasing to women. *My* taste is pleasing to women."

His taste. Wait, as if he knew this from personal experience?! And when Geva shot him a look of sheer jolting disbelief, he returned it with a cold, contemptuous snort. "Ach, *my* taste," he hissed. "I have had women *beg* to suck me. I have had women make themselves *sick* upon my seed, and then crawl back for more."

Something roiled in Geva's belly—surely nausea and nothing more—but her disbelieving gaze had again dropped to that telltale swell at the orc's groin. Which was now far nearer than it had been, impossibly close before her eyes... and damn it, his big hand had moved to adjust it again. His sharp black claws lingering on where there was now a very long, thick, prominent ridge, swelling against the trousers' grey fabric.

"You do not believe me, woman?" he growled, as that hand slowly slipped down the full length of that ridge, until his fingers were casually cupping at the oversized bulge beneath. "You do not believe a proud, prim schoolmarm like you could welcome an orc's sweet seed down her throat?"

Geva's breath hitched, surely with horror and disgust, but she couldn't seem to drag her eyes away as the orc's hand leisurely slid up again. Showing how that ridge had grown even longer and thicker than before, tenting the trousers around it, reaching nearly up to his waist...

"Mayhap we ought to test this, then, woman?" the orc asked, his voice gone a little lower. "See if you can bear my taste, before you swear to this?"

Oh. Geva had fully stopped breathing now, those shocking words swirling through the ever-worsening mess of her thoughts, her eyes still fixed to the sight before her. To the orc's big clawed hand sliding down again, slow and shameless and blatant. Toward where he was shifting his powerful thighs a little apart, so she might better see the true heft of the weights hanging between them, see how plump and heavy they were in his big clawed hand...

"You are not a maid, ach, poppet?" the orc's husky voice asked, even deeper now. "I can smell what, seven other males upon you? Eight?"

Geva twitched, and shot a furious glance upwards, toward

the orc's taunting, flickering eyes. How did this bastard know that, how *dare* he mock her with that? And wait, why the hell hadn't he smelled the other servants coming, if he could apparently smell every damned man she'd ever *touched*?

"I am thirty years old, orc," she snapped at him. "You can't honestly expect a woman to stay celibate for decades on end? Gods, it's not like I was—"

She stopped there, wincing, because where had she been going with that? Yes, she'd sought pleasure and relief with men, but she'd always been very, very careful, and her primary focus at the time had always been her family, and her education. Until—until she'd ended up here, where her contract with the Fitzwalds firmly forbade any kind of male contact whatsoever. And gods, she'd never imagined how much she would miss it, or the... *possibilities* that came with it. The possibilities of her own partner, her own children, her own family...

"Ach, I do not hold this against you, pet," the orc murmured, and wait, that was his big hand, once again settling on Geva's head, tilting her face up toward him. "I only say, you are no innocent, and neither am I. So there is naught to lose in testing this, ach?"

In testing this. In his other hand still stroking up and down that swollen, oversized ridge in his trousers, while Geva blankly watched. Watched as it seemed to grow even longer, fuller, until the upper end had indeed reached the waist of his trousers. And his smooth, steady strokes just kept priming it, plumping it, until Geva caught a glimpse of glossy grey skin, peeking up above his belt, looking impossibly scandalous against his starched white shirt.

"One taste," the orc purred, as his hand slipped up to loosen his belt, and then slid the trousers' fabric downwards. Revealing more and more of that rounded, silken head, with its sliding hood of soft grey skin. With the long, thick, veined shaft beneath, growing fatter and darker as it extended downwards, until it disappeared in a swarm of thick black curls. But then below, there were those twin bulging weights, also covered over in black softness, almost as if they wanted to be touched and cradled and...

And. The orc's trousers had fully fallen to his thighs, now, and the sight of this—of this orc exposing himself, and now again *stroking* himself, in Geva's damned bedroom—was the only truth left in her frantically fraying awareness. Gods, it was big, it was ghastly, it was *gorgeous*. And there was no way it could belong to this orc, and there was absolutely no way Geva was actually *tasting* it, like he'd suggested. Not even with his other hand now petting her head again, as if she were still a favourite skittish pet. And not even with how that glossy tip was now jutting straight out toward her mouth, revealing a thick bead of white, pooling within its deep-cut slit...

"One taste," he said again, or wait, *wait*, that was her, saying these words. "A test. *One*."

And even as she winced, she didn't try taking it back, because yes, damn him, she'd said it, she'd *meant* it. And in return, there was an instant's silence, a sound that might have been an intake of breath—

And then the orc laughed. *Laughed*, making the impossible vision at his groin bob and dance before her eyes. And then his big hand on her hair gently flexed, tilting her head back... and he smoothly brought that hard, dripping head to her mouth.

Geva shuddered all over, her eyes wildly fluttering, as a low, hoarse moan dragged from her throat. Because gods, it had been so, *so* long. And the feel of smooth, virile, hungry male flesh against her lips was a deep, dark thrill she'd very nearly forgotten...

And the taste. Good gods above, the *taste*, it was silky and shockingly sweet. Like syrup, like honey, like the most succulent fruit she'd ever tasted in her life, sparkling and dancing across her tongue, and—

But then, without warning, the orc drew away. Keeping Geva's head in place with his hand, while that glossy head hovered before her eyes, another thick bead of that sweetness slowly pooling in its deep slit.

"So, poppet?" came the orc's voice, and when Geva darted a desperate, wide-eyed glance up, he was looking entirely unaffected, but for perhaps a very faint flush in his grey cheeks. "Shall you be able to bear this, then? For one moon?"

Geva's face felt shamefully sweaty and hot, her thoughts strange and stilted, and her tongue had brushed against her lips, almost as if seeking more. And the orc was watching her, and looking unmistakably *amused* again, his thick brows rising as he waited for her answer.

"I—I suppose," Geva managed, with as much dignity as she could muster, even as her betraying eyes darted back toward the all-consuming sight before her. A sight that was slightly bobbing as it oozed out more, as that pearly white pooled ever thicker, until it dropped into a dangling, growing, glistening strand...

"Good," the orc murmured, as that big hand resumed petting her hair, as if comforting her in her defeat. "Now, mayhap, as a token of your goodwill—as a sign of our new bond—you might wish to drink your first good fill of me, ach?"

Oh. Oh, hell. And he was still watching her, still waiting for her answer, still with that damned amusement in his eyes. And she was not giving this duplicitous bastard an answer, she was *not*...

But all the same, she was... nodding. Nodding, again saying yes—*gods*, yes—as she leaned toward him again, closer, closer. Her tongue just brushing out, until—

Her moan was audible this time, her tongue settling hungry and eager against that slick pulsing slit, and the infuriating orc above her let out a low, indulgent chuckle, even as he shifted a little closer. Easing that smooth slick head further into her mouth, parting her lips wider around it, and she was not truly doing this, was she truly doing this...

But oh, that taste, that impossible sweetness, the feel of such solid powerful male, prodding hard and hungry *inside* her. And with that, the distant, glimmering certainty that he must want this, he *had* to want this, and his other hand had even dropped to stroke the rest of his exposed length, to nestle his silken head a little deeper into her opened mouth.

"Ach, I shall even make this easy for you, my sweet," he purred, as that hand kept stroking, so easy and familiar on that massive veined shaft, jutting out from between her lips. "You only keep a good latch upon me, and keep suckling, ach?"

Geva's distant disbelief was rising again, but she was somehow, again, obliging. *Agreeing.* Sucking harder, nudging her hungry tongue against that pulsing slit, while the orc gave a low hiss, and stroked faster. His long-lashed eyes gone hooded as he watched, his head tilting slightly back, and his other hand tipped Geva's head further back, too. Making sure he could still see her, see himself stuck in her sucking mouth...

"Good, stubborn poppet," he breathed. "So good, to witness you so eager and hungry upon me. Almost there, stay open for me, swallow for me, *ach*—"

With that, the heft in Geva's mouth swelled, shuddered, shook—and then released. Surging out into her mouth with stream after stream of hot, decadent sweetness, while she frantically, furiously swallowed. Dragging it down in deep, desperate gulps, drinking like it was pure priceless nectar, like it was truly a favour, a gift...

And for a strange, staggering instant, as she kept swallowing, staring up at the orc's intently watching face, there was only pleasure, and satisfaction, and peace. She'd shown him, surely she'd pleased him, she'd proven their bond, and finally made everything right between them. Made everything... *good.* And oh, the way he was looking back down at her, those hooded eyes glimmering with such warm, wicked *pride.*

"You drink it all up, poppet," he murmured, patting her cheek. "And then you suck your orc clean, ach?"

Geva twitched a shy, furtive little nod, as she obediently drew out the last of that succulent sweetness, swirling her tongue against his smooth head, making sure she'd caught every last drop—until the orc nodded too, and slowly slid his softened length out of her mouth. But not quite all the way, just holding it there against her swollen wet lips. Wanting to see this, surely, wanting her to press him another soft, open-mouthed kiss before he finally drew away.

"Very good," he said, with a wry, sharp-toothed grin, as he tucked himself back into his trousers. "I should have known you would welcome this, my prickly pet. The sharpest mouths are always the sweetest, ach?"

The soft, curling warmth had strangely shivered, stilled—and for a long, hurtling instant, Geva blinked up at the orc's face, at the laughter in his eyes. The... the mockery. The *triumph.*

It felt like something ice-cold had been dumped over her, even through her multiple layers of clothing, and a hard, bitter shudder wrenched up her spine. What... what the hell. Why had she just done that. Why had she just given this orc that. He'd made his lack of attraction to her very clear, hadn't he? So this had surely only been a—a game to him. A challenge. A *conquest.*

I should have known you would welcome this. The sharpest mouths are always the sweetest.

And surely—another frigid-feeling shudder ripped up Geva's spine—this had even been retaliation. She'd called him names, she'd called his people's intimate practices absurd, outrageous, obscene... so in return, he'd turned around and watched her eat her words.

You do not believe a proud, prim schoolmarm like you could welcome an orc's sweet seed down her throat?

Geva's now-full stomach had begun painfully churning, her gaze dropping to her multiple layers of skirts, while her trembling, tingling hands dragged against her hot face. Gods, what had come over her. Why had she agreed to any of this. What in all the devils' unholy curses had possessed her to suck off an orc, after he'd insulted her, threatened her, destroyed her career, and ruined her entire *life*?! And now she was stuck with him, stuck working for him, for her very *survival*. And what was left, how could she possibly move forward with this, what had she *done*...

"Now, woman," came the orc's voice above her, a little rough. "We ought to leave, you ken? Before these fool men come to seek you again?"

Right, oh gods, *right*, because Geva was still just sitting here in her bedroom with an orc. Waiting to be discovered and ruined even more, and if the servants came back, would they know what she'd just done, oh gods, oh gods...

She belatedly lurched to her feet, angling toward the door, but—gods curse it—she somehow tripped over her damned overstuffed satchel. And once again she pitched forward, flailing her arms, flying straight toward the huge, horrible orc.

But of course the bastard was ready and waiting, easily catching her against him, folding her into his big solid chest. And for a choked, miserable breath, there was the sudden urge to stay there, to cling to him, to beg and shout at him until her throat was raw. Why had he done this, how could he be so cruel, how could one single awful creature have so systematically, single-handedly destroyed her entire *life*?!

"Careful, poppet," said the orc, with a cool lightness that scraped and strained against Geva's heaving stomach. "Are you always this skittish, to be falling over your own feet?"

He was mocking her again, laughing at her again, and Geva furiously shoved away from him, and grabbed unseeing for her satchel. And it was only once she'd turned her back to him, her satchel clutched to her chest, that she could find her voice again, find words to say in the abject, clawing misery.

"One month," she choked. "One month, orc, and then I never, ever want to see you *again!*"

And before he could reply, she stumbled toward the door, and rushed out into the waiting darkness, alone.

8

———————

Geva only made it halfway down the back stairs before she'd slowed to a stop, squeezing her eyes shut, gripping her satchel tighter to her chest.

She had no idea where she was going. No idea where the other servants might be. No idea how she could possibly leave here without raising suspicion, without being seen or caught or...

"Ach, this way is good," cut in the orc's low voice behind her. "I ken those other humans have all gone to the wine-cellar, and there are no more within scenting distance."

Right. So *convenient*, that this horrid bastard could apparently only smell people when it suited him, but Geva nodded, and began moving again. Keeping her gaze straight ahead as she crept down the stairs, and out the servants' side door, into the bright afternoon sunlight.

One month, her whirling thoughts repeated, as she drew in deep, shuddering breaths of fresh cool air. She would put up with this foul snake for one month, and then leave this cursed continent behind forever.

"This way," the orc said, as he brushed past Geva, and strode toward the small patch of overgrown forest—likely once a garden—that surrounded the Fitzwalds' house. "We ought to stay hidden until we are well past the village, ach?"

Geva gave another grudging nod that he couldn't see, and hurried to catch up to his big striding form. "And then where?" she made herself ask, her stiff voice still not her own. "Southwest, you said?"

"Ach," he replied, giving a curt nod over his shoulder as he slipped into the dense line of trees. "It shall take five more days on foot, I ken, to reach Orc Mountain."

Wait. Geva's mouth fell open, and she stumbled to a halt, just within the edge of the forest. "Orc Mountain?" she echoed, her voice shrill. "You're taking me to *Orc Mountain*?!"

A flare of piercing, ice-cold fear flashed up her spine, because this damned devious orc had *not* said anything about Orc Mountain... had he? And while Geva had always attempted to ignore the worst rumours about the orcs, the terrifying tales were already here, swirling through her thoughts with an alarming vividness they'd never carried before. Orc Mountain was a huge, horrifying death-trap, a labyrinth of inescapable tunnels and mines, brewing filth and blight and disease. And of course, it was overrun by countless packs of greedy, violent, slavering orcs, desperate for gold and power and sons.

And once a woman entered Orc Mountain, she would never come out again. *Never.*

"Ach, Orc Mountain," the orc was saying, frowning at Geva over his shoulder. "I told you I travel to the home of my kin, ach? Where else do you ken this should be?"

Geva's mouth was opening and closing, her eyes goggling at his back. "Well—why would *you* assume any woman would volunteer to go to Orc Mountain?" she spluttered. "You can't honestly think I want to risk my *life* for this job? Or that I want to risk getting snatched away from you by some *other* orc who *does* want a son, and then find myself pregnant and trapped in Orc Mountain forever?!"

The orc whirled fully around to glare at her, clearly about

to respond in kind—but then, to her vague surprise, he winced, and glanced away. "Your life shall not be forfeit," he said flatly. "And you shall not be trapped or stolen, or filled with a son. I told you, you shall bear *my* scent, and this shall keep you *safe*. So long as you scent of me, no other orc shall touch you."

Oh. Geva still felt cold and shivery all over, her eyes searching the orc's set face. "But how can you be sure," she managed. "There's only one of you, and likely thousands of them, and—"

She couldn't finish, biting her lip, and before her the orc visibly exhaled, his shoulders sagging. "There is no need to fear, woman," he said, his voice low. "I cannot swear we will face no danger amidst this, but I shall do all within my power to keep you safe. I swear this to you."

His sharp-taloned hand was on his sword-hilt again, flexing with genuine-looking purpose. And Geva found herself blinking at that, and then up at his eyes. At their sudden, surprising determination, dark and distant and strangely unsettling. Suggesting that... this meant something to him. Something important.

"You'll forgive me if I remain skeptical," she replied, her voice still damnably weak. "I mean, you've already threatened to kill me yourself once today, remember?"

The orc's eyes briefly dropped to Geva's throat, while something she couldn't read passed across his face—but then he spun away again, striding deeper into the trees. "I always begin with this threat," he said, over his shoulder. "It makes the work far faster, you ken. Had it gone as I meant today, I would have then bought your silence with some foolish trinket, and we should all now be content."

Wait, really?! Good gods, this utter *cretin*, and Geva glared at his diminishing back, at that huge black cloak billowing out behind him. At where—she blinked—the cloak whirled sideways, and then upwards, into the low branches of a nearby tree. And when he leapt down again, he was now in possession of a huge, heavy-looking leather pack, and—an apple?

"Here," he told Geva, holding out the apple, which he'd apparently stabbed onto his *claw*. "We have much ground to cover before nightfall, ach?"

Geva eyed the apple for an uneasy instant, but then gingerly plucked it off his claw, and took a careful bite. Earning a short, approving grunt from the orc, who then spun and strode off again. Leaving her to stumble along behind him on a narrow but serviceable path, eating her apple, while also trying in vain to keep her voluminous skirts out of the surrounding greenery.

But the apple was helping, Geva could admit, and so was the fresh air, and the quiet forest all around—and maybe, maybe even that fervent-sounding promise of his. *I shall do all within my power to keep you safe.* And she found her breaths steadily coming deeper as she walked, her frazzled thoughts settling back into a grim, resigned determination.

She was looking forward. Doing the next thing. Leaving the Fitzwalds, taking on a new job, and then sailing across the sea. And all she had to do—her eyes narrowed at his steadily striding bulk ahead—was pretend to care for this belligerent orc. For one month. At Orc Mountain.

And the better job she did of it, the more he would pay.

"So if I'm pretending to be your... *mate*," she finally said to his back, her voice unnaturally loud in the silence, "perhaps I should know a little more about you?"

The orc's shoulders instantly stiffened beneath his pack, and he shot a brief, disapproving frown over his shoulder. "Such as?"

Geva bit back her sigh, and gave an all-consuming wave of her hand. "Your background?" she replied testily. "Your family? Your highly questionable life choices? Why you're returning to your home? Gods, even your *name*?"

She felt her face flushing as she spoke, because yes, indeed, she'd sucked him off without even knowing his damned *name*—and she could see his steps faltering, his hand dragging through his hair, as his stiff shoulders fell, and rose, and fell again.

"I am... Rathgarr," he said, quiet. "Of Clan Ash-Kai."

Rathgarr, of Clan Ash-Kai. The name clearly from another language, the *R*s rolling with fluid ease in his smooth, deep voice. Enough that Geva felt a highly unwelcome dip in her belly, her throat swallowing hard, her response rising all on its own.

"I'm Geva," she said, allowing her parents' familiar accent to slip into her voice. "Geva Okoro."

The orc—Rathgarr—jerked a nod, his eyes angling briefly over his shoulder toward her. And for an instant, Geva almost thought he might offer a genuine reply. Might acknowledge, perhaps, that they had this in common. Raised speaking another tongue, hearing tales of another world...

But instead the orc—*Rathgarr*—just kept walking, his steps swift, his face held straight ahead. Not even making an attempt at answering any of her other questions, and Geva drew in a deep, fortifying breath, let it out. One month, and then the sea.

"Perhaps you could tell me more about Orc Mountain, then?" she asked, as steadily as she could. "What is it like? Is it really as awful as all the tales say?"

But Rathgarr didn't even look at her this time, and if she wasn't mistaken, he was walking faster, too. "It is a mountain," he said flatly. "With orcs inside it."

Well, that wasn't promising, and neither was the way he suddenly veered sideways off the path, straight into the thick brush. And Geva doubtfully watched him grow smaller and smaller before she finally gritted her teeth, clutched up her skirts, and picked her way after him through the long grasses and bushes. Which were rapidly thinning again, giving way to—

Oh. A road. The main road leading southwest, perhaps.

And one that was in heavy use, judging by the steady stream of horses, carts, and foot travellers passing by.

"You really mean to travel on the *open road*?" Geva asked, her voice too sharp. "Is that really advisable? Or... *safe*, for an orc?"

Rathgarr shot her a baleful look before striding off again, straight toward the road's dirt-packed edge. "It shall never be safe, if no orc does this," he snapped back. "Do *you* wish to toil through brush and muck for all these next five days?"

Geva couldn't help a pained glance down toward her already-compromised skirts, and then she huffed an exasperated sigh, and hurried to catch up again. Earning a mocking grunt from Rathgarr as she fell into step beside him, though she valiantly kept her chin lifted, her gaze fixed straight ahead.

However, her doubts about this mode of travel soon proved to be entirely justified, because their presence caused an almost instantaneous response from their fellow travellers on the road. Nearly all of them staring stunned and slack-jawed toward Geva and Rathgarr, and several already muttering, or pointing, or both.

"Is that an *orc*?" an approaching man demanded in a shrill, scandalized voice. "With a *woman*? Is that even *allowed*?!"

"Most certainly not," sniffed his companion, an older woman with unfriendly eyes. "He's likely kidnapped her. Ought to be reported to the authorities."

Geva's face already felt painfully hot, her uneasy eyes glancing sideways toward Rathgarr. Who was still staring straight ahead, his jaw taut, his hand now clenched to his sword-hilt. "Pay them no heed," he muttered, under his breath. "Most of them only stare, and prattle thus."

Most of them? Geva's previous irritation toward him was rapidly fading, in favour of sheer incredulous outrage—that peace-treaty *was* still in place, wasn't it?—when from up ahead came the distinct sound of a high-pitched yelp. "It's an orc!" squealed a young woman, while clutching for dear life to a second woman beside her. "With a victim! He's coerced her! *Kidnapped* her!"

And despite Rathgarr's order from only a moment before, Geva could feel his big body stiffening beside her, his breath hissing out in a sound much like a growl. A sentiment she rather found herself sharing, to the point where she glared straight back toward the women, her gaze steady and cold, until they finally averted their eyes, and quickly scurried past.

Next came an older couple, who cringed away as they stared between Rathgarr and Geva, while also grumbling loudly about foul, devious orc kidnappers. And this time, before Geva had quite realized it, she'd slipped her hand around Rathgarr's huge bicep, and flashed the couple a bright smile, together with a careless, friendly wave.

The couple instantly fell silent, and the look of pure aghast shock on their faces offered some degree of grim entertainment, if nothing else. And if Geva wasn't mistaken, Rathgarr had heaved a slow, relieved-sounding exhale—and then even crooked his arm toward her a little. As if instead of a belligerent thief on the run to Orc Mountain, he was an upright, well-mannered man about town, politely escorting his lady to some respectable, mutually-agreed-upon engagement.

So Geva kept holding on to him, greeting the gawking passersby with smiles, waves, and even a few knowing winks. And when she handed Rathgarr her satchel, thereby freeing up her other hand for additional clinging and waving, he still didn't protest or complain. If anything, his stiff arm had seemed to relax beneath her death-grip, and his occasional glances down toward her had begun to look reluctantly amused.

"Already working for your coin, poppet?" he murmured, his brow arching with something that might have been contempt—but Geva purposely ignored it, and gaily waved at a cluster of staring farmhands in a passing wagon. Eliciting the now-familiar expressions of shock, awe, and disbelief, and yet more stunned, blessed silence.

"Yes, I am," she said back, under her breath. "What, would you rather I stop? Did you *prefer* being called a cruel and coercive kidnapper?"

Rathgarr huffed an unintelligible reply, but didn't comment again. Not even once the sky had begun darkening, to the point where he might readily be mistaken for a very large man, rather than an orc. And while Geva should probably have stopped clinging to him, she couldn't deny that his warm shifting strength was oddly comforting in the deepening blackness, especially once she could no longer make out the faces of the various strangers passing by.

"There is an inn just up ahead," Rathgarr finally said, as he fished in his pouch for something—a coin—and pressed it into Geva's hand. "Go eat a hot meal, and hire a room, ach? And order a bath, also."

Geva was decidedly hungry and weary after so much walking, enough that it took a moment to digest what he'd said. He was offering her accommodation overnight... at an *inn*? He wasn't demanding she camp out on a hard forest floor, with gods knew how many insects and vermin? She could have a hot meal, and a *bath*?

"But—what about you?" she blurted out, without thinking. "Where will you stay?"

There was an instant's silence, followed by a low, dissatisfied growl. "I shall stay at the inn," his curt voice replied. "In the room I shall *pay* for."

But Geva's heart was pounding again, her thoughts twisting back to those moments in her bedroom at the Fitzwalds'. When he'd so easily sparked her pleasure, and then so cruelly mocked her. And now she needed to spend an entire night alone with him, in a small bedroom? *Sleeping* with him?

"Could we have two rooms, then?" she ventured, before she could stop it. "Or two beds, at least?"

The question rang between them for an instant, and far too late, Geva heard the implied insult in her words. Like she, too, couldn't bear the thought of sharing a space with an orc. Like she had more in common with all those muttering, mocking travellers than she'd wanted to admit...

But before she could open her mouth, take it back, Rathgarr was growling again, even deeper and more vicious than before. "No, *human*," he hissed, his voice clipped and contemptuous. "Not only do I pay good coin for this room, but I pay good coin for *you*, also. And I shall *have* what I have *paid* for!"

With that deeply alarming statement, he spun off, and stalked away toward the trees—and then whirled around again, his face unreadable in the darkness.

"Go, and gain this room," he ordered. "And when I come to you, you shall be ready."

9

———

All too soon, Geva found herself alone in a small, lamplit bedroom, pacing in agitated circles around a steaming steel washtub.

It was a clean, adequately furnished room, and the process of reserving it—along with eating a hot meal in the inn's dining-room—had proven thankfully straightforward. But Geva had found herself entirely unable to enjoy any of it, amidst the churning miasma of guilt, and fear, and twisting, towering apprehension.

Go, and gain our room, Rathgarr had ordered her. *And when I come to you, you shall be ready.*

And Geva had obeyed, or at least, partly obeyed. She'd lit the candle, inspected the room, ordered the bath, and even turned down the blankets on the bed. The single, disconcertingly small bed, which looked far too tiny for two average-sized humans, let alone a tall, shapely woman and a truly massive orc.

But she'd made herself keep going, doing the next thing. Kicking off her boots, and then peeling off almost all the layers of clothing she'd been wearing, and hanging them neatly away in the wardrobe. And finally, after another moment's warring with herself, she'd even taken down her tightly bound hair, shaking out her masses of coiled black curls around her head.

It left her standing in the room bare-footed, bare-headed, clad in only a flimsy, close-fitting white shift. And while the obvious next step was to take advantage of the waiting bath, she couldn't seem to muster the will to undress any further. To face the near-certain possibility of Rathgarr walking in, and seeing... *everything*.

And truly, where *was* Rathgarr, anyway? A considerable amount of time had passed since they'd parted, and he'd meant he would meet her here... hadn't he? Or, had he perhaps reflected on her earlier insult, and then decided to stay away longer, as some kind of admonition, or retaliation? And gods, perhaps she even deserved it, because after today's experiences on the road, there was no doubt that staying at an inn was a fraught prospect, for an orc. One that could result in suspicion, or ridicule, or perhaps even violence, for the grave sin of being an orc who dared to exist, in public.

Geva groaned aloud and paced faster, dragging her shaky hands down her face. No. No. She couldn't allow her own judgement to become clouded with sympathy, with guilt, with... *commiseration*. By all possible measures, Rathgarr had still been cruel, and arrogant, and selfish. A shameless brazen *thief*, who'd destroyed her entire life in a single damned day. And now he was making her wait for him, ready herself for him, so he could—

A sound. From behind her. And when Geva whirled around to look, the room's heavy oaken door was swinging open—and behind it stood a huge, hooded figure, its shoulders nearly filling the entire doorway, its face shrouded in shadow.

Geva yelped, twitched, attempted to lurch backwards—but then tripped over something solid and unyielding. The bath, the gods-damned devils-cursed *bath*, and her body was already falling, her arms helplessly whirling behind her, no, *no*—

And even as she splashed backwards into the hot steaming

water, something... caught her. Something warm and alive and powerful, its strength circling around her back and her hips. Cradling her with astonishing care, preventing any part of her from hitting the basin's hard steel edge.

"What the—" Geva began, spluttering and flailing against it, against the shock of the sudden liquid heat—but then she met its eyes. *His* eyes. Rathgarr.

The relief swarmed in a dizzying rush, and she felt herself sagging into the heat, into... his arms. His sturdy, massive arms, still curved around her, holding her strong and safe. And now she was soaking wet, damn it, and Rathgarr had to be half-soaked too—but in this baffling, ludicrous instant, Geva could only seem to stare at his face, at his intent, long-lashed eyes. At how—unlike hers—they weren't a deep brown, but a pure, full, unbroken black. So oddly, inexplicably compelling, and she felt herself inhaling, drinking up a rich, familiar sweetness, as he came closer, closer, his parted mouth only a breath away from hers...

But then his eyes squeezed shut, blocking her out—and suddenly he yanked up and backwards, away, as Geva flailed too, scrambling up to her feet. And when the world settled again, she was standing knee-deep and dripping-wet in the bath, while Rathgarr was pressed back against the closed door, his eyes glittering, his claws digging into the dark wood.

"Truly, woman?" he demanded, though his voice sounded hoarse. "You cannot stand next to a *bath* without falling in?"

Geva grimaced, but couldn't seem to move, let alone reply—especially when Rathgarr's glinting eyes dropped, sweeping down her wet, dripping body. Catching on where— she blanched as she followed his gaze—her thin white shift was now fully transparent, and clinging to her like a pale, useless second skin. Blatantly displaying her heavy breasts with their brown nipples, the soft roundness of her belly below, the full strength of her thighs, the hint of darkness between...

"Damn it," Geva gulped, as she clamped her arms over her too-exposed chest. "You could have knocked!"

Rathgarr's eyes guiltily darted back up to her face, his brows furrowing. "I *paid* for this room," he snapped back. "And I told you to be ready for me!"

His gaze again flicked downwards, now holding with baleful disapproval on her wet shift, as if it were somehow offensive to his eyes. And suddenly his words from earlier that day were ringing, echoing with peculiar, powerful meaning through Geva's stunned, stilted thoughts.

You shall need to be bared, and bathed all over in my fresh seed.

And damn it, this was part of her *job*. It was what she'd signed up for, her next step. One month, and then the sea.

So before she could think better of it, her shaky hands clutched for her wet shift. Yanking it up, and off over her head, and then tossing it aside. Leaving herself fully exposed, ready and waiting, for this orc's watching, judging eyes.

And oh, gods, he was watching. His intent, glittering gaze sweeping up, and down, and up again. Catching on the halo of her curly black hair, and then dropping to her full breasts, the ample curves of her belly and hips, the dark patch of hair at her groin. And then back up to her breasts again, lingering on her dark nipples, on how they were jutting out straight toward him...

Geva's heart was hammering in her chest, but she bit her lip and kept fighting through it, holding herself still, her head high. Waiting, waiting, as Rathgarr's throat bobbed, his black tongue brushing against his parted lips. As his big clawed hand surreptitiously slid over, toward... toward where there was a highly visible bulge, swelling beneath his tight-looking trousers.

Wait. *Wait.* As if... as if he *wanted* this?

The sudden awareness of it—the certainty of it—felt almost dizzying, enough that Geva had to briefly close her eyes, gulp down deep breaths of the humid air. No. No. This was surely just about the job. About his scent. Right?

"So?" she made herself say, her voice far too thick. "How... how do we do this?"

Rathgarr's eyes snapped back up to her face, and then quickly away again, fixing on something behind her. While his hand rubbed at his mouth, his claws out, his shoulders sagging.

"You are sure," he abruptly said. "You truly wish to do this? With my seed?"

Oh. He was... asking? He was still *asking*, even after all this, after she'd gone and fallen into the damned bath. And suddenly, somehow, that was the most important thing, the only thing—

"Yes," Geva replied, on a wavering exhale. "I'm sure."

Rathgarr nodded, his hand still rubbing at his mouth, his eyes still fixed intently beyond her. "Ach, then," he said stiffly, as he lurched sideways, and grasped an empty ewer from the nearby washstand. "Then mayhap—mayhap I could spill my seed into this, for your use."

Into this, for your use. Geva fought back the sudden, strangest urge to laugh, because gods, the vision of that was so ludicrous, so absurd, so... *scandalous.* He would empty himself into that, while she watched? And then he would give it to her... and she would pour it out over herself, while *he* watched. She would rub it into her skin, paint herself with it, while he just stood there, and...

"That's—ridiculous," she replied, her voice still not her own. "There must be... an easier way."

An easier way. Gods, what was she even saying, because the easy way earlier today had been him just pumping out straight into her mouth. And yes, yes, he'd followed that, his throat again bobbing, his hand setting the ewer back down with a too-loud *thunk.*

"Ach," he said, his voice low. "Then mayhap... you keep standing thus in this bath. Whilst I..."

He didn't finish, but his meaning seemed clear enough, at least. So Geva nodded, and watched, and waited, as Rathgarr's big hands swung his cloak backwards, out of the way over his shoulders, and then dropped to his belt. Unbuckling it in deft, familiar movements, and then—aided by the weight of the sword still at his side—dropping the loose trousers down to his hips.

And showing—damn. That. That huge, veined heft at his groin, bobbing out long and hungry toward Geva's bared body, and already dripping with thick succulent white.

She stared at it for a stunned, stuttering instant, while a soft, husky moan whispered from her throat. Because oh, *oh*, his hand was already moving to touch it, his big fingers circling its plump base with cool, practiced ease. And then he began slowly sliding up and down, easing that slick head out from beneath its grey hood, its deep slit oozing out even more of that pearly white sweetness...

"You are yet... sure, woman," his hoarse voice said, from somewhere very far away. "You wish to scent of me."

Asking, again. And as unthinkable as it was—as indefensible as it was—Geva felt herself fervently nodding, and biting her lip. Yes. Yes, she wanted this. Wanted to scent of him. Wanted to watch him stroking himself like that. Wanted to see where this went, to again find that place that had so briefly felt so good, so *right*, between them. The place—had it only been earlier that day?—where he'd been so focused, so hungry, his eyes sparkling with such wicked, wild pride...

"Good," he murmured, as his hand kept sliding, so easy, so smooth, pumping out an even thicker bead of white. "If you wish it done faster, then"—he cleared his throat—"mayhap you shall show off those plump teats for me, ach, poppet?"

What? Geva stared at him, momentarily snapped from the heat, from the rising shameful longing—but Rathgarr just raised a taunting brow at her, and then trailed his eyes downwards. Purposefully this time, lingering with undeniable appreciation on her full breasts, on her brazenly peaked nipples. His hand on his leaking cock sliding even faster as he looked, and oh, Geva was *not* considering this, not raising a shaky finger to brush against one of those rigid, straining peaks...

But oh, she was, she *had*. And Rathgarr's breath audibly caught, his hooded eyes fixed to the sight—and somehow, she did it again. Brushing her fingers against it, feeling her own breath catch at the sensation of it, at the way his watching eyes fluttered. And now her other hand was sliding up, too, and carefully stroking around the full, fleshy weight of the other side. Perhaps even lifting it up for him, wanting him to look...

And hell, yes, he was looking. His eyes focused, glimmering, as he watched her hands gaining more purpose, fondling, clutching, caressing. His own hand stroking even faster, smoother, hungrier—until that steadily thickening bead of white finally burst, and fell. Now dangling from his slit in a glossy, lengthening string, swinging back and forth as he stroked.

It was quite possibly the most enthralling sight Geva had ever seen in her *life*, and she heard another helpless moan escaping her parted lips—and then fraying as he stepped closer. His strong thighs straddling wide over the basin, his eyes still fixed to her fervently caressing hands. As his own hand kept pumping, that dangling swinging string now almost reaching the steaming water beneath them...

"Ready yourself," he hissed, hot and rumbling in his throat. "Present them to me."

Geva couldn't even pretend not to know what he meant, and she moaned again as she nodded, cupping her breasts with both hands, holding them out for his viewing, for his approval, for his *use*. For the way he tilted his head back, his breath hitching into a hard, husky growl—

And then his hips bucked, and that strength in his hand... *fired*. Spraying out stream after stream of thick fragrant white, catching and spattering not only across Geva's bared, proffered breasts, but also across her collarbones, her shoulders, her belly. It felt strange and sticky and warm against her skin, and oh, the sight of it still jetting from him, spewing out of that deep slit, was doing powerful, impossible things in her groin. Twisting, tightening, drawing his hooded eyes...

"Address that," he breathed, almost inaudible, as the spurting from his heft gradually slowed, spattering with far weaker intensity against her thighs and knees. "Whilst rubbing in my good seed. This shall... strengthen our scent. Deepen it."

The words sounded laboured, his nostrils flaring, his tongue sweeping over his lips. And Geva was nodding, quick and furtive, sliding down her sticky hand toward where she felt so swollen, so desperately hungry, so—

"Wait," she gasped, as a distant trickle of awareness edged into her thoughts, just in time. "I can't. I'm—"

She held out her sticky, shaky hand toward him, showing him how it was coated with fresh, dripping white seed. With the certain risk of his *son*, damn it. And she could see the awareness flashing through his eyes too, chased by a brief, unmistakable relief.

"Ach," he breathed, squeezing his eyes shut. "No. Even if you wash it off, some may yet remain. Thus—"

"Then... you do it," Geva heard herself whisper, impossible, *appalling*. But she was already stepping closer toward him in the basin, almost near enough to touch... and her sticky, shivering fingers had brushed at his wrist, above his dry hand. Feeling how it shifted forward, into her touch. Wanting this.

And gods, she wanted it too, the furious longing spinning so strong it was consuming all sense, all reason. And when Rathgarr's eyes flicked open again, hot and blazing on hers, he was right there with her, his head jerking a hard nod, his long black tongue again brushing his parted lips.

So Geva guided that big, warm, willing hand toward her, until those fingers nudged against the dark hair between her thighs. Their touch soft and careful—he'd even drawn his claws back in—and she shifted her stance a little wider, easing him lower. Until his warm solid palm was pressed against the curve of her, his big fingers slipping willingly, almost eagerly, beneath.

Oh, it was good, it was that perfect combination of hard pressure and teasing gentleness, and Geva's eyes fluttered, her head arching back, as she pressed him closer. As her audacious other hand slid back up to her spattered-wet breast, streaking the seed against it, just as he'd asked.

That was another growl from his throat, rasping and breathless, his ravenous eyes sweeping between Geva's hand stroking her seed-smeared breasts, and his own hand seeking between her legs. His palm grinding harder, his fingers delving deeper, as if wanting to sink inside...

"Clever thinking, poppet," he breathed, his voice catching. "This shall help, also. With the scent."

Yes, yes, of course, that made perfect sense—and Geva felt herself almost preening as she rapidly nodded, circling his palm a little tighter against her, shuddering out more whirling pleasure. And then, in another unthinkable flash of daring, she released her grip on his wrist, in favour of smearing both hands against her sticky breasts.

Rathgarr hissed another low, approving growl, and his hard palm kept circling, with the exact same speed and pressure she'd shown him. Even as those fingers teased lower, closer, until one settled just *there*, nudging light and tentative at first, but slowly sinking, deepening...

Geva's gasp was more like a shout, her hot, inflamed body frantically clamping against his thick, steady, beautiful invasion. Against him inside her, sinking even deeper, oh, oh...

Her own hands faltered, lost in the impossible tightening tension between her legs—but then they twitched, and began caressing even faster, rubbing him in all over. Smoothing over her slick breasts, slipping down to her belly and thighs, and even up to her neck and shoulders. And in return, it was as though he couldn't decide where to look, his eyes darting between his hand against her crease, her hands streaking in his seed, her breasts now fully coated in shiny sweetness, dripping white from her peaked nipples...

"Ach, thus," Rathgarr breathed, heated and low. "Cover yourself in me. Make yourself *reek* of me, whilst you tremble and *whimper* upon my touch. Ach, thus, woman, *ach*—"

Oh hell, that was it, that was *it*—and Geva's coiling pleasure sparked, and exploded. Flashing and flaring through her groin in pulse after desperate pulse, clamping in furious rhythmic clutches against that finger sunk so deep inside her. Sweeping away all her vision, all her breath, leaving only arching wheeling sensation, devouring her, destroying her...

And wait, wait, there was *more*. More of that shocking spattering sweetness, streaking warm across her breasts and her belly. Because oh, Rathgarr's other hand was *still* pumping his bared length, and he was again spurting out, painting her with yet more thick strings of fresh white. Not nearly as strong as before, but still there, still hers, *hers*.

This time, Geva's hand found it, streaked it wide—and then brought it to her mouth. Slipping her dripping-wet fingers between her swollen-feeling lips, and tasting it. So sweet, so succulent, even richer than before. And oh, he liked it, he wanted it, his eyes wide and arrested as he watched, as his hand between her legs kept stroking, caressing up and down her slick crease with an almost proprietary gentleness. Almost as if he were petting her, approving of her, *rewarding* her, *oh*—

But then, without warning, he was—*gone*. Gone, whipping out of her, away from her, whirling around so fast his cloak flew in a sweeping black arc behind him. Almost catching against where Geva was still standing there, alone and gasping and untouched in the bath, but for the mess of sweet-scented stickiness covering her, and her own finger still caught in her mouth.

Oh. She dropped the finger, and felt herself blinking and

biting her lip, her gaze darting up and down Rathgarr's back beneath his cloak. His huge, heaving back, gone forbidding, distant, cold again.

"That ought to be enough for now," he said, the words quick, clipped. "You may bathe now."

Right. A stark, bitter chill was snaking up Geva's spine, tangled with a strange, stilted awareness. Right. *Right.* To him, this had only been about... *that.* About the scent. The job. And that was all.

And as she was still digesting that, standing there in the chilly humiliating misery, Rathgarr lurched away, toward the door. He was leaving—leaving?!—and Geva couldn't choke back the yelp in her throat, the way her still-sticky hand reached out after him.

"Where—are you going?" she stammered at his stiff back. "You're not—*leaving*?"

But Rathgarr didn't turn around, didn't even glance toward her. And his big hand—the same hand that had just touched her, had been *inside* her—had already grasped for the latch, and yanked the door open.

"Ach," he said, his voice hard. "Our work here is done for the night, and you did not wish to share a bed with an orc, ach? I shall meet you again come morning."

And with that, he strode out the door, and slammed it shut behind him.

10

———

Geva barely slept that night.

It was as though the previously innocuous inn had turned into something dark and menacing, even with the room's heavy door firmly latched, and the lamp still flickering a soft light onto the solid wood walls. And every time she heard a sound in the corridor, her heart leapt in her chest, her ears straining to listen, her eyes fixed on the door.

But it never opened. Rathgarr was gone. Until morning, he'd said.

And gods, why did she even care? Why had she even gotten drawn into that again, allowed herself to trust him again, to *want* him again? He was a cruel, selfish, calculating *crook*, and even if he'd wanted that pleasure with her—or even *enjoyed* it, damn it—that certainly didn't change the truth of it in the slightest.

This was just a job. Just her next step. And Geva needed to keep her distance, keep her focus on her goal. One month, and then the sea.

But it was only cold comfort, and the shivery memories of that fierce, forbidden pleasure kept swinging out, with no logic or warning. The way Rathgarr's hungry, swollen heft had sprayed those streams of sweet seed. The way his finger had delved so deep inside her. The way he'd touched her exactly how she'd shown him, thereby proving himself a more attentive lover than most of the human men who'd shared her bed. An orc. A cold, calculating *criminal*, who otherwise couldn't care less how she felt, or what she wanted.

She only fell asleep after telling herself what felt like a dozen tales, silently reciting them line by line while she clutched at the blanket, and squeezed her eyes shut. The tale of the days when the squirrels ran rampant over the earth. The time when the lizard survived a great flood. The story of the hero who transformed into a shaggy dog and tricked everyone he knew, but for his quick, clever wife.

But even once sleep finally came, wakefulness returned far too soon. And with it, the unmistakable, alarming sound of someone just outside the room's door. Someone jiggling at the latch—lifting it up from the outside—before swinging the door wide open.

Geva yelped and flailed up in bed, yanking the blanket to her neck—but of course, it was only him. Rathgarr. Still dressed in the clothes he'd worn the night before, but—she blinked—they were now far filthier than before, with multiple green and brown streaks across his previously pristine white tunic. And wait, did he have a *black eye*?

"Did you get into a fight?" Geva's voice demanded, before she could possibly stop it, and in return Rathgarr shot her a narrow, contemptuous look, and slammed the door shut behind him. And then he strode over toward her, and promptly began yanking off his clothes, tossing them onto the bed.

Geva kept staring blankly up at him, watching as he stripped off his fur, and then his hooded cloak, and then his stained white tunic. Revealing a broad, powerful, muscled grey chest, with deep grey nipples, and a heavy dusting of thick black hair. And beneath it, a softer-looking abdomen, bisected with a line of more dark hair, thickening as it trailed down toward his low-slung trousers…

Geva dragged her eyes away with effort, gritting her teeth, clamping her hands to fists against the blanket. No. *No.* He was cold. Selfish. A criminal. One month, and then the sea.

She belatedly lurched her own bare body out of bed, shoving past Rathgarr's bulk toward the wardrobe—but then her feet faltered, her breath choking in her throat. Because— those were fresh red *scratches*, down Rathgarr's grey chest and shoulders. Scratches that looked to be from… fingernails. Human fingernails. A woman's fingernails, perhaps.

Had he… met someone else overnight? Had he left Geva alone, for *another woman*?

Something powerful plummeted in Geva's chest, strong enough that she almost retched—and she rushed the rest of the way to the wardrobe, yanking it open, clutching numbly at clothes. Gods, she had to dress in all this again, and what even went where, why couldn't she *think*—

"Ach, poppet," came Rathgarr's voice from behind her, a little tentative. "I can carry some of this today. No need to wear it all again."

Oh. Geva shot a wet-eyed look over her shoulder toward him, and then down toward his pack—where it must have been lying all night—and managed a tight little nod. And then attempted to return her focus to her clothes, yanking on a shift with shaky hands, and then her simplest day-dress, and her stockings and boots.

She'd tied her scarf around her hair to sleep, so she took that out, too, fanning out the tight black curls around her head. And amidst everything else the night before, she'd neglected to oil them—but when she spun back to collect the oil from her satchel, she nearly ran straight into Rathgarr again, damn the gigantic bastard. And damn the way he was still standing here, blocking her with his infuriating bare chest, with all those appalling scratches upon it.

But he still wasn't moving, and his eyes were fixed blankly to Geva—or rather, to her head. And his big hand was slowly, purposefully rising in midair between them, reaching toward her hair. Almost as if he wanted to... to *touch* it. To stroke it like he had in the wardrobe, like when she'd been sucking him, and...

"You do *not* touch my hair," she hissed at him, and she almost tripped as she dodged around him, and began digging frantically through her satchel. Finding the bottle of scented oil—her mother's traditional recipe—and fumbling at the cork, pouring out the familiar liquid into her shaky palm. And then rubbing her hands together, warming it, before combing her fingers through her hair, the way she always did. And *why* was Rathgarr still looking at her like this, looking rather like she'd struck him across the face.

"You did not..." he began, his tongue brushing his lips, as his eyes darted down to where the washbasin was still sitting beside the bed. "You... washed your hair. In water scented of... *this*."

Geva's disbelief surged with staggering, furious force, and she glared fiercely toward him, yanking her hands hard enough through her hair that she winced. "Do you honestly have some kind of problem with that?" she shot back. "It was due for a wash, so I washed it! It's not *my* fault the bathwater was full of your spunk, is it? And even if I *am* stuck working for you for the next month, you still have *no right* to tell me what to do with my own damned hair. *None!*"

Her voice had gone thin and shrill, dangerously close to breaking—and before her, Rathgarr grimaced, and ran a hand through his own hair, too. Which, Geva irritably noticed, was far more mussed-looking than it had been the night before, no doubt due to his overnight trysting with whatever unfortunate woman he'd met. Or more likely, whatever woman he'd gone and *paid*.

"I seek to tell you *naught*, woman," he replied, his voice stiff, his eyes angling guiltily away. "It is only... I did not ken... my scent, on your hair from this, it is..."

Geva kept frowning at him, waiting, still pulling her fingers through her hair, until he grimaced again, shrugging his bare, scratched-up shoulder. "It is very strong upon you," he said. "Very clear, even when blended with the water thus. Mayhap we could..."

His eyes darted back to her hair again, while his hand— damn the transparent bastard—once again dropped to adjust something at his groin. That long, dangerous ridge, highly visible beneath his trousers. And Geva stared for an instant too long before she dragged her eyes away, and gave a loud, brittle bark of a laugh.

"No," she hissed. "*No.* You will not spray that directly in my hair. *Never.*"

And good gods, Rathgarr actually looked disappointed, and wait, was he even *pouting*?! "It shall easily wash out," he said stubbornly. "It washed off the rest of you, did it not? And if you are scented so strongly of me thus, the other orcs may not even question why you have no scent of my seed in your womb, or your rump."

What?! Unbelievable. *Unbelievable.* Geva truly could not speak, her mouth frantically opening and closing—and without thinking, she lunged for the leather pouch still tied to Rathgarr's belt, and plucked out a large gold coin.

"We are *never* discussing this *again*," she spat, as she brandished the coin toward him. "Now, I am going to buy myself a very large breakfast, and some provisions for the day. And *you* are going to pack, and wash and dress yourself, and *fuck off*!"

With that, she whirled around, yanked open the door, and stormed out. And while it should have felt good—wonderful— to tell off the smug cheating bastard, Geva still couldn't deny the thick lump rising in her throat. Or worse, the realization that she'd forgotten to twist her hair up, which would certainly lead to even more wrangling with it later, probably again while that prick watched, and thought about dousing it with his spunk.

Even an excellent breakfast in the inn's dining-room didn't improve her mood, nor did the innkeeper's willingness to trade a large sack of food for Rathgarr's coin. And when Geva finally stalked out the inn's front door, and found a much cleaner-looking Rathgarr lounging against a nearby tree, she strode past him without a word, curtly snatching her satchel from his outstretched hand.

Rathgarr hadn't spoken either, but he soon fell into step beside her, his looming bulk rigid and forbidding. So on they walked, stiffly and silently, both staring straight ahead, and attempting to ignore the renewed pointing and muttering of the various passersby.

"I ought not," Rathgarr's low voice began, making Geva twitch, her eyes angling reflexively toward his hard profile. "To have asked to scent your hair. I ken this was not... part of our plan."

Geva twitched again, but managed a shrug, and kept walking, her eyes again staring straight ahead. Just a job. One month, and then the sea.

Rathgarr made an odd harrumphing noise, but then fell silent, because they were now passing a gaggle of schoolgirls, all of them pointing and gasping and whispering. And abruptly dragging Geva's gloomy thoughts back to poor Cecily, stuck on that horrid trip with the Fitzwalds, much like she herself was stuck on this horrid trip to Orc Mountain.

"You are yet angry," cut in Rathgarr's voice, grating up Geva's spine. "Why? Because I did not stay with you last eve, after you *said* you did not wish for this?"

Geva didn't deign to answer that, so of course the bastard just kept speaking, his voice deepening. "Or mayhap because I did not speak sweet false words to you before I left?" he asked, now with an unmistakable tinge of mockery. "Ach, did you wish me to fuss and croon over you, as if you are the most stunning creature to ever bear my scent?"

Good gods, this utter *cretin*, and Geva shot him a look of purest loathing, and put a good arms-length of distance between them. "No, you ghastly swine," she hissed back. "I'm angry because you ruined my *life*. You destroyed my *career*. You asked me to work for you, you negotiated on what I *thought* were fair terms, you swore to keep me *safe!*"

Rathgarr visibly bristled, his eyes dangerously narrowing, but now that Geva had started speaking, she couldn't seem to stop. "You left me all alone," her voice spat, "in the middle of gods know where, with no food or coin or protection, so you could go off and tryst with someone else! And then you waltz back in this morning, and decide to start up on my *hair*, of all things?!"

She was shaky and breathless by the end of it, genuinely shouting at this awful bastard in the middle of the road, and earning for her trouble an extremely dubious stare from a passing elderly man. But she kept glaring at Rathgarr, who was blinking back down toward her, and looking... confused?

"I did not *go off and tryst*," he replied, his voice clipped. "I would not touch another thus, not whilst I seek to build my scent upon you. This should risk betraying our deceit to my brothers, ach? They well know how jealous you women are, and how closely you guard your mates."

Really? *Really?* Geva's brief surge of highly unnerving relief had already drained entirely away, her mouth fallen open, her hand on her hip—but then she flailed around and kept walking, far faster than before. This prick. This gods-damned, lily-livered, shrivelled-brained—

"I was only out sparring, last eve," Rathgarr's flat voice continued, because of course he'd easily kept pace with her, his face now glowering straight ahead. "With one of Orc Mountain's scouts. He has been... meeting me, when he is near. I have been away from my own kind's best warriors for too long, and thus am not now in strong fettle to fight them, ach?"

Geva's feet tripped beneath her, and she whipped around to stare at Rathgarr again, her disbelief surging higher in her chest. "What do you mean, *fight* them?" she demanded. "Wait, do you think the other orcs will meet your return to Orc Mountain with *violence*?! I thought you said they *asked* you to return!"

Rathgarr's lip was curling, his eyes sharp and contemptuous. "Ach, they *did* send for me," he shot back. "And no, I do not ken they shall seek to attack me thus. But neither do I wish to show myself weak and wrong-footed before them!"

Geva sneered back up toward him, while a grating laugh escaped from her throat. "Oh, so once again, it's all about you putting on a good show, is that it?" she scoffed. "Making the other orcs believe that you're a skilled, desirable, well-adjusted paragon of orcish honour, rather than the smug, smarmy, out-of-shape *crook* that you actually *are*! Do you really think they won't see through all your sad sorry *rubbish*?"

Rathgarr lurched toward her with surprising speed, his hard, rumbling growl vibrating through her chest. "Silence, woman," he snarled. "You agreed to this. You have sworn to help me in this. You *wished* for my seed last eve, and my touch, and then wished me to go away! And when I did this, and now offer you my truth, you snipe and sulk like one of your spoilt brats, and call me a *swine* and a *crook*?"

Geva flinched despite herself, shaking her head, because that surely wasn't what was happening here, was it? He deserved this, he'd been rude and dismissive and presumptuous, he'd wanted to spray in her *hair*, he'd ruined her *life*—

But her anger was already draining away, leaving behind something like regret, or even guilt. Damn it. *Damn* it. She was supposed to be trying to make this work, not insulting him, or yelling at him. Especially, curse her, after she *had* implied she hadn't wanted him to stay last night. That perhaps he hadn't deserved to stay. Because he was an *orc*.

She was already squaring her shoulders, opening her mouth to apologize—when Rathgarr lunged another step closer, his eyes glittering with cold fury. "You are here at *my* whim, woman, for *my* gold," he continued, his growl even deeper than before. "This is all. I shall not treat you as some fine frail goddess, just because you have deigned to touch me and bear my scent! And if you do not wish to be truly left behind all alone, with *none* of my food or gold or guarding"—he jabbed a sharp claw toward her chest—"you shall henceforth be meek, and yielding, and *quiet*. You shall be the hireling you are, and obey me!"

His furious voice rang and echoed in Geva's ears—a hireling, left behind, all alone, *all alone*—and she could only seem to stare back at him, while something cold and sick surged in her belly. Trampling over the guilt and regret, and hurling out raw, staggering *fear* in its stead.

He would... leave her behind? With *nothing*? If she didn't stay meek, and quiet, and *obey*?

Her throat swallowed hard, her suddenly sweaty hands clutching tightly to her satchel. Because yes, yes, he could still leave. He could run off into the forest again, and abandon her here, just like that. With no coin, no clothes, and no help. And what then? What would be left?

Desperation. Destitution. Destruction.

And for a dark, dizzying instant, it was as though she was back in the city again, the day after her parents' funeral. Standing alone in the street, weeping into her hands, and realizing, for the very first time, that she was utterly, entirely alone. No one else would care. No one else would come.

No. Gods, no. Never again. She needed this. She needed the next step. Needed the gold. She needed... *him.*

So she made herself nod, rapid and fervent, her eyes dropped to Rathgarr's feet. One month, and then the sea.

"Then please, sir, I beg your forgiveness," she whispered. "I'm so very sorry. I'll obey."

11

The rest of the day passed with awful, agonizing slowness. With Geva and Rathgarr walking in stiff, stilted silence, and attempting to ignore the incessant onslaught of whispers, glances, and alarm from the ongoing parade of passersby.

At one point, Rathgarr curtly held out his elbow toward her, in a silent but very clear command, and Geva nodded, and obediently clasped her hand to his arm. But she couldn't muster the will to make light of it, like she had the day before, or even to meet the other travellers' eyes.

She was alone. A hireling. One month, and then the sea.

"Do you hunger?" Rathgarr's stilted voice asked her, perhaps around midday, and when Geva managed another nod, he led her a little ways into the woods. To a place that was perhaps familiar to him, a mossy clearing with several large scattered stones, and they sat and ate in more silence, not meeting one another's eyes. And then it was yet more walking, more gawking passersby, while Geva's loneliness and exhaustion kept deepening, dragging down her head and shoulders.

One month at Orc Mountain, obeying silently, without question or complaint. And then the sea.

They finally stopped for the night at another inn, this one noticeably seedier than the night before. And when Rathgarr again ordered Geva to go eat, and then secure them a room and a bath, she dutifully obliged, even as she valiantly fought to ignore the raucous, drunken crowd in the dining-room, and the greasy-faced man at the bar who loudly offered to share her bath.

By the time she'd reached their room for the night—a cramped, candlelit room in the attic, with, predictably, only one bed—Geva was trembling with unease and exhaustion, and clinging to her satchel as though it were a shield. And when a massive, hooded figure abruptly appeared behind her in the doorway, she nearly leapt out of her skin, and scrabbled halfway across the room before realizing it was him. Rathgarr.

"Settle yourself, poppet," he said with a grimace, closing the door behind him. "No need to always be so skittish, ach?"

Geva swallowed, but quickly nodded, and even attempted a wretched smile. Because gods, he couldn't leave her alone in this strange place, and he wanted her obliging and obedient and silent, and—

"Brought your bath, pretty girl," called a sing-song male voice from beyond the door, making Geva jump again. "You alone in there?"

Thankfully, Rathgarr spun back around, yanking his hood down further over his face before swinging the door open. And though the men likely couldn't identify him as an orc in the darkness, Rathgarr's towering bulk clearly spoke for itself, sending them scurrying away with an urgency that might have once been gratifying.

"Pay no heed to those vermin," Rathgarr told Geva, his voice hard, once he'd heaved the full, steaming washtub into the room. "I shall stay here with you tonight, ach?"

Geva's tired eyes darted toward that one small bed again, but she couldn't deny the sheer, staggering relief blooming in her chest. "Th-thank you, sir," she made herself say, her voice unnaturally small. "I am—very grateful, and should be glad to share with you."

Rathgarr's mouth thinned, but he nodded, and then waved a too-casual hand toward the bath. Because yes, yes that was what came next, and even the thought of it was doing strange, sickening things in Geva's gut. Gods, he'd been so enthralling the night before, so compelling, so cruel. And would he want that again, he wanted a silent obedient hireling, he didn't care about her in the least, and—

"Mayhap I shall just scent the bath again," he said now, not meeting Geva's eyes. "Should you wish."

Right. Geva jerked a quick nod, and then she turned away from him, yanking off her sticky, grimy clothes, and then twisting up her hair. While intently ignoring the distinct sounds of rustling fabric behind her, followed by something that had to be... movement. Yes, that had to be him, stroking that heft at his groin. Swelling it to full hardness, bringing out those brimming beads of sweet white seed...

Geva's breath hitched, and she shivered as she stood there, her backside now fully bared toward him, her eyes squeezed shut. And her mouth was not watering—it was *not*—as the visions of him caressing himself, coaxing out that seed, seemed to parade behind her eyelids. Gods, she could even hear his low breaths, could feel that rhythmic stroking, rising and rippling, faster and higher, until—

She twitched at the distinctive sound of liquid spattering against water, strong and sustained and steady. Pouring out, emptying himself, for *her*—but then gradually fading, lessening. Just like when he'd sprayed her the night before, when his breath had caught like that in his throat, his eyes blazing with hunger...

"Ach, it is done," came his voice behind her, and when Geva turned her trembly body around, it was to the sight of him tucking himself away again. Though his hands had clenched on his trousers, his big body stilling, and his heavy, half-lidded eyes were looking at... her. Briefly flicking down her front, catching on her bare breasts and groin, before darting guiltily back up again.

And for a fraught, frozen moment, there was the strongest, strangest urge to slip her hand up to her breast. To touch it again while he watched, to show him what he so clearly desired. To prove that she could be the silent hireling he wanted, the soft, sweet, eager woman he'd said he preferred, the kind of woman he could actually care about...

No. No. *Hell*, no. And before she could think better of it, Geva lurched forward, and leapt into the scalding bath. Where she hissed aloud at the sudden swarming heat, and then again at the familiar, heady scent in the water. The scent of *him*, rich and sweet. The scent she'd perhaps been smelling in her hair all day...

Gods damn it, what was *happening* to her, and Geva gritted her teeth, and set to bathing as quickly as she could. Washing off the grime and stickiness from the full day of travelling, taking care to keep the scented water away from her twisted-up hair. All while intently avoiding looking at Rathgarr, who had yanked off his own fur and cloak and tunic, and sprawled back bare-chested on the bed, his arm flung over his eyes.

"Mayhap you should rather I sleep on the floor?" he asked, once Geva had finished bathing, and had tied her scarf over her hair, and dressed in her most modest sleeping-shift. "To spare you the shame of sharing with an orc?"

Geva squeezed her eyes shut, and shook her head. "Of course I am happy to share with you, sir," she replied, her voice wooden. "You being an orc has no bearing upon it. I am glad to do whatever you wish."

Rathgarr barked a low, grim little laugh, but then eased his big body sideways, and patted the small space he'd created beside him. "Then get in, poppet," he said, as he reached up behind him to snuff out the candle. "I shall savour the taste of your great *gladness*, ach?"

Geva pointedly ignored the mockery in his voice, and stiffly nodded as she obeyed, gingerly easing herself down onto the bed beside him. It was indeed a very small bed, and his body was still far too large for it, making it utterly impossible for them both to comfortably fit. Even when she shifted onto her side, turning her rigid back toward him, she was still pressed into his big bare arm, its warmth emanating through her shift, down into her still-damp skin.

But the bed was soft, if nothing else. And after such an endless, arduous day, and the wakeful night before it, sleep should have come swift and easy—so of course, Geva instead found herself lying there wide awake, and staring off blankly into the darkness. While all the day's combined miseries surged through her thoughts, and an infuriating wetness began prickling behind her eyes.

She was alone. One month, and then the sea.

"Still feeling so *glad*, then?" came Rathgarr's low voice, making her flinch in the darkness. "Ach, poppet?"

Geva flinched again, the bitter despair surging through her chest—but she shoved it back, and swallowed over the obstruction in her throat. "Very glad, sir," she choked out. "And with all due respect, why does it matter to you how I feel, when I'm only a *hireling*? When all you want from me is my obedience, and my silence? Just like my horrible employers at my previous post?"

And wait, this was obviously the opposite of silence, and Geva bit her lip, and rubbed painfully at her prickling eyes. One month. That was all.

There was a long, heavy silence from Rathgarr behind her, enough that she thought he'd fallen asleep—until she felt him shift, creaking the bed beneath him, his breath huffing out in a heavy sigh.

"Ach, woman," he said, his voice very quiet. "Can we not come to peace upon this?"

Geva felt herself stiffening even more—*he* was the one who'd wanted it like this, wasn't he?—and he sighed again, even heavier than before. "Ach, I ought not to have called you a mere hireling today," he continued. "And I ought not to have ordered your silence. But did you not also rage at me over a wrong I did not commit? And say I ought to sleep outside, rather than in a bed? And then call me a *smug, smarmy, out-of-shape crook*?"

It was an exact quote of Geva's words, even spoken in a serviceable likeness of her accent, and she grimaced into the dark. "It was wrong of me, to suggest you shouldn't stay at the inn," she gritted out. "I know how it feels to be treated that way, and I'm realizing I—I clearly still have a lot to learn about orcs. But"—she drew in a shaky breath—"you *do* realize I've faced considerable challenges of my own, too? And you threatened to *fire* me, and abandon me defenseless and destitute in the middle of nowhere, if I didn't stay quiet, and obey you?"

Her voice had gone far too shrill, and she should stop, why couldn't she stop. "And before that," she went on, "you ransacked my employers' house, you ruined my reputation and my career, you made me leave behind everything I've ever known, *again*! And"—she drew in a ragged breath—"I'll never see Cecily again, either, and now she'll *never* stop wondering why I abandoned her, and *stole* those little trinkets from her, and—"

She bit off the words far, far too late, because gods, was she truly still fool enough to be arguing with this orc? While also actually *weeping*, damn it, dripping tears onto the damned bed—and she angrily dashed the wetness away, and bit painfully at her lip. No. What the hell was she doing. He wanted her agreeable and obedient, or else he would *abandon* her, and...

"F-forgive me, sir," she blurted in a rush, as sharp, sickening fear plumed in her gut. "I shouldn't have said any of that. I'm just very tired, and I—"

"Enough, poppet," cut in Rathgarr's resigned voice, and with it, a gentle but unmistakable elbow to her back. "I do not wish for your falsehoods, and I shall not cast you aside for speaking truth to me. I"—his voice lowered—"I ought not to have threatened you thus, this morn. For I swore a vow to you, and I shall keep it. I shall keep you safe, and then I shall see you across the sea. I swear this."

Geva's uneasiness was still surging cold and bitter, and behind her, Rathgarr huffed another heavy sigh. "And I do not wish for your fear, or your silence," he continued. "Nor do I wish to lord over you as your master, woman. I wish us to be... helpmates, in this."

Helpmates? Geva scoffed before she could stop it, the sound loud and betraying in the darkness, but Rathgarr only elbowed her again. "Helpmates," he repeated, harder this time. "For this is what this is, ach? You help me regain my home, and my rightful due from my kin—and I shall do the same for you. This well serves us both, ach? Thus, what good is there in sniping and quarrelling over this?"

Geva clenched her mouth shut, fighting the sudden, almost overwhelming urge to point out that even before all this, he'd mocked her, he'd refused to answer multiple benign questions, he'd wanted to spray in her *hair*—until there was another gentle elbow in her back, another heavy sigh.

"I ken I have not so far shown myself well in this," he continued. "I am not... used to having another to care for, thus. It has been... a long time. I am... sorry."

Oh. Geva's throat swallowed, her body slightly sagging against him. "And why, exactly, should I believe any of this?" she heard herself ask, her voice thin. "Why should I ever risk trusting you? You must realize that you have all the control in this particular situation? All the strength, all the leverage, and all the gold?"

But that was a snort behind her, a purposeful shift of Rathgarr's body on the bed. "Ach, until we walk into Orc Mountain," he countered, "and you hold my every last secret. With a few choice words, you could destroy all I seek to gain. Who shall wield the power then?"

It was a point Geva hadn't at all considered, and for an instant she was caught in it, contemplating it. *Would* she hold the power at Orc Mountain? Could she truly hold that over him? Over this huge, terrifying, enraging orc?

"Helpmates," Rathgarr said again, flatter this time—and without warning, his huge body shifted closer. Enough to make her stiffen all over, but no, he was moving above her, easing himself out of the bed. And with a quick snap, the candle was lit again, illuminating the room with dazzling brightness, and showing Rathgarr kneeling beside his pack, plucking something out of it.

"A token," he said, as he stalked back toward her, and held out the... the *book*? "As a sign of my goodwill toward you."

And wait. Wait. It was *Geva's* book. Her family's book. The book she'd left behind at the Fitzwalds'. And now... Rathgarr had it? He'd brought it? Here?

"Oh," she said numbly, reaching out a shaky hand toward it—and gods, even the feel of it, the truth of its familiar solid weight in her fingers, was a strange, powerful relief. Enough that she abruptly clutched it close, cradling it tight against her heart. Gods, what had she been thinking to leave it behind, why had she agreed to any of this, to him—

Rathgarr snuffed the candle again, and was now settling back onto the bed behind her, his heavy body making it creak and sag around him. And when Geva's own weight tilted a little more into his overlarge bulk as a result, she couldn't find the will to wrench away.

He'd brought her a gift. A token. And he must have taken it before they'd left the Fitzwalds, right after she'd—*tasted* him, and then he'd carried it all the way here. And why would he have done that? As leverage? As a bribe? Surely not as... a kindness?

"Thank you," she said, her voice hoarse. "This book... means a lot to me."

There was an instant's silence, and then the feel of Rathgarr's big shoulder shrugging against her. "Your scent was strong upon it," he replied. "I knew you did not wish to leave it behind."

Oh. Geva couldn't seem to find an answer to that, and behind her, Rathgarr cleared his throat. "It is not in a tongue I have seen before," he said. "Kraitish, mayhap?"

Geva felt a flare of surprise—he could *read,* enough to identify other languages?—and hurriedly swallowed down that particular misconception. "It's in Eziran," she replied thickly. "My parents were both born in Ezira, but they served as state ambassadors in Wolfen. Up until five years ago, when—"

Her voice broke there—gods, she couldn't bear to get into this, not now—but perhaps Rathgarr had followed anyway, giving her a sympathetic-feeling nudge with his elbow. "I am sorry," he said, quiet. "Both my father and mother are laid to rest now also."

Geva couldn't deny another unwilling flash of surprise, an odd lurch of something almost like commiseration, and behind her Rathgarr cleared his throat again, louder this time. "So this... *Cecily,* you spoke of," he said. "Is she also your kin, then? I thought you said you had no kin left to help you."

Right. Geva grimaced in the darkness, but clutched the book closer to her chest, and drew in a breath. "No, Cecily is the Fitzwalds' ward," she replied. "One of my pupils."

There was more silence, and then the feel of Rathgarr perhaps propping himself up behind her, his gaze oddly prickling in the dark. "You did not... *care* for those sulky, spoilt brats at that house?" he demanded, with genuine-sounding astonishment. "Ach, I listened to them whine and wail for only half a day, and by then wished for naught more than to drop them all down a well."

Something far too close to mirth bubbled up in Geva's throat, and she fought the strange, unaccountable urge to turn around, to seek his eyes in the dark. "They certainly weren't easy children to care for," she replied, with a sigh. "But they've had a difficult time of it, too. Their parents barely acknowledged them, let alone offering them any real affection or support or safety. And poor Cecily always got the worst of it, she might as well have been *invisible* to them, and—"

Geva broke off there, because why was she getting into this, either? One stupid apology—one single token—surely did not change the mess this entire day had been, all the ways this orc had hurt her? And surely now he would mock her, or use all this against her, or...

"You are very... fair-minded," came his quiet voice behind her, surprising enough to make her twitch. "These younglings were... blessed, I ken, to have your kindness in this."

Oh. Geva felt her brow furrowing in the darkness, but she couldn't find a trace of sarcasm or mockery in his voice. And he'd again shifted behind her, perhaps turning around—and surely now that was his back, pressing warm and solid against hers.

"So if ever we have the ill luck to meet these fool humans again," he said, "mayhap we shall drop the *parents* down the well instead. And then we shall save the ill-treated human we like best, and keep her warm and safe and content. This is indeed the proper Ash-Kai way, ach?"

The proper Ash-Kai way. Ash-Kai was Rathgarr's clan name, Geva distantly recalled, and his voice sounded almost wistful as he spoke it. Drawing up something deep and shameful in her belly, something not unlike jealousy. Because gods, what it would be like to be *saved*, to be *liked*, to be kept safe and content? And why did this orc keep affecting her like this, he'd been so utterly vile today, he was still a selfish capricious thief, and—

"Now sleep, poppet," came his low voice. "You are weary, and we have much road to travel tomorrow."

He accompanied this with another nudge of his elbow, a shift of his big back against hers. So warm, so solid, so safe...

And despite everything, all the whispering misgivings and misery, Geva finally closed her tired eyes, and slept.

When morning came, it was with the smell of... breakfast?

Geva jerked awake and shoved up in bed, blinking down toward the overloaded tray of food propped on the bed beside her. Piled with fresh boiled eggs, and ham, and greens, and even a pot of steaming tea?!

She shot a searching, disbelieving glance upwards, and found—Rathgarr. Standing tall and broad before her, fully dressed in fine crisp clothes, and flashing her a decidedly smug smile.

"Breakfast," he said firmly, as he settled his huge form down to sit on the bed, and nudged a bowl of eggs toward her. "Eat, poppet."

Oh. Geva certainly wasn't about to refuse, not with so many succulent scents swarming her nostrils—and she accordingly picked up a fork, and took a careful bite of egg. Gods, it was good, and she found herself giving Rathgarr a wary, grateful smile as she chewed.

"This is... unexpected," she said, between bites. "Thank you."

He gave a too-casual shrug, and then stabbed a boiled egg

with his claw before tossing it whole into his open mouth. "As I said last night, I wish to come to peace with you," he replied, once he'd swallowed. "I wish for a happy helpmate, not one who dreams of cutting out my heart whilst I sleep."

Geva's mouth twitched a little higher, almost into a smile—but then Rathgarr purposefully glanced downwards, and nudged something toward her with his claw. It was a heavy silver goblet, filled to the brim with a white, creamy liquid, something Geva's distracted brain had previously identified as milk. But... but...

She frowned and snatched the goblet up to her face, breathing in deep—and gods damn this devious orc, it was... *that*. His... *seed*. Its scent rich and sweet and so, so familiar, and her traitorous mouth was actually watering, her tongue brushing against her lips.

"You put it in a *cup*," she managed, and while she'd meant to sound outraged, her voice came out low, tolerant, almost... amused. "For my *breakfast*?!"

Rathgarr's mouth quirked up, his eyes glinting with satisfaction. "Ach, should you wish," he blandly replied. "Or should you rather suck this straight from my prick, mayhap?"

Geva made a face at him, but curse it, her mouth was still watering, her breath inhaling deep against the goblet's smooth silver rim. And yes, she had agreed to this, hadn't she? He'd said he wanted his scent on her mouth. And the better job she did, the more he would pay...

"How about this, poppet," he said, his eyes still glittering on hers. "For each load you swallow, the more you shall gain. For this, mayhap..."

He plucked a gold coin from his pouch, brandishing it out toward Geva's face, while a smug smirk played on his mouth. "This. And twice this, should you again drink it fresh from its source. And"—his voice dropped, his smirk curling higher—"five times, mayhap, should you be brave enough to drink it straight up your rump."

The hell. This *prick*. This devious, brilliant *bastard*, because this wasn't just a copper, it was a real gold piece. Enough to keep Geva comfortably housed and fed for likely an entire week.

And he was offering twice this much, for... *that*. And five times for *that*?!

"You wouldn't," Geva snapped at him, but her voice came out far too low, too tolerant, as if this appalling little challenge was somehow up for *debate*?! "You said you'll pay me *after* all this. At the end of the month. In a lump sum."

"Ach, did I?" Rathgarr replied lightly, flicking that coin between his claws. "Then test me, poppet. Drink up."

Geva's breath was strangely shuddering, her hand lifting the goblet closer to her mouth—but then she shoved it down again, squeezing her eyes shut. No. No. She couldn't risk sinking deeper into this mess, playing straight into his sneaky, smarmy hands. Or risking what he'd already offered, what they'd already agreed upon...

But Rathgarr was still watching her far too intently, his smirk twisting into something like a grimace. "I do not mean to say you *must* do this," he said, flatter than before. "Or that this should alter aught else we have agreed upon. I have sworn to care for you, and keep you safe, and see you across the sea, and I shall keep my vow. But should you choose to do more"—he shrugged, glanced away—"mayhap a scheme such as this should make matters more... fair, between us."

Oh. So this devious orc offering her extra coin like this was supposed to be a generosity? A kindness?! To make matters more *fair* between them, to his own full and blatant benefit?

But as Geva glanced down at that cup, still sitting so innocuously on the tray, she felt her tongue again brushing her lips, the longing swelling up, shameful and shimmering. Because damn him, maybe she did want this, more than she'd ever imagined possible. And *would* it have felt better, fairer, if they'd had clearer terms in place? If those heated moments between them hadn't felt like a failure, but a gain? A scheme? Or even... a challenge?

He was watching her again, that challenge brazenly glimmering in his eyes—and before Geva could think better of it, she again snatched up the sweet-scented silver goblet, raised it to her mouth, and drank.

And *oh*, it was good. Warm, and sweet, and surely fresh from its... *source*. And she just kept drinking, dragging its succulent honey deep down her throat, swallowing it in gulp after gulp. Until the goblet was entirely empty, and she was tilting it high, willing out one more glorious drop, one more, oh...

She set the empty goblet back on the tray with a clatter, lifting her chin, licking her sweet-tasting lips. All while holding Rathgarr's watching eyes, and perhaps even raising a silent challenge of her own. What would he do now? Would he really just hand over a week's survival, for that?

But Rathgarr wasn't flinching, wasn't dropping his eyes from hers. And in a swift, efficient movement, he grasped for her hand, and pressed the coin into her palm. Its cool weight just lying there, so real and powerful against her skin.

For an instant, Geva couldn't breathe, and instead just sat there, holding his glinting eyes, and feeling the weight of his coin in her palm. The more she pleased him, the more he would pay. More... fair. His... helpmate.

The new, tenuous truth of it—that bright simmering challenge of it—seemed to hover between them as they finished eating, as Geva washed and dressed, now with that precious gold coin tucked into her satchel. And as they walked together out onto the road again, her hand was already curling against Rathgarr's big bicep, her happy-helpmate smile plastered firmly to her face.

She could do this. One step at a time. One month, and then the sea.

"You said you'd pay twice as much," she murmured toward

him, after gaily waving at a cluster of staring passersby, and even stroking her hand suggestively against Rathgarr's bicep for good measure. "If I drink it straight from you again. Why does that matter?"

"This shall greatly strengthen my scent upon you," Rathgarr murmured back, making a show of indulgently patting his big hand against hers, as if he in fact welcomed her over-enthusiastic stroking. "And make it clear to my kin that you have eagerly done this, as a true orc's mate oft would. Most of all if they were not mating the... *customary* way."

He'd angled a brief but telling glance down toward Geva's skirts, and she fought through her irritation to frown at him, chewing at her lip. "And the other orcs will be able to tell we're not doing it the *customary* way, you said?" she asked. "Is that because they can smell it?"

Rathgarr nodded, and then assumed a tolerant, toothy smile as Geva waved toward another passing couple, and even took the liberty of blatantly stroking her hand up and down his chest this time. "Right," she replied. "So perhaps"—her head tilted, her fingers absently spreading wider against his tunic—"perhaps it would be best if we tell your relatives that our unusual—*abstinence*—is at my request. We could say that I'm very nervous about having children, and wanted to wait a while longer, because my mother nearly died giving birth to me. And that part is true, if that helps at all."

Rathgarr's glance toward Geva was surely surprised, and perhaps even... appreciative? "Ach, I ken this *should* help," he said slowly. "Some orcs can sense falsehood, and many more shall feel ill at ease if one's scent does not match one's words. So the more truth we can speak, the more they shall accept this."

That made sense, and Geva gave a slow nod. "So that can be our story, then," she said. "No... *customary* activities, between us. But then, you say, I would otherwise be..."

She shot Rathgarr a regretful grimace, and in return he

grinned again, showing those sharp white teeth. "Welcoming all the other joys to be found with an orc," he said archly. "Painting yourself with my scent. Drinking up my sweet seed. *Begging* me to fill your rump, if I cannot have your womb."

Geva groaned and rolled her eyes at him, but her whispering, uncooperative thoughts had already flicked back to that shiny new coin tucked in her satchel. Twice as much, he'd said. Five *times* as much.

"So in the unlikely event that I *did* choose to drink it straight from you again," she ventured, and gods she was not proposing this, she *wasn't*, "how much effort, precisely, would I need to put into this?"

She was thinking about the unfortunate incident back in her room at the Fitzwalds', and how Rathgarr had at least done most of the work—but predictably, he was now shaking his head, and snorting a hard, dismissive laugh.

"Ach, you humans," he said contemptuously. "How about this, kitten. Just the same as the rest of it, ach? The better work you do when you suckle me, the more I shall pay."

Geva glowered viciously toward his smug, scheming face, and opened her mouth to snap back at him—at least, until a wagon appeared around the bend up ahead. To which she assumed a worshipful smile, stroking her hand up and down Rathgarr's torso, while also letting her fingernails dig in with what she hoped was painful pressure.

"So two coins is the base rate for sucking you?" she asked him, still smiling, sliding her scraping hand rather lower than she meant. "What's the upper end, then?"

The wagon had finally passed them by, and Rathgarr's indulgent smile had soured into something vicious too, his eyes flashing on hers. "Try it," he growled, "and find out, woman."

Geva's stroking hand had somehow—*unthinkably*—slipped even lower, finding that hard, impossible ridge beneath his trousers. Because yes, he wanted her to try him, to *test* him— and suddenly there was a strange, shivery longing, burning low in her belly. He wanted this from her. No matter what rubbish he spouted, he wanted... *her*.

"Fine," she hissed back. "Where?"

Rathgarr blinked at her, and for an instant, his eyes looked very wide—but then he jerked his head toward the nearby forest. "There," he purred, all cold haughty control again. "On your knees in the *dirt*, poppet, with an *orc* stuck in your throat."

He was baiting her, Geva well knew, being the incurable bastard she already knew him to be—and before she could think better of it, she lifted her chin, and spun off toward the trees. She was *not* giving him the satisfaction of winning at this. *She* was going to win, and he was going to pay. Through his smarmy white *teeth*.

But despite her determination, her resolve faltered when she stepped into the trees—gods, it *was* dirty, mucky and swampy, and did she really need to kneel *here* in her clean clothes? But then Rathgarr brushed past her, striding along a narrow path, deeper into the forest. And when Geva irritably followed, it was to the realization that he'd found another dry, mossy little clearing, tucked within the protective shelter of the surrounding trees.

"Still so eager now, my sweet?" he drawled, as he sank down onto a large stone, his knees spread wide, his mouth curled in a contemptuous smirk. "Ready to kneel before your orc?"

Gods, he was horrid, he was so utterly enraging—but he was also still sitting there, waiting, watching her with strange, flickering eyes. And somehow, somehow, Geva was stepping closer, and closer... and then she clutched up her skirts, and sank to her bare knees on the ground before him. Only distantly noting that the moss was blessedly soft and dry— because oh gods, she was kneeling between an orc's thighs. *This* orc's thighs. And what the hell was she thinking, she couldn't truly be doing this, rising to this, *meeting* this...

But the devious bastard was already loosening his belt, dropping that heavy broadsword to the side—and then shoving his trousers a little downwards. Releasing that huge, shocking sight beneath, already ruddy and swollen, bobbing out toward Geva's waiting mouth...

"Ach, poppet?" Rathgarr's low voice murmured, as his clawed hand slid brazenly toward it, stroking up and down that thick, veined length. Casually easing out more and more of its rounded head from beneath that soft grey skin, and oh, she wasn't staring, her mouth wasn't watering, it *wasn't*...

"Ach?" Rathgarr said again, even huskier this time, and oh, that was already a glossy bead of white, pooling in that deep slit, so close to Geva's caught, staring eyes. And she could just lean a little closer, just breathe it in, perhaps just a light little taste...

Rathgarr hissed as her tongue touched it, the sound low in his throat—and Geva moaned too, helpless and hoarse. Because oh, he tasted even better this way, so much better, and she could just keep doing this, just this, drinking more and more, please—

But a distant awareness was lingering, nagging, thudding louder and louder with her heartbeat. The challenge. The *opportunity*. And somehow, without at all thinking, she pulled away again, blinked up at his face with hazy wide eyes.

"Will you—teach me," she gulped. "What you like. So I can—try my best."

Rathgarr was staring at her again, his eyes glittering dangerously in the dappled sunlight, and Geva braced herself, waiting for his response. What if he refused, what if he laughed, what if he fully intended for her to flounder about and make a total fool of herself, so he could cede as little ground as possible, and—

"As you were, then," he replied, his voice gruff. "Soft, at first. Seek into me. Awaken me."

Oh. Oh, yes, Geva could do that, and she twitched a relieved, trembly nod as she again leaned forward, and brushed her mouth against him. Feeling him shudder and swell against her parted lips, oozing more of that honeyed sweetness onto her tongue. Suggesting that... perhaps this really *was* how he liked it, at first. Soft. Seeking. Gentle.

It seemed an odd preference, suddenly, for someone who'd shown himself capable of such astonishing coldness—but in this strange, stilted moment, as Geva kept carefully kissing at him, she couldn't deny that it was still working. The silken hardness beneath her lips swelling even fuller, his smooth head shuddering as it squeezed out more sweetness, and bore deeper into her mouth. Opening her lips wider and wider around him, oh—but she still kept it soft, kept kissing, seeking, awakening.

"Good," Rathgarr said, still gruff, but surprisingly steady. "Now touch. Both hands."

He'd shifted himself a little as he'd spoken, shoving his trousers further down, and heaving out the bulge of his full, heavy bollocks. Surely suggesting he wanted her touching there, so Geva willingly obliged with that, too. Curling one hand around both soft, heavy weights—gods, they were big— and sliding her other hand around the base of his thick shaft. A movement that seemed to please him, given the low grunt from his throat, the swell of that jutting head between her lips.

"Ach, thus," came Rathgarr's impossibly steady voice. "And no clinging to me like a drowning maiden, ach? You pet and stroke and squeeze. Seek to wield all your wiles to soften me. To tempt out my good seed toward you."

Oh. The words—the vision, that *promise*—seemed to bloom in Geva's belly, in her stroking hands, her gently slipping tongue. Seeking to soften him even further, to tempt him, to awaken him. And even if Rathgarr didn't want any more from her than this—*neither should I ever choose to mate you*—he surely couldn't deny that this was still working. That he liked what she was doing, his head tilting back, his eyes hooded and glinting, his chest hollowing with his heavy breaths. The sight of it so unexpectedly compelling that Geva had to close her eyes, breathe in deep—

"*No*," he hissed, snapping her eyes open again, her heart skipping a beat—and oh, his big clawed hand was slipping under her chin, tilting it toward him. "You look at me when you suck me, my prickly poppet," he ordered, with low, heated malice. "I wish to *see* your face, with my prick deep inside it. Ach?"

He gave her chin a purposeful little shake as he spoke, his eyes flashing with cold, imperious command. And instead of arguing with him, or perhaps biting the bastard like he deserved, Geva found herself desperately attempting a nod, and holding his eyes, just as he'd ordered. Watching him watching her, weighing her, *assessing* her.

But oh, it was good, so damn good, and he had to agree, he *had* to see that. Even as he cocked a lazy eyebrow at her, and then settled his free hand to her head, tightening his other hand's grip on her chin. Giving him total control over her movements, and now—now taking full advantage. Drawing her slowly, smoothly toward him, delving himself long and deep into her mouth.

"Ach, thus," he said, his voice catching, as he held Geva there, his hard, dripping head now nudging and flexing against her throat. "As deep as you can without choking, ach? I wish to feel the clutch of your sweet little throat kissing me. Wish to feel it seeking to milk out my seed."

Good gods, this *orc*, and Geva betrayed a harsh, strangled moan, and even delved a little deeper. Doing it, letting him feel her throat convulse upon him, while holding those watching eyes. Knowing he was revelling in the sight of her hot, sticky face, her lips stretched out around him, her throat both accepting and rejecting his deep, inexorable invasion...

"Good, poppet," he murmured. "But this alone is not enough, ach? You must also now seek in earnest for your seed.

You shall suck harder—keep that tight little latch upon me—whilst pumping with your hand and your mouth. *Ach*."

His eyes fluttered as he spoke, because Geva was already attempting it, valiantly trying to stroke and squeeze and fondle, while also keeping the suction, and plunging him deep. Her watering eyes still fixed to his face, her cheeks hollowed and hot, her throat just on the edge of gagging with every desperate thrust. And he just kept looking back, with that cool crackling assessment in his eyes, while she knelt for him, prostrated herself for him, silently begged him to give her this, please, *please*—

The surge of sweet spewing heat came without warning this time, flooding hard and hot into Geva's mouth, and she fervently, frantically gulped it down, still stroking and milking him, holding his stunning, blazing eyes. Yes, he was seeing this, he had to see this, she was proving this, she was—

And suddenly the coiling twist of tension in her belly snapped, juddering out wide—and then her own pleasure was pulsing, reverberating on its own, crushing her beneath its sweeping, towering strength. Oh, it was good, he was *so* good, and yes, *yes*, he was even smiling at her, with such warm, shimmering pride in those watching, approving eyes.

"Hungry little poppet," he purred, his big hand sliding up her face, caressing at her hot, sweaty cheek. "Now suck me good and clean, ach? *Gently*."

Geva furtively nodded, running her tongue up and down his softening length, keeping it light and careful as she slowly drew away. As he again stopped her there on the end of it, just like last time, stroking her cheek with his thumb, watching as she gave his smooth silky head one last, wet, lingering kiss. His other hand's claws somehow carded deep into her hair, and gods, she hadn't even noticed, couldn't notice anything but this...

She'd done it. She'd proven it. And now he would praise

her, he would tell her how quick and thorough and hard-working she was, he would offer his reward, his kindness, his...

But instead, he cleared his throat, and angled his eyes away. Away toward the surrounding trees, to where something seemed to be *moving* amidst the leaves. Something shaped like—Geva startled and froze all over—

It was another person. Or wait, another... another *orc*? And no no *no*, not just one new orc, but *two*?!

"Greetings, my brothers," Rathgarr said toward them, his voice far louder and steadier than before. "Now, I wish you to come, and meet my sweet new mate."

13

There were two more orcs. Here. *Now.*

And holy gods above, Geva was kneeling in the dirt between Rathgarr's sprawled thighs, with his softened head still tucked in her mouth. And the other orcs— the *orcs*?!—were still there, still here, still coming closer. One of them had actually leapt out of a *tree*, his tall, lean form landing with unnatural ease, while his companion, stalking out from beneath the low-hanging branches, was *massive*. Just as big as Rathgarr, in fact, his bare grey chest covered in scars, his dark, dangerous eyes frowning straight toward... *her.*

The panic flashed white and sharp through Geva's stunted thoughts, and she scrabbled up to her shaky feet, her heartbeat thundering, her trembling hands brushing out her skirts. Good gods, these orcs had seen that, had they seen *everything*?!

But wait. *Wait.* Rathgarr hadn't even moved, the deceitful bastard, and he was *still* exposed, that softened, shining-wet sight at his groin brazenly hanging out of his open trousers. As though he wasn't ashamed of this in the least. Almost as though he... he *wanted* these new orcs to see what Geva had just done to him.

And as she gaped at him, frantically digesting that, his big hand snapped out toward her, curling around her wrist. "Peace, my sweet," he said, and though the words sounded light, Geva didn't miss the meaningful clench of his fingers, or the practiced tilt of his smile. "I told you my brother has been coming to see me, ach?"

Oh. *Ohhhh.* So these orcs clearly couldn't know the truth about who she was, right? Which meant this—this horrible, hanging moment, with no discussion or preparation whatsoever—was part of their deception, already. Part of Geva's *job*. And curse Rathgarr, but he could have damn well given her some warning, and he had *not* said anything about... *public displays*, had he?!

"Oh, yes, naturally, of course, I remember," Geva heard herself babbling, her uneasy eyes glancing again toward the two approaching orcs. Who were both staring straight back, the tall, lean one with cool appraisal in his eyes, while the big bulky one just looked hard and grim and forbidding. And perhaps—Geva twitched as his heavy gaze shifted toward Rathgarr—perhaps even downright hostile.

"Brothers, this is my sweet new mate, Geva Okoro," Rathgarr said now, his voice slow and careful on her name, mimicking her own accent with surprising accuracy. "And poppet, this is Killik"—he nodded toward the lean orc, before angling his gaze to the bigger one—"and Ulfarr, both of Clan Skai."

The lean orc—Killik—inclined his head toward Geva, while the big Ulfarr orc huffed a deep grunt, his frowning eyes gone even narrower on Rathgarr's face. A show of blatant suspicion that Rathgarr pretended not to notice, though his hand still around Geva's wrist clenched tighter, his smile a little too fixed on his mouth.

"Ulfarr and I were raised together," Rathgarr continued, with highly unnatural blandness. "Though it has been many summers since we have last spoken, ach, brother? As for Killik"—Rathgarr's smile toward him felt slightly more sincere—"he is one of Orc Mountain's best scouts, and he has been bringing me much news of home. As well as trouncing my portly arse in combat, whenever he can wheedle me into this."

His voice had gone wry and amused, matching the self-deprecating tilt of his mouth—and if it hadn't been for the tightness of his hand still around Geva's wrist, she might have almost believed that he and this Killik, at least, were old, familiar friends. But there was most certainly more to it—especially with Ulfarr still standing there glowering like that—and Rathgarr was clearly still making some kind of statement, and fully expecting Geva to do the same.

So Geva drew in a shaky breath and pasted on a wide smile, before turning and giving Rathgarr's arm a playful little swat. "Your arse is not portly in the *least*, love," she informed him, with what she hoped was an affectionate air, before wrenching her gaze back to Killik and Ulfarr. "And it's very nice to meet you both. I apologize for my agitation, I just didn't expect—"

She flapped her hand toward Rathgarr's still-bared groin with genuine consternation, and his answering smile looked almost relieved this time, or maybe even indulgent. "Ach, my sweet mate is yet new to the ways of orcs," he told Ulfarr and Killik, as he finally released Geva's wrist, and pulled up his trousers again. "Now settle yourself, my skittish sweetling, whilst we share our news. Ach?"

He'd patted his still-spread thigh as he spoke, in another very clear order—so Geva again sucked back a bracing breath, and obeyed. Sinking heavily down onto his solid thigh, while Rathgarr's big arm curled around her waist, and hitched her a little closer. Wanting her to do this. To pretend.

But he wasn't even looking at her now, his deceptively genial eyes again focused on Killik and Ulfarr. Ulfarr still hadn't moved, still frowning with palpable hostility, but Killik sank his lean form down onto a nearby rock, and began speaking. His voice low and rasping, the words in a language that Geva couldn't at all identify.

But Rathgarr easily replied in kind, the strange words deep and rumbling in his close familiar voice. Speaking with careless, casual ease, despite the still-tight clutch of his hand against Geva's waist, and the tension all over his big body beneath her. Betraying his certain awareness of the huge Ulfarr orc still glaring at him, challenging him, *judging* him.

And suddenly, Geva couldn't bear to keep sitting there on him like a lump, like a gods-damned decorative accessory. No. She could do this. His *helpmate*.

"Excuse me, love," she murmured in Rathgarr's ear, perhaps still loud enough for the orcs to hear. And then, without waiting for his answer, she slipped off his thigh, and made straight for his pack. It was lying nearby, and she could feel the prickle of Rathgarr's gaze as she knelt beside it, and began rummaging inside. But he just kept speaking to Killik, smooth and easy, as though he weren't even slightly confused. Almost as though... he trusted her.

So Geva just kept going, pulling out the provisions they'd purchased before leaving the inn that morning—biscuits, and berries, and a good quantity of salted pork. And after yet more digging—gods, Rathgarr had truly obscene amounts of plunder in here, and so many *clothes*—she thankfully found two silver dinner-plates, too. And once she'd arranged a choice selection of food on both plates, she strode over to Killik and Ulfarr, and held out the plates toward them.

"A little something to eat, while you meet with my mate," she said, giving them her brightest smile, and a low curtsey. "Fresh from the inn this morning."

Killik's brows snapped up, and he instantly snatched the plate from Geva's hand—while Ulfarr, who was now looming close behind him, loudly harrumphed, and crossed his huge arms over his chest. "And how do we ken," he said, his voice deep and deliberate, "that these are safe to eat? That this is not yet another devious Ash-Kai scheme?"

Ulfarr's eyes had again narrowed toward Rathgarr, who was

doing a creditable job of conveying blank bewilderment, rather than the fury Geva was sure he felt. And despite her own inward acknowledgement of Ulfarr's point—Rathgarr was most certainly not to be trusted—she squared her shoulders, and mustered up a bemused smile of her own.

"Well, I did watch Rathgarr buy these provisions fresh this morning, so I'm quite certain they're safe," she said, as lightly as she could. "But I will say, he also refused to buy me dessert! That is indeed a devious Ash-Kai scheme, if I ever heard one. Don't you think?"

Killik clearly agreed, smirking as he tossed a piece of dried pork into his mouth, while Rathgarr flashed Geva a broad, approving grin. "You ken it brings me great joy to fatten you up for me, poppet," he purred toward her. "But my Ash-Kai need to steal away your dessert should be far too strong to endure, and"—he gave his own belly a rueful-looking pat—"I am already portly enough, you ken?"

Geva couldn't help a genuine choke of laughter, a roll of her eyes toward him—and in return, Rathgarr laughed too, the sound deep and rich, his eyes crinkling at the corners. The sight of it so suddenly, bizarrely compelling that she couldn't seem to look away, and she only belatedly noticed Killik snatching the second plate from her hand, and thrusting it up into Ulfarr's chest.

"Is good," Killik said, in heavily accented common-tongue, with another tilt of his head toward her. "Our thanks, Ash-Kai."

Ash-Kai. The word shivered strangely up Geva's spine, but she managed another cheery smile before turning and fleeing toward Rathgarr again. And while he didn't thank her, or even acknowledge what she'd done, she could have sworn she felt his big body slightly relaxing as he again pulled her down into his lap, his arm curving tighter around her than before.

The rest of their conversation seemed to flow more smoothly after that, and Geva couldn't help feeling rather smug at the sight of Ulfarr carefully picking his plate clean. Killik, on the other hand, had inhaled his lunch with astonishing speed, and was now standing and stretching his arms over his head, angling Rathgarr a cool, appraising smile.

"Now, brother," he said. "Another sparring match, ach? Me and you, whilst these two judge?"

Rathgarr's reply was something between a laugh and a groan, but Geva could again feel the telltale stiffness in his body against her. Even as he nodded, shifting himself out from under her, and then—her throat convulsed—he began stripping off his clothes, and dumping them into her lap.

First was his usual silver fur from across his shoulders, and then his huge, heavy black cloak. And then, with a quick flick of his claws, he unlaced the neck of his crisp white tunic, and then drew that off, too. Confronting Geva's blinking eyes with the sight of his broad bare chest, somehow looking even more powerful in the bright daylight. What with all that corded rippled muscle, the sheer size of it, the breadth of his massive shoulders...

"You shall not be alarmed by some sparring between us, ach, poppet?" Rathgarr asked her, his voice still deceptively genial, despite the brief flare of command in his eyes. "Killik shall not castrate or kill me. Not today, at least."

"He'd damn well better not," Geva made herself reply, giving what she hoped was a teasing smile as she took the tunic from his hands. "Best of luck, love. I can't wait to see you *demolish* him, as a proper Ash-Kai should."

Rathgarr shot a rather approving smile back, and then—Geva swallowed again—he plucked a string out from his trouser pocket, and began tying up his hair. An action that seemed to reveal his already-familiar face in an entirely different light, and as she kept blinking up at him, it occurred to her that Rathgarr really was a far better-looking orc than either Killik or Ulfarr. What with his rugged but harmonious features, his expressive eyes, that supple mocking mouth...

Geva dragged her gaze away, earning a strange little

harrumph from Rathgarr in return—but when she glanced toward him again, he was already striding off toward Killik. Who was still casually stretching his long arms over his head, his harsh face tilted up to the sun, as though he hadn't even noticed Rathgarr approaching.

But then, in a sharp flash of movement, Killik's lean body launched up into the air, and—*attacked*. His clawed hand sweeping out strong and vicious, swiping straight for Rathgarr's exposed, undefended eyes.

Geva gasped aloud, her hands clapping over her mouth—but somehow, *impossibly*, Rathgarr twisted away, just in time. His big body shifting with unaccountable speed as his clenched fist snapped out, and caught Killik on the shoulder. Striking with enough force that Killik staggered, whipping around with a sly smile on his mouth—and then he launched back at Rathgarr again. His claws furiously flying, moving so fast Geva could barely follow them, and wait, those were brand-new *gouges*, already welling fresh lines of red across Rathgarr's chest.

But Rathgarr hadn't seemed to notice, and shifted on his feet again, his big fists raised and waiting. And one of those fists met Killik's next flying strike, knocking his arm away, while the other fist sank deep into his belly. Making him bend double, in what looked like defeat—until he leapt up and whirled around again, aiming a vicious-looking kick at Rathgarr's groin. But Rathgarr avoided that one too, and landed another powerfully impressive punch, against Killik's chest this time.

Geva's breath still felt caught in her throat, but she felt her heartbeat gradually slowing as she watched, as something almost like admiration began to bloom in her chest. Rathgarr certainly seemed to be holding his own in this, despite all his grand claims of being out of shape. And though he had a very different fighting style than Killik—far less light and flamboyant, relying much more on his weight and his fists—it still seemed to be brutally effective, sending Killik flying on multiple occasions.

But—Geva's head tilted—there was still something... *off* about it. Because while Rathgarr kept smiling throughout, meeting Killik's taunts with lighthearted mockery of his own, she could still see that telltale edge of tension on his form again, hunching his shoulders, pulling on his smiling mouth. Suggesting, quite clearly, that the fighting was just as fraught as the speaking had been. And though Rathgarr never once glanced over at Ulfarr's silent watching form, Geva could almost feel the awareness between them, the implication that this entire little scene was somehow a test, or maybe even a provocation.

"Ach, enough," Rathgarr finally said, his breath heaving, his palms upraised toward Killik. "You may count that as a win, brother. I am already undone, and I must yet walk across half this province today."

Behind Killik, Ulfarr's eyes narrowed, but Killik only twitched a careless-looking shrug, and flashed Rathgarr a complacent smile. "This was not as bad as last time," he replied smugly. "You are better, with a woman to impress."

Rathgarr huffed and rolled his eyes, but he didn't quite look at Geva as he strode back toward her. "Two more days, brother," he said over his shoulder, "and I shall be *demolishing* you in the Skai arena, whilst my sweet mate *laughs* at your doom."

Two more days. Wait, did they only have two more days, before arriving at Orc Mountain? And yes, good gods, Rathgarr had said the trip would take five days, and this was already their third day of travelling, and how had Geva not even noticed?

It took far too much effort to keep the smile fixed to her face, but thankfully Killik and Ulfarr had already turned to leave, Killik giving a casual wave over his shoulder, Ulfarr not sparing a single backwards glance as he stalked into the trees. And finally Geva was left alone again with Rathgarr, who was still copiously dripping with blood and sweat, his breaths heaving, his bare chest gleaming in the bright midday sun.

"What the hell was that about?" Geva asked, her voice low, as she rummaged in Rathgarr's pack for the waterskin, and thrust it out toward him. "And are you... all right?"

Rathgarr took the waterskin without comment, and then heartily drank, before dumping out the rest of the water over his head and chest. "Ach, I am well," he said, with a hard exhale. "And this was only a friendly meeting between brothers, ach? Killik is a first-rate fighter, as are many of his clan."

There was more telltale tension in his voice, and he'd purposefully angled his eyes toward the forest, where Killik and Ulfarr had gone. Very clearly suggesting that they might still be listening, damn it—so Geva thrust down all the bubbling questions she wanted to ask, and instead plastered another worshipful smile to her face. And then, as a proper mate would surely do, she let her eyes linger on Rathgarr's flushed cheeks, his long wet lashes, the water still running down his broad chest in rivulets.

He looked... tired, she realized, as something oddly flipped, low in her belly. He looked... defeated. Like that entire unexpected little visit, whatever the hell it had been about, had taken more out of him than he'd have liked to admit.

His eyes had even fluttered closed again, his shoulders still high and stiff—and without quite meaning to, Geva set aside the pile of his clothes she'd still been holding, and again grasped for his pack. Searching inside for one of the clean rags she'd remembered seeing, and then, in a burst of bizarre, inexplicable daring, she rose to her feet, and wiped the rag against his wet, heaving chest.

She fully expected some kind of snide protest or resistance, but Rathgarr didn't open his eyes, or betray a single twitch. Suggesting, perhaps, that Killik and Ulfarr were indeed still watching, still expecting such behaviour from Rathgarr's devoted mate. So Geva wiped his sweaty chest again, firmer this time, and in return he huffed a shuddery exhale, his shoulders sagging, his face tilting higher toward the sky.

Oh. And maybe that was what a besotted orc—or a tired one—would do in this situation, so Geva kept wiping at him. Drying off his chest, and then around to his back, and up to his neck and shoulders, and finally, even his face. Fighting to ignore the feel of his sharp jaw under her fingers, the heavy ridges of his brow bone and cheekbone, the softness of his full mouth...

Rathgarr still hadn't looked at her, or even acknowledged her in the slightest, so in another flash of inexplicable boldness, Geva plucked up his tunic from the pile of clothes behind them. And after shaking the fabric out, brushing off a bit of debris, she lifted it up, and carefully pulled it on over his head. *Dressing* this devious orc, good gods, as though she had every right to do this, as if he *wanted* her to do this...

But again, Rathgarr didn't seem even slightly disconcerted, sliding his arms obligingly into the tunic's full sleeves without even looking. So Geva took the liberty of pulling the tunic down, smoothing it out over his powerful chest and arms, and then against his softer belly, before tucking it properly into his trousers. And then—her face was heating, now—she tied up the tunic's laces at his neck, taking care to leave them a little loose, the way he seemed to prefer. Just enough to show the smooth grey skin of his upper chest, the smattering of black hair beneath.

Rathgarr still hadn't moved, beyond another slow, heavy exhale, so Geva kept going, next reaching for his huge black cloak. And once she'd thrown it over his shoulders, she couldn't resist fussing with it, smoothing and shifting until it hung in even, heavy folds, its thick cord pulled firm—but not too tight—across his collarbones. And last was his grey fur, and she fussed with that, too, until it also looked just as it should.

"There," she told him, her voice thick. "All good again, but for your hair. Unless you'd like that dealt with, too?"

She'd been eyeing his hair rather too much throughout all this—it had half-fallen out from where he'd tied it back, with multiple sweaty strands clinging to his face and neck. And to her distant surprise, Rathgarr shrugged, the movement sweeping out his beautifully arranged cloak. "Should you wish," he said gruffly. "There is a comb in my pack."

Geva remembered seeing it earlier, and accordingly knelt and dug it out again—a lovely, human-made silver comb, with the kind of close-set teeth she'd never be able to use on her own hair. But once she'd moved behind Rathgarr, and pulled down the rest of his hair, she could soon see how well the comb worked for him, how it smoothed out the thick black strands into a beautiful glossy sheen.

"Do you cut it yourself?" she heard herself say, her voice still unaccountably thick, as she eyed the line of it across the bottom. "Or are there orc barbers you can visit, perhaps?"

Rathgarr made a low scoffing sound, and very slightly shook his head, as if not wanting to disturb Geva's combing efforts. "No," he said. "And I cannot cut it straight myself, or risk visiting a human shop to do this. I most oft ask a bedmate to tend it, when I can."

Oh. Geva froze in place, her heart skipping a beat, while the sudden, staggering vision of Rathgarr with a *bedmate* swarmed through her thoughts. It would be a sweet, beautiful woman, no doubt, quiet and obliging, just the way he preferred, coming apart beneath his clever hands. And afterwards, perhaps as they dressed the next morning, she would *tend* to his hair with this exact silver comb, and he would flash that smile at her, and ask if she would—

Oh, hell, no. *Gods*, no. And far too late, Geva stumbled away from him, lurching back toward his pack. Thrusting the comb deep inside, and then packing up everything else, too. Doing her damned job, because Rathgarr was her employer, and that was *all*. This was pretending, and nothing more, not that she would ever want more from him anyway. One month, and then the sea.

When Geva stood up again, she'd steadied her breaths, and assumed what she hoped was a distant, dispassionate smile. Holding her eyes very carefully on a place past Rathgarr's head, where she didn't need to look at his face, or envision the beauty of his last bedmate, who'd taken such care with his hair.

"So?" she made herself say, quiet, through gritted teeth. "Are they still watching?"

Rathgarr drew in a long, purposeful-looking inhale, and then shook his head. "I ken they are gone now," he replied, just as quiet, as he reached for the pack, and slung it up onto his shoulder. "I can no longer smell them."

Geva jerked a curt nod, and then spun away, moving too quickly back toward the road. "And can we really trust your so-called sense of smell?" she asked tightly, over her shoulder. "Shouldn't you have at least"—she felt her steps faltering, while a grim, belated comprehension flashed across her thoughts—"smelled them approaching, while we were...?"

Gods, she couldn't even say it, the simmering fury and frustration surging higher into her throat—until something caught her arm, and drew her to a halt. Rathgarr's... hand. Turning her around to face him, as if he wanted her to see his eyes.

"I did not smell them there," he said, grimacing, "until we were well in the midst of it. And by then, it seemed a waste to stop. This was"—he paused, rubbed at his face—"this was a good showing, poppet, and I ken it helped me more than aught else so far, ach? It is all to my gain, if the Skai—and most of all Ulfarr—see me as an addled, lovestruck fool, and not as a true threat."

Geva blinked at Rathgarr for a choked, frozen moment, while too many thoughts swarmed her head at once. He'd thought that was a *good showing*? That, with the suffocating tension, the lost match, the visceral malice from Ulfarr? And he thought what he'd done with her—all that warm, indulgent approval—had been the behaviour of an *addled, lovestruck fool*?!

"So why," Geva managed, desperately groping for the real questions, damn it, "would you present a *true threat* for them? When you're only one orc, and you haven't been home in *years*? And you apparently can't even beat Killik—who must be *half* your size, by the way—in combat?"

She couldn't deny the petty-sounding mockery in her voice, but Rathgarr didn't even argue it, just grimaced again, and gave an unfairly elegant shrug of his shoulder. "My blood-kin once stood in high esteem, amongst the Ash-Kai," he said finally. "We once bore great wealth, and power, and gifts. And now that I seek to return..."

His voice trailed off there, but Geva was still staring at him, her heartbeat rising in her chest. "Now that you're returning, you're a threat to what?" she demanded. "To *who*?"

Rathgarr shrugged again, his gaze angling away, but he drew in a breath, let it out. "To the new captain of Orc Mountain, mayhap," he said flatly. "Grimarr, of Clan Ash-Kai. A hard, ruthless, single-minded orc, from a long line of the same. And like his father before him, he bears no dissent, and no rivals for his place."

Wait. *Wait.* Geva's mouth had fallen open, her thoughts spinning, flailing between comprehension and disbelief. *No rivals.* So was Rathgarr truly saying that the orcs' own *captain* might actually see him as a rival? And this captain—Grimarr—had apparently sent Killik and Ulfarr out to *spy* on him, to *spar* with him, to gauge the likelihood of him being a true threat? When Rathgarr had said—yes, he'd *said*—he didn't expect any actual violence from the other orcs? Hadn't he?

"I told you, there is naught for you to fear, woman," Rathgarr's stiff voice said, as if he'd too neatly followed Geva's thoughts. "If they wished to maim or kill me, they would have done so many days past, ach? I have a strong plan in place, and

I shall face their mistrust with ease. Grimarr and his attack dogs shall *not* find a threat in me, you ken?"

Geva couldn't stop gaping at him, while yet more understanding flashed through her thoughts. Rathgarr had a *strong plan*. Which meant that little sparring match with Killik just now—the match he'd supposedly lost—had *that* been on purpose, too? More pretending? Part of the *plan*? And he hadn't bothered to tell her, *again*?

"So if your own people don't actually want you, or trust you," Geva snapped, "then why the *hell* did they ask you to come back, then? And why the hell did you agree to it, if you need to put on an act like this the entire time? If everything you show them is going to be a *lie*? Including *me*?!"

She could see her own rising frustration reflected in Rathgarr's narrowing eyes, in the hard set of his mouth. "Ach, do not question me in this, woman," he shot back. "I have already told you all this. And *you* agreed to help me!"

Geva blinked, and snapped her mouth open to reply—but Rathgarr lurched a sharp step closer, his huge body looming over her, his eyes cold and glittering on hers.

"But here it is again, poppet," he hissed. "I shall show myself *settled* upon my visit home, with a sweet devoted mate by my side, and mayhap a sweet little brat soon on the way. I shall smile, and tease, and lose all my sparring-matches, and flaunt all the gold and goods I can carry. I shall be an obedient brother, a harmless Ash-Kai, and a boon to my kin. And thus"—his voice had deepened into a growl—"I shall *never* let the Skai or their foul *usurper* captain see what I truly think of them!"

Geva's voice had entirely vanished in her throat, her eyes staring wide and blank up at Rathgarr's face. This... wasn't just pretending, then. This wasn't just about making a good impression after a long absence. This was about politics. About enemies. About *power*.

And for what? Revenge? Conquest? That position of *Captain of Orc Mountain*?!

And before her, Rathgarr barked a harsh, sudden laugh, his eyes blazing on hers, his hand gripped tightly to his sword-hilt. Making another silent, but very real threat. Making it clear that he was a threat. He *was*.

"And neither shall *you* betray me, my pretty *poppet*," he growled. "Until my ends are met, and my price is paid!"

And with that, he spun around and stalked away, his cloak whirling out black and furious behind him.

14

For a wild, panicked moment, Geva stared after Rathgarr, her heart lurching in her chest.

Of course there was more to all this than he'd let on. Of course he had ulterior motives. *I have good cause to show myself settled. I could be well-served by a... deception.*

And staring at his diminishing back, at that huge billowing cloak behind him, Geva felt an odd, distant whisper of... fear. Perhaps she should have been more afraid of him, all this time. Perhaps the Rathgarr she'd met that first day—the terrifying orc who'd so easily threatened to kill her, and gloried in the taste of her blood—perhaps that had been the real Rathgarr, after all. Not the one who'd wanted her to dress him just now, not the one who'd praised and petted her, not the one who'd brought her breakfast in bed this morning.

Because this Rathgarr was... powerful. He had enemies. He was playing a political game, and he'd wrapped Geva up in it, and he hadn't even told her, he didn't even care...

But suddenly his long strides halted, his head tilting toward the sky, his shoulders sagging beneath his cloak. And then he turned around, and... held out his hand. Toward her.

Geva blinked at him, swallowed as her eyes dropped to his

hand, and then flicked back to his face. To where he again just looked… tired, his mouth thin, his brow creased, his hand still outstretched. Waiting for her. Asking her.

Wanting her.

Something lurched in Geva's chest, and she felt herself nodding, her feet tripping toward him. Not thinking, not questioning, not refusing. Because this was still just a job… right? Still just one month, and then the sea…

"I do not know," Rathgarr said, his big hand clasping hers, "all that awaits me at Orc Mountain. But I yet know"—he cleared his throat—"I do not mean to stay long. I have no wish to steal the place of captain. And I have sworn to care for you, and keep you safe there, and I *shall*."

His voice was smooth, his words very careful—but glancing at his face, there was yet more awareness swarming Geva's thoughts, more sweeping swirling mess. "But you also just told me," she replied, her voice wavering, "that orcs can smell falsehoods. So I'm sure it's all part of your *plan* to keep telling me what you think they'll want to hear, right? To make sure I won't give you away?"

Rathgarr didn't immediately reply, and Geva's frustration was already surging again, escaping out her mouth. "Even though I've already proven to you," she continued, waving sharply toward the clearing behind them, "that I can do this. I can be *good* at this. My parents were ambassadors, I know politics, I know diplomacy, I know *all* too well how to deal with multiple spoiled arguing *children*! And if you could just be honest with me for once"—her voice was rising, harder and shriller—"and tell me the *real* reason why you're dragging me all the way across the realm to Orc Mountain, maybe I could actually *help* you!"

Rathgarr was still frowning at her, not speaking, but Geva was too caught in this now to stop. "You said I could earn more, the better job I do at this," she hissed at him. "Do you think that's meaningless to me? This is my *life*, Rathgarr. This is my *survival.* I will work myself to the *bone* for you, and make your enemies believe whatever the hell you want, if you'll just give me a chance, like you damn well *promised*! I'm supposed to be your *helpmate*, remember?!"

Her voice had gone far too loud, surely risking far too much, and Rathgarr clearly realized it too, his eyes darting at the forest all around them, his hand clenching tighter on hers. And without another word, he tugged Geva away, back toward the road. Back toward Orc Mountain, toward all his refusals and his secrets and his *lies*, and—

"I have... a brother there," he said, abrupt and low. "A blood-brother. Kesst."

He... *really*? Geva's feet faltered at the edge of the blessedly empty road, her eyes blinking uncertainly toward Rathgarr's profile. Catching on the tightness in his jaw, the deep crease in his brow, the thick swallow of his throat.

"I have not seen nor scented Kesst in sixteen summers," Rathgarr continued, even lower. "For half his life. I... wish to see him now. I have stayed away"—his throat convulsed again—"too long."

Oh. He'd been away for *sixteen years*?! And Geva could feel the strain in his voice, the hesitation, the... shame. The suggestion that this, suddenly, was truth, and it was truth he hadn't wanted to tell.

"Kesst is my highest aim in going home again," Rathgarr added, his voice hardening, as he drew Geva to a walk again, his hand still gripped to hers. "Above all else."

Geva was still eyeing him, studying his grim mouth, the bitter, betraying set of his jaw. "But there's obviously still... *more* to your trip home, right?" she tentatively asked. "Beyond just your brother?"

Rathgarr huffed a heavy sigh, his eyes briefly closing. "Yes. No. I do not know. I need"—he sighed again—"I must see how Kesst fares. What he says. What he wishes from me. And then..."

He jerked a shrug, surely suggesting that there was little he wouldn't do, if his brother asked. That this entire visit home might still very well be about politics, about... *revenge*. About that position of captain. *That foul usurper.*

"So why *have* you stayed away from home for so long, then?" Geva asked slowly. "You couldn't have gone back for a visit now and then, even just to see your brother?"

Something spasmed in Rathgarr's cheek, and he shook his head. "No," he replied, clipped. "No. I could not."

He clearly wasn't keen to elaborate, and perhaps Geva should have pushed it, demanded more explanations and answers. Because there was obviously so much more to this, Rathgarr might have done something truly awful, he might be genuinely loathed or feared by his people...

But he clearly cared about his brother. Missed his brother. And Geva had asked for the real reason for his return home, and he'd given it.

"So what's your brother like, then?" she asked, quiet, into the taut silence. "Do you two have much in common?"

There was a twinge of surprising softness on Rathgarr's face, a wry little smile curling on his mouth. "Naught at all," he replied. "But Kesst is... a delight. Quick, and clever, and bright. You shall like him, I ken."

Oh. Geva felt oddly caught in that warmth on Rathgarr's face, enough that it took an instant to digest what he'd said. He thought she would *like* his brother? And wait—something flipped in her stomach—had he meant that as a *compliment*?

She made herself glance away, back toward the still-empty road ahead. "So... can you at least tell me what's changed, then?" she asked, choosing her words carefully. "To make you return home now, after so long? Or, wait"—she felt her eyes widening, darting back toward Rathgarr again—"when you said *they* sent for you... was it actually *Kesst* who sent for you?"

The softness had rapidly drained from Rathgarr's face, and he barked a curt, hollow-sounding laugh. "Clever, poppet," he said, in a jovial voice that wasn't jovial at all. "Ach, this was the *one* summons that should have dragged me back there. And with Kesst's message, they sent a vow from the *captain* himself, swearing my warm welcome upon my return."

There was a heavy thread of sarcasm in his voice, suggesting just what Rathgarr thought of this so-called vow, and Geva considered that too, adding it to the rest of the churning mess in her thoughts. "So are you thinking," she ventured, "that Kesst might have been... compromised, some-how? Or"—she winced, shot Rathgarr a regretful look—"that he might have been convinced to... betray you?"

She braced for Rathgarr's certain retaliation, for the abrupt and angry end of this conversation—but to her distant aston-ishment, he only laughed again, still too loud and cold. "I have wondered this each day since," he replied flatly. "I wonder this each time Killik comes to me, and pretends I am his brother, and not his target. And now that *Ulfarr* has joined him"—he paused, and actually spat on the road at their feet—"I wonder this even more, for of all the orcs in that curst mountain, *he* is mayhap the one who should laugh loudest at my downfall, and I at his!"

A chilly, unpleasant shiver snaked up Geva's back—so *should* she have been more concerned about her safety, all this time?—but Rathgarr's eyes angled toward hers, his hand's warm grip tightening against her fingers. "I cannot believe Kesst would eagerly ally with an orc like Ulfarr, or wish me real harm," he continued, with a grimace. "I should not now be going back there, if I feared this. But I yet cannot afford to be careless in this, or a fool, ach?"

Right. And as Geva kept walking, considering it, his hand still clamped in hers, she felt something much like understand-ing, or perhaps even commiseration, coiling in her chest. Of course Rathgarr would want to be careful about this trip, then. And of course it made sense for him to appear harmless and settled, only there for a short, innocuous visit to his brother, so he could gain the space and time to evaluate the situation. To evaluate his brother's choices, perhaps, and make his own choices from there.

"So how much of your plan," Geva began, "is meant for *Kesst*, then? Some of the plunder you're carrying is meant as gifts for him, I presume? And you bringing me with you... should I be particularly..."

Targeting Kesst, she might well have said, but her wince surely conveyed it, all the same. And beside her, Rathgarr gave a dismissive-looking shrug, together with a rather betraying twitch of his fingers.

"Ach, mayhap," he said, too casually, with another unconvincing shrug. "Kesst always liked women. Our mother doted upon him, and he worshipped her."

Geva should have been fully focused on that first point—because wait, had Rathgarr really hired her in part to impress his *brother*?!—but instead she seemed stuck on the second. On how there was yet more of that tension in his voice, in his clammy-feeling fingers. *Our mother doted upon him.*

"And how about *you* and your mother, then?" Geva heard herself ask. "You didn't worship her the same way, I take it?"

Rathgarr barked another too-loud laugh, even emptier than before. "No," he said. "I did not. My mother and I were never... in accord. Too much like my *witless, brute orc father*, she liked to say."

His voice had slipped into a distinct northern accent, suggesting that these were indeed his mother's exact words, in her own voice. And gods, Geva couldn't imagine her own warm, generous mother *ever* saying such an awful thing, and suddenly there was just more commiseration, more sympathy, tightening in her chest.

"Well, your mother clearly did *not* know you very well," she said firmly, nudging Rathgarr's elbow with hers. "Because no matter what kind of act you put on, you are quite possibly the most devious, calculating person I've ever met in my *life*. Why, if I didn't know better, I'd have thought you and Killik were the best of friends today! And I really *did* think you'd lost that match, fair and square."

Her blatant attempt at distraction was rewarded with a deep but tolerant-sounding huff, a quirk of Rathgarr's brow toward her. "Ach, you played a good game in this also, poppet," he replied, his voice far lighter than before. "I almost believed you *wished* to kneel for me in the dirt, and tend to my every need."

Of course he would go straight there, the slimy bastard, and Geva gave an irritated groan, even as she flashed him her broadest, sweetest smile. "I *did* do a good job of that, didn't I?" she said smugly. "So good, in fact, that I think you should increase my payment to *five* coins."

Rathgarr scoffed, but now his mouth was twitching up, too. "Five is for that pretty, plump rump of yours, poppet," he replied. "We agreed upon three, for your mouth."

Geva's breath caught for an instant—he thought her arse was *pretty*?—but she quickly composed herself, and shot him another sickly-sweet smile. "And we also agreed that you'd pay me more for good performance," she airily pointed out. "And you yourself just admitted that I gave you a truly excellent performance, didn't you?"

Rathgarr's mouth was still curving up, into something almost like a grin. "Mayhap I shall further ponder more coin for this," he purred, "*if* tonight, you prove to me you can recall *all* you have learnt today, ach?"

Geva spluttered and flailed at him, but it was an unfairly effective challenge, and one that seemed to hover powerfully between them for the rest of the day's journey. And despite Geva's best attempts at distraction—including her usual loved-up charade for the passersby, as well as stilted discussions about the weather and the road—she found her traitorous thoughts wandering toward that challenge again and again. Toward how he'd caressed her, when she'd been kneeling between his thighs. How he'd watched her with such approving, glittering pride. *Good poppet*, he'd said. *Good.*

By the time they'd finally settled into their room for the night—again, predictably, with only one bed—Geva was nearly vibrating with tension, and she was almost certain Rathgarr was similarly preoccupied. A suspicion that was only reinforced by the fact that he hadn't ordered a bath this time, and instead—Geva's breath choked—after sweeping off his fur and cloak, he promptly sprawled his big body back on the too-small bed, and began unbuckling his belt.

"Come, then, poppet," he drawled, patting the bed beside him, as he brazenly reached down into his trousers, and drew out—*that*. Already swollen and veined and dripping, and shuddering even fuller against his casually stroking fingers. "Time to show me what you have learnt, ach?"

And curse her, but Geva's mouth was already watering, and she swallowed hard, and attempted a chilly smile. "You know, you are the *worst* employer," she informed him, even as she stepped on shaky legs toward the bed, and climbed up to kneel between his sprawled thighs. "Greedy, and cheap, and shameless, and unappreciative, and—"

But her voice broke off into an enraged growl, because Rathgarr had cupped his big hand around her head, and abruptly dragged her downward. Straight toward that waiting swollen heft, prodding purposefully against her lips, and then—oh, *hell*—delving its way into her mouth. Sliding deeper and deeper, until her lips were stretched wide around him, and his hard rounded head was jutted up tight and close against her swallowing, convulsing throat.

"Ach, much better," Rathgarr coolly informed her, with a smug, infuriating grin. "You are so much sweeter, poppet, with a good fat prick blocking your ungrateful little mouth."

Geva glared viciously up toward him, and—oh gods, what was she *doing*—let her teeth clamp against the swollen flesh filling her mouth. Not hard, but certainly enough that he could feel it, his body stiffening beneath her, his eyes flashing with mingled amusement and disbelief. And without warning, he whipped her head up and off him, grasped the base of his shaft... and used it to *swat her across the face.*

Geva's shock was genuine, her mouth still half-open, her cheeks gone far too hot—and in return, Rathgarr flashed her a taunting, satisfied smile. "That is what wilfulness shall gain you, poppet," he said. "Now *behave.* Show me how good you can be."

He'd nudged that slick head back against her lips, and oh, gods, Geva was already kissing at him, softly this time, just the way he liked. Holding her blinking eyes to his, in something that felt too close to contrition, to *eagerness.* And perhaps he even saw that, his big hand caressing down the side of her face, his mouth curving up.

"Good," he murmured. "Now, do you remember how to please me? Or have you already forgotten all your lessons, my prickly little schoolmarm?"

Geva managed an irritable groan, and even a creditable roll of her eyes at the smug bastard—and this time, he drew back his big hand, and gave her cheek a light, gentle slap. "I said, *behave,*" he growled, in a voice that shot an unaccountable surge of heat into her lower belly. "Else you shall be licking your seed off this filthy *floor,* poppet."

Geva's breath choked, her mouth grimacing around his slick head with too-visceral disgust, and Rathgarr laughed, the sound low and rolling, his hand patting her cheek. "Now get to work," he purred, flaring another flush of heat deep into her groin. "Show me what I have paid for, poppet. Impress me."

And damn the infuriating menace, but Geva wanted to impress him, she did—and without at all meaning to, she was holding his eyes, and doing it. Kissing him, caressing him, soft and gentle at first, coaxing him to full hardness against her lips and tongue. And then adding both hands, stroking and sliding, and delving down to find his heavy bollocks, rolling them gently in her fingers. While keeping her gaze to his face, watching his eyes flutter, his nostrils flaring, his lips parting with his breaths...

"Now deeper," he ordered, with infuriating steadiness, and a slight roll upwards of his hips. "Milk me with your throat until you *choke*."

Good gods, this ungrateful *cheat*, but Geva was desperately nodding, and taking him deeper. Gouging him into her throat, while also hollowing her cheeks, tightening the suction, just the way he'd taught her. And then putting it all together, sucking and stroking and fondling, revelling in the silky sweetness now oozing into her mouth. Milking even more of it out of him, showing him, *impressing* him...

And yes, there was that look in his eyes, the glittering gathering *pride*. His fingers spreading against her sweaty cheek, his black tongue slipping out, as his cock swelled even fuller between her already-stretched lips, prodding even deeper into her convulsing throat. All hot sweet invading heat, slick and sliding, closer and closer, his bollocks tightening, his breath catching, his—

His release flooded out in a rush, pouring with furious force down Geva's blocked, desperately gulping throat. Surging so strong that she couldn't stop herself from gagging on it, *damn* it—until he yanked himself out, away. Leaving her coughing and dragging for air, and reflexively spitting out a full mouthful of thick sticky sweetness.

But at least she hadn't spat onto his clean white tunic, because Rathgarr had snapped both his big hands toward her face, cupping them beneath her spitting, dripping mouth. Catching nearly all of that viscous, sweet-scented white, but for a few strands already slipping between his fingers.

"Drink it," he breathed, an order, or perhaps a plea—and amidst her hammering heartbeat, the heated flush pulsing through her entire body, Geva accordingly bowed her head, and... licked at it. Licked at this, at his own hot fresh sweetness, cupped here in his own hands, for her. Feeling almost like a gift, an opportunity, a reward...

Her face was smarting painfully now, but she kept licking, drinking up everything he would give her. And when there was no liquid left in his big palms, she licked them clean too, and then his big fingers, one by one...

"Look at me," he hissed, because curse it, she'd forgotten that, in the heated closeness of his hands—so she instantly obliged, holding her wide, ashamed eyes to his, as she licked and sucked his fingers, feeling how their claws were drawn fully in, their touch warm and indulgent against her lips. And even if she couldn't quite read his eyes now, it surely wasn't disappointment, at least, was it?

"And now?" he asked once she'd finished, a distinct challenge in his voice. Dragging Geva's thoughts back to the lesson, to what he'd told her he liked, and she nodded, licked her lips. And then bent down over his groin again, and slipped his softened, still-slick heft into her mouth. Sucking it slow and gentle, using her tongue to clean off the last sweet smears of seed, to delve beneath his sliding hood, into his slit. And when she slipped off again, he was glossy and clean, looking strangely soft and innocuous against his thatch of thick black curls.

"Good?" she whispered, again licking her swollen-feeling lips, while a tenuous thread of longing seemed to tighten against her chest. She'd done her best, she'd offered what she'd thought was a good performance, and what if he disagreed, what if he hadn't liked it, if he...

"Good," he murmured back, with a rueful little smile, a firm pat of his hand against her cheek. "Ach, I am impressed, my sweet. Very good."

Oh. Well. Geva felt herself swallowing hard, her head slightly ducking, and when his big hands guided her up again, it felt almost too easy, too natural, to rise up over his face, to hold his shimmering eyes. To perhaps lean a little closer, to where his lips were parted, his tongue brushing very brief against them—

But then, he—turned his face away. The movement quick and purposeful, its intention suddenly, staggeringly clear, as his eyes fixed intently on the wall.

He... didn't want to kiss her. Oh. Right. Because this was just—a job. And Geva felt herself flinching backwards again, squeezing her eyes shut, shaking her head. *No true mating between us. Only play-acting...*

And Geva knew that, how did she keep forgetting that, and suddenly she couldn't bear to look at him, or even be in the same bed with him—and she frantically scrabbled away, lunging for her satchel, for her nightclothes. And then she swiftly, shakily changed, and then tied up her hair in her scarf, keeping her back turned firmly toward Rathgarr in the bed. One month, and then the sea...

"Ach, poppet," came Rathgarr's low voice behind her. "I could... say more sweet things, should you wish."

Geva's hands froze on her scarf, her eyes staring at the room's dingy wall, and she could hear him shifting on the bed, clearing his throat. "How clever and pretty you are, mayhap?" he continued. "How your hair is that of a sun goddess, mayhap, and your skin like purest shining bronze, new from the forge. How your hunger lights you from within, and shines in your bewitching brown eyes, and—"

"*Gods*, no," Geva choked out, frantically flapping her hand, because damn it, hearing him say these things, when he clearly didn't mean them, was somehow even worse than him not kissing her, worse than him not saying anything at all. "Please, no. Not from you."

There was a slow, resigned-sounding exhale behind her, the sound of his body shifting on the bed. "Then come," he said, quiet, "and tell me what you should wish for instead."

Geva shot a suspicious look over her shoulder toward him, but his eyes were strangely serious, flickering in the candlelight. And he'd even shoved up onto his elbow, his hand patting the empty space he'd made beside him.

And it wasn't as though there was anywhere else to go, so finally Geva sighed, and stalked over and dropped herself into the bed, twisting to face away from him. But instead of turning away from her in kind, like he had the night before, his big arm pulled her stiff back up against his front, his body far too big and warm against hers.

"Now, what should you wish to speak of," came his low voice behind her, as his hand reached up—snuffing out the candle—before drawing her close again. "What brings you peace, in the deep of the night."

Geva's swallow was audible, her shoulder jerking up. "Well—tales," she blurted out, before she could say something else she'd surely regret. "My family—we always told tales together at nights."

Rathgarr's hand clenched, his breath seemingly stilled in his chest. "Tales," he repeated, in a voice Geva couldn't at all read. "What sort of tales."

Geva jerked another shrug, but this was something, anything, to focus on, and she drew in a deep breath. "All kinds," she replied, speaking too quickly. "The book you brought from the Fitzwalds' was full of them, but they're usually spoken aloud. In Ezira, each family has different tales they pass down and expand upon, so when we meet, we always have something new to share with each other."

But gods, even this was painfully twisting in her chest, because yes, her parents had repeatedly taught her this—but would her tales truly be welcome in Ezira? Would *she* be welcome there? How long would it take to find her parents' family, to fit in, to make a new home?

Behind her, Rathgarr now felt almost as stiff as she did, his breath still not moving in his chest. "Tell me one," he said. "One of these tales of yours."

Oh. Geva briefly thought about refusing, but what was the

point, so she sighed, and launched into one of Cecily's favourites. The tale of the peevish porcupine, who longed for a shell. Like all the tales from Geva's mother's side, it was more about the fun than the lesson, reeling from one absurd scenario to the next. Until the hapless porcupine finally set aside his last shell—a heavy hippopotamus skull—and accepted his prickly pointy self.

Rathgarr hadn't spoken or interrupted throughout, and his silence afterwards stretched so long that Geva thought perhaps he'd fallen asleep. But finally he cleared his throat, and shifted on the bed behind her.

"This was…" he began, and then he cleared his throat again. "Delightful, poppet. It has been a long time since I heard such a well-spun tale. Since I…"

His voice trailed off, his chest filling and emptying. "My brother Kesst," he said slowly, "oft told tales, also. Great, sprawling tales, so real they came to life behind my eyes. This was… his gift."

Oh. Truly? And before Geva could muster a coherent reply, Rathgarr drew in another long, shaky-sounding breath. Almost as if… as if he was *weeping*?

"And Kesst was so quick and bright and watchful," he continued thickly, between breaths. "He oft knew if I was vexed or downhearted, even before I did. And he would follow me all about the mountain on his skinny little legs, and spin me these wild, merry tales, and laugh with me until we wept. He was such a great gift to me, and I have never cared for another so deeply, it was as if he was my—my own—"

He broke off there, his breaths shuddering against her, and Geva's own breaths felt unnaturally laboured, too. "I'm so sorry, Rathgarr," she whispered back. "You must have missed him so much, all these years."

Rathgarr didn't reply this time, but his breaths were coming even heavier than before, and Geva could hear the hard, sustained swallow in his throat. Sounding unmistakably like loss, like grief, like regret. Sixteen *years*.

"Although," she made her wavering voice say, "it seems utterly unfathomable to me that such a lovely person would be related to *you*. I mean"—her hand gave a shaky, helpless-feeling wave in midair—"you just gave me more genuine compliments about my silly porcupine story than all my other work for you today, including sucking you off *twice*! All of it done *impeccably*, I might add."

She could feel Rathgarr's body abruptly sagging behind her, his heavy breaths breaking into a choked, relieved-sounding laugh. "You can call your work *impeccable*, poppet," he replied, far more steadily than before, "when you can swallow a full load each time you suck me, without wasting a single drop."

Gods, he was such a vile snake, and *why* was Geva's mouth watering like this, damn it—and now the great bastard had gone and slipped his big hand up to the side of her arse, giving it a blatant, too-familiar squeeze through the thin fabric of her shift.

"Or, mayhap," he purred in her ear, "when you swallow my good full load up *here*. Tomorrow, mayhap?"

Geva twitched all over, and jabbed back at his infuriating bulk with a sharp elbow. "You are such a vulgar arrogant *lecher*," she hissed at him. "Such a greedy, overbearing, ungrateful—"

But without warning, the lecher's huge hand gently clapped over her mouth, and his chuckle behind her was low, maybe even indulgent. "Settle yourself, my prickly poppet," he drawled. "Should you agree to this, I shall make it as easy for you as I can, ach? As I did our first time with your mouth."

That was *not* even slightly comforting, and Geva elbowed him again—but he still didn't seem to take any notice, and just settled a little closer behind her. "And after this, mayhap you shall have only praise and worship for me," he mumbled, "and when we reach Orc Mountain the next day, all my kin shall see this, and believe it as truth."

Right. Orc Mountain. In two days. And blinking out into the room's darkness, it occurred to Geva that—despite everything, despite *him*—she'd almost been... growing accustomed to it. That compared to her tedious, grating life at the Fitzwalds, this whole orc-induced adventure had been surprising, and stimulating, and sometimes even... *enjoyable*?

"Do you really think the orcs there will believe it?" she asked, over that disconcerting thought. "They won't suspect that we're pretending?"

Rathgarr yawned again behind her, his fingers stretching wider against her belly. "Not once you fully scent of me," he said drowsily. "Now sleep."

And perhaps Geva should have argued, but she did feel strangely relaxed, and warm, and there was something inexplicably soothing about Rathgarr's big body behind her like this, his heavy arm slung over her waist. So after a massive yawn of her own, she curled a little closer, and sank into the warm quiet darkness.

15

Geva awoke to the feel of warm sunlight across her face, a warm heavy arm over her waist... and a long, distinctive warm ridge, prodding hard and hungry between her arse-cheeks.

Her eyes snapped open, blinking at the room's wood-panelled wall, while her body jerked a strange, reflexive shiver. The movement settling her closer against that inexorable pressing ridge, making it swell back against her. And even through the fabric of her shift, it felt far too powerful, too *alive*, too...

"You like it, poppet?" came Rathgarr's lazy voice, close in her ear. "Like to feel a little more of it, mayhap?"

Geva was not replying to that, she was *not*—but she'd shivered again, her breaths too audible in the silence. And behind her, Rathgarr huffed a low, satisfied laugh, as he gave a slow, purposeful roll of his hips, grinding that pulsing length even deeper between her arse-cheeks. As if it wanted to be tucked in there, caught, sunk as deep as it could go...

"See?" said his husky voice from behind her. "It shall not be such a hardship to earn your coins, ach?"

Her coins. Geva froze all over, full wakefulness finally

flaring through her body—and before she realized it, she'd tumbled out of the bed, and halfway across the room. Well away from that voice, that warmth, that... *temptation.*

"I meant this, when I said I shall make it easy," Rathgarr's voice continued, and when Geva darted a furtive glance over her shoulder, he was still lying there languidly on the bed, one hand propping up his head, the other blatantly adjusting the highly visible tent in his trousers. "Our early seed is a great help in this, and as I said, I only need to do this long enough to scent you. And"—his voice hitched lower—"you are not new to this either, are you?"

Geva blanched, and purposefully whirled away from him, yanking off her shift. New to this *either*, he'd said, suggesting that he'd clearly done this before. And of course he had, if he was so adamantly against having children, right? And even worse—she grimaced as she began to dress—how had he known *she* wasn't new to this? Her damned smell again, no doubt?

"I can scent this upon you," Rathgarr supplied, as if she'd spoken her question aloud. "But only one man, ach?"

Geva couldn't suppress another grimace, because yes, yet again, this devious orc had the right of it. And that particular man had pushed and wheedled and rushed, to the point where she'd sworn never to do it again, but—

"Not good then, poppet?" came Rathgarr's too-perceptive voice behind her, now tinged with contempt. "More fool him. *I* should never leave a bedmate regretting our pleasure together."

It was thankfully enough to twist Geva's head around, glaring at where Rathgarr was flashing her a smug, ingratiating smile. "Oh really?" she demanded. "I regret you deeply, orc. *Deeply!*"

But he only kept grinning as he shoved out of bed and strode past her, giving her arse a firm little slap on the way by.

And then—Geva's mouth fell open—he halted before the chamber-pot, and promptly began relieving himself into it.

Geva huffed an affronted gasp, even as she desperately fought to ignore her lips' reflexive twitch upwards. "You are the *worst*," she continued toward his back, though there wasn't nearly enough heat in her voice. "You are an ill-nurtured, outrageous, utterly insufferable *ingrate!*"

She winced at the sound of the insults escaping her mouth, at the memory of him truly being insulted in return—but this time, he barked an amused-sounding laugh as he shook himself off, and tugged up his trousers again.

"Ach, natter all you wish, my silver-tongued schoolmarm," he drawled at her, coming a step closer. "Or mayhap"—he waggled his eyebrows, and reached into his pocket—"this shall suffice to quiet you?"

He tucked something into Geva's slack hand, and her heart skipped a beat as she blinked down toward it. It was... a ten-piece coin. The equivalent of ten coins. *Weeks* of survival, of life, of freedom. Just... here? Just like that?

"But," she managed, "this is more—far more—than we— agreed on. And we haven't even—"

She couldn't seem to finish, still blinking down at that shiny coin in her fingers, and before her, Rathgarr cleared his throat, and gave a dismissive-looking shrug. "Ach, I ken you have earned it," he said gruffly. "For... *good performance.*"

That last bit was in her accent, her words, and Geva found herself swallowing, and meeting his eyes. Catching on how their mockery had faded, in favour of something almost... earnest.

But then he cleared his throat again, and spun and stalked away, toward the washbasin. Grasping for one of the nearby washcloths as he leaned over it, and frowned mightily at his reflection in the tiny looking-glass.

"You do not mind if I wash, ach?" he said. "Or shave?"

Geva's stilted thoughts had still been trapped on the coin,

on the *good performance*—but she waved away his question, and blankly watched as he dunked the washcloth, and began washing himself. An activity that she hadn't seen him do before, and it felt strangely, unexpectedly intimate to be standing here witnessing it, watching him clean his face and neck and ears, giving particular care to his ears' elegant pointed tips. And then moving down to his hairy underarms, and then—Geva was blatantly staring now, but he didn't seem to notice—again shoving down his trousers, so he could scrub his groin. Lifting and manipulating himself with careless, purposeful ease, scrubbing up and down and even deep behind, until he seemed satisfied.

"Will you find my shaving-blade?" he asked absently, now running both wet soapy hands against his face, which did seem to have more stubble than the night before. "And my comb?"

Geva nodded and went to dig in the pack, where she found a human-made razor, and his comb. And though Rathgarr accepted the razor with a grunt, he gave the comb a sidelong glance, and then casually nudged it back toward her again.

Oh. He meant... he wanted her to tend to his hair. He'd... *liked* that. And perhaps that wasn't actually a surprise after yesterday, but something still flipped in Geva's belly as she eased around behind him, drew back all his thick black hair, and carefully began drawing the comb through it.

Rathgarr hadn't even slightly acknowledged this, his eyes now fixed to the looking-glass, his hand scraping the blade down his jaw in smooth, swift strokes. But there was again something almost like... *trust* in it, in how his head tilted a little backwards as she worked, his breath exhaling in a slow sigh.

"One thing I shall be glad of, when we reach Orc Mountain," he said, now scraping the blade up his bared neck, "is their tools. I shall welcome a proper shaving-blade, and shears, also. Mayhap"—his eyes met Geva's in the looking-glass—"you shall even trim my hair for me there? *If* you swear not to saw it all off in a fit of pique?"

Geva's mouth twitched up before she could help it—he would really trust her to do that?—and she gave his hair a light little tug with her comb. "You would deserve it," she said primly. "Having the world's most horrifying haircut would do wonders for your unbridled vanity."

Rathgarr's flash of a grin in the glass was surprisingly stunning, and far too devious, too. "You ken what shall be even better for my vanity," he said slyly. "My scent. Up your—"

Geva yanked the comb again, eliciting a deeply satisfying yelp from his throat—and she felt herself laugh, without at all meaning to. "Maybe I'll consider it," she said, "*if* you behave yourself today. Though knowing you, my expectations are *very* low."

Rathgarr snorted, though his mouth was still curving up. "Ach, I can behave for you, my prickly schoolmarm," he drawled. "You shall see."

And to Geva's genuine surprise, it turned out that Rathgarr was indeed on his best behaviour for the rest of the day. Not only continuing to play along with her loved-up charade for the passersby, but also carrying on an unprecedented amount of steady conversation between them.

It was the first time they'd managed to maintain a full discussion like this, and it occurred to Geva that it was greatly helped by a concerted avoidance of personal topics. No more questions about his brother, or his past, or even—despite Geva's temptation to ask—Orc Mountain. And instead, they talked about lords and politics, about the latest news from the capital, about the realm's ongoing grain shortage. And then, to Geva's surprise, even about the state of orcs' acceptance throughout the realm, and what the recent peace treaty had—or hadn't—changed.

"Even three summers past, I could not walk in the open thus without risking attack," Rathgarr told her, with a wave at the road ahead. "Now, as you have seen, the humans mostly only snipe and mutter, thanks to the threat of redress from their own lords. But this does not yet mean orcs are welcome or safe, ach? We must be always on our guard."

Geva nodded as she considered that, her eyes on a cluster of passing, whispering young men. "But at least it *is* slowly improving, then?" she asked. "And honestly, it seems remarkable that the treaty has remained in place for this long, and is still endorsed by the realm's lords and Council. Who, from all I've seen, are a pack of greedy backstabbing snakes. At *best*."

"Ach, the lords would be Captain Grimarr's doing," Rathgarr replied, with a grimace. "Trapping all those fools in his thrall is the *one* credit I shall grant him, ach? And mayhap"— he grimaced again—"the pamphlets, also."

The pamphlets? Geva opened her mouth to ask, but Rathgarr was already reaching around to pull something from his pack. It was a tightly folded piece of paper, and when she opened it, she felt her brows rising, her mouth pulling up.

ORCS ARE FRIENDLIER THAN YOU THINK, it read in large block letters, with a slightly alarming illustration of a broadly grinning orc. *If you're ever in need of a strong helping hand, just ask!*

"The orcs are... *distributing* these?" Geva asked, her voice high-pitched. "And surely this isn't... is this an *innuendo*?"

Rathgarr harrumphed as he plucked the paper out of her hand, and stuffed it back into his pack. "It hinges upon the mind of who reads it," he said dryly. "I have indeed spent fewer nights alone from this, but not a week passes without a sweaty human waving a shovel or a pickaxe at me."

Geva couldn't help a bright burst of laughter, despite the alarming twist in her belly at the thought of Rathgarr being propositioned for a *helping hand*—and worse still, *accepting* it. "And do you actually help them?" she asked. "I mean, digging holes in people's gardens, and the like?"

"*Ach*, no," Rathgarr replied, his lip curling. "This should soil all my garb for the day, you ken? But"—he sighed—"if I can, I send them to one who will. Some orcs have now built whole trades, thanks to this."

Geva laughed again, though she felt her head tilting, her eyes searching his profile. "And you said that Captain Grimarr is behind this?" she asked. "The orc you said was cruel and ruthless and single-minded? The one who sent Killik and Ulfarr to spy on you?"

It didn't seem to add up, but Rathgarr nodded, scowling at the road ahead. "Ach, him," he said flatly. "I said, I give him his due for the pamphlets. But he is yet a cold, selfish orc, who sets himself above the rest of his kin, and pretends he is king of our kind. And gives not a *thought* for the many, *many* orcs who yet live and work outside that mountain!"

Huh. "So how do *you* know all this, then?" Geva asked carefully. "If you haven't actually stepped foot in Orc Mountain in sixteen years?"

Rathgarr gave a jerky shrug, and shot her a dark, baleful look. "I have my ways, woman," he said. "You ken I am too witless to learn news of my own kind? Or"—his frown deepened—"you do not believe what I tell you as truth?!"

Gods, just when they'd been getting on so well, and Geva rolled her eyes at him, even as she gave his arm a tight little shake. "I believe you, Rathgarr," she said firmly. "I'm fully on your side, all right? I just want to learn as much as I can, so I can do the best possible job for you. Earn all my coins, remember?"

The steadily rising tension in Rathgarr's body abruptly seemed to soften again, and his glance toward her was almost resigned this time. "There are... places," he said, with a sigh. "Places where orcs can meet and share news, oft in secret, where names are not needed. In truth, the inn I wish to visit tonight"—he nodded at the road up ahead—"is one of these."

Oh. Geva glanced up at the gradually darkening sky—how had an entire day passed so quickly?—and felt herself smiling up at him, and squeezing his arm. "Of course," she said. "I'm looking forward to it."

Rathgarr snorted, but also gave a mollified-looking nod, and soon they were indeed entering yet another inn. From the outside, it looked like any other inn, with a busy drive, and warm lamplight spilling out its small windows. But instead of Rathgarr sending her in first to make the arrangements, and then meeting her afterwards, this time he just pulled his hood low over his face, and walked through the front door beside her.

There were only two other orcs obviously present in the bustling dining-room, and Rathgarr was already earning a few wary glances from other patrons—but the elderly human barman was looking over too, and giving a curt little nod. And soon he was ushering Geva and Rathgarr into a cozy little back area, which was mostly shielded from the rest of the room by thick, dark oaken dividers. And in the smattering of booths, there were indeed multiple other orcs and humans—men and women both—dining and talking together, as though this were a perfectly ordinary thing to do.

Several of the unfamiliar orcs nodded at Rathgarr, some of them pressing their fists against their hearts, clearly in some kind of greeting. And Rathgarr made the same gesture in return, bowing his head toward each of the orcs, before sliding into the empty booth the barman had indicated, and waving Geva in opposite.

It meant that he and Geva were actually sitting across from each other at a table, in a public inn. And it was a surprisingly lovely feeling, and Geva felt herself relaxing back into her booth, and even giving him a small, genuine smile across the table.

"This is nice," she told him, once the barman had brought them both frothing glasses of ale. "Back in the capital, there were places like this for Ezirans, too. Places where we could go and just... be ourselves. Pretend like we belong."

Rathgarr's head tilted, his brows furrowing. "Ach, you humans," he said, taking a long swig of his ale. "I cannot fathom how *you* do not belong here, poppet. You look human. You smell human. You speak a human tongue and wear human clothes and know human ways. What more can the other humans wish for?"

Geva gave a humourless little smile down toward her ale, and attempted a careless shrug. "Well, I know I still have a lot to learn about orcs," she began, "but I'm beginning to realize that maybe *you* aren't really that different, either. You speak the language, you dress beautifully, you've apparently lived among humans for sixteen *years*. Should it matter that you have some different customs, or different skin and fingernails? But yet"— she met Rathgarr's eyes, her brows raised—"here you are, hiding, fearing for your life, only able to walk on the road for the past three years? Relying on suggestive *pamphlets* to keep us from killing you?"

She'd lifted her chin a little, holding his eyes—but to her genuine surprise, Rathgarr inclined his head, and raised his glass toward her before taking a long, gulping drink. As if he'd believed her, or even conceded her point, and Geva blinked blankly toward him, before taking a bracing drink of her own.

"And at least *you* can walk to your home," she continued once she'd finished, with a sigh. "There's a whole *mountain* full of people who share your culture, and look just like you. Whereas *I* need to go off and take an appallingly expensive sail into the unknown, across the damned gigantic *sea*."

Rathgarr had set down his half-empty glass with a thunk, his eyes flinty and narrow on hers. "You have not gone to Ezira before?" he asked, his voice suddenly sharp. "And they would not be expecting you?"

Geva couldn't suppress a deeply betraying flinch, but she gripped her glass of ale, and raised her chin higher. "No," she said thinly. "But what else do you expect me to do? I'm a criminal now, remember? And *you* were the one who didn't want me to risk going back to the capital!"

Rathgarr visibly winced, and then took another long, sustained drink of his ale. Again clearly choosing not to argue her point, and Geva rubbed at her eyes, and let out a slow, shaky breath. Gods, why was she getting into this now, when they'd finally managed to pass such a pleasant day together? When they'd almost begun to feel like... friends?

"And look, I'm very capable of taking care of myself," Geva continued, steadier than before. "I have a plan. I have a job. And my employer"—she gave him another too-sweet smile— "isn't even quite as horrible as I'd first supposed."

She was rewarded with a telltale glint in Rathgarr's eye as he knocked back the rest of his ale, fully emptying the glass. And then—she blinked—he slid the empty glass down under the table. Wait, under the *table*, where his other hand had begun purposefully... stroking?

"What are you *doing*?" Geva demanded, her voice shrill— but Rathgarr, the unbelievable bastard, only grinned lazily back toward her, and settled himself a little more comfortably against his bench. While that arm under the table just kept steadily moving, up and down and up again. As if he was—he could *not* be—

"Showing myself a good *employer*," he replied coolly, "and granting you a chance to earn yet more of that sweet coin you long for."

For an instant, Geva was struck fully speechless, her eyes darting uneasily toward the booth nearest. Thankfully, its chatting orc occupants hadn't seemed to take any notice of Rathgarr's audacious behaviour, and when Geva glanced back at his face, he was actually *laughing*, the sound low and husky in his throat.

"Even if they see, they shall not care a whit," he murmured. "Mayhap you might even wish to kneel beneath the table, and remind me how much you learnt from your lessons yesterday?"

Good gods, this *orc*, and Geva rapidly drained the rest of her ale, willing its coldness to lower the palpable heat in her cheeks. "Absolutely not, you great menace," she hissed. "I am not risking that in public, *again!*"

But Rathgarr's eyes were still far too warm, dancing with genuine amusement. "Ach, ach, my prickly poppet," he drawled at her, as his hand kept casually stroking away beneath the table. "Since I am such a good *employer*, I shall make this easy for you, yet *again*—"

With that, his breath caught, his lashes fluttering, his body gone taut and rigid—and then he groaned, long and low, his head tilting back, his hand moving slower, slower, slower. Clearly pumping himself out, milking himself dry beneath the table, in *public*, for *her*.

Geva truly could not move, or stop staring—not even when Rathgarr's movements had finally stilled, and his body sagged heavily back into the booth. His eyes gone lazy and sparkling, his lips parted, his cheeks flushed. Looking utterly debauched and sated and *amused*, because—because—

"Here, poppet," he purred, as he lifted his hand out from beneath the table again. And in it—Geva audibly choked—was his previously empty glass, now filled to the brim with rich, frothy, creamy whiteness.

"Drink up," he ordered, sliding the full glass across the table toward her. "Warm and fresh, just for you."

Geva gaped at the glass, at his smug waiting face, and then at the glass again. *Warm and fresh, just for you.* And she'd agreed to this, oh gods had she agreed to this, she could do this, she was allowed to do this, right? For the scent?

Her hand snaking across the table toward the glass felt damnably willing, even eager—and oh, now the glass was in her fingers, and it indeed felt warm to the touch, for her. And as she drew it closer, she could already smell it, full-bodied and sweet, curling into her nostrils, tugging deep in her groin...

And Rathgarr was watching, he was waiting, his eyes still

glittering, intent. And that was his long black tongue, brushing brief against his lips, perhaps in encouragement, or accord. Enough, somehow, just enough, that Geva's shaky hand lifted the glass, and brought it to her mouth.

Her moan was reflexive, unthinking, unconscionable—but damn it, Rathgarr *liked* it, he was still smiling like that across the table, with such wicked, insolent approval. So she just kept drinking, swallowing down his thick, succulent richness—fresh, for *her*—in gulp after heavy, dragging gulp.

But suddenly, they were interrupted by the presence of the barman, bearing two steaming plates of supper. Prompting Geva to hurriedly set down her half-empty drink on the table, her face burning hot—and while the barman didn't seem to notice, it felt even more absurd to have it just sitting there, beside her damned plate, as if it were an innocuous glass of milk, and not—*that*.

But somehow she managed to eat, even if the excellent food tasted impossibly bland, compared to her careful, intermittent sips of Rathgarr's sweetness. And each time she drank, Rathgarr's eyes would angle sharply toward her, his full lips parting, his hand spasming on his fork. So much that he once even dropped a whole forkful of food back to his plate, while Geva smiled smugly toward him, and made a show of finally, finally, finishing off the glass, and licking its last sweet, frothy remnants off her lips.

"Enough, poppet," Rathgarr growled at her across the table, his eyes blazing with fury, or perhaps heat, or both. And when his hand clutched around her wrist, she was already sliding out to stand before him, meeting his flashing, commanding eyes with something almost like excitement.

And damn it, she knew what he wanted, and it was just as inappropriate as that drink had been. *Five coins are for that pretty, plump rump of yours. I shall make it as easy for you as I can...*

But even so, her steps felt undeniably eager as she followed his long strides to the bar, and then up the stairs to the room he'd reserved. Where he swiftly lit the lamp, slammed the door shut, and yanked off his fur and cloak and sword. And then he spun and met Geva's eyes, his brows raised, his hand hovering at his belt. Asking a silent question, waiting for her answer.

Geva swallowed hard, but then twitched a furtive nod. Saying yes, *yes*, and she fumbled to undress too, yanking off her outer layers, until she was left standing there in her shift, her heart thundering, her tooth biting her lip. He'd said he would make it good, he would make it quick, *I only need to do this long enough to scent you...*

"Only a little, right?" she heard her shaky voice say. "Just enough to... get the... *scent*?"

Rathgarr's nostrils flared, but he nodded. "Ach, only a little," he replied, husky. "Should you wish."

Right. Right, then. Geva swallowed again, raised her chin— and then, before the terror could properly rise and take over, she whirled around, and clambered to kneel on the bed. Facing away from him, so her still-covered arse was jutting out toward him, and was she really doing this, oh gods, she was really doing this—

"Very well," she whispered. "I'm ready."

16

Geva couldn't have said how long she waited there, trembling on her hands and knees. Desperately fighting the urge to turn and look at him, what was he doing, was he second-guessing this, would he mock her or laugh or—

When finally, there was a touch. A warm, gentle touch against her hip, over the fabric of her shift. His hand.

And then his other hand settled to the other side, and together they slowly, carefully began sliding the shift up. Up, and up, and up, scattering tingling gooseflesh across her skin. Until her bottom half was fully exposed, her arse facing out bare and brazen toward him.

Geva fought the urge to cower, to hide, to yank her shift back down again. And she could almost feel his gaze prickling on her skin, looking at this, as his warm hands gently gripped tighter, and drew her arse-cheeks a little further apart. Making her face burn even hotter, her heart pummelling her chest, until...

Oh. That. That hot, pulsing strength of him. Settling in lightly against the length of her crease, skin sliding against skin.

Geva quivered and gasped, her body tensing, waiting—but there was no pushing, no demanding. Just that warm heavy weight, now easing back and forth along her open, exposed crease. Feeling smoother and slicker with every slow, gentle stroke, and wait, that was because it was—wet. He was—preparing her. *Our early seed is a great help in this*, he'd said.

Geva's breath shuddered out, her body relaxing again, and in return she could feel that thick sliding weight swelling even fuller, its strokes gradually deepening, lengthening. Sinking a little further between her bare arse-cheeks, closer, oh...

"Good, poppet?" his husky voice came from behind her. "Ready for more?"

With that, he'd let himself catch, just there, oh hell, just against Geva's tight knot of heat. Just nudging, just kissing, warm and wet and soft, waiting for her to open, to welcome him...

"Just—a little, right?" she managed, breathless. "Just—like this?"

This was the way his slick rounded head was very gently nudging deeper, just beginning to open her around it—and oh, even as Geva's body clutched back, there was no pain, no resistance. Just this soft steady prodding, a slick jut of smooth warm flesh eased just slightly into her actual *arse*, oh hell.

"Ach, just this, if you wish," he replied, perhaps a little breathless, too. "And then the seed. And after, you shall scent so strongly of me, no other orc shall *think* to question this."

His voice had hardened into something dangerous, almost triumphant—and in response, a full-body shiver rippled up Geva's spine, clamping her powerfully against him. *Against him*, because he was *inside* her—but he was still waiting, still asking, and she would scent so strongly of him, reek of him...

"Right," she gulped, her voice only slightly quavering. "Do it, then. Give me—your seed."

There was a strange, guttural groan, surprisingly close in her ear—and then the feel of his hand, dropping down between them. Moving, surely, along the rest of his shaft, stroking up and down, and Geva could feel him shuddering harder inside her, pulsing, squeezing out drop after drop. And she was pulsing and shuddering back, feeling the rising gathering tension, the growing curling heat, the way his body was stiffening behind her, his breath catching low and hot...

"But first, you find your pleasure for me, also," he hissed, so close. "This shall make the scent stronger. More real."

More real. With his fingers nudging at her arm, in a silent but very salient command. And oh, Geva was eagerly nodding, shifting her weight onto one hand, so she could slide the other one down, toward her pulsing, aching groin.

And oh, it felt so, so good. Her body rocking against the tight firm pressure of her fingers, against that prodding, leaking heft inside her. And *yes*, she could feel him stroking himself faster, smooth and deliberate, pumping himself, for her. The movement nudging him a little deeper with every single stroke, and gods, he had no right to feel so gentle, so *good*. And the longing, the craving, was curling and coiling, higher and closer, but it wasn't enough, it wasn't, not yet—

"Need—more, first," Geva's breath choked, all on its own, before she'd even formed the thought. "Just—a little."

She grimaced at the sound of it, her eyes shamefully squeezing shut—but behind her, Rathgarr hissed a low growl, and then his big hands were gripping tighter against her arse, pulling her further apart. So he could ease just a little further inside, open her just a little more...

And yes, yes, that was it, and Geva was breathing hard, her head nodding, her tongue brushing her lips. And she was dropping her other shaky hand back to the bed again, so she could arch her back, and open wider. Feeling that nudging, jutting hardness sinking even deeper, swelling even fuller than before, stretching her out around him.

But there was still no pain, not yet, and maybe that was because of the still-pulsing liquid, easing the way. Or maybe it was because Rathgarr wasn't pushing or pressuring with it, or taking more than she could give. No, he'd said he would make it good, make it easy, and he was actually keeping his word. And the blazing, craving heat churning in Geva's belly flared even higher at the thought, her back arching more, pushing a little deeper...

She could feel his answering shudder inside her, *inside* her, because oh, that's where he was now, her body clamping tight against solid, rigid thickness. Against that huge, uncompromising invasion of him, holding her wide open around him. And when she moaned again, clenching him even tighter, he instantly pulsed back, in a silent, dizzying response. In accord. Or maybe, maybe even in... a challenge.

And oh, he was *not* going to win with this, and amidst the swelling surging heat there was suddenly determination, certainty, relief. She could do this, she could arch and soften even more, she could welcome the feel of him slipping a little deeper, filling her even fuller. She could hear him gasp, hoarse and low, she could toss her head, and ease back a little more...

Her hair had been pulled up into a twist, one that was already falling out—and she scarcely noticed Rathgarr's hand moving up to gently tug at it, freeing her coiled black curls around her head. And oh, he actually groaned as both his hands gripped her arse again, drew her even further apart.

"Good?" came his rasping voice from behind her. "More?"

Geva furiously nodded, because hell, yes, she wanted more—and now he was the one prodding, challenging, sinking in bit by bit. That hard intruding flesh gliding in ever further, while she arched more, opened wider, met him, matched him. Feeling impossibly full now, fuller than she'd ever felt in her life, stretched and bared and split wide open around that huge plunging sliding strength, until—

Until there was skin, warm, new, alive. Because he was in, oh he was all the way in, and his hips were settling tight against her arse, his full bulging bollocks swelling close against her wet, swollen heat below. Just where Geva most desperately craved his touch, oh—and she cried out, hoarse and fervent, as she clutched against him, ground against him, encased him hot and whole. Still needing more, more, and that was surely the sound of a muttered low curse behind her, the feel of his hand slipping down, around, and...

"Fuck," Geva gasped, as that warm hand settled firm and familiar against the curve of her, against her swollen, shuddering, dripping-wet heat. Pressing just perfectly, as two blunt-tipped fingers nudged up beneath. As—she gasped again—they slowly slid up inside, while his big palm kept circling, grinding with slow, beautiful pressure. Just—just the way she'd shown him, damn him, *bless* him. And in retaliation—or reward—she drew away a little, and then ground back against him, upon him, even deeper than before.

He hissed and cursed again, his touch stuttering against her—but then it was back again, and he was circling his hips too, moving that massive heft inside her, actually fucking her now, oh, oh. And she was meeting him, taking him, wanting him, impaling herself upon him again and again. She was so open, so exposed, so hungry and frantic and full, she needed it, she needed him, please, *please*—

And with one last, heated thrust, a choked shout from her throat, she was flying, flaring into the abyss. The relief and the ecstasy seizing in hard, furious pulses, milking that straining, invading heat again and again—and oh, oh, now he was shuddering out, too. His strength inside her swelling and spasming, erupting out stream after stream of rippling warmth. Painting her with him, scenting her from the inside out, oh gods above, oh, *oh*.

When he finally stilled behind her, inside her, Geva was still trembling all over, and gulping desperately for air—and perhaps so was he, his hands gripped too tight on her hips, his breaths hot and harsh against the sweaty skin of her back. And for a strange, dangling moment, it almost felt like satisfaction, like—victory. Like they'd both met the challenge, and surpassed it, and now they could revel in it, and in one another.

But just as Geva had twisted her head a little, making to look back toward him, she felt his body stiffening behind her, even as his strength jutting into her notably slackened. And as his hand—gods, he'd still had his fingers *inside* her—swiftly pulled away, its warmth utterly vanished. And then he was drawing himself out of her, that softened skin sliding away, breath by breath, despite her desperate, helpless clutches against it.

But it was too fast, too soon, and for an instant, there was the bizarre, overpowering urge to beg him to stay. Beg him to keep going, to let her have this, to perhaps do it all over again...

But he was already slipping out, escaping her frantic, pleading clutch with a humiliating little squelch. And where he'd been—Geva squeezed her eyes shut, gritted her teeth— she was... *leaking*. His sticky wet heat pouring out in a rush, streaming liberally down her trembling parted thighs. And there was no way to stop it, her body stretched and lax and blown wide open from him—and was he looking, was he watching, surely he was, oh *hell*. And what should she do, the bedding, the mess, his seed—

She'd finally twisted to find his face, perhaps his reassurance—but instead, she found only his darting-away eyes, his hands rapidly fastening up his belt. Because wait, he'd still been fully *dressed* all this time, while she was here on her hands and knees, her messy hair loose, her body gaping wide open and leaking his fresh seed.

But Rathgarr wasn't even looking at her now, though that was surely a flush on his cheeks, a sheen of sweat on his brow. "Good—good work, poppet," he said, his voice husky and thick. "Very good. This was—"

He glanced briefly toward her face, a wild look in his eyes— but then his eyes shuttered again, and he pushed off the bed, and fumbled in his trouser pocket. "Here," he said, as he drew out a large, glinting gold coin. "Your payment."

With that, he flipped the coin in his fingers, and then... tossed it toward the bed. Where it briefly rolled in a shimmering circle, before settling to stillness beside her.

It was another ten-piece coin. Ten coins, for that.

And Geva should have been crowing aloud, rejoicing at her victory—but for a long, horrible breath, she could only seem to stare down at it, and then up at him. Her payment. Her *payment*. For what they'd just done. Not a challenge, not an adventure together, not a victory.

No, no, it had been about *work*. About plots, about scent, about impressing and influencing his people at Orc Mountain, and that—that was all.

Only play-acting. Neither should I ever choose to mate you...

"Mayhap I shall go gain us a—a drink," Rathgarr said now, still not meeting her eyes. "I shall return in a spell, ach?"

Geva somehow nodded, her eyes blinking hard, but he hadn't even waited for her response, striding swiftly to the door, and slipping out beyond it. Leaving her here, alone, bared and exposed and forgotten on her knees, still with that glinting gold coin beside her.

And before she could stop it, before she'd even seen it coming, she sank to the bed, buried her face in her arms, and wept.

17

———

By the time Rathgarr returned to the room again, Geva was dressed and curled up tightly in the bed, the blanket yanked up to her eyes.

This was just a job, she'd told herself again and again, as she'd slogged through the highly humiliating cleanup, and then scrubbed herself all over at the washbasin. One month, and then the sea.

Even so, she'd felt almost sick as she'd gingerly picked up that ten-piece coin from the bed, and stuffed it deep into her satchel. Her stomach curdling and churning, while the memories of what they'd done—what she'd done—kept flaring behind her eyes. *Need more*, she'd gasped, as she'd brazenly arched herself toward him. *Give me your seed.*

And gods, what had come over her? She could have stopped—should have stopped—far earlier, and still achieved the exact same result. So why had she kept pushing it, pushing past the boundaries they'd both set, they'd both agreed upon? When she knew this was just a job? When she knew exactly how he really felt about her?

And she couldn't even blame him for walking out like that, because he'd repeatedly been very clear about what this was, hadn't he? And he'd even paid her extra for her efforts—or more likely, as a cover for her mortification. He'd been kind, he'd been a good employer, and damn it, he'd absolutely been the better person—the winner, even—in this entire horrible scenario.

So when she finally heard Rathgarr entering the room again, the wooden floor creaking beneath his steps, she couldn't seem to move, let alone look at him, or speak. Not even when she heard him halt beside the bed, heard the sound of something hard setting against the nightstand. The drink he'd promised to bring, perhaps.

And thankfully, he didn't push it, or try to speak. Instead, there was only the sound of shifting fabric, and then the feel of the bed sinking under his weight. And then his big bulky warmth, easing under the blanket, his broad back shifting close against hers.

It took far too long to fall asleep, and Geva again resorted to silently telling herself tales, dragging her thoughts from one to the next. The tale of the falcon and the chicks. The mosquito and the ear. The disobedient daughter who married a skull...

She must have fallen asleep at some point, but when morning came, it felt as though she hadn't rested at all. And unlike the day before—she wrenched around—there was no Rathgarr in bed, no warm arm around her waist. And instead, he was already up and dressed, his face freshly shaven, his hair smooth and gleaming.

Geva's stomach inexplicably plunged—gods, as if she'd wanted him to wait for her help?—and she shoved up in bed, rubbing at her bleary eyes. "So sorry," she said thickly. "I didn't mean to oversleep."

But Rathgarr waved it away, his eyes not quite meeting hers. "No matter," he said. "I have already packed, and readied us to go. And I hope you shall not take offense, but I have..."

He trailed off, and gave another too-dismissive wave, this

time toward the end of the bed. Toward where there were... clothes, carefully laid out upon it. *Her* clothes.

And blinking down toward them, Geva realized that they were the best, finest clothes she'd brought. A slim shift, in silk so thin it was almost transparent. A deep blue dress, with a plunging neckline. And a light wool black cloak, far too costly for actual daily use.

And as she glanced back toward Rathgarr, she noticed that he was dressed in surprising finery, too. In a new-looking white tunic, also cut far lower than usual, showing off the strength of his chest. And below that were very tight trousers, fitted so close that she could easily make out the telltale bulge beneath. And rather than the simple cord he usually wore on his cloak, he'd put on a gleaming, braided gold chain, with large, beautifully carved clasps at each end.

Oh. Of course. Because—today was the day. The day they would reach Orc Mountain. And now that Geva was fully... scented of him, he wanted her to dress for him, too. To join him in putting on the show, in presenting the best possible face. For his kin, and his long-lost brother, and his enemies.

And yes, this was what she had agreed to, so she jerked a nod, and quickly washed and dressed. Desperately fighting to ignore the feel of Rathgarr's eyes on her bare body as she changed, and the temptation to wonder if he was looking at her arse. On where it was still slightly tender, but not nearly as much as she would have expected, and she squeezed her eyes shut at the flash of memory, and the accompanying surge of nausea in her gut. Just a job. The next thing. One month, and then the sea.

"There," she said, as she turned to face him again, smoothing out the front of her dress. "Does this look all right?"

Rathgarr's eyes had, unnervingly, been lingering in the vicinity of her arse, but they instantly flicked up, briefly meeting her gaze, before sliding down again. Holding for perhaps too long on the ample cleavage displayed by the blue fabric, and then down to how the dress curved over her waist and hips, before glancing back up, and giving a curt little nod.

"This is—good," he said, glancing away again. "And also"—he winced—"your hair. If you should wear this unbound today, I should be—grateful."

Oh. Because, damn it, he liked her hair. He thought the other orcs would like her hair. And while a distant part of Geva wanted to take offense again, she felt herself exhaling, nodding, as she reached up to the headscarf she'd slept in, and untied it.

Rathgarr kept intently looking away as she shook it out, and then carefully separated the curls that had become tangled overnight. And once she'd finished, she stood there, waiting, her chin held high, until he looked back again. His eyes sweeping down and up, lingering for only a very hurried instant on her hair, before glancing down again. And then holding, oddly, on her hand.

"One last thing," he said, with a twisting grimace, as he knelt beside his pack. And when he rose again, he was holding out something small, and red, and... glittering?

Geva stepped forward, blinking toward it—and then froze all over, her breath locked in her throat. It was a ring. A fine gold ring, with a huge, sparkling, square-cut red gem attached. A ruby, perhaps.

"What?" Geva gulped, her eyes wide, maybe even aghast, on Rathgarr's blank face. "You're not—*giving* this to me? Not as—as *payment*?!"

And as stunningly beautiful as the ring was, the nausea was once again rising, churning in her stomach. He couldn't give her this, not as payment, oh gods, oh *gods*—

"It is only—a loan," Rathgarr said hurriedly, with another grimace. "Only—some women expect this from a mate, ach? My own mother never forgave my father for not gifting her a wedding-ring, and I should not wish—anyone—to think me remiss, in this."

Oh. He meant... his brother would notice. *Kesst* would

notice. Of course. So Geva swallowed hard, and jerked a nod, and thrust out her hand toward him.

But wait, wait, that was clearly the wrong way to go about this, as if she wanted him to put the ring on himself, like some sort of *bridegroom*—but before she could yank her hand away again, Rathgarr had caught it lightly in his warm, strong fingers. And then, keeping his eyes very intently on what he was doing, he slid the ring onto her finger.

Geva stood stock-still as he did it, feeling the cool circle of the gold, the strange weight of the gem, the surprisingly perfect fit. It had been so long since she'd worn any jewelry, and she couldn't seem to look away from it, from the way it sparkled, the way it looked against her hand, beneath the careful touch of Rathgarr's black claws.

"Is it—a ruby?" she asked, foolishly—but Rathgarr nodded, his claws again adjusting it on her finger.

"A good, proper Ash-Kai stone," he said, a little hushed. "I thought it should look well, against your skin."

Right. Well. He wasn't wrong, Geva could admit, because it did look beautiful, almost painfully so. And it took almost all her willpower to draw her eyes back up to his face again, to attempt some semblance of a smile.

"Well, I'm sure they'll be impressed," she said, though her voice wavered. "It's very lovely."

Rathgarr twitched another nod, and then jerked away, and snatched up his pack. "Ready, then?" he said stiffly. "We shall reach Orc Mountain by afternoon, I ken."

By afternoon? That soon? A cold chill rippled up Geva's back, but she made herself smile again, and silently followed him downstairs, and out into the bright morning sunlight.

But she couldn't seem to shake the strange, stilted feeling in her chest, the tension coiling in the air, the unfamiliar weight of that beautiful ring on her finger. And it was only after they'd passed several staring, gossiping passersby that she even remembered to clutch at Rathgarr's arm, and resume her usual friendly display, though it too felt forced, heavy, tense.

And beneath her hand, Rathgarr felt unnaturally stiff too, his eyes held straight ahead, his steps steady and deliberate. And the further they walked, the slower his steps became, until they'd crested over a hill, and—

And there it was. Orc Mountain. A huge, hulking mass of craggy grey stone, looming over the surrounding hills, and streaming multiple plumes of thick black smoke into the sky. And as he stared toward it, Rathgarr's face had begun to look markedly ashen, his throat bobbing, his hand clutching the sword-hilt at his side.

"Oh," Geva heard herself say, her own hand gripping far too tightly at his bicep. "So that's it, is it?"

Rathgarr barked a harsh, humourless laugh, his steps faltering to a halt beside her. "Ach," he said. "That is it."

He clearly wasn't inclined to continue, and Geva shot him a searching, sidelong look, even as her heartbeat kept rising, her hands clammy and cold, her breaths ever shallower in her throat. He'd sworn she'd be safe there. One month, and then the sea. One month.

"Is there anything I really should know about it?" she made herself ask, glancing again at his hard, bleak face. "Anything you would have told me, if I truly was your real... mate?"

Gods, she could barely say the damned word, and in reply Rathgarr winced, his eyes still fixed to the sight of it looming ahead. "It is... very large," he replied, his voice wooden, as he jerked to a walk again. "With many rooms and tunnels, both above ground and below."

Geva swallowed, but she nodded and kept pace with him, angling him another sidelong look. "And how many people live there?" she asked, as carefully as she could. "And is it all orcs, or are there some women, too? Or children?"

"Hundreds of orcs still live there, I ken," Rathgarr replied, still without inflection. "And some humans now also, Killik says, and a few orclings."

Geva couldn't deny a small twinge of curiosity at that—she'd never seen an orc child before—and it was enough to bring up another question, and then another. And thankfully Rathgarr just kept answering, all in that same empty voice, even as that massive smoking mountain loomed closer, and closer, and closer.

And though Geva had been trying to keep an open mind about Orc Mountain—she'd sworn to live there for an entire month, after all—she had to admit that it didn't sound even slightly appealing. It sounded dark, and damp, and dreary, with mazes of convoluted corridors, no actual lighting or provisions for humans, and an alarming amount of quarrelling, brawling, and backstabbing between the five different orc clans.

Her unease kept growing as Rathgarr spoke, gnawing deep in her chest, until she couldn't seem to ask any more questions at all. And then it was just walking, and walking, and walking, down a road that had now gone entirely empty, but for them.

"I scent—" Rathgarr finally said, his voice thin and strained, as he roughly brushed back his hair, and tugged awkwardly at his cloak. And despite Geva's quivering heartbeat, she pulled him to a halt, and turned him to face her. And then she straightened out his cloak with shaky hands, making sure it fell in even, heavy folds around his broad shoulders. And then did the same with his hair, smoothing it back neat and straight.

"You look perfect," she managed, her eyes searching his wan face. "I'm sure they'll be delighted to see you."

But Rathgarr didn't reply, and he didn't move, either. Just standing there, his big body so taut and tense, his hand once again clenched to his sword-hilt. And when Geva risked another glance at his eyes, they looked upset, unnerved, unnatural. Almost... afraid.

"Poppet," he whispered. "I ought—ought to tell you, I—"

Geva's own fear kicked in her chest, her breath inhaling

sharp. There was something else he hadn't told her? Something important, surely, something dangerous, something that could change *everything*—

But just then, two unfamiliar orcs stalked around the corner up ahead. Two huge, hulking orcs, both bare-chested and bulging with muscle, with gleaming steel swords strapped to their sides.

And with a carrying, terrifying shout, the orcs kicked off, and sprinted straight toward them.

18

———

It took all Geva's willpower not to whirl around, and run. To run, and run, and run, until Orc Mountain was a dim, distant, meaningless memory, never to rise again.

But she managed to hold herself braced and still, her teeth gritted, her heartbeat wailing in her chest. Waiting, and waiting, as the two attacking orcs pounded closer and closer, their eyes blazing, their black braids streaking out behind them. Their huge bodies rushing straight toward Rathgarr, and...

Embracing him?

Geva choked on her breath, her mouth dropping open, her feet staggering beneath her. Yes, these two terrifying orcs were both piling onto Rathgarr at once, speaking loudly and rapidly in the orcs' language. Or, rather, one of the orcs—the smaller of the two—was speaking, while the other bigger orc hadn't yet said a word. Instead, his eyes had squeezed shut, his huge fist thumping Rathgarr's back again and again.

And to Geva's continued astonishment, Rathgarr was actually *laughing*, his arms fervently yanking the two orcs even closer. "Ach, ach, my brothers," he said, with surprising warmth in his voice, in his shining, crinkling eyes. "Ach, it is so *good* to scent you both. Though Sig, I can scarcely breathe thus! How is it that you are even *more* of a boulder than before?!"

The bigger orc drew slightly away, a wide smile on his sharp-toothed mouth, and Geva realized that he was indeed even larger than Rathgarr. His huge sloped shoulders were packed with muscle, his broad chest a solid-looking wall of strength, his blunt features heavily marked by scars. While the smaller orc, though still scarred and muscular, bore a leaner build, his face slimmer and more delicate, and remarkably handsome, too.

"And look at you, Abjorn!" Rathgarr said with a grin, clutching both his hands to the smaller orc's shoulders. "I should never have placed you, but for your scent. A born warrior if ever I saw one, ach?"

The orc's cheeks visibly reddened, and he flashed a swift, stunning smile up at Rathgarr's face. "Ach, you ken?" he asked, now speaking in the common tongue, though it was heavily accented. "I have trained and fought much these past years, and oft with the Skai and Bautul also! Though I have nursed many grievous wounds, and thus wasted far too many days in the sickroom. And"—his smile went a little wry—"it is only the gods' own luck that the Ka-esh have not yet disowned me, you ken?"

He'd been speaking so quickly that Geva almost couldn't follow, but Rathgarr and the other orc clearly had, and they groaned in unison, shaking their heads. "Gammon, *kærasti*," said the big orc, his deep voice slow and measured. "You bring great honour to your clan. You have well earned your rank as one of our mountain's most able warriors. As a truly named *lieutenant*."

The smaller orc briefly ducked his head, wildly waving away the reassurance with both hands, but Rathgarr gave his shoulders another purposeful little shake, his brows raised high. "What is this, Abjorn?" he demanded. "A *lieutenant*?"

Abjorn was grinning up at Rathgarr again, and then

making a face at him, and bobbing a little on his feet. "Ach, this is mostly for show, I ken," he said quickly. "You ken how it is, with you Ash-Kai. Good to have a weak Ka-esh as a—"

But before he could finish, Rathgarr had yanked him into another powerful-looking embrace, swaying him back and forth. "You well deserve this," he said fervently, into the orc's neck. "It brings me such joy to hear this, brother."

The orc—Abjorn—sagged into Rathgarr's chest, his eyes fluttering closed, his mouth still curved in a stunning little smile. And as Geva watched, she felt herself swallowing hard, while something strange and bitter surged in her chest. Something that felt suddenly, alarmingly close to... jealousy.

She hurriedly wrenched her gaze away, and found herself looking straight toward the bigger orc. Who was giving a slow, wry little shrug, with an expression rather like indulgence on his broad features. As if this... this *intimacy* between Rathgarr and this effusive, handsome orc was both expected, and *familiar*.

Geva's stomach horribly plunged—gods, she did *not* care, Rathgarr was her employer, one month—and she belatedly plastered on a smile, and thrust out her hand toward the big orc. "Hi, I'm Geva," she said, over the lump in her throat. "And you must be a friend of Rathgarr's."

The big orc angled a meaningful glance toward Rathgarr, who was now hurriedly extracting himself from Abjorn, and giving a quick, narrow-eyed nod. To which the big orc nodded too, and then carefully reached to shake Geva's proffered hand, his huge grip warm and gentle.

"Ach, I am Sigarr, also of Clan Ash-Kai," he told her, in his slow, measured voice. "Welcome to our clan, woman. I am sure our brother shall keep you safe and hale and content."

Now it was Geva's face flushing, but her smile felt somewhat more genuine this time. "Er, thank you," she told him, but before she could say anything more, Abjorn had shoved himself in close beside Sigarr, his own hand outstretched toward her.

"Please forgive our rudeness, woman," he said, fixing her with the full force of his unfairly stunning smile. "We are so honoured to meet you. Any woman of Rath's is most welcome among us. I hope he has been good to you, and spared you the worst of his overbearing bluster? Or his ill temper? Or his obstinacy?"

Geva desperately fought down another rising surge of jealousy—they called him *Rath*? And by *any woman*, did he mean Rathgarr had brought other women here before, too? But she kept the smile pasted to her mouth, and rapidly shook Abjorn's hand. "I see you know my mate very well," she said, with a valiant attempt at a teasing glance toward Rathgarr's watching, unreadable face. "But yes, he's been very good to me. I'm a very lucky woman."

Abjorn seemed outwardly convinced, at least, glancing back and forth between her and Rathgarr with every impression of delight. "Ach, we well know Rath is the lucky one," he replied, as he winked toward Geva. "And mayhap soon we shall meet a strong Ash-Kai son?"

A strong Ash-Kai son. Geva felt herself twitching, her mind gone curiously blank—good gods, what had they agreed to say about this?—but luckily, Rathgarr had stepped a little closer, his big hand spreading against her back. "Ach, mayhap," he said lightly. "But my sweet mate's mother faced many trials upon her birthing, so we wished to give this some time."

Right. That. Geva's smile toward Rathgarr surely betrayed too much of her relief, but thankfully Abjorn was still smiling too, his eyes shining with warmth. "Then you must meet our midwife, and my cleverer Ka-esh kin, who have studied this at length," he said firmly. "And most of all, you must meet Efterar! He is a worker of miracles, ach? Together with our midwife, he has now helped birth dozens of orclings, and has not lost a single woman or orcling yet."

Oh. They had a midwife here? And a *physician*?! And though Geva was already nodding, her smile toward Rathgarr had gone rather fixed. And Rathgarr's smile looked just the same, and Geva could almost see him searching for a way to deflect this, to offer some kind of appropriate response...

"Efterar," he repeated. "Is this a new orc? I have not before heard of him."

It seemed a perfectly innocuous question, but before them, Sigarr and Abjorn had gone suddenly, strangely still. Both of them staring at Rathgarr with genuine-looking shock, before glancing toward one another. And Sigarr's previously genial face had hardened into something dark and grim, while Abjorn's still-present smile rapidly shifted between apologetic, uneasy, and sad.

"Efterar is... your kin-brother, Rath," Abjorn said. "He is Kesst's bonded mate. For many summers now."

Oh. Rathgarr's brother Kesst had taken a *mate*. Another orc. Which seemed like an important point, surely? And Rathgarr... hadn't known?

But no, no, surely he hadn't, because Geva could feel his body's sudden stiffness against her, the way his breath had stilled in his chest. The way his hand on her back had begun... trembling.

But he didn't speak—perhaps he couldn't speak—and finally Geva cleared her throat, and squared her shoulders. "We would dearly love to see them," she said. "I don't suppose they might be nearby, by any chance?"

And thankfully Abjorn nodded, relief flaring bright in his eyes. "Ach, they are," he said, with another stunning smile. "So come. We shall be glad to take you, and welcome you home."

19

———————

For the rest of the short walk to Orc Mountain, Geva could almost taste the strain in Rathgarr's body, the taut agitation thrumming through his hand against her. The hand that hadn't actually moved from her back, almost as if he needed some kind of stability, some means to keep him from falling.

But Geva didn't feel even slightly stable either, not between these two disconcerting new orcs—Abjorn kept flashing them careful smiles from where he and Sigarr were walking ahead—and that revelation that Rathgarr's brother had had a mate. For *years*. And Rathgarr hadn't known about it.

And why hadn't Rathgarr known about it? When he'd known about politics, about places to share news, about *pamphlets*? And most of all, when he'd spent all that time talking to Killik? They'd had multiple meetings, right? Hadn't he bothered to ask how his own *brother* was faring?

And gods, maybe Rathgarr really was that selfish, or that guarded, or that uncaring. He'd barely spoken to Geva of Orc Mountain either, had he? And despite how they'd managed to get along these past days, he'd still done some truly horrible things, too. He'd stolen from the Fitzwalds, and from Cecily. He'd ruined Geva's career. Destroyed her life.

And once again, she felt that too-familiar whisper of alarm, of fear. She was walking straight toward Orc Mountain, together with this devious, untrustworthy orc. She'd agreed to stay in Orc Mountain with him, pretending to love him, for an entire month. And—her breath choked as they rounded a corner—they'd arrived. Here.

At Orc Mountain.

She only distantly noticed the few small outbuildings scattered about, because her eyes were casting up, and up, and up. At the massive looming wall of rugged, jagged grey stone, towering over them like a brooding, vengeful, ravenous beast.

And at the base of it, directly here before them, there were—more orcs. Two more orcs, standing arm in arm, and clearly waiting. Waiting for them.

The nearest orc was big and bulky, with heavy, harsh, scarred features, and long hair that was pulled tightly back. And though he briefly nodded toward them, his eyes were already angling sideways, toward the orc beside him.

And this orc—Geva's heart skipped, her throat swallowing—this orc *had* to be Kesst. Rathgarr's long-lost brother.

And yes, yes, he had the same shade of grey skin, the same symmetrical, finely carved features. The expressive eyes, the straight nose, the full mouth. Even the same thick, shining black hair, hanging long and loose down his straight back.

But unlike Rathgarr, Kesst was slimmer. Leaner. Visibly younger. And along with tall black boots and a pair of tight leather trousers, he was also wearing a dangling, black-jewelled pendant, multiple earrings in both pointed ears, and a variety of glittering rings on his long fingers. Fingers that were all clutching tightly to the bigger orc beside him, his claws digging into skin. And the bigger orc didn't seem even slightly bothered by this, but only drew Kesst closer, and fixed Rathgarr with a rather sharp, demanding glare.

And wait, that was because Rathgarr was just standing there beside Geva, and staring blankly at Kesst. While Kesst stared straight back, his chin lifting, his long-lashed eyes rapidly blinking. Looking suddenly, unmistakably uncertain, uncomfortable. Perhaps even vulnerable.

But Rathgarr still hadn't moved, damn him, his big body frozen in place beside Geva, his empty eyes fixed to Kesst's face. And as surreptitiously as she could, Geva slid her hand up to his back, and gently shoved him forward.

He went, thank the gods, though his feet briefly stumbled, his usually graceful big body seeming suddenly too large and cumbersome. But he'd closed the space between himself and Kesst, at least—and with another jerky, jolting movement, he reached out, and yanked Kesst into his arms.

Kesst clearly hadn't expected it, his eyes gone wide, his body very stiff against Rathgarr's much larger form. A silent signal that Rathgarr obviously hadn't missed, and he hurriedly drew back again, giving a surreptitious, shaky wipe at his eyes with his arm. Almost as if he was... weeping.

"Ach, little brother," he croaked. "Look how handsome you are. How tall you have grown."

Kesst visibly blanched, his throat bobbing, his claws again digging into the arm of the orc beside him. But then he smiled, a careful, practiced smile that didn't at all reach his empty eyes.

"Yes, well, it *has* been sixteen years, hasn't it, big *brother*?" he said, in a smooth, pleasing voice, lacking even a trace of Rathgarr's accent. "How *delightful* to discover you're actually not dead, after all this time."

Rathgarr must have heard the sarcasm in Kesst's voice, but he only gave a jerky nod, and then a wavering smile. "Ach," he said, hoarse. "I have missed you greatly, little brother."

Kesst returned this with a careless toss of his head, and a brittle, tinkling little laugh. "And that's why you sent *so* many letters and messages, of course," he replied smoothly. "I felt positively *smothered* with affection, you must know. Why, if I hadn't had Eft here, I might have even *expired* from it. Or, wait"—he tapped a claw against his pursed lips—"was that all my murderous masters trying to *kill* me, while you were off gallivanting about the countryside?"

Wait. Was Kesst saying... he'd had *masters* in Rathgarr's absence? Masters who'd tried to *kill* him? But yes, yes, clearly he was, based on Rathgarr's visceral, full-body flinch, the way he'd nearly lost his footing. The way his hand was already gripping his sword-hilt, his mouth opening, and closing, and opening again. As if he wanted to ask, wanted to demand if this was some kind of cruel joke, if it was... true.

But he was forestalled by another toss of Kesst's head, another tinkling little laugh. "But luckily, Eft came along, just in time," Kesst continued, with a sideways glance toward the orc he was still clutching. "And he's actually been here for me ever since, unlike *some* people, hmmm?"

There was another instant's horrible, hanging stillness, broken only by another full-body flinch from Rathgarr—but then he snapped his fist to his heart, and bowed his head toward this orc. This... *Eft*. Or, perhaps, *Efterar*, Abjorn had said.

"Then I am most grateful to you, Ash-Kai, for your good care of my brother," Rathgarr said thickly. "I have already heard of your great skill as a healer. And I ken"—he rapidly glanced between Efterar and Kesst, his shoulders squaring—"from the smell of you, I ken you and Kesst are scent-bound, also? I am most deeply glad of this."

Geva didn't recognize that term he'd used—*scent-bound*—but there was something oddly hopeful in Rathgarr's voice, in his unnaturally bright eyes on Kesst's face. But in return, Kesst was looking suddenly incredulous, and furious, and perhaps even vicious.

"Well, you can take your gladness and *choke* on it, Rath," he hissed, jabbing a sharp finger toward Rathgarr's chest. "I only smell this way thanks to some quite frankly *impossible* interventions. In truth, the notches on my requisite belt—or, let's be honest, on my abused arsehole—likely rival *yours*."

There was another awful dangling stillness, ringing through the too-thin air, through Geva's shocked, stilted thoughts. Was Kesst—really saying this? That he'd—he'd—

But Kesst was already laughing again, the sound cold, taunting, horribly hostile. "Let's compare, then, why don't we, deadbeat brother dearest?" he continued, the smoothness in his voice at total odds with the rage still flashing in his eyes. "How many new lovers do I smell on you since we last met, hmmm? Surely"—he inhaled deeply, his nostrils flaring—"well over a hundred, at least?"

A... *hundred*. That wasn't possible, it couldn't be possible, could it?—but Rathgarr wasn't speaking, or moving, or arguing this. No, no, he just kept standing there, staring blankly toward Kesst. And his hand—the hand he'd used to make that greeting to Efterar—was still hovering limply against his chest, as though he'd entirely forgotten it.

"Well, even so, I've still got you beat," Kesst blithely continued, with another brittle, awful smile. "Or wait, they had *me* beat, didn't they? I'd like to say I enjoyed it, but you know how these things go. When you're young and weak and beautiful, and trapped, terrified and alone, without *any* protection, in a mountain full of ravenous orcs?"

Oh. Oh, gods above. And amidst the mass of chaos now churning in Geva's thoughts, the uppermost truth was horror. Sharp, sickening horror, because Rathgarr had left home, left Kesst without any protection for sixteen years, and then *this* was what had happened in his absence? Kesst had been attacked? Abused? *Forced*? By *hundreds* of orcs?!

And the only saving grace—the only tiny, desperate piece of hope—was the way the last of the colour had drained from Rathgarr's face. The way his hand was still hovering fruitlessly in midair, still as though he'd meant to do something with it, but couldn't remember how. And the way he was breathing, the sounds heavy and laboured, far too loud in the dead, empty silence.

He hadn't known. He couldn't have known. As obtuse and infuriating as he could be, there was no way he was pretending. Not with this.

And suddenly Geva couldn't bear it for another instant, and she rushed forward to stand beside Rathgarr. Clutching at his still-hovering hand, yanking it into hers, squeezing as tightly as she could.

"He didn't know," she choked at Kesst, frantically shaking her head. "He would never have borne it, if he'd known such vile things were happening to you. He's spoken of you so often, he's missed you so much, and this is so completely horrifying to hear. We're so, *so* sorry."

It was unquestionably foolish, and surely out of place, inserting herself where she had absolutely no business being— but Kesst had blinked at her, once, twice. And suddenly his face was twisting into something much like chagrin, or regret.

"Ah," he said, with a wincing little smile. "Right. Welcome to Orc Mountain, sweetheart. Aren't you glad you came?"

20

———

*A*ren't you glad you came.

For another fraught, frozen instant, Geva blinked at Kesst, her heart hammering against her ribs, her voice locked in her throat. Until he smiled again, even more regretful than before.

"There's no need to look so stricken, sweetheart, I swear," he said, with an obvious attempt at lightness. "Things are much better around here these days. And at least I was of age, and luckily"—his eyes angled toward Efterar beside him—"I *love* fucking. The bigger the better, hmmm?"

Efterar twitched an affectionate little smile back toward Kesst, but there was an unmistakable sadness in his eyes, too. Suggesting, perhaps, that what Kesst had faced in Rathgarr's absence had indeed been just as horrifying as it sounded, and that Kesst diminishing it, downplaying it like this, was perhaps nothing new.

And beside Geva, Rathgarr was looking as though he'd followed that too easily too, his face gone even paler, his mouth opening and closing. And gods, they had to say something, Kesst wanted them to say something, *something*, and Geva gulped down air, and gave Rathgarr's cold, clammy-feeling hand a tight, sustained squeeze.

"Er, so, I'm Geva," she managed, her voice someone else's. "Geva Okoro. It's so lovely to finally meet you."

"*So* lovely, I'm sure," Kesst said, but there was no malice in his voice now, only that same dry regret. "I'm Kesst, Rath's surly little blood-brother, as I'm sure you've realized. And this"—he nudged at the big, heavy-featured orc beside him—"is Efterar. My mate, and Orc Mountain's Chief Healer."

Geva briefly considered extending her hand, but instead clenched it against her heart, the way Rathgarr had done. "Very happy to meet you, Efterar," she said, pronouncing the unfamiliar name as carefully as she could. "Are you from the Ash-Kai clan, as well?"

Efterar's thick brows rose, but he nodded, and made the same gesture in return. "Yes, I am," he said, also without any trace of an accent whatsoever. "But I was raised in Salven, rather than here at the mountain. How about you? Where are you from?"

Geva swallowed down her reflexive twitch at the too-familiar question, which so often carried pointed undertones, and attempted another smile. "I was born and raised in Wolfen," she replied, "but I've spent the last few years living in the north of Tlaxca, and working there as a governess."

This Efterar gave a nod and a careful smile at that, though his eyes had angled back toward Kesst, who was eyeing Geva with rather unsettling intensity. "Wait, you're a *governess*?" he echoed. "You really mean to tell us that *Rath* actually fell in love with a *schoolteacher*?"

He was jabbing his claw at Rathgarr again, who—despite having regained a little more colour in his face—was still an unmoving, unhelpful lump beside her. And once again, Geva had to shove down that ridiculous twist of uncertainty, of misery, he'd had a hundred lovers, one month, this was her job, *damn* it—

"Believe me, I was just as surprised as you are," she finally said to Kesst, her voice passably light. "But I was trapped working at a truly terrible post, for absolutely abhorrent employers. And Rathgarr"—she shot a smile toward his stiff, still-frozen face—"saw my distress, and offered to help me."

Rathgarr gave no indication of actually having heard her, but that was surely interest in Kesst's eyes, or maybe disbelief. "Really?" he demanded, with palpable skepticism. "So what, Rath, you've spent the last sixteen years jaunting willy-nilly around the realm, searching for lonely, down-on-their-luck women to 'rescue'?"

There was an unmistakable edge on his voice, and Geva bit back her wince, her unnerving realization that she still had very little conception of what Rathgarr had actually done with himself, all those years. Had he truly spent the entire time running about stealing? Seeking out unsuspecting women to share his bed?

But Rathgarr still wasn't speaking, his eyes still arrested on Kesst's face, so Geva cleared her throat, and desperately attempted a wry smile. "Er, well, I'm quite sure he had no intention whatsoever of rescuing me, at first," she said, with what she hoped was a teasing glance toward Rathgarr's immobile profile. "But the more we got to know each other, the more we began to appreciate one another. He says it's the proper Ash-Kai way, to find the ill-treated person you like best, and keep them safe and content."

There was another instant's silence, in which Kesst and Efterar exchanged a long, unreadable look—and then Efterar snorted, while Kesst let out a choked, reluctant laugh. "Right, I suppose we'll give you that, Rath," he said, raising his chin as he glanced toward Rathgarr again. "Well, do you have anything else to say for yourself, then?"

But beside Geva, Rathgarr still hadn't moved, or spoken. And when she gave him another surreptitious little nudge, he seemed to snap all over, yanking awkwardly for his pack, and fishing furiously around inside it.

"Ach," he said, in a strangled-sounding voice, as he thrust something out toward Kesst. "A gift, brother."

It was a small, long, narrow item, tightly wrapped in cloth, and Kesst carefully took it, a wary, watchful look in his eyes. And once he'd flicked off the cloth with his claws, Geva realized it was the dagger. The beautiful, jewel-studded dagger that Rathgarr had stolen from the Fitzwalds.

"Oh," Kesst said, his voice blank. "Father's, isn't it?"

Rathgarr fervently nodded, a sudden, strange twist on his mouth—but then Kesst swiftly re-wrapped the dagger, and shoved it back toward him. "No, thank you," he said smoothly. "I have no desire whatsoever to brood over gaudy heirlooms from our witless brute father. I think you'd be better off keeping this for yourself, *brother*."

Geva couldn't hide her grimace, her uncertain glance up toward Rathgarr's face. Toward where he looked truly ill now, and he hadn't even reached to take the dagger back. And gods, were they truly going to fight over this too, and Geva somehow reached and plucked the dagger from Kesst's hand, flashing him an apologetic smile.

"Perfectly understandable if this isn't your preference, of course," she said. "I know Rathgarr's brought you a variety of other gifts as well, since he very much wishes to—"

"No," Kesst hissed, not even looking at Geva now, his eyes again narrow and flinty on Rathgarr's face. "No gifts. No bribes. *No coin*. You need to know"—he raised his chin higher—"there is *nothing* I need from you, Rathgarr. Nothing I haven't found on my own, these past sixteen years. You know, you're damned lucky"—Kesst's voice deepened into something darker, colder—"I'm even lowering myself to *speak* to you right now. Not a single apology? Not one explanation? *Nothing*?! It was sixteen *years*, you useless *arsehole*, without one letter, without even a damned *Farewell, good luck, I hope you don't DIE!*"

The words felt almost like blows, striking powerfully against Rathgarr's faintly flinching form, but Geva was almost resigned to his ongoing choked, desperate silence, to the horrible, visceral misery contorting his face.

"I am—sorry," he gulped at Kesst, too loud, far too late. "I am sorry. I—"

But Kesst was raising his hand and whirling around, his black hair flying out behind him. "No," he hissed again, without looking. "No more of your rubbish, you great greedy prick. I am *finished* with you, *forever!*"

And with that, he grasped Efterar's arm, and stalked away toward Orc Mountain, without looking back.

21

————————

For all Geva's previous impending dread of Orc Mountain, it turned out that she scarcely noticed it as she stiffly strode beside Rathgarr through its wide, lamplit stone corridors.

They were following Sigarr and Abjorn again, who—much to Rathgarr's obvious embarrassment—had unfortunately been present for that entire disastrous little scene. And who were now casting uncertain glances over their shoulders toward him, as though he was now liable to forever abandon *them* at any moment, too.

"Here you are," Abjorn said, his voice falsely jovial, as he waved toward one of the many tall doors cut into the thick stone walls. "We were told this room shall be yours, for as long as you wish, and you have this whole corridor all to yourselves, also. Should you like to join us for a meal soon? Or mayhap a tour? I ken the captain and his mate are most eager to see you both."

The captain. That had to be the captain Rathgarr hated, surely? And Geva couldn't suppress a compulsive shiver at the thought of yet another catastrophic meeting, especially with Rathgarr still in such an utterly incompetent state.

"That sounds very lovely," Geva replied, as brightly as she could, sparing only a glance toward the well-appointed, lamplit room around them. "But I'm afraid we've been travelling all day, and I'm completely dead on my feet! I would be very grateful for an opportunity to rest and refresh myself, and perhaps we can visit more thoroughly in the morning? I'm sure there is so much to see, and I would love to be properly awake to enjoy it all."

At this, Sigarr betrayed a dubious-looking frown, but thankfully Abjorn was already nodding, his eyes warm and sympathetic. "Ach, ach, we follow," he said firmly. "There is a latrine down the way if you need this, and if you should like to wash, the Skai bath is not far from here—you yet ken where this is, Rath? Is there aught more you might need?"

Geva didn't even bother looking at Rathgarr for an answer this time, and instead gave Abjorn and Sigarr her best, biggest smile. "I'm sure we'll be fine," she said firmly. "We're so grateful to you both for all your kindness."

Abjorn broadly smiled back, but it rapidly faded as he glanced toward Rathgarr again. And evidently, Rathgarr had finally deigned to take some notice of his surroundings, because he abruptly grasped for Abjorn, and yanked him close into his chest.

"Thank you, my brother," he whispered, his voice cracking. "More in the morn, ach?"

Abjorn was looking thoroughly gratified again, sinking into Rathgarr's embrace with easy familiarity, and Geva once again found her teeth clenching, her eyes flicking away. And catching once more on Sigarr, who was again meeting her gaze, and giving a wry, tolerant shrug. As if to say, *what can be done about this*, but Geva's patience was already badly fraying, her temper rising far too close.

"Well, goodnight, then," she said loudly, through her gritted teeth. "See you soon!"

Thankfully Abjorn took the hint, even if Rathgarr couldn't,

and he gave Geva a quick, sheepish wave as he hurried to follow Sigarr out the door. And finally, *finally*, Geva and Rathgarr were alone again, and she could whirl around to glare at him, her fury flashing sharp and white behind her narrowed eyes.

"What the hell, Rathgarr!" she breathed, as quietly as she could, under the circumstances. "What in all the gods' scorched stinking earth was *that*?!"

For a brief, alarming moment, Rathgarr just kept gazing at her, long enough that she felt a faint, genuine flicker of fear. Perhaps all this had truly shattered him, somehow? Perhaps seeing Kesst had broken something forever? Perhaps this was already over?!

She reflexively stepped forward, gripping at his arm, giving it a little shake—and at the touch, Rathgarr seemed to shake himself awake again too, the movement jerky, strangely uncontrolled. "Why—why do you say this," he said, his voice still not quite his, but that was surely him behind his eyes again, in that contemptuous curl of his mouth. "I am here. Is this not enough?"

"No!" Geva spluttered at him, snatching her hand away again. "No, damn it, it isn't! I thought you wanted to reconcile with Kesst! But instead you barely speak a *word* to him, or to his mate?! Wait"—a horrible suspicion was dawning—"is it because you're upset his mate isn't a *woman*?"

It was unfortunately an all-too-common sentiment, though luckily Geva's own parents had refused to tolerate such narrow-minded judgements—and Rathgarr visibly balked, and then spun and stalked away from her, pacing across the small, stone-walled room.

"You ken I am vexed over *that*?!" he demanded, as he whirled around, and stalked toward her again. "Ach, I have known Kesst since he was an orcling, and I should only be vexed if he *had* gone off and mated a woman!"

Oh. Well. Geva allowed herself a brief moment of relief, but then pulled herself up taller, folding her arms tightly over her chest. "Well, if you know him so well, why did you try to give him that damned dagger?" she shot back. "Did you not notice that he wasn't wearing any weapons, the way Sigarr and Abjorn were? He was wearing jewelry! Surely you still have any *number* of other pilfered baubles you could have offered him?"

She shot an uneasy glance down toward her own wedding-ring, and Rathgarr had surely noticed, angling her a dark, baleful look from where he was still pacing back and forth, now yanking at his hair. "This has no bearing upon you, woman," he snapped. "It is none of your concern!"

Geva couldn't help a shrill, wild-sounding laugh, a desperate shake of her head. "This *is* my concern, and you know it!" she growled at him. "This is my—"

But before she could finish, Rathgarr had clapped his hand powerfully over her mouth, his big restless body shifting far too close. "Hush, woman," he breathed in her ear, his voice hot and low with menace. "Should you keep speaking of this here, and risk ruining *all* for me, I shall happily *gag* you!"

Oh *would* he, the utter bastard, and Geva felt herself bristling, hissing through her teeth. "You will not," she breathed back. "You have no right *whatsoever* to—"

But her voice again broke off, this time because Rathgarr had snapped up his hand—and in his claws was a shiny gold coin. Another ten-piece, damn him to hell and back, and Geva's traitorous eyes stared at it for an instant too long. To which Rathgarr gave a grim, harsh little laugh, and tossed it onto the bed.

"Undress," he growled at her. "Now."

Undress. And curse it, Geva should have argued, fought it, thrown his infuriating coin straight back in his infuriating face. But instead, she was looking at that face, which—angry as it was—still looked like... him. Like the Rathgarr she hadn't seen, perhaps, since the night before.

"Fine," she snarled back at him, as she began unfastening

her lovely blue dress, and yanked it off over her head. And then she hurled it straight toward him, an action that should have been satisfying, but for how easily he caught it, folded it, and draped it over a nearby chair. And then he impatiently snapped his claws toward the rest, the great greedy brute, so next Geva went for her boots and shift and stockings, and threw all that toward him, too.

It had the effect of flashing more cold anger across his eyes, but Geva found that she didn't quite care—at least, until he shoved her back toward the bed behind her. The touch far rougher than he'd ever used before, sending her sprawling onto the soft furs, and when she yelped and flared up, shoving back against him, he hurled his huge heavy body down onto her, his massive clothed thighs straddling her bared hips, trapping her firmly to the bed.

"*Behave*," he growled at her, as he swiftly clutched her wrists with one hand, and pinned them to the bed behind her head. "Now what shall it be? Your mouth again, or your rump?"

He was leaning over her face, too close, and he was even baring his teeth, vicious and deadly. "Answer me!" he barked. "Your mouth? Or here?"

Here. *Here*, with his legs already shifting again, shoving her bare thighs apart, and settling down hard and purposeful between. And then, his eyes still blazing on hers, he blatantly ground his hips up against her wide-open crease, making sure she felt that long, powerful ridge beneath his too-tight trousers.

And damn her, but Geva had stopped struggling, and a hard, hoarse moan escaped her throat. The sound far too loud, too betraying, and in return Rathgarr threw back his head and laughed aloud, rich and deep and cruel.

"Ach, poppet, this is better," he drawled at her, as his other hand went down to his trousers, and loosened them with a few quick tugs. And oh, now that huge pulsing length was bobbing out, hovering so close over Geva's exposed crease, dripping a string of thick white liquid down toward it...

Geva's eyes widened at the sight, and above her Rathgarr glanced down, too—and for an instant, they'd both somehow stilled, just looking. Looking at how she was split wide open for him, her bared, swollen heat visibly clenching, again and again. As if it desperately wanted that dangling white seed, wanted to swallow it deep inside, and then perhaps the rest of him, too...

Rathgarr cursed through his still-bared teeth, his eyes glancing at Geva's rapidly heating face with sudden bitter fury—and in another flare of movement, he grasped his big hands to both her thighs, and shoved them up and back. Pressing them almost into her shoulders, bending her nearly double, so he could—

Geva moaned again at the touch, at the shocking feel of that slick rounded head nudging just there, against her tight knot of heat. And Rathgarr laughed again, pushing her thighs back even further, trapping her beneath him, exposed and immobile and helpless...

And gods, how this looked. Geva's thighs split wide open, pressed tight to her torso, her belly and breasts bulging up full and fleshy between them. Surely the most unflattering position one could possibly be seen in, and she felt her face flaming even hotter, her uncertainty surging—and wait, Rathgarr was looking too. Looking at her squashed, bent-double body, and— she gasped—licking his lips, as that slick, prodding heat shuddered and swelled against her.

"Better," he said again, and when his eyes flicked back to hers, they were smug, satisfied, wicked. "Ready for more, my pretty poppet?"

Geva was inhaling in hard, reedy gulps—he liked this, he liked *her*—and found herself nodding. The movement rapid and fervent, earning another low, mocking laugh from Rathgarr, before his eyes dropped again. To where she could just feel that slick rounded tip of him, nocked close against her... and now pressing a little harder. Easing just slightly further inside, just beginning to open her around him...

"Oh," Geva gasped, her eyes fluttering, her head tilting back—because despite a faint lingering tenderness from the day before, it still felt so damned good, and perhaps even easier, too. Easier to relax against him, to feel that slick, gentle prodding strength sliding deeper, deeper. Carving its way inside, opening her wider and wider around him. Around where he seemed to be throbbing fuller with every breath, with every tight answering flex of her body against him.

Geva couldn't suppress her gasps now, or the furious, full-body shudders beneath him. And as he kept sinking deeper, filling her more and more, it felt as though time had stuck, somehow, like that steady, dizzying slide of slick skin into gripping slick heat would never, ever stop—

Until it did. With Rathgarr's solid hips pressing hard against her arse, the rest of him buried all the way inside. And oh, it felt even fuller like this, so powerful, so visceral, so unyielding, and Geva's moan was more like a steady cry, her back arching, her body clutching and clamping on him, oh, oh...

And above her, Rathgarr's head had tipped back, his tongue sweeping against his lips—but he was watching her again, and oh, that was more satisfaction, more cruel wickedness, in his smug blazing eyes.

"Ach, this *is* better, is it not?" he asked, as he very slightly ground himself deeper—and when Geva cried out again, he actually laughed, his shoulders shaking. "I knew it, poppet. Knew this pleased you, last eve."

Geva could only seem to groan and glare at him, her thoughts whirling in a stilted, stunted mess. Gods, he was awful, and gods he felt good, and why was he bringing this up about last night? Didn't he want to keep it professional, to keep his boundaries, and she had to try, say something, anything—

"And then," she gulped at him, her voice breaking as he ground deeper, "you threw a coin at me, and left!"

He laughed again, damn him, and then drew out just a little. The movement making Geva cry out again, her body uncontrollably clutching him, almost as if to hold him there—but the bastard just kept going, deliberate and agonizingly slow, taking this away from her, no, no—

"Ach, and this time," he said, raising his brows as he kept moving out, away, "I have paid you before, so mayhap you shall not sulk at me over this after. Or"—his voice hardened—"pretend as though I am not even there!"

Gods damn him, he was nearly free of her now, and Geva fought down the rising surge of emotion, something that felt almost like anguish. "I was trying," she gasped, too high-pitched, too close to the edge, "to stay professional! To do a good job for you. To—impress you, and be what you want, and earn your—"

Oh gods, oh gods, what had she been about to say—not coin, surely?—and she clamped her mouth shut, and wildly shook her head. And above her, Rathgarr was blinking at her, his head cocked, his backwards movement stilled, his strength held just at her edge...

And then, oh hell, it began to ease back in. Moving slow but sure, wrenching her even tighter around it, clinging to the stunning sparkling power of it, the sheer reassurance of it, he still wanted this from her, if nothing else, he still wanted this...

"Ach, this is what I wish," he murmured, as he finally sank deep again, his hips grinding against her arse, his thick strength locked all the way inside. "I wish for an eager, hungry helpmate, who *longs* to draw out my good seed."

Oh. Geva felt caught, suddenly, held, pierced to stillness upon him, beneath his eyes. And he huffed a satisfied little laugh, and then shifted himself, holding back her thighs with one arm, so his other hand could slip lower. Down to—she choked and hissed—there, to her slick, swollen crease, still held wide open above where he was jutted inside her.

"I wish," he purred, as his fingers began stroking, circling, "for a prim, proper schoolmarm, whimpering and trembling upon my touch. I wish to make her screech and squirm beneath me. Wish to feel her sucking my good fat Ash-Kai prick up her plump, tight little rump."

Oh hell, Geva's moan was almost a cry again, her body reflexively clamping against him—and then wrenching all over at the feel of a strong finger settling close, slipping a little inside.

"I wish," he breathed, as his hips ground tighter, his finger sinking deeper, "to feel her come undone for me. Wish to taste the strength of her joy for me, whilst she milks out my good seed, and *screams* my name."

His voice was a husky heated hiss, crashing up against the teasing taunt of those fingers, against the fierce inexorable invasion of him deeper below. Grinding in even harder, swirling up swarms of sheer screeching sensation, and she was swelling, surging, cresting to the edge—

And then it exploded, lit up, flashed out in stunning, staggering light. In Geva's entire body blazing up in it, in him, around him, here, hers—

"Rathgarr," she gulped, and oh, he was swirling up too, his body locking tighter against her, his fingers stilling, his breath catching. "Oh, Rathgarr, please, Rathgarr, *yes!*"

His groan was more like a shout, his hand holding her hips slipping, slamming to a fist on the fur—and then he was pouring out inside her, his strength spasming again and again, spraying out rhythmic spurts of hot, gushing release. Filling her with it, flooding her with it, as her own still-shuddering pleasure kept milking out more, and more, and more. Until she could feel it straining, squeezing out its last dregs, as deep as it could go.

And then... stillness. Shivery, silent stillness, broken only by the occasional slight shudder of Geva's body, and the faint, answering flares of his softening strength inside her. Still there, still here, not leaving. Not yet...

But it wasn't exactly a comfortable position, with her legs shoved up like this, and she shifted a little, wincing—and then blinked as Rathgarr's strong hands gripped her, lifted her leg, and tilted her onto her side on the bed. But also easing himself around behind her, so that—somehow—they were both lying on their sides, Geva's back to his chest, his softened cock still jutting up slightly inside her.

It was—strange, but also warm, and maybe even… comforting. Reassuring. And while Geva couldn't quite seem to touch at some of those memories—his mockery, her misery, his praise, *please, Rathgarr, yes*—he was still here. And even more importantly, still himself. Still the wicked, mocking, arrogant orc she knew, and not the blank, broken shell.

Or—was he? Because behind her, his previously silent breaths had gradually begun to sound thick, choked, laboured. His chest swelling and emptying almost convulsively against her back, his hand spasming against where it gripped to her waist.

And Geva knew, with strange, stilted certainty, that this wasn't about her. Wasn't about what they'd just done. No, it was surely about today. About the utter disaster today had been, despite what had obviously been Rathgarr's best efforts, in the face of his grief, and his guilt.

And perhaps she should have pretended to sleep, or make some excuse, seek out that latrine—but there, suddenly, were more memories, clearer memories, from amidst all that. *As though I am not even there. I wish for an eager, hungry helpmate…*

"How would you feel," she ventured, very quiet, "about a tale? I always tell them to myself, when I can't sleep."

Behind her, Rathgarr stiffened, his breaths gone silent—but then he sagged again, his hand slackening against her waist. "Ach, mayhap," he croaked, conspicuously offhanded. "Should you wish."

So Geva drew in breath, and launched into another one of Cecily's favourite tales. The one with the warrior and the seven-headed spirit, full of lighthearted, increasingly preposterous adventures. And while Rathgarr didn't speak once throughout, she could feel him listening, his body sinking closer against hers on the bed.

"Another?" she asked afterwards, into the quiet darkness, and she could feel his nod, his head tucking into the mess of her hair. And damn it, she'd forgotten to put up her hair, and she would pay for that come morning—but she couldn't seem to muster the will to draw away. And instead, she told another tale, and then another, and another. Until Rathgarr's body had gone fully slack against her, and that was unmistakably the sound of a soft snore, close in her ear.

But Geva finished the tale anyway, her voice fallen to a whisper. And then she stared into the darkness, and carefully thought of nothing at all, until sleep finally, finally came.

22

———

When Geva's consciousness returned, she was alone in the bed, her bare body sprawled wide across its soft, cozy fur. And where Rathgarr had been—she twitched as she reached around—there was only what felt like a rag, tucked up close against... well.

She carefully pushed herself upwards, taking care not to dislodge the rag, and blinked at the room around her. Gods, she'd scarcely even noticed it the night before, and it was a good size, walled in smooth grey stone, with a variety of large, sturdy wood furnishings. Not only the bed, but a wardrobe, a chair, a nightstand with an oil lamp, and even a small, rocking cradle.

Geva's eyes lingered too long on the cradle, something odd clutching in her chest, and she yanked her gaze away again, searching upwards this time. Up toward where there seemed to be light, somehow, coming from—she blinked—a small, intentional-looking slit, cut across part of the otherwise smooth ceiling, and letting in what appeared to be actual *daylight*.

"Awake, poppet?" came Rathgarr's voice, and when Geva twisted to look, he was striding in from around a corner. From what must have been a second attached room, she realized, as her eyes darted back to the bedroom's main door, which even had a full-length velvet curtain strung across it.

"Y-yes," Geva replied, noticing with a wince that Rathgarr was once again fully dressed, in yet more fine-looking clothing she hadn't seen before. While her own clothes—she glanced around the room again—were apparently nowhere to be seen.

"Er, where are my clothes?" she ventured. "And... the latrine?"

Rathgarr smirked, his eyes purposefully angling down toward her arse, but then he strode for the wardrobe, and yanked out one of her shifts. "Here," he said, tossing it over toward her. "And whilst we are here, should you choose to only wear this—or naught at all—no orc shall mark this, ach?"

Wait. No one would notice if she didn't *dress*?! Geva gaped at him as she grasped the shift, her mouth uselessly opening and closing, and Rathgarr stepped a little nearer, raising his brows toward her. "Except, mayhap, to envy me," he added, as he dropped a hand, and gave her bare breast a brief, proprietary squeeze. "And these plump pretty teats of yours."

Geva ought to have been highly offended, alarmed, something—but instead she ducked her hot-feeling face and yanked on her shift, firmly pulling it down before standing up and stalking past Rathgarr toward the door. "The latrine," she managed. "Please."

Thankfully, he didn't argue, and escorted her out into the wide, lamplit corridor. Which, Geva now noticed, steadily tilted upwards, and it again featured smooth stone walls, studded with more open doors, and clean-looking stone floors that felt soft and surprisingly warm under her bare feet. Suggesting, perhaps, that the floor was even *heated*?

"In there," Rathgarr told her, waving her toward another curtained door, and giving her arse a gentle slap. "I shall meet you back in our room, ach?"

Geva nodded, and soon found herself marvelling at what turned out to be a clean, spacious latrine. Featuring not only a covered toilet, but also a washbasin, a looking-glass, a flickering lamp, and a variety of clean rags and towels. And after a moment's studying the empty washbasin, she noticed a small steel lever on the wall above it—and when she pulled it, the spout above the basin poured out fresh, clean water.

All combined, it made washing up an actual pleasure, even despite Rathgarr's copious mess, and her still-tender arse. And when Geva stepped back into their room again, she felt clean and fresh all over, and far more optimistic about Orc Mountain than she'd ever thought possible. She could do this. One month.

"Rathgarr, this place is—" she began, stopping short at the sight of the empty room—but wait, there was a sound behind the corner, where he'd come out from earlier. And when she went over to investigate, it was indeed an entire second room, its entrance cleverly tucked into the back wall. It was only slightly smaller than the main bedroom, but instead of bedroom furnishings, it boasted multiple large chests, cases, and shelves, scattered about with a variety of glittering items.

"You survived, poppet?" Rathgarr asked over his shoulder, from where he was arranging things on a shelf. And after a moment's blinking at him, and around at the room, Geva realized that he was... unpacking? Yes, that had to be it, his familiar pack now lying half-empty at his feet, while around him, this was... his plunder.

And while she recognized some of it—much of it—from the Fitzwalds', there was still so much more. Piles of coin. Clusters of glinting gold and jewels. Small shiny carvings and baubles. And tools, and weapons, and flasks, and goblets... and even those two shining silver dinner-plates, now standing proudly on a shelf, with four more to match.

Geva couldn't seem to stop gaping at it, at all this shocking wealth just scattered around this little room—and suddenly she felt dizzy, enough that she had to put her hand to the stone wall beside her. Gods, no wonder Rathgarr hadn't cared about throwing her all those ten-piece coins. No wonder he hadn't balked at paying for her passage across the sea. Compared to all this, she was... cheap. A... bargain.

"This is... all yours?" she made herself say, though it came out sounding faint. "And this your... dressing-room, or something?"

"Ach, this is all mine," Rathgarr replied, without looking up. "And this is a proper Ash-Kai trove-room. Kept safe just beyond where the Ash-Kai sleeps, and serving to flaunt his wealth, and his strength, and his standing among his clan."

Oh. Of course. So it was another part of the show, then. And yes, Rathgarr had even mentioned the flaunting, and Geva had known very well he was carrying excessive quantities of plunder in that gigantic pack of his. But even so, seeing it all out like this, seeing just how much there was, was clutching with surprising misery at her belly.

"Right," she said weakly. "Well. Perhaps I'll—dress, then?"

"Ach, should you wish," Rathgarr said absently, as he combed through a messy pile of jewelry with his claws. "The red dress today, mayhap."

Oh. The red dress. Because he'd clearly unpacked her clothes too, and therefore knew which ones were the finest. And wait, he'd done this yesterday, too, hadn't he? Choosing her clothes for her, as if she were another trinket. Another thing... to *envy*.

But this was Geva's job, damn it, and she jerked a nod he couldn't see, and went back into the bedroom to dress, and wrangle with her hair. Which turned out to be just as painfully tedious as she'd expected, but finally she was groomed and ready, clad in the close-fitting red dress, and waiting.

But Rathgarr still hadn't emerged from his trove-room, and when Geva went to look again, he was still bent over the jewelry. Plucking out piece after piece with his claws, turning each one over, bringing it to his nose—and then shaking his head as he put it away again.

"Rathgarr?" Geva asked, and when he didn't respond, she stepped closer, her eyes caught on his stiff shoulders, the hard set of his jaw. "What are you doing?"

He still didn't look at her, but she could see his throat bobbing as he yanked out a long gold earring, sniffed it, and tossed it away again. "Seeking a new gift for Kesst," he replied, without inflection. "You were right. He wore jewels, not weapons."

Oh. Geva winced, and her hand reached for him, gently gripping against his arm. "But Rathgarr," she said, quiet, "Kesst said he didn't want any gifts. Remember?"

Rathgarr didn't seem to have heard her, yanking out a big gold bangle, and Geva sighed as she watched him sniff it, turn it over, sniff it again. "Kesst said he wanted an apology," she continued. "Or an explanation. Perhaps you could try starting there?"

Rathgarr's shoulders hunched higher, and he hurled the bangle away, hard enough that it bounced on the stone floor, and rolled away under a shelf. "Kesst does not wish to hear from me," he said, his voice hard. "He said he is *finished* with me. Forever."

Geva winced again, her hand squeezing tighter against his arm. "Yes, but sometimes people say things they don't mean," she replied carefully. "Especially when they're hurt, or surprised, or distressed."

She could feel Rathgarr's muscles flexing beneath her touch, and suddenly he laughed, the sound echoing harsh against the stone walls. "Ach, but he too called me a *useless arsehole*, and a *great greedy prick*," he said, in a perfect imitation of Kesst's accent. "You cannot ken he did not mean this? Not when *you* have oft called me much the same, poppet?"

Gods damn it, and Geva made a face, drew in a deep breath. "Well, you know *I* don't actually mean any of it, either," she replied, without quite looking at him. "Don't you?"

There was an instant's dangling silence, the feel of Rathgarr's intent eyes on her face. Because what *did* she mean, if she didn't mean all that? Surely it didn't mean... she liked him? *Wanted* him?

"And besides," she added, too quickly, glancing briefly at his unreadable eyes, "how are *you* one to judge other people for not meaning what they say? Let's see, since the first moment we met, I've been"—she pulled away to begin counting on her fingers—"your *poppet*, your *sweetling*, your *angel*, your *kitten*, your *pet*, your *prickly little schoolmarm*... am I missing any?"

She raised her brows imperiously toward him, and was deeply gratified by a faint twitch at the corner of his mouth. "Ach, you ken I do not mean all this, poppet?"

"Of course you don't, you sleazy cheat!" Geva retorted, but she was half-smiling, too. "You do it so you don't need to remember any names, or worry about calling any of your lovers the wrong one by mistake!"

And though her stomach twisted at the thought—*hundreds*, Kesst had said—it had still been worth it, because Rathgarr's mouth curved higher, that familiar wickedness glinting in his eyes. "Ach, you ken I could forget you, *Geva Okoro*?" he purred at her, again pronouncing her name with deliberate care. "Or how sweetly you screech *my* name, when I empty my bollocks deep into your tight little rump?"

Oh, hell, because Geva's face instantly flooded hot again, her throat swallowing hard enough that she could hear it. And in return Rathgarr laughed, his big hand swatting her rear, even giving it a firm little squeeze. "Ach, we both know this pleased you, my hungry little pet," he drawled. "Now, today, mayhap you shall..."

Geva's breath caught, her eyes damnably eager on his—but he'd suddenly gone still, the words fading to silence in his throat. And something had passed over his face, turning it cold and empty, almost—Geva shivered—just the way he'd looked the night before.

And then, a sound. A rap, perhaps, near the door. And

Rathgarr wasn't moving again, still wasn't even blinking—and rather than argue it this time, Geva just drew away, and went out to the door. Yanking the curtain aside, and finding—two orcs. Two new orcs, one of them bulky and green-skinned and genial-looking, and the other tall and sharp, with his arms crossed over his bare chest, and murder in his flashing black eyes.

"Greetings, new Ash-Kai woman," said the greenish orc, with a swift little bow. "The Captain of Orc Mountain seeks the presence of you and your mate at his table. At once."

23

———————

The Captain of Orc Mountain. At once.

It took far too much effort for Geva to smile, to keep her eyes warm on the genial orc's face. "Of course, we'd be happy to oblige," she replied, as smoothly as she could. "If you could just grant us a moment to ready ourselves?"

Fortunately, the orc nodded, so Geva thanked him, dropped the curtain, and went back to Rathgarr again. He was still standing there in the trove-room, still in the exact same place she'd left him, still with that same empty look in his eyes. And after an instant's studying him, she put her hands to his shoulders, and began smoothing out his tunic with easy, gentle strokes.

"We've been invited for a meal, love," she said, because those two damned orcs were still waiting, and no doubt listening, just beyond that door. "Would you like to wear your cloak, or your sword? And perhaps I can comb your hair?"

Rathgarr slightly twitched beneath her touch, his eyes shifting, his head jerking what might have been a nod. So Geva finished smoothing out his tunic, tucking it more tightly into his trousers, before guiding him back out into the bedroom again. And after a moment's quick searching—his cloak was in the wardrobe, his sword propped in the corner, his comb on the nightstand—she was back before him again. Fussing first with his cloak, and then huffing a laugh at the damned heaviness of his sword, and how she could scarcely lift it, let alone put it into his belt.

But thank the gods, Rathgarr's awareness had seemed to keep returning throughout all this, and his hand jerked to hers, helping her lift the sword, and sheath it into place. And then Geva moved around to his hair, combing it out slow and careful, until she could feel his head tilting back, his breath shuddering out, his shoulders gradually sagging beneath his cloak.

"Almost done," she murmured, letting her hands slip back to his shoulders, squeezing them, easing out the tension even more. "What do you think, love?"

At that, Rathgarr exhaled again, and jerked a curt little nod. So after another brief moment's rubbing his shoulders, Geva took his hand, and drew him out into the corridor. To where the two orcs were still waiting, the friendly one still smiling, the angry one still looking murderous.

"Thank you so much for waiting," Geva told them, with the biggest smile she could muster. "Proper grooming is *so* important, you know. I'm Geva, and this is my mate Rathgarr, of Clan Ash-Kai. It's so lovely to meet you... er...?"

The greenish orc's smile had gone rather bemused, but he nodded, and gave a brief little bow. "I am Baldr, of Clan Grisk, Left Hand to our captain," he replied. "And this is Drafli of Clan Skai, my mate, and our Right Hand."

Oh. That surely sounded important—though wait, Clan Skai was the same as Killik and Ulfarr, right? The clan Rathgarr had called the captain's *attack dogs*?

But Geva kept the smile fixed to her mouth, and aimed it toward this alarming, lethal-looking Drafli. "It's such an honour to meet you," she said brightly. "I've already had the pleasure of meeting several of your Skai clan-mates. Killik, and Ulfarr? Killik is a very impressive fighter."

There was no forthcoming reply, only more of the murderous glare, and Geva's helpless glance toward Baldr found him clearing his throat, his smile sheepish this time. "Drafli does not oft speak aloud, the way we do," he said. "But he is one of our mountain's best scouts and warriors. And he is also"—his chest puffed out—"the father of our son, to be born this summer."

Geva blinked at that, glancing uncertainly down at Baldr's very flat bare waist—but then firmly congratulated him on his forthcoming son. And then, after another sidelong glance at Rathgarr's immobile form, she loudly proclaimed how hungry she was, and how lovely it was to be invited to dinner, or perhaps this was rather breakfast?

Luckily, Baldr took the hint, and soon he and Drafli were leading Geva and Rathgarr through the broad, lamplit corridor. Which was now twisting and turning more than before, and tilting even further upwards. And as they walked, Geva felt her trepidation steadily rising too, her hands again clinging to their usual place on Rathgarr's arm.

They'd been summoned by the captain of Orc Mountain. The orc Rathgarr hated most, the orc he most wished to deceive. The orc who'd possibly turned Kesst against him.

A foul usurper, Rathgarr had called him. *A hard, ruthless, single-minded orc, who bears no dissent, and no rivals for his place.*

And glancing again at Rathgarr's set face beside her, Geva realized that she had no conception of how he wanted to play this. He wanted to show himself settled and harmless, but what did that mean? How did he want her to behave? What were his goals for this damned meeting, and how could she possibly follow his lead, when he could scarcely seem to speak?

But there were no answers forthcoming, not even a single sideways look. And as Baldr and Drafli halted outside one of the corridor's doors, Baldr again smiling as he waved them toward it, Geva drew in breath, and squared her shoulders. Bracing herself, for...

A cozy, firelit room, with a large low table in the middle, and two people seated behind it. One was a tall, capable-looking woman with fair skin and dark hair, dressed in what appeared to be... men's clothing? While beside her, there sat quite possibly the most alarming orc Geva had seen yet. He was perhaps even bigger than Rathgarr, his bare chest huge and strapped with muscle, his heavy-browed face harsh and brutally scarred.

But in the orc's massive arms, he was holding—a child. A small, grey-skinned, pointy-eared orc child, who was waving his chubby little arms, and giggling.

And that—Geva's eyes followed the little orc's delighted gaze—was because the big orc was using his clawed hand to cast a shadow on the opposite wall in the firelight. Making it look like an excitable little dog, perhaps, bouncing around and wildly snapping at the shifting, flickering sparks.

It was something Geva had often done back at the Fitzwalds', especially with Cecily—and a strange, stilted lump rose in her throat as she watched. Enough that it took a full moment to digest that this was the cruel, ruthless orc captain Rathgarr hated? The foul usurper? *Him*?!

"Ach, enough for now, my son," the usurper was currently telling the little orc, in a deep, steady voice. "Let us greet our new guests, and welcome them to our home."

At this, both he and the little orc looked up at Rathgarr and Geva, with near-identical considering expressions on their faces. And Geva couldn't help an impulsive, genuine grin, and a curtsey toward first the orc and his son, and then the woman. Who was already standing and striding over to meet them, her hand outstretched, a warm smile on her face.

"Welcome to our mountain," she said, with a firm shake of Geva's hand, and then a nod toward Rathgarr's still-stiff bulk beside her. "I'm Jule, of Clan Ash-Kai, and this is my mate

Grimarr, Captain of Five Clans. And this"—her smile softened as she glanced toward him—"is our son, Tengil. And I presume you've already met Baldr and Drafli?"

Baldr and Drafli were indeed still here, striding around to sit at the table together, on the side nearest Grimarr. "Yes, thank you," Geva replied, smiling between them both, and then back toward this Jule. "And I'm Geva Okoro, and this is my mate Rathgarr. We're so grateful to you for welcoming us here, and inviting us to your home and table."

Jule flashed her another warm grin in return, and then angled a brief, curious glance toward Rathgarr. "It's our pleasure, of course," she said. "Kesst is a dear friend of ours, and I've been so eager to meet his brother, after so long."

It was clearly an opening for Rathgarr, a conversational offering, and Geva could have groaned at the sight of his still-blank face, the very faint curl of his lip. "Yes, it's certainly been a while," she interjected, with a brief, purposeful clench of her fingernails into Rathgarr's arm. "But I know you're very eager to catch up again too, love, aren't you?"

To her great relief, Rathgarr finally twitched beneath her, and inclined his head toward Jule. "Ach," he said stiffly. "Greetings, Ash-Kai woman. And"—his eyes slid toward Grimarr, his head bowing—"Grimarr. My regards upon all your great gains, these past years."

Grimarr bowed his head in return, but his eyes remained decidedly wary, even as he waved for them to sit down across from him at the table. A silent order that Rathgarr seemed entirely disinclined to obey, so Geva surreptitiously drew him forward, and tugged him down beside her. And then—after desperately searching for some distraction—she found one in the little orc, who was still eyeing her suspiciously from his father's arms.

"Hi, Tengil," she said, with a cheery little wave. "I'm Geva. I like funny shadows, too."

She wasn't sure if Tengil would have followed that—he

looked to be a little more than a year old, at least by human baby standards—but his eyes narrowed at her, before glancing toward the now-empty wall. A blatant hint if Geva ever saw one, so she twisted sideways, and raised her hands up into the firelight. Not doing the dog, like Grimarr had done, but rather the horned, fire-breathing dragon her mother had taught her.

"I am the great and hungry spirit-dragon Amhalia," she said in her best dragon voice, making the huge shadowy figure dance and sway upon the wall. "And I love to eat... mosquitoes! Yum yum!"

Her dragon had snapped at a little spark, munching away with gusto, and to Geva's distant relief, Tengil gave a brief but delighted-sounding gurgle. So she kept on going, making Amhalia messily eat mosquito after mosquito, until Tengil was giggling uncontrollably, his wriggling little body collapsed into his father's arms. Looking so adorably gleeful that both his parents were smiling, Baldr was laughing aloud, and even Drafli looked slightly less murderous than before. And— perhaps the greatest victory of all—next to Geva, Rathgarr was looking almost like himself again, his eyes focused on the wall, a small smile quirking at his mouth.

"So full!" Geva made Amhalia groan, writhing back and forth. "So—many—mosquitoes! Must go poo—and sleep! Bye-bye!"

With that, Amhalia flailed away, leaving Tengil still wildly shrieking with laughter, interspersed with something that sounded suspiciously like *"poo"*. And Geva was grinning too, even as she gave an apologetic wince across the table. "The poo jokes, I tell you," she said. "Every single time."

But Jule was laughing too, and exchanging a knowing glance with Grimarr beside her. "You've spent a lot of time with children, I see," she said wryly. "We actually heard that you're a trained governess?"

Geva blinked for an instant, but right, that had come up the day before, hadn't it? "Yes, for quite a few years now," she replied, "and before that, while I was studying, I often worked as a tutor as well. I've always loved children and teaching, although"—she half-grimaced, half-smiled—"I could do with less poo, I'll admit."

Jule laughed again, and then asked Geva where she'd worked, and how many children she'd taught. And soon they were deep in conversation on the subject, and Geva had once again told the entire tale of her awful employers, and of Rathgarr's highly heroic rescue.

"But you cannot have known one another long?" Baldr interjected at this point, his head tilted. "Your scents upon one another, they are just"—he gave an apologetic smile—"quite recent."

Damn it. There was an instant's hitching silence, in which Geva couldn't help a sideways glance at Rathgarr, who was suddenly looking rather pale around the mouth. *Some orcs can sense falsehood*, he'd told her. *The more truth we can speak, the more they shall accept this.*

"No, that part of it—is fairly new, for us," she replied carefully. "But we've known each other for some time now, and I just wanted to wait until"—she waved her hand at them, showing her ruby ring—"we had a proper commitment, and a serious plan for our future. I've had some—difficulties, in the past, and I'm still quite nervous of childbirth, besides."

The words carried at least some ring of truth, enough that Baldr thankfully appeared mollified—and luckily, Geva was spared any further questioning by the arrival of several more people into the room, all of them carrying heaping plates of food. Two were older-looking orcs, but the last was a young, pretty blonde woman, clad in an astonishingly revealing ensemble that proudly displayed her pale, rounded belly.

"Hi!" she said under her breath to Geva, as she set down a plate in front of her. "I'm Alma, and we're so happy to have you! I'm looking forward to—"

But before she could finish, a clawed grey hand had

clamped around her wrist, and yanked her sideways. And though Alma yelped with surprise, she was also smiling, and willingly following the hand's pull. Landing straight in... Drafli's lap?

"My lord," she murmured, her face prettily flushing, her eyes downcast. And to Geva's rapidly increasing shock, Drafli's murderous expression had entirely faded into something soft, or maybe even affectionate. As his hand caressed wide and protective against Alma's belly, his other hand casually flicking the hair off her neck...

And then, without warning, he swiftly bent his head into her neck, and... *bit down.* His sharp jaw flexing as his teeth clamped into her slim neck, and his throat began *swallowing.*

Alma shuddered and gasped in response, but there was no visible pain or discomfort on her face. And blinking toward her, Geva realized that there were multiple other faded bite-marks on her neck, too. And—she shot a furtive glance around at the room's other occupants—on Baldr's neck, also, and even on Jule's?

And yet more disconcerting, no one else at the table seemed even slightly alarmed by this behaviour. Jule only spared Drafli and Alma a fondly amused glance before tucking into her food, while Grimarr was ignoring them altogether, in favour of carefully tearing up strips of meat, and placing them into Tengil's little waiting fingers. While Baldr, in a rather stark contrast, was blatantly watching Drafli and Alma, his black tongue brushing against his lips, and Rathgarr—an odd chill wrenched up Geva's back—was watching, too. His gaze heavy and half-lidded, and unmistakably... hungry.

Geva's eyes dropped, while her swirling thoughts made multiple rapid, equally unpleasant points. The... *biting* had been one of those tales about orcs, and clearly it hadn't been wrong after all, had it? And also, clearly Rathgarr again hadn't seen fit to inform her about this, or prepare her, although a certain memory from the wardrobe was now looming far more vividly than before. And—worst of all—of course Rathgarr liked watching this. Liked seeing just the kind of soft, sweet, eager woman he preferred, pliant and willing and minimally dressed, and freely gasping in her lover's arms. The kind of woman an orc would want to have *sons* with.

There shall be no true mating between us. I shall have no surprise son from this. Neither should I ever choose to mate you...

Geva couldn't help a relieved exhale once Drafli finally pulled away from Alma, prodding her to her feet with a gentle slap to her arse, before returning his full attention to his plate. But wait, now *Baldr* was reaching for her instead—and drawing her down for a slow, sensual kiss. One hand spreading against her rounded waist, just where Drafli's had been, while the other sank deep into her hair.

Oh. So they both—*oh*. And suddenly Baldr's comment about the son was making far more sense than before, especially once Drafli's hand snaked sideways again, grasping at Baldr's groin beneath the table. Making Baldr gasp and moan helplessly into Alma's mouth, while Drafli kept eating his meal with his other hand, his expression now one of smug, self-composed satisfaction.

It took almost all Geva's willpower to draw her attention back to her own plate, and the admittedly delicious meal upon it. And she couldn't even seem to say a thank-you as Alma finally waved goodbye and walked out again, her face flushed, her pretty blue eyes sparkling with pleasure.

"So how are you two finding your room?" Jule asked now, speaking rather quickly, perhaps as if she'd caught more of that than Geva might have hoped. "Will it be adequate for your needs?"

Rathgarr had apparently reverted to stony silence again, his eyes darting a narrow glance toward Geva's face, so she drew in a breath, attempted another smile. "Oh, yes, very comfortable indeed, thank you," she told Jule. "Near such a well-appointed latrine, too. And the trove-room was a very nice touch."

It seemed like an utterly innocuous statement, but suddenly the room snapped to a taut, ringing silence. In which Baldr grimaced, Drafli's expression went murderous again, and Grimarr's eyes bore into Rathgarr's, something heavy and dangerous behind them.

"Forgive my ignorance," Jule said into the silence, her voice deceptively light, "but what's a trove-room?"

Oh, damn, Geva had somehow botched this, and she couldn't hide her wince, or her apologetic squeeze to Rathgarr's knee. But he was busy staring straight back across the table toward Grimarr, his brows low, his jaw tight and set.

"A trove-room is where a strong, worthy Ash-Kai guards his goods," Rathgarr replied, his voice unnaturally steady. "It is how he shows he can keep and care for his kin. Grimarr well knows this, for his father"—Rathgarr's mouth curved into something not at all like a smile—"once held the greatest hoard in mayhap all the realm. I well recall how oft you boasted of its wealth and strength, ach?"

Geva's hand squeezed even tighter on Rathgarr's knee, because Jule was looking both surprised and confused, and Grimarr's gaze had gone nearly as murderous as Drafli's. "Ach, this was a long time past," he replied flatly. "Much has altered, since then."

Something spasmed on Rathgarr's mouth, but his eyes hadn't moved from Grimarr's face. "Ach, it has," he said smoothly. "So now you keep your hoard secret, mayhap? Unseemly to boast, I ken."

With that, his gaze had briefly, tellingly glanced toward Jule—implying that Grimarr was *lying* to her, good gods—and that was unmistakably a growl, rumbling from Grimarr's throat. "There is no secret," he hissed. "I spent my father's hoard. *All* of it."

Rathgarr blinked, once, though his mouth was already curving up again. "You *spent* all this," he repeated, the skepticism heavy in his voice. "Upon what?"

Grimarr growled again, but his eyes stayed heavy on Rathgarr's, glittering with hard, intent purpose. "On aught that was needed," he said flatly. "Grain. Salt. Seeds. Ore. Cloth. Boots. Pay for fair work. Meed for early deaths. Amends for past wrongs. Gifts to each clan's heads, so they could again build their own trades, and gird their homes within the mountain."

Rathgarr blinked again, and Grimarr kept glaring at him across the table, with unmistakable challenge in his glinting eyes. "I gained the place of captain not by my trove-room," he hissed, "but by my strength, and my deeds, and my fealty to my kin. By feeding and housing all my brothers, and keeping them *safe!*"

The last word echoed through the room, ringing with certainty, with conviction. Until it was broken by—laughter. Rathgarr's laughter, the sound deep and rich, and almost, almost real.

"Ach, keeping your brothers *safe*," he repeated, his voice a dragging drawl. "I have heard how well you have kept Kesst safe, *Captain*. Now, in calling me here, mayhap you seek to further this for him? To *finish* this?"

Curse it, Rathgarr was surely not supposed to be risking this right now, and Geva flinched at the all-too-palpable rage, flashing up fierce and vicious in Grimarr's glinting eyes. "I have done all within my power for Kesst," he snarled. "Ach, even bearing *you* here. Swearing your safety. Your *welcome*."

He gave a furious wave at the table, at the elaborate meal before them—but Rathgarr laughed again, the sound brittle and cold. "You truly dare to claim this?!" he demanded across the table. "When Kesst says he has borne a hundred orcs he did not wish for? When he says he had no surety, and no safety? When he says he was kept *trapped, terrified and alone, without any protection, in a mountain full of ravenous orcs?*"

He'd again spoken in a perfect echo of Kesst's voice, down to the exact lilt of his accent, and Geva could see Grimarr blinking, his brows furrowing low. His mouth opening, as if to make some kind of explanation, but Rathgarr barked a growl, his hand sharply sweeping through the air.

"No," he hissed. "No more lies, Ash-Kai. You failed my brother. You failed *me*."

Grimarr was still frowning, though it was different now, perhaps almost defensive, or even confused. "I have done naught to you, Rathgarr," he said slowly. "And I should never harm Kesst, or *fail* him. I have—"

But beside Geva, Rathgarr let out another deep, angry growl, loud enough that the hairs on her neck stood on end. "No—more—Ash-Kai—*lies!*" he hollered, and he leapt up to his feet, his cloak swirling out around him. "I shall mayhap hear you, Captain, when you offer us your *meed* and *amends*, from this trove-room you have so helpfully *forgotten!*"

With that, he spun around, and swept for the door—but when Geva jerked to follow, he thrust out his hand toward her. Stopping her. Not—wanting her?

"No, poppet," he said, his voice harsh. "Stay. Eat. I shall meet you later."

And without another glance, he strode out the door, and was gone.

24

———————

For a horrible, hurtling moment, Geva sat there numb and unmoving, staring at the door, while her thoughts screeched in a dozen directions at once.

Why had Rathgarr told her to stay? Was he angry that she'd brought up the trove-room, and set off yet another disastrous scene? Or did he truly want her to stay, and perhaps spy for him? To try to learn what Grimarr had done?

And what *had* Grimarr done? Why hadn't he protected Kesst? And why had Rathgarr seemed to believe that it had been Grimarr's obligation to do so, while he himself had stayed so intently away, for sixteen years?

No, he'd said, when Geva had asked about him visiting Kesst. *No. I could not.*

And why hadn't Rathgarr just told her what had happened? How the hell did he expect her to be a good mate—a good helpmate, damn it—if she still didn't know why he'd made the most devastating decision of his damned *life*?

And worse—Geva grimaced as she looked back at the table's occupants again—how did Rathgarr expect her to follow a departure like that? What was she supposed to say, without betraying his confidence? He'd wanted to impress them, right?

To show himself settled? Harmless? To never let the Skai or their foul usurper captain see what he truly thought of them?

"Um," Geva said into the stillness, her voice wavering. "I'm sure Rathgarr just needs—a few moments. I know it's been quite—difficult, for him, coming back here, after so long. Kesst was very"—she grimaced again—"eloquent, in his initial reception yesterday. Understandably so, of course."

She glanced uneasily around the table, bracing for their responses—Jule had called Kesst a *dear friend*, hadn't she?—and she was vaguely startled by Jule's answering laugh, the wry shake of her head. "I can only imagine Kesst's *eloquence* on the subject," she said. "I would have loved to see it. Almost as much as I would have loved to see Grimarr strutting around boasting of his vile father's ill-gotten hoard! *Really*, Grimarr?"

To Geva's increasing astonishment, Grimarr was looking decidedly shamefaced, or perhaps even contrite. "I was young, and sullen, and easily vexed," he said, with a sigh. "And Rathgarr is *deeply* vexing, ach?"

Jule laughed aloud, even as she shot a brief, regretful glance toward Geva. "I'm sure you're right, and he just needs some time," she said firmly. "And I'm sure Kesst will come around with time, too. Now"—her eyes angled toward Grimarr again, holding there for an instant too long—"why don't we finish eating, and then I'll take you on a tour of the mountain, Geva? Let these three reminisce for a while, perhaps?"

Her eyes had flicked toward Drafli, who was very casually picking at his food, and Geva realized that both Grimarr and Baldr were eyeing him, too, the room gone unnaturally silent. So she accordingly finished eating as quickly as she could, and then followed Jule out into the corridor.

"Well, I'm sure we're all glad that's over," Jule said brightly, hoisting Tengil up onto one hip. "Now, what would you like to see first?"

Geva was still feeling decidedly off-kilter, but she drew in breath, and attempted a smile. "I'd love to see it all, of course," she said. "Everything I've seen so far has already been so fascinating."

Jule seemed suitably pleased by this, and soon Geva found herself in the midst of a comprehensive tour of Orc Mountain. Beginning at the top of the mountain in the Ash-Kai wing—each clan had their own designated area suited to their needs, Jule explained—and steadily working their way downwards, through an ever-expanding maze of twisty stone corridors.

And while it was certainly dark, and convoluted, and seemed to indeed house hundreds of orcs, Orc Mountain was once again not at all what Geva had expected. While some areas were pitch-black, many others were well-lit, with either lamps or fires, and the floors were dry and clear, the rooms cozy and well-furnished. A large number of the rooms also seemed focused on some productive purpose, and by the time they'd left the Ash-Kai wing, Geva had already seen a trading-post, a shrine, and a bright, bustling forge. Not only that, but along the way Jule had introduced her to at least a dozen new Ash-Kai orcs, nearly all of them big and scarred and bare-chested—and all of them, to Geva's surprise, remarkably friendly.

"Rathgarr's mate, ach?" said one of the smiths, smiling toothily at Geva between steady strikes of his hammer. "Welcome, woman. It is good to see our brother back and settled again."

This had seemed a common sentiment among the new orcs Jule had introduced so far—an immediate recognition of Rathgarr's scent on Geva, as well as some sort of genuine-seeming pleasure upon his return. And once again, Geva smiled and curtsied at the orc, and thanked him for his kindness, and then desperately attempted to embed his name and face into her memory as they continued on their way.

"Now, this is the Skai wing," Jule said, waving Geva into a narrower corridor, with distinctly dimmer lighting than before.

"The Skai are typically excellent fighters and spies. They're very loyal, and committed to keeping our mountain safe."

Geva couldn't help comparing that to Rathgarr's far less complimentary references to the Skai clan, but before she could ask, Jule began eagerly waving at several figures down the corridor. "Hey, Maria! Come meet Geva, will you?"

This Maria turned out to be a striking, golden-skinned, heavily pregnant woman, dressed only in what appeared to be a very large tunic, with a gleaming dagger strapped to her side. And stalking over to stand behind her—Geva blanched—was a frowning, truly gigantic orc, who Maria cheerfully introduced as her mate Simon. He was the most massive orc Geva had seen yet, and certainly the most terrifying—at least, until a small, dark head poked up over his shoulder.

"That is new human," said a small, high-pitched voice. "She smell different. *Look* different."

Geva blinked, because yes, it was another little orc, maybe eight or nine years old, clinging to Simon's shoulders with small, pointy claws. And Simon was reaching back to pat the orc's head, and giving a slow, inscrutable nod. "Ach, little brother," he said, his voice deep and firm. "Humans have many smells and colours, just as with orcs. Just as with"—his eyes flicked up the corridor, his hand giving a purposeful wave—"Kalfr and us, ach?"

When Geva turned to look, she indeed found another orc striding up the corridor, glancing between them with mild, curious eyes. But unlike the rest of the orcs she'd seen so far, with their greyish or greenish skin, this one's skin was a deep pearly charcoal, contrasting beautifully with his careful, sharp-toothed white smile.

"Ach, what are we, Simon?" he said politely, with a little bow toward Geva. "And welcome to our home, woman. The whole mountain has been abuzz with news of Rathgarr's return, and his stunning mate."

Geva felt herself flushing and waving it away, to which

the orc gave an apologetic smile, and glanced inquiringly toward Simon again. Who was now firmly clasping Kalfr on the shoulder, and turning him toward the little orc on his back.

"You ken how Kalfr looks and smells different than we do, also?" Simon asked the little orc, with another gentle pat to his head. "How he is Bautul, and we are Skai, but we are yet brothers? It is just the same with humans. You have only not met all the other human clans yet."

The little orc frowned intently toward Geva, his nose wriggling, and she felt herself giving him a quick, genuine-feeling smile. "Your—big brother—has the right of it," she said. "My family is from a clan called Ezira. We usually look like this, with brown skin and curly hair. And we're often known for our stories, and art and music, and dancing."

The little orc's eyes brightened at that, darting eagerly between Geva and Maria. "Maria *love* dancing," he informed Geva, with an authoritative nod. "This is how she please Simon, you ken, and earn her keep."

Simon was quirking a rather devious smile at that, and nudging purposefully at Maria. And after a groan and a roll of her eyes, she indeed kicked up, grasped her heavy-looking belly, and launched into an actual *jig*, right there in the middle of the corridor.

Geva couldn't help laughing with the rest of them, but after watching Maria for a moment, she did her best to join in, adding a syncopated hand-clap for good measure. An effort that shot a gratifying flash of delight across the little orc's watching eyes, and soon he'd scrambled down to join them, too. Adding a few stomps of his own, not quite in the rhythm, but Geva grinned at him anyway, and attempted to stomp along. Until all three of them were flushed and laughing, and poor Maria had finally collapsed into a fond-looking Simon's arms.

"I am too pregnant to keep doing this, damn it," she

mumbled into his chest, to which Simon swept her bodily up into his huge arms, and pressed a kiss to her flushed forehead.

"You honour me, my Maria," he said firmly. "Come, and I shall care for you. Bjorn, mayhap you shall..."

He'd glanced uncertainly toward Geva and Jule, but Geva was already smiling again, and nodding down at Bjorn. "Jule and Tengil are taking me on a tour of the Skai wing," she told him. "Perhaps you'd like to join us? I'm sure, being a Skai yourself, you would have a lot of knowledge to share."

"This is truth," Bjorn immediately replied, even as he eyed Kalfr beside him, and then grasped his wrist with his little hand. "And then, I help Kalfr show you the Bautul wing, too. Ach, Kalfr?"

Kalfr stilled for an instant, but then gave a slow, indulgent smile, and allowed himself to be pulled along. And soon Geva was once again engrossed in discovering this astonishing mountain, now with additional amusing—and often cheeky—commentary from Bjorn, tempered by more measured explanations from the kind, soft-spoken Kalfr.

It turned out that the Skai wing was smaller than the Ash-Kai one, but it also included a truly marvellous bathing-pool—the bath Abjorn had mentioned the night before—fed by an actual rushing waterfall, pouring out from the stone above. It also featured a huge, echoing fighting-room—the Skai arena that Rathgarr had mentioned—full of orcs battling and wrestling together. Luckily, after seeing Rathgarr and Killik's *sparring*, this wasn't as shocking as it might have otherwise been, but Geva still winced at the sight of one orc kicking another one in the head, and then crowing with laughter as his hapless opponent slammed sideways into the nearest wall.

"Get him, Joarr!" Bjorn shouted gleefully, and beside him, even Kalfr was dangerously grinning, with a rather feral-looking light in his eyes. While Tengil, who had previously been squirming in Jule's arms, was now sitting straight up, watching the goings-on with focused, vivid attention.

"Yes, I think we've gotten a good look," Jule said dryly, turning toward the door again. But before they'd stepped outside, the head-kicking orc had bounded over beside them, his arm hooking over Kalfr's neck, his black brows waggling toward Geva.

"You go next to Bautul garden, new Ash-Kai?" he said with a grin. "See my witch?"

Geva shot an uncertain glance at Jule, who was giving an amused nod. "Yes, we were headed there next," she said. "Coming along too, then, Joarr?"

This Joarr was already pulling Kalfr ahead of them down the corridor, giving a supremely smug smile over his shoulder. "We have snacks," he said. "You like."

It turned out that the garden did have snacks, and it was truly a marvellous place, surrounded by tall stone walls, and tucked in against the mountain's south side. And though it was now well beyond the regular growing season, the garden still boasted an astonishing variety of plants, trees, fruits, and berries. And working within it were two more new women—the first one tall and dark-haired and slim, but for the prominent swell at her waist, while the other was shorter and plumper, and cradling a small, sleeping orcling against her pale chest.

"Oh, he's adorable," Geva said, and the woman beamed back, her hand stroking at his thatch of downy black hair.

"He is, isn't he?" she said in a soft, pleasing voice. "His name is Skoll, and he's two months old. And I'm Stella, of Clan Bautul."

"And I'm Gwyn," said the taller woman, with a grin. "Mated to that one"—she jerked her head sideways, toward where Joarr was now hanging from a nearby tree by one hand, an apple in his mouth—"and I'm also our mountain's resident midwife. If you ever feel like being subjected to a barrage of personal questions about your reproductive health, you know who to ask."

"Oh, nonsense, Gwyn," said Stella, though the words were softened by her warm, grateful smile toward Geva. "She's a wonderful midwife, and you really ought to set up a consultation with her, especially if you're thinking about having a child of your own."

She was still stroking her adorable orcling's downy head, and Geva felt herself swallow, her stomach unaccountably tightening. "I'd like to," she said, suddenly far too aware of this Joarr still dangling there, listening. "But my mother had a very hard time birthing me, so I'd like to wait a little longer."

She half-expected some kind of judgement, or hesitation—especially since these women all clearly wanted children—but Gwyn's easy, reassuring smile hadn't faltered in the slightest. "Of course," she replied firmly. "In that case, I'd usually recommend a good course of silphium, but unfortunately, it's not nearly as efficacious with orcs. But now that you're here, Efterar is a very gifted healer in these matters, and I know he'd be happy to help you."

Oh. Efterar again. Kesst's mate. And Geva couldn't help her wince, the slight shake of her head. "Um," she said, "I don't think that's the best idea. I'm not sure we're all... comfortable yet."

Kesst's words from the day before were ringing through her thoughts—*I am finished with you, forever*—but all three women were looking at her oddly, now, and Jule snorted, shaking her head. "Look, no matter what's going on between Kesst and Rathgarr," she said, "Efterar would *never* deny you care. In fact, why don't we go consult with him after our tour?"

Geva couldn't seem to find a compelling reason to refuse, though she found herself desperately wishing, not for the first time, that Rathgarr would suddenly emerge from around some corner, and offer some kind of guidance or reassurance. *I shall meet you later,* he'd said, but it had already been quite some time, with no sign of him whatsoever. And would he really be comfortable with her going off to visit Kesst's mate, without him?

That uncertainty seemed to hover over Geva for the rest of the tour, even though she fought to push it away, and focus on what was before her. The rest of the garden was delightful, and so was the rest of the Bautul wing, which included another forge, a trading-post, and a huge sunken fighting-pit. And then, at the lower edge of the Bautul wing, there were two stunning, in-ground pools for swimming and bathing, and then a large, well-appointed kitchen. Where they once again encountered Alma, who apparently worked out of the kitchen as the mountain's housekeeper. And after yet more introductions, including to the two smiling, silver-haired cooks—an orc named Gegnir, and a human woman named Olga—Alma offered to lead their tour of the Grisk wing.

"The Grisk clan is the largest of the five," Alma cheerfully explained, as she led them into its broad, well-lit corridors. "And so we have the largest wing as well. You'll definitely want to visit our storage-room, and you're welcome to come worship or meditate in our shrine at any time."

The Grisk shrine turned out to be lovely, with colourful silks lining the walls, and a row of beautiful carvings depicting both humans and orcs. And inside the shrine, Alma introduced a variety of her Grisk friends. Another smiling, scantily clad human woman was named Ella, and she was mated to Nattfarr, a huge, genial-looking orc who was heavily adorned with jewels and piercings. They also had a small son, Rakfi, perhaps six or seven months old, who had been wildly squirming between the other four Grisk orcs in the room—Thrak, Thrain, Dammarr, and Varinn.

"Makes you wan' your own, doesn' it?" said the tall, spiky-haired Thrain with a chuckle, as he juggled Rakfi in one hand, while trying to keep from spilling a goblet in the other. "Dozens of 'em. Most important thing, y'know."

At that, the orc named Varinn—who was shorter and

bulkier than Thrain—loudly scoffed, and then stepped closer, and swiped the goblet out of Thrain's hand. "This again, Thrain?" he demanded, wrinkling his nose, and firmly setting the goblet aside. "Ach, you ken *you* are worse than any orcling, with your ceaseless need for tending!"

Thrain's grin faltered, his gaze dropping—but then he laughed again, the sound even more jovial than before. "Just givin' you practice, Varinn," he said, clapping him on the shoulder. "F'r when you're *crawlin'* with 'em. You'll be the best father, ach?"

Varinn's brow creased, but Thrain was already glancing away, and giving a purposeful jerk of his head toward the shrine's door. Toward where a shadowy figure had been hovering—a shorter orc, perhaps?—and Varinn turned to look, his expression softening, his hand giving an easy wave.

"Come along, Timo," he said. "I am sure our new sister wishes to meet you."

The Timo orc tentatively stepped inside, and Geva reflexively smiled, because he, too, was a younger orc. Perhaps about thirteen or fourteen, with smooth grey skin, long gangly limbs, and nervous but curious eyes.

"Geva, this is our little brother Timo," said Varinn, slinging his bulky arm around Timo's shoulders. "And Timo, this is Geva, our newest Ash-Kai. Can you scent aught more about her?"

The nervousness in Timo's eyes had slightly faded, and Geva could see him inhaling, his gaze gone distant. "Ach, a little," he replied shyly. "She has just come to our mountain yesterday, and she scents very strong of Ash-Kai. Much like Kesst, I ken, but"—his nose twitched, his head tilting—"it is not Kesst, is it?"

"Very good, little brother," Varinn said approvingly, ruffling Timo's hair with his claws. "She is mated to Kesst's elder brother Rathgarr, who has only just come home. And we wish her to be most welcome here with us, ach?"

At that mention of Rathgarr, something clenched in Geva's chest, but Timo was still smiling toward her, and she made herself draw in a deep breath, and give a genuine smile back. "It's so lovely to meet you, Timo," she said. "You clearly have a very impressive sense of smell."

Timo's cheeks and ears visibly flushed, his head ducking, while Varinn gave Geva a broad, grateful smile. "Ach, he does," he said firmly. "With more training, our Timo may well become one of the best noses—and the best fighters—among us."

That seemed like high praise, and Geva willingly told Timo so, earning another shy smile, along with an approving, appreciative nod from Varinn. And then Varinn glanced down toward Bjorn, who had been standing quietly beside them, watching all this with carefully unaffected attention.

"I will be good fighter also," Bjorn's little voice interjected, his shoulder shrugging, as he drew a circle on the stone floor with his foot. "And mayhap even good nose. With more training."

"Ach, you shall, Bjorn," said Varinn. "Mayhap you might now wish to come practice scenting with Timo and me? We could"—he glanced over toward Ella, who had a look of resigned fondness in her eyes as she watched a happily screeching Rakfi crawl after Tengil around the room—"play at hunting the orclings about the mountain, if their mothers should spare them for a spell?"

"Yes, *please*," Jule instantly replied, exchanging a grateful glance with Ella. "*Bless* you, Varinn. Now, Geva, how about the rest of that tour? We only have the Ka-esh wing left, and I promise, it's usually *very* quiet."

Geva chuckled and nodded, and after a round of farewells, she followed Jule out to where the corridor was tilting more sharply downwards, the lights dimming with every step. It felt very far away from the Ash-Kai wing, suddenly, and Geva's stomach twisted at the thought of Rathgarr, gone gods knew where, doing gods knew what.

"You know, the children—the orclings—really seem very lovely, though," she made herself say, her voice a little thick. "I'm ashamed to say that I would have perhaps expected something quite—different. But really, compared to my last set of pupils"—she winced at the thought—"they seem very empathetic, and well-adjusted. Well-loved."

Jule's smile was swift and genuine, but there was a twinge of sadness in it, too. "I'm so glad to hear that," she said. "We've really been trying to do our best for them—it's been a lifelong goal of Grimarr's, and one of the reasons he fought so hard against his vile father. But we've really only begun, and there's just so much left to do. So many ways we could be better supporting those orclings, if only we had the guidance and resources. And even more importantly, the leadership."

Geva could well appreciate that, and she felt herself considering it, her head tilting. "Do you have any kind of schooling set up currently?" she asked. "Or training, apprenticeships, that kind of thing?"

Jule sighed, and shook her head. "Not yet. The Bautul have recently put together a nursery, staffed by trained volunteers, which has been a great help. But until now, our most pressing priority has been safety. Making sure every orcling— and orc—is safe, fed, and accounted for. Making sure we learn from the failures of the past, and do better in the future."

She shot Geva a wincing, pained-looking glance, and too late, Geva realized that perhaps... perhaps she wasn't only talking about orclings, but about Kesst, too. About all those horrors he'd faced, after Rathgarr had left.

"But now, our next priority is absolutely education," Jule continued, her jaw set. "With that awful war raging on for so long, so many orcs now aren't equipped—or able—to give their sons everything they need, through no fault of their own. So we need to step up, and offer our young orcs consistent structure and support. If we can encourage their mental, physical, and emotional development, we'll make this mountain a better, safer, and more nurturing place for all of us."

Her voice had gone flat and determined, her eyes glinting with purpose. And this time, her glance toward Geva was questioning, or perhaps... pleading? As if she was asking...

But before Geva could find a reply, a small, whirling, yellow-topped figure swept out from a nearby door, and bounced excitedly before them. Another... woman?

"Oh, how exciting!" the bouncing woman exclaimed, her blue eyes sparkling. "Jule's finally found us a new teacher! You *will* say yes, won't you?!"

25

Geva couldn't stop blinking at the new arrival, her brain desperately struggling to catch up. Yes, this was a woman, a pretty, petite blonde woman, wearing a long belted tunic, a slim gold choker, and a beaming smile on her face. And in her ink-stained fingers, she was clutching a giant stack of papers, hugging them almost reverently to her chest.

And... she thought Jule wanted Geva as their new teacher? And she wanted Geva to say *yes*? As in... *permanently*?!

"Ah, Geva, this is Rosa," Jule was saying now, with a wince, and a rueful smile toward the blonde woman. "And Rosa, this is Geva, Rathgarr's mate, as you're obviously well aware."

"Yes, indeed!" Rosa replied brightly, fixing her delighted gaze back on Geva's face. "You're *all* the mountain is speaking of today, you know. And truly, how *serendipitous* is it that a qualified educator should arrive, just when we most desperately needed one?! If I weren't far too well-informed to believe in all that foolishness about omniscient peeping gods, I would truly start to wonder."

She concluded this with another bright, expectant smile

toward Geva, while Jule winced again, and gave a frantic flap of her hands. "Er, thanks, Rosa. The thing is, though, Geva just arrived yesterday, and while it is indeed very exciting to have a qualified educator among us, she's under no obligation whatsoever. And it's becoming quite evident"—she cleared her throat, her smile gone distinctly apologetic—"that I was coming on rather too strong with this. My apologies, Geva—too much time spent with orcs, you know."

Geva laughed despite herself, waving it away, but Jule's expression had gone sober, her eyes intent. "If you would be interested in offering some guidance, or even doing some teaching," she said, with a heavy emphasis on the *if*, "even on a trial basis, of course we would be very happy to discuss it, together with an offer of fair wages. But again, there is no obligation, and no hard feelings if you refuse. *Right*, Rosa?"

This Rosa was looking decidedly subdued, her ink-stained hands clutching tighter at her papers. "Yes, yes, of course. But"—she bit her lip, her pleading eyes turning to Geva again—"only imagine how *convenient* it would be! You see, I'm our mountain's resident librarian, and for almost a year now, I've been teaching adult classes in common-tongue and Aelakesh—the orcs' language, you know, it's *fascinating*—but there's the greatest need for more, especially for those orclings. And there are still so many orclings hidden all over the realm, where it still isn't *safe*, and we know offering an accessible education for them would be a *crucial* incentive in finally bringing their families here. But I've just had a son of my own, and my mate is already run off his feet, so we just haven't had time to expand into—"

"*Rosa*," Jule said again, now with a heavy note of warning in her voice—and Rosa accordingly broke off, her eyes dropping, her slim shoulders sadly slumping. To which Jule visibly blanched, her gaze darting around, until it settled on the papers in Rosa's hands.

"So, is that a new pamphlet, Rosa?" she asked. "From your

hand-press? Perhaps you'd like to demonstrate it to Geva, while we're touring down here."

Rosa immediately straightened again, her eyes brightening. "Oooh, yes, it's my latest!" she exclaimed. "Although I still need to improve distribution in Tlaxca, and"—she plucked out one of the papers she was holding, and brandished it toward them—"I can't decide if this is too much?"

Geva instantly recognized it as a similar pamphlet to the one Rathgarr had shown her on the road, complete with block letters and a detailed illustration. But this time, the broadly grinning orc appeared to be... brushing his *teeth*?

ORCS: HEROES OF HYGIENE, the letters declared. *Bathed, brushed, and sweetly scented, pleasing to even the most discerning of tastes!*

"I really feel this could be our next big breakthrough," Rosa was blithely saying. "Do you know how many humans have *abominable* personal hygiene? We had no conception *whatso-ever* what we were missing!"

Geva's mouth twitched up, her thoughts lingering pointedly on Rathgarr's excellent grooming, while beside her, Jule was already giving a gleeful grin, and clapping Rosa on the shoul-der. "Brilliant, Rosa, as always," Jule said. "Let's paper the realm and see what happens, shall we?"

But that caught at something in Geva's thoughts, and she felt her smile fading as she studied the pamphlet. "Though you know, it might be worth consulting with the orcs living outside the mountain," she said slowly. "Rathgarr mentioned that some of the pamphlets have had unexpected... side effects. I'm sure he could offer some advice, at least? And he might know some places to distribute in Tlaxca, as well."

Both Jule and Rosa were looking surprised by this—Rosa's head cocked like a bird's, Jule's forehead furrowing. "Really?" Jule asked. "Our scouts haven't mentioned anything about... side effects?"

Geva awkwardly shrugged, her gaze back on the pamphlet.

"Well, the scouts likely aren't making their entire lives out there, like Rathgarr was, right?" she said. "It seemed to me as though he had quite a large network, and knew a lot of goings-on."

Jule had begun to look unmistakably intrigued, while Rosa was delightedly smiling again, and bouncing on the balls of her feet. "We will most certainly consult with him," she said firmly. "*Serendipitous*, I tell you. Now, do you really want to see my hand-press?"

Geva did, of course, and soon found herself admiring Rosa's large, complicated-looking contraption, which was surrounded by neat stacks of pamphlets. And once Rosa had finished her demonstration, she eagerly escorted them around the rest of the Ka-esh wing, which turned out to have the most varied collection of rooms yet. There was a laboratory, a small medical clinic, a clever sunlit reading-nook, and even a lovely little library, which apparently was managed by Rosa and her mate John, who served as a leader among the Ka-esh orcs.

And along with the new rooms, Geva was also surprised to find herself faced with multiple instances of orcs... *enjoying* one another. Pressing each other into walls, biting at bared necks, groping blatantly down into trousers. And even—Geva had to take a moment to recover herself—one orc holding another orc over the hot burning forge by his *hair*, while pounding again and again into his bare, bent-over backside.

"Er, so is that kind of thing... typical, around here?" Geva asked Jule and Rosa, once they'd gone some distance down the corridor again. "In... public?"

Her thoughts had unhelpfully darted back to the memory of herself on her knees in the forest, bent over Rathgarr's groin, when Killik and Ulfarr had found them... or the night at the inn, where Rathgarr had so blatantly given her that *drink*, and told her the other orcs wouldn't even notice. Or even how Rathgarr had told her—just that morning?—that she didn't need to bother *dressing*.

"Oh, yes, that's orcs for you," Rosa blithely said, her hand waving it away. "It can indeed be shocking at first, but you'll soon become accustomed, I'm sure. Oh, and if you're worried about the orclings barging in, apparently they have a very distinct scent, even at a distance, so it's quite easy to avoid them—but just in case, we've recently implemented some new safety criteria, haven't we, Jule? No obvious activities in the corridors until after nightfall, and any more *intense* pleasures are always enjoyed in scent-marked rooms, which require particular permissions to enter, like the Ka-esh pleasure-den. Would you like to see, Geva?"

Geva's thoughts were straining to keep up with all this— had she just said they had a *pleasure-den*?—but Rosa was still looking at her expectantly, waiting for an answer, so she squared her shoulders, and jerked a shaky nod. She was doing this to learn, wasn't she? To try to be the best possible helpmate for Rathgarr? Even if there were... *pleasure-dens* involved?

It had clearly been the right response, because Rosa was looking ecstatically pleased again, and excitedly waved Geva and Jule down yet another corridor. Until she'd halted outside the door of a dimly lit room, and gestured for them to come look inside.

And it was—well. A... pleasure-den. A room clearly dedicated to physical enjoyment, and to all the games one could possibly play to gain it. There were chains, and shackles, and a stunning variety of distinctly shaped implements, many of them strapped to the solid stone walls—and among them, *using* them, were orcs. Perhaps a half-dozen moaning, gasping orcs, writhing and driving against one another with shameless abandon. Wielding mouths, hands, claws, *teeth*.

Thankfully, it was difficult to make out most of the orcs' faces, due to the fading light from the guttering fire—at least, until Geva's eyes caught on the orc nearest them. He was bent over a bench, his head bowed, his shaky hands holding himself up on muscular arms—while behind him, another large, vicious-looking orc slammed his hips powerfully against his bared backside. And wrapped around that orc's hand was a thick, heavy chain—and when he yanked on it, the kneeling orc's head snapped up, revealing his flushed, sweat-streaked face, his gasping mouth, the thick steel cuff clasped around his corded neck.

Geva blinked, and then froze all over, because wait. *Wait.* Good gods, she recognized this orc. It was—

"Abjorn?" she gasped, without at all meaning to. "*Really*?"

But yes, it was most certainly him, Rathgarr's eager, cheerful Ka-esh friend. And to her ongoing astonishment, Abjorn's mouth twitched into a brief but delighted smile, one of his hands lifting to give her an enthusiastic little wave. An action which prompted the orc behind him to growl and yank fiercely at his chain, making Abjorn's head snap back again, his throat hissing deep and low. And then he was clearly lost in it again, his eyes fluttering, his handsome face rapt with mingled pain and pleasure.

"Er, thanks, Rosa," Geva choked out, her feet stumbling backwards into the corridor, her hands rubbing at her eyes. "That was—very—enlightening?"

Beside her, Jule laughed, and gave her a bracing clap on the back. "See anything you like?" she said cheerfully. "Perhaps you and Rathgarr can pay a visit later?"

Geva's mouth opened and closed, her face flushing hot, and suddenly there was only a deep, sickening misery, clutching in her belly. *Did* Rathgarr enjoy such things? *Could* that be another truth he hadn't told her? Especially if such a close friend clearly partook of it, very freely?

But wait, no, Rathgarr liked soft women, sweet women, quiet women, who did what they were told. And gods, Geva didn't know whether that was better or worse—or curse it, why she even cared. This was just a job, working for an arrogant orc who couldn't even be bothered to meet her, the way he'd promised. One month, and then the sea.

And damn it, Jule had likely caught some of that, because she quickly cut in to thank Rosa for the tour, and was soon ushering Geva back up the corridor again, toward the rest of the mountain. Toward where perhaps Rathgarr would finally reappear, and explain what had possibly been so important, and why he hadn't come, all this time...

"Do you still want to stop in to see Efterar?" Jule asked now, her voice careful. "It will only take a moment, I imagine?"

"Might as well," Geva said, with a failed attempt at a smile, and therefore soon found herself entering yet another unfamiliar, firelit room. It was clearly a sickroom of sorts, and it was beautifully appointed, boasting multiple metal-framed beds separated by dividers, along with a variety of shelves and cozy-looking furniture. Several of the beds were occupied by sleeping orcs, and bending over one of them was Kesst's mate Efterar. And—Geva froze—striding out from a back room was Kesst himself.

He was just as smartly dressed as the day before, wearing close-fitting leather trousers, long dangling earrings that glittered in the firelight, and a gleaming, intricate cuff around his bicep. But his handsome face was looking more drawn than before, and there were dark, heavy circles beneath his eyes.

"Oh," he said, his lean body jerking to stillness, his tired eyes narrowing on Geva. "Hello. Where's Rath? Already run for the hills again?"

Beside Geva, Jule cleared her throat, and gave Kesst a meaningful look. "Be nice, Kesst," she said. "And we're actually here to see Efterar, if he might have a moment?"

"Oh, of *course*," Kesst icily replied, as he waved furiously toward Efterar, and then whirled around, and stalked off again. Disappearing into wherever he'd come from, and Geva winced, and nearly made to call after him—but Efterar had quickly come over, and asked how he might be of assistance.

Geva's throat felt horribly tight, her eyes still angling after where Kesst had gone, but thankfully Jule once again jumped in, and explained why they'd come. How Geva still wasn't feeling quite ready for a son yet, and would appreciate his help in gaining a little more time.

"Yes, I'd be happy to help," Efterar said, with genuine-seeming firmness, as his big hand slowly reached out, and hovered in the vicinity of Geva's waist. And deep inside her, she could feel something tickling, shifting, *moving*.

"There, that should do it," Efterar said after a moment, drawing his hand away. "Now just come back when you'd like it reversed, all right? And feel free to let me or Gwyn know if you have any questions or problems at all."

Jule was smiling and thanking Efterar, as if this were all an entirely ordinary occurrence, but Geva was struck stunned and silent again, gaping at Efterar's scarred, genial face. How the *hell* had he just done that? Had he just—was he—why hadn't Rathgarr *said*—

"Er, th-thank you," she belatedly stammered. "I'm very grateful for your help."

Efterar waved it away, though his eyes were perhaps a little too knowing on hers. "Is there anything else I can help with?" he asked mildly. "Any other questions?"

And gods, Geva needed to pull herself together. Needed to do a good job of this. To be a good helpmate, even if Rathgarr damn well didn't deserve it. One month, and then the sea.

"Er, y-yes, actually," she made herself say. "Rathgarr and I—we would very much love to spend some time with you and Kesst, and talk through some things."

Efterar blinked, his brows rising, but he didn't speak, so Geva drew in a breath, and soldiered on. "I know it's all been very difficult, and of course we understand if Kesst isn't ready to meet, or discuss it yet. But I also know"—her voice steadied, strengthened—"how much Rathgarr missed him, and how much he's grieved being away from him, all this time. He was completely horrified by everything Kesst told us yesterday, and while he knows he can't make amends, he will do whatever he can to try."

Efterar was watching her very closely, his eyes wary but considering—and then he glanced, purposefully, toward the back corner. "Sweet-Fang?" he called. "Will you come, for a moment?"

There was an instant's silence, and then Kesst stalked around the corner again, his mouth pursed, his shoulders very stiff. And when Geva opened her mouth to say it all again, he frantically waved his hands, and lurched into the circle of Efterar's waiting arm.

"Yes, yes, I heard," he snapped. "And if Rath really feels that way, why couldn't he have come to ask me himself?"

Geva couldn't hide her wince, and felt her hands twisting together in front of her. "Rathgarr thinks you don't want to speak with him," she said. "He wants to respect you, and your wishes."

Kesst barked a harsh laugh, not a laugh at all. "Does he, now," he drawled. "So considerate, my deadbeat brother is. So *respectful*. Well, sweetheart"—he jabbed a clawed finger toward her—"you can tell him that he has *one* more chance to speak to me. Tomorrow morning, in the Ash-Kai common-room, where all our entire damned *clan* can hear. And he can either choose to tell us everything—*everything*—or *else*."

Gods damn it, *damn* it, and Geva's hands were wringing tighter together, her unease surging, shuddering into something not unlike fear. Kesst expected Rathgarr to tell him *everything*? In front of his entire *clan*?!

"Or—or else?" she heard herself stammer, too high-pitched. "How—how so?"

But Kesst's face was grim, flinty, far too vicious. "Or else Efterar will make Rath suffer, until he does tell it," he said coolly. "Won't you, Eft? If I ask you?"

Oh. Oh, hell. And Geva's pleading eyes had gone to this

Efterar—this *magician*, curse it, who could alter things inside you without even a touch—and found him grimacing, his eyes squeezing shut, his arm drawing Kesst closer into his side.

"Yes," he said, quiet. "Yes, I suppose I will."

26

By the time Geva stepped back into the room she shared with Rathgarr, she felt stiff, clammy, and utterly drained.

Gods, what a day. What an endless, exhausting day. But she'd done it, she'd been the best helpmate she possibly could, she'd held it together while meeting dozens of unfamiliar orcs, and taking a full tour of Orc Mountain, and visiting a *pleasure-den*. And even if the tour had ended with that highly alarming threat, Rathgarr *had* wanted to speak with Kesst, hadn't he? Wanted to tell him the truth? And Geva would tell him now, and perhaps they would work out a plan, and—

And then she stopped short, blinking around the dark bedroom—because Rathgarr wasn't here. The room was silent. Untouched. Empty.

"Rathgarr?" she tentatively called, as she lit the lamp, and then made her way toward the back room—but it, too, was empty. Even though it seemed to have been significantly tidied in her absence, all the jewels and plunder now organized and carefully displayed on the room's many shelves. And among them were a few books, including—Geva peered closer—her own book of tales, set in a place of obvious honour atop one of the shelves.

Something twisted in her belly as she looked at it, but she swallowed hard, spun around, and went back into the bedroom. And then just stood there, gazing helplessly around at it, until her eyes caught on the crack in the ceiling, and the pitch-black darkness beyond it. So it really was evening, and should she try to sleep, or perhaps seek out a much-needed bath, or...

When without warning, the curtain at the door swept aside, and Rathgarr strode in. The sight of his big cloaked body suddenly so blessedly, beautifully familiar that Geva almost felt faint, and she had to fight back the urge to rush over toward him, and fling her arms around his waist.

"Where have you been?" she made herself say instead, her voice cracking. "I thought you were going to meet me later?"

She couldn't quite read the expression on Rathgarr's face, the shifting in his eyes. "Ach, I did," he said, as he shot a sharp, meaningful glance toward the curtain behind him. "And thus, here I am."

Geva's stomach twisted again, and she shook her head, crossed her arms tightly over her chest. "It was all day, Rathgarr," she managed, as quietly as she could. "You left me alone and unprotected in Orc Mountain *all day!*"

Rathgarr's eyes were still shifting, his lips thinning. "I knew where you were, ach?" he said coolly. "And you did not seem in much need of me."

The disbelief swarmed through Geva's chest—he'd known where she was all day, and he hadn't even said hello?—but before she could speak, Rathgarr came a swift step closer, his cloak flaring out behind him.

"All day long I heard tales of you," he continued, his low voice even colder. "Dancing in the halls. Playing in the garden. Peeping in the Ka-esh dungeon. Visiting my *brother*. All of this with the mate of my sworn *enemy!*"

What?! Geva's disbelief was clashing against a sudden surge of fury, and she clamped her hands to fists, and shook her head. "But *you* left me with them, and *wanted* me to do all that!" she hissed at him. "I was trying to learn and make friends, and do my best to represent you! To be a good—a good helpmate!"

There was an instant's dangling silence, and then Rathgarr huffed a hard, bitter laugh, the sound clutching deep in Geva's churning stomach. "A good *helpmate*," he shot back, "would not cozy up to a woman like Grimarr's! A woman who surely seeks to use you to gain my weakness, and my defeat! She was once the wife of Lord Norr, who was the cruelest lord in the realm, you ken?"

She *what*? Jule had been married to a *lord*? And suddenly more of the distant tales about orcs were shifting, snapping into place, because there *had* been rumours of orcs seducing lords' wives, hadn't there? And Lord Norr had met his untimely demise under highly mysterious circumstances, and...

"Then why didn't you tell me that, damn it?" Geva demanded, her voice rising. "If I'd known, I'd have been far more on my guard! But even so"—she dragged in a shaky breath—"I *liked* Jule, Rathgarr. She was lovely to me, and very hospitable. And she barely said a single word about you all day!"

Rathgarr curled his lip and scoffed, harsh and mocking— like he didn't believe her?—and in response, Geva barked a short, strangled-sounding laugh, her hands clamping even tighter at her sides.

"She didn't, Rathgarr," she hissed. "If anything, she was far more interested in my teaching experience. She even offered me a position *working* here, if I wanted it!"

The thought of it was suddenly a strange, bizarre comfort, or even something to cling to. Jule had recognized her training and experience, and offered her a job. An important job, doing important things, that would make a real difference.

But before her, Rathgarr was blinking, a fleeting flash of something like *fear* in his eyes. Or perhaps astonishment, or incredulity, or... rage.

"*What*?!" he thundered, his voice vibrating in Geva's chest. "Grimarr's mate seeks to pay you *coin* to work for her?! *You*?!"

A bitter, brittle rebellion surged in Geva's throat, and she jerked a curt little nod. And in return, Rathgarr's rage only seemed to flash higher, his teeth bared, a low growl rippling from his throat.

"Ach, I ought to have known you would welcome this, woman," he snarled, his voice scathing. "For you will do *aught* you are asked for a bit of gold, will you not?"

Oh. *Oh.* It felt like a slap, like raw, visceral hurt flashed across Geva's face, powerful enough that she nearly retched, the room stuttering around her. *You will do aught you are asked, for a bit of gold.*

And surely, he was referring to the night before. To how he'd ordered Geva to undress, and pinned her onto the bed, pushed inside her most intimate place. And how she'd begged for it, pleaded for it, and screamed his name. Just like... like he'd wanted.

And now he was judging her for it, mocking her for it, and Geva was staggering beneath the humiliation and the misery, her eyes swimming too much to see. But somehow, somehow, the unfairness of it, the gods-damned injustice of it, was enough to make her raise her chin, and find her breath.

"I *didn't* agree to work for Jule," she whispered, her voice thick and choked. "I didn't make any kind of commitment whatsoever. And I'll remind you, *sir*"—her chin lifted higher—"that *you're* the one who hired me. *You're* the one who brought me here, and asked me to do all this work for you, and left me alone all day, without any kind of instruction or reassurance. I kept looking for you all day, wondering what had happened to you, but I kept trying my best for you, doing everything I possibly could to help you!"

There was no answer from Rathgarr, and Geva's eyes still couldn't seem to focus on his face, her clammy hand now rubbing against her trembling mouth. "And instead of thanking me," she gulped, "you return my efforts with anger and mockery and contempt? Do you"—she choked down another breath—"do you even *want* me to work for you anymore, Rathgarr?"

Her voice had gone small and shaky by the end, betraying her weakness, her shame. Her fear of what he might answer, even now. Would he mock her? Remind her of her place? Throw her a coin or two?

And before he could do it, any of it, she lurched away, and staggered toward the door. And then hesitated, her eyes squeezing shut, her hands again clamped in fists at her sides.

"Oh, and I made you an appointment with Kesst," she said, her voice wavering. "Tomorrow morning, in the Ash-Kai common-room, with the rest of your clan. And you're going to go, and tell him *everything*, and *beg* for his mercy, or *else!*"

And without waiting for an answer, she pushed unseeing through the curtain, and fled.

27

Geva staggered down the empty corridor on unsteady legs, her eyes blinking hard, her hands still clutched to fists.

She shouldn't care. It shouldn't matter. This was just a job, and she knew very well what Rathgarr was. A cold, greedy thief, who only cared about himself. One month, and then the sea.

But gods, why did it hurt so much. Why had she spent all this endless day searching for him, thinking of him. Why was she still *helping* him like this, with Kesst. Why did she keep thinking he was—they were—

"Poppet," came a voice, Rathgarr's voice, too close—and when Geva flinched and glanced sideways, he was there. Here. His eyes unreadable on hers, his big hand circling around her wrist, pulling her to a halt beside him. "Where do you ken you are going?"

Geva flinched again, and yanked her wrist away. "For a bath, in the Skai wing," she gritted out, as she strode down the corridor again. "It's been a long day."

Despite the emptiness of the corridor, she was suddenly very aware of the dark, gaping doors cut into the stone around them, hiding any number of possible listeners. And surely Rathgarr was thinking of it too, his body lurching closer beside hers, his eyes darting uneasily at the walls around them.

"Ach, you need not go alone," he said, a little too loudly. "It should grant me great joy to bathe you, my pretty pet."

It was such a blatant lie, and Geva's body reflexively recoiled, her sideways look at Rathgarr feeling almost wounded. "I shouldn't wish to trouble you," she managed. "I'll be quite all right, I'm sure."

Rathgarr betrayed a visible grimace, his head shaking, and his hand again slipped around her wrist. "I yet wish to come," he replied. "I wish to keep you content, and safe."

His fingers had purposefully squeezed at the word *safe*, his gaze again angling around the corridor, and suddenly Geva was fighting the urge to shout at him again, to shove him off and sprint away into the darkness. "Oh, yes, I know you're *so* concerned about my safety," she replied, as blandly as she could. "As you're such a kind and *attentive* mate."

Rathgarr grimaced again, and darted another look at the darkened doors around them. "Ach, your safety is of greatest import to me, sweetling," he said, his voice only slightly clipped. "This is why I am so pleased you spent all this day with the captain's mate and son, who are surely the best guarded in all this mountain."

Oh, so *that* was his explanation for abandoning her all day, then, and Geva glared at him, and walked faster. "Is that so?" she replied, surely with too much coldness in her voice. "I think you may have forgotten to mention that as well, *love*."

Rathgarr's jaw had gone very tight, his mouth pursed, his hand spasming against her wrist. "I hope you shall forgive my lapses, poppet," he said. "I should never wish to leave you baffled, or vexed, or afraid."

Geva nearly laughed at that, but bit her lip, and stalked faster down the corridor. They were surely in the Skai wing by now, and if she turned here, that waterfall bath should be around...

"I speak truth in this, poppet," Rathgarr's low voice continued. "I wish you to be... happy, here, with me."

Good gods, that was nearly worse than all the rest, and Geva furiously shoved off his hand, and spun sideways into her destination. The cool, airy Skai bath, with the rushing waterfall pouring out of the ceiling, pooling onto the stone floor beneath.

Like the corridor, it was thankfully empty, with no other orcs to be seen, but when Geva stalked over to the edge of the pool, Rathgarr immediately followed, his big body restless and far too close. "Please, poppet," he said, his low voice almost drowned out by the steady thunder of the water. "I am... sorry. I ought not to have said this, about the coin."

Geva's fury surged again, her head whipping back and forth. "But you did, Rathgarr," she hissed back at him. "You said it, and you *meant* it! You judged me for working hard for you, for doing my best for you! You made it *very* clear"—she jabbed a shaky finger toward his chest—"that you only see me as a greedy, shameless *hireling*, ready to sell out to the highest bidder!"

Her voice had gone far too frayed, her eyes painfully prickling. And before her, Rathgarr winced, and shook his head. "I do not truly see you thus, woman," he replied, with a heavy exhale. "I was only angry, and afraid you should rather accept *her* offer of work, rather than mine."

Geva barked a too-loud laugh, and whirled away from him, yanking off her dress with shaky hands. "Well, maybe I *should* accept Jule's offer," she shot back, without looking. "She was kind and considerate toward me, and respected me, and explained things when I had questions! She wanted me to feel comfortable, and prepared, and *valued*!"

She made to hurl her dress away, but Rathgarr lunged around before her again, catching the dress in his hands. While a strange, urgent light flashed in his eyes, looking almost like… panic.

"Please, poppet," he breathed. "Geva. Please, do not leave me for other work. Mayhap I—I can pay you more gold. Double what we first spoke of. This shall please you, ach? You shall stay?"

What? Geva's mouth fell open, her heart plunging horribly in her chest, and the sound she made could have been a laugh, or a sob. "You—your response to all that is to offer me *more gold*?" she choked at him. "*Really*, Rathgarr?!"

Rathgarr only stared back at her for an instant, his shoulders rising and falling. And suddenly Geva couldn't bear to look at him anymore, and she scrabbled to yank off her shift, and her boots and stockings. To at least escape him in the bath, to feel a blast of merciless, ice-cold water streaming against her hot, miserable face.

"Poppet," Rathgarr hissed, his hand again catching on her wrist, and Geva yanked it away—only to find it there again, even tighter than before. "*Wait*."

Geva flailed and yanked away again, but again he was close before her, his huge body blocking hers in, his hand still clutching her dress, and somehow her shift, too. And even as she made to reel backwards, her eyes caught something— moving, at the door behind him. Something *walking in*.

It was—more orcs. Two more orcs. And not only that, but they were both… familiar. Killik, and *Ulfarr*. The huge, angry Skai orc from the forest.

And damn it, because Geva was standing here completely undressed, and only shielded from the orcs' view by Rathgarr's big body, hovering between her and the door. Blocking her, she realized, because he'd smelled them coming, damn it, *damn* it.

"Greetings, brothers," Rathgarr called over his shoulder, his voice deceptively light, even as he gave Geva a wincing little grimace, his body easing closer toward her. "How fare you two, this eve?"

There was a loud, heavy harrumph from Ulfarr in reply, and when Geva shot an alarmed glance toward him, he was leaning against the wall beside the door, his eyes contemptuous, his huge arms crossing over his bare chest.

"You ken this is the Skai wing, Rathgarr," Ulfarr replied, in a deep, dangerous voice. "What do you wish here among us?"

Rathgarr grimaced again, but his answer over his shoulder was still light, even casual. "Just what it seems, Ulfarr. I wish to bathe with my sweet mate."

Ulfarr's answering scoff was loud and mocking, his eyes flicking between the water, and Rathgarr's fully clothed body. "There is no *bathing* here that I see," he replied coldly. "Mayhap you have rather come to seek Skai gold, ach?"

Something flashed oddly in Rathgarr's eyes, even as he outwardly laughed, the sound easy, almost amused. "Ach, no," he said. "And Skai have gold now? I should never have fathomed this."

Ulfarr instantly growled, and beside him Killik was frowning now, too. "Do not dare to mock my clan, Ash-Kai," Ulfarr hissed. "Most of all whilst you stand here within Skai walls, and speak false to us of why you are here! Now either bathe, or *get out!*"

Gods curse it, because even Killik wasn't arguing this, only leaning casually back against the wall beside Ulfarr, his brows raised. Suggesting that they were indeed going to keep standing here, *watching,* while Geva and Rathgarr bathed.

And before Geva, Rathgarr's expression was aggrieved, and annoyed, and... regretful. His shoulders heavily sagging, his exhale prickling against Geva's bare skin. "Do you yet wish to bathe?" he asked, quiet, as he angled a glance down toward her clothes, still clutched in his hand. "Or shall we go?"

Geva searched his eyes, her thoughts uselessly spinning, because she *did* still want to bathe, damn it—and Rathgarr was still staying here, shielding her, blocking her from their view. And had he guessed that they might follow her, that she truly might not be safe here alone? *Your safety is of greatest import to me...*

And as she kept blinking at his waiting, resigned eyes, it occurred to her that leaving now would just lend credence to what Ulfarr had said. That it would only increase the animosity between them, and make all this that much worse. And she did not owe Rathgarr anything, especially after today, she did not...

"No, I'd still like to bathe," she heard herself say, with a desperate attempt at a smile toward Rathgarr's face, and then over toward Killik and Ulfarr. "As long as our generous Skai hosts are sure they don't mind?"

Ulfarr's expression hadn't changed in the slightest, but Killik shrugged, and gave a careless, magnanimous-seeming wave of his hand. Telling her, very clearly, to proceed.

Geva drew in breath, and nodded, and met Rathgarr's eyes again. "And you said you'll bathe with me, right?" she said, her voice almost pleading. "Please?"

Rathgarr's throat bobbed, his mouth thin, his eyes still quiet and regretful on hers. Looking almost sorry, almost sad—but then he jerked a nod, and brought his hand to her face. Tilting her chin up, his thumb gently brushing her cheek, in a gesture that felt suddenly too raw, and far too meaningful.

"Ach, my lovely poppet," he murmured. "I should be most honoured to bathe with you."

Of course it was another lie, another act, but even so, Geva's cursed face was heating, her gaze dropping. Only distantly noticing as Rathgarr carefully tossed her clothes toward one of the benches lining the nearest wall, and then began pulling off his own clothes, and tossing them over, too.

Geva's eyes reflexively darted back toward him, catching on the sudden, still-unfamiliar sight of his broad bare chest. Of his smooth grey skin, heavily dusted with thick black hair, and then thinning to that single line down over the relative softness of his abdomen below. Far softer than Killik's or Ulfarr's, Geva realized, and her uncertain glance back up at Rathgarr's face showed it slightly reddening, as if he was very well aware of that fact.

And suddenly Geva was very conscious of her own nakedness, too. Of how she'd just been standing here, brazenly displaying her own full breasts and belly to the room. And though Killik and Ulfarr surely still couldn't see through Rathgarr's bulk—not much, at least—Rathgarr most certainly could, and had been, all this time.

But as Rathgarr's hands dropped to his belt, and shoved his trousers downwards, the sight behind them was... slack. Uninterested. Hanging there small and innocuous, as though he hadn't even noticed Geva standing here naked before him.

The hurt bloomed swift and sharp in her chest, the heat again prickling behind her eyes, and gods, what was wrong with her, why did she care? Why was she even doing this, why did she keep giving him this, when he just kept—

"Ready, poppet?" Rathgarr's low voice asked, as he kicked off his boots, and tossed the trousers away. Leaving him standing here fully undressed before her, for perhaps the very first time in their acquaintance—but Geva's eyes were blinking too hard to notice. "Now come, and prepare to be frozen, ach?"

He'd clasped Geva's hand in his, his touch almost tentative, now. And then, keeping his big body between her and the door, he led her into the pool, and straight beneath the pouring, rushing stream of water.

Geva couldn't help a little yelp, her body cringing away, shivering at the impact—but Rathgarr was already moving closer, the warmth emanating through his skin, through his big hands now rubbing against her shoulders. "Ach, even colder than I remember," he murmured, as he reached around her to grasp for something—a bar of actual soap—from the stone wall behind them. "But should you stay close, and allow me to wash you, mayhap this shall help."

Geva fervently nodded, without at all meaning to, and

Rathgarr's big hands rubbed the soap to a lather before setting the bar aside again. And then he drew her a little outside the streaming water, and brought his warm soapy hands to her shoulders, before sliding them slowly down her arms.

Geva kept her eyes firmly lowered as he did it, fighting to ignore the way the water was still running down his chest, sticking his hair to his skin. And the way his big warm hands were sliding up again, now coming up to skim over her collarbones, her neck—and then slipping back down her front, slow, until they found her heavy breasts, and curved gently around them.

Geva's breath caught, the sound somehow audible amidst the rush of water, and Rathgarr's touch stilled, just slightly. Enough that she couldn't help a quick, ashamed glance up at his watching face. At where he still looked rueful, almost regretful.

But then, holding his gaze on hers, he caressed her breasts again. His hands still sliding so careful, so gentle, lifting their heavy weights, his thumbs brushing against her hard, peaked nipples.

"So plump and pretty, poppet," he murmured, as something warm and rigid began nudging, swelling, against her thigh. "Mayhap the prettiest I have ever seen, ach? So full, they cannot even fit in my hands."

And he was demonstrating, damn him, his hands spreading wide over both brown breasts, bulging them between his fingers, as his palms pressed against her hard nipples. "So bewitching," he said, his voice catching, as that telltale warmth against her thigh nudged again, swelling fuller. "Just like you, my sweet. With your sun goddess hair, and your burnished skin, and your deep speaking eyes. And"—his throat convulsed, his gaze still steady on hers—"with how kind and generous you are. How hardworking. How fair-minded."

Geva swallowed, her head slightly shaking, because he was surely only saying all these lies for Killik and Ulfarr's benefit, only as part of the job, the game—but Rathgarr was shaking his head too, his hands giving her breasts a gentle, proprietary squeeze.

"You are, poppet," he continued, sounding almost grave, now. "Ach, even today, you walked through this mountain without fear, and made friends of all you met. I could not move three steps, but for being told what a good, brave, stunning woman I had found, and what hale, hearty sons she should make for me."

He'd grimaced at the last bit, suggesting that this part was true, at least—and Geva couldn't quite breathe as his big hands slid downwards, now curving over the softness of her belly. Caressing it, almost as if treasuring it, while that hardness against her thigh gave a strong, sustained shudder. Almost as if he was saying... surely he wasn't saying...

And no, no, surely not, because he'd startled a little, his eyes gone wide and alarmed—and then his hands clenched, and snapped away entirely. Back to the soap, Geva realized, rubbing it to a lather, before returning this time to her hips, her thighs. And then around to her arse, cupping that in his big hands too, squeezing it, drawing her closer against him. Against that ever-swelling ridge at his groin, now prodding hard and demanding into her belly, streaking warm wetness against her skin.

And Geva was not considering this, *no*—or was she, because one of her hands had skittered down toward that swelling hardness, just brushing against it. And in return, it instantly leapt at the touch, pressing powerfully against her. Wanting her, perhaps, after all, even for just a moment...

Another brief glance up at Rathgarr's face found his eyes gone half-lidded, his nostrils flaring, his hands clenching tighter on her arse—and oh, oh, Geva was doing it again. Gently stroking up the full heavy length of him now, feeling the softness of his skin, the hunger swelling beneath. The way that deep slit was already oozing more wetness into her palm, and she felt her other hand sliding around too, coming up to feel that, to feel his slick liquid pulse out against her fingers...

Rathgarr's breath hitched, his grip clamping tighter on her arse, and she felt her irrational bravado rising as she stroked harder against his full length, her other hand still brazenly lingering at his slit. Feeling that slick glossy skin, how it nudged and gripped against her touch, as more slippery wetness spurted up, painted against her fingers. And when she stroked a little deeper, it gushed out even more, its silken heat such a compelling contrast to the cold water still splashing down beside them.

And was Rathgarr easing her closer toward the cold rushing stream, yes he was, maybe so it didn't feel so strange, so shameful. So it felt more hidden, perhaps, more natural, to be blatantly toying with an orc's body in public like this. To remember his heated instructions, from what felt like an age ago. *Awaken me. Seek to wield all your wiles to soften me. To tempt out my good seed toward you...*

Rathgarr's hands were stroking harder, too, now, moving against her with firm, deft familiarity. One of them slipping with blatant ease between her arse-cheeks, oh gods, against where he'd taken her—twice—while his other hand slid around to the front. Sliding straight down the curve of her, delving deep between her swollen, heavy-feeling folds, drawing them apart for his touch. For that purposeful brush of his finger, finding its place, oh hell...

And then—Geva gasped and shivered—that finger sank slow and easy up inside. As his other hand kept gently prodding behind, he was not doing this, not while they were watching this, but he couldn't stop, he couldn't—

She choked and trembled as he sank deep, driving up into both places at once, as his swollen, leaking hunger kept straining and sputtering against her. Against where her own hands were brazenly touching him now, caressing and exploring, as if she had every right to, as if he was *hers*. As if he truly wanted this, his hips bucking helplessly into her touch, his palm pressing tighter against her front, grinding where she most craved it, as his long finger swirled and stroked deep inside.

And his *face*, his gasping mouth, easing down, closer, closer. His breath inhaling, his nose nudging the wet hair away from her *neck*. So that—Geva shuddered against him, upon him— his lips could touch there, against the curve of her throat. As if he were tasting her, *kissing* her, but it was too open to be a kiss, too aggressive, too audacious—and Geva moaned and writhed as she felt teeth, settling sharp and close and intent, scraping against prickling, untouched skin. Just like in the wardrobe, just like what she'd seen on Jule and Alma and Baldr, he wanted to bite her, to leave his marks on her, *forever*—

"Oh," Geva gasped, her body arching up, tightening, clamping furious against him, baring itself for him. "Oh, gods, Rathgarr, please, Rathgarr, *please*—"

She'd barely noticed her hands still pumping him, milking at him like they were starving—but suddenly he bucked and moaned, the sound vibrating deep, straight from his mouth into her throat. Enough to wrench her tighter, higher, her body desperately clamping on his fingers—

And then she was convulsing all over, the pleasure storming and blazing, as he finally blew out into her hands. His hot white liquid wildly surging and pumping, spraying up between her fingers, all over their close writhing bodies. Painting thick pearly stripes up across Geva's arms, her belly, her breasts, her face. Even... her *hair*.

But the awareness of that felt stunted, dense, distant. Lost in the way Rathgarr's groan was slipping into something husky and low, his rhythmic spurts steadily weakening, until they'd faded to a slow, oozing drizzle. And then his body sagged against hers, his fingers gently easing out of her, the hot, sharp press of his mouth drawing away from her throat.

But in its wake, Geva couldn't seem to feel any blood, or any pain. Suggesting that perhaps he hadn't actually bitten her, after all—and surely she should have been relieved, or even grateful. But instead, there was a strange, shifting discontent, one that only seemed to deepen as he drew fully backwards, and began to rub at the sticky white he'd painted on her skin, scrubbing it away into the frigid, still-pouring water.

"I did not mean to catch your hair, poppet," he murmured with a wince, as he reached a hand toward it, and quickly dropped it again. "I swear this."

But Geva couldn't seem to respond, let alone move, though she distantly realized she was shivering, her teeth chattering from the cold. And she'd perhaps begun to feel rather light-headed, too, the room slightly tilting around her—and after a narrow, searching look at her face, Rathgarr quickly drew her back toward the pool's edge. Where he plucked up a thick cloth and began drying her off, his strokes firm and swift on her trembling body, and very, very tentative on her hair.

"I ken we have chilled you, sweetling," he said, as he swiped for their clothes—or rather, for his heavy cloak—and swung it around her shoulders, enfolding her in its weight, in its lingering sweet scent. "Can you feel all your limbs? Can you move your fingers? Do you ken you might need a healer?"

His voice was rapidly rising, his hands yanking the cloak closed, his eyes searching her face. Looking almost genuinely concerned, or even alarmed, and Geva felt herself quiver all over, a wan smile pulling at her mouth. "I-I'm fine," she managed, through her chattering teeth. "J-just chilled, as you said, I think."

Rathgarr loudly huffed, and then swiped for the rest of their clothes, and threw them over his shoulder. And then, before Geva had quite realized what was happening, he swept her up into his powerful arms, clasped her close into his warm chest, and stalked out of the room.

Geva only vaguely noticed Ulfarr and Killik on the way by—Ulfarr still glowering, Killik's expression more considering—and Rathgarr didn't show any sign of having seen them at all. His eyes frowning straight ahead, his forehead deeply furrowed, as he strode down the corridor, and finally back into their familiar bedroom, still lit by the light of the dim, flickering lamp.

He set Geva down on the bed with obvious care, pulling his cloak more tightly around her, before turning to the wardrobe, and yanking something out of it. His fur. The big silvery fur he'd so often worn travelling, large enough to wrap fully around her entire upper body over the cloak.

"Is there aught else I can do to help?" he demanded at her, from where he was now pacing restlessly beside the bed. Still with his hair streaked long and wet against his skin, pasted against where he was still fully bared, without even a stitch of clothing.

And despite his huge size, it almost seemed... vulnerable, somehow. Especially with that softness of his belly, and the slack heft dangling at his groin. And with the way his eyes on her were still tentative, uneasy, fearful.

"I'm really fine, Rathgarr," Geva managed, and she could admit that she *was* feeling better, the warmth easing back into her limbs again, the heavy cloak and fur oddly comforting around her shoulders. "Thank you. Although I should have"— she reached a hand out, tentatively touching at the wet mess of her hair—"damn it."

She was trying very hard not to think of how he'd sprayed in her hair, and how they had most certainly not washed it out properly—and she could almost feel him thinking the same, his expression still uneasy and alarmed. But then he squared his shoulders, and stood a little straighter, his eyes narrowing on hers.

"Then you shall allow me to address this," he said flatly. "Tell me how best to tend it. You use this oil, ach?"

He'd again lunged for the wardrobe, and when he whirled

around again, he was brandishing her familiar bottle of oil toward her. "You comb this in, ach? With your fingers?"

Geva warily nodded, and watched as he plucked out the stopper with his claws, and poured some oil into his palm. And then he rubbed his palms together, just the way she always did, before stepping closer, and settling down behind her on the bed.

"You shall speak if this pains you, ach?" he said, as she felt his fingers cautiously touching at her hair, stroking the oil in—and then almost instantly catching, stilling, on a tangle. "And ought I to—pull through this? Or cut it, with my claw?"

Geva winced, and shook her head. "No pulling, and *especially* no cutting," she said. "But if you can carefully work at it, maybe from the bottom…?"

It was perhaps asking more than he'd wanted to commit to—no doubt he'd thought it like his hair, needing only a quick comb through—and she was distantly, genuinely surprised at the feel of him actually… doing it. Carefully picking at the knot from the bottom, and then reaching for more oil from the nightstand.

It took a good while, but he did eventually accomplish it, his fingers now gently drawing through that section without any resistance, his claws lightly scraping against her scalp. The touch entirely unexpected, and feeling so suddenly lovely that Geva gasped, her entire body shuddering beneath the cloak.

She half-expected Rathgarr to laugh, to mock her, something—but instead, he just kept going. Finding another knot, and teasing it out, too. And this time, his claws lingered longer against her scalp as they combed through that section, sending another glorious, prickling shudder up her spine.

And then he did it again, and again, and again. Using more oil than Geva would have ever used herself, but she couldn't seem to find the will to care. Especially once he'd finally detangled all of it, his hands now carding easily through the full masses of her hair, his claws dragging slow and beautiful down the length of her scalp.

"I ken this is yet not how you wear it," he murmured, and she could feel one of his hands gingerly patting the side of it, where it had to be sticking nearly straight out, now that all the curls had been separated into a fluffy, voluminous mass. "What ought I do next?"

Geva found herself oddly swallowing, her shoulder giving a quick little shrug. "I would usually pull it back, or twist it, or put it in two braids," she said, her voice hoarse. "Just something to keep it protected, especially while I sleep."

If she expected Rathgarr to refuse, she was once again surprised, because he was already pulling her hair into two sections over her shoulders, and then drawing his claw down the centre of her scalp. "Ach, I can do braids," he said. "I oft braided Kesst's hair, when he was small."

Oh. Geva couldn't seem to find a reply, but she nodded, and shivered again at the feel of him shifting to one side, and using his claw to part that into smaller sections, as well. And then, starting at the top of her head, he began to slowly, carefully braid downwards, drawing in more sections as he went, keeping it close against her scalp. Just the way Geva would have done herself, the way her mother had always done, and she felt her breath catching at the feel of it, her body utterly still.

"Ach, no," he muttered at one point, and then tugged out what felt like a large section, before resuming it again, moving slower than before. But Geva still didn't care, didn't move, because gods, she would sit here and let him do this all night, no matter how long it took.

"What should you think," he ventured, once he'd reached the base of her skull, "of some beads here? Kesst always wished for these."

Geva's breath caught again—she hadn't worn hair beads since her mother's passing—but she managed another nod, and in return Rathgarr gave a satisfied-sounding huff. "Hold this," he said, nudging the braid against her, and once she complied, she could feel him standing, and striding off. Over toward his trove-room, where she could hear him rummaging around, and then coming back again.

His braiding felt different this time, and she could feel him sliding the beads onto the strands as he went, perhaps using his claws. Until finally, he gave a grunt of satisfaction, and carefully draped his new braid over Geva's shoulder.

She couldn't help twitching a hand to touch it, craning her head to look. The sight choking her breath in her throat, because the braid was neatly, evenly done, and the beads studded within it were—beautiful. Perfectly rounded, shining gold beads, gleaming in the lamplight.

They were surely very valuable, and Geva couldn't seem to look away, or stop blinking her wet eyes. "You—didn't have to do that," she said, her voice hoarse. "You don't."

There was an instant's silence behind her, and then the feel of Rathgarr moving to the other side of her head, parting her hair the same way with his claws. "Ach, I wish to," he said. "Wish to be a better... helpmate to you. Wish you to feel... *valued.*"

Right. Of course. This was a way of him trying to still keep her, to make sure she didn't dump him over for Jule's teaching post, and ruin all his carefully laid plans. Just like how he'd offered her more coin earlier, and apologized, and said all those lovely, empty things in the bath. *How kind and generous you are. How hardworking. How fair-minded. Bewitching. The prettiest I have ever seen.*

And perhaps he'd followed that too, because he sighed, the feel of it prickling against the nape of her neck. "I am sorry, for speaking to you as I did tonight," he said, quieter. "You have done much good work for me, even when I have not deserved this. I do not wish to lose your help."

Something sank in Geva's chest—yes, yes, it was only about this, again—but she twitched a silent little nod. Because even if she could take on the teaching job, she still wanted to leave in a month, right? She still wanted to sail to Ezira, to her real home... right?

"I have been dwelling more upon this," Rathgarr continued, even quieter. "And should you truly wish to do this teaching work whilst we stay, I should not stop you. Not so long as you shall yet keep working for me, ach? It is only natural that you should want to gain as much gold as you can, for your journey across the sea."

Oh. Right. Of course. And this was him attempting to be generous, to help her, his claws nudging her scalp as he kept braiding, kept shuddering heat and pleasure up her spine.

"Thank you," she said. "I'll... think about it."

Rathgarr didn't reply, just kept working at her second braid, now sliding on more beads, one after the other. Until finally, it too was finished, and he was carefully draping the second braid over her shoulder.

It was identical to the first, studded with those same glinting gold beads, and Geva fingered at them without thinking. Feeling the smoothness of them, their gentle heavy weights, the way they felt steady and soothing and so very *there*, with even the slightest tilt of her head.

"Thank you," she said again, and she meant it. "They're lovely."

Rathgarr gave a pleased-sounding grunt behind her, and a satisfied pat to her shoulder. "Ach, I ken," he said smugly. "Now get into bed, and I shall further warm you, ach?"

Geva again couldn't seem to argue, not even when Rathgarr had doused the lamp and yanked her close under the fur, curling his naked body snugly behind hers. Even entwining his legs with hers, so that she truly did feel enveloped in smooth silken warmth, in soft, cozy safety.

"Good, poppet?" he murmured, tugging her a little closer— but then he slightly stilled, and gave a little cough against her neat new braids. "Or—ach. Should you rather I call you Geva?"

Right. So he'd remembered that from earlier, then. And suddenly, this all felt far too tenuous, too dangerous, his body entwined with hers, his ring on her finger, his braids and gold beads in her hair, his scent all over her, *inside* her. And she should have been alarmed, appalled, but he couldn't take it away from her, not now, not yet...

"N-no, poppet is fine," she stammered, too quickly. "And the rest. As long as they're only for—me."

She winced as she said it, painfully biting her lip—even as behind her, Rathgarr's big warm body seemed to soften, curling even closer. "Ach, then, poppet," he purred, with a brief, proprietary squeeze against her bare breast. And then his hand just stayed there, curled gently around its heavy weight, as though it belonged there. Just like his braids, his ring, his...

"So did you know that Efterar has *magic*?" Geva asked, too loudly, in a desperate attempt to block the rest of that thought. "And that he can change things *inside* you, without even touching you?"

The words had the desired effect of stiffening Rathgarr behind her, his warm, tempting softness gone wary and rigid again. "Ach, I had wondered this," he said, after a moment. "It is an old Ash-Kai gift, borne by all the great healers of ages past. Kesst shall have a long, healthy life, I ken."

He sounded truly pleased by this, though perhaps a little wistful, too. And while Geva could have brought up the blatant lack of warning on this crucial point of orcs having *magic*, she couldn't seem to find the will, or the words.

"Kesst bears a great gift also," Rathgarr continued, still with that quiet wistfulness in his voice. "With his tales. I spoke to you of this before, ach?"

Now it was Geva's turn to stiffen, because wait, yes, he had. *This was his gift,* he'd told her. *Great, sprawling tales, so real they came to life behind my eyes.*

"When you spoke of Kesst, before this," Rathgarr continued, his voice almost inaudible against Geva's hair, "was this truth? That he wishes to see me, come morning?"

Geva gave a slow, careful exhale, her eyes blinking into the darkness. "Yes," she replied. "But... he made it very, very clear that he wants the truth from you, Rathgarr. All of it. *Publicly*. Why you left, why you didn't contact him, why you didn't come back for all those years."

She could hear Rathgarr's hard swallow, could feel his body gone even more rigid behind her. "I—cannot," he began. "Poppet, I—"

But suddenly all the overwhelming chaos of the day was swarming, collapsing, pooling in on this single, infuriating point. "No, actually, Rathgarr, you can," Geva snapped back. "Kesst deserves it. And good gods, after all this time, *you* deserve it, too. And if you don't tell him, I damn well will!"

Rathgarr's body betrayed a palpable spasm behind her, his breath stilled in his chest, his claws prodding into her skin. "What," he hissed, his voice heavy with menace, "shall you tell him."

Geva dragged in a long, fortifying gulp of air, and then huffed it out. And let herself think about it, really think about it, about everything she'd seen, everything Rathgarr had said and hinted at. Even everything from today, how Rathgarr had made it very clear that Kesst had been *Grimarr's* responsibility. That promises had been made. Promises that hadn't been kept.

"Well, I'll start by telling him it wasn't your choice," Geva began, quiet but sure. "I'll tell him you didn't want to leave, and you didn't want to stay away all that time, either."

Rathgarr still wasn't moving behind her, or even breathing, but Geva was feeling her way through this, more and more certain with every breath. "You had to stay hidden," she continued. "You couldn't send messages. You couldn't even"—a memory flared, from how he'd described that last inn they'd stayed at—"use your name. Gods, you didn't even want to tell *me* your name, when we first met. Did you?"

There was still no sound or movement from behind her, but Geva kept grasping for it, finding it, speaking it into truth. "And you couldn't talk about Kesst, either," she breathed. "Even when Killik came to see you, multiple times, and you obviously had plenty of opportunities to ask how Kesst was doing—you didn't. You didn't know how he'd been treated while you were gone. You didn't know he'd taken a mate. You didn't know his mate was a healer. Gods, you didn't even know his mate had *magic*, until this very moment!"

The words seemed to slice between them, sharp enough that Rathgarr's body flinched, his breaths now far too audible against her hair. But Geva wasn't stopping now, couldn't stop now, because...

"It wasn't your choice," she said firmly. "Someone made you leave, Rathgarr. So the question is just who, and how, and *why*."

Rathgarr flinched again behind her, his breaths still so close, so harsh. And Geva's breaths suddenly felt short too, her thoughts whirling, tumbling, turning over and over again.

"You thought it was Grimarr," she said, faster now. "But I think you're wrong. I don't think he knew. I think he meant it, when he said he wouldn't have hurt Kesst on purpose—which means he wouldn't hurt *you*, either. And sure, maybe he still could have paid you to go away, but he said he wanted to use his gold for good, remember?"

There was another hard, jolting spasm behind her, perhaps in response to the implication that Rathgarr would have disappeared, for the right price—but Geva was still too caught to care. "But today, after you left that meeting," she continued, "Grimarr looked at Drafli. As if he thought *he* knew something about it. As if... the *Skai* knew."

Her thoughts had flashed back to Ulfarr and Killik in the bath, in the forest, and then to the way Rathgarr had spoken of the Skai. *It is all to my gain, if the Skai—and most of all Ulfarr— see me as an addled, lovestruck fool, and not as a true threat. I shall*

*never let the Skai or their foul usurper captain see what I truly think
of them...*

Geva's breaths had gone just as shallow as Rathgarr's, now, her body just as stiff. "And you just said Skai don't have gold, right?" she whispered, into the darkness. "So what did they do? What did they threaten you with? What kind of threat has enough power to make you—"

But there was a sudden, frantic flailing behind her, a hard clap of a hand to her mouth. And Rathgarr's breath was shuddering in her ear, his body heaving, as though he couldn't find enough air.

"Please," he gasped. "Please, do not. I swore—a vow, upon this. To the *death*."

A vow, to the *death*. Those horrifying words suddenly ringing and echoing between them, vibrating, menacing. *To the death*.

And both Geva's hands were trembling on his, pulling it down from her face. "But—you said they swore your safety, coming here," she whispered. "And you... swore mine. So..."

The noise from Rathgarr behind her sounded almost like a sob, like something was choking his throat. And it was choking Geva, too, the cold, bitter horror of it clamping tight and close and sickening.

"They threatened to hurt *Kesst*?" she whispered. "That's how they made you leave?"

And even as she spoke it, she realized perhaps she'd already known. That it was the only way it made sense. The only way Rathgarr would have left, or stayed away so long. The only way he wouldn't have sent a single message, or asked a single question, or spoken a single name. A vow, to the death.

"I'm so sorry, Rathgarr," she breathed, blinking into the darkness, curling her fingers around his wrist. "I'm so, so sorry."

But there was only more silence, more empty, echoing bleakness, broken finally by a hard, convulsive swallow behind her. "Would you, mayhap," he choked, "tell me a tale. The porcupine?"

And somehow, Geva swallowed too, and fervently nodded, clutching tighter at his hand. And then she spoke, and spoke, and spoke, until her voice was raw, and Rathgarr's gasping breaths finally steadied, and faded into sleep.

28

———————

Despite Geva's exhaustion, it took far too long to fall asleep, to stop thinking about the horror in what Rathgarr had told her.

He'd been run out of his home. He'd been forced to abandon his brother, his only family. He'd gone sixteen *years* without any news, without any contact, without even using his own damned name.

And gods, no wonder he hadn't wanted to come back here. No wonder he'd wanted to pretend as though he was harmless, and *settled*. And how he must have agonized over this, over the danger of doing this, the possibility of slipping up, the risk not to his own life, but to *Kesst's*.

Even when Geva finally slept, it was fitful and fleeting, full of dreams of her own parents, her own grief. And all too soon—she jerked awake with a start—there was a faint light from the crack in the ceiling, and Rathgarr was shifting behind her, and easing out of the bed. Striding away toward the wardrobe, and Geva felt suddenly, inexplicably lost without his warmth, his solid strength behind her.

"So do you think Kesst is still in danger?" her scratchy voice asked, toward where he'd already opened the wardrobe, yanking a pair of trousers up over his bare arse. "Do you think the threat against him is still in effect?"

Rathgarr's shoulders sagged, his hand running through his hair. "I do not know," he said, his voice cracking. "And mayhap it is the height of selfish foolishness for me to now return here, and bring such risk to him. But"—he gave a helpless-looking wave—"to hear that he had sought me out, and sent for me, after so long, this was—"

He didn't finish, but Geva pushed to sit up in the bed, and nodded at his back. "I think it was the right choice," she said quietly. "Kesst deserves to know the truth, and you deserve to be free again. It's not fair for either of you to live like this, estranged from your only family for reasons you can't even talk about. You're"—she had to take a breath—"you're so *lucky* to still have family, Rathgarr. I would do *anything* to have mine back again."

Rathgarr's shoulders sagged even more, his eyes angling her a glance that might have been knowing, or sad. Because maybe—maybe that was exactly what she was doing here, wasn't it? Selling herself to him, sacrificing herself, maybe not just for survival... but for the hope of a *home*.

You will do aught you are asked, for a bit of gold.

"And besides," Geva quickly added, over the misery catching in her throat, "Kesst is an adult now, and no doubt he's very capable of taking care of himself. If nothing else, surely *Efterar* can help protect him, right? I mean"—she grimaced at where Rathgarr was now pulling on a tunic—"if he can prevent me from having children without even *touching* me, what else—"

But at that, Rathgarr whirled around, the tunic hanging crooked and forgotten over his shoulders. "What?" he demanded. "You mean to say Efterar... *did* this, for you?"

Geva swallowed, but attempted a careless shrug. "Er, yes?" she replied. "I know how strongly you feel about children, so I just—wanted to make sure. Just in case."

Rathgarr was still gaping at her, his eyes flaring with something she couldn't quite identify. "But—*you*," he said, his voice hard. "Do *you* not want children? A way to make your own family again, once this is done, in three weeks' time?"

Wait. In three weeks? And now Geva was the one staring, her hands clutching at the fur. "I thought…" she began, her voice hollow. "I thought we agreed on a month? Or… one moon, you said?"

Rathgarr's eyes shifted downwards, his focus now very intent on straightening and tucking in his tunic. "Ach, one moon," he said, his tone unreadable. "We have now been here two days, and before this, we spent five days in travels, ach? So this leaves twenty-one days left."

Oh. That was… short. Less than Geva had thought. Three weeks, before she'd be making that trip across the sea. Alone.

"Right," she said, over the catch in her throat. "Well. Efterar said it was fully reversible, so as long as I visit him again before we leave, I should still be fine to have children of my own. Once I'm… home."

Rathgarr still wasn't looking at her, but he nodded, and then swiped for his belt and sword, strapping them on with fumbling hands. "Ach, then," he said thickly. "I must—shave. Meet me in the latrine, once you have dressed?"

Geva gave a nod he couldn't see, and clutched tighter at the fur as she watched him stride out the door. One month—three weeks—and then the sea.

She sat there for longer than she meant to, staring at the wall, her thoughts curiously blank. And it was only once she realized she was absently stroking her new braids—her new beads—that she winced, shoved out of bed, and dressed as quickly as she could. Three weeks.

She indeed found Rathgarr in the latrine, glowering into the looking-glass, and swiping his shaving-blade down his face with unsteady-looking strokes. And then hissing aloud as the blade caught on his lip, and a spot of red welled in its wake, only to disappear under an impatient brush of his black tongue.

"Here," he said curtly, thrusting out something toward her. "If you would."

Geva blinked at him, and then down at the item in his hand. It was—oh. A pair of shiny, new-looking shears. For his hair. *Mayhap you shall even trim my hair*, he'd said, teased, what felt like an age ago. *If you swear not to saw it all off in a fit of pique.*

And perhaps Geva should have been offended by his presumption, by the command. But instead, something was swooping in her stomach, and she silently took the shears, and glanced around for his comb. Which yes, he'd set just there, on the edge of the washbasin—so she plucked it up, eased around behind him, and drew his hair back over his shoulders.

She couldn't seem to speak as she carefully combed it out, and neither did he, his focus still intent on his work in the looking-glass. But even so, she was certain she could see his shoulders slowly relaxing, his breaths exhaling deeper with every smooth slide of the comb.

His hair was indeed just a little ragged along the bottom, and Geva's stomach swooped again as she made a careful first cut, as the thick black wisps fell to the floor at her feet. And when Rathgarr didn't betray even the slightest flinch, she cut again, and again, and again, not missing how his own hand had steadied on his blade, moving with far more speed and ease than before.

Again, almost as if he liked this. Trusted her to do this, just the way he'd done it for her last night. Helpmates.

So she kept going, making it as perfectly straight as she could, and then brushing off his clothes, and disposing of the clippings down the latrine. And then, once he'd finished shaving, she took the liberty of turning him around, smoothing out his tunic, fixing the laces at his neck.

"Very handsome," she told him, with a smile. "Are you ready?"

But even that was enough to bring back the tension in his shoulders, his mouth twisting, his eyes dark and surprisingly bleak on hers. "No," he said, after a heavy sigh. "What if Kesst again rages at me? Or mocks me? Or spurns me before all our kin?"

But Geva shook her head, smoothed his tunic down against his chest. "You can't control what Kesst does, or how he feels," she replied firmly. "But you *can* control yourself. You can finally be honest with him. You can tell him the truth, after all this time, and you can decide to be patient with however he responds to that. You can do your part to try to rebuild your relationship, one step at a time. All right?"

Rathgarr was still grimacing, but his throat convulsed, and he jerked a quick, erratic nod. His eyes on hers warm, almost... grateful.

"And mayhap you shall... help?" he said, very quiet. "If I need this?"

Geva's hands hesitated against him, her heart skipping a beat, but she nodded, too. "Of course I will," she said, with as much certainty as she could muster. "Helpmates, remember? Even if you *are* still the single most enraging creature I've ever met in my life."

At that, Rathgarr's mouth curved up, into a hint of a smile— and without warning, he stepped forward, and bent his head low over hers. And then—Geva stilled, caught, breathless—he very gently touched his mouth to her braided hair. As if... he was kissing it. As if he liked it. Liked this. Liked... her.

It was something to cling to, perhaps, as he silently took her hand, and led her out the door. Taking her up the corridor, past a variety of doors, until he paused outside a new room, one Geva hadn't yet seen. Surely, the Ash-Kai common-room, where Kesst had wanted to meet. Where Rathgarr would tell his clan everything.

It turned out to be a large, open room, with a crackling fire at one end, and a variety of tables, benches, and chairs scattered about. While beneath Geva's bare feet, the floor was softly carpeted in furs and animal skins, and even more furs and skins lined the stone walls around them. Creating an overall effect of warm, snug coziness, apart from—Geva's body had stilled along with Rathgarr's, just inside the door—the fact that there were well over a dozen people already inside the room, all staring straight toward them.

There was Jule, with Grimarr beside her, and Tengil in her arms, while on Grimarr's other side were Drafli and Baldr, with Alma curled into Baldr's lap. And there was the midwife Gwyn with her mate Joarr—Gwyn giggling as Joarr nibbled at her ear—and Stella, nursing her tiny orcling, while she herself was cradled by a huge, hairy orc Geva hadn't yet met. And there was Rosa, with yet another lean, unfamiliar orc—surely her mate John—who was also holding a tiny, squirming orcling, and next Ella and Natt and Rakfi, and Simon and Maria, and Sigarr and Abjorn. And—Geva stiffened all over—even Killik, and *Ulfarr*, frowning with deep disapproval toward them.

But most importantly of all, there, in the very middle of the room, stood Kesst. Once again tucked close into Efterar's side, and again impeccably dressed in his jewels, boots, and tight trousers. Though his eyes looked even more tired than the day before, and they'd already snapped to Rathgarr's face, holding there with a strange, shifting intensity.

Beside Geva, Rathgarr's body was still frozen in place, his previous ease utterly vanished, his eyes locked on Kesst's face. His mouth opening, closing, opening, nothing coming out, and oh gods, this wasn't going to happen again, please...

"Skeeto! Poo!" said a small, clear voice, making both Geva and Rathgarr jump—but oh, it was just Tengil, scrambling down from Jule's arms, and toddling over toward them with wide, careful steps. "Hi. Poo!"

Geva laughed, the sound rather shrill, and before them, Kesst jerked away from Efterar, and strode forward to sweep up Tengil into his arms. "Rude, Bitty-Grim!" he said, gently tapping his claw against Tengil's little chest. "You cannot greet other people by saying 'poo'. It just isn't *done*."

But thankfully the room's curdling tension had seemed to collapse all at once, and Geva was laughing again, and grinning at Tengil's wide, perplexed eyes. "It's all right," she told Kesst. "It's my own fault. I brought out the poo jokes yesterday, and now they'll never be forgotten, *ever*. Right, little fella?"

Tengil was looking very stern, suddenly, and giving a small nod of his little head. Enough that Geva laughed again, and when Tengil reached out toward her with his chubby arms, she willingly took him from Kesst, propping him onto her hip. "But still, we should come up with something new," she informed him. "How about moo. Or boo?"

"Boo!" Tengil said, excitedly hiding his eyes with his hands. And soon Geva found herself playing peek-a-boo with an eager, giggling orcling, while Kesst watched, with a reluctant, amused smile on his tired-looking face—and beside Geva, perhaps Rathgarr looked just the same. His body slightly relaxing again, his soft eyes flicking between Geva and Tengil, and then back to Kesst. And then just holding there, glimmering with something between longing, and pleading, and grief.

And Kesst had surely felt it, his eyes snapping up, and instantly shifting back to cold, brittle distance. "Well, get on with it, then, Rath," he said flatly. "You supposedly wanted to talk, so talk."

But beside Geva, Rathgarr's body had gone even stiffer, his eyes darting around the room. Catching on Grimarr, and then on Drafli, and on Simon, and on Killik and Ulfarr. On... the captain, and his Skai. His *attack dogs*, Rathgarr had called them, who had threatened to *kill* Kesst if Rathgarr returned, or even spoke his *name*.

"Before we begin," Geva heard herself cut in, her voice too loud in the silence, "we would appreciate some reassurance that there will be no consequences or retaliation for Rathgarr speaking truthfully today. No threats, and no harm done. Either toward him, or—anyone else he cares about."

She didn't miss the murmurs and glances around the room, clearly following the implications behind such a request—but then, thank the gods, Grimarr rose to his feet, and put his fist to his chest. "No harm shall befall you, or any of yours, for speaking your truth to us, Rathgarr," he said. "This I vow to you."

None of the room's other occupants seemed surprised by this—most of all Kesst, who just raised an impatient brow toward Rathgarr, and irritably waved for him to continue. While Rathgarr himself was looking stunned again, his throat bobbing, something not unlike panic flaring in his eyes.

But Geva kept rubbing at his back, letting her fingernails dig in—and even, in a moment of daring, letting her hand slide down to his rounded arse, giving it a blatant squeeze. And it was enough to angle his eyes toward her, toward where she was giving him a firm little nod, and a small, encouraging smile. Saying, *I'm with you. Helpmates.*

And in return, Rathgarr gave a little nod too, his shoulders rising, and falling. "Ach," he said, his voice hoarse, his eyes angling back toward Kesst again. "Ach, little brother. The truth."

Geva kept rubbing at Rathgarr's back—*I'm with you, help-mates*—and he angled another glance toward her, hauled in a breath, met Kesst's eyes again. "When I left here," he began, "left *you*, sixteen summers past... this was not my choice."

Kesst didn't reply, just kept watching with that brow raised, and Rathgarr drew in more breath, heaved it out. "You were yet—young," Rathgarr continued thickly. "Mayhap fifteen summers, ach? And you ken how our father, long before this, was not—himself. Not—there, in his mind."

That was news to Geva, and she felt her head tilting, her fingers stroking a little harder. While before them, Kesst jerked a stiff nod, his brow still arched, his arms folding over his bare chest.

"It was never—easy, here," Rathgarr said, his voice cracking. "But with our father lost thus, leaving us without his help or guarding, it was no longer—safe. Not beneath the former captain's rule."

As he spoke, his eyes glanced sharply toward Grimarr, as if expecting him to argue this. But Grimarr only kept looking back, his mouth tight and grim. While Tengil—who was still propped on Geva's other hip—was blinking between Rathgarr and his father, and then he squirmed to climb down, toddling over toward Grimarr's waiting arms.

"I feared most of all for you, little brother," Rathgarr continued, his shoulders again rising and falling, his gaze back on Kesst's face. "I knew you would never be a fighter, and you bore great gifts, which brought you great risk. Thus, I wished to take you and our mother, and run from the mountain. But"—his mouth thinned—"she would not hear of this. No matter how I fought or pleaded."

Something shifted in Kesst's eyes at that, suggesting that perhaps he hadn't previously known this—but he still didn't speak, and Rathgarr drew in another deep breath. "She thought it too great a risk," he continued, "to take you out into the realm, whilst we were yet at war with the humans. She said that if I dared to run away with you, she should claim I had stolen you, and send the Skai after us, to drag us back. She said you were her son, and not mine, and that she had plans of her own. That she had bought you safety in—other ways."

Kesst's face had gone a little paler, his body again leaning close into Efterar's, but he still didn't interject, and Rathgarr kept speaking, now without any inflection in his voice. "So I kept our mother's wishes. I did not go. I sought to care for you and guard you however I could. But I yet made my own plans in secret, in hopes that she would relent. In hopes that we could some day... vanish."

There was still no answer from Kesst, only his pale face and staring eyes, and Rathgarr barked a blank, brittle laugh. "And then she died of fever," he said. "And this next night, after you had wept yourself to sleep, the band of armed Skai came to our room. Ofnir, Skaap, Balgarr, Alfver, and Falgr. And they said"—Rathgarr's jaw flexed, his mouth twisting—"either I would vanish that very night, or I would watch you die."

Kesst's body startled against Efterar's, his lips parted, his eyes gone blank. But he still wasn't speaking, no one was speaking, and Geva's uneasy glance around the room found a mixture of shock, and sympathy, and—on Grimarr's face, and several of the other orcs', too—a grim, unsurprised resignation.

"There were terms," Rathgarr continued now, his voice still wooden and empty. "I could not speak aloud my name, or yours. I could not come within scenting distance of the mountain's furthest tunnels. I could not seek to send word or letters to you. I was to forever vanish, alone. And as long as I kept to this, they vowed not to harm you, and to keep you safe. So"—he brought his hand to his eyes, rubbing hard—"I obeyed. I took these plans I had made for us, and I left. Alone."

The room had gone utterly still and silent, as if blanketed with a sickening, suffocating chill—until it was abruptly broken by the sound of a scoff. By *Kesst*, his head whipping back and forth, his mouth contorted into something like a laugh.

"A solid attempt, Rath," he hissed. "But you've *always* been rubbish at telling tales, you know, and *none* of this makes any sense. *Everyone* here admired and respected you, you were strong in battle, you were an *asset* to our clan and this mountain—so why would they even care about getting rid of you? And honestly, even if they *did* want to get rid of you"—his eyes flashed, and he lurched away from Efterar, came a step closer—"why wouldn't they have just *killed* you, and been done with it!"

There were a few audible hisses from around the room, and

beneath Geva's still-stroking hand, Rathgarr's body had gone fully rigid again, his face drained of all colour, his eyes locked to Kesst's. Looking like Kesst had just slapped him, and oh, he was even swaying on his feet, as if it might truly reel him back, fell him where he stood—

"Leave him be, Kesst," cut in a low voice, and when Geva glanced toward it, it was Grimarr. And suddenly he just looked tired, his gaze angling briefly down toward Tengil, who was now tucked close into his arm, his big eyes now intent on his father's face.

"I ken your brother is not speaking false," Grimarr continued, with a sigh, and a grimace toward Kesst. "And you ken, just as well as I do, that Rathgarr *was* a threat to some orcs here. Most of all, mayhap, to my own father. To what my father saw as my own rightful place as captain, after him."

Kesst shot Grimarr a sharp, betrayed look, but Grimarr frowned back, and gave a slight shake of his head. "Before his infirmity, your father was a wealthy, powerful orc, from a long line of esteemed, gifted Ash-Kai. And his eldest son"—Grimarr sighed, gave a vague, irritable-looking wave toward Rathgarr— "was well set to surpass him. As you have said, Rathgarr was a strong fighter, who was admired and favoured amongst our kin. He well knew how to speak and dress and carry himself, and he made friends and wooed women with ease. He had much to credit him that I did not."

He gestured downwards at his own simple ensemble, which admittedly was far less polished-looking than Rathgarr's, and then at his scarred, heavily marked face, which also stood in stark contrast to Rathgarr's even, handsome features. And Geva could see Kesst looking between them too, his brow furrowed, his mouth gone very thin.

"So if Rath really *was* such good competition for you, Grim," Kesst said coldly, "then why not just kill him?"

Rathgarr flinched again, his face so vividly pained that Geva actually slid her arm around his waist this time, squeezing him close. While Grimarr gave Kesst another disapproving frown, and then a slow, resigned sigh.

"Because of your father's gold, mayhap," he said heavily. "If Rathgarr had died without a son, this would have fully been yours, Kesst, after your father's passing. But since Rathgarr ran, and thus spurned and disavowed his clan—and abandoned you to the clan's care—my father could then reclaim the wealth as that of the clan's, and make it his own."

Oh. Oh, how *vile*. So not only had Grimarr's awful father apparently gotten Rathgarr out of the way for good, but in the process, he'd also found a way to steal his family's wealth, too. To steal it from... Kesst. Kesst, who was now looking markedly paler than before, his eyes blank hollows in his suddenly stark-looking face.

But he'd gone silent again, and so had Grimarr, and Rathgarr was still slightly swaying against Geva's body, against her arm still tightly around him. But there were still so many questions, damn it, and Geva drew in a breath, and found herself glaring down at Grimarr's face.

"So how much did *you* know about all this, then?" she demanded at him. "How involved were you in this horrible plan of your father's? And did you spend all of their inheritance, too?!"

But Grimarr didn't even blink at this, his eyes steady on Geva, and on Rathgarr. "I knew naught of it," he said, "until we spoke yesterday, and I understood that there must be more to this than we knew. Kesst and I are near in age, and I was too caught in my own trials at the time to follow all my father's schemes. I ken I must have seen or scented the gold after all this, but I cannot recall. If it was in my father's hoard"—he shrugged, and sighed—"it is gone. I am sorry."

His eyes flicked to Kesst now, too, shifting as they held to his stark, staring face. "Had I known this, there is much I would have altered," he said, on another heavy exhale. "You deserved far better from us, brother. From *me*."

But before them, Kesst twitched, his hands flailing up into the air. "Oh, no you don't, Grim," he snapped, his voice wavering. "Don't you *dare* take this one on yourself, too. Other than Eft, you have done more for me than anyone else in this damned entire *mountain!*"

The words seemed to swing through the room, echoing and shuddering, striking without thought or care where they landed. Without caring that Rathgarr could hear them, Rathgarr who had loved Kesst, who'd fought and failed for Kesst, who'd lost everything, for Kesst. And Rathgarr, who felt like a rigid teetering stone beside Geva, like he was one breath, one more word, away from falling.

"Well, it seems to me," Geva heard herself cut in, the words clipped and cold, "that there are multiple victims here, and that there ought to be a proper investigation into all this. In particular"—she lifted her chin, narrowing her eyes at Drafli— "around who *did* know, and who was responsible for enforcing and continuing this ongoing mess. Quite a few Skai, perhaps."

Drafli was shaking his head, frowning back at her with deep dislike in his glittering eyes, and beside him, Simon cleared his throat, his gaze steady on Rathgarr's. "We also did not know the full truth of this," he said flatly. "And all the Skai Rathgarr have named are now dead. Many by our own hands, for their misdeeds."

Oh. That stopped Geva short for an instant, but it was beside the point, damn it, and she drew in another breath, and lifted her chin. "Well, despite that," she continued, her voice even harder, "it still seems very obvious that Rathgarr's name ought to be cleared at once, and the record publicly set straight. And even if his father's gold is gone forever, Rathgarr should be reinstated as one of his father's heirs, in case any of it ever comes to light again. In case"—she felt her lip curling as her eyes swept across the room—"he can *ever* manage to move past all this suffering and devastation, and even *consider* having sons of his own, after having essentially his first one *stolen* from him!"

The room had gone fully silent again, every eye in it firmly and perhaps warily on Geva—but she still didn't care, because the only thing that mattered was Rathgarr. The way Rathgarr was still so rigid, still gone somewhere else, and gods only knew when he would return. And he didn't deserve this, they didn't deserve to see him like this, she was done, done, *done.*

"And I think that's enough of this for today, thank you," she told the room at large, as she turned and bodily steered Rathgarr around, toward the door. Not sparing them another single look, not one, until—

"Bye-bye," said a small voice behind them, and when Geva spun around again, she found Tengil looking at her from his father's lap, his head tilted, his eyes very grave.

And Geva was blinking hard, her throat swallowing, her mouth attempting some broken travesty of a smile. "Bye-bye," she said, with a shaky little wave. "We'll see you again soon."

And with that, she lifted her chin and stalked out the door, dragging Rathgarr's staggering body close behind her.

29

———————

Geva stalked down the corridor without thought, without intention. Just needing to get Rathgarr out of there, away from there, from all those appalling memories and secrets and lies.

His own people had destroyed his life. They'd stolen his rightful inheritance. And even if the stolen inheritance was another point that Rathgarr had surely known, and could surely have mentioned, Geva's indignation was still surging far too strong to dwell on it. Gods, no wonder he was so strange about gold. No wonder he was so strange about *sons*.

And—Geva shot a helpless look backwards, toward where he was dragging behind her, his eyes gazing blankly ahead— no wonder he was like this sometimes. Like the darkness was consuming all his thoughts, all his awareness, and leaving room for nothing else.

And now that she'd hesitated, Rathgarr had stopped too, just staring at the wall. His body so hard and stiff again, as if perhaps the darkness had snatched away even his ability to walk, or speak. And this time, when Geva tugged on his arm, he didn't move, just kept standing, staring, silent and blank and empty.

She shot a helpless glance back down the corridor, where the common-room's entrance was still just in view, where the rest of them might walk out and see him like this at any moment. And suddenly she couldn't stand even the thought of it, and after frantically searching the corridor around them, she powerfully shoved Rathgarr sideways, into what she hoped was an empty room.

Thank the gods, it was indeed empty, the dim lamplight from the corridor showing only bare stone walls, and a few low benches pushed close against them. So Geva dragged Rathgarr further inside, well out of view of the door. And thankfully he didn't resist this time, and followed her into the darkness, where he then just stood, gazing at nothing, lost.

And blinking at him, Geva's thoughts were lurching back to that room, to how he'd described his father. *Not himself. Not there, in his mind. Lost.*

"Rathgarr," she ventured, into the uneasy, eerie silence. "Can you hear me? Are you all right?"

His big body didn't move, his eyes still staring unseeing toward the wall, and Geva felt a twinge of panic, clamping in her chest. "Rathgarr," she said. "It's all right. You're all right. You're safe."

But there was still no response, no recognition that she'd even spoken—and Geva tried again, louder this time. "Rathgarr. You're all right. You're *safe*. Can you hear me?"

Still nothing, not even a flicker in his eyes, and the panic was surging higher, escaping in Geva's fluttering hands, her short, shallow breaths. "Rathgarr, come back to me," she said, pleaded, at his empty eyes. "You're fine. We're fine. You're working through this. One step at a time. *Please*."

Her trembling hands had settled to his shoulders, squeezing against their rigid strength—and in return, she could feel just the faintest shudder, wavering back through her fingers. And wait, wait, when he'd been like this before, touching had helped, hadn't it? And it had even helped back in that meeting, right?

So Geva kept her hands to his shoulders, stroking them up and down as firmly as she could. Again feeling them shudder back against her, so she deepened her strokes, made them longer, smoother. Moving lower, down his muscled arms and back up again, and then even higher, over his broad collarbones, up to his bare neck.

At the first touch of skin to bare skin, something shifted in his eyes—so Geva kept stroking there, tracing her fingers against the strength of his neck, the hard line of his jaw. Just touching him without thinking, wherever her hands wanted to go, while her gaze stayed fixed to his face, to that hint of awareness behind his eyes. To the way his head had perhaps tilted, very slightly, into her touch.

Right, then. Right. Geva's thoughts were spinning now, her head fervently nodding—and then, in a burst of bravado, she reached down, yanked out Rathgarr's tucked-in tunic from his trousers, and slipped both hands beneath. Sliding them up his soft bare belly, her fingers spreading wide against the warm silken smoothness of his skin.

And yes, yes, that was working even better, his body twitching a little more into her touch, leaning closer. His eyes still shifting—perhaps even beginning to refocus again—as Geva drew up more courage, and slid her hands around to his bare back beneath the tunic. Stroking up and down, and then even slipping down further, into his trousers, over the hard, muscled curve of his bare arse.

He definitely jerked at that, his breath hitching, so Geva kept going, even harder and bolder than before. Clutching both hands to his arse now, and then his hips, and...

"Please, Rathgarr," she breathed, her body easing closer. "Come to me."

And yes, she could hear his breath catch, could feel his hard, full-body shiver against her—and then his hand jerked forward, clamped rigid and clammy around her wrist. Flaring sheer, shuddering relief up her arm, all down her own trembling body, because he was touching her, he was here again, with her again. And she didn't even pretend to resist as he drew her hand closer, guiding it around to his front, pressing it... oh. There. Between his legs.

It still felt soft and uninterested beneath the trousers, but instead of feeling insulted, like she had last time, Geva felt her breath quickening, her heartbeat picking up speed. Her hand willingly caressing him there, stroking, lingering, feeling him faintly shudder in return.

But damn it, it needed more, she needed to do this properly—and before she'd even realized it, she was fumbling at his belt, unfastening it, yanking the trousers downwards. And yes, there he was, still soft and slack in her fingers—but already she was stroking again, caressing, meeting him as he was. *Awaken me. Seek to wield all your wiles to soften me. To tempt out my good seed toward you...*

Rathgarr's breaths had begun to deepen, the focus now shifting in and out of his eyes, so Geva kept touching, just the way he'd taught her. Gentle and careful at first, and then as he slowly shuddered and swelled, moving harder, firmer, smoother. Feeling him awaken in her fingers, responding to her, rewarding her. And the hunger of it, the power of it, felt almost dizzying, stunning, swirling the dim room around her—

And suddenly she was spinning, too. Whirling around beneath the grip of big, powerful hands, hands that were turning her away from him. So she was facing toward the stone wall, while behind her, Rathgarr was...

There. Here. Aware. His body huge and warm and close, his hips grinding hard and purposeful against her arse. His hands sliding down to her hips, gripping her skirts, yanking them up, so he could—

"Oh," Geva gasped, as she felt his long, breathtaking hardness settling against her bare crease. As it began stroking up and down, easing itself deeper between with every cant of his hips—and oh, she could feel the liquid smoothing and slicking his strokes, could smell that telltale sweetness in the suddenly thick-feeling air. And she shuddered all over as those strokes kept deepening, oh hell—but now drawing away, and angling even lower. Lower than they'd ever gone before, because...

She startled at the sound—the *feel*—of him kicking at one of the low benches, pulling it over with his boot, positioning it between them on the floor. And then—Geva choked—he lifted her up onto it, settling her feet onto the solid wood. And then he swiftly spread her legs wide apart, tilting her upper body forward, toward the wall before them. Meaning that she was raised up and bent over for him, fully exposed and opened for him, so he could—

"Ohhh," Geva groaned again, her hands now flat to the wall, as that hard, relentless ridge now slid long and slow between her spread thighs, dragging along the full length of her open, pulsing heat. Against where he'd never touched her like this before, not with that, ever—and she could feel her slick, hungry body clutching at him, kissing at him, as he slowly slid past. And then he did it again, and again, vibrating harder and fuller against her with every stroke...

And when he bent her a little further forward, and let himself notch, just there, just into her wet waiting sheath, Geva shuddered and moaned, her back arching, her body eagerly angling out toward him. Holding him there, wanting him there, he couldn't stop, not now, please...

"Please," she choked, straining for him, begging for him. "*Please*, Rathgarr."

There was a harsh, hitching exhale behind her, a clench of his hands on her hips, settling closer—and then he bore down. Pressed in. Slid that hard, throbbing strength slow and deep inside her, breath by agonizing breath. The movement so smooth, so easy, parting her willing clenching hunger around him, piercing her full of firm, rigid flesh. And firing out swarms of impossible heat, of pleasure, leaving her helplessly trembling and gasping as he pushed in more and more and more, there couldn't possibly still be more left, there was so *much* of him, he was—he was—

There. There. Sunk all the way inside her, his hips pressed to her thighs, his heavy bollocks bulging full and close. Just holding there, jutting strong and deep inside, while Geva writhed and whimpered and gasped, stuck whole and firm and unrepentant upon a huge, hungry orc.

"G-good, poppet," came his husky voice behind her, as his hips ground harder, closer. Even circling a little, shifting that rigid pole inside her, wanting to make her feel it, make her thrash and moan upon it. "I had hoped you could swallow all of me, ach?"

He'd hoped. Oh, gods, he'd hoped, he'd *thought* about this, and Geva moaned and nodded, her body gripping back upon him, clutching at him, craving him, like she'd never craved anything in her life.

"Yes," she whispered back, desperate. "All of you, Rathgarr."

His growl was dark, approving, alive, his hips circling deeper, his big warm hands spreading wider on her bare flanks. "Yes," he repeated, breathless. "Good. And now…"

Geva strained to hear him, waiting, her heartbeat hammering, her breaths sharp and short, her body convulsively pulsing upon him with every gasp. "And now?"

A long, sustained shudder inside her, a heated laugh from behind. "And now," he said, deeper, steadier, "I shall finally fuck you, my sweet."

Geva's moan was frantic, hopeless, her head vehemently nodding—and he was already drawing out, slow, smooth, stunning. Dragging it on, making her wait, because now, now he was going to—

His sharp slam inside felt like light, like a revelation, like the entire world flashing white behind Geva's fluttering eyes. Like an empty, echoing ache finally filled, finally alive again, sparked and sustained by the deep driving thrusts of a hungry, powerful orc. By him making her his, in a way he'd never done before, filling her and feeding her and stoking the flame. Plunging in again and again, whipping it higher and hotter between them, his breaths rough and guttural, hers rising to choked, frantic moans. And then breaking into shouts as his hand slid around her front, found her, hurled one last breath on the flame—

Geva's release flashed raw and staggering, ripping through her in a burst of fierce, blazing brightness. Clamping her again and again on the solid strength still filling her, feeding her—when suddenly it was erupting, too. Blasting out deep inside her with sharp, shattering surges, flooding and dousing her with wave after wave of molten heat.

Geva trembled all over as she took it, met it, welcomed it. As her own echoing shudders kept rippling through her, melding and fusing with his, milking out that liquid surging heat in long, lingering clutches. Until the blaze slowly, softly faded, settling into something shivery, almost sweet.

She could feel the shaky heave of Rathgarr's exhale, his hands spasming against her hips. And even though she was already expecting it, dreading it, she winced at the feel of his softening strength drawing out, away. Until it fully dropped from her with a slick-sounding pop, and—Geva winced again—that liquid heat poured out after it, splattering on the bench and the floor beneath her.

Her face was burning, now, her eyes squeezing shut, her body trembling, waiting, until it finally slowed into a thick, oozing trickle. And Rathgarr had exhaled again, his hands clenching tighter on her hips, before she felt him stepping away, leaving her leaking, exposed, untouched.

"I—I did not think—to bring a rag," he said, his voice hoarse. "Should you wait here for a short spell, I shall go fetch one."

Right. Geva's face was still flaming, something plummeting

in her belly, but she swallowed hard, and nodded. And then she could hear him walking away, could hear the faint rustle of fabric as he went, because of course he'd been dressed throughout all that, *again*. And when he came back, would he offer her a coin, too? Maybe a bonus, for her foresight in now making this kind of pleasure possible, too?

She heard herself groan at the thought, and leaned heavier against the wall, buried her face in the crook of her arm. No. *No*. This was still just a job. Just about the coin. And knowing all of Rathgarr's horrible history didn't change a thing, did it? He'd been so clear, again and again and again, and gods, even with that apology of his last night, she still knew how he truly felt, didn't she? One month—three weeks—and then the sea.

It was at least enough to hold Geva's body steady and silent as Rathgarr came back in, as she felt the careful brush of a damp cloth against her upper thigh. Wiping up in firm, gentle strokes, mopping the wetness away.

But he didn't speak this time, not even to offer any coins. And he just kept going, cleaning her in strange, stilted silence, until he'd finally finished, tugging her skirts back down over her bare, still-sticky thighs, and nudging her toward the door.

It clearly meant he didn't want to talk about it, or acknowledge it, or ascribe to it any kind of meaning whatsoever. And gods, why would he, why did she care, a job, nothing more...

"So what now?" Geva heard her scratchy voice say, once they were again walking side by side down the corridor. "Any plans for the rest of the day?"

Rathgarr cleared his throat, his arm shifting against hers, guiding her hand back into its usual position against his bicep. "Ought to find some food, and take this to the laundry," he said offhandedly, raising the now-wet rag still in his other hand. "And as I was gaining this, Abjorn found me, and asked if I might wish to come sparring, for a spell."

Oh. Of course. So now Rathgarr would go off sparring with

Abjorn, and leave Geva alone, again. And damn it, she did *not* care, her eyes were not prickling, just a job, three weeks...

"But only should you wish," Rathgarr added, more quickly now. "I ken this is likely not pleasing for you, to be trapped in a small room, watching sweaty orcs pummel one another."

Wait. Did he mean... he meant he was asking? He wanted her to come *with* him?

Geva risked a glance up at his face, searching for reluctance, mockery, something—but it was just a waiting, wary watchfulness. As if he really was asking. Inviting her.

So Geva managed a furtive little nod, and accompanied him to the kitchen, where he dropped off the rag at the adjoining scullery, and wheedled a quick lunch from a shrewd-looking Olga. And then they made their way up to the Ash-Kai sparring-room, which was distinctly smaller than the Skai and Bautul ones, but still had the same style of an open ring, surrounded by rising benches cut straight from the stone.

"You came!" Abjorn exclaimed, as he rushed over to meet Geva and Rathgarr at the door, and broadly grinned back and forth between them. "Ach, I am so glad. I should not have blamed you if you wished to hide all the rest of the day, after—"

His eyes abruptly widened, his mouth snapping shut, and behind him, Sigarr had strode over too, his hand clamping to Abjorn's shoulder. "It shall be good to spar against you again, brother," he said to Rathgarr, in his deep, measured voice. "Do you wish to face me first, or Abjorn?"

Abjorn was all but bouncing in his eagerness, and Rathgarr smiled back toward him with warm, indulgent affection. "Ach, Abjorn, I ken," he said. "Though it is all his fault if I am too winded to face you after this, Sig."

Abjorn returned this with a delighted smile, and soon he was dragging Rathgarr off toward the ring, leaving Geva and Sigarr behind. And once again, Geva found herself fighting that odd hitch in her chest, and the highly unwelcome prickle behind her eyes.

"Shall we sit, sister?" Sigarr asked beside her, and when Geva darted a look toward him, he was settling his big body onto one of the nearby stone benches. "I am sure Rathgarr shall wish to show off for you."

The words might have been teasing, but his voice and eyes were almost concerned, and Geva couldn't hide her wince as she nodded, and sat. Staring out blankly toward where Rathgarr was stripping off his tunic, the sight of his broad bare chest again catching, stinging behind her eyes.

"This may not be my place to speak, sister," Sigarr began beside her, his voice deliberate, "but after all this today, I ken you ought to know. Even if Kesst does not well recall this"—he exhaled, heavy and slow—"Rathgarr *was* Kesst's father, in all but blood and name. It was only he who cared if Kesst ate, or washed, or slept. It was he who dressed Kesst, and guarded him, and tracked where he went, and with whom he had gone. It was he who did not rest for three days when Kesst once was lost in the old Ka-esh tunnels, and could not be found."

Oh. Geva found that she could easily believe that, and she nodded and attempted a smile, despite her still-stinging eyes—but now Sigarr was waving his big hand toward where Rathgarr and Abjorn were now circling each other in the ring. "And it was not only Kesst," he continued, his voice deepening. "Rathgarr was oft this for Abjorn also, ach?"

Wait. Really? Geva's head tilted, considering that, even as her eyes searched Sigarr, the soft ruefulness in his smile. "Abjorn never well fit with his own clan, or his own father," he said. "He followed us about like a lost, loud, lonely little pup. But Rathgarr never pushed him away, or called him small or weak, or told him he would never be Ash-Kai, ach? He praised him, and watched over him, and taught him to fight. And thus"—Sigarr's smile had gone almost sad, now—"Abjorn shall now worship him for life, ach? Even after all these years apart."

There was unmistakable wistfulness in Sigarr's voice, in his eyes back on Abjorn again, and Geva felt her breath exhaling, the tension loosening just slightly in her chest. So it was like that, then, between them. And suddenly she could see it, in the way Abjorn was excitedly laughing, dancing around Rathgarr and throwing wild, playful punches, while Rathgarr indulgently grinned back, and praised Abjorn's aim and his form, and then—Geva's mouth twitched—even made a show of stumbling back onto the floor after one of Abjorn's punches, his limbs sprawling wide.

"Victory!" Abjorn called toward them, his face flushed and shiny with sweat, his arms thrown triumphantly into the air. And when Sigarr grinned and gave a purposeful jerk of his head—clearly saying, *come here*—Abjorn obligingly trotted over, and willingly accepted the waterskin that Sigarr had somehow produced, and thrust into his hand.

"That was fun," Abjorn said brightly, once he'd taken a long, gulping drink. "I forgot about those fists of Rath's. Slow, but deadly."

Rathgarr's hand raised in a rude gesture from where he was still lying on the floor, and Abjorn glanced over and laughed, and took another drink. "He is yet not truly seeking to defeat me, though," he said, with a sigh, and a disgruntled smile toward Geva. "These Ash-Kai, they all ken they do you a favour when they pull their punches and play-act for you, ach? Who wants this?"

Geva's heart skipped at that telltale term *play-act*—Abjorn couldn't *know*, could he?—even as she felt her mouth curving into a sincere-feeling smile. "Indeed," she said lightly, with a glance over toward where Rathgarr had pushed up on his elbow to frown at them. "Especially when you call them out on their rubbish, and then they behave as though it's all *your* fault."

"Yes!" Abjorn crowed, raising the waterskin toward her.

"Just so, sister. See, Sig, *she* understands. You Ash-Kai are all the same."

Sigarr was now the one looking disgruntled, even as his big hand rubbed up and down Abjorn's sweaty back. "Ach, we are not," he countered stubbornly. "I do not do this. Do I?"

Abjorn rolled his eyes, his genial smile fading. "Ach, you do, Sig," he said archly. "You yet coddle me as though I am your lost, lonely little pup, in constant need of tending."

Geva's mouth was twitching again, especially since Sigarr's hand—which had reached to rummage in a pack beside him—had now re-emerged holding a fresh-looking bun. And now both he and Abjorn were looking down toward it, Sigarr betraying an unmistakable wince, while Abjorn sighed, rolled his eyes again, and snatched the bun from Sigarr's hand. And then gingerly settled down onto one of Sigarr's spread knees, where he began munching away at the bun with all apparent gusto.

Sigarr shot Geva a helpless-looking glance, and at her answering wry smile, he seemed to rally a little, squaring his bulky shoulders. "Ach, but you do not mind this, *kærasti*," he told Abjorn, his brow heavily furrowed. "It oft pleases you, to be cared for thus."

Abjorn shrugged and sighed, his eyes once again on Geva's. "Sometimes," he said, with a shrug, between bites of his bun. "And sometimes, you only wish to have your chain yanked, and your rump pounded until you can no longer sit fully upon it."

Sigarr's eyes narrowed, glancing purposefully down toward where Abjorn was still carefully perched on his thigh. While Abjorn gave a smug, bitter little smile, and tore another large bite from his bun. "Without," he drawled, his voice hardening, "being reminded of how this is not safe, or seemly. Or of how larger orcs should never harm sweet small Ka-esh. Or how it is *my* failing for wishing for this."

With that, he tossed the rest of the bun into his mouth, and stalked back toward the ring. While Sigarr stared morosely after him, his hand rubbing at his set, flushed-looking face.

"Ach, sister," he said abruptly, without looking at her. "Have you ever wished to learn to fight?"

What? Geva stared at him in genuine horror, her mouth fallen open. "Oh, gods no," she said. "I'm a *governess*. And I'm too big, and ungainly on my feet. Just ask Rathgarr"—she attempted a smile—"I can't even stand next to a *bath* without falling in."

But Sigarr's glance at her was odd, and perhaps a little too knowing, too. "Then all the better reason to try this," he said firmly. "The less skill you bear at first, the more room you have to improve, ach?"

Geva's horror at this hadn't decreased in the slightest, but Sigarr gently elbowed her, and gave her a plaintive little smile. "You should honour me by trying this with me," he said, quieter. "Please, sister?"

And damn him, damn the way he was looking at her, for all the world as though *he* were the lost, lonely pup in need of tending. And finally Geva groaned, and threw up her hands, and waved him toward the ring.

It was large enough to accommodate all of them, though both Rathgarr and Abjorn were already warily eyeing them, even as Abjorn delivered a vicious-looking kick to Rathgarr's gut. But Sigarr's attention seemed fully focused on Geva, his mouth drawing up into a patient, encouraging smile.

"First, there are many ways to do this," he told her. "And it is always best if you seek your own way. You have no doubt seen how Rathgarr uses his weight and his fists, ach? Whilst Abjorn"—Sigarr nodded toward where he was again kicking furiously at Rathgarr's belly—"is lighter and faster, so he uses this to his gain. Now you"—his head tilted, his brow furrowing—"shall have your own strength. Mayhap... how about this *dancing*, Rathgarr spoke of?"

Dancing? They had heard of her dancing? From *Rathgarr*?

But when Geva glanced over at him, he was again fully focused on Abjorn, as though he hadn't at all heard. And she felt herself shaking her head, giving Sigarr a pained, regretful smile. "Dancing is not at all the same as fighting," she said. "There's a beat to keep you going, and..."

But Sigarr was already stomping his foot, raising his brows in a silent challenge, and beckoning Geva toward him. "Then use this beat," he said, as he kept stomping. "Attack me. Seek to strike me with your fists, mayhap, and use your full form to drive them. As if you are Rathgarr, but much lovelier."

Beside them, there was a rather sharp-sounding growl from Rathgarr, but when Geva glanced sideways, he was glaring at Abjorn, his fists hovering at his chin. Pretending, perhaps, as though he hadn't noticed. As if he didn't care, as if nothing else today had even happened. Three weeks.

So Geva sighed, and gritted her teeth, and assumed the same stance. And then let herself sink into Sigarr's beat, which was surprisingly steady and even, despite his shifting body, and his careful, encouraging smile.

Her first punch went far too wide, missing his face by a truly humiliating degree, but Sigarr's smile only broadened, his head nodding, his foot just keeping up that steady beat. So she tried again, and again, and again, and found herself sinking into it, into the rhythm and the flow of it, into Sigarr's approving nods, into his head now ducking out of her way.

"Good, sister," he said, again and again. "Good. Ach, this is it. Close! *Very* good."

That time, Geva had actually grazed his cheek, the impact horribly stinging her knuckles—but she was grinning back at him, and trying again. Catching him almost in the nose this time, close enough that he had to dance backwards, losing the beat with his foot. And even as Geva winced away too, expecting some kind of retaliation or displeasure, Sigarr only seemed delighted, flashing her another broad, toothy grin.

"Ach, very good, sister," he told her. "And not ungainly at

all, you ken? Next time Rathgarr tells you this, you may safely ignore him, and punch him in the nose."

Geva actually laughed at that, the mirth rising far too easily amidst the strange, sweaty exhilaration—and she was surprised to discover that Rathgarr was standing close behind her, and glaring fiercely toward Sigarr. "I have never called you *ungainly*, poppet," he snapped. "Only skittish, ach? And only in need of soothing, now and then."

With that, he swiftly slipped his arm around Geva's waist, and drew her against his front. And then—she froze all over—he bent his head, and gently *nibbled* at her *neck*.

And this was not soothing, it was *not*, as Geva should have firmly pointed out—but instead, she was shivering, and leaning back into his strength. Into his solid, powerful touch. Into that slick teasing warmth at her neck, into his play-acting, surely. Into where it felt so close, so real, he'd fucked her, he'd wanted her, he...

"Ah, here you are!" cut in a voice, a new voice, behind them—and when Geva guiltily whirled around, it was Jule. Jule, with Tengil once again on her hip, both of them wearing a very similar, eager expression on their faces.

"We just wanted to let you know," Jule said, "that for the rest of the day, we'll be hosting a proper Ash-Kai party. And as a token of our gratitude, and our welcome"—she gave a fluid little bow toward Rathgarr and Geva—"we invite you to join us, as our esteemed guests of honour. Will you come?"

30

———————

Ashort time later, Geva found herself ensconced in her bedroom with Rathgarr, readying herself for the party.

It turned out that a proper Ash-Kai party was an important event, especially when one was the guest of honour. And—according to a muffled-sounding Rathgarr, as he dug inside the wardrobe—apparently these parties often led to deaths, or mutinies, or both.

"You really don't mean to participate in a mutiny, Rathgarr," Geva said, as lightly as she could. "Do you?"

Rathgarr was pulling on a silk tunic so fine it might as well have been transparent, and he frowned at her as he yanked it down over his chest. "You were in this meeting this morn," he said flatly. "Did you not hear all they did to me? To *Kesst*?!"

The fury was again rising in his eyes, and Geva reflexively strode toward him, batted his clawed hands away, and smoothed out the silk tunic over his stiff chest and shoulders. Taking a vague satisfaction in the way his muscles relaxed again, his breath exhaling through his nose.

"Yes, I heard it all, love," she told him, wincing at the last bit, and dropping her attention to tying up the laces at his neck. "And yes, it was vile, and they ought to be falling all over themselves to attempt some kind of amends for you both. But it also seemed quite clear"—she risked a brief glance back up at his face—"that none of them were actually involved in doing it to you. Right?"

Rathgarr huffed a low growl, and jerked up his shoulder. "None of them *did* this, mayhap," he replied. "But I cannot believe Grimarr knew naught of it. He knew *naught* of a plan that was fully meant to ensure *his* gain, and his gain only? And for the Skai to also play-act as though they are now all blameless, blinking babes, caught in the cruel schemes of their dead fathers? This is beyond all fathoming, poppet, and I shall not be swayed by their tricks and *lies!*"

Geva winced again, and focused on tucking the tunic into Rathgarr's tight, too-revealing trousers. "I'm not arguing that you don't have plenty of cause for suspicion," she said, as her thoughts darted back to that moment at breakfast with Drafli, that suggestion that he knew more than he'd wanted to admit. "But... if they're lying to you, or trying to trick you somehow, why would Grimarr have welcomed you here in the first place, let alone swearing your safety? I can't see how that would benefit him, especially when he truly seems to care for Kesst? And when Kesst seems to trust Grimarr completely, and credits him with—"

She broke off just in time, but Rathgarr was already stiffening again, damn it—and before she could think better of it, she began adjusting the tunic beneath his trousers, letting her fingers linger down there in entirely unnecessary ways. "What do you think they actually want from you?" she asked, raising a brow toward him, as her audacious wandering hand gave the bulge at his groin a gentle little squeeze. "What do any of them have to gain, by lying to you about this?"

Rathgarr's expression was oddly shifting now, his breath

heaving in and out, and his gaze darted away toward the wardrobe. To where he next reached and yanked out a belt, and began swiftly looping it on around Geva's still-exploring hand.

"Ach, and what do *you* have to gain from me, my pretty poppet?" he said coolly, in a very clear bid to change the subject. "Mayhap you wish to suck out some good seed, before this party? Or mayhap"—his eyes shifted again—"you shall offer up that sweet, deep little womb for my ploughing again?"

Oh, hell, he had not just said that, and Geva snatched her hand out of his trousers, while her muddled thoughts choked and churned. Had he just admitted—yes, yes, he had—that he'd *liked* that? That he wanted it again?

"Later, then," he said smoothly, with a wicked-looking quirk of his mouth, as he finished fastening the belt. "Now, what shall you wear for this party? Should you not yet wish to walk about bare for me, mayhap you shall at least show off more of your pretty form for me? Whilst making this ploughing easy for me, also?"

Geva's face was burning now, her mouth fallen open, her thoughts charging between disbelief, and frustration, and worst of all, *amusement*. "You didn't seem to have any trouble earlier, you ingrate," she hissed at him. "Now stop trying to distract me, and answer my damned questions!"

At that, Rathgarr grinned at her, swift and stunning, and purposefully tugged up on her dress. "Mayhap if you behave, poppet," he drawled, "and allow me to dress you, as a good mate should."

And damn him, why was Geva's breath catching like this, why was she suddenly clutching at her dress with fumbling hands, and yanking it off. And then her shift and stockings, too, leaving her standing there entirely naked and exposed before him, her chin lifted, her eyes defiant.

"Better," Rathgarr purred at her, as his gaze deliberately raked up and down her body, lingering on her peaked, heavy breasts. "You are so pretty when you are angry, my prickly schoolmarm."

Geva rolled her eyes at him, and purposefully crossed her arms over her breasts, hiding them from view. To which Rathgarr laughed, the sound low and almost indulgent, before finally turning back toward the wardrobe, his hands carding through the various fabrics hanging inside.

"So?" Geva asked, tapping her bare foot on the floor. And though she could hear Rathgarr's groan, his shoulders stayed low and relaxed, his mouth pursing as he plucked out one of her most form-fitting silk shifts, and sniffed at it.

"Ach, ach," he said, with a sigh, thrusting the shift into Geva's hands. "I have good cause to believe that there is... more to this. For of the five Skai who came to me that night, one of these—Alfver—was Ulfarr's father."

Oh. Geva considered that as she yanked the shift on over her head, and then watched as Rathgarr began fussing at it, frowning with a surprisingly critical eye. "You think Ulfarr knew what was going on, then?" she asked. "Or that he was even involved in getting rid of you, somehow?"

"Ach, I do," Rathgarr curtly replied, and then he turned and stalked off to his trove-room, the distinctive sound of tinkling metal emanating from beyond the door—and when he stalked back, he was holding several long, glittering gold chains. "You cannot think Ulfarr has shown himself *guiltless* so far, in this?"

His voice was incredulous, and Geva grimaced as she kept considering it, thinking it through. Because yes, Ulfarr had made it exceedingly clear that he was spying on Rathgarr. That he didn't trust Rathgarr. *Mayhap you have rather come to seek Skai gold, ach? Get out.*

"So... what does that change, then?" Geva asked, searching Rathgarr's eyes, as she twisted her ruby ring on her finger. "What are your goals here, for these three weeks?"

But Rathgarr wasn't quite meeting her gaze now, his eyes

focused on where he was holding up one of the gold chains against her shift. "Kesst is yet my highest aim in being here, always," he said, his voice very steady. "And"—his eyes flicked to hers, and down again—"you have not told him, or any others, about the three weeks, ach?"

Oh. Wait. Rathgarr hadn't told Kesst this was just a visit? He hadn't told *anyone*? And Geva's thoughts were scrambling back, and back, because no, he hadn't, at all, right?

And was that... was that to reduce suspicion? So Rathgarr could come here and... what, damn it? Steal from the Skai? Attack Ulfarr? Wreak some horrible revenge, and run away again?

"I think... you should tell Kesst, Rathgarr," Geva said thickly. "If you really want to have any hope of rebuilding your relationship, you need to be honest with him. Not only about your timeline, but about"—she swallowed, raised her brows—"your other possible motives in being here."

Rathgarr grimaced, and his throat bobbed, his head jerking a nod. "I shall tell him," he said, quiet. "Only... not yet. I cannot bear to hurt him any more than I already have, ach? He has borne so much, and I have failed him so much, and I..."

He was squeezing his eyes shut, his chest rising and falling, and his throat convulsed again, again. "I keep failing him," he said heavily. "Ach, today, it was not I who thought to seek that vow from Grimarr for his safety, but *you*. And mayhap you do not know the weight of this, but when the captain makes a vow thus"—his eyes opened, found Geva's again—"this also binds all who swear fealty to him. So in doing this, you have broken any vow that the Skai might have been clinging to upon this, ach? You have gained Kesst safety from this curse, forever."

Oh. Well. Geva's eyes were prickling, suddenly, and she attempted a smile. "I'm happy it helped," she said. "And just— promise me you *will* tell Kesst the truth? When you're ready? And before you do anything... dramatic?"

Rathgarr's mouth twitched up, his eyes gone unmistakably warm on hers, or perhaps even grateful. "I ken not what you mean, poppet," he said lightly. "Ash-Kai are never *dramatic*."

Geva laughed aloud at that, and poked him in the chest. "Nice try, but Abjorn had it exactly right about you," she said, just as lightly. "Play-acting. Pulling your punches. Thinking you're doing everyone around you a *favour*."

Rathgarr was fully grinning, now, and he gave a wry shake of his head. "Ach, and you are not counted in this, kitten?" he scoffed. "You play-act with the best of us, you ken. Who should have thought such a prim, upright schoolmarm could fight thus, or fuck thus, or command a whole room of vengeful orcs to her whims?"

Oh. Well. Geva's face was heating again, and Rathgarr's grin had faded into something softer, almost unguarded, as he glanced down at the chains still in his hand—and then he lifted one up, and settled it carefully around Geva's neck. "Here," he said, a little rough. "I ken these shall look well upon you, ach?"

Geva's stomach flipped, her eyes dropping to the intricate, gleaming chain he'd placed around her neck, to the way he was already slinging the other, larger chain around her waist, and tying its loose ends together with his claws. Creating a belt of sorts, its thick gold links cinching against the curve of her waist, its shimmering ends cascading down over her hip.

"Now this is how a true Ash-Kai mate ought to dress for a party," Rathgarr said offhandedly. "Should you wish."

Geva was still looking downwards, taking in the shift's low-cut neck and narrow straps, the way the gold sparkled against the white silk. A shocking ensemble to wear in public, to be sure... but at the same time, it still fell to her knees, and was thick enough to conceal everything beneath. And the gold chains perfectly matched the beads in her hair, and—she glanced down to its red sparkle on her finger—her wedding-ring, too.

And even if Rathgarr was still keeping secrets from her, still being his devious, vengeful Ash-Kai self, somehow... somehow, this felt like enough. For now.

So Geva drew in another breath, and met his waiting, shimmering eyes. "Very well, then," she said, with a smile. "Let's go."

31

The Ash-Kai party was... astonishing.

Geva truly hadn't known what to expect, especially given all the tension from the meeting that morning—but it certainly wasn't for Rathgarr to be swept along in a sudden sea of enthusiastic embraces and back-thumping. With apparently every orc in the loud, bustling room coming over to offer welcomes, praises, and congratulations.

And even more surprising was how Grimarr soon strode over too, with Jule and Tengil at his side, and loudly called the room to silence. And then, amidst a low thrum of steady drumbeats, he drew Rathgarr close and embraced him, before the room of watching orcs.

"Today, we welcome back our long-lost Ash-Kai brother Rathgarr!" Grimarr called out, his voice loud and carrying, his arm still around Rathgarr's shoulders. "For no fault of his own, he was betrayed and cast out by our fathers, and his birthright stolen from him and his kin. Together, we grieve these wrongs, and restore our brother to his rightful place among us!"

Rathgarr's initial expression of shock had smoothed into an easy smile, a grateful incline of his head toward Grimarr—at least, until Grimarr held out something toward him. Something that looked like... a bag of coins?

"A token," Grimarr's deep voice announced. "For all you have borne, brother."

A token. The word bizarrely blurring in Geva's thoughts, with her memory of Rathgarr back in the inn, saying these very same words to her, handing her that book of tales. And for an instant, Rathgarr again looked just as stunned as she felt—but then he smiled again, almost genuine this time, as he... shook his head?

"I—thank you, Captain," he said, with only the slightest hitch in his voice. "But if he shall accept it, I should rather this token be granted"—his eyes angled sideways—"to my beloved blood-brother Kesst, who has been failed most by these great wrongs."

And yes, he was looking at Kesst, who was standing with Efterar against a nearby wall, his gaze unreadable on Rathgarr's face. On where Rathgarr was giving him a careful little smile, before turning back to Grimarr again. "And should you truly wish to make amends to us, Captain," he continued, his voice deeper, steadier, "you shall also do as my faithful Ash-Kai mate has asked you, earlier this day. You shall swear that our birthright shall be granted back to us, if ever it is found. For our amends, and mayhap someday, for our sons."

Oh. He was making Geva's request... for their *sons*. And making a very public challenge of it, here, before all these watching orcs. And Grimarr clearly saw the challenge for what it was, his eyes shifting with surprise, and consideration—and then, perhaps, a rueful, resigned amusement, as he tucked the bag of coins back into his pocket again.

"We hear your call, brother," he said firmly. "Should your father's wealth ever come to light, it shall be yours. Welcome home!"

This was promptly met by more loud, raucous cheers, echoing through the room. And soon the drums were thudding loud and merry, and the room had surged back to life again, swelling with noise and laughter and dancing. With even more orcs coming over to greet Rathgarr, and congratulate him on his return home.

And to Geva's ongoing surprise, Rathgarr kept her close the entire time, his big warm arm slung around her waist as he spoke and smiled and laughed. As he introduced her to multiple unfamiliar orcs, calling her his sweet mate, his pretty poppet, his quick, clever schoolmarm.

It was all coiling strangely in Geva's chest, and even more so when Bjorn came over, tugging at her arm, and demanding why she wasn't dancing yet. And after a quick kiss to Rathgarr's cheek, Geva accompanied Bjorn toward the drums, where she joined a smiling Maria and Simon, and a growing group of young orcs, all of them dancing and clapping together. And it felt so easy, so natural, so... *right*, to talk and laugh and dance with all her new friends, to mimic their movements, to sweep up Tengil when he toddled over, and dance about with him, too.

"Gods, these orclings already all adore you, sister," Jule said, once she'd come over to grin at Tengil, tickling at his little belly as he happily wriggled in Geva's arms. "I don't suppose you've given any more thought to our job offer, then?"

Right. That. Geva's eyes reflexively glanced back toward Rathgarr, who was still surrounded by well-wishers, and talking and laughing with animated ease. Looking almost... relaxed. At peace. As if all of this—that proclamation of Grimarr's, the restoration of his birthright, and this party in his honour—had perhaps meant something to him, after all. Even in the face of that conversation earlier, with its looming threat of secrets, of vengeance, of death.

And somehow, it seemed to settle something in Geva's thoughts, in her chest, and she gave a firm, purposeful little nod. "I will... accept your offer," she said to Jule, on a heavy exhale. "But only on a term basis. And"—her thoughts flicked back to the Fitzwalds, to Cecily—"I'll need support from you. Real, substantial support."

Jule was already nodding, her eyes alight, and Geva drew in another breath, felt the strength of the drums beneath her feet, the warmth of Tengil's watchful little body in her arms. "Not just for planning schedules and curriculum," she continued, "but for implementing those plans, too. Making sure we give these orclings the most relevant, most well-rounded education we can offer them. And making sure it's sustainable, and that it will continue long-term, no matter who's in charge."

She was trying not to think of that nagging three-week deadline, the very real possibility that she'd be establishing all this just to turn around and leave again—but thankfully Jule was still nodding, still with that eager glint in her eyes. "Absolutely," she said. "Excellent, sister. I'll start pulling together a cross-clan committee to support you at once. Did you have anyone in mind you'd particularly like to work with?"

Geva considered that for a moment, her eyes glancing around the crowded room—and then catching on the sight of Varinn, who was cheerfully chatting to an animated Timo, while a rather unsteady-looking Thrain clung to his shoulder. "Varinn might be a good choice, if he's interested?" she replied slowly. "And you said the Bautul have already established a nursery, so we really ought to coordinate there as well. Would Kalfr be able to help, perhaps?"

Jule fervently nodded, looking even more delighted than before. "Perfect, sister," she said. "Leave it with me, and I'll set up a meeting to work out the details together. First thing in the morning, perhaps?"

Geva nodded too, her mouth twitching into a bemused-feeling smile—to which Jule gave a gleeful cackle, and spun off across the room toward Grimarr. Leaving both Geva and Tengil blinking after her, Tengil's head tilted, his little lips pursed.

"Poo," he said, with utter seriousness, as he transferred his frowning gaze back to Geva. "Poo."

Geva chuckled, even as an unpleasant comprehension slowly began dawning, together with a telltale wafting scent in the air—when thankfully, someone strode up beside her, and plucked Tengil out of her arms. Someone who was—Kesst?

"Not again, you stinky little menace," he said flatly, poking Tengil in the chest with his finger. "That's what, your tenth diaper today?"

Tengil's serious gaze had flicked to Kesst's face, his head giving a grave little nod. "Poo."

Kesst laughed at that, the sound surprisingly genuine—and then his eyes angled toward Geva, his smile gone a little fixed. "Well, I'm off to change him in the scullery, then," he said offhandedly. "Unless... you'd like to come?"

Geva blinked, and then shot a swift glance over toward Rathgarr, who was still laughing in the midst of a knot of orcs, Sigarr and Abjorn among them. And perhaps she should consult with him first, but this was crucially important, damn it—so she belatedly nodded toward Kesst, and gave him her best smile. "Of course," she said. "I'd love to."

But Kesst didn't smile back, his attention now focused on signalling at Grimarr and Jule across the room, clearly conveying his diaper-changing plans. And then he turned and strode out of the room, while Geva hurried along behind him, the party's bustle and drums and voices trailing away down the corridor.

Kesst didn't speak again as they walked, and when Geva glanced toward him, his handsome face was held straight ahead, his shoulders stiff, his mouth tightly set. Looking eerily reminiscent of Rathgarr, suddenly, when he was anxious, or tense, or upset.

"So you and Tengil must be quite close, then, are you?" Geva made herself ask, into the stilted silence. "He seems very comfortable with you."

Kesst betrayed a noticeable twitch, but then he shrugged, and huffed a short laugh. "I suppose we are close, aren't we,

Bitty-Grim?" he said, rustling at Tengil's hair. "Never thought I'd end up being the nurturing type, but life is full of alarming surprises, isn't it?"

There was a thin, unmistakable bitterness in his voice, and as Geva searched his hard profile, she felt her determination settling again, circling tight in her chest. Whatever rubbish Rathgarr was plotting, Kesst was still his greatest priority here. And she was Rathgarr's helpmate, and Kesst's... sister, even if just for now. Three weeks.

"This all must have been so horrible for you," she told him, her voice low. "I can't imagine how you must be feeling, after learning all that earlier today. About how you didn't just lose Rathgarr, but your inheritance, too."

Kesst gave a hard sigh, another jerky shrug of his shoulder. "Well, I suppose it could be worse," he said thinly. "At least now I know why Rath left. Even if he didn't do squat afterwards for *sixteen years.*"

Geva couldn't seem to find a reply for that, and Kesst sighed again. "And as for the gold," he said, his voice hitching. "I barely even remembered it, let alone realizing it should have been his. *Mine.*"

Geva swallowed, her own eyes fixed on the corridor ahead. "I hate to say this, but maybe it's better that you didn't know," she said. "My family was quite comfortably situated, before— well. And it wasn't easy, having that life, and then losing it, you know?"

Kesst made a face, and absently hoisted a watching Tengil closer to his chest. "And then, you got to babysit spoiled brats for a living," he replied, with an obvious attempt at lightness. "Including Rath. My condolences, sister."

Geva laughed, gave a wry shake of her head. "Like you say, it could always be worse," she said. "Luckily, I really do love children and teaching, and Rathgarr has been—"

Her voice unexpectedly caught at the end, enough that Kesst angled her a sharp, too-aware look as he turned and strode into the kitchen. "Rath's been what?" he said, his voice careful, as he waved a halfhearted greeting toward Olga and Gegnir, and led Geva back into the scullery. "Selfish? Arrogant? Secretive? Greedy?"

Geva couldn't hide her wince, but Kesst had already turned away, smoothing out a large cloth onto the scullery's stone counter, and setting Tengil on top. And then proceeding to change him with a deft, matter-of-fact ease, suggesting this was a routine they'd done many times before.

But Geva could feel Kesst's attention still on her, waiting, wanting to hear her answer. And suddenly, she couldn't bear to lie, or even to make an attempt. Kesst had borne enough, hadn't he? He deserved the truth, from both Rathgarr, and from her.

"I won't say it's always been perfect, between us," she said carefully. "But Rathgarr has been very... generous. And he can be very fun, sometimes, and we joke and tease quite a lot. He likes to hear my tales. And he always makes sure I'm fed, and clothed, and looked after. He makes me feel... safe."

Kesst had turned on a stream of water above a large nearby sink, and was intently washing out the cloths, and then scrubbing his hands. "That... sounds like Rath," he said, his voice nearly inaudible. "He did your braids, too, didn't he? I'm... happy for you."

But even once he'd turned off the water, he didn't turn around again, his clawed hands gripping the sink's edge, his shoulders rising and falling. And Geva was almost sure she could hear a short sniff, and then a slow, shaky exhale. Again sounding far too much like Rathgarr did, when they were alone in the dark, and he was lost in the memories, the grief.

"Look, I know it probably doesn't help," she continued toward Kesst's back, through her own thickening throat. "But I know Rathgarr will never forgive himself for any of this. He's missed you so much, and he hates how deeply he's hurt you."

There was another sniff from Kesst, a visible clench of his hands against the sink. "Then why didn't he *try*," he said, his voice plaintive. "It was sixteen *years*. Why didn't he try one damned *message*. He just took it, and sat there, and let them ruin our lives for all that time? Just like that? Gods, you know Rath, he's such a stubborn relentless *arse*, why the hell did he just *give up*?!"

Geva's throat convulsed, and she gave a shaky shrug Kesst couldn't see. "I don't know why he made the choices he did," she whispered back. "But if you asked him, I think he would tell you. I *know* he would."

Kesst huffed another unsteady exhale, and then plucked up Tengil, who had been watching from the counter with solemn, patient eyes. "Fine, then," Kesst said, as he stalked toward the door, angling a wet-eyed glance over his shoulder toward Geva. "Let's go ask him."

Geva froze in place—Kesst was going to ask Rathgarr, *now*?—but then nodded, and rushed after him out into the corridor. Trying to keep her breaths even, her thoughts steady, as she walked in silence beside him. Surely she hadn't been wrong. Surely Rathgarr would welcome this, and be honest. Surely...

Even so, she nearly stumbled at the sight of Rathgarr's big, familiar body stalking around a corner up ahead. Briefly hesitating at the sight of them, his head tilting, but then he strode straight toward them, with something much like relief shimmering in his eyes.

"There you are," he said, his sweeping hand encompassing Kesst and Geva both, as a tentative, wary smile pulled at his mouth. "I wondered where you had gone. Is aught amiss?"

Geva found herself drifting toward him without quite meaning to, sinking into the feel of his warm arm slipping around her waist. "We just went to change Tengil," she told him, sliding her own hand against his back. "Perhaps I ought to take him back to Jule, while you two catch up?"

But neither Rathgarr nor Kesst gave any response to this, Rathgarr's hand only clenching tighter against Geva's waist,

Kesst clutching Tengil a little closer. And both of them now just looking at one another, Rathgarr's face still wary, Kesst's suddenly hard, cold, defiant.

"So, Rath," Kesst said, clipped. "I can understand, now, why you left. Why you didn't say goodbye. But"—his mouth thinned—"I can't understand why you didn't come back sooner. Why you didn't even *try*. And what the hell you even did, all that time, that was so much more fucking *important* to you!"

Beside Geva, Rathgarr's body had snapped to that telltale taut stiffness, his hand gripping almost painfully to her waist, as his mouth opened, and closed, and opened again. While before them, Kesst's eyes were already flashing with impatience, and then with a fierce, rapidly rising anger.

"You know what, never mind," he hissed at Rathgarr. "I am so damned *sick* of giving you chances, you great—"

"*Wait*," Geva cut in, her voice too loud, too strained, her hand firmly stroking against Rathgarr's rigid back. "Please. He's just—he just needs a moment, all right?"

Kesst blinked, his forehead furrowing, his eyes angling suspiciously back toward Rathgarr again. While Geva kept blatantly stroking, rubbing from Rathgarr's shoulder down to his arse, while her other hand gripped to its usual place against his arm.

"I know he wants to talk," she told Kesst, almost pleading. "He wants to tell you anything you'd like to know. Don't you, love?"

She'd nudged herself harder into Rathgarr's side as she spoke, her hands squeezing even tighter against him. And she nearly shuddered with relief when he glanced down toward her, his rigid body spasming, and then perhaps slightly relaxing, beneath her touch.

"You want to be honest with Kesst," she repeated, holding his eyes. "About what you did, all these years."

Rathgarr jerked a hard nod, his gaze snapping back to

Kesst's, and she could feel him fighting for breath, for words. For a way through this.

"I... survived," he finally replied, his voice not his own. "I oft moved, from place to place, so I could not be known, or found."

He paused there, gulping for more breath, and Geva kept stroking, waiting. "I learnt all the places where orcs live and hide in secret," he continued, a little faster. "I stayed for a long spell with the southern Bautul clans, and also in the north, with the bands of orcs who run deep beneath the humans' capital. I lived also with a long line of human women, and I traded pleasure for food and shelter and coin, until they tired of me, or I of their demands."

Oh. Geva's hand stroking him had abruptly faltered, her eyes gone blank on his grim, drawn face. Rathgarr had... truly done that? Traded coin for pleasure, and submitted himself to their demands? Just like... just like...

"But amidst all this, I sought to stay in the shadows," his wooden voice continued. "To leave when any got too close. I learnt to lie and wheedle and steal, to smile amidst my rage, to say only empty words and vows. I spent much of my coin on wine and ale, until I forgot who and where I was. I became... a ghost."

A ghost. And gods, Geva could almost see it, the bleak, blank, endless misery of it swarming to life behind her eyes. Rathgarr alone, hiding, inebriated, leaving, lying, lost. Trading his big, beautiful body for food and coin and shelter. Surviving. A ghost. For *sixteen years*.

And standing before them, with a silently watching Tengil still in his arms, Kesst was looking just as unsettled as Geva felt. His grey skin pale, his swallow bobbing in his throat.

"Well, that sounds delightful," he said, with a forced-feeling lightness. "I must say, it seems unfathomable to me that *you* would choose to live like that, for so many years, without even making an *attempt* to return to your kin, or your home? Or to send a message, or a letter? Maybe a cryptic clue or two?!"

Rathgarr's body was again stiffening under Geva's touch, and she belatedly resumed her stroking, felt him slightly softening, struggling to draw in air. "I could not," he choked out. "I could not risk this. It was only this—this dream of you, safe, happy, at home, that made my days bearable. And even when"—his body shuddered against Geva's touch—"I began to wonder this, to question this, to dream of ways to see you again—I could not face the risk of it. Not only that I might harm you, and destroy all I had fought so hard to keep, but that I might find I was—wrong. That I had done all this, to me, and to you, for so long... for naught."

His voice was badly wavering now, his eyes blinking hard, holding, pleading, to Kesst's drawn face. "And now, this is truth," he whispered. "It is all my worst fears come alive, at my own foolish, craven hand. I failed you, little brother. And I shall now never rest until I do all that can be done to mend this. To avenge this. To take back what is *ours*."

Kesst's face was looking even paler than before, his eyes squeezing shut—and then he shook his head, a sharp laugh escaping from his mouth. "Gods, Rath, I don't want your vengeance," he snapped, his voice cracking. "Any more than I want your coin or your gold or your jewels, whether through you, or Grim! If you really want to make amends to me, you'll—"

He broke off there, wincing, still shaking his head. And Rathgarr lurched a step forward, reaching for him, but then pulling away again, just in time.

"What, little brother," he pleaded. "Only say what you wish, and I shall do it."

But Kesst grimaced again, his eyes dropping to Tengil's watching, wide-eyed face, and darting away again. "Nothing," he hissed. "Forget it. It's fine. I just—"

He clamped his mouth shut, furiously flapping his hand, and then spun away, and stalked back up the corridor. Leaving Geva and Rathgarr staring after him, Geva's hand still clutched to Rathgarr's stiff back, while his throat convulsed again, and again, and again.

"What did he mean by this," he whispered, sounding more lost, more forlorn, than Geva had ever heard him. "What did he wish for?"

Geva's throat was convulsing too, and she leaned a little closer, both arms circling around his waist on their own. "You'll find out, love," she said, as steadily as she could. "One step at a time, remember? And you two are speaking again, and you told him the truth, and he accepted it. That's incredible. A huge step forward."

Rathgarr didn't reply, but at least he was breathing again, his stiff shoulders sagging lower with every heavy exhale. "Ach," he said. "I... thank you, poppet."

Geva's heart skipped a beat, a low, whispering warmth curling in her belly—but she waved it away, as casually as she could. And then twitched a hopeful little smile up toward him, clasping his hand in hers.

"Back to the party, then?" she said lightly. "You owe me a dance or two, I think."

Rathgarr huffed an exasperated-sounding groan, but there was no real malice in it, and once they reached the party again, he willingly followed Geva up toward the drums. They were thudding slower and deeper than before, and glancing around the much-dimmer room, Geva realized that all the orclings—including Tengil, and Kesst along with him—had now vanished, and that the party had taken a far more... intimate turn. There were orcs grinding together on the benches, several of them blatantly bared, and Geva could just make out Grimarr, pinning Jule purposefully to the wall across the room, his face buried in her neck.

Rathgarr was glancing around the room too, his eyes catching—and narrowing—on where a big, unfamiliar orc was yanking a smiling, flush-faced Abjorn by his wrist toward the door, while Sigarr frowned from the bench opposite. But then

Sigarr shoved up to follow, his gaze briefly meeting Rathgarr's as he strode out after them—and Geva could feel Rathgarr relaxing again, his eyes angling down toward hers, one brow arching up in a silent, meaningful question.

Geva's face felt hot, suddenly, and she dropped her gaze to his chest, felt the steady warmth of the low, thudding drumbeat. Let it coil around her, and then sinking deeper into it, following where it led. Into the rhythmic, easy sway of her hips, the flow of her turning feet, the lightness of her arms, rising over her head.

She could feel the touch of Rathgarr's eyes as she spun, circling into the beat—and once she'd turned to face him again, she met his watching eyes, felt her mouth curve into a soft, teasing smile. And then felt the warmth shudder all through her, even deeper than the thudding beat, as his hand slipped to her hip, his fingers spreading wide against it, following it as she moved.

And that meant he was moving too, spinning along with her, his other hand finding her waist, clenching close and proprietary against it. But in contrast to her fluid, easy movements, his were harder, more forceful, his hair swaying out sharp behind him, his booted foot stomping along with the beat.

It was similar to the way the other orcs had danced—even Bjorn and the orclings—and now that she knew it a little better, Geva found herself drawing from it, her body spinning faster, harder, her feet driving against the stone floor, meeting the drumbeats as they rose. As her arms settled light and familiar on Rathgarr's broad shoulders, her fingers catching into his hair, her hips eagerly tilting into his touch. Into the stunning, astonishing sensation of his hand slipping around to her arse, and yanking her closer, harder, hotter. Their bodies moving almost as one, now, their hips pressing tight, rocking together again and again. And Geva was distantly but powerfully aware of the swell at the front of his too-tight trousers, the way it kept growing steadily larger, hungrier, with every touch, every sway of her hips...

And then—Geva's breath caught—Rathgarr's big hands snatched her up, pressed her close, just there, oh hell, there. Their eyes meeting, holding, as they ground tightly together, and it was as though the crackling shimmering hunger had shattered, suddenly, raging and reeling between them—and with one swift, purposeful movement, Rathgarr was striding off, toward the nearest bench, with Geva still clutched in his arms, clinging to him with all her strength.

He sank down onto the bench with a low hiss, his nostrils flaring, his black tongue brushing his parted lips. Because oh, she was now straddled over his lap in her shift, her knees spread wide, her body still swaying to the beat still swelling all around them. And Rathgarr's eyes were flashing with devious, daring defiance, as his hands purposefully snapped down to his straining, bulging trousers, and began... *loosening his belt.*

Geva's awareness suddenly lurched to life again, her body stilling over him, because *wait.* They were—at a party. In public. And even if other people were doing similar things around them—her gaze caught on the sight of Varinn, now sprawled down the bench with tightly closed eyes, while Thrain's hand moved in his trousers—that didn't make this acceptable. Respectable. Did it?

"Ach, do not pretend I cannot scent you, my pretty poppet," Rathgarr was murmuring, as he kept drawing his belt apart, and then began sliding his trousers downwards. "I ken what you wish for, ach?"

Oh, gods damn him, because the trousers were already easing lower, lower. Revealing first his lower belly, then that dense black hair. And then—Geva had to bite back her gasp— that glossy head, atop that length of ridged, hard grey flesh, more and more of it, until—

It bobbed out all on its own, springing up between them, exposing itself for the entirety of the surrounding room.

Standing there long and thick and dripping, jutting up straight and swollen... and then pulsing even fuller against the light touch of Rathgarr's easy, stroking fingers.

Geva truly could not move, because he could not be doing this, not in public, not with an audience—and yes, oh hell, there was already an audience, several orcs settling on the bench's other side to look, several more perhaps milling about behind, their prickling gazes far too palpable on the back of her neck. While Rathgarr, the devious underhanded cheat, just kept looking at her, his eyes so warm and wicked, brimming with the blatant, brazen challenge of this moment.

"You ken you can take this, poppet?" he murmured, as his audacious hand kept stroking, pumping out a growing bead of thick, pearly white. "Can you again swallow it whole inside you?"

Geva's whole body shuddered, her face flaming hot, her eyes locked to his, to his provocation, his audacity. And as her shocked, stilted thoughts desperately fought to regroup, there was suddenly a new awareness, a truth she'd nearly forgotten. This was her job. What he'd hired her for. A show. Play-acting. Pretending to be his sweet, eager mate.

And instead of the choked, bitter misery that so often accompanied that thought, this time, looking into Rathgarr's wicked, provocative eyes, it almost felt like—relief. Like... permission. This was a show, a challenge, and he was damned well not going to win. Not after everything today. Not like this.

"Oh, but I don't know if I can, love," she heard her voice say, sounding impressively plaintive, or even uncertain, as her eyes briefly dropped to the huge, hungry sight between them. "It's just so... big. And... messy."

And oh, the way Rathgarr's nostrils flared again, his sly grin leaping on his mouth. "Ach, but I have brought a rag this time," he replied, patting with obnoxious satisfaction at his rumpled trouser pocket. "And only think of how good it shall feel, ach? Of how your tight, deep little womb longs to be filled. How it craves a good, strong, fat orc-prick to kiss and milk and seize upon."

Oh, gods curse this outrageous menace, because Geva's swollen, slick-feeling body was indeed clutching, seizing, gripping at nothing. Longing to be filled, damn him, and when she fought for her most vicious glare, he actually laughed, the sound rich and delighted, perhaps easier than she'd ever heard from his mouth.

"Ach, you are so pretty when you sulk, my prim little schoolmarm," he drawled, as his hand on that huge heft kept stroking, pumping up, squeezing out more liquid white, until it oozed down the length of him in a thick, glossy rivulet. "But I must yet needs empty myself, ach? So if you shall not offer up your womb for my filling, mayhap you shall grant me your sweet sucking mouth, or your plump, pretty rump?"

Geva's shock wasn't even slightly put-upon this time, especially when Rathgarr purposefully glanced down the bench. To where both Varinn and Thrain were now openly watching too, Thrain's hand still deep inside Varinn's trousers.

"You ought to see her rump," Rathgarr coolly informed them, giving her arse a blatant squeeze over her shift, "after I have split it wide open upon me. As if it is *begging* to be ploughed again and again. To swallow up as many good, fat loads as I shall deign to feed it."

Geva's mouth fell open, but no words came out, and her shock only whirled sharper at the sight of Varinn's lips parting, his eyes gone glassy and dazed, while Thrain shifted closer against him, his face easing into his neck. "You think that about me, Varinn?" he breathed, husky, as Varinn's eyes squeezed shut, a pained look flashing across his face. "Want to feed me all your good seed?"

There was truly no possible answer to this, other than to glare back at Rathgarr's smug, appalling face, to see the light and the laughter dancing in his eyes. "I ken you long for it, poppet," he purred, his hand still on her arse guiding her closer, gently crumpling her shift in his fingers. "And in this, you shall not even need to bare yourself, ach? Now come. Sit."

Geva's lips were still parted, her eyes darting between his groin and his face, her thoughts distantly circling around those words. She wouldn't need to bare herself, because yes, she was still wearing her shift, just like he'd wanted, just for this. And yes, she could just ease a little up and forward, and... and...

"Ach, my sweet," he murmured, his eyes shifting again, flickering between the challenge, the craving, the... longing. "Sit deep upon me. Make me your own, whilst all my clan bears witness. Should... you wish."

The last part was so low, so soft, a whispered caress just for her, beneath all the hungry watching eyes, the steady, sensual thrum of the drums. And Geva could still so easily refuse, she could easily make some petty excuse, get up, and run away...

But instead, she was holding his eyes, and giving a brief, furtive little nod. And then shifting up, closer, her legs straddling wider over his, while an unmistakable astonishment—and then a fierce blazing heat—flared across his watching eyes.

"Good, poppet," he breathed, as his big hand came to the bottom of her shift, lifted it up just enough for him to slip that swollen, leaking cock beneath it. "Find me. Open up wide for me."

And oh, she already was, they were finding each other, his smooth, slippery head nudging up against where she was so wet, so wide open, so exposed. So ready for him, oh gods, her hungry heat clutching at him, scattering out streams of shuddering warmth as he swelled even closer, eased a little deeper. His breath catching, his lashes fluttering, as his hand slipped out from beneath to join the other on her arse, cupping tight and firm over her shift. As if locking her in place above him, upon him, so he could...

Slide her down, as he slid in. As that slick delving hardness sank up slow and smooth inside, splitting her apart upon him, as he kept plunging deeper, deeper, deeper. And between the drive and the drums and the sheer screaming sensation of it, Geva scarcely heard her shrill, shaky cry, or his answering low, guttural growl.

But he was still watching her, his gaze glittering on her face, with something much like triumph, or perhaps even greed. "Ach, my stubborn schoolmarm," he breathed, as his claws pricked at her arse through her shift, drawing her down even deeper. "You take my good fat Ash-Kai prick inside you. You suck it up deep, swallow it whole for me. You kiss it, and drink it, and tell me how it is all you shall ever need."

Oh, gods, Geva couldn't stop shuddering, gasping, her hands clutching at his shoulders, because oh, he was everywhere, filling her, consuming her. That still-driving hardness swelling even fuller, opening her even wider. Conquering the very core of her, breaking her apart, the ecstasy already near enough to taste...

"Ach, not yet," Rathgarr hissed, his eyes glinting with command, as his hands convulsed against her arse, holding her still. "You speak this first. Use your clever words for me, and then I shall grant you relief."

And oh, how was he doing this, flashing out so much frenzied craving that Geva felt faint, her body frantically seizing at where he'd indeed stopped moving, jutted up almost all the way inside her. Feeling so good, so perfect, his eyes, his hands, his safety...

"You feel—so good, love," she gulped at him, between deep, desperate breaths. "Nothing has ever felt so good. I need— more of you. All of you."

She nearly sobbed at the feel of that invading strength swelling fuller at her words, straining against her wildly clamping grip, his claws digging a little deeper into her arse— but his eyes hadn't changed, still glinting with that danger, that greed.

"Not enough, poppet," he told her, lazy and smug, as one of his warm hands gently slipped around, slid up her bare thigh beneath her shift. "Make me believe this as truth, my sweet. Only then I shall plough you again, and grant you the sweet seed you long for."

Geva's groan was guttural, broken, her fingernails digging into his shoulders, her eyes fixed on his watching, enraging face. "I need it, Rathgarr," she gasped, pleaded. "I need to feel you inside me. I need to swallow you whole, and drink your seed, and anything else you'll give me."

And yes, yes, his eyes were shifting again, his sharp tooth biting his lip, as that hand under her shift slipped up further, further, skating over their joined bodies, finding her pulsing, straining peak, just above where she was stretched out wide around him...

"Better," he breathed, as his hard thumb ground against it, as his swelling heft began sinking a little deeper again. "More."

More, oh he wanted more, just as she did, and she fervently nodded, clung tighter to his shoulders, shook all over at the feel of him moving deeper, filling her again, yes, yes. "More, Rathgarr," she begged. "More. I need you. Need anything you'll give me. Your seed, your hands, your gifts, your tending. Your"—she dragged in air, her body writhing all over as he finally sank all the way, skin pressing to hot skin—"your trust. Your truth. Your *sons*."

And oh, the way he groaned at that, his lashes fluttering, his teeth bared, his eyes flaring between fury and craving. While inside her, his strength viciously swelled, and then canted up sharp and deep. And a greedy, gleeful part of Geva was shouting at it, glorying in it, because oh, she had him, she'd known there was something in that, she was clutching and arching and writhing into his touch. Into his sudden hard, angry thrusts up, his hand on her arse driving her down again and again, his other hand grinding at her peak, just how she'd shown him. Swarming her with roaring raging sensation, overwhelming all else in its fierce flashing vehemence, the pleasure arching up in jagged, juddering bursts, higher and higher, until—

Geva screamed as he overcame her, as her writhing body capitulated, collapsed into surge after surge of shaking, shattering relief. Seizing at him, swallowing him, as he stilled, stiffened, cursed under his breath—and then he was shoving up harder, driving up deeper, and pouring out inside. Filling her, rewarding her, giving her all he had, all she'd ever wanted, here in swell after swell of sweet spraying heat.

Geva couldn't have said when it stopped, when the dizzying euphoria shifted into something else. Something she could scarcely catch in his watching, blinking eyes—but there it was too, in the way his hand's touch under her shift jerked away, as if it had been stung. As if... as if...

"Very nice, woman," he said smoothly, as that hand rose to pat at her cheek, the touch distant and firm. "I always knew you secretly longed to beg and plead for my seed, and my sons. You women are all the same, ach? All too easy, by far."

His tone was light, teasing, as if this was all still part of the game, the challenge—but it was almost as though that hand had slapped her across the face. As if yes, she'd gone too far with the sons, and now this was his retaliation, his vengeance.

And worst of all, he'd done it here, in front of all these watching orcs, who were obviously waiting for some kind of response. Some kind of lighthearted jest in kind, but how could Geva possibly speak with her eyes smarting like this, with the horrible betraying waver on her mouth, with his softening heat still cradled deep inside her?

"Indeed, love," she finally managed, desperately bringing a smile to her mouth, if not her blinking, prickling eyes. "We well know what a great honour it is to earn an Ash-Kai's true favour and affection, and to bear him hale, hearty sons."

There were a few approving murmurs from behind her, suggesting she'd at least kept up the appearance of it, thank the gods. But she couldn't bear to look at Rathgarr anymore, and her eyes had dropped, to his trousers, to where he'd said he'd brought the rag, this time.

And yes, he was already fishing for it, yanking it out of his pocket with a rather unsteady-looking hand. And perhaps Geva should have been caught on the fact that he'd thought to bring it, that he'd so clearly wanted this, planned this, with her—but instead, she could only seem to snatch at the rag, press it up between her thighs as she abruptly drew up and away from him. As his softened heft fell from her, slapped down wet and thick against his belly.

"Well, I'm off to clean up, then," she gritted out, perhaps not for Rathgarr's benefit, but for any of the orcs still listening around them. "I'll see you after, all right?"

She didn't wait for his answer, just turned and shuffled toward the door, unthinking, unseeing. Only needing to escape, to get away from him, from all those watching orc eyes. This was just a job, one month—three weeks—and then the sea.

But that thought only made her eyes prickle harder, a large lump now caught in her throat, and she rushed faster through the corridors, clutching awkwardly at the rag, stumbling over her shuffling feet. Until she finally reached their latrine, and staggered inside.

The cleanup was just as messy as ever, full of painfully vivid reminders of how it had gotten that way, and by the time she'd finished, she could only seem to sag back against the stone wall, her hands over her face. While her awful, traitorous thoughts just kept spinning, sinking, dragging her down in their despair.

Gods, what had she been thinking. What, Rathgarr had been kind to her for a whole single day, and suddenly she'd started to have all these delusions of this being something it so clearly wasn't? She'd actually believed he'd be above such a petty public attack, above throwing her into that horrible posi-tion, under such high stakes, while all his clan had watched?

After she'd already given him so, so much, not only in that, but all damned day? After she'd worked so hard to help him, to support him, to do her very best for him?

The first sob escaped her throat without warning, echoing through the small stone room, and suddenly the sobs were consuming her, wrenching out her throat in bitter, painful gasps. And gods, what would she do now, did she need to go back to that party? To keep smiling and lying, and perhaps thanking Rathgarr for being cruel to her, for mocking her before all his clan after she'd begged for him, and...

And suddenly something swept into the room. Something huge and dark and terrifying, looming over her with vicious, furious malice.

Geva screamed.

32

———

Geva's terror was a living thing, roaring up white and raging inside her. Escaping in her wildly scrabbling hands, her staggering feet, the room spinning and wheeling—and then juddering to a skidding, horrifying halt, as something warm and familiar clapped over her mouth.

A hand. His hand.

"Poppet!" hissed a voice, Rathgarr's voice, close and urgent in her ear. "It is me! Only me!"

Geva's heart was thundering in her ears, her body trembling all over, and she couldn't breathe, couldn't seem to find her feet. And suddenly both Rathgarr's warm familiar hands were on her shoulders, holding her in place, keeping her upright.

"It is me," he said again, harder this time. "I am here. You are safe."

But Geva was whipping her head back and forth, he was supposed to be safe but he wasn't, he wasn't, he'd mocked her and humiliated her and he'd—

And then he'd swept her forward against him, into him, folding her tight into his strong warm arms. And his big hand was stroking her head, her hair, petting her, again and again and again.

"I did not wish—to startle you," he breathed, his voice thick. "I only wished to tell you, I—"

Geva's body had slightly sagged against him, but she was still trembling all over, her breaths shuddering shallow, as she waited for him to continue. But he didn't, and somehow she sucked back enough air to form words, to speak.

"What," she hissed at him. "That I'm not good enough for you? Too easy? Too cheap? Too greedy? Just the same as every other woman, apparently, even all those awful ones you lived with for all that time, the ones who used you, and *hurt* you?"

She could feel Rathgarr's breath catching, his body snapping rigid against her, his hand stilling against her hair. As if she'd again cut too close, gone too far, but in this moment she didn't care, she *didn't*...

"Or maybe you've come to throw me another coin, and put me in my place," she choked. "To remind me that I only have three weeks left to be here, to please you, while you keep all your real plans secret from me. Or maybe you'll remind me that you'd never actually *want* a woman like me, or sons with me, even after I was the one who went and made sure those sons would never, *ever* happen! Because I knew that's what *you* wanted!"

Her voice had gone shaky and shrill, even muffled like this into his shoulder, and she could feel his sharp, full-body shudder against her, his chest fighting to draw in breath. His hands squeezing her closer, hard enough to push her own breath from her lungs.

"I—I ken, poppet," he said, into her hair. "I ken. I am—sorry."

Geva shook her head against him, felt his hands clutching tighter in return, his claws gently pricking through her shift. "I ought not to have said this," he said. "I did not—think. To speak of sons amidst this, I cannot—I cannot bear this. Even in jest, in our play-acting. But it was yet—wrong, to strike back at you, as I did."

Geva didn't reply, couldn't, and she could feel him dragging in another breath, his hand again stroking fervently at her hair. "You are not cheap, or easy," he whispered. "And if aught is truth, it is that you are too good for me, ach? You have been such a gift to me, all this day. All these many days. And should you not wish for my coin as thanks, mayhap you shall accept— ach. Mayhap..."

He'd drawn away a little, his eyes oddly shifting on her face—and then, without warning, he... sank down. To his knees. Kneeling, on the stone floor, here in this damned latrine, his head tilted up, his eyes shimmering on hers in the lamp- light. And as Geva gaped down at him, unthinking, unmoving, he put his hand to the hem of her shift, and began slowly, purposefully sliding it up.

"Mayhap this," he murmured, so soft, his breath a warm kiss of air against her bare hip. "I ken this shall please you, ach?"

There was truly no way to move, to breathe, to follow this— at least, until he slid the shift up a little higher, and leaned in closer, closer. Until his eyes fluttered closed, and—he kissed her. *Kissed* her. *There.*

Geva almost lost her footing again, her body staggering back toward the wall behind her, but Rathgarr's big hands were firm on her hips, holding her steady, safe. And then even guiding her a little backwards, propping her carefully against the wall, spreading her legs a little apart...

And then, oh hell, he kissed her again. His mouth soft and hot and impossibly sweet against that curve of her, not even seeming to notice the thick hair, the certain remnants of his own mess. And instead, his kiss was deepening, his lashes flut- tering as he again glanced upwards, and—Geva gasped, nearly staggered again—he touched her with his *tongue*. His long, slick, sinuous tongue, snaking deeper down her crease, shattering out impossible flares of heat with every soft, slippery stroke.

"Oh," Geva choked, on another fervent, full-body shudder, her eyes shocked wide and disbelieving on his face. On where he was still looking up at her beneath those long lashes, as that mouth kept gently kissing, licking, caressing. Apologizing. Making amends. Making, perhaps... a trade.

I traded pleasure for food and shelter and coin, until they tired of me, or I of their demands.

And no, Geva couldn't stand it, couldn't bear it, and she shoved him off, stumbled away, rubbed her hands painfully at her hot, sweaty face. No. She wasn't. She couldn't.

But when she dropped her hands, Rathgarr was still there, still on his damned knees on the floor, still studying her with strange, shimmering, heavy-lashed eyes. "It is not good, then?" he said, sounding almost... hurt. "You do not like it?"

Geva groaned aloud, and gave a furious, bracing shake of her head. "Gods, Rathgarr," she gulped, and suddenly she felt in stark, sudden accord with Kesst, back in that corridor. "I don't want your pity, or your payment, or whatever the hell this is! Damn it"—she dragged down another breath—"you just compared me to those women you lived with, who only wanted this from you. You can't really think that's what *I* want from you now, too? That I want to make you relive something like that?!"

Rathgarr's shoulders rose and fell, those lashes still fluttering long and low over his eyes, and Geva's own traitorous eyes felt caught on them, on his flushed-looking cheeks, his visibly wet mouth, his full, plump lips.

"No, my sweet," he murmured, as his hand reached back toward her, curved gently around her calf. "I ken you do not expect or demand this of me. And this is why I wish to do it, ach?"

Geva was again caught short, her eyes frozen on his face. On where he looked so earnest, so serious, suddenly, so... vulnerable.

"You have not once asked for this," he said, still so quiet. "Even though it should only be natural, for an orc to bear his mate's fresh scent on his mouth. Most of all if he could not please her the *customary* way, ach?"

Oh. Geva still couldn't speak, her thoughts hitching, catching, twisting—and his hand on her calf slid a little higher, circling around her thigh. "Instead, you have always given," he continued. "Even when I have not deserved this. You ask me how you can please me. How you can help me. And then, you have done this, again and again. You keep granting me all the power over you, and"—his voice faltered, his eyes shimmering on her face—"it is all the sweeter when you fight me for it first, ach?"

Oh. Wait. So he was saying... he really did like this? This entire... arrangement that they'd made, between them? The coin, and the commands, and the challenges?

And wait. Wait. Was... the rest of it part of that, too? The three weeks? Maybe even the secrets? The revenge?

But no, no, surely not... surely? But Geva still couldn't stop looking at his flushed, watching face, perhaps seeing him with entirely new eyes. No matter what else he said, what else he did, he truly did like this. What they had. What they'd made together. He liked *her*.

And even if she should have been furious, suddenly there was something almost like eagerness, like *hope*, rippling up her spine. He liked this. And yes, if she was honest, she liked this, too. Too much. And maybe. Maybe...

"Gods, that's just so damned *typical*," she made herself say, her voice not nearly her own. "Do you really mean to tell me that you've been depriving me of my rightful due as an orc's mate, all this time?!"

And oh, the way the surprise flashed across Rathgarr's eyes, instantly chased by a bright, beautiful warmth. Affection. *Appreciation*.

"Rubbish, my ungrateful little schoolmarm," he purred, his

eyes alight, his hand slipping a little further up her thigh. "How many times now have I freely granted you my good, fat Ash-Kai prick, and all its sweet bounty of seed? Ach, and how many times have you not even *thanked* me for this?"

Geva's affronted disbelief rose far too easily, and even more so when Rathgarr's hand gripped her thigh a little harder, and yanked her back toward him. "You are such a greedy, overbearing *lech*," she replied archly. "As if I'm going to *thank* you, for giving you exactly what you want!"

But Rathgarr's grin was still lighting up his face, his hands spreading her legs apart. "Ach, yes, you shall, my stubborn sweetling," he drawled, as he leaned closer and inhaled, his nose gently nuzzling into the hair at her groin. "You shall thank me so loudly, I shall feel it deep in my own tongue."

And with that, he closed the last small space between them, and again pressed his mouth against her. Kissing her so soft, so sweet, his lips and tongue so slick and warm and close. And it felt so, so good, it felt indecent, impossible, obscene, and Geva was already trembling all over again, a low moan escaping from her throat.

In return Rathgarr chuckled against her, the sound vibrating into the very core of her—and she trembled harder, gasping for air, sagging back heavier against the wall behind her. To which he took full advantage, spreading her thighs further, shifting in closer. His hot, wicked mouth opening wider against her, kissing deeper, as that silken tongue licked and stroked, slipping between, settling in hungry and intent...

And as he held her gaze, his eyes glimmering, his lashes fluttering against his flushed cheeks, that slick, slippery tongue slid *inside* her. Inside her, into where he'd poured out only moments ago. And surely he was tasting it, swallowing it, and what was he thinking, what did it taste like, why was he groaning as that glorious tongue sank deeper, as if to drink her from the inside out...

"Oh *gods*," Geva said, or perhaps sobbed, her tingling hands scraping at the stone wall behind her, and the tension was already rising, swelling, surging closer. Coiling into her wet, invaded heat clutching at him, kissing back at him, closer and closer, oh it was so good, so, so *good*—

But then, suddenly, horribly, it was gone. He was gone, leaning back and away, looking up at her with those heated, long-lashed eyes. And his face was shiny and slick, with her, with *them*, and the bastard was licking his lips, letting her see that long sinuous tongue, the tongue that had just been *inside* her...

"So, my ungrateful sweetling?" he purred at her. "What do you say? Shall you now behave for me?"

And damn him, bless him, because Geva's awareness was gone, lost, forever vanished into the rapture of his succulent tongue, his beautiful eyes. "Th-thank you, Rathgarr," she said, shuddering, searching, grasping at his head, his hair. "Please don't stop, oh gods don't stop, *please*."

His smile was like a light, like a stunning shattering gift, and so was the gentle touch of his hand, patting against her shivering thigh. "Better," he murmured. "You keep speaking thus, poppet, and mayhap I shall grant you your reward."

Oh, gods, yes, Geva was furiously nodding, and fighting to drag his head closer. And he was laughing, openly and blatantly laughing, as he held his eyes to hers, and again put his mouth between her thighs.

"So good," she gasped at him, as that mouth opened, deepened, his tongue already snaking out again, seeking up inside. "Don't stop, please, please. It's so good, you're so good, you're so gorgeous, I need you so much, please, Rathgarr, please—"

And it was so close now, her hands clutching in his hair, grinding him against her, as that slick slithering tongue sank deeper, the command already far too clear in his watching eyes. "Just—that," she gulped. "Just—you. Oh, yes, like that, don't stop, please *don't stop*—"

And he wasn't, he didn't, because he was so good, so stunning, the way he kept going, his tongue moving just that same way, driving her winding her breaking her apart—

She shouted and staggered as the pleasure crashed over her, whirling raw and fierce and dizzying, her desperate craving body clutching again and again on his stroking tongue. On where he was holding it still, making it stay, watching her writhe and whimper and gasp upon him. Until there was truly nothing, nothing left, and she collapsed back against the wall, destroyed, utterly spent.

It was only then that he drew out his tongue, but even now it was still lingering, kissing, caressing. Making sure she could feel it, making sure she knew who'd done this, who she owed for this. *You shall thank me so loudly, I shall feel it deep in my own tongue...*

"Thank you, Rathgarr," she whispered, as he slowly drew away, that beautiful tongue again sweeping over his swollen lips, his wet, slick face. "That was... incredible."

His swift quirk of a smile was undoubtedly smug, but also soft, and perhaps even a little shy. "Good, poppet," he said, low. "I always knew this should please you."

It was a strange, stilted echo of that moment back at the party, when he'd mocked her about the sons, but this time felt... different. Real. As if... he truly did mean it.

And Geva should have said something, some clever quip about being deprived or bamboozled, perhaps, but she could only seem to blink down at him, at her hands still sunk into his thick black hair. And finally he eased up to his feet again, once more looming over her, his body so big, so warm, hers. He liked it. Liked this. Liked her.

"So what do I need to do," she whispered, "to get that again?"

And gods, the way his eyes warmed again, the way he smiled. As though this was exactly what he wanted, exactly how she should please him. Exactly the kind of challenge he needed. Three weeks...

"Mayhap you shall keep behaving for me, this night," he murmured. "Thanking me, as is my due. And"—his brows rose—"sucking out as much of my good seed as you can swallow, ach?"

And yes, yes, Geva was already nodding, meeting his challenge, facing it head-on. "Hell, yes," she breathed. "I'll do my best."

33

Geva scarcely slept that night.

It was as though they'd broken through some barrier she hadn't known existed, crashing over it with pure, barrelling hunger. With Geva willingly caressing at Rathgarr, grasping at him, sucking him deep in the dark, shivering all over his huge, beautiful body.

And gods, she hadn't at all realized that he could be so generous, so indulgent, so willing—but now that she fully understood what this was, what he wanted, it made so much more sense. He craved that control, that upper hand, perhaps because it was the opposite of what he'd so often had before. But he also didn't want her to lie down and take it, he wanted her to fight him for it, to make him earn it.

It meant that she glared at him as she sucked him, scraping him with her teeth. It meant that she kicked and struggled as he turned her over and pounded her into the bed, hard enough that her teeth chattered, until she pleaded and begged for it. And it meant that when his slick, dripping-wet strength slid purposefully up her crease, prodding hard and demanding against her tight resisting heat, she cursed loudly and eloquently toward him, even as she willingly arched her back, and opened up as wide as she could, as he slowly, surely sank all the way inside.

"I knew you loved this, poppet," he hissed at her, his claws scraping light but purposeful down her back. "You love naught more than having a strong Ash-Kai orc ploughing your plump little rump, feeding it full of good seed."

Geva was cursing at him again, even as she desperately clutched and clung to him, and he gave her arse a firm, stinging little swat. "*Behave*," he ordered her, dark and dangerous. "Else I shall need to plough it again straight after this, ach?"

But Geva kept fighting him this time, calling him every awful name she could possibly think of, because oh, she wanted him to do it again, needed it so much it ached. And once he'd poured her full, and drawn out of her with a messy, humiliating squelch, she nearly preened at the feel of him touching her tender body with his fingers, holding it wider open, greedily looking at the mess he'd made...

"Again, then," he'd said, so cool, so casual, firing impossible flashes of craving all through her body. "And *behave* this time."

So Geva did behave, begged and pleaded and thanked him, until both her throat and her rump felt reddened and raw. And once she'd collapsed down onto the bed, utterly exhausted, she couldn't help shivering all over at the feel of him gently wiping her up, tending to her, caring for her. Without a single mention of coin, or twenty-one—twenty—days, or the sea.

"G'night, love," she whispered at him, once he'd gathered her close, his big body in its usual place against her back. "Thank you."

He chuckled into her hair, his body rhythmically vibrating against her. "I ken you are fuck-drunk and seed-sick, poppet," he murmured in her ear. "You shall be cursing me again, I ken, come the morn."

But when morning came—and with it, the feel of Rathgarr easing out of bed, going to the wardrobe—Geva somehow still felt more awake, more aware, than she perhaps had since first arriving in this mountain. Like all the truths she'd learned last night were twining with everything that had come before, shifting into something she hadn't been able to see until now.

Maybe... maybe there was another way. Maybe it didn't need to be revenge, and twenty days. Because it was very clear that Grimarr was making an effort, the Skai were making an effort, and even Kesst had said he didn't want vengeance, right? He wanted something... else. And maybe there *was* something else to all this, something here. Something... new.

So instead of just lying there, or asking pointed questions about where he was going off to this time, Geva slipped out of bed, and followed him over to the wardrobe, to where he'd already yanked on trousers and a tunic. And when he spun around to face her, his tunic askew, she reached up and straightened it out, pulled it smooth over his familiar broad shoulders.

"So I accepted Jule's teaching position," she told him, as lightly as she could, ignoring the sudden stiffness of his body beneath her fingers. "Just on a term basis. Not for the coin, but"—she glanced up at his watching, already-narrowed eyes—"because I really do agree with what she's trying to do. Those orclings need to be supported, educated, kept *safe.*"

Rathgarr's body was slightly relaxing beneath her touch, so Geva kept going, tying up the laces of his tunic, tucking it into his trousers. "So I intend to help develop a plan, and a curriculum," she said, flashing him an easy, teasing smile as she let her fingers linger against that lovely bulge in his trousers. "And I was wondering if you might have any advice? If you'd had the chance to implement a curriculum for Kesst when you were raising him, what would you have liked to see included?"

Rathgarr was blinking down at her, now perhaps more suspicious than disapproving, but he shrugged, and reached into the wardrobe for his belt. "Mayhap not just this reading and writing, I ken," he said slowly, as he shoved the belt into Geva's hands. "Kesst should have liked to learn music, or art, or mayhap how to sew clothes, or forge fine jewels. Or"—his brow furrowed—"he ought to have been taught the clan's tales, rather than needing to seek them out all over, as he did."

Geva's head tilted with genuine interest, her hands gone slack on the belt. "Do you mean your clan has its own tales, too?" she asked. "Ones that are passed down orally, rather than in writing?"

"Ach, each clan has these, I ken," Rathgarr replied, with another shrug. "Tales of our gods, and our forebears, and their journeys and conquests. Amidst all this war, most orcs have not had time nor peace to mark these all down in books to carry about, as you humans have, ach?"

This was highly intriguing, and Geva eagerly nodded, and gave him a grateful smile. "I'd love to include that," she said, as she belatedly slid the belt around his waist. "Anything else you can think of?"

Rathgarr was looking truly thoughtful now, his eyes faraway, his mouth pursed. "Ach, mayhap," he said. "Kesst ought to have learnt how to fight, and defend himself. I sought in earnest to teach him this, but it so oft ended in weeping and shouting that I could not bear to push it further. But mayhap with another teacher, one who is mayhap more patient, and can alter this to suit each learner's strength. As mayhap with…"

"Sigarr," Geva finished for him, with a grin. "That's a magnificent idea, love. He was a wonderful teacher yesterday."

Rathgarr's eyes had gone unmistakably warm on hers—and then even warmer as they glanced downwards. To where he was now fully dressed, while Geva, much to her sudden chagrin, was still completely bare, her brown skin liberally covered in thick white streaks, several in the distinct shape of his big hands.

"Very pretty, poppet," he purred at her, with a gentle slap at her rear. "But this, today, if you must."

His voice had gone a bit too casual as he reached into the wardrobe, producing yet another one of her shifts. And rather than arguing it, or questioning it, Geva twitched a nod, and a rueful smile toward him. Earning another gentle slap at her arse, lingering for an instant too long—but then a purposeful glance away, a clearing of his throat.

"I have a few matters to attend to, this morn," he said. "Shall you be well, on your own? I shall again keep track of your scent, and"—he shot her a smirk—"it shall be even easier now, you ken."

Oh. Geva fought to ignore the sudden plunge in her belly— he was really still leaving her alone again, no doubt so he could pursue his nefarious plans?—and desperately attempted another smile. "And you'll come find me, after?" she said, the hope too tenuous in her voice. "I was wondering if maybe... maybe you'd come dancing with me again, if we can find some music?"

And yes, yes, that was warmth flashing again in his eyes, or perhaps even the same affectionate indulgence as the night before. "Still seeking to earn more of my tongue, poppet?" he said lightly. "Ach, we shall find some music for this, I ken."

Geva's answering grin was bright and delighted this time, and she impulsively leaned up, and pressed a quick kiss to his cheek. "I can't wait," she said. "See you then."

At that, Rathgarr gave an uncertain-looking smile, and then made a rather hasty exit. But as Geva cleaned up and prepared for the day, dressing in the shift he'd chosen, she found her determination circling even closer, settling quiet and deep. They could find another way. Something new.

That purpose stayed with her for the rest of the morning, even once Jule had come to collect her, as promised, for the first-ever meeting of the Orc Mountain Educational Congress. The title had been chosen by an ever-enthusiastic Rosa, who proudly presided over the meeting in her library, smiling beatifically at the attendees as they entered. In addition to Jule and Geva, this included a bemused-looking Kalfr, a mild-eyed Varinn, and a smaller, remarkably handsome Ka-esh orc named Tristan, who softly introduced himself as one of Rosa's closest kin-brothers.

"It's so *wonderful* to have you all here to discuss such an important priority for us all," Rosa said, once they'd all been seated around a large table. "Now, Jule, if you could—"

But she stopped there, frowning up at the door, to where another tall, narrow-eyed orc was striding in. It was—*Killik*? *Ulfarr's* friend?

"What are *you* doing here?" Rosa asked, eyeing Killik with undisguised suspicion. "You *do* realize this is a library, right?"

Killik had already dropped his lean body down into the last empty chair at the table, his arms crossing over his bare chest. "No, is it?" he replied coolly. "I have become lost, then, for I thought this was the Skai arena."

Beside him, Jule loudly coughed, and gave him an apologetic smile. "We thought we should have some Skai involvement as well," she said, "and Killik was kind enough to volunteer. Thank you, Killik."

Wait, he'd really volunteered, to be on Geva's *educational committee*? And across the table, Rosa was looking just as flummoxed as Geva felt, her mouth pursing. "Aren't you the one who told Simon reading is a waste of time?" she demanded. "Time that could be better spent sparring, or sharpening your weapons?"

Rosa accompanied this with a pointed glance toward Killik's hair, which was bound in a messy knot on top of his head—and which, Geva now noticed, had two gleaming crossed *knives* stabbed into it.

"Ach, and this was truth," Killik said, as he settled further into his chair, and propped his booted foot on the edge of the table. "Thus, who better to tell you how to teach small, squirmy Skai, without losing them all to the arena on this first day?"

It was a fair point, Geva could admit, and even Rosa wasn't arguing it, her disgruntled gaze now fixed to Killik's boot on the table. While Jule again loudly cleared her throat, and smiled at the table's assembled occupants. "Yes, so thank you all for joining us," she said. "As you're probably all aware, we've been wanting to do better by our orclings, and make this mountain a safer, more nurturing place to raise them. And since Geva has worked quite extensively as an educator, we're hoping that she can guide us in accomplishing this. Any opposed?"

No one immediately argued, but Kalfr was shifting uneasily in his chair, and giving Geva an apologetic grimace. "I do not mean any insult," he said, tentative, "but we have only just met our new sister, ach? How can we be sure she is a safe human—the best human—to guide and care for our sons?"

It was another fair question, even if it was at Geva's expense, but before she could attempt an answer, Jule gave a regretful smile, and a wave of her hand toward Killik. Who in turn sighed, rolled his eyes, and then stretched out further in his chair.

"Geva Okoro was birthed in Wolfen, thirty years past, to Ginika Okoro and Chijioke Equiano, well-liked ambassadors from Ezira to Wolfen," he said, in a bored-sounding voice. "She studied for many years at the Wolfen Ladies' School for Language and Decorum, where she finished first among her peers. Her tutors wrote that she is clever, forthright, and kind, and well suited to a political appointment, to follow in the role of her sires."

Geva's breath was suddenly choking in her throat, her eyes frozen, or perhaps even pleading, on Killik's face. And though his glance at her was almost too brief to catch, she could see a shift in his body, a barely visible shrug of his shoulder.

"After her mother and father's passing, she moved south, and worked for a family in Tlaxca for four summers," Killik continued, his voice still blandly distant. "There, she taught first three, then four younglings, with lessons in three tongues, mathematics, music, drawing, and dance. Before her, no other teacher had stayed there for longer than half a year, and whilst these younglings were not well inclined to learn, three of them yet wept after leaving her."

Geva couldn't stop staring at Killik, her mouth dropped open, her heartbeat thundering in her chest. How—how the hell had he learned all this? And three of the Fitzwald children had wept over her? Cecily she could well believe, but—*three*?!

Killik glanced over toward her again, his eyes entirely unrepentant. "It is the work of the Skai, to learn such things," he said. "We do our work well, ach?"

His *work*. So wait, he was essentially admitting—confessing—that he *had* been spying on her? And obviously on Rathgarr, too? Together with Ulfarr, no doubt?!

"Thank you, Killik," Jule was saying, with a half-smile, half-grimace toward Geva. "We appreciate the Skai's efforts in keeping us safe. Now, any other questions about Geva's qualifications? Or Geva, is there anything you'd like to add?"

Geva's thoughts were still wildly spinning, her clammy fingers twisting her wedding-ring beneath the table, but she gulped for air, fought for focus. Anything she wanted to add, about this. About her work. Her chosen profession, despite all—that.

"Well," she managed, squaring her shoulders, casting her eyes around the table. "I'm happy to offer what skills I have, and help to teach this mountain's orclings to the best of my ability. However"—she drew in another bracing breath—"I also can't do it alone. Children need support and guidance and role models beyond just their teachers. They need a community of involved, invested people—especially parents and consistent caretakers—who are committed to helping them, and doing their best for them. If I decide to step back in three weeks, they still need to be taken care of."

Her heart was still thundering, her mouth twisting at even the thought of those three weeks—but thankfully, no one seemed to notice, and she felt her determination settling again, her breath exhaling. Another way. Something new.

"I also obviously have no experience teaching orc children," she continued. "But I believe very strongly that their education ought to reflect their own culture, and not just that of the world around them. I greatly benefited from learning my own family's history and customs, and I have no interest in implementing a curriculum that separates orcs from their own. And to start"—her thoughts flicked back to that conversation with Rathgarr—"I'd like to suggest instruction in orc art, music, metalworking, and oral history. As well as training in self-defense."

There was still no protesting from the table—if anything, Jule was wearing a self-satisfied smile, and even Killik was jerking a curt nod. Although, Rosa and Tristan were exchanging uncertain-looking glances, and finally Rosa drew in a breath, and smoothed out the fresh sheet of paper she'd set before her.

"We absolutely respect that, of course," she said firmly. "However, we Ka-esh are very united in the belief that orcs need to learn to read, write, and speak common-tongue, as well as Aelakesh, and that instruction needs to occur on a daily basis. It's a crucial element of being able to connect to the women they're seeking to mate with, the women they need to birth and help raise their sons. It's vital to the very *survival* of this species. And even if orcs don't learn human cultures as their own"—she fixed her glinting gaze on Killik—"you still ought to learn about them. Knowledge is power. Knowledge is *everything.*"

But Killik only rolled his eyes again, and lounged even more languorously in his chair. "You shall not see the Skai stand against this," he replied, toward where he was picking at his claw. "We now accept that this helps with our work, and our sons. But"—he glanced up to frown darkly at Rosa—"this is only together with orc ways, as our wise Ash-Kai sister says. And for Skai, this is not only learning how to fight, but how to watch, and listen, and stay *silent.*"

Rosa loudly sniffed, clearly taking this as the insult it was intended to be, while beside Killik, Kalfr leaned forward a little, his claws thoughtfully drumming on the table. "The Bautul should endorse all this, I ken," he said. "But young orcs also ought to learn to hunt, and make skins and furs, and grow food for our kin."

Beside him, Varinn was nodding, his eyes thoughtful. "And we cannot forget scenting, and tending to our home," he said. "These are oft seen as only Grisk gifts, but they ought to be learnt by all the clans."

"Yes, indeed," said Rosa, who was still eyeing Killik with obvious dislike. "And from the Ka-esh side, we'd add drafting, mathematics, and basic medical skills. So if anything happens to us, you won't all *die* of completely preventable infections, while the mountain crumbles to dust around you!"

Killik actually snarled at that, prompting Jule to bark a surprisingly sharp growl of her own, her hand snapping out between them. "And on the Ash-Kai side," she loudly interjected, "I know we'd also welcome training in strategy, logic, and current affairs. Perhaps we need a list, Rosa?"

"Ooooh, yes, of course!" Rosa replied, apparently forgetting her ire, in favour of drawing a neat-looking table on her paper. "And a schedule. What do we say to starting each day with reading and writing, followed by an alternating rotation of each clan's priorities, with a different guest on each day? Starting with Ka-esh, perhaps?"

"With Skai," Killik pointedly countered, but it sounded halfhearted, and he angled a sharp glance toward Geva. "Or, mayhap the trained teacher ought to decide this? There may be much to ponder we have not yet thought of?"

Geva shot Killik a surprised but pleased smile, and soon found herself leading an intense—but unexpectedly respectful—discussion around orcling interests, sleeping patterns, and energy levels. And most importantly, the ages and number of anticipated students, from across all five clans. The number turned out to be lower than Geva had expected—about twelve to begin, if Tengil and Rakfi were included—but, Varinn explained, the numbers would likely increase once word began spreading further beyond the mountain.

"Many, many orcs still fear to bring their mates and young sons here," he said, earning multiple nods of assent from around the table. "If we can prove ourselves well able to support and care for their young, this shall be a great help in drawing them home again."

Geva was nodding too, her thoughts again on Kesst, on Rathgarr. On finding another way. And after another round of intense discussion, they'd roughed out a draft schedule, as well as a plan for the younger orclings—their caretakers would bring and supervise them, with the Bautul nursery offering support as needed. They'd also worked out a slate of possible guest tutors, including everyone currently at the table, as well as Geva's recommendations of Sigarr and Kesst. It also turned out that Tristan was currently helping Rosa teach reading and writing to adult orcs, and he readily offered to assist with Geva's daily instruction, as well.

"I ken I should struggle to keep excitable orclings in order," he said in his soft voice, smiling shyly at Geva across the table. "But I am glad to help teach them to read and write, if this might be of use."

"Of course you'll be of use," Rosa cut in, with a militant glint in her eye. "Tristan is quite possibly the most gifted and patient teacher in all of this mountain, isn't he, Jule?"

Tristan visibly flushed at this, but Jule roundly agreed, and even Killik only shrugged, and shoved up from the table. "Tomorrow, then," he said, reaching over to tap Rosa's schedule with his claw. "Find a room, and we shall come."

With that, he spun and stalked out, his long strides silent on the stone floor. Leaving the rest of them to blink at each other, until Jule rose up too, giving the table's remaining occupants a swift, satisfied grin. "Thanks, all," she said. "Now, how about that room, Geva? I wonder…"

She was tapping her chin, her eyes thoughtful, and then, perhaps, distinctly devious. And soon, she was eagerly ushering Geva up the corridor again, and then into... the sickroom. To where Efterar was intently working over an unfamiliar sleeping orc, while Kesst—who had been murmuring and rubbing Efterar's back—was already glancing up, his tired eyes narrowing on the sight of Jule and Geva at the door.

"So it turns out that we need to find and prepare a schoolroom," Jule announced toward Kesst, without preamble. "For tomorrow. And I have a few other commitments today, so I was hoping you could help Geva arrange it? She's going to serve as our teacher for the next few weeks."

Geva didn't miss the faint flare of interest in Kesst's tired eyes, followed by an unmistakable suspicion as he strode over toward them. "And you just couldn't find anyone else to help her, hmmm?" he asked Jule, his brows raised. "What about Rath?"

At that, Geva's chest tightened—what *was* Rathgarr doing, anyway?—but Jule was already shrugging, and thoroughly dismissing Rathgarr with a careless flap of her hand. "Busy," she said vaguely. "And don't deny it, Kesst, you're truly the best there is at choosing and outfitting rooms. Your room is perfect, isn't it, Geva?"

She shot Geva a brief but meaningful look at that, and wait, was she saying—*Kesst* had chosen and prepared their room? With the natural light, the adjoining trove-room, the generously sized wardrobe and bed? The... cradle?

It took Geva an instant to recover herself, but she nodded, and flashed Kesst a warm, grateful smile. "Our room *is* perfect," she said. "All the small details were so thoughtful. I'd be so honoured if you'd be willing to help with the schoolroom, too."

She could almost see Kesst softening, though it was accompanied by a piercing glance toward Jule. "We'll need trading-credits to buy what we need from the storage-rooms, then," he said archly. "And no complaints from you or Grim, if you don't like what we choose."

"Done," Jule said, with a satisfied grin, as she spun toward the door. "Later, then!"

Kesst watched her go with his mouth pursed, and a half-amused, half-aggrieved look in his eyes. But then he sighed, and stalked back over to Efterar, briefly murmuring in his ear before waving Geva after him toward the door.

"Well, what are you looking for, then?" he asked, a little stiff. "How many students? And what will you be doing in it?"

So Geva explained as well as she could, telling him about the Orc Mountain Educational Congress, and the plans they'd developed so far. And to her vague surprise, Kesst seemed genuinely interested, especially in the idea of a more unconventional curriculum, tailored specifically toward the clans' needs. "Those orclings *should* be learning art and music and medicine," he said decisively. "And oral history, you said? Like tales?"

"Yes, exactly," Geva said, smiling toward him. "And we were actually hoping that you might be willing to consider teaching a few sessions? Or perhaps serving as our principal advisor on the subject? Rathgarr says you're a wonderful tale-teller, and that you used to seek them out all over. You must have an incredible collection to share."

Kesst's grey cheeks had slightly pinked, though his sideways glance at Geva was sharp, searching. "Rath told you that, did he?" he said, his voice far too casual. "What else has he said about me?"

Oh. And glancing toward him, toward that uncertainty in his eyes, there was once again that quiet, certain determination, settling in Geva's chest. Another way.

"All kinds of things," she replied. "He said you're quick, and clever, and bright. That you used to know if he was upset or unhappy before even he did, and how you would always comfort him, and help him. How much he loved your tales, and how they used to come to life behind his eyes. How he's never cared for anyone else so deeply. How he considered you his own son."

Kesst was looking straight ahead now, his jaw very tight, and Geva drew in a breath, drew up more of Rathgarr's words. "And how nervous and terrified he was, when you sent for him," she added, quieter. "How much he feared for your safety, but how he couldn't bear to refuse. How he *had* to see you again. How you were the only thing that would have brought him back here again."

Kesst's gaze was still fixed on the corridor ahead, but Geva didn't miss his little sniff, or his palm rubbing at his eyes. "And then, when he finally waltzes back in here," he said, with a sigh, "first he shoves that dagger in my face, and now he starts railing on about *vengeance*. As if he's completely forgotten everything about me! Next thing I know, he'll be nagging at me to go sparring with him, so I can improve my self-defense skills, or some other such rubbish!"

Geva's mouth reflexively twitched, her thoughts flicking back to Rathgarr's words from just that morning—but then she made herself consider it, turning it over in her thoughts. Something new.

"Well, if you *were* to do something together with Rathgarr," she ventured, "what would it be? Was there anything you both enjoyed? Anything you had in common?"

She winced as she spoke, because only now was she also remembering Rathgarr saying he and Kesst had nothing in common at all—but to her vague surprise, Kesst was sighing, and running a hand through his hair. "I don't know, a good meal, maybe?" he said. "Or shopping? Rath always had good taste. In clothes and jewels, at least, because his taste in women was truly appal—"

He broke off there, angling Geva an alarmed glance, as if he'd just remembered who he was talking to. "Sorry, sister," he said, with a grimace. "I assure you, you're very much out of his usual line. Or what used to be his line, anyway."

But Geva's heart was erratically beating now, her thoughts darting back to Rathgarr's too-present, too-powerful words from what felt like months before. *Why should I not wish for a soft, sweet, eager woman to share my bed. Neither should I ever choose to mate you...*

"And look, that's a good thing, all right?" Kesst added, rather too quickly, his eyes angling toward hers. "If Rath wasn't off running roughshod over some sweet, obliging, unsuspecting creature, he was falling all over women who obviously only wanted his prick, his gold, or the thrill of bedding an orc. Honestly, to see him swearing vows to a thoughtful, capable, self-possessed *governess*, of all people"—Kesst shot her another sidelong look, perhaps a little suspicious this time—"it's just... surprising, that's all."

Geva felt herself flushing at the praise—Kesst thought she was thoughtful, capable, self-possessed?—and she desperately flailed for an appropriate answer. "Well, I do think Rathgarr has... changed, in some ways," she said. "And I know he'd absolutely love to share a meal with you, or go shopping together. Tomorrow, maybe? Although wait"—she felt her brow furrowing—"is shopping actually something you can do here?"

Kesst gave a small, too-aware smile, a wry shake of his head. "Yes, it is," he said. "And if Rath actually wants to do it, you can tell him to come ask me himself. Now"—he'd paused outside the door to a room, and waved her inside—"what do you think of this, for your schoolroom?"

Geva blinked at him, and then around at the corridor—they'd come all the way back up into the Ash-Kai wing—and then stepped into the room. It was a large, low-ceilinged room, and it was surprisingly well-illuminated, thanks to the long, jagged opening cut into the opposite wall, showing a strip of bright blue sky. And while it was very chilly, there was an empty fireplace against another wall, as well as what appeared to be adjoining doors, one on each side wall.

"There are smaller rooms attached on either side," Kesst said, leading Geva over to look into one. "It's the biggest set of unoccupied rooms in the mountain, and the whole thing actually used to belong to Kaugir—Grim's vile father, the one who ran Rath out. But after Grim offed his father, he had the rooms cleared, and ever since, he's refused to step foot in—"

"Wait," Geva interrupted, her hand hovering aimlessly in midair. "Did you just say—Grimarr killed his own *father*?"

Kesst was giving her an odd look now, and a slow, wary nod. "Yes, of course," he said. "Very graphically. I'm not usually one for violence, but Kaugir was a steaming pile of putrid *scum*, and he deserved every moment of it. He even went after my poor damned *mother*, and she had to pretend like she cared about him, pretend to be his sweet obliging mate, but—"

Kesst bit his lip, wincing, and then jerked a quick shake of his head. "Look, I'd never say Grim's been perfect," he continued, "but he saved us, when no one else could. And ever since then, he's kept trying his best. Doing everything he can to make this mountain a better, safer place for all of us."

There was a fierce glint in his eyes, as if he expected Geva to argue, or refuse. But her thoughts were already darting back to all the things Jule had already said, while her eyes again swept over the large, lovely, well-lit space. Her schoolroom.

"I love it, Kesst," she said, and she meant it. "This is perfect. It has light, heating, plenty of room to spread out and grow. And maybe using this as a schoolroom"—she gave him a hopeful half-smile—"maybe it's a bit poetic, then, isn't it? Turning it from a place of oppression, into something new?"

Kesst's answering grin was swift and stunning, and unmistakably relieved, too. "Yes, exactly, sister," he said. "Especially since it's *you*, you know? They tried to get rid of Rath forever, but now"—Kesst drew in a breath, his eyes flaring with strange, sudden meaning—"he's finally come home again, for good.

And his faithful mate will fill his enemy's old, empty rooms with life and hope again. With *joy*."

Oh. Something bright and powerful surged up in Geva's chest, her blinking eyes held to Kesst's sharp, glittering gaze. Held to his certainty, his determination, his... vision. *Home again, for good. With joy.*

"Yes, brother," she whispered, over the longing in her throat. "Let's get started."

34

———

For the rest of the day, Geva and Kesst bustled around the mountain, preparing the new schoolroom for the next day's arrival of twelve new orcling students.

Kesst continued to be incredibly helpful, what with his intimate knowledge of the mountain, and his instant awareness of how to find whatever items Geva needed. Ranging from quills and charcoal and paper—held in large supply in the Ka-esh storage-room—all the way to toys, decorations, and furnishings. In addition to the storage-rooms, it turned out that multiple rooms around the mountain contained unused furniture, and soon they'd collected a variety of shelves, tables, and mismatched chairs.

It also turned out that Kesst seemed to know every single orc in the mountain by name, and he was all too willing to make cheerful introductions, amidst a steady stream of clever, highly amusing quips and anecdotes. To the point where Geva's belly soon hurt from laughing, and she found herself becoming increasingly inured to the more shocking sights they encountered along the way, framed as they were by Kesst's casual, lighthearted commentary.

"I can see you're busy, Abjorn," he blithely said, perhaps

mid-afternoon, once they'd inadvertently walked in on the alarming sight of a gasping, bloody-faced Abjorn being pinned to a table by his neck, while a huge, unfamiliar orc viciously slammed into his upraised arse. "But we really need this table. Could you please go get yourself annihilated somewhere else?"

To Geva's ongoing astonishment, Abjorn shakily nodded, and signalled at the huge orc behind him. Who then bodily threw him onto the floor, before kneeling behind him and continuing on, as though nothing out of the ordinary was occurring.

"Thanks, brother," Kesst airily replied, as he plucked up the blood-streaked table, hanging it over his back as he turned toward the door. "And make sure you go see Eft after you've come down again, hmmm?"

Abjorn somehow managed a wave goodbye, before choking out a sound much like a cry. And despite Geva's ever-increasing tolerance toward these matters, she still found herself warily eyeing Kesst as they walked up the corridor again, her face gone decidedly hot.

"Er, I don't wish to judge," she said uncertainly, "especially when I'm still learning about orc culture and practices. But do you really think that's... safe?"

She was distantly relieved at the sight of Kesst's grimace, the swift shake of his head. "Abjorn's always been reckless," he replied, "but it's definitely been getting worse these days. Attention seeking, no doubt. Trying to get a certain taciturn Ash-Kai to take notice."

He shot Geva a knowing half-smile as he spoke, but she found herself blinking, and frowning back toward him. "You don't mean... Sigarr?" she asked, blinking again at Kesst's answering nod. "But just yesterday, Abjorn was complaining that Sigarr was too overbearing and overprotective."

But Kesst only gave a merry laugh, and another shake of his head. "That sounds like exactly what you *would* say," he informed her, "when you want the object of your lifelong worship to bend you over his knee, and have his filthy way with you."

Geva laughed too, but she still wasn't even slightly following. "But—Sigarr said Abjorn always worshipped *Rathgarr*," she replied. "Because Rathgarr was always—kind to him."

The amusement rapidly faded from Kesst's face, and he shrugged, shifting the table on his back. "Yes, well, and then Rath left," he said, clipped. "And luckily, Abjorn had someone else to turn to. Someone else to take care of him."

Right. Geva winced, the apology already rising on her mouth, but Kesst fervently waved it away, nearly dropping the table in the process. "Look, I'll get over it," he said flatly. "Eventually. I always do. And I *have* had a lot of support these past years, all right? And now that I have Eft"—his voice visibly softened—"he's always been there for me, and done everything he can to keep me safe. *Always*."

Oh. Geva couldn't seem to look away from his face, her thoughts again catching on Rathgarr, and all his cryptic, secretive plans, whatever the hell they were. Against Ulfarr, and Grimarr, and the Skai. *To avenge this*, he'd told Kesst. *To take back what is ours.*

"I'm so glad to hear you have support now," she told Kesst, her voice fervent. "And look, it's probably not my place to say, but"—she drew in a breath—"I think Rathgarr just wishes he could have been that for you. He wasn't able to be here to keep you safe, so now he wants to make up for that, however he can."

"Well, I'm sorry, but he's too late," Kesst replied, though there was no malice in his voice, only a cold, clipped certainty. "Eft and Grim have already been cleaning up around here, for *years*—and even the Skai have done a hell of a lot, too. So if Rath really wants to reconcile with me, he can forget the vengeance, and forget the gold. *Forever*."

Geva nodded, even as she took a bracing breath, gave Kesst another sidelong glance. "So there's really no one here you have… issues with anymore?" she asked, very carefully. "Not even someone like… Ulfarr?"

Kesst shot her a sharp look, but then shook his head. "No. I mean, yes, Ulfarr's often been a raging cretin, and he's always underfoot when you least want him—but that doesn't mean I want Rath to run off and kill him. Believe me, sister"—a rather unnerving glint flared in his eye—"the orcs I wanted dead? They're *dead*."

Right. That was perfectly, impeccably clear, then, and once again, Geva felt her own certainty settling, coiling even firmer than before. And she earnestly threw herself into the rest of the day's preparations, which culminated in a whirlwind jaunt through the gigantic Grisk storage-room, picking up all the last little items on her wish list. And when they returned to their lovely little schoolroom again, they found Jule and Tengil standing in the middle of it, and staring around at it with matching expressions of disbelief in their eyes.

And following their gaze, Geva felt her mouth curving up, her cheeks warming with a flushed, eager pride. The room had been set up with multiple tables, each with a few chairs clustered around it, and one wall was lined with shelves, which were filled with as many orcling-appropriate toys, tools, and games as they'd been able to find. One corner was covered in soft furs and pillows for reading or resting, and a lively fire was crackling in the fireplace, its light dancing on the bright, elaborately patterned tapestries they'd hung around the room.

"You—devious—Ash-Kai," Jule's breathless voice finally said, her eyes darting between Kesst and Geva with incredulous awe. "This is—unbelievable. Grimarr is going to be—"

She was blinking hard, her mouth pulling into a rather weepy, wavering smile. "It's so thoughtful," she said, on a strange little gulp. "Thank you. Both of you. Gods, I—"

She didn't finish, flapping her hand at her face, while Tengil, still in her arms, had begun to look visibly alarmed, giving a high-pitched little mewl. Prompting Kesst to stride over and pluck him out of Jule's arms, even as he gave her a companionable-looking bump with his shoulder.

"You like it too, Bitty-Grim?" he asked lightly. "Will you come in here every day and poo all over the place?"

Tengil brightened at that, his eyes darting meaningfully toward Geva, and then toward the wall opposite the fire. And Geva gave a shaky little laugh of her own as she brought up Amhalia, and made her roar to life in the firelight.

"I have returned!" she announced in her deep dragon voice, as Amhalia's huge shadow writhed triumphantly upon the wall. "I have found a new room, with even more delicious mosquitoes to eat! Yum yum!"

Tengil was already squealing with contagious glee, wriggling in Kesst's arms. And after watching for a moment, his mouth slowly twitching up, Kesst thrust Tengil back toward Jule, and then joined in. Roaring up with a huge, flailing, sharp-toothed dragon of his own, complete with a showy head-dress—Kesst's claws—on top. But of course, Amhalia was highly offended by competition for her mosquitoes, and soon the two dragons were wildly out-competing one another, each one's antics more ridiculous than the next.

It went on until they were all laughing too much to speak, and Tengil's wild shrieks had begun to verge close to meltdown territory—so Geva made Amhalia say a showy farewell, and then trot off for her poo and nap. And it was only then, with Tengil still delightedly giggling, that Geva caught sight of Rathgarr leaning against the schoolroom doorway, where he'd perhaps been watching all this, his eyes glimmering strangely in the firelight.

The room had gone starkly silent, and Geva belatedly smiled, and strode over to meet Rathgarr at the door. "There you are, love," she said, as she leaned up to press a kiss to his warm cheek. "How was your day?"

Rathgarr still had that strange look in his eyes, and he slipped his arm around her waist, drawing her close. "Not near as gainful as yours, I ken," he said, with an unmistakably appreciative glance around the room. "You have done all this today?"

"Yes, with Kesst's help," Geva replied, flashing a grateful grin over toward him. "Your brother is a force to be reckoned with, love."

Rathgarr's warm eyes had followed hers toward Kesst, as a slow, affectionate smile curved on his mouth. "Ach, I ken," he said softly. "Thank you for helping my mate thus, little brother."

Kesst waved it away, though his cheeks were unmistakably flushed. "Of course," he replied. "She's lovely, and it still beggars belief that she's voluntarily mated to *you*. Now I'm late for Eft, so—"

He stepped toward the door, his brows meaningfully raised, and both Geva and Rathgarr hurriedly moved aside, so he could pass through. But once he was in the corridor, he turned back toward them, his shoulders squared. "I'll stop by tomorrow to see how you fare, sister," he said. "As for *you*"—he exhaled as he glanced at Rathgarr, his mouth very slightly quirking—"don't get seed on the orclings' clean new furniture, it's in *very* poor taste."

With that, he spun and stalked off down the corridor, followed closely by Jule, who gave Geva's hand a quick little squeeze on the way by, her eyes still unmistakably bright. "We'll be here tomorrow too," she said. "Thank you again, sister."

It left Geva and Rathgarr standing alone in the schoolroom, Rathgarr's hand spasming against Geva's waist. And when she glanced up toward him, he was looking back down at her, again with that strange shifting meaning in his eyes.

And then, without warning, he grasped her waist, spinning her around—and then he bent her double over the nearest table, his hands yanking up her shift, lingering on her bare arse.

"What," Geva gulped at him, "the hell, Rathgarr! This is a *schoolroom!*"

But oh, that was a low, lazy laugh from behind her, the feel of his booted foot bumping her leg sideways. "Ach, and all the orclings are now down at dinner," he drawled at her, as he slid her other leg out, too. "And any good Ash-Kai would wish to mark his mate in a newly christened room thus, and thus stake his claim. Most of all"—his voice deepened—"in a room that was once his enemy's."

Gods curse him, because Geva could already feel that silken swelling hardness, seeking warm and hungry between her now-parted legs. Enough to make her gasp and shudder all over, nearly losing her footing—and with another firm grip of his hands, Rathgarr lifted her knees up onto the table, spreading them wide apart, while she scrabbled to find balance on her hands.

"Even better," he murmured, as his finger gave a slow, proprietary swipe down her open, already-slick crease, followed by an audacious little nudge inside. "Your hungry little womb has missed me this day, ach, poppet? It has longed for my tending and filling?"

There was truly no answer to this, not when she was bared and spread wide on a schoolroom table, with an orc shame-lessly stroking at her clutching, wide-open heat. And saying these things, why was he still saying these things, as if other orcs were listening—but they weren't. Were they? It was just—them. Just this. Something new.

"Of course not," Geva managed, as steadily as she could, as she felt Rathgarr tilting her out more toward him, replacing his finger with a much larger, much rounder press of heat. "I barely thought of you at—*fuck!*"

He'd slammed inside with a hard, powerful thrust, plunging all the way to the hilt in one devastating cant of his hips. And then he stayed there, sunk deep, circling slow and dizzying inside. "This is it, my stubborn schoolmarm," he said approvingly. "You curse and squeal and beg for me upon this table, and take joy in your deep Ash-Kai ploughing."

Joy. That word pulling strangely in Geva's belly, her body desperately grasping at his invasion inside her—and of course, that was when he chose to draw out, dragging that slick hard heat slow and relentless from her desperate clinging clutch.

"I said beg, poppet," he drawled, with a gentle slap of his warm hand at her arse. "Tell me how much you have missed me. How you have craved my touch and my taking. How you long for me to claim you here, and make you *reek* of me."

Oh, how did he keep doing this, Geva's frantic heat gripping at the hard prodding end of him, now jutted just slightly into her slick soft wetness. And when another slap stung at her arse, rang through the roiling craving, she cried out, her back arching, her body fighting to sink deep, to swallow him whole...

"I missed you all day, Rathgarr," she gasped at him, between her strangled breaths. "Needed your touch and your taking. Needed you to claim me, and make me *reek* of you."

And yes, that low hissing growl was just what she wanted, what she craved, that stunning hardness sinking just a little deeper, back where it belonged. "Need you to take me like this," she breathed. "Need you to tend me, plough me, make me yours. In the room of your enemy."

Rathgarr's groan hissed deeper, rumbling harsh and low, and he slammed the rest of the way inside, filling her with his hot hard strength, making her shake all over. "Because he's gone, but you're—still here," she gasped, as he drew out, and slammed in again. "Making this room—ours. Making—a new way."

Rathgarr was taking her in earnest now, hammering in again and again, and Geva needed it so much, needed to gulp it down and drown in it. He wanted her, he wanted to make her his, to stake his claim and scent this entire room of them and—

And oh, he was already grinding in and surging out, his invading heft thrumming and shuddering as it sprayed his seed deep, pouring her thick and messy and full. As he marked her, claimed her, here—and suddenly that felt strangely, impossibly meaningful, almost like an indulgence, a gift. Acknowledging her efforts, her full day's work, and rewarding her, by filling her with his sweet fresh scent, by claiming this room, making it theirs.

"Thank you," she breathed, before she could possibly stop it, as she kept arching for him, drinking him, milking out every-thing he would give her. As she could finally feel him slowing, settling, softening again. "You're such a good Ash-Kai. So good to me."

She didn't think she imagined his hard, choked gasp, the brief flaring shudder of that heat still inside her—until he swiftly, suddenly drew out. Leaving her gaping, empty, untouched, the wetness already beginning to spill, but for...

"Ohhhh," Geva moaned, because oh, oh, something else was there instead. Something slick and soft and glorious, pressing warm and sweet against her wet dripping heat. Some-thing... new. Rathgarr's *mouth.*

She again shuddered all over, so fierce she nearly lost her balance, because, oh, sweet gods, he'd fallen to his knees on the floor behind her, so he could tilt his head up, press his hot, open mouth up against her shivering, leaking crease. So she could pour out his own mess back into his mouth, feeding him with his own gushing seed, oh this wasn't actually happening, it wasn't—

But it was, damn him, it was, his glorious tongue even slip-ping up into her slick spurting heat, as if he was licking it, welcoming it, sucking it out of her. And she could hear him swallowing, could hear the lurid slick sounds this was making, as if he was feasting upon her, making their fresh rich scents his own...

Geva's release flashed sudden and shocking, trampling over her in throb after throb. And oh hell, Rathgarr actually chuckled as he kept licking, kept swallowing, kept moving that tongue just the way she needed it, until the impossible wheeling pleasure slowly faded, into the quiet sweetness of his open, softly seeking kiss.

"Do you have any more for me, poppet?" he breathed, between gentle swipes of his tongue, making Geva instantly clamp upon it—but yes, yes, there was more, oozing out from inside her, into his warm, waiting mouth. And then a little more, and a little more, squeezing from her in hard dizzying pulses, until nothing more would come, and she was finally, fully empty.

She waited, still gasping, revelling in every surreal instant, as she felt him gently licking her clean. Until he gave her one last kiss, and then drew away, and pulled her shift down again.

Geva hauled in one more deep, shaky breath—and then, without thinking, she furiously flailed around to find him. To clutch at him, to put her hands to his stunning, watching face, to see the light and the amusement shifting like that in his eyes.

"What in the—sweet—shrieking—*gods*—" she stammered, but it wasn't even making sense, and in return Rathgarr laughed, and blatantly licked at his wet, shiny face with his long black tongue. Making her groan again at just the sight of it, her vision spinning hard enough that she had to fall back onto the table, and draw in great gulping gasps through her mouth. Damn him. *Bless* him.

Rathgarr was still laughing, the sound husky and approving, and in a sudden movement, he dropped himself onto his back on the table beside her. Making it creak slightly beneath his weight, but thankfully it seemed sturdy enough to hold them both—though in this moment, Geva would not have cared if it completely collapsed beneath them.

"That was—" she began, but words had utterly failed her again, her trembling hands dragging at her hot face. "*Gods*. Th-thank you."

Rathgarr laughed again, and gave her elbow a companionable-feeling bump with his. "I did not wish to spill any seed in your pretty new schoolroom," he replied lightly. "Kesst was right, this should be in very poor taste."

Geva could only reply with a laughing groan, a shake of her head on the hard wood, as Rathgarr gave her elbow another little bump. "This room is good work, poppet," he said, sounding suddenly almost serious. "I am... amazed, in truth, that Grimarr should allow the Ash-Kai throne room to be overrun by orclings."

The Ash-Kai throne room? Geva opened one eye to look at Rathgarr, whose head was tilted, looking back toward her. His forehead furrowed, as if he was genuinely confused by this.

"Well, as far as I've been able to tell, Grimarr hated his father, and everything he stood for," Geva replied, her voice somewhat steadier than before. "Did you know he actually *killed* him? And Kesst said Grimarr's refused to step into this room ever since. He thought it would be fitting, to make this into a schoolroom, and a place of joy."

Rathgarr didn't reply to that, his mouth pursing, and Geva took another slow, bracing breath. "I really don't think Grimarr is your enemy, Rathgarr," she said. "Kesst seems to care about him very deeply. And"—she pulled in another breath—"today, Kesst again made it very, *very* clear that he doesn't want any vengeance, against anyone, ever. Not against the Skai, or even Ulfarr. He said the Skai have actually been *helping* to clean things up around here, these past few years. He said that any orc he wants dead is already dead."

Rathgarr still hadn't spoken, his eyes now intent on the stone ceiling above them, his jaw very tight. Clearly not wanting to talk about this, and Geva exhaled a heavy, resigned sigh, her body tilting toward him on the table, her hand snaking over his waist. Another way.

"Also, Kesst would like you to ask him out for a meal tomorrow," she said, as lightly as she could. "And a shopping trip. Which I didn't realize was possible here, but then I saw the

Grisk storage-room! That place is bigger than any shop I've ever seen in my *life.*"

At her mention of Kesst's invitation, Rathgarr instantly jerked to stiffness—but then he slowly softened again beneath her gently stroking touch. "Ach, I have heard about this new Grisk hoard," he said. "But"—his eyes narrowed at her—"they would not freely give their goods away, so how did *you* shop there? You did not spend your coin on this?! I thought you meant to save this for the sea."

His voice had gone very sharp, and Geva reflexively flinched, her eyes focusing back on the stone ceiling, the fire-light still flickering upon it. "No, I didn't spend anything," she said thinly. "Jule gave us a very generous allowance of trading-credits for all this. On top of the salary she's offered, too."

There was a brief silence from Rathgarr, and then a strange-sounding harrumph. "Ach, this woman seeks to curry your favour with gifts and flattery, I ken," he said. "This is a long-standing Ash-Kai scheme, ach? It is clear that she has been sharing Grimarr's bed for too long, and has been well tainted by his seed."

Geva bit back her groan—gods, had he not heard *anything* she'd just said about Grimarr?—But she made herself focus on the second part of that statement, fighting to keep her voice light. "You don't actually think women can be *tainted* by orcs' seed, do you?" she asked, attempting an incredulous smile toward him. "And what, then they take on all their orcs' worst tendencies?"

"Ach, indeed," Rathgarr replied grimly, though his mouth was curling up again, too. "Have you not met that Skai woman, Maria? Or that Grisk, Ella. Or"—his eyes glinted, and he propped himself up onto his elbow to peer down at Geva's face—"this Ka-esh chit Rosa. She cornered me today down in the Ka-esh wing, and would not leave me be until I had read a dozen of those pamphlets, and told her all I had ever thought upon them! And then she claimed this was upon *your* advice, poppet!"

Geva's mouth was opening and closing, though her smile felt far easier than before. "Well, given all your experience, I knew you would have valuable guidance to offer," she said, a little defensively. "Which I'm sure you did, didn't you? And also"—she tried for a glare back up toward him—"that doesn't even slightly prove your point about the—*seed-tainting!*"

"Wrong, poppet," Rathgarr countered, with an imperious arch of his brow. "Rosa is as though Abjorn had moulted into a small, shrill female, who is only consumed by pamphlets, rather than fighting. Whilst *you*, my devious pet—"

He broke off there, grimacing, but Geva couldn't stop grinning up at his face. "Are you telling me that I've already been tainted, too? And what, the longer I stay with you, the more smug and sneaky and greedy I'll become?"

Rathgarr was looking both annoyed and amused now, but perhaps the amusement was winning out, because he barked a choked, reluctant-sounding laugh. "Just so, poppet," he said, with a sigh. "Just so."

But looking at his eyes, at that warmth quivering on his mouth, it occurred to Geva that he didn't truly seem to mind. That perhaps—perhaps he just needed more time. Needed to look forward. One step at a time. Something new.

That thought again stayed with her throughout the rest of the evening, as she and Rathgarr first straightened out their clothes, and then went for a late supper in the kitchen. And then, much to Geva's astonished delight, Rathgarr indeed led her back up to the Ash-Kai common-room, where they danced until they were both sweaty and gasping, their bodies again grinding up hard together in the deep thrumming firelight.

And this time, when Rathgarr led her to the bench, he gently but purposefully guided her down onto her knees, between his sprawled-wide legs. Kneeling, on the floor, in a room full of watching Ash-Kai, while he deliberately unfastened his belt, and drew out that rigid, swollen length, already leaking a thick bead of white.

"You are overdue for a good thick load in your belly, sweetling," he said coolly, the words firing a shocked flare of heat to Geva's groin. "I should not wish my clan to think I am not well feeding my mate, ach? I must make you hale and fat for me."

Oh, gods curse him, because Geva's tongue was already brushing her lips, even as her eyes darted uneasily around at the busy room, at the increasing feel of prickling orc gazes on her back. "Um, I don't think I need any—help, in that department," she stammered, which was absolutely the wrong point, most definitely. Or was it, because Rathgarr had raised a challenging eyebrow toward her, and slid his warm strong hand around the back of her neck. Drawing her closer, as he aimed that flushed, leaking head straight toward her mouth.

"You shall take as much help as I wish to give you, poppet," he ordered, with a rather dangerous glint in his eye. "Now suck. Show them how pretty you are, with your Ash-Kai deep in your throat. Show them how well you can please me."

And oh, he was nudging it up against her mouth, brushing that sweet silky seed against her lips. And at the first taste of it, Geva felt herself groaning, nodding, agreeing—and then hurling herself into it, perhaps harder than she ever had before. Sucking him just the way he liked, just the way he'd taught her, her mouth soft and sweet at first, her eyes on his, until she was slurping and caressing him with desperate abandon, his hands buried in her hair, his flesh jammed in her throat.

And despite her certain awareness of their watching audience, all that mattered was that look in Rathgarr's eyes, that affection, that appreciation, that approval. Perhaps just for the other orcs' benefit, but it felt so strangely, sharply intimate, his body buried hard and deep inside her, pulsing and flaring and leaking for her, priming itself to pump out for her. To fill her, and feed her, and fatten her for him, and—

She moaned a muffled cry as he finally surged out, bending double over her as he streamed hot plumes of seed into her throat. As he moaned, too, the sound deep and guttural and raw, his hands clutched hard to her head, holding her there for him, making sure she swallowed every last hot, succulent drop.

When he'd finished emptying himself, and Geva had carefully sucked him clean, she could scarcely seem to meet his eyes anymore, her body trembling on the floor between his knees. At least, until his warm hand slid around to her hot cheek, tilting her face back up toward him.

"Good, my pretty poppet," he murmured. "Very, very good. You make me so proud, ach, my clever schoolmarm? You have learnt your lessons so well, that you have mayhap now gained the sweetest mouth I have ever known."

Oh. Damn. And again, perhaps he'd just said it for the others' benefit, to make sure they believed the charade—but that warm, affectionate approval stayed in his eyes as he drew her up onto her shaky feet, and escorted her from the room. And after a brief stop by the Skai bath, where they both quickly washed up, he guided Geva back into their bedroom, wrapped her in his fur on the bed, and plunked what appeared to be a basket of snacks into her hands.

"I have ruined your braids, I ken," he said from behind her, a little offhandedly, as she felt a gentle tug on one damp, beaded end. "Mayhap I shall do them again, to ready you for your first day's teaching?"

Geva was certainly not about to refuse, flashing him an eager, shy-feeling grin over her shoulder. And soon she was contentedly curled up on the bed, sampling the fruit and nuts from the basket, while Rathgarr's gentle, deft hands combed and oiled her hair, and massaged her scalp. And this time, he put in multiple smaller braids, taking far longer than before, but there wasn't even a thought of moving or complaining. Only sitting there, feeling his hands move, feeling the prickles of pleasure with each careful touch.

It was so easy to fall asleep after that, tucked into her usual place against his chest, his big hand spread wide over her belly. And when morning came, this time he was still there, his breath hot on her neck, his warm hand slipping down to her thigh, and pulling it up high, so his heavy pulsing hardness could slip up in between, while his fingers eased around to her front.

He took her just like that, grinding in again and again while his clever fingers circled and pressed, until Geva cried out her pleasure, and he'd surged up deep inside. And without thinking, she reached up for his head, twisting around so she could breathe him in, his soft, supple lips just a whisper away…

But then he pulled backwards, clearing his throat, his eyes darting intently away. And for an instant, there was a sudden, crashing surge of disappointment, because he still couldn't even kiss her, after all that? Still?

But no, no, she was doing this. Something new. One step at a time.

"Will you come see me off in the schoolroom this morning?" she asked, as easily as she could. "Wish me luck surviving all those orclings?"

She could hear Rathgarr's swallow, but then he nodded, his eyes still fixed beyond her. "You shall more than survive, poppet," he said. "You shall have them all eating out of your pretty Ash-Kai hands by the end of the morning, you ken."

Geva made a face at him, but it suddenly felt easy to smile again, and to turn her focus toward preparing for the day. Cleaning up in the latrine, and then dressing in the thick black shift Rathgarr handed over—no doubt, the best possible choice among them for the day, if she was continuing to forego regular dresses. And then, after stalking into the trove-room, Rathgarr reappeared with what seemed to be a large, coiled gold cuff—and then he carefully drew all her new braids back into it, clasping them together at the nape of her neck.

"To spare them from any grabby orcling fingers," he said gruffly. "Now, are you ready?"

Geva gave a shaky-feeling nod, but as they walked up to the schoolroom together, she felt her fingernails digging into his arm, her heartbeat rising with every step. Gods, what if she had no idea what she was getting into. What if she mucked this up. What if she—

"Enough of that, poppet," Rathgarr abruptly said, as he drew her to a halt, just down the corridor from the schoolroom. "You shall be a good and clever and patient teacher for these orclings, and they shall be blessed to have you on their side. Ach?"

Geva attempted a nod and a smile, which he returned with a sharp little growl, and a gentle slap at her arse. "You dare to question me, my sulky schoolmarm?" he demanded. "You ken this is how you shall earn more of your mate's hungry tongue, once you are done with your day's work?"

Oh. Geva's face instantly heated, her breath escaping in a choked little gasp, and Rathgarr grinned as he brazenly grasped at her arse. "You will behave," he purred at her. "You will show your Ash-Kai how good you are. Ach?"

It was... another challenge. Another game. And Geva was nodding and smiling again, but it felt genuine this time, her body leaning into his touch. "I'll try," she murmured. "I'll do my best."

"Good," he replied, with a satisfied gleam in his eyes. "Now, get to work, poppet. Impress me."

35

———

Even despite Rathgarr's challenge, Geva fully expected him to turn around, and disappear for the rest of the schoolday. At least, until they stepped into the schoolroom, and found Jule, Tengil, Rosa, and Tristan already all there, and all eyeing them with eager anticipation.

"Oh, Rathgarr's come to help, too!" Rosa exclaimed, her hands clasped to her heart. "And how *convenient*, because I've brought along new drafts of the pamphlets, with all the edits we discussed! I'm sure you won't mind reviewing them for a moment?"

Rathgarr angled Geva a wry, meaningful look, but then he sighed, and gave Rosa a surprisingly tolerant smile. "Ach, I should be glad to help," he said. "What have you altered, then?"

Soon he was embroiled in what appeared to be an involved discussion with an excitedly chattering Rosa, the expression on his face very similar to the one he wore around Abjorn. While Geva smiled to herself, and turned her focus to putting the finishing touches on the room, and readying it for the morning's first arrivals.

Her goal for the day was really just to meet all their new students, make them feel comfortable, and offer them a fun taste of what was to come—so together with Jule and Tristan, she set out a variety of possible activities, including paper and charcoal, some dice-games she'd found in the Ash-Kai storage-room, and a variety of toys and carvings, including a perfectly carved set of building-blocks from the Skai storage-room. She'd also kept the wall opposite the fire clear, and after drawing a few mosquitoes, spiders, and butterflies on the wall with chalk, she set the basket of chalk nearby, hopefully to tempt some orclings who might like to draw, too.

Her heartbeat had begun rising again as she'd worked, her palms clammy and hot, and she couldn't help whirling around, and perhaps even slightly staggering, at the sight of someone walking through the door. It was Varinn, who was first on the guest teaching schedule, and he was blinking around at the room with unmistakable awe in his eyes—and then grinning down toward Timo, who was hovering close behind him, together with a similar-aged orc Geva didn't recognize.

For an instant, Geva stood there frozen, her breaths locked in her chest—when suddenly, a warm, familiar body eased up beside her, a hand slipping around to her back. Rathgarr, giving her a rueful little smile as he nudged her forward, toward the door.

And again, it helped. Enough that Geva could smile and step forward, welcoming Timo and Varinn, and then introducing herself to the new orc, a light-eyed, grey-skinned Grisk named Trygve. Who, Timo proudly informed her, was a brilliant fighter, and likely to become an excellent Grisk nose, as well.

Geva warmly congratulated Trygve on his impressive-sounding skill, and invited the two of them to choose a table, and perhaps to think of a scenting game they could play with the younger ones, after Varinn had led the day's lesson. A suggestion that was thankfully well-received, and soon Timo and Trygve were chattering together at a table, and sketching out complicated-looking plans with the paper and charcoal.

They were soon followed by a smiling Ella, with a squirming Rakfi perched on her hip, and three more young Grisk orcs hovering shyly around her. All of them were perhaps between six and eight years old, and once Geva had knelt to greet them, they introduced themselves as Bram, Njal, and Tyr. They were all cousins, it turned out, and their fathers had recently moved to the mountain together, now that—according to a very solemn Bram—they weren't likely to be sent off to war by the heartless, horrible Ash-Kai.

Geva's smile felt a little fixed at that, her eyes angling uneasily toward Rathgarr, who had still been hovering close nearby. And to her genuine astonishment, he came over to kneel beside her, and produced what appeared to be three small, slim wooden swords, with thick strands of softening cloth wrapped around them.

"Ach, we Ash-Kai now ken this was a great wrong," Rathgarr said, his voice just as solemn as Bram's had been. "So now, we only seek to spar for fun amongst ourselves. Should you like to play with these, and try this?"

The three small orcs eyed Rathgarr with wary, wide-eyed suspicion, but then Tyr snatched one of the swords from his hand, swiftly followed by Bram and Njal. And soon the three of them were racing around the room, chasing one another between the tables and laughing with shrill, delighted glee.

"Rathgarr!" Geva hissed at him, once she'd found her voice again. "You can't just give weapons to children in the schoolroom! And most of all as an *apology* for the Ash-Kai sending them to *war*?!"

But Rathgarr appeared entirely unconcerned, his eyes watching the racing orclings with surprising fondness. "You shall be thanking me once they are tired enough to sit and listen for a spell," he said, with a shrug. "And better to give them safer swords now, rather than waiting for them to bring their own. One time, I near killed Sigarr with a sharp table-leg I had found, ach?"

Geva shot a helpless look toward Ella and Varinn, both of whom were still standing nearby. Ella with similar-looking commiseration on her face, watching Rakfi frantically crawl around the room, while Varinn was following the shouting orclings with distinctly fond eyes, too. "Ach, orclings are sturdy, and they know enough not to harm one another," Varinn told Geva, with a good-natured shrug. "But if you are truly vexed over this, mayhap we can keep them penned in over there?"

He'd nodded toward one of the adjoining rooms, which were both still currently empty, so Geva finally threw up her hands, and agreed. Which was just as well, because there were already more orclings arriving, spilling with their caretakers into the room. First were three small, adorable Ka-esh named Isak, Ulfrik, and Erik, followed by two preteen Bautul blood-brothers named Hagen and Hauk, both wearing matching pendants with teeth around their necks. And then, a smiling Maria brought in Bjorn, followed by Killik and—

"Ulfarr?" Geva gasped with genuine dismay, glancing toward where Rathgarr had been setting up the three small Ka-esh at the table with the building-blocks. And yes, Rathgarr was visibly stiffening too, his eyes cold and narrow on Ulfarr, who was frowning back toward him with equal hostility. At least... until Ulfarr's gaze dropped back down toward where a slim figure was stepping out from behind him, his pointy chin uplifted, his black claws gripping deep into Ulfarr's meaty arm.

It was—another orcling. Or rather, another half-grown orc, perhaps around the same age as Timo and Trygve. And Geva belatedly pasted on a smile, and lurched over to welcome him and introduce herself. But the new Skai didn't speak back, only regarding her with a wary, uncertain gaze, until Killik stepped up beside him, clasping his hand to the young orc's slim shoulder.

"This is Sune, of Clan Skai," Killik said smoothly. "He is staying with us as our ward, for a spell."

Their ward. Wait, *Killik and Ulfarr's* ward? But based on the vicious glower from Ulfarr's eyes, and the heavy clap of his big hand on Sune's opposite shoulder, this indeed seemed to be the case. And suddenly, blinking at this young orc's uneasy face, Geva was painfully, powerfully reminded of Cecily, lost and lonely and parted from everything she'd known.

"Welcome to our schoolroom, Sune," Geva said, pressing her fist to her heart in the now-familiar greeting the orcs seemed to prefer. "We're so glad to have you with us."

This Sune orc blinked at her, but then he also put his fist to his heart, and gave a slight bow of his head. Prompting Killik to give his shoulder a companionable little shake, his eyes flicking toward Geva with something that might have been approval.

"Sune favours speaking with his hands, ach?" Killik said coolly. "It is oft how Skai speak, and we should not ask him otherwise, should he not wish."

"Of course," Geva said, her voice firm, her fist again pressing to her heart. "Though I'm afraid to say I'm not currently familiar with Skai sign language, but I'll certainly do my best to learn."

This earned her another brief, approving nod from Killik, and a skeptical-sounding grunt from Ulfarr. Who, much to Geva's alarm, was again glowering toward Rathgarr at the Ka-esh table—and unsurprisingly, Rathgarr was glowering straight back, his body taut and rigid all over.

"So Sune, have you met Timo and Trygve?" Geva hurriedly asked, gesturing toward where they were both watching with wary eyes from their own table. "If not, perhaps I can introduce you? And"—she glanced back toward Killik, and then Ulfarr, too—"you two are welcome to stay, but we'll likely finish around noon, if you'd rather come back then?"

Killik curtly nodded at that, angling toward the door—but when Ulfarr showed no sign of following, Killik rolled his eyes, grasped at his belt, and yanked him out after him. A development that seemed to reduce the room's growing tension by a significant degree, and Geva bit back her sigh of relief in favour of smiling again at Sune, and waving him after her toward Timo and Trygve. Who were still looking distinctly uneasy, but after Geva's overly enthusiastic introduction—including the crucial bit about the sign language—Timo gave Sune a tentative smile, followed by a few careful movements of his slim hand.

"Oh, you know sign language too!" Geva exclaimed, with genuine pleasure. "Perhaps you could help teach us, Timo?"

It had perhaps been the wrong thing to say, based on the frantic shake of Timo's head, and the deepening flush in his cheeks. "Only a little," he said. "Baldr has been showing me some, as he and his mates oft speak thus, also."

Well, that was still very helpful, and Geva firmly told Timo so, while silently resolving to enlist Baldr for a few teaching sessions. And once she returned her attention to the rest of the room, it was to the realization that everyone had somehow been settled at the tables. Even the three young Grisk, though they were all clinging tightly to their new swords, and Rathgarr was now sharing their table. His body almost comically large in contrast to theirs, his brows lifting as he held Geva's gaze.

Show your Ash-Kai how good you are, he'd said. *Impress me.*

And perhaps Geva had even nodded at him, her own mouth drawing up, her eyes sweeping over the room's assembled, bright-eyed students. Fourteen of them in total, including Tengil and Rakfi, even more than they'd hoped for. One step at a time. A new way.

And again, it felt almost easy, natural, to step to the front of the room, her head high, her shoulders back. "Hi, and welcome to Orc Mountain's first school!" she told the class, with a genuine grin. "We're going to have so much fun learning and playing together, right?"

Her words were met by a round of enthusiastic shouts and stomps, Rathgarr very prominent among them, and Geva's smile toward him might have been almost weepy this time. But again, it made it easy to finish introducing herself, and then to go around and introduce everyone at the tables, as well. And then to talk through their plans and schedule, including how they would spend some time reading and writing each day, followed by a rotation of special guests from across the five clans.

"And on your clan's day, we'll be especially happy to have your help," Geva told them. "To start, today we're going to focus on the Grisk. And our special guest Varinn will teach us about scenting, right, Varinn?"

Varinn had already come over to stand beside her, smiling easily at their watching audience of orclings, some of them already squirming in their seats. "Ach, thank you, sister," he replied. "For this first lesson, we shall try tracking each other's scents. But... amidst some hindrances. Alma?"

He'd glanced expectantly toward the door, where a smiling Alma was indeed striding in, holding a large platter before her. A platter that was piled high with an abundance of fresh-looking tarts and cakes, and even Geva could smell their sweet, mouthwatering scents wafting through the room.

The orclings all instantly snapped to attention, their faces turned toward the treats, and one of the smaller Ka-esh had even slipped out of his chair toward them—until Varinn laughed, and put up his hand. "Not yet," he said. "We shall all get a treat, but first, we must earn it. Now, who should like to go first?"

Multiple orclings shouted and waved their hands at once, and Varinn called up one of the Bautul brothers, Hauk. And then he tied a thick strip of cloth over Hauk's eyes, before waving over the three small Ka-esh, and placing a cake into each of their outstretched little hands.

"Now, no eating yet," he said firmly. "And I need one more orc for Hauk to find, one whose scent he does not well know. Bjorn, mayhap?"

Bjorn willingly sidled forward, though his eyes were very wary on Varinn, and then on the cakes. But Varinn returned this with another encouraging smile, and knelt down to Bjorn's level. "Now, I need you to be a good Skai," he said, "and sneak quietly about this room *without* a cake, whilst Hauk stays here, and seeks to follow your scent. And whilst"—he grinned at the three waiting Ka-esh—"our three hindrances also run about with their cakes, and seek to draw him from finding you."

The three small Ka-esh excitedly murmured at this, and soon the entire room was gasping and shouting and laughing, fully invested in the game. In the three little Ka-esh gleefully running about while Hauk stood there blindfolded, inhaling deeply as he pointed around the room, attempting—but not always succeeding—to follow a very quiet, watchful Bjorn, who was slowly sneaking about the tables.

"Good, brother!" Varinn said, once Hauk could consistently follow Bjorn's scent. "Now, you take a cake, and become a hindrance for us, whilst one of our Ka-esh takes your place. But first, he can eat his cake, ach?"

He winked down toward little Isak, who was excitedly bobbing in front of him, his cake already half-eaten in his tiny claws. And then they did it all again, and again, and again, and between each round Varinn loudly explained how to sharpen one's focus on the most important scent at hand, and how distracting other scents could be, especially when they were something the orc found very appealing.

"My kin-brother Nattfarr has a very good nose," he told them, with a teasing glance toward where Ella was smiling from a table, while Rakfi crawled in circles around her chair. "But when Nattfarr first... *met* our sister Ella, he was nearly killed by men, so caught he was in the thrall of her scent. We do *not* wish to be Nattfarr, ach?"

Geva laughed along with the rest, from where she'd been sitting at the Grisk table with Rathgarr—though it occurred to her that he was very intently not meeting her eyes. As if this scent-distraction was something he'd also experienced before, and would rather not admit—and suddenly her thoughts were swirling with the memory of the first day they'd met. With the wardrobe. With how he hadn't smelled the men approaching, despite claiming he could easily do so.

It was one more thing to add to the rest, maybe even one more step. And truly, so was the fact that Rathgarr was even still here, still staying with her, helping her, supporting her. And even, a little while later, nudging her, squeezing meaningfully at her knee, when Kesst and Grimarr appeared at the door.

Grimarr was standing very still, blinking toward the mass of shrieking, running, cake-strewn orclings, while Kesst's mouth was already twitching into a grin, his eyes sparkling with delighted amusement. And after a companionable bump at Grimarr's shoulder, Kesst strode over toward Geva and Rathgarr, and dropped down into Bram's recently vacated chair.

"Well, this has become a terrifying hellscape," he said, with another amused glance toward the surrounding chaos. "You two still surviving in here?"

Rathgarr's body had inevitably jerked to that familiar stiffness, his hand now clutching almost painfully at Geva's knee, but she easily touched at it, caressing him, as she grinned back toward Kesst. "What, you're not looking forward to your turn?" she said lightly, pointing toward the schedule they'd affixed to the wall. "You're coming up soon, you know."

Kesst rolled his eyes, though his smile toward the nearest screeching Ka-esh looked genuinely fond. "Oh, I'm planning to tell them a highly involved tale about falling asleep," he said, a little offhandedly. "Rath used to love that one, didn't you, Rath?"

Rathgarr's hand spasmed against Geva's knee, but she kept stroking, perhaps squeezing a little too hard, and she could see him drawing in air, letting it out. "Ach, that was a good one," he finally replied, his throat bobbing. "I have missed it, little brother. As I have—missed you. Do you ken"—he glanced briefly at Geva, and then back again—"might you have time to spare for a meal with me today? Or mayhap a shopping trip?"

Kesst shot Geva a wry, knowing look, but then sighed, and shrugged. "Fine, why not," he said dismissively. "Now?"

Rathgarr's glance toward Geva was hesitant this time, but she was already smiling back at him, and firmly patting his hand. "You should definitely go, and enjoy yourself," she told him. "You've been such a help, love, truly. Thank you."

His smile back was warm, and a little apologetic, and once he'd stood to follow Kesst, he even bent to press his mouth to her head. "Later, then, poppet," he murmured, soft. "Be ready for my tongue, ach?"

Oh, gods, it was just what she'd needed—and perhaps hadn't needed—to hear, but it seemed to provide another much-needed burst of energy to push through the rest of the day. To help wrap up Varinn's game, fervently thanking him and Alma for making it so much fun, and then helping Timo and Trygve—and a silent but observant Sune—guide the still-frantic orclings through their own game, which involved even more screeching and racing about the room. And by the time the adults began returning, most of the orclings seemed genuinely worn out, and little Isak instantly fell asleep on his bemused-looking father's shoulder.

"I ken Ash-Kai are not all so bad after all, Papa," Bram was gravely saying, to his big, scarred Grisk father. "They did not even seek to send me to war!"

Geva had thankfully thought to tuck away the wooden swords prior to this, promising they would safely await the Grisks' return in the morning, and she waved goodbye to Bram and his father with as much innocence as she could muster. And soon nearly all the orclings were gone, and Geva was saying goodbye to Sune, using the palm-out *farewell* sign Timo had shown her amidst the hubbub.

"Thank you so much for coming," she told him, angling an uneasy glance up toward a forbidding, frowning Ulfarr. "It was so lovely to have Sune with us. And, he was the best in the class at hiding his scent! Not even Timo could consistently find him, right, Timo?"

Timo, who had been heading out the door with Varinn and Trygve, turned back long enough to make a purposeful-looking sign toward Sune, almost like a challenge. "Tomorrow, brother," he said cheerfully. "My Grisk nose shall defeat your Skai sneaking yet, you shall see."

Sune's blank, inscrutable face hadn't betrayed any kind of response to this, but at Ulfarr's heavy hand settling on his shoulder, he twitched a little nod. And finally, Ulfarr and Sune turned and walked out too, leaving Geva alone with Jule and Grimarr, Grimarr now holding a boneless, softly snoring Tengil against his chest.

"That was spectacular, sister," Jule told Geva, with a warm, beaming grin. "They loved it, and you are *incredible* at this, you must know. I can't tell you how much we appreciate it."

Beside Jule, Grimarr was giving a slow, serious nod, his eyes glancing around the cheerful, messy room. "Ach, we thank you, sister," he said, his voice very low. "This is... a great gift. One I would not have hoped to see, in my lifetime."

Well. Geva's throat felt too thick to speak, suddenly, though she managed a watery-feeling smile. To which Jule gave a knowing smile back, and then waved Geva toward the door. "Now, we'll clean up," she said, with that familiar stubborn glint in her eyes, "while you go revel in your accomplishments, all right? And maybe have a well-deserved nap?"

Geva attempted to refuse, but promptly found herself being escorted out of the room in Jule's surprisingly powerful grip. And in truth, a nap did sound wonderful, and once she'd staggered back to their bedroom, she almost instantly fell asleep on the soft, warm furs, their sweet scent of Rathgarr drifting deeper with every breath.

When she awoke again, the faint daylight from above was gone, replaced by the soft orange light of the lamp, and the bed was sagging, as if beneath a heavy weight. Beneath Rathgarr's weight, it turned out, and Geva yawned as she rolled over toward where he was sitting on the bed, and smiling down at her with surprising softness in his eyes.

"Weary, poppet?" he asked. "I have brought you some supper, should you wish."

Geva perked up at that, and soon found herself sitting across from him on the bed, eating from the large bowl of remarkably delicious fried meat and vegetables he'd brought. "So how did it go with Kesst?" she asked him, between bites from her fork. "Did you two manage to get along?"

"Ach, this was the best so far," Rathgarr admitted, with another disarmingly soft smile. "We made a meal together—this is some of what was left over—and then went to the Grisk storage-room. Those Grisk, poppet, given a few years of freedom and peace"—he gave a wry shake of his head—"they have gathered a hoard even greater than my father's. And they say Ash-Kai are greedy!"

Geva consciously refrained from glancing toward his trove-room, and instead smiled back at him, and took another bite. "Did you buy anything, then?" she asked. "A new gift for Kesst, maybe?"

Rathgarr sighed, and shook his head again. "He would not hear of it," he said. "And thus it seemed ill-judged to buy for myself, so"—he grimaced—"instead, we chose gifts for you."

"Gifts for me?" Geva echoed, her voice unaccountably high-pitched. "Really? Like what?"

Rathgarr shrugged, his eyes now carefully intent on Geva's supper. "A few more frocks," he said, with an offhanded jerk of his head toward the wardrobe. "And... this."

His hand had reached into his pocket, and re-emerged holding—Geva's breath choked, her fork dropping into her bowl—something large, shiny, and glittering. A gold cuff, she realized, made of multiple intricate twining strands, with a stunning, sparkling red ruby set into it.

"Kesst thought it should match your wedding-ring," Rathgarr said gruffly, as he thrust it into Geva's slack hand. "He thinks very well of you, ach?"

Oh. Geva couldn't stop blinking at the cuff in her hand, feeling its heavy weight, watching that ruby flash and sparkle in the lamplight. "But this—this must have cost you a fortune, Rathgarr," she managed, over her very tight throat, and gods, it was so stunning, and she couldn't pretend it was hers, she couldn't. Any more that she could pretend the wedding-ring was hers, either, and—

"Ach, I have the gold," Rathgarr said, a little too dismissively. "And Kesst says I ought to be gifting you more jewels, to keep you from running off, once you learn the truth of me."

He accompanied this with a rueful half-smile, but Geva truly couldn't move now, her panicked eyes darting between the cuff and his face. "But—you'll want me to give it back, after?" she whispered. "Like the ring? When—we leave here?"

Gods, it almost hurt to say it, to bring that up again—and her faint, whispering hope that Rathgarr might argue it was decisively dashed by his careless, too-casual shrug. "We can speak of it then," he said. "We yet have nineteen days, ach?"

Geva's hard swallow was surely audible, her eyes entirely unable to meet his, but she made herself nod. Nineteen days. One step forward at a time...

But even once Rathgarr had set aside the bowl, and once again put his tongue to staggering, spectacular use, Geva still couldn't stop thinking of it, not even as her body trembled with the aftershocks of his pleasure, his reward. Nineteen days. For his secret schemes, whatever they were. For his vengeance.

"Have you... made any progress, then?" she ventured, quiet, once Rathgarr was again curled up behind her in the dark. "On your... dramatic plans?"

Rathgarr's body had gone still against her, his breath exhaling slow against her hair. But he didn't reply, and the silence seemed to keep expanding, deeper and heavier between them. He didn't want to tell her. Didn't, perhaps, want to lie.

"You can trust me, you know," Geva's voice said, sounding far too plaintive. "I've kept all your secrets so far, haven't I? Kept up our... *deception*?"

She winced at the word, at the continuing, thickening silence behind her, smothering all else between its weight. Until Rathgarr huffed a sigh, and drew her a little closer against him.

"You have been... perfect, poppet," he said finally, his voice just as thick as the silence. "It is not... you, ach? It is just... all humans. All women."

The hurt was burrowing into Geva's belly, into her frantically blinking eyes, because he should know her by now, he should—and he sighed again, heavy and hot against her hair. "When I was small," he said, "I longed to be just like my father, with his fearless strength and great riches. So one day, in secret, I began to build my own tiny hoard. Full of pretty rocks, and broken jewels, and shavings from the forges. My father even let me choose a few trinkets from his own hoard for this. And I did not think my mother would like this, but I was so proud of what I had done, that she soon saw my glee, and asked what I had been keeping secret from her. So I brought her to see my little hoard, and..."

The silence was sprawling again, twisting in Geva's stomach, and Rathgarr laughed, not a laugh at all. "She took it from me," he said, his voice hard. "She told me I had become a *greedy, secretive hoarder*, just like my father. And if I ever did this again, she would forbid me from seeing Kesst, for she would not have him swayed into becoming a *piggish, plundering orc pillager*."

His voice had kept tipping into that distinctive northern accent, suggesting that these were his mother's exact words, and Geva's wincing hiss was drowned by his brittle, angry laugh. "I was mayhap Bjorn's age," he said flatly. "And Kesst like one of those eager little Ka-esh today. He spent half his days riding around the mountain on my shoulders, chattering to me of all he saw. And"—his voice cracked—"my mother would have *stolen* this from us? Just as she stole my little hoard?"

Oh, how vile. Geva's fury was lurching up hot and bitter, even as her stomach twisted with more stark, sinking misery. Rathgarr truly couldn't think she would ever hurt him like that? Threaten him? Betray him?

"I ken you are not her, poppet," he said now, with another heavy sigh. "I ken. I only mean to say... I learnt very well to keep my secrets close, after this. Most of all when a pretty woman smiles at me and asks for them, ach?"

Right. There didn't seem to be a way to answer that, suddenly, or even a way to even attempt an argument, because what could she possibly say? What words would possibly sway him, without sounding like just the kind of manipulation he expected? The kind of betrayal he feared?

The misery was twisting even tighter now, shifting into something much like despair, and Geva fervently fought for her focus, for her plan. Looking forward. The next step. He'd told her this, he'd at least been honest about this part of it, and it was still something, something new...

"I understand," she said, through the catch in her throat. "And before I forget, I was wondering if you might—come with me tomorrow, again. It was really—really helpful, having you there today."

But perhaps that was even worse, the way Rathgarr laughed again, the sound hard, heavy, mirthless. "Ach, was it," he said, but when Geva didn't reply—couldn't, through her blocked throat—he sighed again, and drew her a little closer. "I shall think further upon this, my sweet. If *you* shall tell us a tale, and then settle yourself, and sleep."

But it was perhaps the worst challenge yet, because even as Geva's voice launched into the most entertaining tale she could think of—the goat and the dancing potato—the misery kept rising, churning, sticking in her throat. Nineteen days. And then the sea.

And even once Rathgarr was softly snoring behind her, she stared blankly into the darkness, twisting her wedding-ring on her finger, blinking back the wetness behind her eyes.

36

———

If Rathgarr noticed Geva's red eyes and puffy face the next morning, he didn't acknowledge them. Instead, he silently handed over a plate full of hot, steaming breakfast, along with—Geva's eyes widened—a silver goblet, full of distinctive scented whiteness.

Her glance up toward him was perhaps both accusing and amused, earning a small, smug smile in return. "I told you, my kin shall be expecting me to fatten you for me," he said lightly. "There is naught for it, I ken."

Geva rolled her eyes at him, but her smile felt warmer than before, and she willingly sipped at it as she ate, as Rathgarr watched with glinting, satisfied eyes. And once she'd finished, he drew her up out of bed, and dressed her in one of the new "frocks" he'd bought the day before—another simple, full-coverage black shift, admittedly ideal for teaching in—and then he insisted she wear her glittering new cuff, as well.

"I have some matters to attend to, this afternoon," he said, a little offhandedly, as he slid the cuff up her arm, and then tilted it side to side, as if admiring his handiwork. "But I shall again come with you to the schoolroom this morn, ach?"

Oh. Geva's delight at that was almost enough to drown out

the twinge of lingering bitterness about his secret plans, especially once Rathgarr had again escorted her to the schoolroom. Where he helped her welcome back their new students, greeting them all by name, and surreptitiously slipping the small Grisks' new swords into their eager little hands. And then he even signed a hello to Sune, while also balefully glaring up toward Ulfarr behind him.

Today, Geva's goal was to introduce some writing instruction with the soft-spoken Tristan, and it turned out that Rathgarr was a great help with that, too. Not only emphatically calling the rambunctious class to order for Tristan, but then helping Geva manage the students throughout the lesson, as well. Keeping them in their chairs, showing them how to sharpen their charcoal with their claws, and even assisting some of them in drawing their letters.

As a reward, the day's clan-focused activity was sparring, led by Sigarr in the nearby Ash-Kai sparring-room. And as Geva had expected, Sigarr proved to be a patient, flexible, and indulgent instructor, with a consistent eye toward awareness and safety. Though it turned out—much to Geva's reluctant amusement—that he fully expected both her and Rathgarr to participate in any demonstrations, along with an effusively eager Abjorn, who'd somehow been enlisted to help as well, despite still sporting an alarmingly cut-up face and a magnificent black eye.

But it ended up being great fun, and Sigarr led them in a highly interactive show, with a variety of comparatively safe exercises and drills for the orclings. And the orclings clearly loved every moment of it, even the three small Ka-esh, who despite their own reluctance to fight, intently followed Abjorn about with wide, mystified eyes.

"He cannot be Ka-esh," little Isak firmly pronounced, once he'd watched Abjorn flip entirely sideways, catching Sigarr in the head with a spectacular kick. "This is not what Ka-esh do."

"But he *smells* Ka-esh," interjected Bram, after a series of careful sniffs. "Timo, do you smell this?"

Timo was already nodding, from where he'd paused his nearby sparring with Sune to watch. "He is *wonderful*," he said to Bram, with palpable reverence. "The most wonderful Ka-esh I have ever seen in all my *life*, ach, Sune?"

At this, Sune huffed and rolled his eyes, and gave an admittedly impressive kick of his own into Timo's side. And soon they were all fully invested in their own sparring again, even the little Ka-esh, who mostly focused on finding creative ways to avoid each other's tentative jabs.

It turned out that the session went far longer than planned, to the point where the orclings' caretakers began turning up in the sparring-room to collect them. And when Geva attempted a breathless apology toward Varinn about the confusion, while fanning at her sweaty face, he waved it away, and smiled as a grinning, equally sweaty-looking Timo tripped over toward them.

"We can always smell our kin, ach, Timo?" he said, rustling his hand in Timo's hair. "Even Thrain should not fail, in this."

He'd cast a rather disgruntled look toward Thrain, who had unsteadily followed him into the room, his usual goblet still in hand, his eyes suffused with red. "Me, fail?" he exclaimed, with a not-quite-convincing grin, a dramatic clasp of his hand to his heart. "At *scenting*? You have wounded me, Varinn. *Again*."

But Varinn's mouth thinned, his gaze angling purposefully away, and he swiftly guided Timo out of the room. While Thrain stared after them, and gulped down the rest of his goblet with alarming speed. And once he noticed Geva watching, he flinched and lurched toward the door, nearly bumping into a huge, frowning Ulfarr on the way by.

Geva had learned a few more signs over the course of the day's lessons, at least enough to say a proper thank-you and goodbye to Sune, and she didn't miss the faint flicker of surprise in Ulfarr's eyes before he silently guided Sune away again. Which Geva was taking as a compliment, damn it, and she was still smiling as she went back over to Sigarr, and thanked him for his help.

"Ach, I was honoured to," he said, with a distracted-seeming wave of his clawed hand, as he sank down onto the bench, his eyes focused on where Rathgarr and Abjorn were still playfully sparring together in the ring. "Good, Abjorn!" he called. "Again!"

Abjorn hesitated long enough to grin beatifically over toward Sigarr, his black eye horrifically on display, before ducking around to aim a kick at Rathgarr's back. While Sigarr visibly cringed, his hands rubbing at his mouth, his eyes darting guiltily toward Geva, and away again.

"Rath is already much improved, ach, sister?" he said, in an obvious attempt at a diversion. "It shall be no time, I ken, before he is once again one of the deadliest fighters in the mountain."

Now it was Geva's turn to wince, her thoughts once again back on the nineteen—eighteen—days, and on all Rathgarr's secrets. Secrets that surely still had plenty to do with the Skai, and with Ulfarr... and maybe even with fighting like this. With *death*.

"Do you—do you really think Rathgarr is that... *deadly*?" she said, too quickly. "Surely there are plenty of excellent warriors here? Say, Grimarr, or Ulfarr?"

Sigarr vaguely nodded, his eyes once again fixed on Abjorn. "And Simon and Drafli also," he said absently. "And there are many Bautul I should not wish to meet in armed combat. But Rath was always among the best, ach? Once, in a pitched battle, I watched him kill three fully armed human men with only his fists."

He *what*? Geva's horror was rapidly rising, her hands clapping over her face, but thankfully Sigarr seemed too focused on the match to notice, hissing through his teeth as Rathgarr's fist grazed Abjorn's cheek. And without another word, Sigarr leapt up and strode over toward them, roughly knocking Rathgarr aside, and then giving a purposeful jerk of his head toward Geva.

And gods, she was probably still looking perfectly aghast, her heart still trampling through her chest, while horrifying visions of a bloody murdering Rathgarr swarmed behind her eyes. And yes, damn it, Rathgarr's head was tilting as he studied her, and after a clipped word to Abjorn, he swiftly strode over toward her.

"Are you well, poppet?" he demanded. "Is aught amiss? Are you in need of a rest?"

Geva firmly waved it away, and attempted a reassuring smile toward his worried face. "Er, just a bit hungry, I think," she managed. "How would you feel about a late lunch?"

Luckily, Rathgarr didn't attempt to argue this, though he kept angling Geva uneasy glances as they walked down the corridor toward the kitchen. While she desperately attempted to shove it all away, the secrets and the vengeance and the eighteen days, and ended up blurting out the first thing she could think of.

"So, Kesst thinks Abjorn is acting out for Sigarr's attention," she asked. "It seems to me like it's working rather well, don't you think?"

The concern on Rathgarr's face had somewhat faded, giving way to a warm, glinting amusement. "Ach, mayhap," he said. "Matchmaking, are you, poppet? This is a very Ash-Kai pastime, you ken."

Geva's swell of surging relief made it almost easy to raise her chin, and fix him with her most affronted look. "Well, you can't really blame me, can you?" she said primly. "It's not as though I get to enjoy a happy relationship of my own, stuck as I am with a vengeful, murderous, greedy—"

Rathgarr cut her off with a harsh, sudden growl, though that glint was still there, sharpening in his eyes. "Ach, what is this?" he demanded. "I have granted you my tongue *three times* this week, my spoilt little schoolmarm. And I have cared for you, and given you gifts, and fed you countless loads of good Ash-Kai seed! And even helped you tend all those orclings in that loud little room! Twice!"

And curse her, but Geva was actually frowning back at him, right here in the middle of the corridor, her hands on her hips. "That *loud little room* was once the Ash-Kai throne room, thank you very much," she said archly. "And also, any scheming Ash-Kai pastimes I might undertake are all in fact all *your* fault, because you've irrevocably tainted me with all that devious Ash-Kai seed!"

Rathgarr's brief, delighted grin was almost staggeringly stunning, though it was instantly replaced with a mighty, ferocious scowl. "You dare to bemoan my good seed?" he hissed at her. "Do you not know what happens to greedy, ungrateful schoolmarms like you?"

Geva tossed her braids and scoffed at him, her chin still lifted. "Oh *noooo*," she scoffed, "the big scary Ash-Kai is angry at me, whatever will he—"

She broke off with a yelp, because Rathgarr had bodily plucked her up into his arms, and stalked toward the nearby kitchen. Fully ignoring the sight of Gegnir, Olga, and Alma working inside, in favour of striding toward the nearest blank wall, snatching Geva up, and shoving her firmly against it.

"Now, my unruly poppet," he drawled at her, as he hoisted her legs around his waist, and yanked up her shift. "Here is what your angry Ash-Kai shall do with you, ach?"

One of his hands had snapped to his trousers, thrusting them down in a sharp jerk—and suddenly his hard, pulsing strength was there, shoving up between her legs, ramming its way deep inside. Making Geva yelp and moan upon it, her wide eyes glancing toward their watching audience, while Rathgarr tilted back his head and laughed, rich and bright and approving.

"Ach, this is better," he purred, as he eased into a hard,

steady rhythm, plunging in again and again as Geva desperately clung to him, and fought to bite back her screams. "Where are all your clever words now, my sweet?"

Gods damn him, because there was truly no way to speak, not with that raw, reckless pleasure sinking deep again and again, swallowing all else in its strength. And with Rathgarr grinning at her like that, so warm and wicked, wanting this, enjoying this, revelling in this, oh—

"This pleases you, ach, my sweet?" he crooned at her. "You long to be caught in my clutches, with my Ash-Kai prick buried deep inside you. You shall wield all your wiles to woo me, and soften me, and"—his breath hitched, his eyes shifting distant, strange—"tempt me to grant you my sons, ach?"

Geva froze all over, her eyes snapped wide—and then, without warning, her release charged through her. The waves of pleasure slamming into her again and again and again, making her wildly cry and tremble against him, while Rathgarr's eyes widened too, his mouth parting, a low, guttural groan escaping his throat—

And then he pinned her even more powerfully to the wall, his face ducking deep into her neck, as that hot liquid surged out deep inside. While Geva just kept clinging to him, gasping into his shoulder as the ecstasy kept reeling and roiling between them. And gods curse him, damn him, why the hell had he brought up the sons, and...

Once he pulled back, she wasn't even slightly surprised to see him purposefully glancing away, his shaky hand fishing in his pocket for a rag. And she silently took it, surreptitiously tucking it into place as Rathgarr drew away, and settled her down onto her unsteady feet. His eyes still intently held away from hers, toward—oh. Their watching audience. Which consisted of a rather stunned-looking Gegnir, a gleefully grinning Olga, and a kindly smiling Alma.

"You like that, Gegnir?" Olga said archly, slapping his shoulder with her wooden spoon. An action that made him visibly startle, before angling her a hungry, watchful look. While beside them, Alma was still smiling, and giving a purposeful little wave of her hand toward Geva.

"Perhaps you'd like to come back to the scullery to wash up properly, sister?" Alma asked, in her soft, lilting voice. "I always keep extra rags on hand."

Geva willingly followed Alma toward the rear of the kitchen, not quite looking at Rathgarr as she went, or Gegnir and Olga, either. But as Alma ran fresh water over a clean rag, and then handed it over, there was no judgement whatsoever in her eyes, only a warm, teasing commiseration. "I'm so happy for the two of you," she said, as she headed for the door again. "It's obvious Rathgarr cares for you very much."

Geva attempted some semblance of a smile at that, and then began furtively scrubbing, until she was fully clean again. While all those words kept jumbling, mashing together in her thoughts. *You shall wield all your wiles. Tempt me to grant you my sons. It's obvious Rathgarr cares for you...*

And when Geva walked back out toward where Rathgarr was waiting, she smiled at his unreadable face, slipped her arm into its familiar place against him, and leaned in close. Breathing him in, feeling his warm familiar strength, his safety. Even stronger than the eighteen days, the looming impending doom. One step at a time.

"So lunch next, then, love?" she asked, as lightly as she could. "Also, I was wondering if you might come with me to the schoolroom again tomorrow morning?"

She still couldn't at all read the look in his eyes, the very slight movement on his mouth. But she waited, waited, her heart thundering louder with every beat, until finally he nodded, his breath exhaling out slow.

"Ach," he said. "I shall come."

37

Rathgarr came to class the next day, and the next, and the next.

Geva was truly grateful to have him there, guiding and settling the orclings, and running interference whenever she, Tristan, or their clan guests needed it. And so far, with his support, the daily clan visits had been an unqualified success—they'd had a lesson in seed sprouting from Kalfr, a demonstration on moving silently from Simon, and a session on basic first aid from a tall, cheerful Ka-esh medic named Salvi, who also turned out to be Tristan's mate.

In addition to the daily clan guests, Geva and Tristan had also continued to add more focused lessons on reading and writing, in both common-tongue and Aelakesh—however, this had inevitably resulted in copious amounts of squirming, wriggling, and whispering, especially from the younger orclings. To the point where Rathgarr began rotating each table into wrestling sessions in the side room, where he'd spread out soft furs all over the floor.

"If we truly wish them to sit through logic or mathematics, or even music," he told Geva after the fourth day, "we ought to make sure there is wearying activity before this. Can you not add this to your schedule?"

It was a good point, Geva could admit, and she wheedled Rathgarr into explaining it to the Orc Mountain Educational Congress the next day—a planned day off—at their first follow-up meeting. Prompting Killik to smirk smugly over toward Rosa, his arms folding with satisfaction behind his head as he crossed his booted feet on the table. "Ought to run about outdoors each day, I ken, along with all the rest," he said. "We shall order this, ach, Rathgarr?"

To Geva's vague surprise, Rathgarr didn't argue this plan, and the next morning, they began the day out on a stunning little alcove near the top of the mountain, beneath the bright beaming sun. The alcove had sheer stone walls rising on each side, some steeper than others, and Killik and Rathgarr had attached multiple knotted ropes across the top. And then, while the orclings watched with awestruck fascination from below, Killik swept up the longest rope, climbing hand over hand as his feet lightly leapt up the ledges lining the wall.

"Wow," squeaked Isak, who, like the other small Ka-esh, was wearing an adorable little eye-mask that Rathgarr had brought, on accord of Ka-esh eyes being extra sensitive to sunlight. "But Killik is Skai, ach? We Ka-esh cannot do this."

"You can, Isak," Rathgarr said cheerfully, with a gentle shake at his shoulder. "You remember your clan brother Abjorn, ach? Now, you three are with me, on this smaller wall. You younger Grisks, also."

Soon the orclings were collectively squealing, laughing, and scurrying up the walls, with varying degrees of success. Unsurprisingly, Sune and Bjorn were the most nimble, with their lean Skai bodies, but Hagen and Hauk, the two Bautul brothers, were highly impressive as well. And by the end of it, all the orclings had succeeded in climbing at least one wall, their faces bright and flushed with delight.

It turned out that they were indeed far more attentive to

Tristan and Geva's reading instruction after that, and also to the day's clan-focused activity. It was a drumming session with a burly, smiling Ash-Kai named Othan, who came in laden down with an armful of round wooden hoops and dried animal-skins. "First we must make the drums," he told the class, "and then we shall learn to play them, ach?"

It was a truly fascinating lesson, in which Geva learned that drum-making was a uniquely Ash-Kai trade, and that Othan currently served as the resident expert on the subject. And apparently even Rathgarr had learned a little drumming in his youth, and it did strange, simmering things to Geva's insides to watch him lead the drumming circle with Othan, a steady beat thudding out from beneath his big capable hands.

"You were very good also, poppet," he told her afterwards, raising his brows toward her. "I should almost think you had studied this at length, ach?"

Geva flushed at that, and quickly explained that the kind of drumming she'd learned was entirely different, on a pot drum, rather than a skin drum. Which then prompted Rathgarr to demand a full explanation, and after having gained it, he cocked his head sideways, his brow thoughtfully furrowing.

"I ken I saw a drum like this in the Grisk storage-room," he said. "Come along, poppet."

Geva readily obliged, and soon found herself staring in awe at a large, lovely Eziran pot drum. It was built rather like a huge metal bottle, with a rounded base and a slim neck, but also with a small circular hole cut into the side. And once Rathgarr had fetched some water to pour into it, Geva settled down onto the nearest available chair, placed the drum between her knees, and began to play. Patting out a light, easy rhythm at first, brushing her fingers against opposite sides of the drum, and then adding layer after layer. Until her hands were flying over the pot, her palms striking at the hole, while its smooth, intricate sounds rippled through the room.

When she finished, Rathgarr was eyeing her strangely, his

mouth pursed. And without a word, he picked up the drum and strode with it to the counter, where he briefly consulted with the Grisk porter, and then began counting out coins.

"You... you didn't need to do that, Rathgarr," Geva stammered at him afterwards, as he carried it up the corridor. "That was a lot of coin, and it's so big and heavy, I couldn't possibly..."

Take it with me, she should have said, but she couldn't seem to find the words, because they were already down to twelve days. And though she'd been very intently trying to avoid thinking of that ever-encroaching deadline, it still seemed to loom higher every morning she awoke in their lovely little room, curled close into Rathgarr's chest.

"Ach, we shall keep it in the schoolroom, where the orclings shall welcome it also," Rathgarr replied, a little too casually, as he strode back into the schoolroom, and set it down beside a table. "And should you wish to thank me, you well know how to do this, ach?"

The gratitude was surging far too strong in Geva's chest, and she beamed up at him as her hands swiftly found his belt, and she nudged him down into a chair. Where she knelt between his sprawled legs, working over his groin with furious abandon, until his head arched back, his fist striking the table, as he poured his thick sweetness deep down her desperately swallowing throat.

Once she'd sucked him clean, just the way he liked, Rathgarr bent over toward her, his hands shaky and gentle on her face. Tilting it up, almost, *almost*, as if he might kiss her—but then he abruptly sagged back again, his eyes squeezing shut, his hands sinking deep into his own hair.

It was a familiar theme by now, his consistent pulling away whenever things became too close, creating distance between them with either his words or his actions—or still, far too frequently, his secrets. And once again, Geva fought through the whispering hurt, the ever-rising fear and dread and disappointment, and attempted a smile, and a change of subject. Looking forward. One step at a time.

"So I was talking to Kesst, when he stopped by earlier," she said, as lightly as she could. "And he mentioned that maybe we'd like to join him and Efterar for supper tonight? And then dancing?"

Rathgarr easily agreed, as Geva had known he would—he always accepted every possible invitation that Kesst would offer, many of them gained through her own mediation, and the occasional slight falsehood, too. A fact that she'd felt consistently guilty about, until that evening found her and Efterar standing together in the kitchen, and watching Kesst and Rathgarr bickering over how best to bake the cake they wanted for dessert.

"Oh, I think they need as much of our help as they can get," Efterar wryly replied, once Geva confessed that the invitation had actually been entirely her doing. "They're both far too stubborn and suspicious to get through this all on their own. And maybe"—his eyes on Kesst had softened, gone a little sad—"maybe they've both been hurt too much, too. They both need time to trust and heal again."

Geva could heartily agree with that, and in the following days, she threw herself into being the best mate, and the best teacher, she could possibly be. Doing everything she could to bring Kesst and Rathgarr together, while fighting to ignore all those quiet, nagging uncertainties. The way Rathgarr would pull away again and again. The way he kept disappearing for long stretches of time, without offering any kind of explanation where he'd gone. The way he still glared at Ulfarr every day he brought Sune to class. The way he spent more and more time in the sparring-room, battling with Sigarr and Abjorn, until the previous softness in his belly was nearly almost gone, replaced with ridges of hard, solid muscle.

Geva's efforts at ignoring all this were considerably helped by the fact that Rathgarr still kept coming to class every day, not only continuing to support her daily teaching with Tristan, but also leading an imaginative variety of exercise activities each morning. In addition to the wall-climbing, he and Killik had arranged tree-climbing in the garden, swimming lessons in the pools, and hide-and-seek around the mountain, along with more mundane tasks like weeding, tidying, and mopping floors. And one morning, he'd even brought Othan in again, and had had Geva and Othan play their drums together, while he and the orclings danced merrily around the tables, stomping their feet as the beats bumped and swirled around the room.

The daily clan-led activities had continued to become even more intriguing as well, often building on what had come before, or combining several clans' skills together. Alma and Baldr taught a Skai sign language class, which helped so much in communicating with Sune that Geva asked them to continue it every week. Another Skai-Grisk class turned out to be pet care, led first by Ella, who apparently had three adorable little dogs, and then by a young, laughing Skai named Tryggr, who introduced an ornery black cat named Cat.

And afterwards, if Rathgarr disappeared without explanation for the rest of the afternoon or evening, Geva bit back the lingering questions, and fought instead to keep showing him. To keep supporting him, doing her best, seeking that new way. Focusing on how he kept tending to her, feeding her, choosing her clothes, braiding her hair. How he kept asking for her tales, when they were together in bed in the dark. And how they kept taking their pleasure together, sometimes multiple times each day, with ever-increasing shamelessness, on both Geva's part, and his.

"I wish you over my lap, poppet," he told her late one afternoon, as they finished tidying up after the end of the schoolday. "Rump up. Now."

He'd been sitting sprawled sideways in one of the schoolroom chairs, and Geva made a face at him, even as she scrambled to comply. Bending herself over his spread knees, her upper body uncomfortably propped on the nearby table, while he began sliding up the short skirt of her shift.

"But wait," Geva gasped, her head jerking up. "I'm expecting Tristan to come back with Rosa, we need to review the lesson plans for—"

But Rathgarr's firm slap at her bare arse stunned her to silence, and so did the way his hand lingered, caressing her stinging arse-cheek before slipping lower between. "Behave," he murmured, dark and low. "Tristan shall smell this long before they come, and should they wish to stay away, they shall."

Geva could only splutter and gasp, writhing against the feel of his smoothly stroking fingers, slipping up and down her crease. Not moving with any sort of urgency whatsoever, just teasing and taunting her, bringing her helpless gasps higher and higher, until—

Until Tristan and Rosa indeed strode in, both of them with large stacks of paper in their hands. And neither of them seemed to take any notice of Geva's highly compromised position, even when they both pulled over chairs, and sat down across from Rathgarr at the table.

"So before we begin, I'd love to ask Rathgarr a few more questions about pamphlet distribution routes," Rosa was blithely saying, glancing between Geva's flushed face on the table, and Rathgarr up behind her. "If you two don't mind, that is?"

Geva truly could not speak, while Rathgarr, utter bastard that he was, chose that exact moment to finally slip his finger up inside her slick, quivering heat. "No, not at all," he replied easily, as his finger blatantly swirled, making a wet squelching sound. "Our schoolmarm may yet need some time, before she is able to speak."

Gods curse him, because both Tristan and Rosa again glanced toward Geva's flushed face, Tristan with a soft ruefulness, Rosa's with a rather delighted deviousness. "Well, that's really *quite* serendipitous, because I actually have quite a lot to get through," she said brightly. "Now, do you have any contacts near Kentnek?"

Rathgarr drawled some sort of answer, but Geva couldn't hear it through the ringing in her ears, and the feel of Rathgarr settling a second finger close, and slipping it up inside, too. And then blatantly circling and scissoring them, bringing up more wet, obscene sounds, while she helplessly gasped, and Rosa just kept on asking incessant pamphlet-related questions, each one more elaborate-seeming than the last.

"Fuck," Geva gasped, without even slightly meaning to, as Rathgarr's thumb—which had been sliding up her crease— gently, purposefully prodded at that tight clutch of heat, while his fingers kept moving below. And in answer, his other hand again gently slapped her, hard enough that she could feel the soft flesh jiggling, feel the heat stinging across her bared skin.

"I said, behave, poppet," ordered Rathgarr's low voice. "It is in very poor taste to disrupt our meeting with your cursing, most of all in a schoolroom, ach?"

Oh, gods damn him, but she was painfully biting her lip, because that thumb was slowly circling, pressing its way inside. "You must forgive my unruly mate," Rathgarr blandly said to Tristan and Rosa across the table. "She only loves to be filled by her orc, and cannot contain her joy at this, ach?"

Geva's fury was wildly flaring, and with it, oh, oh, was the sheer, sharp surge of release, rocking and reverberating through her trapped, trembling body. Clamping her again and again around Rathgarr's invading fingers, the sounds even more obscene than before, while he kept himself held deep, and huffed a low, satisfied laugh.

"There, there, poppet," he purred, as he drew everything out, and gave another gentle slap at her arse before pulling her shift back down again. "All better, ach?"

Geva glared bitterly back toward him, but in return he

flashed her his most stunning grin, wide and warm and wicked. And then he drew her back onto his lap, settling her close, his arm curling around her waist, as his head bent down, and gently kissed her forehead.

It was enough to throw her off-kilter once again, to the point where she could still scarcely speak throughout the rest of the meeting. And it wasn't until Tristan and Rosa had finally left that she seemed to find her voice again, even if it was still choked and thick in her throat.

"You—unbelievable—ingrate," she hissed at him, elbowing him in the stomach. "What—in all the gods' unholy *names*—do you think you were doing?"

But there was the grin again, so dazzling it set something flipping in her belly. "I knew Rosa had more to ask me of these pamphlets, ach?" he said. "If I was bound to endure all her questions, I thought I ought to find *some* joy in this."

Oh. Well. Geva fought to muster up at least a little more outrage, glaring at him with sharply narrowed eyes, but he just laughed, and shook his head. "Do you wish to teach me a lesson, my prim little schoolmarm?" he drawled at her, as he nudged her up to her feet. "To punish me for all my misdeeds, mayhap? Mayhap someday. If you are very, *very* good."

Someday. Very good. Those words catching, clawing, in too many impossible ways, holding her still and staring, as Rathgarr's smile went a little wry, his head again shaking. "Now, I am off for a spell," he said. "I shall meet you later for supper, ach?"

Geva could only seem to nod at him, and then stare at his retreating back as he strode out the schoolroom door. Her breaths heaving harsh, her hands clutched almost painfully to the edge of the table, while something reckless and hopeful swirled in her chest.

Because that—that had been another challenge, with an unspecified end date. A challenge that hadn't included a single mention of their seven remaining days. If she was good. One step at a time.

So when Rathgarr reappeared some time later, again without offering any explanation about where he'd gone, Geva crushed down the ever-present impulse to ask, and instead smiled, took his arm, and accompanied him to dinner, which she'd again arranged with Kesst and Efterar. It had begun to feel like a familiar routine, though tonight Kesst had decided to cook in the Bautul garden. So after some good-natured arguing between Kesst and Rathgarr in the kitchen over the menu and ingredients required, they all headed outdoors, into the garden's clean, chilly evening air.

It turned out that there was a small firepit available to use, with low stools surrounding it, and dry stacks of firewood nearby. And while Geva and Efterar watched from their stools, Kesst and Rathgarr bustled about above them, working together with easy efficiency. Rathgarr starting and banking the fire, while Kesst set up the pan over it, and then began slicing and frying the ingredients as Rathgarr handed them over. And Geva found herself exchanging a companionable glance with Efterar, who was looking just as fondly amused as she felt.

"You two are so good at this," Geva said lightly, earning equal, almost comically suspicious glances from both Rathgarr and Kesst. "You must have spent so much time cooking together, growing up."

It was a blatant attempt at getting them talking, they all well knew, but it worked more often than not, and Geva was distantly gratified when Rathgarr shrugged, and cleared his throat. "Ach, we oft had to fend for ourselves back then," he said. "The clans did not come together to freely serve a meal each day, as they do now. So if we did not make food, we did not eat."

Truly, their upbringing sounded more and more grim every time Geva heard of it, because how old had Rathgarr been when he'd been driven out, again? In his early twenties? And Kesst had been about fifteen?

"Wouldn't your parents have provided meals for you?" she asked tentatively. "Even at some point, when you were younger?"

Kesst's mouth pursed, his hand chopping faster, and again it was Rathgarr who replied, his voice lower than before. "I ken our father did, a little. But then he… could not remember how. And our mother… she was…"

Kesst's head snapped up, fast enough that his hair flew out behind him. "Don't you dare imply Mother was useless, Rath," he shot back. "As if Father was any better? That witless brute even forgot how to *walk*, by the end. The week before he died, he thought I was *you*. Which of course I wasn't, because you"— he jabbed his knife at Rathgarr—"weren't *there*!"

Beside Geva, Efterar hissed through his teeth, and she could see Rathgarr's body stiffening, that telltale tightness pulling up his shoulders—but he was still breathing, his eyes fixed on Kesst's face. "Ach, I was not there," he said, quiet. "And neither was our father. But our mother *was*, for these first fifteen years of your life. Why could she not have fed you, now and then? Why could she not have found you clothes, or cared for your hair? Why did she always cast blame upon *me* whenever you wept, or shouted, or ran away?"

Kesst was still glaring at Rathgarr, bitter and vicious. "Mother was *suffering*," he snarled back. "She had to deal with all the rubbish from our fool father, and Kaugir, and this entire damned mountain!"

But Rathgarr just kept looking back, his shoulders still rising and falling. "Ach, and we did not?" he asked. "We did not need to face all this, for all those years, when we were not even grown? And had our mother been granted her way, little brother"—Rathgarr exhaled, heavy—"we would not even have had each other, amidst it all."

For a long moment, neither of them spoke, but then Kesst

twitched a visible shudder, his head jerking back and forth. "It wasn't that bad," he said, though he didn't sound entirely convinced. "Mother didn't *hate* you, Rath."

Rathgarr's laugh sounded more like a choke, and his head shook, too. "No?" he said. "So why did she so oft say she did? Ach, not long before I was run out, she told me she hoped some heroic man would soon kill me in battle, so I might finally leave her in peace about *you*!"

What? Geva's body flinched on her stool, her hands rubbing painfully at her face, while Kesst had gone very still, his eyes now firmly on the fire. And oddly enough, Rathgarr glanced down at Geva, holding her gaze, as he drew in another shaky breath, and looked at Kesst again.

"I ken you loved her, little brother," he said, quiet. "But she was not a good mother, not even to you. She wished to keep you forever down in that stinking little room in the Ka-esh wing, telling her your tales, and helping her weave her petty little plots, until she forgot all else. Until she was just the same as our father."

Kesst still wasn't looking up, though his mouth twisted, his hand spasming on his knife. "You had plots, too," he replied. "And *you* loved my tales just as much as she did! If not more!"

But Rathgarr didn't even blink this time, his eyes steady on Kesst's face. "Ach, I did," he replied. "But I loved you more, little brother. You were"—his throat convulsed—"the light of my days. The son of my heart. And I would have gladly never heard another of your tales again, had it meant you were fed, and happy, and *safe*."

Kesst didn't reply to that, or look up from the fire, but there was a strange, choked little sound, escaping from his mouth. And within an instant, Efterar had leapt to his feet, and folded Kesst tightly into his arms.

Kesst didn't resist, just clung to Efterar as he sobbed, his face buried in his chest. And Geva felt her own eyes prickling too, and then catching on Rathgarr. Who was helplessly looking at Kesst, his big body again gone rigid, his claws extended sharp from his fingertips.

For a long while, no one spoke or moved, but for Efterar's firm hands, running up and down Kesst's back. Until Kesst finally hiccoughed and drew away, wiping at his face with unsteady hands.

"Well, isn't this fun," he said, though his voice was thick. "And we've only just begun! Who else has some horrifying trauma to share? Eft? Geva?"

Efterar was twitching an almost painfully affectionate smile down toward Kesst, his hand still stroking his back, and Geva felt herself drawing in a shaky breath, and glancing at Rathgarr's stiff, still-staring body. *Someday. If you are very, very good.*

Seven days. The next step. The...

"Well," she said, on a strange, choked gulp of air. "A few years ago, my family's house burned to the ground, with everything we had still inside it. Including—my parents. If that counts?"

38

Geva almost instantly regretted her confession, her mouth wincing, her hand spasming over her face. While above her, Kesst's mouth had fallen open with shock, Efterar was looking deeply alarmed, and—

And Rathgarr. Rathgarr was staring at her, utterly unmoving, his eyes shadowed hollows in his blank, empty face.

Damn it. *Damn* it. That was obviously not the kind of help he'd meant, she was not supposed to be disrupting this meaningful moment with her own damned rubbish, what if she'd ruined this, ruined everything...

Kesst was the one to recover first, squaring his shoulders, and striding over to drop down onto the stool beside her. "You know, that might be one of the worst ones I've heard yet," he said lightly. "Unless *you* set the fire yourself, by chance?"

He was eyeing Geva with blatant mock suspicion, and suddenly she was so relieved, so horribly, desperately grateful, she almost felt faint. "No, it wasn't me," she managed, valiantly attempting to match his tone. "It was just—a horrible accident. Started in a bakery down the street. And I'd been away for a few days tutoring, and when I came home—"

All three orcs were staring at her now, waiting for her to continue, and gods, Geva couldn't bear it, her eyes dropping to the crackling, snapping fire. "It was gone," she whispered. "Everything except what I'd taken with me. All of it. My life. My *future.*"

There was only a dank, dangling silence, waiting, waiting, as if there was more to say. But there wasn't, really, and Geva attempted a smile toward the fire, but didn't at all succeed.

"So I wrapped up our affairs as best I could, and then started searching for work," she said thickly. "And ever since, I've just kept looking forward, doing the next thing. Saving up my coin. One step at a time. Right?"

She felt herself glancing up, searching their eyes, pleading for them to see it, to agree, to understand. But Efterar was still looking appalled, and Kesst was furiously blinking again, and Rathgarr—Rathgarr hadn't yet moved, his eyes still those empty, unseeing hollows in his stark, still face.

"Um," Kesst finally said, into the awful, ringing silence. "Right, sister. One step at a time. You've obviously—really— overcome this. Very well."

Geva couldn't help another wild, grateful look toward him, a frantic, fervent nod. "Right," she said. "Just looking forward. Working as hard as I can. It has to work out, in the end. I mean, I'm still here. Still surviving. Right?"

There was again a horrible, empty silence, as though she'd said something completely wrong, as though she'd completely misread this—and yes, surely she had, based on that look on Kesst's face, on Efterar's, on Rathgarr's.

She felt herself painfully blanching, her hand flapping at her face, her body leaping up to her feet. "I'm—very sorry," she gulped. "I didn't mean to—interfere. I'll just—go, and you three can—"

She'd already spun away, dodging toward the mountain behind them—but oh, oh, gods, she'd tripped over the damned stool. And now she was soaring sideways, her hands flying out, and finding—

Oh. Rathgarr. His big solid body catching her, enclosing her tightly against his strong, familiar chest. His arms wrapping around her, his head bent close over hers, his breaths heavy in her braids.

"No, my skittish poppet," he whispered, his voice wavering. "No. Stay. You ought to eat. And mayhap"—she could feel his head shifting, looking up—"mayhap Kesst shall tell us a tale?"

His voice hitched again, gone almost pleading, and behind her, Geva could hear Kesst clearing his throat, and then the sound of a slow, heavy exhale. "Yes, of course," he said, his voice carefully light. "What kind do you think, Rath? Princesses? Angels? Proud, powerful warriors who fall into a deep, dreamless sleep, only to awake the next morning with all their demons defeated, and their kin safe and whole?"

That one must have been something Rathgarr recognized, his body shuddering against Geva's, his hands clamping even tighter around her back. "She likes—funny ones," he said, his voice still strangely choked. "Oft—with animals. There is this one with a porcupine, who lost his shell. Or the wisecracking fox. Or the—roaming rat, and his troublesome tongue."

There was another moment's strange silence, another shaky exhale of Rathgarr's body around Geva's. And then a huff of laughter from Kesst, and the sound of movement, the clank of the pan over the fire.

"I have clearly been missing out, sister," came his voice, from a little further away. "I'm afraid my animal repertoire is shamefully slim. But I do have one about a lovely maiden and a skunk?"

Despite everything, Geva felt herself twitch with interest, her head tilting toward his voice, and against her Rathgarr laughed, the sound unmistakably relieved. "This sounds most apt, brother," he said, his voice soft. "We should be honoured to hear it."

There was a satisfied-sounding huff from Kesst's direction, and another clank of the pan. And then a gentle, purposeful movement from Rathgarr, drawing Geva downwards toward the stool, curling her into his lap. His hands so warm, so gentle, tilting her toward the crackling fire, and toward Kesst's smooth, easy voice, as he launched into the tale.

And it was... wonderful. It told of a sad, lonely maiden, who was trapped in a cruel twisted labyrinth, with no hope of escape. It told how she wandered, frantic and forgotten, until she caught the rank, rotten scent of a skunk, and mindlessly followed it, deeper and deeper and deeper. Becoming ever more ill, alarmed, and alone, until she finally caught up to it, and discovered—

That it wasn't a skunk at all, but a friend, who'd known she needed help, and who'd gained her attention the only way he knew how. A friend who then took her hand, and guided her out of the labyrinth, into the light again. Into hope, and peace, and joy.

The tale seemed to hang there long after Kesst had finished, resonating in raw, stunning stillness. In Geva caught rapt, unblinking, in Rathgarr's arms, while the tale kept circling, sweeping, soaring behind her eyes. Into hope. Peace, and joy. Joy.

When the world seemed to stop again, settling quiet and still, Geva found that her face was wet, her breaths still coming in short little sniffs. While behind her, Rathgarr's breath was heaving harder than she'd ever heard it, his body shivering all over, his eyes rapt, reverent, on Kesst's wryly smiling face.

"This was—" he began, his mouth crumpling, his head shaking. "Even better than I remembered, brother. More— beautiful. You have become—a master. A true Ash-Kai galdr-spinner."

Kesst's smile twitched a little higher, his expression rueful, almost shy. "Well, it still wasn't a porcupine, though," he said lightly, as he fumbled with his pan, and shook some of it out into a bowl. "Here, Rath. She should eat."

Rathgarr rapidly nodded, swiping the bowl from Kesst's hand, and thrusting it into Geva's chest. "Here, poppet," he said firmly. "You ken it shall be perfect, if my brother made it."

Geva couldn't seem to argue, and obligingly took a few careful bites. And Rathgarr was right, because it was mouthwateringly delicious—soft, flavourful venison, with sweetly seasoned fried greens. And as she ate, she finally found the wherewithal to smile up at Kesst, in a desperate attempt to convey her awe, and appreciation.

"That really was spectacular," she managed, between bites. "And so is this. Thank you, brother."

Something she couldn't read passed across Kesst's eyes, but then he was smiling again, though it almost looked sad this time. "Anytime, sister," he said. "It's the least I can do."

The rest of the meal felt a little stilted after that, as if no one could think of anything else to say. And when Efterar carefully suggested that Geva and Rathgarr could retire early, and leave the cleanup to him and Kesst, Rathgarr instantly thanked them, and all but swept Geva up to her feet, and back into the mountain.

He didn't speak again until they were back in their bedroom, with the curtain firmly closed. And suddenly he was hovering close before her, his body edgy and restless, his eyes flashing strange and sharp on her face.

"Was this—truth?" he hissed at her, low and demanding. "About your parents?"

Geva blinked blankly at him, her throat painfully convulsing. "What—what do you mean?"

He towered even closer before her, his hands grasping her shoulders, squeezing a little too tight. "Was this truth!" he repeated, his voice even harder. "What you said, about the fire, and your birthright. Or was this only another plot, to push

Kesst and I together? Another way to please me, and win my favour, or my coin?"

Geva's shock surged sudden and painful, sharp enough to sway her on her feet. "What?" she croaked. "No. No. Of course not. You don't"—she hauled in a breath—"you don't really think I would *lie* about something like that? For *coin*?!"

The bitter disbelief kept twisting tighter, dark and miserable in her belly, because Rathgarr wasn't even denying it. Was still just looking at her like that, like he didn't believe her, like he didn't even know her, after all this time…

"Then why did you speak false until now," he hissed at her. "Why did you keep this hidden from me!"

Geva's breaths were very short, suddenly, gulping in and out, her eyes frozen on his face. "Well, you never asked, did you?" she shot back. "You've barely asked me anything about my past at all! Why would I tell you, when I knew you wouldn't even *care*!"

Rathgarr visibly flinched at that, and his shoulders hunched, his hands clenched at his sides. "I thought you did not wish to speak of the past," he said, very stiff. "You have not oft pushed me to speak of mine, and I was—grateful, for this. I should never have thought"—his voice cracked—"*this* was why you wished to work for me? Because you lost all else you had?"

He grimaced, shaking his head, rubbing his hand over his eyes. As if he was genuinely hurt by this, offended by this, and the unfairness of that was surging up, scraping at Geva's tight throat. "Why the hell does it matter?" she croaked back. "What the hell difference does it make? It was *years* ago, Rathgarr. And I needed a new job, you offered me one, I took it. End of story!"

But damn him, Rathgarr was looking almost wounded now, his hand again dragging against his eyes. "After I broke into your schoolroom, and threatened your life?" he said. "After I near stole your tiny hoard from you?!"

Oh, so now it was all about *him*, and his own damned guilt about taking advantage of a poor helpless governess, and Geva felt her fury surging up even harder, her head whipping back and forth. "You did not coerce me into anything, Rathgarr," she replied, as hard as she could. "I *wanted* this. I *chose* to work for you. I made a logical, practical decision for myself, for my own damned future. You could have been a snivelling illiterate *ghoul*, and I still would have done it! For *myself!*"

And it sounded right, it should have been right, it shouldn't have flashed even more palpable hurt across Rathgarr's watching, blinking eyes. Eyes that were carefully looking away, now, focusing on the opposite wall.

"Ach, I see," he said, very even. "So it *is* all for the coin, then."

Wait. Wait, how had he gotten there, and suddenly he was whirling around, and striding for the door. He was going to leave, just like that—and even as Geva lunged after him, he spun back around to face her again, his mouth twisted and thin.

"My only question, then," he said, his voice so cold and brittle now, "is why you keep seeking to make me stay. Why you keep seeking to enmesh me here, and turn aside all my plans. Why you so eagerly wish to make me into this settled, harmless, useless *failure* I pretend to be!"

What? A cold, jolting chill raced up Geva's back, her mouth fallen open. He—he *knew* she'd wanted him to stay, all this time? And he thought—he thought he was a failure? Settled, harmless, *useless*?!

And gods, he was smiling now, but it was hard, grim, not nearly reaching his eyes. "Ach, is that the coin too, poppet?" he asked, his voice silken and deadly. "You ken if we stay here, and my father's hoard comes to light, half of it shall then be yours, as my mate? This should be far more than a simple payment from your *employer*, ach?"

Another chill was racing up Geva's back, and finally she seemed able to move again, her hand clutching at Rathgarr's arm, her head whipping back and forth. But he was nodding, and still smiling like that, so wrong, wrong, wrong on his mouth.

"And mayhap the sons are part of this also," he continued, so smooth. "Mayhap you wish to lull me into ease upon this, until I finally relent, and agree to ripen your womb. And then, when my hoard comes to light, you only need to find a way to be free of me, ach?"

Good gods, he was not truly saying these things, he couldn't actually believe these things, and he was still just looking at her like that, mocking her, waiting for an answer. But how could she possibly answer this, how could she make him see, how had they even gotten to this, this was—

His harsh bark of a laugh cut through her thoughts like a knife, and he made to whirl away again—and somehow, somehow, Geva managed to clutch at him, clinging as hard as she could, keeping him here, please, anything, please—

"No, Rathgarr!" her voice finally gulped, toward his rigid shoulder. "Gods, no! How could you possibly think such things?!"

His hand made a sharp slicing movement, as if to shove her away—but then it halted, just in time, his eyes squeezing shut. His body utterly still, now, even as he laughed, and shook his head.

"Ach, how could I not?" he drawled, the words striking, staggering, with impossible strength. "You thought you were so clever, poppet, with all your devious little plots. You ken I did not see how hard you worked for me, and sought to gain my trust? How you altered yourself to suit me, and learnt how best to please me, and soothe me, and make me feel at home? How you shamelessly sought to draw out the depths of my hunger, in a way no other bedmate has *ever* sought to do?"

No, no, damn it, no, and Geva couldn't stop clinging to him, wildly shaking her head. "No, Rathgarr," she croaked. "No. I did all that because—"

She couldn't say it, she couldn't, not with him looking at her like that, with that judgement and mockery and contempt in his eyes. Just the way he'd looked at her the first day they'd met, and no, no, no...

"I did it because I love you, Rathgarr," she whispered. "And because—I want to stay."

39

———

Even as Geva spoke those strange, betraying words—*I love you, I want to stay*—she knew Rathgarr didn't believe them. Could see it in the flash of his eyes, the sharp, sudden sneer on his mouth.

"Ach, this is a good one, poppet," he said, after a beat of silence, with a smile that might have almost been approving, if it weren't so menacing. "But if you truly wish me to believe it, mayhap you ought to wail and weep a little. Or mayhap throw yourself at my feet, or beg me to spray into your hair?"

Good gods, this *orc*, and Geva groaned aloud, her hands digging painfully into his arm. "Oh, fuck off, Rathgarr," she growled at him, suddenly breathless, thoughtless, with rage. "Just because you see nefarious plots around every corner, that doesn't mean they actually exist! Is it so hard to believe that yes, I may have started doing this for the coin, but"—she sucked back a breath—"the more I got to know you, the more I liked you?!"

But Rathgarr was snarling back at her, shaking his head. "I have heard this tale before," he hissed. "And I know it was a falsehood, for I was *there!*"

Geva's fury felt almost dizzying, and she glared back up into his infuriating face. "Yes, and so was I, and it was *weeks* ago!" she snapped back. "And even then, it was already coming true, and you damn well know it!"

Rathgarr opened his mouth to reply, but Geva flapped her hand between them, and fiercely shook her head. "Because yes, you're smug and devious and *extremely* enraging," she growled, "but you're also funny, and clever, and quite possibly the most generous person I've met in my life. You've fed me, and cared for me, and danced with me, and braided my hair, and given me multiple very thoughtful gifts. And you've given me shocking amounts of advice and help in the schoolroom, and you are *brilliant* with those orclings, and you *enjoy* spending time with them, and don't even try to *pretend* otherwise with me!"

She was panting by the time she'd finished, the room slightly flickering around her, but she drew down more air, more of the churning rage. "And has it not occurred to you," she gasped, "that maybe I *like* children? Maybe I like teaching them, and maybe I'd like to have some of my own? Maybe I'd like to have them with a generous, considerate, and *settled* part- ner, who's already proven a dozen times over that he's a damned good father, and that his first son loves him very, *very* much?!"

Rathgarr's scowl had slightly faded, though his brows were still furrowed, his head shaking—and Geva's laugh sounded far too shrill, her finger jabbing into his chest. "Kesst loves you," she hissed. "And he wants you to forget the hoard, forget the revenge, and *stay*. Just like I do. And in case you've been too dense to notice"—she waved sharply toward that cradle, still sitting innocuously beside their bed—"*he* wants us to have a son, too!"

There was still no answer from Rathgarr, so Geva laughed again and shoved away from him, her hands flailing aimlessly in the air. "And honestly," she choked out, on another shrill, strange-sounding laugh, "even if my nefarious plot *was* to have your son, and thereby somehow steal away your nonexistent hoard, why the hell would I want to get rid of *you*? When you keep giving me everything I've ever damn well *wanted*?!"

The words rang through the room, her breath finally gone, her rage shuddering one last time—and then sputtering out. Sinking into a bleak, dragging misery, because gods, that look in his eyes. The way he was holding himself. Not with the stiff, unseeing, unnerving emptiness, but just the way he looked at Ulfarr. With the dislike, and the mistrust, and the resentment, as he looked first at her face, and then down at her clothes, her jewels, her *wedding-ring*.

"And when I stop giving you what you wish for?" he asked, in a voice she'd never heard before. "Will you keep my son from me? Will you put him at risk, because you only care for what you want? Will you then find a clever way to *get rid of me*?"

His voice had shifted into a human accent at the end, and something sharply roiled in Geva's stomach, her head wildly shaking, no, no, *no*—and she made herself jerk a step backwards, away. Putting an arms-length of distance between them, and swallowing hard, and fighting to keep her prickling eyes on his.

"How can you even *think* that, Rathgarr," she hissed at him, though her voice cracked. "I have worked so, so hard for you. I have given *everything* I have to help and support you, again and again and again. And after all that"—she had to gulp down another breath—"you still don't trust me? Still?"

And Rathgarr... didn't deny it. Just stood there looking at her like that, with such strange, unsettling blankness in his eyes. As if he perhaps wasn't even seeing her, but every other woman who had hurt him, and betrayed his trust.

"Is there anything," Geva managed, between heavy breaths, "that I can do to convince you, Rathgarr. To show you that I mean it, when I say I'm not here for the coin. I—I'm here for you. *You*."

He remained still for another long, hanging moment, but

finally something moved, deep in his eyes—and then came another laugh, low and mirthless on his mouth. "You truly ken I should tell you how to convince me?" he asked, his voice so thin. "And then, as with every other time I have told you what I wish, you shall go forth and do this, so flawlessly I can no longer tell up from down?"

Damn it, damn it, Geva's eyes were swimming, her thoughts desperately flailing for solutions, ideas, anything, but finding nothing, nothing. Only just standing here in silence, staring at him. Only an arms'-length away, but suddenly feeling like a vast, empty chasm was racing out between them.

"I'm not going to apologize for working hard for you," she bit out, into it, against it. "Or for not telling you about my family, when you didn't even ask. But if you want the truth"—she made her blinking eyes hold to his—"I didn't tell you because I couldn't bear for you to feel sorry for me, or to feel you'd taken advantage of me. I didn't want to lose what we had. Didn't want to"—the word broke into a sob—"to lose you, too. To lose this life with you, when I've only just found it."

She had to keep dragging for air, trying to breathe through the lurking sobs in her throat. And there was no way to say anything else now, not without breaking down and weeping before him, just the way he'd told her to, if she wanted to try to convince him. And oh gods, how had it come to this, how could she have prevented this, no, forward, no—

"I need—some time," his voice broke in, sudden, wooden, as his clawed hand dragged through his hair. "Alone. I shall—come to you. With an answer."

And without another word, or even a look, he strode to the door, and left.

40

Rathgarr didn't return that night.

It had been weeks since they'd spent a night apart—since their very first night travelling together—and Geva had almost forgotten how it felt to sleep without him, without his safe, familiar warmth curled up against her. And even worse, without the heady release of their usual evening pleasures, turning her sated and boneless and peaceful beneath his clever, easy touch.

And as she lay there in their bed alone, she couldn't stop thinking backwards, sifting through the past few weeks, desperately searching for where it had gone wrong, what she could have done differently. Should she have been less attentive, less obliging? Should she have argued more, ignored more, refused to accept his coins or his praise or his tongue? And surely she shouldn't have tried to sway him the way she had, to show him why he should stay—but clearly he wouldn't have been any more willing to consider her honesty, either? And he'd been the one to keep pulling away, to keep putting those walls between them, to keep all those damned secrets.

I learnt very well to keep my secrets close. Most of all when a pretty woman smiles at me and asks for them.

Geva somehow fell into a fitful, miserable sleep, jerking awake again and again at every sound in the corridor, until finally the faint morning light from above was enough to drag her out of bed, and over to the wardrobe. To where she hadn't opened it in days—weeks?—because Rathgarr liked to choose her clothes, and it had been one more way to oblige him. And—she could admit—another way he'd made her feel special. Cared for.

And even now, she still found herself blinking hard as she carded through the neat rows of clothes inside. There were so many new shifts, ones she didn't even recognize, in multiple cuts and colours—and even here, at the very back, was a cloak she'd never seen before. A thick, warm-looking, well-made cloak, with a soft, fur-lined hood. And it was far too small for Rathgarr, and it was here in their wardrobe, so...

She felt herself fingering at her wedding-ring, the one he'd chosen for her, because he'd thought it would look well against her skin. And he'd chosen the cuff for her too, and the belt and the necklace, and the beads and clasp for her hair. And why had he done all that, why would he have bothered, if he hadn't cared?

He'd needed to think. And that wasn't a no. Was it?

Geva kept repeating that thought as she dressed in one of the new shifts, with his cuff, and his hair-clasp. And as she walked up to the schoolroom, she felt her heartbeat rising, her hope swelling higher with every rapidfire beat. Maybe he would meet her here. He hadn't missed a day yet. Surely he would come.

But when she stepped into the cozy, familiar schoolroom, she was dismayed to find only Killik and Ulfarr with Sune, the three of them rapidly signing together, even as Killik glanced up toward her. "Rathgarr sent word that he cannot come today," he said. "So Ulfarr shall help me lead the morning's game out in the trees, ach?"

Oh. Geva fought through the plunge in her belly, and

managed a nod, and a signed *thank-you* toward Ulfarr. Who eyed her with blatant suspicion in return, and she was deeply grateful for the abrupt arrival of Hauk and Hagen, followed by the three small Ka-esh. And it turned out that Erik had forgotten his eye-mask, requiring her to rush around to make a new one, and then the three Grisk were excitedly pulling over a brand-new, plump little orcling, with two neat braids in his hair, and wide, long-lashed eyes.

"Miss Gee!" exclaimed Tyr, tugging the orcling forward. "This is Vragi. He is new today, and his father has brought him all the way here from Bairia, so that he might come learn with us!"

Oh. Geva felt herself giving the first genuine smile of the day, and knelt down to introduce herself, and welcome Vragi to the class. And though he seemed very shy at first, he was soon running around shrieking with the rest of them, until Killik— instead of Rathgarr—called for the orclings to follow him outside.

"Is Rathgarr not here?" Timo asked Geva, with an uncertain twitch of his nose, as a few other orclings lingered back, clearly wanting to know, too. "I cannot smell him nearby."

"No, he had another commitment today," Geva made herself say, as lightly as she could, as she cheerfully waved him toward the door. "But I hope he'll be back soon."

Timo didn't seem convinced, still eyeing Geva with his nose twitching, but after a meaningful grunt from Ulfarr, he scurried toward the door. Leaving Geva behind with Ulfarr, of all people, and she lurched forward too, while desperately hoping he would follow along far, far behind.

But there was no such luck, of course. And somehow Ulfarr had even fallen in step beside her, angling her a narrow look out the corner of his eye.

"Where has your Ash-Kai really gone?" he asked, in a deep, deadpan voice. "Plotting again, mayhap? Digging deeper, this time?"

Geva startled, and couldn't help a wide, wet-eyed glance toward where he was frowning at her, his heavy brow deeply furrowed. "If Rathgarr was wise," he continued, "he would leave this, and welcome the gifts he has. He would look forward, rather than back."

Something shivered up Geva's spine, but she lifted her chin, gave him her haughtiest look. "I'm not surprised you would think so," she said crisply. "That would benefit you very well, wouldn't it?"

And damn it, perhaps that was betraying far too much, risking exposing all Rathgarr's secret plans, but Ulfarr didn't look even slightly surprised. "No," he said flatly. "This would benefit *him*."

Well, that was unsettling, and Geva couldn't seem to shake off the ever-rising unease, even once they'd reached Orc Mountain's front entrance, and Ulfarr had stalked off to help Killik with the game. It was a very Skai hide-and-seek amidst the trees surrounding the base of the mountain, and while usually Geva would have laughed and cheered as she watched, or maybe even participated, she could only seem to stand there with her arms folded, her eyes glancing again and again toward the bulk of the mountain behind her.

There was still no sign of Rathgarr as they all traipsed inside again, the orclings flush-faced and chattering with pleasure. And despite Geva's best attempts to focus on Tristan's morning's teaching—writing simple words in Aelakesh—she finally had to set down her quill, and focus hard on breathing through her nose. It hadn't been a no. Forward...

"Are you all right, sister?" interrupted a familiar voice, and when Geva glanced over, it was Kesst, pulling up a chair to sit beside her. "Where's Rath?"

His eyes looked sharply suspicious, suddenly, almost as if he somehow knew about their fight, and Geva desperately attempted a shrug, a casual wave of her hand. "He just had a few things to sort out this morning," she said, fixing her gaze back to where Tristan now had the orclings verbally translating sentences for one another, their little voices clamouring loudly through the room. "Are you ready for your first teaching stint, then?"

It was finally Kesst's day to lead the clan-focused activity, in their very first session on oral history. Which, before today, Geva had been eagerly anticipating—but now that she was again thinking of Kesst's wonderful tale the night before, there was only more deep, dragging misery in her belly. It hadn't been a no. He'd said he would come back...

Kesst was giving her a very odd look, now, but Tristan had clearly had enough, blinking bemusedly around at the room of now-shrieking orclings, and Geva lurched to her feet, and called for the room to quiet down. And then she waved Kesst up to the front of the room, introducing him as enthusiastically as she could.

"Along with our reading and writing, spoken stories and tales are a very important way to learn and share with one another," she told the watching class. "And our brother Kesst is a very gifted tale-teller. A true Ash-Kai galdr-spinner. And I can't wait to hear what he has for us today."

She beamed toward him, in perhaps her second genuine smile of the day, which Kesst returned with another sharply suspicious look, before sighing and flicking his gaze back to the room. "Right, then," he said, leaning back against the nearest table. "We'll begin with Edom and Akva. Our furthest fore-bears, and the founders of our mountain."

On its face, it sounded like a far less compelling story than the skunk and the maiden—but soon Geva was just as rapt, just as caught, as the night before. Lost in the twisty, turbulent tale of a lonely, runaway elf, betrayed by his own kin, and cast away from his home. And when he ran, sailing to a new realm across the sea, he soon found refuge in a new home—a great, sprawling mountain, which in return for his care, granted him shelter and safety from his enemies.

But the more settled Edom became, the more lonely he grew, too. He'd lost all his kin, and he longed for a companion, a friend. And so, he sought out a mate, and found one in a brave, beautiful human woman named Akva. She soothed him and comforted him, and offered him peace and pleasure—and in his gratefulness and affection, Edom marked her as his own, and swore he would never seek another. And together, they raised five sons, who became the five clans of orcs. Ash-Kai, the strongest, then Bautul, the bravest. Then Skai, the swiftest, and Ka-esh, the wisest. And finally, Grisk, the kindest.

Kesst stopped speaking there, but just like the night before, the tale seemed to keep sprawling in the silence, settling out wide across the room. Where more than a dozen rambunctious orclings sat in hushed, enthralled stillness, their bright eyes rapturous and glittering on Kesst's face, on the way his clawed hands were hovering in midair, as if holding up the spell, the story, for all of them to see.

When his hands dropped, it was as though a rushing little ripple swept through the room—and then the orclings began shifting and stirring again, some of them whispering to each other, some just blinking in stunned, spellbound awe. And Geva felt her throat swallowing hard at the sight of Vragi, who was staring with unabashed wonder toward Kesst, while a shiny drop of wetness streaked down his plump little cheek.

"Another!" called a familiar voice beside Geva, and when she jerked to look, it was Jule. And when she'd come in, Geva couldn't have said, but she was wryly smiling from the nearest chair, with a silent, wide-eyed Tengil in her arms. "Kesst is a wonder, isn't he?" she asked. "I'm so glad you suggested this, sister."

Kesst had obviously overheard, rolling his eyes toward them, but then he shrugged, and launched into another tale. This one a far lighter story about the two brothers Bautul and Skai, and their friendly but steadily escalating rivalry. One that culminated in Skai enlisting Ka-esh's help to flood Bautul's favourite part of the mountain, which had the unexpected result of creating a rich, loamy garden on the Bautul side—a garden Bautul then used to grow delicious food, which he flatly refused to allow Skai to eat.

"But finally, they came to a truce," Kesst's light voice said, his hands still fluttering in midair, "when swift, watchful Skai travelled all over the realm, seeking out the rarest, most succulent plants and seeds. And when he returned, he freely granted them to his brother Bautul as a gift, and swore to guard his garden, and keep his great bounty safe. And thus, the two brothers were forever reconciled, and Skai never went hungry again."

This time, the tale's end left the orclings smiling and giggling, the Skai and Bautul casting proud, bashful glances toward one another. And at their collective urging, Kesst then told another tale, and another, and another.

It was a truly wonderful way to spend a morning, and at one point Tengil crawled over into Geva's lap, his little body curling up warm and reassuring against her. And it was almost—almost—enough to make her forget Rathgarr, forget the unease and the misery, in the quiet, perfect peace of this moment.

But then at some point, Sigarr and Abjorn came in, ready for the day's scheduled sparring session. And suddenly the spell was broken, and Geva was blinking between them and the door, and feeling the misery surge even stronger than before. Rathgarr still hadn't come. Forward...

It took nearly all her willpower to get up and thank Kesst, and then to start directing the class toward the Ash-Kai sparring-room. But finally they were there and settled, happily throwing themselves into Sigarr's first exercises of the day, and Geva sagged down onto the nearest stone step, her fingers twisting her wedding-ring again and again. Her eyes blankly watching where Sigarr was demonstrating a specific kind of throw, pinning a squirming Abjorn firmly down beneath him, his knee digging deep into his belly. While Abjorn choked and gasped, his eyes gone curiously blank, before he flailed up again, kicking at Sigarr's solid, unyielding back.

"They'll figure it out one of these days," interrupted a light, familiar voice, making Geva jump—but it was only Kesst again, giving a wry smile as he sank down to sit beside her. "At least, we can only hope. For the safety of the orclings' eyes, if nothing else."

Geva managed a wan smile in return, glancing back at where Abjorn was wildly wriggling away from Sigarr's crushing grip—at least, until Sigarr launched onto him again. Pinning him face-down to the floor this time, while Abjorn helplessly arched and growled beneath him, his eyes rolling back.

"Is there a reason they can't just talk to one another?" Geva said, wincing at the obvious wistfulness in her voice. "Be honest with each other, and work it out?"

Kesst huffed a mirthless laugh, and then jerked a too-casual shrug. "We're Ash-Kai, sister, remember?" he replied. "Well, not Abjorn, but close enough. And why would we ever expose ourselves to that kind of potential pain and loss if we don't actually need to? At least this way"—he nodded at where Sigarr was pulling Abjorn up again, giving his shoulder a firm little squeeze—"they know they have this much. Here. Right now. No matter what rubbish comes tomorrow."

Oh. And blinking over toward them, watching Abjorn grin delightedly up at Sigarr's face, the heaviness seemed to plunge harder, deeper, into Geva's stomach. Because... she'd perhaps done that too. Hadn't she? She hadn't wanted to risk talking to Rathgarr, being honest with him about what she wanted, and how she felt. She'd kept it to herself for so long, and then of course he'd been shocked and confused. Of course he'd struggled to believe her.

"So really, sister, what is it?" came Kesst's quiet voice, his knee gently nudging at hers. "It's Rath, right? What happened?"

Geva twitched, but Kesst was still here, waiting, giving her a light, encouraging smile that didn't quite meet his eyes. "What, did last night set him off somehow, then?" he continued. "Did he go souse himself in ale? Or, maybe he sat there like a lump and stared at the wall and ignored everything you said, until you finally came to your senses, and told him you'd had enough of him?"

Geva couldn't help a sharp look toward Kesst this time, but then she grimaced, rubbed painfully at her face. "He can't... help that," she replied, more defensively than she meant. "It's just... something that happens, sometimes. He just needs time, that's all."

There was a brief flare in Kesst's eyes, something almost like satisfaction, even as he grimaced, too. "I know," he said, with a sigh. "It's only—Father used to do it, too. Sometimes for days, or weeks. And seeing Rath like that, it's always been quite uniquely horrifying, you know? Especially since"—he drew in a breath, his eyes dropping—"Eft says it's not something he can just heal, either. Not like that."

Right. Geva felt herself nodding, wilting a little against the solid stone beneath her. And then glancing back toward the door, to where there was still no sign of Rathgarr, still.

"So what set him off, then?" Kesst prodded, with another companionable bump at her knee. "Was it all that discussion about Mother and Father last night? All those lovely, heart-warming memories?"

Geva winced, but Kesst clearly wasn't letting this go. And at least he wasn't truly close to the real reason yet, because surely he thought Rathgarr had already known what had happened to her own parents, right? And surely she could tell him something, at least some piece of the truth...

"That was—part of it," she finally replied, on a heavy exhale. "I know he finds it—difficult, to trust. Humans, and women, especially. I mean, your mother, she..."

Her voice snapped off there, her thoughts reeling backwards in a sudden, stilted jolt. Back to what Rathgarr had said the night before, when he'd looked at her with such strange, angry resentment in his eyes.

Will you keep my son from me, he'd said. *Will you put him at risk, because you only care for what you want.*

Will you then find a clever way to get rid of me.

And how... how he'd said that, mimicking the accent. Not Geva's accent, that time. But a distinct northern accent, one she'd heard him use several times before.

His... his *mother's*.

A vicious, cracking ice was shattering up Geva's spine, because—no. *No.* That wasn't possible. Rathgarr had been run out after his mother's death, he'd said. *After.* And surely their mother wouldn't have wanted to leave Kesst alone and unprotected like that... right? Surely she'd realized on some level what Rathgarr had been for Kesst, how he'd kept him safe... right?

But Geva's heart was slamming against her ribs, now, her hands clutched clammy to her knees, her eyes staring unseeing toward the front of the room. Toward—toward Kesst's hand, waving in front of her face.

"Sister," he was loudly saying from beside her, and he was gently shaking her shoulder, too. "Hey. Are you in there? Are you pulling a Rath on me? Do you need help?"

Geva was blinking, blinking, but she couldn't quite seem to focus on Kesst's face. On where he was smiling, yes, but he was looking pale, suddenly, too. His bones standing out stark beneath his skin, those dark circles somehow seeming deeper under his eyes...

"Kesst," she whispered. "Your—your mother. Did she want the inheritance to go to... to *you*?"

And in return, there was... silence. Silence, with Kesst just sitting there staring, unmoving, the entire world choked and still. *Will you find a clever way to get rid of me.*

And in a sharp, sudden movement, Kesst leapt up, and fled for the door.

41

––––––––––

Geva sat there for another numb, dangling moment, staring at where Kesst had gone. Staring, and staring, while her thoughts turned over again, and again, and again.

Their mother. Their *mother*. And suddenly, all the things Rathgarr had said about his mother were crashing together, careening into a horrible, harrowing mess.

My mother and I were never in accord. Too much like my witless, brute orc father, she liked to say. A greedy, secretive hoarder. A piggish, plundering orc pillager.

I wished to run... but she would not hear of this. She said she should send the Skai after us. She had plans of her own. She had bought your safety in other ways.

She hoped some heroic man would soon kill me in battle, so I might finally leave her in peace about you.

But—*why*. Why would their own mother have gone to such lengths, such risks, for an inheritance that was so precarious? Kesst had said their mother had been entangled with Grimarr's vile father Kaugir, right? So surely she would have known what Kaugir might do with their inheritance? How it might then be forfeit to the clan, for Kaugir's own gain, like Grimarr had said?

But... had Grimarr *known* that, for certain? No. No, he'd said he hadn't known his father's plan. He didn't remember there being a vow to swear Kesst's safety. He didn't remember seeing their family's hoard. And Geva had naturally believed Grimarr's assumptions, believed the hoard was gone, that it didn't exist...

But had *Rathgarr* ever said that? Gods, what *had* Rathgarr said? *You shall swear that our birthright shall be granted back to us, if ever it is found. You ken that if my father's hoard comes to light, half of it shall then be yours, as my mate...*

Was the hoard... *still here?*

Geva's stomach was roiling again, her bile rising, her heart hammering so hard she felt faint. And without thinking, she leapt to her feet, fast enough that the room spun around her— but there was suddenly only one thing, one drive, one goal remaining.

She needed to find Rathgarr.

"Sigarr," she said, as steadily as she could, as she lurched over to the side of the ring. "Have you seen—or scented—Rathgarr today? Or last night?"

Sigarr instantly paused his coaching of Hauk and Hagen to come over, his heavy brow furrowing. "No, sister," he replied. "Have you not? Is aught amiss?"

Damn it, *damn* it, and Geva shook her head, and attempted a casual wave of her hand. "We've just had a slight—misunderstanding," she said, "and I'd like to check in with him, but—"

"I can help," piped up a familiar voice, and when Geva jerked to look, it was Timo, with a cautious smile on his mouth. "I am sure I can follow Rathgarr's scent through the mountain, as long as it is quite fresh."

Oh. Geva couldn't deny the flare of hope in her chest, her eyes angling helplessly toward Sigarr. Who, gods bless him, was nodding, and waving them toward the door. "You go, then," he said firmly. "Abjorn and I shall handle the rest of this today."

Geva fervently thanked him, and then said a quick round of

goodbyes to the orclings, with a particular thank-you to Vragi for joining them. And then she rushed after Timo toward the door, only to discover that there were two more teenage orcs lurking behind her. Trygve, looking slightly guilty, and Sune, with chilly, blatant defiance in his eyes.

"Ach, yes, Miss Gee, they must come also," Timo said, with a quick sign toward them that Geva couldn't follow. "I shall need their help, you ken."

Geva couldn't be bothered to protest, and swiftly led the three of them over to her and Rathgarr's room. Knowing, now, after weeks of classes, that scent-tracking was most effective when the tracking orc had a clear starting point, and an approximate time.

"So Rathgarr left from here last evening, a while after sundown," she said thickly. "I didn't see which way he went, after that."

Timo was carefully sniffing around the door, with Trygve close behind him, while Sune stood a little off to the side, his slim arms folded, waiting. Until Timo's eyes glanced up, his head cocking sideways, down the corridor toward the Skai wing. "Rathgarr went that way," he said, with certainty. "Down into the mountain. And he was... unhappy, ach?"

Geva swallowed hard, but she knew that strong emotions sometimes helped with tracking too, and she twitched a nod. Earning a satisfied nod back from Timo, and an airy wave down the corridor. "Come, then," he said. "This way. Mayhap bring your lamp, ach?"

Geva quickly fetched the lamp, and soon they were all following Timo through the mountain, heading steadily downwards. Passing through the Skai wing, and then the Bautul, and the Grisk. Going deeper and deeper through the mountain, without stopping, without even any kind of hesitation from Timo. His face held straight ahead, his breaths inhaling steady and slow.

And as they kept walking, Geva felt her dread rising, tightening with every single step. Why would Rathgarr have come all the way down here? What would he want down here? Except for, maybe, maybe, *that stinking little room in the Ka-esh wing...*

And yes, yes, they were in the Ka-esh wing now, and still going deeper. Not to the library, or the laboratory, or any of the frequently used Ka-esh rooms, but beyond, and below. Deeper than Geva had ever gone, to where there were no lamps, and no other orcs. Only dank, narrow, twisty corridors, lined with empty, abandoned rooms. The walls often rough and cracked, the floors tilted and uneven, sometimes with wet patches—and Geva blanched at what looked like a dark bloodstain, pooled out across the full width of the corridor.

"Are we close?" she ventured, as she gingerly stepped over the bloodstain, but Timo shushed her, and then ducked into a nearby empty room. One that had a few old, dusty furnishings, mottled with damp and age, but Timo ignored them and instead ran his hands against the cracked, uneven walls, breathing in slow and deep.

"Not here," he muttered to himself, and then moved to the next room, and the next. Walking around that room's walls three or four times, before doubling back to the first one, and repeating it all over again. While Geva clutched her lamp tighter and tighter, her breaths shallow, her dread now a sickening weight churning in her belly.

Until finally, Timo jerked to a stop in the middle of the dank, unlit corridor. His nose twitching and wrinkling, his eyes casting uneasily about in the shadowy light of Geva's lamp.

"Rathgarr's scent is... muddled, here," he said, with another unhappy twitch of his nose. "He has oft been here, walking here, over and over again, for many days and weeks. So much that I cannot tell where he has now gone, or how."

Oh. Geva's stomach roiled again, and she shot a helpless, desperate glance around the dim, eerie corridor, all its shadowy doors looking rather like gaping hungry mouths in the guttering lamplight. *This* was where Rathgarr had been secretly spending his days? *This* was what he had been doing? Walking down here, over and over again, for *weeks*?!

"There must be something else we can do," Geva's voice said, hollow and thin in the damp, close corridor. "Someone else who could help. Varinn, maybe?"

Timo grimaced and shook his head, his nose still twitching. "Varinn has gone north with Alma and Ella for the day," he replied. "I should next say Baldr, but his scent is not now in the mountain, either. But... mayhap we could try Thrain?"

Geva frowned at that, vaguely remembering how Varinn had gently mocked Thrain's scenting capabilities—but beside her, Trygve was firmly nodding. And after a swift sign from Timo, Trygve rushed away up the corridor, while Timo gave Geva a shrug, and an apologetic smile.

"Thrain is indeed hopeless, when he has had a few drinks," he said. "But if you can catch him before this, he is one of our best, ach?"

Oh. Geva certainly wasn't about to argue, though she couldn't seem to stop moving, pacing a little up and down the dank corridor. While the unease and the dread kept rising, heaving, why had Rathgarr done this, why had he never said...

She absently spun around, and found she'd nearly careened into Sune, who was also apparently pacing, looking far more agitated than she would have expected. And amidst her own rattling edginess, she managed to sign him an apology, and then, after another look at his eyes, one of the simple questions they'd learned. *Is anything amiss?*

Sune visibly flinched, and now Timo was stepping over too, his head tilting, his nostrils flaring. "Ach, what is it, brother?" he said. "Only the close walls? Or... something you scent?"

In return, Sune's eyes purposefully flicked away, but Timo stepped over beside him, and bumped him with his elbow. Until finally Sune signed something, very quickly, something that made Timo's head tilt further, his breath again inhaling deep.

"Ach, I scent him now," he said thoughtfully. "Not far from here. That is... odd."

Geva's stomach leapt again, her eyes widening, but Timo quickly shook his head, and gave another apologetic smile. "Not Rathgarr," he said. "But Sune's heart-father is near here, also."

Sune's... *heart-father*. Geva's brief flare of hopefulness had horribly plunged, her eyes frantically glancing between Timo and Sune. "Killik?" she demanded, because please, please, maybe he'd gone scouting down here, or hunting, or...

"No, Killik is his blade-father," Timo absently replied, and he was already sniffing again, wandering a little way down the corridor. "It is Ulfarr, here."

Ulfarr. *Ulfarr* was near here. Near here, with Rathgarr. And Geva's heart was racing now, screeching and shrieking through her chest, because—Rathgarr wanted vengeance on Ulfarr. Rathgarr probably wanted to kill Ulfarr. Sune's... *heart-father*?! Who'd told Geva just today, what felt like ages ago, that Rathgarr should... forget the past. Look forward. For his own benefit.

And gods curse it, Geva needed to run, to scream, to kick something, to do something—when oh, thank the gods, Trygve jogged back down the corridor, with a tall, spiky-haired Thrain at his heels. And Geva would never have dreamt she'd be so happy to see him, and she bobbed anxiously on her feet as he curtly nodded toward her, and then began sniffing at the wall, trailing his sharp claws against it.

"Och, I follow why you're baffled, brothers," he said. "This is a mess. Almost as if they were both on this side, but also... inside the wall."

They. *Inside* the wall. Geva's heart kicked again, her throat swallowing hard. "They?" she asked, her voice faint. "Who?"

Thrain had leaned back to look at the wall, frowning, his

hands on his hips. "Rathgarr, and Kesst," he said. "And do I smell *Ulfarr*, too?"

Damn it. Rathgarr, and Ulfarr, and *Kesst*. Kesst, who'd rushed off like that... to come *here*?! And Geva could not move, could only stand here and stare at Thrain's thoughtful face, his slowly shaking head. "We need a Ka-esh," he said. "John isn't far from here, if you would fetch him, Trygve?"

Trygve nodded, spinning off down the corridor again, while Thrain beckoned Timo after him back into the nearest room. Where they again began tracing their hands against the wall, now talking back and forth with incomprehensible terms like age decay, and scent-tails, and kin-threads.

Geva's surging agitation was now nearing panic, and she nearly yelped at the sound of more approaching footsteps. Trygve again, this time accompanied by Rosa's handsome, stern-faced mate John, his sharp brows raised in silent inquiry.

"John," Thrain said, waving him forward. "We're seeking a way behind this wall. The scents beyond it are fresh in this room, but then they also fade off"—he pointed his claw downwards—"toward the east, as if following a passage. There are no recent Ka-esh scents on the passage, not even your usual surveyors, so we ken it's been blocked, and forgotten."

John was already nodding, his mouth pursed, his eyes casting over the wall, and then the floor. "The grain and weight of the stone here should not allow for a cut," he said flatly. "It would need to be..."

His eyes were travelling upwards, and then downwards, narrowing as they fixed on the cracked, mottled stone floor beneath the musty old bed. On where—Geva's throat caught— there was a slightly raised stone. And when John stomped on the stone, grinding down with his heel, there was a very faint, distant scraping sound—and then, from up above, a very short, rusty chain lowered down, dangling from one of the cracks in the ceiling above.

Thrain was looking too, and in a swift movement he

jumped up onto the bed, reaching up, yanking on the chain. And with another strange, scraping creak, the cracked ceiling somehow... opened. Part of it shifting aside, revealing a jagged black hole, perhaps big enough for a person to fit through.

"There we go," Thrain said, grinning with supreme satisfaction up toward it, as though it wasn't a horrifying hidden tunnel, leading to gods knew where. "Though how do we get up? Damned difficult to use it like this, so—"

"Reach up inside," John said curtly, eyeing the tunnel with marked dislike. "And this is mayhap not safe, so you go first."

If Thrain was offended by this, he didn't let on, and instead grunted as he awkwardly hung from the chain by one hand, while attempting to grope around up inside with the other. Until beside Geva, Sune gave an impatient-sounding huff, and then leapt up too, shoving Thrain out of the way—and with a hard swing off the chain, he was hanging off the edge of the hole itself, and dragging down something from inside.

It was another chain, but this time it was shaped like... a ladder. One that Sune was already scrambling up, his lean body disappearing into the hole above.

"Sune!" Geva gasped, but damn it, Timo and Trygve were already shoving past Thrain to climb up, too. And then Thrain was shrugging, and doing the same, leaving Geva standing there staring in alarm at John, who waved her up with a sharp flick of his hand.

"If it did not fall on Thrain, it ought to be safe," he said flatly, as he reached to pluck the lamp out of her hand. "My forebears did not bear shoddy work, ach?"

It wasn't much comfort, but Geva's panic was truly screeching now, and she awkwardly nodded and shuffled up the ladder, while John held it taut beneath her. And when she neared the top, Thrain's strong hand yanked her up into the darkness, her feet skittering against a surprisingly solid-feeling floor.

"What is this?" she croaked, but John was already climbing

up behind her, with the lamp hanging off his arm. And in its light, she could make out yet another damp, twisty tunnel, even narrower than the one below.

"Just what we were seeking," Thrain said, inhaling deep. "Come. They went this way."

Geva nodded, and followed after Thrain, Sune, Trygve, and Timo through the passage, with John behind. His lamp casting large, shuddering shadows on the rough-cut walls, as Geva's heartbeat wailed even louder, her hands cold and clammy, her eyes furiously blinking. Rathgarr had come this way. And Kesst. And *Ulfarr*.

And gods, the awful little corridor felt like it went on forever, twisting, turning, twisting again. Now breaking into occasional forks, the paths dark and sinister in the lamplight. And Geva had to drag for air, hauling it in shaky and deep, fighting to stay upright, to keep her feet moving. Rathgarr was in here. Kesst. Ulfarr.

Until finally, ahead of them, Thrain and Timo both startled at once, and rushed toward a wall. A wall that looked like any other wall here, damp and rough and stained with age—but John was striding forward, and pushing at a sharp-looking piece of stone on the wall.

And with another rough, grating, painfully loud creak, the wall slowly tilted open. Revealing something else behind it, something that glinted bright and yellow in the flickering lamplight.

The gold.

42

———

Rathgarr's inheritance was here.

And as Geva stepped inside, blinking stunned and shaky toward it, she realized just how naive she'd been. How foolish. Because this wasn't anything like Rathgarr's little trove-room, with its display of assorted treasures. This was... a hoard. A blatant, shocking display of wealth like Geva had never seen, had never once thought to imagine in her life.

There were coins. Gems. Jewels. Sculptures, statues, suits of armour, weapons. Furniture. Mirrors. Wardrobes. Trunks with clothing and furs. And even just huge stacked chunks of rough-cut stone, with glittering seams of colour inside them.

And they say Ash-Kai are greedy, whispered a voice, Rathgarr's voice, into Geva's stunned, shaking thoughts. *Those Grisk have gathered a hoard even greater than my father's.*

But Rathgarr wasn't here... or was he? And Geva's eyes were desperately scanning the glittering room in the dim lamplight, catching on the mass of furniture—and then she flinched all over, because no, yes, that was Rathgarr's voice speaking, hard and loud and close.

"You *knew* this was here," it growled. "You Skai plotted with my mother against me, to steal my birthright, and *destroy* me!"

Geva flinched again, hard enough that her feet staggered, sliding on a loose gold coin. And suddenly she was sprinting forward, further into the room, toward the pile of furniture, and around behind it—

And there. Here. Was Rathgarr. With his huge sword drawn, his body big and rigid and so stunningly, blazingly familiar that the room spun. He was here, he was safe, alive— and even as the relief crashed through Geva, there was also fear, surging and screeching, even higher than before.

Because... Ulfarr was here, too. Huge, bare-chested, terrifying, with a curved, shining scimitar held in his huge clawed hand. And his eyes were fixed on Rathgarr, flashing with pure, contemptuous rage.

"The Skai sought *naught* against you, Rathgarr," Ulfarr was growling back. "If you wish to cast blame, you ought to cast it upon your own clan. Your own kin!"

With that, his eyes darted furiously sideways, toward— Kesst. Toward where Kesst was here too, standing half-hidden in the shadows, his arms tightly crossed over his chest. And surely Rathgarr had already known he was there, casting a sharp glance toward him, his body easing a little closer in front of him, as if to block him from Ulfarr's view.

"I shall not blame Kesst for my mother's sins," Rathgarr snarled back, his voice even harder than before. "It was the Skai who carried out her foul wishes. It was *you*. I knew you were part of this, Ulfarr. I *knew* you were yet my enemy, no matter how you and the Skai play-acted that you were not!"

Ulfarr barked a rough, loud laugh, and shook his head. "And what do you ken we gained from this?" he demanded. "For these past sixteen summers, I was doomed to guard *your* blood-brother! A sly, surly, sneaking Ash-Kai, who ran wild wherever he wished, spoke false with every breath from his mouth, and did *naught* that he was told! Do you ken it was easy, tending to him all this time?"

He'd shot an angry glare toward Kesst, who was glowering back just as viciously, his arms clamping tighter against his chest. "You know, I told Rath not to take vengeance on you," he said, his voice very silky, "but maybe it's high time I changed my mind, hmmm?"

The look in Rathgarr's eyes was almost feral, suddenly, and he moved a swift, smooth step closer toward Ulfarr, his sword lifting. "And how *dare* you claim you guarded my brother, Ulfarr," he growled, "when you so deeply *failed* at this. When you allowed Kesst to be harmed, and taken against his wishes!"

But Ulfarr loudly scoffed, his own sword rising, his huge body shifting into a deep, settled stance. "We only vowed to keep your brother close, and alive," he hissed. "Naught more. I ken your sulking, scheming mother *wished* him to use his pretty form and silver tongue to gain power and gold, just as *she* did!"

He'd given a sharp, furious sweep of his scimitar at the room—at all the obscene, glittering wealth—and behind Rathgarr, Kesst visibly flinched, his hand clamping over his mouth. While Rathgarr roared with fury, his huge body leaping into motion, lunging straight toward Ulfarr's crouching, waiting bulk—

When suddenly, from behind Geva, there was a strangled little yelp—and even as she clutched toward it, no, no, too late, too late, a slim, dark-haired figure was sprinting forward. Rushing straight out in front of Rathgarr's upraised sword, and hurling his arms around Ulfarr's waist.

It was—Sune.

"No," he choked, the first words Geva had ever heard him speak. "No. *Papa.*"

43

P *apa.*

Rathgarr reeled up just in time, his sword swinging high toward the ceiling in a sharp, deadly arc. His eyes frozen on Sune, his face suddenly pale, his breath dragging in deep—

And then he spun toward Geva. Toward where she was still standing stock-still in the shadows, her eyes shocked wide, her heart wildly pounding in her chest.

"Poppet?" he said, his voice wondering, strange—and then he whipped around further, blinking back behind her. Back toward where a fearful-looking Timo and Trygve were hovering too, with Thrain and John both frowning behind them. And—Geva startled—Killik?!

But yes, that was indeed Killik, casually sauntering forward through them all, his own scimitar held loose in his clawed hand. "Ach, I have been missing all the fun," he said lightly, as he strode over toward where Sune was still clinging to Ulfarr. And once Killik had firmly clamped his hand to Sune's shoulder, he eased close in front of him, just the way Rathgarr was again doing with Kesst. "Now, was there more, mayhap?"

Another low growl hissed from Rathgarr's throat, but he

didn't move, his eyes narrow and flinty on Killik's face. "Ach, mayhap," he said coldly. "If your clanmate shall keep speaking such vile falsehoods of my brother!"

But Killik just kept looking blandly back toward Rathgarr, his brows upraised. "Which part is the falsehood?" he asked coolly. "The part where Ulfarr was pushed into a secret vow he did not wish to make? The vow he yet kept, even when all its other speakers were dead? The vow that bound him to guard *your* brother? Who, ach, was not an easy orc to care for, after he lost both his mother and the blood-brother he so worshipped?"

Rathgarr angled a brief, uncertain glance toward Kesst behind him, but Kesst was glaring at Killik, his arms still crossed tightly over his chest. "I never asked for the Skai's guarding," he spat. "I did not need their rubbish *help*. And if I'd known that was what was going on, I would have immediately refused, especially from the likes of *him*!"

He'd shot a dark, baleful look toward Ulfarr, whose heavy jaw was very set, his hand visibly tense on Sune's shoulder. And Killik had glanced back too, his breath exhaling, his shoulder giving a slow, rolling shrug. "Ach, we all ken Ulfarr is not fault-less," he said flatly. "But he now seeks in earnest to make amends for his past wrongs. And I ken"—he looked down his nose toward Kesst—"keeping you alive was not one of these."

But Kesst was shaking his head, barking a sharp, shrill laugh, and suddenly Rathgarr was laughing too, the sound not unlike Kesst's, but richer and deeper. "Ach, Ulfarr seeks to make *amends*," he drawled. "And we ought to trust you *Skai* to watch over this."

At that, Killik's expression had hardened, and he tossed his scimitar to the other hand. "Ach, you ought," he said, his voice very cold now. "Our Enforcer Simon is the strongest orc in this mountain, and our Right Hand Drafli is mated to our best nose, and has the ear of the captain each day. If there is *one scent wrong*, they shall know this, and the transgressor shall be punished. Why do you ken"—he stepped forward, glaring at

Kesst and Rathgarr—"none of the other Skai who made this vow to your mother now live? Because we *Enforced* them, for all their sins against our kin!"

No one spoke, and Killik glared between Kesst and Rathgarr, and jabbed his scimitar-tip toward Ulfarr's chest. "Ulfarr's sins were far less than theirs," he continued, "but do you ken he has been spared in this? Do you ken he can spawn sons of his own blood now? Do you ken he should have been granted leave to raise Sune, without me as his keeper?!"

Killik was spitting out the words by the end, showing more emotion than Geva had ever seen from him. And blinking at them, and at Sune, who was still clinging to Ulfarr with visceral fear in his wide dark eyes, it was as though something suddenly snapped to life inside Geva, shaking her awake again. There were children here, damn it, children she was responsible for—and she lurched forward, her hands up, her breaths still heaving in unsteady gulps.

"Look, can't we just—put the weapons down, and have a reasonable conversation about all this?" she said, her voice wavering. "Perhaps we can all agree that the people most at fault for this mess aren't actually here?"

She was vaguely surprised to see Rathgarr following her gaze toward Sune, and slightly lowering his sword—but behind him, Kesst was still glaring at Killik, who was curling his lip in return. "Not yet," Killik replied sharply. "I am weary of you Ash-Kai casting blame and slander upon the Skai, and then standing there sly and silent whilst we suffer for this. So"—he smiled, vicious and deadly—"which of you wishes to tell the rest of this tale?"

He was pointing his scimitar straight out now, swinging it back and forth between Kesst, and Rathgarr, and... Geva. Catching her breath cold in her already-frozen body, her eyes blinking uneasily at his cruel, smiling face.

"None of you?" Killik said, as he swung his sword back toward Rathgarr and Kesst—toward where Rathgarr was frowning, and Kesst was suddenly looking pale again, and rather tight around the mouth.

"Ach, then," Killik said smoothly, with a dangerous flash in his eyes. "Even the telling of this tale shall fall upon us, keeping in true Ash-Kai manner. Let us begin at the start, ach?"

44

Killik's tale began with an orc in love.

His name was Reykur, and he was a proud, powerful warrior, with a fair face and a silver tongue. He was born from a long, esteemed line of Ash-Kai, many of them bearing the great gifts of farsight, galdr-spinning, and healing, and his family's wealth rivalled that of the greatest human lords in the realm.

And for his mate, Reykur had set his heart upon a merchant's daughter named Katya. A beautiful, ambitious woman who refused to be wooed by an orc... at least, until she learned of Reykur's grand, glittering hoard. And in true Ash-Kai fashion, Reykur stole her away, drew out her hunger, and swore his vows, all in one night.

But it was an ill-fated match, for Katya's affections were fixed upon Reykur's hoard, rather than on Reykur himself. She disdained his loves of good food, pleasure, brawling, and brotherhood, and she scorned his skill as a warrior, and his unthinking loyalty to his cruel Ash-Kai captain. A captain who sent him out again and again to lead raids and battles against the humans, until Reykur's wounds began to wear upon not only his body, but his mind.

This left Katya even more discontented than before, trapped in a mountain with hordes of orcs, and now having borne her first son, a hale, strapping orcling named Rathgarr. He was a son much like Reykur himself, and Reykur doted his deepest affections upon him, having long since lost all love for his cold, unhappy mate.

As Reykur's battle-wounds grew, so did Katya's discontent—most of all when her womb was once again filled with child. But when the second son was birthed, he was a clever, beautiful child, and he eagerly clung to Katya, and soon earned her affections in return. And as her second son grew, Katya saw his many gifts, and the deep power that lay within them. The power not only to lead, but to gain Reykur's hoard itself.

Thus, Katya found a new aim, one she embraced with wholehearted zeal. When she began to draw the eye of the cruel Captain of Orc Mountain, she did not seek to escape, or gain refuge at Reykur's side. Instead, she welcomed the captain's cruelties, and looked away as her mate grieved in shame, and his mind began to fall fully into darkness.

Katya did not mourn her mate, but instead plotted and preened, and eased ever closer to the power she wished to wield. A power that was often grim and heavy to bear, so Katya often prevailed upon her youngest son to serve and comfort her, to grant her succour and peace and relief.

But amidst all this, without their forebears following this, the two sons had found one another. The elder son now fulfilling what Reykur had once done, feeding and clothing and caring for his brother, while the younger freely offered his gifts, his devotion, and his loyalty. And as their captain's cruelties grew and festered, the elder guarded the younger, keeping him safe from the ever-encroaching darkness, until the darkness came too close, and the elder sought to take his mother and brother away.

But this ran counter to Katya's aims, and all her careful plans. And when Rathgarr pushed this, again and again and again, she girded herself with gifts and vows and freedoms from the cruel captain who shared her bed, and began to plot against her son. First hiring the Ka-esh to make a safe, secret place to hide Reykur's hoard, and then moving it there, piece by piece, with help from the Skai her captain had gifted her. Doing this with such care and leisure that Reykur, now bound deep in his darkness, did not note its loss.

Emboldened, Katya then turned her eye to other orcs, and other hoards, within the mountain, pilfering their wealth as her own. And when these losses were marked, the blame fell only upon the captain, who had only grown in his cruelty and his greed, and cared not for the complaints of his kin.

But as the years passed, Katya's son Rathgarr remained her greatest fear, and her greatest foe. Not only prodding her upon her second son's safety again and again, but he had also begun to ask after the hoard. After the wealth he knew ought to one day belong to him, and his brother.

So Katya made another plot, for her second son's gain. She would wield her faithful Skai servants, locking them into the vows they so fiercely revered, to send Rathgarr away, and ensure he never returned. She would do all within her power to break the two sons apart, and destroy their bond with betrayal and grief.

And she would keep the hoard hidden, and her second son safe and close to power. So that he might gain his birthright, and wield it, when the time was right.

"But then, mayhap, the gods saw this great wrong," Killik's voice continued, in his smooth, easy cadence. "They brought sickness upon Katya, and then her doom. And the same vows that bound her Skai also bound them from speaking this truth to her second son, even as they carried out her wishes, well beyond her death. But they oft wondered"—Killik's voice lowered—"if the second son already knew. If he was only waiting, as his mother wished, until the time was right."

Killik stopped speaking there, his eyes now narrowing

toward Kesst. While the room seemed to ring with a loud, quivering silence, echoing with Killik's question, his implication. Had Kesst known his mother's awful plans? Had he only been waiting, until the time was right?

Geva was staring at Kesst too, and so was Rathgarr, and every other orc in the room. Looking at how Kesst's face had gone even paler than before, his mouth very thin, as his throat bobbed, again, again.

"I didn't know Mother's plans," he whispered, his eyes too bright on Rathgarr's face. "At least—not at first. I knew she was involved with the hoard, and with Kaugir, and the Skai. I knew she liked it down here in the Ka-esh wing, and maybe even that there was something odd going on with the Ka-esh. But she never once came out and said, and after she died, and Rath left, I never even thought of the hoard again."

There was a distinct scoffing sound from Killik, but Kesst shook his head, his fingers rubbing at his eyes. "I couldn't bear to think of you, Rath," he whispered. "Or Mother, or any of it. Ever. And if someone had asked me what happened to the hoard, I suppose I'd have said you probably took it, or Father wasted it, or Kaugir stole it, like Grim said. Either way"—he gulped down a breath—"what good would it have done me, here alone in this mess? What would have kept any of these bastards from just taking it from me, like they took everything else?"

Rathgarr was rubbing at his eyes too, and then angling another furious glare toward Ulfarr and Killik. Who were both frowning back, Killik still with a cold, glinting light in his eyes. "Ach, so if you knew naught about this," he drawled, "where do you ken you now stand? The arena, mayhap? The library?"

Both Kesst and Rathgarr growled back at him, but then Kesst sighed, and pulled himself a little straighter. "I didn't think of it again," he said flatly, "until I asked Grim to send for *you*, Rath. And you betrayed yourself, at our very first meeting!"

He was jabbing his shaky-looking finger toward Rathgarr,

who was now blinking blankly toward him, his sword now held slack at his side. "How had I..." he began, and then his voice trailed off, his hand again rubbing at his eyes. "Ach. The dagger."

"Yes, the dagger," Kesst snapped back, though his voice wavered. "From Father's hoard. One of his most prized possessions, supposedly forged by Ash-Kai himself. Not even Kaugir would have let that go, and Grim wouldn't have, either. And when *you* left"—he jabbed his finger at Rathgarr again—"it was *still here!*"

Rathgarr was still rubbing at his eyes, shaking his head, and Kesst tossed his hair over his shoulder, his own eyes flinty and narrow. "So *you* miraculously having it, Rath," he hissed, "meant that either you'd been in contact with someone here, or you acquired it somewhere out there. Either way, something was off, and *somebody* had been pilfering from that hoard!"

His glare snapped back toward Killik and Ulfarr, to where Ulfarr was still glowering, and Killik was carelessly shrugging, and scraping at his claw. "As part of your mother's terms," he replied, "each Skai bound by the vow could take one piece from the hoard, with each summer that passed. How was Ulfarr to know this dagger had worth to you Ash-Kai? It is useless for fighting, and humans will pay senseless sums for such old, crusty orc-forged trinkets."

Now both Kesst and Rathgarr were glaring at Killik, and this time it was Rathgarr jabbing his finger toward him. "And if this vow Ulfarr made with our mother was so binding, that he could not even tell *Kesst* about his *own hoard*," he snapped, "then how do *you* know all of this?!"

A decidedly smug expression was creeping across Killik's face, and he nibbled at his claw before scraping it this time. "Followed him here," he said, a little too casually. "Then made him tell me, over many days."

Rathgarr made a face, while Kesst made a distinctive gagging sound, which he abruptly broke off as he glanced over at their listening audience. "*Anyway,*" Kesst continued, frowning back toward Rathgarr, "it was questionable enough that you even *had* that dagger, Rath. But then to try to give it to me, on our first meeting, after sixteen years?! It was a *trick*, you great arsehole. You were *testing* me!"

Wait, he was? Geva's overwhelmed brain was desperately fighting to follow, and she was already shaking her head, because that dagger gift had just been Rathgarr's thoughtless fumbling... right? So why was Rathgarr grimacing like that, his shoulders sagging, his hand again rubbing at his eyes...

"I was not seeking to trick you, little brother," he replied, heavy. "But ach, I did not trust you. I could not fathom how this dagger had left the mountain, and I wished to see what you should say. That you had sold it, mayhap. Or it had been stolen from you. I hoped"—he sighed and exhaled—"that you had found the hoard, and a way to wield it."

Kesst barked a hard laugh, and shook his head. "Well, I didn't," he shot back. "And it soon became very clear to me that *you* knew something about the hoard. *You* knew Mother was hiding it here, even if you didn't know exactly where. And you latched onto my invitation to come here, and pretended to want to reconcile with me, so you could find it, and claim it as *yours!*"

Geva's stomach plunged, her eyes searching Rathgarr's face with sudden, frantic disbelief. Because no, no, he'd come here to reconcile with Kesst, he'd said multiple times that had been his highest aim in coming here... right?

But Rathgarr was still squeezing his eyes shut, his hand now dragging through his hair, while visible pain spasmed across his face. And suddenly Geva was remembering that welcome-party in the Ash-Kai common-room, when Rathgarr had publicly made that demand toward Grimarr. *You shall swear that our birthright shall be granted back to us, if ever it is found...*

"I wished to claim the hoard as *ours,*" Rathgarr finally said, his voice thick. "*Ours*, brother. Not only mine. I wished to reconcile with you, and I wished to claim my birthright, and I wished to seek vengeance upon those who had stolen it from us. On those who kept me apart from you, and away from my home and my birthright, for all those endless years!"

It sounded like truth, and it looked like truth, the way Rathgarr was glaring over at Ulfarr again, his hand flexing on his sword-hilt. But beside him, Kesst barked a strange, choked laugh, his head whipping back and forth, sending his hair flying out behind him.

"A fair attempt, Rath," he said. "But you're forgetting how you kept all this secret from me! You made me figure it out on my own! You didn't say, *Ach, little brother, did you ken our hoard is still here, let us seek it together!*"

But that was the sound of Rathgarr's groan, deep and exasperated, his hand again dragging through his hair. "Ach, I ought to have told you," he replied. "I see this now. But when I first came here, and you spoke so fiercely of how you had been harmed, I could not bear to add more to this! Do you ken I wished to tell you I had good cause to believe our mother stole from not only our father, but from half the orcs in this mountain? That she hid away your own birthright from you, and thus made you needlessly suffer, so that she might gain more power through you, *when the time was right*?!"

His voice had risen to mimic a shrill northern accent, and he groaned again, and shook his head. "And the more I learnt here," he continued, "the more I began to wonder if it was *she* who also plotted my exile, to part me from you, and keep you all to herself. And I thought if I found the hoard, I should learn this for certain—and ach, after many weeks of searching, now I have! And had I not met you here, I would next have..."

But the words trailed off there, his head tilting, his eyes studying Kesst's face. How Kesst was looking very haughty, and very pale, and very... guilty.

"Yes, yes," he said, his voice very even, his head slightly

tossing. "I found it weeks ago. Your not-so-subtle gift attempt was a *great* help."

Geva's mouth had fallen open—Kesst had *known* about the hoard being here, all this time?—and now it was Rathgarr's turn to look shocked, and then wounded, and then... then just sad. His shoulders sagging, his head bowing, as if the fight had drained out of him all at once.

"Ach, I see," he said, quiet. "I had... broken your trust in me, brother. It is only natural that you should have wished to keep this secret from me, and keep the hoard safe for yourself."

Kesst blinked, and then twitched all over, his eyes suddenly incredulous on Rathgarr's face. "What?" he demanded. "Of course not, you great lout, I wasn't trying to take the loot from you! I just wanted"—he grimaced—"I just wanted to spend more time with you! Before you found what you came here for, and then *left* again!"

There was more ringing, hanging silence, with Rathgarr again blinking at Kesst's face, his eyes strangely bright—and then he nodded, jerky and fervent. "Ach, little brother," he said, his voice choked. "I wished to spend more time with you, also."

But Kesst had again tossed his head, his arms folding tight against his slim chest. "Is that so?" he replied, very steadily. "So you *aren't* planning to leave here again, as soon as you possibly can? As soon as you found the loot?"

Rathgarr stilled again, his mouth betraying a telltale wince, while Kesst gave a low, brittle laugh. "I'll grant you, brother, you kept that one fairly secret," he said flatly. "But then Jule went and let it slip that your mate would only be teaching for a few weeks. And *whyever* would that be the case, I wonder? Unless you were just planning on turning around and leaving again?"

He raised his eyebrows at Rathgarr, who was wincing again, his eyes darting uncertainly toward... Geva. As if *she* had some-thing to do with this, something he didn't want to admit—and she blinked back toward him, twitched a reflexive shake of her head. While Killik gave another light, dangerous laugh, the scimitar still in his hand now angling back toward her.

"Ach, shall we now hear the rest of this tale?" he said. "Who wishes to tell it?"

Geva swallowed hard, her eyes again searching Rathgarr's, but she couldn't read his expression, suddenly, couldn't follow what he meant. Could scarcely think, now, through the mess churning in her thoughts. Rathgarr had known about all this gold, about his mother, he'd tried to trick Kesst, he'd tried to trick her...

"Once again, then," Killik said, with a sharp edge on his voice. "Our tale next finds our captain sending a call to Rathgarr, welcoming him safely home again, upon Kesst's wishes. This summons was delivered by my own hand, for when I learnt of the job from Drafli, I had also just learnt of the vow and the hidden hoard from Ulfarr, ach? Thus, I wished to help him, and learn what else I could of this—and I did not hide from Drafli that there was good cause to grant me this job. And since Skai *trust* other Skai"—he narrowed his eyes between Kesst and Rathgarr—"he sent me."

Geva swallowed, her eyes again glancing at Rathgarr, who was now looking decidedly grim. As though this had answered one question for him, at least—but he didn't speak. Just kept watching Killik, waiting for the rest.

"So I watch Rathgarr, all these next days," Killik continued coldly. "I watch him plot and scheme around his return, in true Ash-Kai manner. I watch as he begins to journey home, and how each day, he seeks out plunder to steal. He raids manors and houses and shops, in breach of the treaty we have all given so much to gain."

His lip was curling at Rathgarr, who in turn was looking warily at Kesst. At where Kesst's mouth had fallen open, and then clamped shut again. "Of course it was all stolen, as a scheme to impress us with your trove-room, and make us think you were perfectly content with your wealth," he snapped. "Of *course*, damn you. Gods"—he winced, shook his head—"how could it not have been? As if *you* were out there doing honest work all that time, when you could have been blatantly violating our peace-treaty instead?!"

Rathgarr grimaced, but didn't even attempt to defend himself, and Killik kept frowning between them both, his eyes contemptuous. "And to make these thefts easier for him," he continued, "Rathgarr took care to choose places that were either empty, or only held lone women inside. And once he had pressed the woman to help him, he would either pay her to stay silent, or take her to bed. Or both."

What? Now it was Geva's mouth falling open, her eyes jolting to Rathgarr's face, while the shock—and yes, the hurt—recoiled in her belly. He'd targeted isolated, unprotected women like her on purpose? He'd bedded them on purpose?!

Rathgarr's eyes were looking rather hunted now, glancing between Killik and Geva and Kesst. "I only did this, for the treaty!" he said, too quickly. "I ken you see me only as a self-seeking thief, but I yet care for my kind, and did not wish to draw the lords' and magistrates' eyes toward us. This way, these women helped hide my deeds, ach? And you can be sure"—he curled his lip at Killik—"*none* of them were left grieving our time together!"

Killik rolled his eyes at that, but Geva was suddenly just feeling sick, her stomach seething, her eyes blinking toward the floor. She'd just been another target. Just like the rest of them.

"But next," Killik's inexorable voice continued, "he meets *this* woman. Geva Okoro, a poor, mistreated governess. This woman helps him with his raid, and grants him his father's dagger. And when men come near to finding him, she hides him away, and keeps him safe. So when he learns the truth of her despair, and her fear that she will be blamed for his deeds, he offers her a job. One month, play-acting as his mate at Orc Mountain."

The words landed like a stone, like a swinging, staggering

strike, deep in Geva's belly. They'd known. They'd known. And gods, of course they had, and why hadn't she suspected it, when Killik had spouted off her entire life's history in that damned first Educational Congress meeting? They'd so obviously been spying on her—gods, Killik and Ulfarr had walked straight in on her and Rathgarr in the forest—and why hadn't she put it together? How could she have been so foolish?

Her hands had clapped over her mouth, her eyes frantically, helplessly staring at Rathgarr. At how his jaw was very set, his eyes dark and bleak, as he swallowed hard, and glanced at Kesst beside him.

And Kesst looked—stricken. Sick. The hurt and the disbelief flashing across his eyes, as his mouth quivered, and his shoulders slowly slumped, his hands dropping heavy to his sides.

"Right, then," he said dully. "Well, you did get me on that one, Rath. Though honestly"—he cast a sharp, searching look over at Geva—"I suppose I did guess, didn't I, sis—"

Geva's stomach dropped, because he'd broken off with a wince, his face hardening, his eyes darting back toward Rathgarr again. "I *did* guess," he hissed at him. "I *knew* something was off. I knew she was way too good for you, I knew *you* would never actually pick out someone decent and hardworking and *responsible,* and then do something ridiculous like swear *vows* to her, or have *sons* with her!"

Now Rathgarr was wincing too, glancing at Geva with distinct guilt in his bleak eyes, and Kesst's answering laugh was painfully shrill, scraping through the room. "Oh, so the rubbish about not being ready for a son was part of it, too," he growled. "You lied to *Eft* as part of your horrible little scheme? You had him *help* you trick me?!"

And suddenly Geva couldn't stand it, couldn't bear it for another breath, and she lurched closer toward them, her hands wildly flailing in midair. "No!" she gulped, her voice a broken rasp in her throat. "No, Kesst. I wasn't trying to trick you. I wasn't ready for a son. I *wasn't*."

She was desperately searching his face, silently pleading toward him, but he was giving her a sad little smile, a grim shake of his head. "Of course you weren't, sweetheart," he said, very smoothly. "Since Rath was your employer, not your mate, and he only gave you a month to do the job! Or"—something shifted, flared in his eyes—"maybe that was *you*, was it, sweetheart? Didn't want to end up being stuck at Orc Mountain permanently, hmmm?"

Geva blinked blankly back toward him, fully about to refuse—but then her eyes caught on Rathgarr again. On where he was wincing, and rubbing at his mouth, looking even more bleak than before. As if... as if he thought *she* had wanted that? As if he'd thought the month was *her* doing?!

But as she cast back, and back, searching for the truth of it, the certainty seemed to keep slipping away, escaping through her fingers. *One moon, mayhap. I do not seek to stay long. You would most certainly be the very last orc in the realm I would choose...*

"She wished—to journey across the sea," Rathgarr finally said, his voice a low sigh in the silence. "To find her true kin again. I did not wish... to take this from her."

Gods damn it. Damn it. Damn him, damn her, damn this entire awful mess they'd made. And suddenly Geva just wanted to weep, to sink to the floor, to disappear, away from all this misery, all the secrets and lies.

But she was still here, still with all these eyes staring at her, and she had to keep moving, forward, forward...

No. No, damn it, no. She had to face the past. She had to try. She had to.

"If you'll listen to one more tale," she whispered, "I'll tell you everything."

45

Geva's tale was quite possibly the most incoherent one she'd ever told. Her voice rushed and broken, her words tripping over themselves, her memories surging far too strong, and often in an entirely different light than before.

But somehow, somehow, she managed to cover it all. How Rathgarr had broken into the Fitzwalds', and then made her that offer. How they'd spent the next five days travelling together, getting to know each other. How Rathgarr had told her, again and again, that his first priority in going home was Kesst. How deeply Rathgarr had missed Kesst. How he'd wept at Geva's tales in the dark.

And how Orc Mountain had been—a surprise. How she'd truly enjoyed meeting the other women and orcs, spending time with them, getting to know all the orclings. How Jule had offered her the teaching job, and how she'd willingly accepted it, because she'd loved spending time with the orclings, and had wanted to help.

And, too, how much she'd liked Kesst. How she'd hated seeing him and Rathgarr like that, mistrustful and at odds with one another, when she knew how deeply Rathgarr grieved it.

How she'd done everything she could—even those small false-hoods—to bring them together.

And finally, how much she cared for Rathgarr. How with every day that passed, she'd wanted and appreciated him more. How they'd unexpectedly had so much in common, from their tastes in clothes to their affection for children. How she'd wanted to convince him to stay, but hadn't once spoken of it, because she'd been afraid of what he would say. So how instead, she'd just kept working harder, being the best mate she could be, trying to show him, to sway him, to gain his trust.

"It was like—what you said with Sigarr and Abjorn," she gulped, her prickling eyes fixed on Kesst's blank, watching face. "I didn't want to lose—what I had. But in doing it, I only made Rathgarr mistrust me more. It was part of our deal, you see, the better job I did, the more he would pay me—so he thought I was only doing it all for the coin. He thought"—she glanced at Rathgarr, a new, bitter awareness curdling with all the rest— "he thought I'd learned about the hoard. He thought I wanted it, like your mother did. And now..."

She swallowed hard, shaking her head, because what now? What happened next? Was there even a way out of this anymore?

"Now, I don't know if we'll ever be able to trust each other again," she said, her voice dropped to a whisper. "Not after so many lies and secrets. He'll never, ever stop wondering if I only want his wealth. And gods"—something caught in her throat, and she had to wipe the wetness from her eyes—"I still don't even know if he *likes* me."

The room had gone entirely silent around her, except for the sounds of her own faint, muffled sniffs. Her throat swallowing again and again, fighting against the lump steadily rising inside it. And she couldn't even bear to look at Rathgarr now, or Kesst, or any of them, because what must they think of her, after she'd lied to all of them?

"Ach, Miss Gee," cut in a voice across the room, and when

Geva blinked toward it, it was Timo. Still standing there with Trygve and Thrain and John, and witnessing her utter, humiliating defeat.

"Ach, Rathgarr likes you, Miss Gee," Timo said, his voice serious, his eyes surprisingly grave. "You ought to scent him, whenever he is around you, or whenever he looks at you. When you dance with him, or play your drum, he—"

Thrain's hand abruptly clapped over Timo's mouth, and he flashed Geva a rueful little smile. "That's enough, Timo," he said lightly. "We've all scented this, ach?"

Oh. They were saying—oh. And the surge of sudden, bittersweet gratefulness was so strong that Geva felt faint, and she felt her eyes furiously blinking, her shaky hand signing, *thank you. Thank you.*

Timo gave a small smile back, but then his eyes flicked beyond her, toward Sune. To where Sune was swiftly signing something up at Ulfarr and Killik, who were now exchanging a meaningful look, before both glancing at Geva again.

"Ach, well, we thank *you* for your tale, Ash-Kai," Killik said, with a distinct emphasis on the *you*, and a slight bow of his head toward her. "So what comes next in your tale? What shall our sly Ash-Kai brothers do, now that they have finally clutched all this gold in their greedy claws?"

Right. Because now the gold was theirs. Rathgarr's, and Kesst's. Grimarr had promised it, publicly, before what must have been a hundred orcs. And Kesst was blinking blankly around at the room full of treasure, as if he hadn't quite seen it before, and Geva didn't miss the sight of him swaying, slowly tilting sideways—but suddenly Rathgarr was there, catching him, holding him steady and firm.

"We must send for Efterar," Rathgarr said, his voice flat and thin. "Timo, Trygve, could you fetch him, please? And some food and fresh water, also?"

Timo quickly nodded and dashed toward the door, with Trygve close behind him. And after a purposeful little nudge from Killik, Sune took off too, disappearing out the door after them. While Thrain, who had been watching all this with his mouth pursed, went to grab one of the hoard's many chairs—a beautiful, polished specimen of smooth black wood—and stalked over, setting it in front of Kesst with a *thunk*.

Kesst gazed unseeing down toward it, as if he couldn't quite follow what was happening, so Rathgarr carefully eased him down into it, his hands grasping brief but firm on Kesst's shoulders, and then pulling away again. But as he did so, Kesst visibly flinched, his body twitching back toward Rathgarr's, his eyes squeezing shut.

Rathgarr kept blinking down toward him, his eyes suddenly so bright, so sad. And with a careful, tentative movement, he brushed his hand against Kesst's hair. Gently, briefly combing it with his claws, before drawing away again.

But Kesst had again twitched at the loss of it, his head tilting back just slightly toward Rathgarr behind him. So Rathgarr did it again, combing a little deeper this time, drawing out the long, silken black strands through his fingers.

Kesst audibly exhaled at that, his stiff shoulders very slightly sagging, and Geva could see Rathgarr's throat convulsing, his body moving closer behind Kesst. And then he began combing in earnest, drawing his claws down the full length of Kesst's shining black hair, again and again. Moving with an easy, thoughtless familiarity that suggested they'd done this many, many times before.

"Should you mayhap find me some beads, poppet?" came Rathgarr's low voice, making Geva startle—but yes, yes, he was looking at her. His eyes so dark, so sad, almost pleading on her face. As if this was about far more than just some beads, and Geva managed a curt little nod, and lurched on unsteady feet back toward the other part of the room. Toward where Thrain and John were standing, watching, but she fought to ignore them as she began searching through the mess of jewels and coins and gold, seeking out some beads.

It was something to do, if nothing else, and Geva could distantly appreciate Rathgarr's kindness in offering her that, even as another part of her couldn't stop marvelling at the shocking abundance beneath her trembling, searching hands. There was just so much, so many jewels and gems and coins, and she could have laughed at the sight of her hand accidentally knocking aside a haphazard pile of ten-piece coins, just the kind Rathgarr had taunted her with, the kind she'd worked so hard to earn. But she just kept searching, moving through the mess, until she finally found a basket full of beads. Of multiple different sizes and colours, metal and glass and even shells, surely worth multiple years' salary, just pooling around her fingers.

But this was for Kesst, her—no, not her brother, maybe even not even her friend anymore. And she felt her eyes prickling again as she picked out some beads, one by one by one, until her hand was full.

"What do you think of these?" she asked Rathgarr, her voice stilted, once she'd gone back over to him, her eyes on her hand. "I thought the silver colour might look well, against his skin."

Rathgarr's hands slightly faltered against Kesst's hair, against where he'd already parted it, folding strands carefully over one another. "Ach, these are good," he said, very quiet. "Thank you, poppet."

Geva nodded, still not looking up at him, but still not seeming able to move, either. Just watching, her eyes still blank and prickling, as Rathgarr's deft, familiar hands kept braiding Kesst's silken, shining hair, piece by piece.

"So have you thought," Rathgarr's quiet voice continued, "of what you might next wish to do? Or what you might wish to ask for?"

Geva's breath drew in and out, her throat swallowing, her eyes still held on his braiding hands. While a resigned, distant part of her noted that maybe he'd sent her into the hoard to make sure she'd seen it. To test what she would say next.

Whether she would maybe begin negotiating, demanding part of it, as was her due. *The more help and plunder you grant me, the more I shall pay you.*

And even if it was all destroyed now, Rathgarr still had the plunder. She'd still helped him with this, surely, even if only with that request she'd made of Grimarr. *Rathgarr should be reinstated as one of his father's heirs, in case any of it ever comes to light again.* And by rights, she could demand a percentage of it. She could become a very wealthy woman, living in a beautiful, well-appointed house, and never work a day as a governess again.

But gazing down toward the beads, glinting in her fingers, there was only a stark, sinking sadness. The hoard was tainted. It had been stolen, used to tear an entire family apart. It had destroyed their trust in one another, and perhaps their ability to trust anyone else, too. To the point where, perhaps, plots and agreements and terms were the only way they could bear it.

And as much as it had hurt to hear of all the ways Rathgarr had lied to her... he *had* kept to the terms they'd agreed upon, at the start of all this. He'd never faltered in caring for her. He'd kept her safe and fed and clothed. He'd been... generous. Kind. A good father, and a good teacher to her orclings. A helpmate.

And now, he was offering her the payment. Just as he'd promised.

"Then... I'd like to establish terms," Geva finally replied, quiet. "A new agreement, between us."

Before her, Rathgarr's hands hadn't even twitched, and he plucked a bead out of her hand, and carefully slid it onto a folded strand of Kesst's hair with his claw. "Ach, I thought you might wish for this," he said, just as quiet. "And what shall you ask for?"

Geva hauled in a shaky breath, let it out. "I want you to stay here at Orc Mountain for at least a year," she said. "I want you to keep teaching the orclings, every day. And, I want you to use some of your wealth to make sure they receive the best education you can possibly offer them. Whether that's travelling, or materials, or hiring more support. Whatever you think is best. I trust your judgement."

Rathgarr's hands were still working on Kesst's hair, now placing on bead after bead, though perhaps moving a little slower than before. "And where," he said, very carefully, "shall you be?"

Geva swallowed hard, her eyes blinking, as she considered that crucial question. Where would she be. *Here*, part of her wanted to shout, deep and miserable inside. *I want to stay here, with my lovely little school, with my students, with all my new friends. With... you.*

But it was too late, this had already gone too far, well beyond repairing. Rathgarr would never, ever stop wondering about her motives, his mother, and all that he'd lost. He would never be able to trust her with a son.

"I... don't know yet," Geva finally said. "But I do know"— she squared her shoulders, took another breath—"I want to return to the Fitzwalds' house."

At that, Rathgarr's hands slipped on his nearly finished braid, and when she risked a wet-eyed glance upwards, he was glowering thunderously toward her, his lips curled back to show his sharp teeth. "You shall never work in that grim, garish house again," he hissed. "And I shall *never* swear a vow that allows for this!"

Geva rapidly flapped her free hand, and then rubbed at her eyes, shaking her head. "Not—to *work* there," she said thickly. "But as part of my payment, I want you to grant me everything you stole from the children, and the servants. I want to take it all back. And also, I want"—she exhaled, slow—"to leave letters for the children, and especially Cecily. I want to tell her I love her, and I miss her, and I regret not being able to say goodbye in person. I want her to know I didn't abandon her without even a farewell."

There was a moment's silence from Rathgarr, his hands

now fully stilled on Kesst's hair. "Ach, I see," he said, his voice very low. "And after this, where shall you go? Across the sea to Ezira, as you wished?"

But a distant part of Geva had somehow been thinking about this for days, perhaps even weeks, and she shook her head. "No, I don't think so," she said slowly. "I've been so focused on pushing forward, all this time. Looking ahead, rather than back. And going across the sea just seemed like the next obvious step, but after all this"—she could hear herself swallow—"I'm not sure I actually *want* to go there anymore."

Rathgarr didn't reply to that, his hands still unmoving on Kesst's hair, and Geva drew in another breath. "So along with the Fitzwalds' plunder, I'd like to ask you for enough coin to live on, for a year," she said. "What you originally planned to pay me for that passage across the sea. And then I can—take some time. Think about it. Being here has reminded me how much I love children and teaching, so maybe I can look for another teaching job, or maybe even a way to start a school of my own. But without the added pressure of possibly starving on the streets."

She'd attempted to make it sound light, but when she risked a glance up at Rathgarr, he was frowning again, his eyes flickering oddly on hers. "You cannot only want this, woman," he said flatly. "You are due far more than this."

But Geva cast an uncertain glance over toward the piles of plunder, and felt something circling, settling, deep in her chest. "I... appreciate your generosity," she said, quiet. "But I... don't actually want it, Rathgarr. It's not my hoard. And I've only worked for you for a few weeks. A year's salary seems more than fair."

But suddenly Rathgarr was baring his teeth again, his eyes flashing, as a low, dangerous growl burned from his throat. "Ach, I see your tricks, woman," he hissed at her. "You wish to guilt me into paying you more. You wish for me to lie here fretting about you, lost and starving alone. You wish me to follow you weeping, and beg for you to come back, so you can gain our hoard as your own!"

What? Geva flinched and startled, opening her mouth to attempt some kind of protest, but Rathgarr cut her off with a hard snap of his teeth, and another deep, bitter growl. "Or you shall plan to dawdle and linger," he snarled, "wandering about the mountain, saying tearful farewells to all you have met, until they all descend upon me, begging me to keep my sweet mate, if only for the orclings' sake! And then you shall play your part so flawlessly, that I shall grant you my son, only so that you might steal him from me, with all my gold!"

Geva stared at him for a stunned, endless moment, as those words rang through the air. He truly still thought she wanted to trick him? To manipulate him? To lie to him, so she could steal his son, and his gold?

The disbelief was kicking and surging, tangling with something much like rage, and Geva felt her head whipping back and forth, her hands clutched to fists. "I don't deserve this rubbish from you, Rathgarr," she hissed at him. "I *don't.* I've helped you. I've supported you. I've kept all your secrets. I've worked so, so hard for you. Just the way you wanted. Just the way you *asked* me to!"

But he didn't even reply, his teeth still bared viciously toward her, and Geva dragged back another deep, staggering breath. "I have proven to you again and *again* that you can trust me," she continued, her voice cracking. "And meanwhile, here you were, hiding something like *this* from me, all this time? Because you really think I want to *steal* it from you?!"

She'd waved her shaky hand around at the hoard, at all the riches he'd known about, and lied about—but it was as though he hadn't even heard her. His mouth still contorting, his head shaking, his eyes flaring with strange, fervid fury. With... mistrust.

And blinking up toward him, Geva suddenly felt her own anger sagging, the misery plunging dark and deep. Into the horrible, harrowing vision of just what this hoard would keep doing to him. How it would keep clawing at his pain and his paranoia and his greed. How he would perhaps never be able to love or trust anyone again, not with all this gold silently screaming at him, reminding him of his miserable parents, and of all he'd lost.

"You're wrong, Rathgarr," she said, through the pain clamping in her throat. "You're so, so wrong. I have no desire to hurt you, or be part of this. I gave you my terms, so if you'll accept them, I'll now be on my way."

But in return, Rathgarr finally—laughed. The sound hard and brittle and painful, grating through the room, scraping up Geva's shivering spine.

"Ach, I accept your terms, *poppet*," he sneered at her. "So now, what shall you do?"

And gods, he really did still think it was a lie. He really believed she cared about the gold. He really believed she would betray him, just like his mother.

"Well, I'll say goodbye then, I suppose," she managed, lifting her chin, and then glancing down to Kesst's distant, shifting eyes. "Kesst, it's been such an honour meeting you, and I'm so sorry I didn't tell you the truth from the start. And if you'll take these"—she carefully poured her beads into his slack hand—"I hope you'll keeping having Rathgarr braid your hair, because he's very good at it, and the beads do look lovely on you."

Kesst was still blinking blankly at her, as though he couldn't quite hear her, and Geva bit back the sudden sob lurking in her throat, and wiped at her eyes. "Maybe we can—write," she whispered. "I'll send you some animal tales, how about that?"

But Kesst only kept staring at her, the sight so painfully unnatural, and Geva was deeply, profoundly relieved by the sudden sound of more people, spilling into the room. And thank the gods, the first one was Efterar, sprinting over toward them at full speed, reeling to a stop on his knees before Kesst, his steady hands already cupping Kesst's face with gentle, familiar care.

"There, there, Sweet-Fang," he murmured, though his voice sounded hoarse. "I'm here. You're safe."

And bless Efterar, because Kesst's eyes had already begun refocusing, blinking down toward his face. "It's a mess, Eft," he said plaintively. "The most ghastly *disaster*, and now Geva is *leaving*. Because—did I say this hoard is a mess?"

Efterar shot a brief, resentful glance around at the glittering room, as though it deeply offended him—but then he blinked, and frowned up at Geva beside him. "You're leaving?" he asked. "*Permanently*?"

Geva gave a numb-feeling nod, and attempted a wretched smile toward him. "Yes, I'm afraid so," she replied, as smoothly as she could. "I think it's—for the best. It's been so good meeting you though, and I'm very grateful for your kindness."

Efterar kept frowning at her, but then he exhaled heavily, and reached up his hand, hovering it in the vicinity of her waist. "Well, that's your pregnancy prevention gone, all right?" he said, already turning back to Kesst again. "So make sure you use alternate protections, as needed. And"—he shot her another brief glance over his shoulder—"it really has been a pleasure, Geva. I won't forget all your generosity toward us. Thanks."

Right. Geva gave a shaky nod he couldn't see, and then swallowed hard, and clasped her hands together. So this was it, then. Leaving. Leaving, forever, because Rathgarr had accepted her terms. And suddenly she couldn't bear to look at him, and instead she jerked around toward Killik. Toward where he and Ulfarr were still watching, both with darkly disapproving expressions on their faces.

"So am I to understand," Geva choked out, "that you two are still... on this *job*, then?"

Killik nodded, arching his brow, so Geva drew in more

breath, and grasped desperately for focus. Leaving. Permanently. Today.

"Might you be so kind, then," she said, "to escort me back to the Fitzwalds'? I would be happy to pay you for your time."

And to her astonishment, Killik actually... grinned. A swift, sharp-toothed grin, with no smugness or malice in it, only sheer, glittering glee.

"Ach, Ash-Kai," he said. "No payment needed. Ready your goods, and we shall go."

46

I t didn't take long for Geva to pack her belongings, and ready herself to go.

She found her old satchel tucked into the bottom of the wardrobe, and even before she'd begun packing it, Jule showed up at the door. Holding Tengil in one arm, and a large, sturdy-looking leather pack in the other.

"Are you sure?" Geva asked her, with a grimace. "I won't be able to return it."

But Jule waved it away and set Tengil down on the bed, so she could start helping to fold the stacks of Geva's clothes. "Consider it part of your teaching salary," she said firmly. "Also"—she reached into the pack, and held out a small, clinking bag—"here's the rest of it, too."

Geva only seemed able to stare at it, swallowing hard over the ever-present lump in her throat. And she should have said something, some kind of thanks, but there were truly no words to say, amidst the guilt, and the regret. Because Jule had been one of the people to rush into that hidden room with Efterar, along with Grimarr, and Drafli, and Simon, and Ella's mate Nattfarr. And Geva had been appalled to discover that they'd all known, too. Not about the hoard, no—but about her. About how she'd pretended to be Rathgarr's mate, for coin.

But now they did know about the hoard, too, and Geva would never forget the way they'd all looked around at the room packed full of treasure. Grimarr with a dark, glinting fury, surely knowing Rathgarr had tricked him, while Drafli had looked coldly contemptuous, Simon stiff and stern. And Nattfarr had walked over to a shelf with strange, stilted steps, and picked up a heavy gold cuff, studded with deep green emeralds.

"My father's," he'd said, with an odd harshness in his voice. "I had thought it stolen by humans, upon his death."

But amidst it all, Jule had only looked pale, and then sad, her eyes on Geva, and then on Kesst. And she'd spoken kindly to Geva as they'd crept out that horrible tunnel again, and now she was here helping her, working in swift silence until both the pack and the satchel were full, with all Geva's possessions inside. Including not only her book of tales, and all the clothing she'd come here with, but also the children's and servants' plunder from the Fitzwalds'. Which, after some searching in the trove-room, Geva had found stuffed together into the bottom of a shelf, well apart from the rest of Mr. and Mrs. Fitzwald's gaudy loot. Almost as if Rathgarr hadn't wanted to think about how he'd stolen from children and servants, either.

"Is that all, then?" Jule said, surveying Geva's stuffed satchel and pack, while Tengil looked on with unhappy eyes. "Is there anything else that's yours? Anything from the schoolroom, maybe?"

But Geva couldn't bear the idea of seeing the schoolroom again, let alone taking anything from it, and she shook her head. "No," she whispered. "But thank you. You have been... so generous. Especially since you knew, all that time, about my... my..."

And gods, she couldn't even say it, through the misery and the regret surging up into her throat, and suddenly Jule caught her into her arms, squeezing her tight, swaying back and forth. "Oh, sister," Jule said, into her shoulder. "Maybe I should have said something. I thought—I hoped—that you two really did care for each other, and that you'd end up staying, after all. These orcs have a way of growing on you, and Kesst just wanted Rathgarr here so much. So we tried not to interfere, and instead did everything we could to make you feel comfortable and welcome. Hoping you'd decide to stay."

Oh. So maybe Jule had been part of the Ash-Kai plotting web too, then. And while Geva should probably have been offended by that, she suddenly just felt a strange, surreal commiseration, or perhaps even appreciation.

"Well, you almost succeeded," Geva said as she drew away, giving Jule a sad, watery smile. "I really loved being here. And the orclings"—she gulped back a sob—"I'll miss them so much. I so desperately want to say goodbye, but I promised Rathgarr I wouldn't linger or dawdle, or say tearful goodbyes in the corridors, so—"

"So we'll make it quick, then," Jule said firmly, with a watery smile of her own. "And I don't think you'll need to go far."

Geva blinked, mystified, until Jule ushered her out the door—to where a large cluster of people were waiting, milling around in the corridor. Not only Killik and Ulfarr, but also Sune and Timo and Trygve, and Ella and Rakfi, and Maria and Bjorn, and Hagen and Hauk. And even, poking out from behind them, were all the younger Grisk and Ka-esh orclings, all of them looking at Geva with wide, glimmering eyes.

"You are not leaving, Miss Gee?" asked Bram, his little mouth quivering. "But what about our school? And our swords?"

Geva's answer was half-laugh, half-sob, and she knelt down before him, and tried for a smile. "Rathgarr is going to keep teaching you," she replied, as steadily as she could. "And Killik and Ulfarr too, and Varinn and Kalfr and Baldr and Alma, and so many of our other friends. I know you'll have such a wonderful time with them."

But Bram didn't look at all convinced, and now it was Isak slipping forward to frown fiercely up at Geva's face. "You ought to be there also," he said flatly, with a jab of his little clawed finger toward her. "You are good teacher. *Our* teacher."

It felt almost impossible to keep smiling, but Geva made another fervent attempt. "Thank you, Isak," she whispered. "It's been such an honour, getting to teach you. All of you."

Isak didn't look convinced either, his bottom lip jutting out, his eyes far too bright. And Geva blinked helplessly down toward him, utterly lost, until she felt a sudden, familiar prickle, quivering up her spine.

And even before she blinked up, she knew who she'd find. Rathgarr. Standing stiffly at the end of the corridor, his arms folded tightly over his chest, his eyes flashing with something much like disapproval, or rage.

Geva's stomach plummeted, her thoughts suddenly crumpling, screeching with the memories of some of his last words toward her. *You shall plan to dawdle and linger, saying tearful farewells, until they all descend upon me...*

So she snapped upwards, backwards, away, waving shakily toward her audience, and fixing what felt like a genuine smile to her mouth. "I know you'll have so much fun with Rathgarr," she said, and it sounded truthful, it did. "I'm so grateful to have gotten to spend so much time with you all. I'll miss you so much, and I'll never forget you. Thank you."

And with that, she spun around, and rushed unseeing up the corridor, away, away. Not stopping, or thinking, or breathing, just going, leaving, permanently, forever...

When something—touched her. Making her flinch and flare and flash around, her body shivering all over, because she knew that touch, she longed for that touch, she was on the verge of weeping at that touch, warm and heady and solid against her skin.

Him. Rathgarr. Here. But even as she turned her face up toward it, toward him, she was wincing back, amidst the grief, the unease, the fear. She needed to leave. At once. Permanently…

And Rathgarr's hard, glinting eyes were saying it, shouting it, and Geva was cringing further away, whipping her head back and forth. "I'm—going," she gritted out. "I'm not trying to linger and dawdle, and draw out—farewells. I'm going. I am."

But suddenly a strong, familiar warmth circled around her wrist, drawing out her hand. And then something sank into her fingers, heavy and final and firm. A bag. Coins.

"Your payment," said Rathgarr's gruff, curt voice. "As promised."

And blinking down toward it, Geva wanted to weep, to scream, to hurl it straight back in his face. To holler that she didn't want his payment, she'd have done it all without a single damned coin—

But this was the agreement. This was the terms. This was the only way Rathgarr might someday accept that she hadn't been using him, hadn't had an ulterior motive, hadn't had any designs on the rest of his hoard. She'd done her job, he'd paid her, and that was all.

"Th-thank you," she said, and she even met his eyes, drinking up the sight of his familiar face, one last time. "It's been a pleasure working with you."

And before she could break down any further, or perhaps begin begging, she clutched her payment tightly in her fingers, and left.

47

———————

Geva followed Killik out of Orc Mountain as quickly and quietly as she could, her head down, her hands gripped to her satchel. Leaving. At once. Permanently.

And gods, she'd never imagined it would hurt so much. That she would so fervently want to run back to Rathgarr, and clutch at him, and beg him to listen, to understand. To make him see that she hadn't cared about his gold, she'd cared about him. About his kin. His home.

But she just kept walking, leaving, one foot in front of the other, until Killik led her out into the bright afternoon sun. To where—she reeled back, her hand over her squinting eyes—the orclings were waiting? Her students?

And wait, it wasn't all of them—not the three smallest Ka-esh—but yes, there was Timo and Trygve and Sune, and Hauk and Hagen, and Bjorn, and Bram and Njal and Tyr. And behind them stood a frowning Ulfarr, and Varinn and Thrain, and Kalfr, and even Abjorn, all of them wearing cloaks and boots, with large packs and bags slung onto their backs.

"What—what is this?" Geva asked, through her closed-off throat. "You're not all—coming?"

"We are coming on a scenting and scouting adventure!" replied Timo, with a broad, cheerful grin. "As part of our schooling. We shall follow the trail you left coming here, and thus find our way back to where you wish to go!"

Oh. Geva blinked, and then felt herself slowly smiling, because it did sound like a delightful adventure for them, and an excellent learning experience—and now she'd be able to spend a few more days with them, too. "That's such a lovely idea," she said thickly. "As long as you're sure you'll all be safe? And your caretakers have approved this? For such a long trip?"

"Ach, the younger ones shall only come part of this way, and then their fathers shall meet us and fetch them," replied Killik smoothly. "And we shall take great care to scent for humans, and stay hidden whenever they are near. The Grisk shall be a great help in this. And the Bautul will lead us in hunting and food-finding, also."

He'd jerked his head toward Kalfr, Varinn, and Thrain, who were all smiling back toward Geva. "Thus, we shall blend learning from three clans at once," said Kalfr. "This seemed like a plan that should please you."

"And do not forget sparring practice!" interjected Abjorn, with a grin. "And mayhap even a few Ash-Kai tales as we travel, too."

He'd winked at Geva at that, suggesting that *she* could tell the Ash-Kai tales—and she felt her eyes prickling again, her smile shaky but sincere. "That sounds wonderful," she said, and she meant it. "Thank you."

And as they set off, following the main road away from the mountain, Geva felt her heaviness lightening, just a little. She didn't need to say goodbye forever, just yet. And instead of the long, lonely, miserable journey she'd been expecting, she'd now be able to spend it with these lovely, laughing orclings, learning and exploring alongside them.

"Was this your idea?" she asked under her breath toward

Killik, who'd fallen into step beside her, with Ulfarr just behind. "If so, thank you. Truly."

But Killik replied with his typical careless wave, and a casual shrug. "It is good learning for them," he said, nodding toward the gaggle of eagerly chattering orclings ahead. "Also"—he gave a satisfied smile—"it grants me great joy to think of how vexed your mate shall be, by this."

Geva's stomach flipped, and she couldn't help shaking her head, angling Killik a dubious look. "He's not my mate," she said thinly. "And I can't imagine he'll be very vexed, either. Not now that he has the fortune he always wanted."

Her voice had gone flat and bitter, and she was distantly surprised to hear Killik's contemptuous-sounding laugh. "You think wrong, Ash-Kai," he said. "You ken all this gold shall ride his prick, or comb his fancy hair, or keep his bed warm at nights? No. He found a good, clever, hungry mate to please him, and he wasted this for his fool Ash-Kai greed. Mark me, woman, he shall be vexed."

His voice had gone smug and scathing by the end, his smile decidedly complacent. "I should never waste a good woman thus," he continued. "Nor should you, Ulfarr, ach?"

He'd said this with a too-casual glance over toward Ulfarr, who was now walking on Geva's other side, and frowning straight ahead. "No," he said flatly. "But neither shall I ever gain one, now that I have been judged for my past sins. I cannot beget sons, ach?"

On Geva's other side, Killik snorted, though Geva couldn't help noticing his eyes were very intent on Ulfarr's face. "And so?" he asked. "Not all women wish for this. And ach, you have had your troubles with women, but I ken you should yet welcome a tight womb to plough, and soft cuddles at nights. And mayhap a mother for Sune, also."

Ulfarr didn't reply, only looking straight ahead toward where Sune was cheerfully signing back and forth with Timo and Trygve. And it occurred to Geva, not for the first time, that

Ulfarr truly did care about Sune—and maybe even about Rathgarr, too. Because what had he said, just that morning? *If Rathgarr was wise, he would leave this, and welcome the gifts he has.*

"Ulfarr," she said now, tentatively, "you didn't actually *want* Rathgarr to find the gold, did you?"

Ulfarr visibly exhaled, his frown deepening. "Ach, no," he said, his voice grim. "That hoard was tainted from the start, and ought to have died with their scheming mother. And Kesst…"

His voice trailed off, his huge shoulders rising and falling, his jaw flexing in his cheek. "Rathgarr was right to say that I failed his brother," he said heavily. "I did not spare the time nor the patience to follow all Kesst needed, or all he kept hidden. But"—he sighed again, his eyes fixed back to Sune—"now Skai-kesh has charged me to make amends, not only for this, but for all my past sins. And I seek to obey. I seek to regain my place as a true Skai son."

Oh. Skai-kesh was the Skai clan's patron god, Geva now knew, and her sidelong glance over at Killik found him grinning again, with easy satisfaction on his mouth. "And thus, Ulfarr has been curst to tend not one, not two, but *three* stubborn, wayward Ash-Kai," he said cheerfully. "Compared to all this, Sune is a delight, ach?"

Ulfarr grunted his ready agreement, leaving Geva to stare open-mouthed between them, because wait, were they including *her* in this three-Ash-Kai curse?! "Excuse me," she said, as haughtily as she could, "but how have *I* been any trouble?"

In return, Killik rolled his eyes, and waved at the orclings up ahead. "You show us for many days how well you play-act," he said, "and then you turn about and seek to spend your days with our orclings? I ken the captain and his mate thought this a clever Ash-Kai scheme, but we Skai should not leave our sons at risk thus. Do you ken I *wished* to be part of this *Orc Mountain Educational Congress*, and bossed about by haughty chattering Ka-esh?"

Oh. And even as Geva's disbelief swelled—Killik had done all that to spy on her, too?—she felt her appreciation rising, a small smile curving on her mouth. "It was very responsible for you to look out for them like that," she said. "And honestly, you're really very good at it, and the orclings love you. I hope that after this, maybe you'll consider continuing with it? Maybe even teach some Skai tales, too? You're quite the storyteller, you know."

But to her vague surprise, Killik returned this with a dark, disapproving scowl. "I ken your scheming Ash-Kai ways, woman," he said flatly. "Should you truly wish for my help, you shall not flatter me with empty words. You shall instead cease to give me grief, and be an easy travel-mate, with no fussing or moaning. And, mayhap"—his frown slightly faded, his head tilting—"when your mate comes after you begging, you shall make him sweat. And suffer. And weep. This shall offer some small reward for all our pain, I ken."

Geva was smiling now despite herself, even as she shook her head. "Rathgarr isn't going to come begging," she said, with a sigh. "And he's not my mate."

But Killik rolled his eyes again, and then cast an exasperated frown down Geva's form. "Ach, and this is why you yet wear his clothes," he snapped. "And his gold in your hair. And his *wedding-ring*."

Wait. One of Geva's hands had fluttered up to her hair—to where it was indeed still studded with Rathgarr's beads—while her other hand snapped out before her eyes, her fingers spread wide. And yes, damn it, she'd somehow completely forgotten about her ring—his ring—still there on her finger, its red ruby sparkling and shimmering in the bright sunlight.

"It's not—a wedding-ring," she made herself say, though it sounded rather choked. "It was just..."

"A ring he chose for you?" Killik drawled. "A ring he placed upon you, as proof of your bond? A ring you did not even think to leave behind? Ach, woman, I thought you Ash-Kai are meant to be clever."

Oh. It left a strange, shifting sensation in Geva's gut, and maybe—maybe even something abominably like hope. Something that kept whispering and simmering, even as she sought to quash it, to shove it firmly away. Rathgarr didn't care about her. Rathgarr cared about his gold. And even if by some miracle he did follow her, or beg for forgiveness, she would never be able to trust him again, right? She would never again be sure that he didn't hold secret suspicions about her. Especially since he'd already held so much from her, hidden so much, lied so much.

But that quiet, nagging question still made the rest of the day more tolerable, somehow. Made it easier to chatter and laugh with the orclings, to tramp through the forest alongside them, to ask questions as they alternately followed her and Rathgarr's scent, and hunted for game, and foraged for roots and mushrooms. And upon the orclings' enthusiastic request, she even found herself telling them tales as they walked, one after another. Sinking into the familiar comfort of the porcupine, the reckless roaming rat, the seven-headed spirit, the maiden who married the skull.

By the time they stopped for the night, Geva's voice was hoarse, and she was truly exhausted—so much that the prospect of sleeping on a hard cave floor with a dozen orcs wasn't nearly as daunting as it should have been. And she even slept the whole night through, despite Ulfarr's loud snoring, and the fact that she'd somehow collected all three of the younger Grisk orclings, curled up against her in their little cloaks.

It turned out that she wasn't the only one—Thrain, Timo, and Trygve all seemed to be piled atop Varinn, and both Sune and Killik were using Ulfarr as a pillow. While the rest of them were a haphazard mass of hair and furs and limbs, though Geva could just make out a wistful-looking Abjorn, his arms folded behind his head, his eyes fixed on the rough-cut ceiling above.

Of course, the almost-peaceful silence was soon shattered by wakeful, well-rested orclings, full of energy and enthusiasm for the day. And after a morning lesson in hunting—in which Geva was subjected to the alarming sight of all her adorable orclings eagerly gobbling up raw venison—they were on their way again, now travelling mostly off the road, well out of sight of any humans.

It certainly made for a slower, more exhausting day, and more than once, Geva found herself longing for Rathgarr's style of travelling—on the road, sleeping in comfortable inns, enjoying hot meals and baths. But she was determined to be a good travel-mate, damn it, and once again she kept her attention on the orclings, on making their adventure as fun and educational as she possibly could.

They had visitors late that afternoon—Simon and Maria, Joarr and Gwyn, and all the young Grisks' fathers—and spent a delightful evening of tales and laughter around a large, blazing bonfire. And while Geva desperately wanted to ask after Rathgarr, and Kesst, and the treasure, she again made herself focus on the orclings, on being a good teacher, a good travel-mate. On savouring every moment of this while she could, until it was gone, forever.

She again wept saying goodbye to the younger orcs the next morning, but at least it was a proper farewell this time, with a chance to speak to each of them in turn. And afterwards, the day's travels did go faster, with a few deeper conversations, too. She learned that Sune's blood-father was still alive, but that he was no longer able to care for Sune, due to wounds that sounded much like the ones Rathgarr's father had suffered. She also learned that Timo's father had died when he was young, but he'd been mostly raised by Trygve's father Eyarl, with support from a variety of other Grisk, especially Varinn.

And most astonishing of all, late that night around the fire, she learned that *Kalfr* had a son. A four-year-old son named Svein, who lived alone with his mother about a day's journey east of Orc Mountain.

"And... do you see Svein often?" Geva ventured, toward where Kalfr was staring blankly into the guttering fire, his face shrouded in shadow. "Have you brought him to the mountain, to meet the rest of your clan?"

Kalfr shook his head, and Geva could see his throat convulsing, his eyes dropping to his clawed hands. "No," he said. "I... did not well handle this, when first we met, and now she loathes and fears me, and will not allow me to speak to him. I leave them food and goods when I can, but beyond this, I seek to honour her wishes."

Across the fire, Sune had begun signing something, with sharp disapproval in his eyes, while Timo fervently nodded beside him. But on his other side, Ulfarr huffed a heavy sigh, and shook his head. "It is not this easy," he said flatly. "Kidnapping is one of the terms of this peace-treaty with the humans. Were Kalfr to do this, he should then break the treaty, against the wishes of all five clans, and we should be bound to return the son to his mother. This would also cause great distress to the son, ach?"

It was without question a valid point, but Geva couldn't stop studying Kalfr's blank, miserable face. "Do you think she might reconsider," she ventured, "if perhaps we approached her? If we explained in detail what we're offering for schooling, and how it would benefit her son to attend? Surely she would want Svein to be educated, if nothing else?"

But Kalfr gave a grim shake of his head, a sad little smile. "But you are leaving us, sister," he said, quiet. "And she shall not speak to an orc, or even allow one into her house. Let alone to think of us teaching *her* son."

There was palpable bitterness in his voice, and not for the first time during this journey, Geva felt the stark, sudden urge to beg to turn around again. To go back to Orc Mountain, to her little school, to the work she'd loved doing. To a world where she and Rathgarr could travel to meet Svein and his mother, and offer support and reassurance, and do everything within their power to reunite Kalfr and his son again.

But she couldn't, she couldn't. She'd promised Rathgarr she would leave. These were the terms they'd agreed to. And despite what Killik had said, there'd still been no sign whatsoever of Rathgarr. It was over. Permanently.

It felt more difficult to smile and laugh the next day, despite her very best efforts to focus on the orclings, and their interests and needs. And while she was deeply grateful for Abjorn and Varinn and Thrain, and their obvious attempts to engage her in cheerful conversation, she knew she was an increasingly gloomy, morose, and uninspiring travel-mate. And by the fifth day of travelling, she found herself needing to frequently make excuses, so that she could go off into the woods alone, and weep into her trembling hands. She needed to do this. She'd sworn to do this, she wanted to do this. To return to the Fitzwalds', return the children and servants' coin, leave the letters. And then...

"We shall reach the house early this eve," Killik told her, once she'd returned to the rest of the party again, her face dry but surely swollen. "I have sent Ulfarr and Varinn to scout ahead, to watch for humans, and learn how best to gain entry."

Geva nodded, and attempted a thank-you—but then it was swallowed by more sharp, staggering misery. "Should I be saying—my goodbyes, then?" she gulped at him. "For good, this time?"

But Killik waved it away, his eyes shifting away, too. "Ach, not yet," he said, with that telltale casualness on his voice. "Later."

And it was something to cling to, something to keep her going, even as they drew closer, closer. As Ulfarr and Varinn returned early that evening, and reported that the Fitzwalds were indeed still away on their trip—though they were due to return soon—and luckily, it appeared to be the servants' day off, as well. Meaning that gaining entry to the house would be a simple, straightforward task, without even a need to rush.

"This is a sign from Skai-kesh, you ken," Killik told them with extreme satisfaction, his eyes lingering a little too long on Ulfarr's face. "He sees our aims this night, and grants us his blessing."

Well. Again, it was something, and finally, with her satchel in her hand, and her heartbeat thundering in her throat, Geva walked with Ulfarr up to the Fitzwalds' side door, and followed him inside. And once he'd shoved a lit lantern into her hand, she quietly crept up the stairs, back to the servants' quarters. To where she hadn't ever, ever imagined returning.

It was even more dismal than she remembered, the rooms tiny and cramped, smelling of dampness and mould. But Geva moved through them as quickly as she could, putting back the servants' stolen plunder as best she could. Cook had hidden hers under the floor. The first vile footman had kept his in his sock-drawer. The butler under the bed.

And once that was finished, next were the children's rooms, and the letters. Geva had already written out the letters to all four children, using paper and charcoal that Killik had managed to acquire along the way. And in each letter, she'd mentioned a few of her favourite memories, and shared her regrets at the sudden farewell, and her best wishes. She'd even offered a means of exchanging letters in the future, if they wished, thanks to some clever connections the Ka-esh had set up within the human-run postal service.

Cecily's was the last letter to deliver, and Geva lingered for too long in the little room, blinking around at Cecily's few prized possessions. The frilly pink dress that didn't fit anymore, the doll with the missing eye, the collection of mismatched rocks. Until she shook her head and forced herself out the door, closing it tightly behind her. Her mission here was finished. Complete.

It meant she should have left, hurrying away for the side door where she knew Ulfarr was waiting. But instead, she took a strange, shaky breath, and crept back up the stairs. Back toward the schoolroom.

It clearly hadn't been touched since the day she'd left, the children's belongings still strewn all around, Dolly still lying forgotten on the floor. And for a long moment, Geva only stood there in the middle of the room, gazing blankly around at the mess. While the wetness that had been gathering in her eyes finally spilled over, streaking down her face.

Gods, this room. This life. She'd been so, so miserable here, so trapped and lonely and helpless. And then Rathgarr had come, and threatened her, and deceived her, and ruined her life, and perhaps—

Saved her. Rescued her. Showed her a glimpse of a new life. A new calling. A new home.

And gods, what now? What next? How could she keep looking forward, doing the next thing, when she'd found what she'd so desperately wanted? When now it was gone, forever?

What did that leave? What would she do next? How could she possibly say goodbye?

"There you are," cut in a harsh, husky, familiar male voice, curling deep into her belly. "You did not truly think you could escape me?"

Geva leapt and whirled around, her mouth fallen open, her hand clutched to her wildly hammering heart. Because it was—it was—

Him.

48

―――――――

Rathgarr was here. In the Fitzwalds' schoolroom. *Again*.

Geva's heart was still reeling in her chest, her eyes frantically sweeping up and down. Drinking in the impossible sight of him, just standing here before her.

And he looked... tired. Rumpled. There were dark circles beneath his eyes, new lines around his mouth, heavy stubble shadowing his cheeks. And his silver fur had twigs stuck in it, his cloak was visibly torn at the bottom, his boots stained with mud and ash.

But he was—here. *Here*. And he was looking at Geva with an odd, shifting meaning in his eyes, as his tongue swept swift and sudden against his chapped-looking lips.

"What the hell," Geva finally gulped, "are you *doing* here, Rathgarr?!"

The words seemed to flash something else across his eyes, stark and almost feverish—and he lurched a step closer, his clawed hand clutched to his sword-hilt, so tightly his knuckles were white.

"I am here," he replied, his voice dark and menacing, "to claim my mate. *You*."

What? To claim *her*? His... *mate*?! Geva's heartbeat flared even faster, her head whipping back and forth. "You—you didn't want me!" she stammered back. "You wanted—the gold. Remember?"

But Rathgarr hissed a low growl, his huge body lurching a step closer. "I ken what I wish for, poppet," he hissed, as his clawed hand slipped downward, and blatantly adjusted the front of his trousers. "And tonight, I am here for *you*."

For you. A stark, dizzying thrill surged up Geva's spine, her eyes wide on the bulging sight beneath that clawed hand—but she shook her head again, fought to collect her thoughts, to drag her eyes back to his face. "You can't mean it, Rathgarr," she snapped, though her voice hitched. "You don't trust me. You barely even *like* me. You would never want to make me your mate. You *said*."

Rathgarr's scoff was sudden and sharp, and oh gods, his hands had dropped, he was unbuckling his belt, the movements slow but certain. "Ach, and *you* said I should be the last orc in the realm you should choose," he hissed back, so low, so deadly. "But this was not truth either, was it, my pretty poppet?"

Geva had entirely lost the ability to speak, her breaths heaving hard, her eyes still frozen on the sight of Rathgarr's hands. On where he was deliberately drawing the belt open, and then easing his trousers downwards, until...

His cock bobbed out thick, swollen, hungry, already leaking with thick white. And oh, his big hand was circling around the base of it, stroking it, pumping it out to a rich dangling string, swaying back and forth...

"Do you wish for me, my sweet?" he growled. "Do you wish to swallow me deep inside you, and be flooded with my good fresh seed? With my *son*?"

And oh gods, what was happening, why wasn't Geva moving, why was her tongue brushing against her lips. He wasn't really offering this, to give her his fresh seed, his *son*...

But somehow, that almost seemed to break the spell, and

she jerked a step backwards, up against the schoolroom table behind her. "You don't trust me to have your son!" she managed. "You think I'll use him against you. You think I was spying on you, and lying to you, and *using* you!"

That shot a very faint wince across Rathgarr's mouth, so Geva kept going, gulping for air, for rational thought. "And you also made it very clear that you would *not* follow me," she hissed, "because that was apparently part of my dastardly plan to entrap you, and steal away all your gold!"

But oh, he was stepping closer again, his hand still leisurely pumping up and down, his eyes crackling with strange, stark intensity. "But now, my fair angel," he drawled, "you can do none of this. And we shall know if you have spoken truth to me, ach?"

It still wasn't making sense, it wasn't, except for the way he'd closed the last space between them, trapping Geva between him and the table. And she could still shove him, still scramble away, make her escape... so why was she still standing here, her breaths hitching short and shallow in her chest.

"We shall now learn, my pretty poppet," he continued, hot and harsh, "what you truly wish for. Ach?"

He'd raised his brows at her, his hand still just blatantly stroking like that, as if this was another test, another challenge—and oh, hell, his other hand had reached out, spreading wide against Geva's hip, and then slipping up, up, up. And she still wasn't moving, or even breathing, as that hand slid up over her side, her waist, until it found her full breast beneath her shift. And why was she still wearing his shift, his clothes, his wedding-ring...

But maybe this was why, the way his hand gently gripped her, as though she were his. Squeezing, caressing, slow and deliberate, his thumb brushing her already-hard nipple—and then, oh, he reached down inside. Pulling her full, heavy brown breast out over the low neckline of her shift, so he could watch himself tweaking and squeezing it, his tongue again brushing his lips.

"You aren't—making sense," Geva choked out, far too late, even as she felt herself gasping, perhaps even leaning into his touch. "You don't—want this. You don't want *me*. You think I want your gold. That stupid damned *hoard!*"

But oh, hell, suddenly Rathgarr was smiling at her, all sharp teeth and terrifying eyes. "But this is the snare, poppet," he breathed at her. "The hoard is gone."

Gone. *Gone.* The word ringing like a bell through the room, like flying wings trapped in Geva's belly. The hoard was *gone?*

And was he trying to trick her, was he lying, what the hell was this, why couldn't she think, damn it, *think.* "What do you mean, *gone?*" she gasped at him, her body still arching into his touch. "Where?"

Rathgarr was still smiling, stroking, caressing, and now his other slick, seed-coated hand was easing up too, and pulling out her breast on the other side. Flagrantly putting them on display for him, full and shameless, and he leisurely tweaked her nipples, kept giving her that taunting, treacherous smile.

"I gave it to Grimarr," he replied, his voice very even. "To the mountain, for the gain of all our kin."

What? No. *No.* He wouldn't have, he couldn't have—but he was still here, nodding, holding her eyes, waiting for her response. "This hoard was stolen," he continued, harder. "It was tainted. Cursed. Kesst and I, we agreed upon this. We did not wish it"—his eyes shifted, flicked away—"to keep coming between us. To keep tearing us apart."

Geva couldn't stop searching him in return, her body shaky and breathless beneath his touch, her disbelief screaming through her thoughts. He'd—given the hoard away. To *Grimarr*. For the gain of all his kin. He and Kesst had *agreed.*

And suddenly Rathgarr was laughing again, and crowding even closer, enough that Geva had to scrabble back up onto the table—and oh, that was just what he'd wanted, his huge body looming close between her legs, his strong hands drawing her thighs apart.

"*Gone*, poppet," he hissed, harder, as he yanked her shift up, exposing her bare, trembling body beneath. "So now, what shall you do? Shall you make pretty excuses? Call for your loyal Skai to help? Cringe away from your true mate, and seek to run? To betray me?"

And gods curse him, it was another *test*. It was him spreading her out like this on this table, opening her thighs even wider, exposing everything between. Exposing her for him, for his taking, because oh, he was so close, that hard, dripping head only a breath away from her parted, quivering heat. Poised and ready to fill her with his seed, and his son.

And they both knew Efterar's magic was gone. Knew the deep, fundamental, irrevocable risk in what he was offering, what he was challenging.

His son. With no coin, no hoard, no more secrets between them.

Geva's body was shuddering all over, her thoughts screeching and swirling, her eyes still desperately searching his hard, taut, waiting face. This was a test, and a challenge, and… a gift.

And suddenly, she was nodding. Nodding, fervent and frantic, clutching at his back, his shoulders, his hair. Yes. *Yes*.

"Yes, Rathgarr," she breathed. "Yes. Fill me."

49

―――――

For one more fraught, frozen moment, Rathgarr gazed down at Geva, his lips parted, his eyes blinking. Looking almost dazed, suddenly, as if she'd struck him straight across the face.

"You—wish for this," he said, in a whisper. "For me. For my son."

And Geva was still nodding, still clutching desperately at him, fighting to yank him closer. "Yes," she gasped. "You, Rathgarr. *You.*"

But he was shaking his head, suddenly, and his huge hands were fumbling, catching hers above her head, pinning them to the solid table. "You cannot," he gasped back, between hard, dragging breaths. "I have—spoken false to you. I have mistreated you. Mistrusted you. Falsely accused you. You deserve—better, than this. Than me."

Geva was still gasping for air, and maybe she was even still nodding, holding his eyes. "But you're still—mine," she choked back, without thinking, without even hearing the words. "*Mine*, Rathgarr of Clan Ash-Kai. You gave me your scent, and your care, and your wedding-ring, and your best clothes and jewels. You took me before your clan again and again, and praised me, and drank fresh from me, as I drank from you."

And why was she saying this, why did it sound almost like a vow, like a tale whispered in the dark, secret and sacred between them. "You already bought me, Rathgarr," she breathed. "And you sold yourself to me in return. And now"—she yanked her hands out from his loosened grip, clutched them to his face—"if you're still willing to give it, I want your good Ash-Kai seed. I want your son. And I am entitled to it, Rathgarr, because I *am* your mate, whether you admit it or not!"

And oh, the way he groaned. Long and guttural, his lips parted, his eyes fluttering. And when Geva yanked at him again, he didn't resist this time. That swollen, leaking, shuddering heft settling just there, nocking into her, finding its place. While she kept nodding, kept clinging to him, feeling him opening her up, parting her around him, his gaze vehement and glittering on hers...

She shouted as he drove inside, sinking full and deep, impaling her whole in a single smooth stroke. And then holding himself there, stabbed all the way inside her, watching with those glinting, shifting eyes as she gasped and writhed upon him, around him, already lost.

"I ought to have known, poppet," he said, and that was even a trace of a true smile, teasing on his mouth. "You always took far too much joy from this."

Geva fought to scowl back at him, kicking at him with her feet, even as she arched and moaned. "You intolerable—ungrateful—*ingrate*," she gasped, as he slowly drew out again, breath by breath. "You ought to be—"

But he'd plunged in again, breaking off the words, filling her with heat and strength and sharp, staggering pleasure. And then again and again and again, carving into her with furious flaring strokes, his hips snapping swift and powerful, his heavy bollocks slapping with every forceful thrust. As if he couldn't stop, suddenly, as if he was being driven on by some desperate unknowable urge, as if the need to take her, to fill her, had swallowed all else. Just the same way Geva couldn't stop clutching at him, arching for him, her fingernails scraping down his back, her pummelled invaded heat still seizing for him, milking at him. Needing his fresh seed, craving it so hard she felt faint, more, more, *more*—

"Please, Rathgarr," she was gasping at him, begging him. "Please, grant me your seed. Pour me full. Empty yourself for me, give me everything you have, show me you trust me, Rathgarr, *please*."

And oh, he was nodding, he was doing it, obeying it, because she was his mate, she'd earned this, and he was *hers*. His strong legs shifting up to kneel beside hers on the table, his hands again shoving hers above her head, holding her firmly in place. Trapping her here beneath him, pinned on all sides, as he buried his face in her neck, his teeth seeking sharp against her skin...

And as he kept driving into her, slamming into her, his huge body heavy and hot and desperate. Fully focused on the goal, the prize, the conquest, here, within his grasp—

His teeth sank down, flashing out a fierce, fleeting pain as he groaned, deep into her very skin—and then, then, with one last furious drive inside, he exploded. Spraying out into her with shuddering, shattering force, so hard that Geva's entire body writhed beneath it, shouting, fully consumed by him, claimed by him, by her own deadly, stunning mate, *hers*—

Her own relief roared through her in raw, reckless waves, convulsing down the full length of her mate buried so deep within her, drinking up more of him, more, *more*. Swallowing all he would give, all she could possibly draw from him, until his shudders gradually began to fade, wringing out his last, lingering pulses inside her.

And when the world slowly, shakily returned again, it was with the bizarre, unthinkable sensation of Rathgarr's teeth drawing out from her neck. And then a soft, careful warmth caressing where his teeth had been, kissing and stroking with gentle lips and tongue. Almost as if he was—cleaning her, the way he liked her to do with him.

But then, his lips… trailed upwards. Up her neck, to her jaw, her cheek… and then, so gently, finding her mouth. His lips warm and soft, tasting of iron and salt, and an exquisite, familiar sweetness. And Geva moaned as she kissed him back, as she finally, finally learned how her mate tasted. So good, so impossibly, desperately decadent, laced with languid, luxurious hunger, with a longing she hadn't known she'd felt, until this moment.

When they slowly drew apart again, he brushed one last kiss to her mouth, and then to her nose. And then he dropped his head to the wooden table beside hers, his body sagging heavier, closer, as he dragged in deep, shuddering breaths.

"Ach, poppet," he finally whispered. "This was the wrong order, I ken. Ought to have kissed you, before seeking to spawn my son upon you."

Oh. Their son. This. Because yes, yes, that was what this had been. It had been Rathgarr challenging her about the gold… and then her challenging him about the son. *Grant me your seed. Give me everything you have. Show me you trust me.*

And perhaps he'd followed her hesitation, because he'd jerked up over her, his wide eyes searching hers. "You *did* wish for this," he demanded. "Ach? Even without the gold?"

But Geva was already nodding, and smiling at him, though her mouth slightly quivered. "I do want it," she whispered back. "Even if you *are* still the most enraging person I've ever met in my life."

Rathgarr's eyes had instantly softened, his lips curving up—but then he exhaled, and twitched a shake of his head. "I am—so sorry, poppet," he said, quiet. "I have so deeply wronged you. Misjudged you."

Geva wasn't going to argue that, her throat swallowing hard, and Rathgarr huffed a laugh, without any humour in it. "You have been such a gift to me, Geva Okoro," he continued, his voice low. "You have freely granted me so many gifts. Your laughter. Your hunger. Your tales. Your wisdom. Your kindness. Your goodness toward me, and toward all my kin. Your own trust, even when I did not deserve this. And I"—he drew in another shaky breath—"I spurned this. I forgot this. I forgot all you had given me, all you had shown me, in favour of my own grief, and my greed."

Geva still wasn't arguing this, just watching, listening, and he exhaled again, his eyes fluttering closed. "I longed to tell you of the hoard," he croaked. "I very nearly did, just before we reached the mountain. But then, all this happened with Kesst, and with Grimarr, and you learnt how much I had not told you, even without this. And I"—his eyes opened again, held on hers—"I was a coward, poppet. I was... afraid."

Geva felt her head tilting, considering that, as Rathgarr grimaced, shook his head. "I was so afraid you would wish for my hoard, more than you wished for me," he whispered. "I was so afraid that beneath all your goodness, you would yet be just like my mother. When I was small, I thought her the cleverest, most stunning woman to ever walk the realm—and by the time of her death, I would have happily spat upon her corpse, so deeply did I loathe her and her greed. And I could not bear to think of you learning of this hoard, and then becoming just the same. I could not bear to think of losing the one woman who had brought me such joy, and such peace. Who not only made this curst visit home bearable, but... worthwhile. Fulfilling. *Happy.*"

Geva blinked at that, and Rathgarr's hand came to her cheek, stroking gentle but firm. "You did, poppet," he said. "You listened to me. You soothed me. You welcomed my touch and my care. You kept all my secrets. You never once mocked me or belittled me, even in my weakness and shame. You made friends of Kesst and his mate. You cared for all these orclings, and did this so freely, and so sweetly. You were so good, and so kind, that I"—he drew in another deep breath—"I fell to my fear, even amidst my own falsehoods. I was sure you had somehow learnt of the hoard after all, and that this was what had made you so good. *This* was why you pleased me so much. I thought it had to have been, ach? For no woman does all this, and gives all this, for *me*."

Geva's increasing disbelief must have been clear on her face—surely *someone* had cared for him, at some point?—because he huffed a brittle laugh, gave another shake of his head. "Not for *me*," he said, harder this time. "For my face, mayhap, or my form, or my prick, or my gold. For how I could please them, or command them, or beg. For how I could give what *they* wished from me. And in return, I sought to gain what I wished from them. There was no truth in this. *I* was never in this."

Right. And then their own relationship had begun in much the same way, perhaps, with the payment, the coin—but perhaps Rathgarr had followed that thought too, his eyes so intent on hers. "But what we made between us, with the coin, this was... freeing," he continued slowly. "I held the power in this, for once. And though you could have taken this from me, you never did, poppet. You made this... *safe*. And thus, there was no need for me to hide, or play-act, or learn how best to please you, to gain what I wished. Instead, *you* learnt how to please *me*. Not only this, but"—he drew in another deep breath—"you play-acted *with* me. You were my true helpmate, poppet. And I never knew how much I longed for this, until I tasted it. Until I began to fear the loss of it. Until I began to think you had done to me, what I had always done to *them*."

Oh. Geva's hand had slipped into his hair, stroking softly against his scalp, and he leaned his head into her touch, his breath exhaling. "I was wrong," he whispered. "I was afraid, and a fool, and a greedy, selfish *ingrate*. I was so full of my own misbeliefs that I could no more see beyond them. And when you told me this grim truth of your parents, I blamed you, instead of myself. I used this to tell myself that you had spoken false to me, that you kept secrets from me—when I had done so much worse to you. I was so cruel, poppet. I am so sorry."

Geva still couldn't seem to speak, though she felt herself nodding, acknowledging this, agreeing with this. And he was nodding too, hard and fervent, a wretched little smile pulling at his mouth. "And after all this," he said, "you threw those terms upon me. And I was so sure they were a trick, I was so sure you yet sought a secret path to my gold. Until you left, and Kesst finally came to himself, and..."

He huffed a short, humourless chuckle, shaking his head against Geva's fingers. "He laughed at me," he continued. "And then began shouting that I was a fool, who was not worthy of you. For instead of suiting yourself with your terms, you helped *me*. You helped *us*."

Geva felt her mouth twitch up, and Rathgarr flashed her a wry, regretful little smile in return. "This was very Ash-Kai of you, poppet," he said. "You bound me to stay. You bound me to keep running your school, and tending the orclings you so cared for. You even took my coin, so I could not hold this against you, or claim I had been wronged. All this, even after I"—he grimaced—"I again mocked you, and spurned you. I pushed you away. I cruelly stole even these small farewells from you, and thus threw upon those blameless orclings what had been thrown upon Kesst, when I left."

Geva didn't hide her grimace at that, and Rathgarr grimaced too, gave another shake of his head. "Kesst told me I had become worse than our mother and father combined," he said heavily. "With my bluster, and my short-sightedness, and my secrets, and my greed. And he was not wrong, ach? He is so clever, my little brother. So quick and wise."

The smile was again curving at his mouth, his eyes flickering fond and rueful. "And after this, Kesst and I... spoke," he continued. "We spoke for nearly all the day, with no more of these lies and tricks and secrets between us. I learnt much of him, and of how he spent our time apart, that I had not known before. I learnt much about how Grimarr and Efterar—and ach, mayhap even Ulfarr—had looked after him, when I could not. And by the end of this"—he shrugged—"neither of us wished for this hoard. Neither of us wished to gain from so much suffering."

Oh. Geva was smiling back, her relief surely shining in her eyes, and his own smile pulled higher, his head tilting further into her touch. "And by giving this hoard to Grimarr, and the mountain," he said, "I have offered some amends for his kindness—not only in caring for Kesst, but in welcoming me there without deceit or reserve, even when he knew I was plotting against him. Also, he has sworn to return all my mother stole to its rightful owners, as Kesst and I both wished—and once this is done, in keeping with your terms, he shall put the greater part of what remains toward our school. So that all our kin may gain from this. So our young orcs shall be cared for, and kept safe."

Geva couldn't seem to stop smiling, and her other hand had come up to caress against Rathgarr's familiar, beautiful face. "It's perfect," she whispered. "I'm so, so glad."

Rathgarr's grin back was quick and stunning, and perhaps a little smug, too. "I thought this should please you, poppet," he said lightly. "And you shall also be pleased, I ken, to hear that I have kept a few things. Some heirlooms from my father, and some shiny trinkets and goods and clothes for you. For I well know how you like to be spoilt, ach?"

Geva made a face at him, and uselessly kicked at his back with her foot, and in return he laughed, the sound tender and affectionate, his eyes sparkling on hers. "Do not pretend to deny this," he purred. "I know what a greedy little Ash-Kai schoolmarm I have caught for my mate. I know what you long for, my sweet."

Geva fully intended to argue this, eventually, once her

swirling thoughts fully digested those impossible words—*my mate*—on his mouth, in his voice. When suddenly he pushed up and backwards, a teasing, devious glint flashing in his eyes, as his hand slipped down between them, pressing tight over the curve of her. And then he drew out his softened length, even as his other arm firmly encircled both her thighs, hoisting them out and up toward him. Meaning that Geva's arse was tilted up, propped high against his chest, her legs over his shoulders, as he ducked his head deep between...

And then, oh glorious gods, was his mouth. His warm, wet, open mouth, obliterating all else, as it latched tight between her legs. Catching the furious rush of his own hot seed as it surged up and out of her, his throat rapidly, audibly swallowing, his hooded eyes held to hers. And damn him, that was his tongue, slithering down deep inside—and then thickening, lingering there, almost as if to block the rest of it from escaping, to keep it held within...

And oh, yes, that was exactly what he was doing. His half-lidded eyes angling down to her belly, to how he was tilting her bottom half up, as if to ensure all that thick, dangerous seed was settling deep, finding its home. As if she were a cup, and he was making sure she stayed full, until she'd drunk all she could of him. Until she'd made his son.

He hoisted her up higher against him, his eyes now sharp and almost challenging on hers, as his tongue drew a little out again. Enough to release a thick rivulet of seed from the cup he'd made, but he leisurely licked it, caught it, and then delved in again for more. Tasting from it, skimming from it, deliberate and calculating, being careful not to spill it, not to take too much...

And surely, Geva could have been alarmed, or offended, because they'd still only known each other a few weeks, they'd tainted it with coin and secrets and lies. And not only had he pinned her to a schoolroom table, and brutally had his way with her, but now he was blatantly, shamelessly soaking her with his fresh raw seed, doing his utmost to spawn his son upon her. While he licked her like this, taunted her with his beautiful eyes, challenged her to dare fight him on this.

But there was no need to fight him, not when she herself wanted it so much, when her sheer craving was clutching desperately back at him, kissing at his slick lips and tongue. Wanting him to know he could do this, because she'd earned this, she'd seen all of him and she still needed more, needed everything he would show her, all he would give her. Her own fierce, greedy, vicious Ash-Kai mate, covered in a deceptive veneer of smooth manners, impeccable grooming, and exquisite, well-fitted clothes.

But even deeper, perhaps, beneath the ravenous orc who was so shamelessly gaining himself a son, was just... him. The Rathgarr who'd wept at her tales at nights. The Rathgarr who'd so deeply grieved his lost brother. Who'd knelt before her, and whispered, *It is not good, then? You do not like it?*

And somehow, Geva had reached both hands back to his hair, sinking her fingers deep. "You're so good, Rathgarr," she whispered. "So strong. So clever. So generous, to grant me your seed like this. To help me spark your son."

His groan was instant and deep, vibrating into the very core of her through his still-tasting tongue, so she kept caressing him, stroking him, adoring him. "I want you so much," she continued, between gasps, as his tongue slipped a little deeper. "I need you, Rathgarr. Need your pleasure, and your care, and your trust. Need your scent all over me, inside me, until it'll never, ever fade away."

And oh, he was still groaning, his cheeks flushed, his long lashes furiously fluttering, and his tongue stroked harder, deeper, just there, there. Wringing up the taut, trembling anticipation, the already-pulsing pleasure, the greedy kisses against his plunging tongue...

"Please, Rathgarr," she gulped. "Give this to me. Make me yours in every possible way. Please, Rathgarr, please!"

And yes, yes, he was here, with her, his eyes blazing, his mouth sucking and slurping, his tongue plunging and kissing and rewarding her. Meeting her challenge, making her his, and him hers, doing this, sparking this, *I am here for you, my mate...*

The pleasure shattered out even fiercer than before, ringing and raging through the totality of Geva's awareness, and crushing her beneath its sheer, staggering wonder. Swerving out again and again and again, curling her up toward him, pulling at him, desperate for him, while he just kept kissing her there, sucking and slurping upon her, latched to her, burying his face deep. As if he craved nothing more than to drink her dry, to gorge himself on her until he drowned.

Geva was trembling and tingling all over when he finally drew away, his face flushed and slick, his eyes searching, uncertain, perhaps even uneasy. His throat swallowing again, and then again, his mouth twitching into a smile that wasn't a smile at all.

"You are yet... sure, poppet," he said thickly. "This was not just... the hunger, after all these days apart."

But Geva's tingling hand had found his mouth, her eyes utterly certain on his. "I want this, Rathgarr," she said. "I want you. I want to stay with you. I want to raise my son with you. You're *mine.*"

The strange fierceness was in her voice again, ringing with sureness, with truth—and drawing up something much like relief in his blinking, shimmering eyes.

"Ach, I am yours, Geva Okoro," he whispered, so soft. "And thus, I grant you my favour, and my sword, and my fealty. I shall keep you safe, and fed, and filled, so long as I am able, and so long as you shall wish."

He spoke it with a quiet, lilting cadence, as if the words weren't only his, but drawn from well beyond him, perhaps from a tale she didn't yet know. But it sounded like truth, like something that could never be unspoken. And when he slowly bent down, and pressed his mouth to hers, it felt like it was rushing and gathering between them, flinging out fiery cords and filaments, binding them in the depth of its spell. In the taste of both him and her on their twining tongues, in the way his sharp teeth bit gently but purposefully at her lip, and then at his own. Sealing the vow with blood as well as seed, with tang and salt and sweetness, freely gained, freely given.

When he slowly drew away, and rested his forehead to hers, they were both breathing hard, their faces flushed and sticky with sweat. Both perhaps just sinking into the strange, surreal truth of this moment, of this being… settled, finally, between them. No more secrets, no more lies. Just… this. Them.

At least, until Geva's tongue brushed against where he'd bitten her lip, and found that there was—no pain. No taste of blood. Not even a scratch. And when she frowned up at Rath-garr, still nudging her tongue against it, he gave a wry half-smile, a small shake of his head.

"I carry a touch of the old Ash-Kai healing, I ken," he said, husky. "Not enough that I can wield it at will, or heal true wounds. But"—his mouth quirked higher—"mayhap just enough to soothe my sweet mate, when I wish for this. Or mayhap to help open her pretty rump for me, also."

And gods damn him, it was one more thing he hadn't told her—but he bent down again, and very gently nipped at the same spot on her lip. "I did not even think to speak of this, poppet," he said firmly. "It is naught, ach? Your own gifts of telling tales, and dancing and drumming, and charming innumerable younglings, are far greater than this. Even your sun goddess *hair* puts this to shame."

Despite herself, Geva was smiling back at him, shaking her head. Her thoughts darting back to that memory of the night in the inn when he'd flattered her, praised her hair and her skin and her eyes. And maybe he was thinking of it too, his mouth twitching even higher, his eyes soft and affectionate on hers.

"I always thought this was stunning," he whispered. "From this first day we met. *You* were stunning. And quick, and clever, and brave. I could scarce think, through your beauty, and the sweetness of your scent. And then, after you flooded me with your scent in that wardrobe"—he chuckled, low—"you *undressed* before me. Flaunted your plump, lovely form for me, without even a trace of shame. As if I could bear to let you go, after this?"

Geva blinked up at him, and again shook her head, her disbelief rising. "And then you told me you preferred soft, sweet women," she pointed out. "And that you would never mate me. Or want to have a *son* with me."

But Rathgarr just chuckled again, and shook his head, too. "Ach, and then *you* sucked me," he countered. "And all your rancour vanished, and you swallowed every last drop, and kissed me so sweetly, and worshipped me with your soft, bewitching eyes. Should you have refused to come with me, after this"—he raised his brows at her—"I should have bound and carried you, ach?"

Gods, he was infuriating, and why was Geva shivering like this, and slowly smiling up at his face. As if he'd said something truly delightful, rather than showing her another glimpse of his vicious, devious, greedy Ash-Kai self.

But in this moment, she couldn't seem to make herself care... and maybe, maybe, she didn't. It was part of him. Just the same as the generosity, the vulnerability, the impeccable grooming. Hers. Her mate.

"Are *you* sure?" she asked now, without quite meaning to. "About having a son?"

She was thinking of how adamant he'd been against it, how he'd threatened to refuse her payment if it happened. And surely he was thinking that too, exhaling as he nodded, his mouth twisting. "Ach," he said. "I have... longed for this, you ken, even as I feared it. I could not bear to think of failing with my own son, as I failed with Kesst."

Geva had perhaps already known all that, and she nodded, stroked at him, as he drew in a breath. "But when Kesst and I spoke," he continued, quieter, "he swore to help me in this, and to treat our son as his own. And should the worst befall me—or you—he and Efterar shall do all within their power to keep our son safe and cared for. This was... a great comfort to me."

It was a genuine comfort to Geva too, and she felt her smile deepening, her body relaxing even more beneath him. "I'm so glad," she said. "And so grateful to Kesst for offering."

Rathgarr was smiling now too, with a distinctive faraway affection in his eyes. "Ach, the gods have blessed me with Kesst, far more than I deserve," he replied. "I yet cannot believe that we are together again. Or that he has forgiven me, as he has. Ach, well"—he half-grimaced through his smile—"he said he shall only offer his full forgiveness once I have brought my mate back home, and you freely swear to him that I have earned your trust again. Stubborn little Ash-Kai."

The affection was again almost palpable in his voice, and Geva was fully grinning at him now, feeling his words ring and resonate into her chest. His mate. Home.

"So you will come now, ach?" he asked, so soft, his eyes shimmering on hers. "Come home with me again, not only as my helpmate, but my sworn bondmate, also?"

And Geva couldn't stop smiling, couldn't stop the joy from escaping in a bright bubble of laughter. "Yes, Rathgarr," she said. "I'll come."

50

Leaving the Fitzwalds' was an entirely different experience this time. What with Rathgarr first drawing Geva to her feet, and then straightening out her clothes and hair with surprising care, before thoroughly checking her over for any mess or injury.

"Ach, I have not spilled a drop," he said cheerfully, once he'd run his hands up the insides of her thighs, letting them linger for longer than was surely necessary. "In poor taste, you ken, in a schoolroom."

Geva laughed and shook her head, which had the unintended result of lurching Rathgarr closer, his eyes peering disapprovingly down into her hair, before he plucked out a little piece of leaf. "Ach, did Killik not even offer you a hot bath, poppet?" he demanded, as he disdainfully flicked the leaf away. "Shameful. We shall stay in an inn tonight, where you shall bathe, and rest, and eat to your heart's content."

That did sound absolutely wonderful, Geva could admit, but before she could reply, Rathgarr spun around, and stalked for his pack. Which she hadn't even noticed until this moment, and from which—she blinked—he was plucking out a very large piece of thick cloth, and spreading it out over the table.

"What are you—" Geva began, but he'd already strode over to the wall, to... her favourite painting. The one she'd mentioned to him as being valuable, that very first day they'd met. And in return, he'd said, *You ken I wish to jaunt about the realm with some great scribble strapped upon my back?*

But as Geva stared, incredulous, he plucked the painting off the wall, and carried it to the table. Where he carefully began wrapping it up in the cloth, folding it over again and again, before next yanking out some long strips of leather from his pack, and firmly wrapping them around it, too.

"I am stealing this painting," Rathgarr said, with supreme nonchalance, as he kept tying it up, securing the leather strips tight. "You wished for it, so now you shall have it. For our own schoolroom, mayhap."

Oh. Well. And surely Geva wasn't condoning even more thievery, or was she, because she wasn't making any effort whatsoever to stop him, and there was a fierce, glimmering pride in her chest, a warm smile still on her mouth. Her mate. Hers.

"Is there aught else you should wish to take from here?" Rathgarr asked now, as he slung the massive wrapped painting onto his back. "Any goods or treats for the orclings, mayhap?"

And damn him, maybe Geva *did* want to take a few more things, and soon she'd helped him stack up a variety of paper and inks, some paints that she'd always had to wheedle the children to use, and an assortment of seldom-used books and toys. Until Rathgarr's pack was nearly full again, and he was grinning approvingly down at her, and nudging her toward the door. Toward where—Geva twitched, but Rathgarr's hand was already there, steady on her waist—Killik was standing in the doorway waiting, his arms folded, an impatient glint in his eyes.

"Ach, frittering about *thieving*, whilst we guard you, and clean up your mess," he said scathingly, pursing his lips. "You tiresome Ash-Kai are all the same. And you did not even make him weep, woman! Or beg!"

With that, he threw up his hands, and stalked off down the hallway, irritably beckoning for them to follow. And though Geva meekly obeyed, she couldn't help a covert glance toward Rathgarr behind her. Finding him giving an odd little smile back toward her, his hand gently gripping at her arse.

"You were to make me weep?" he asked, under his breath. "And beg?"

"Ach, later, Ash-Kai," Killik cut in, a little too loudly, as he jerked his head toward the door. "For we have a small... setback, first."

A setback? Geva blinked at Killik, and then at Rathgarr, her mirth rapidly fading, twisting into a sharp, sudden fear. A setback. Like—one of the servants? Or had the Fitzwalds returned? Damn it, had the others been caught? Compromised? Endangered?!

But Killik was already shoving open the side door, striding blithely out into the dark night beyond. And Geva drew closer to Rathgarr's solid strength as she followed Killik outside, to where Ulfarr was already waiting, together with Timo and Trygve and Sune, and...

A small, weeping figure, dressed in tattered, muddy clothes. A figure who glanced up, gasped aloud, and then rushed forward, straight into Geva's waiting arms.

It was—Cecily.

51

———————

Cecily was... here? Alone?

"Miss Gee!" Cecily was gulping, between hoarse, hiccoughing sobs, as her small arms clamped tightly around Geva's waist. "You're here! You're alive! But—there are orcs! So many orcs! We're *doomed*!"

Geva's eyes were already blinking hard, and she hugged Cecily as tight as she dared, swaying her back and forth. "Oh, sweetheart, you're all right," she replied, though her own voice was choked, too. "The orcs won't hurt you. You're safe. I promise."

She could feel Cecily's little body slightly sagging against her, though she was still gulping for breaths, and darting a petrified glance over her shoulder. Toward where Ulfarr was giving an admittedly terrifying frown, while Timo, Trygve, and Sune all looked just as alarmed as Cecily did, Timo with distinctly watery eyes. In contrast to Killik, who was now leaning against the nearby house and observing all this with a mild curiosity, and Rathgarr, who was watching with his head tilted, his eyes shifting with genuine concern.

"The orcs are here with me, sweetheart," Geva continued, stroking at Cecily's hair with as much reassurance as she could muster. "They're—my friends. Here, why don't I introduce you?"

Cecily gulped and sniffled, but warily turned a little toward them, even as she kept clinging to Geva's waist. So Geva made a quick round of introductions, which did seem to help, especially when Timo offered Cecily a wavering smile, and a fluid little bow. "We should never harm you, Miss Cecily," he said. "Or Miss Gee, either. She is our new teacher, you ken, and we would never wish to lose her."

Geva could feel Cecily's quiver of surprise at that, and then she sniffed again, wiping at her eyes. "Miss Gee is my teacher, too," she whispered, with an uncertain glance up toward her. "Or... she was. Are you... leaving, Miss Gee?"

Geva had to swallow down the lump in her throat, but she made herself nod. "I'm so sorry, Cecily," she whispered, as she drew her close again. "After you left, I was offered a new job, and"—she cast a wobbly smile up at Rathgarr—"I fell in love with it, and with Rathgarr. And I actually returned here mostly to say goodbye to you, sweetheart, because I know I'll miss you so, so much."

But Cecily gulped another choked sob, and she shook her head, whipping her tattered little braid back and forth. "Oh no," she gasped, as tears streaked down her cheeks. "Oh, I should have known, of course you want to leave, my aunt and uncle are so *awful*. When we were in the city, I accidentally offended one of their guests on the very first day, so my aunt locked me in the cellar every time they had company, and then they forgot about me down there, and—"

She broke off into more gasping, desperate sobs, her face now buried into Geva's shoulder. And Geva found herself gradually digesting all that, blinking down at Cecily's messy little head—which looked caked with mud—and then around at the otherwise silent darkness. At where there was no sign of the Fitzwalds, or a horse and carriage, or... anyone?

"Cecily," she said thickly, "did you… run here alone? All the way from the city?"

Cecily fervently nodded, her face still in Geva's shoulder. "I'm sorry," she sobbed. "I'm so sorry. I know I should have stayed. I know it was dangerous. But I couldn't bear it there any longer, Miss Gee, I *couldn't*."

Oh. Oh, gods. And the horrible Fitzwalds had locked her in a *cellar*? And why hadn't they come after her? Surely they should have been deeply concerned, and returned home at once—or at least sent word to the house for the servants to keep an eye out, in case she might return?

"How… how long were you travelling, sweetheart?" Geva whispered. "And… do any of them know you're here? Your aunt and uncle? The servants?"

Cecily furiously shook her head, and drew back to stare up at Geva with weeping, pleading eyes. "Please don't tell anyone," she gulped. "Please. The servants have barely been here anyway. And I left the city more than a week ago, I was so worried someone would catch up to me, because I just left the way we came, but"—she gulped again, wiped at her face with a grubby hand—"they haven't."

Gods above. Geva's fury was crackling now, her eyes glancing helplessly toward Rathgarr. Toward where he was looking just as angry as she felt, his gaze sweeping up and down Cecily's small, weeping form.

"Here, little one," he said, his voice deceptively calm, as he carefully held out something toward her—a golden, fresh-looking bun. "You look half-starved. You ought to eat."

Cecily was still eyeing Rathgarr with fearful eyes, but then she quickly snatched the bun from his hand, and began to eat. And gods, she did look starved, and neglected, and lost, and perhaps the rest of the orcs thought so, too. At least, Ulfarr was frowning with vicious-looking disapproval, and Timo's eyes were still far too bright.

"We found her hiding in the barn," Timo told Geva, very quiet. "We ken she was eating the animals' food."

Geva didn't think her rage could have surged any higher, and thankfully Rathgarr handed over another bun, since Cecily had already polished off the first one. "It is not safe for you to stay here alone thus, little one," he firmly told her. "I ken you ought to come with us for now, so we can be sure you are cared for."

Wait. Really? Geva's heart leapt, her eyes searching Rathgarr's set face, but as he glanced up toward her, his expression was flinty, stubborn, set. "We cannot leave her thus," he said flatly. "I shall not allow it. She was locked in a cellar? What sort of caretaker does this?"

There was a beat of silence, and then Timo fervently nodded, and came a step closer. "Sune and I both have caretakers also," he said to Cecily, his voice soft, as he gestured between them. "But ours have never locked us anywhere, and always feed us and tend to us. Ach, just today, Sune wished to eat a fish, so Ulfarr half-drowned himself in the river, just to catch one for him! Skai are rubbish swimmers, ach?"

Killik and Ulfarr both growled with disapproval at this, and even Sune was rapidly signing his displeasure—but Cecily was very slightly smiling at Timo, and wiping at her eyes. "What's a Skai?" she whispered back. "And I'm a rubbish swimmer, too."

Timo's smile twitched higher, and he gave a teasing glance over his shoulder toward Sune. "The Skai are mayhap our fiercest orc brothers," he said. "And this is no matter about your swimming, for if you come with us, you can learn this with us at our new school. With Miss Gee."

Cecily's wet eyes angled up toward Geva, but they looked uncertain now, rather than fearful. And looking back down at her, Geva suddenly felt a deep, staggering longing, clutching in her chest. Cecily could come. Cecily should come.

"But—what about the kidnapping law?" she made herself say, her voice hoarse, her eyes darting helplessly between

Ulfarr, and Killik, and Rathgarr. "Wouldn't we be—breaking the treaty? Risking retaliation?"

Killik's mouth pursed, his eyes catching on Ulfarr's. "Mayhap not," he said slowly. "Not if she has already run away herself, with naught of our hand in it. What fault is it of ours, should she wish to keep running away with us? Most of all if she is *sure* she has not been followed, and that there is *naught* to link her to us?"

He frowned back at Cecily, who was still clutching to Geva, though she was standing a little straighter, the fear almost fully faded from her eyes. "I'm quite sure," she whispered back. "I think—my aunt probably thinks I'm still *sulking in the cellar.*"

Her voice had shifted into a very serviceable echo of her aunt's grating voice, and Geva shuddered, even as Rathgarr loudly grunted with displeasure. "Then it is settled," he said flatly. "You shall come with us, little one, and we shall care for you. And should you wish, you shall also come to our school, and learn to swim with Timo and Trygve and Sune, along with much else."

Cecily's eyes on Rathgarr were blinking, shifting between something like awe and hope and uncertainty, and he abruptly swept over, and knelt down before her. "But only should you wish, little one," he said, softer. "And mayhap we shall only agree to a month, so you can see if this suits you. But should you choose to stay, I shall vow to keep you warm, and fed, and *safe*. And I ken my mate shall eagerly support me in this, ach?"

He'd glanced up toward Geva, but she was already frantically nodding, and clutching Cecily even closer. "Of course," she said, her voice cracking. "Of course, sweetheart."

Cecily blinked up toward Geva's face, her eyes bright and wondering—but suddenly she was nodding too, while more water streaked down her little face.

"Yes," she said, on a shaky, gulping laugh. "Yes, Miss Gee. Let's go."

52

———

For the rest of the evening's journey, Geva, Cecily, and Rathgarr walked together on the road, while the rest of their party again travelled through the nearby trees. The arrangement had been at Rathgarr's suggestion, and Geva had agreed that it was a good one—not only to account for Cecily's obvious tiredness, but to give her some quiet time to adjust to all this, as well.

Thankfully, despite the faint moonlight, it was also now dark enough to preclude any irritating comments from passersby, which meant that they were able to speak freely, without interruption. And at Cecily's request, Geva first told her the entire tale of her own adventure to Orc Mountain, and then—with Rathgarr's help—she answered every single follow-up question Cecily asked. About whether Orc Mountain was cold, or dark, or dangerous, and what kind of food they ate, and where they slept, and whether they might allow pets?

And while Geva had already appreciated Rathgarr's skill and patience with children, she found herself marvelling at the honesty and thoughtfulness of his answers. Even admitting, without the slightest hesitation in his voice, that he himself did not want a pet, since he already had his kin and a school to look after—but that if Cecily was willing to bear all the responsibility for a pet, he would do his best to find her one.

"But not in our room, ach?" he said, with a grimace over Cecily's head toward Geva. "A dog might mess on our furs. And a cat might scratch our linens and clothes. And, I have kept some tapestries for our walls from the hoard, poppet, but what shall a cat do to those?"

He was beginning to look distinctly distressed, and Geva laughed and shook her head. "No pets in our room, sweetheart," she told Cecily firmly. "But there are plenty of empty rooms along our corridor, and I think you'll be very comfortable in one of those. Rathgarr's brother Kesst is a marvel at arranging rooms, and I'm sure he can set you up with as many pet-proof furnishings as you need."

This thankfully seemed to mollify everyone, and Geva felt warm and shivery all over when Cecily huffed a happy little laugh, her thin body clutching closer into Geva's side. "It sounds wonderful, Miss Gee," she whispered. "Thank you."

Geva swallowed hard, pressing a kiss to the top of Cecily's head, and then glancing over at Rathgarr, who was watching with surprising fondness. Not looking even slightly concerned about the fact that they'd unexpectedly acquired a child, and Geva found herself smiling at him, slow and true. Her helpmate. Her bondmate. Hers.

They stopped for the night at a familiar inn—the very same one, in fact, that Geva and Rathgarr had used on their first night of travelling, weeks before. But this time, Geva reserved two adjoining rooms, and soon Cecily was fast asleep in her own bed, curled up tight beneath Rathgarr's fur.

"Are you sure about this?" Geva asked Rathgarr, once she'd latched the door between their two rooms, and settled beside him on the bed. "I'm sure you didn't actually want another entire person to look after, did you? And what if it ends up being... forever?"

It almost felt too precarious to even speak it aloud, but

Rathgarr loudly harrumphed, and bodily yanked Geva over onto his lap. "I told you weeks ago, that if ever we had the means, we should steal her away," he said firmly. "And you"—he exhaled, pressed a kiss to her hair—"you have granted me such help with Kesst, poppet. It is only right, and mayhap even a gift from the gods, that I can now help you."

Geva gave him a watery-feeling smile, and sank closer into his strong, solid embrace. Feeling him circle his arms even more tightly around her in return, wrapping her up in warm, sweet safety.

"And most of all," he continued, quieter, "now that I know what befell your own mother and father. This must have brought you such grief and fear and unease, ach? And then I came to you, and threatened you, and sought to steal what little you had worked so hard to gain. Ach, poppet"—his voice hitched—"no wonder you feared me as you did, and sought in such earnest to help me. No wonder you were so skittish around me, when you are otherwise so poised and graceful."

He kissed her hair again, and then gathered her even closer, his hands running up and down her back. "I wish to make amends to you for all this, my sweet," he murmured. "I wish to grant you peace, and ease, and safety."

The words seemed to settle in Geva's chest, soft and certain, and she nodded as she curled up closer, drank him in. And when there was a sudden, sharp knock at the room's main door, she barely even twitched, not even when Rathgarr gave an approving little slap to her arse, and then slid her aside onto the bed, and went to answer the door.

It turned out to be Abjorn, smiling halfheartedly back and forth between them, and holding up a basket of what appeared to be fresh-picked berries. "The orclings wished to send these for the human girl's breakfast," he said. "And Killik wished me to ask if there is aught else you need?"

"No, thank you, brother," Rathgarr replied, as he set the berries on the nearby nightstand—although he was studying

Abjorn oddly, his head tilting sideways. "But is there aught *you* need?"

Abjorn was shifting from foot to foot, his eyes not quite meeting Rathgarr's. "Naught... really," he said, with a jittery shrug. "I only thought... I thought mayhap Sig had come with you. Thought mayhap... I caught his scent."

Rathgarr's smile was warm, and perhaps a little too understanding, as he clapped Abjorn on the shoulder. "Ach, you did," he said, "for Sigarr did come with me. He said"—his smile went rather wry—"he did not yet trust me to roam around the realm alone."

Abjorn gave a wretched little smile too, though he was bobbing even faster on his feet. "Then why," he said, sounding almost plaintive, "did he not come to say hello? Or ask where I had gone?"

Rathgarr kept giving Abjorn that fond smile, along with a bracing little shake to his shoulder. "Ach, well, he told me you did not say goodbye, or even tell him you meant to leave," he said. "So mayhap he thought you did not wish to see him."

Abjorn's mouth thinned, his eyes now fixed intently on the wall behind Rathgarr's head. "Oh," he replied, his voice small. And then he just kept standing there, staring at the wall, until Rathgarr gave his shoulder another little shake.

"Should you wish me to call Sigarr for you, then?" Rathgarr asked gently. "I ken he meant to wait nearby."

Abjorn returned this with a brief, dismissive-looking shrug, and a careless flap of his hand. "Ach, no matter," he said, with unconvincing casualness. "Only should you wish."

Rathgarr studied Abjorn for another long moment, as if he might actually let this go, damn him—and without at all meaning to, Geva huffed a heavy sigh, and cleared her throat. "Well, *I* would like to see Sigarr," she said pointedly. "If you could be so kind as to call him for me, Rathgarr?"

She didn't miss the unmistakable flare of relief in Abjorn's eyes, or the amused ruefulness in Rathgarr's, but he accordingly shrugged, and strode to the nearby window. And after shoving the window open, he put a hand to his mouth, and gave a long, shrill whistle, loud enough that Geva had to cover her ears. But clearly it had worked, because only a few moments later, there were heavy footsteps outside the room's door, and then Sigarr strode in, too.

He looked nearly as disheveled as Rathgarr had, his long black hair falling out from his braid, his grey trousers streaked with dirt and ash. And though he'd surely smelled Abjorn inside the room, he still halted upon catching sight of him, his big hand rubbing at his mouth before carefully shutting the door behind him.

"What is it, brother?" he said, his eyes very purposefully holding on Rathgarr, rather than Abjorn. "What do you need?"

For an instant, no one spoke—Abjorn was also very intently looking at the wall—and finally Geva sighed again. "Actually, Sigarr," she said pointedly, "I think Abjorn has something to say to you."

Abjorn's eyes snapped very wide, his head giving an urgent little shake. "What?" he squeaked, his gaze darting between Sigarr and Geva. "You are mistaken, sister! *You* wished to see him. *You* called for him, not me. Ach?"

Geva gave Abjorn her most imperious glare, but he only shook his head again, and stumbled a little backwards. "I should not wish to see him," he said thinly, "for *he* does not wish to see *me*!"

Sigarr's huge shoulders hunched, his brows furrowing close together. "No, *kærasti*," he snapped, and then grimaced. "*You* did not wish to see *me*. You left to run halfway across the realm, and did not speak one word to me of this! You did not ask me if I wished to come, and you did not even say farewell!"

Abjorn's throat bobbed, and he attempted a smile, though it didn't reach his eyes. "I was only in a hurry," he said offhandedly. "I did not need coddling, or a stern speaking-to of how this would not be safe!"

Sigarr stared at Abjorn for a long moment, but then jerked a curt little nod, and spun toward the door again. But his hand was again rubbing at his mouth, his eyes squeezing shut, and suddenly Geva couldn't bear another instant of it, another single word of these frankly ridiculous Ash-Kai secrets and lies.

"Wait, Sigarr," she snapped, as she lurched to her feet, from where she'd still been sitting on the bed. "I actually do need something from you. Abjorn's wild behaviour has been increasingly out of control lately, and very unsafe. I can't help but feel that he needs to be put in his place, by a very firm hand. And"—she raised her brows at Sigarr—"since he's your *kærasti*, it seems to me that you've been gravely shirking your duty in this, hmmm?"

The room had snapped to utter, ringing silence, all three orcs now gaping at her, even Rathgarr. But then Sigarr's stunned face very slowly turned toward Abjorn, who was suddenly looking very guilty—and then he twitched, and gave a loud, nervous little laugh.

"I... she knows not what she speaks of!" he said, his eyes wide on Sigarr's, his voice very high-pitched. "We both ken how you are about sweet small Ka-esh, with all your *care* and *coddling* and tiresome *safety*, ach?"

Sigarr still hadn't moved, still staring at Abjorn like that, and Geva heard herself give a smug, satisfied little laugh. "Yes, precisely," she interjected. "Which is exactly why Sigarr ought to be the one to handle you, hmmm? He ought to be very capable of meting out appropriate discipline, while taking proper precautions to ensure your overall wellbeing."

There was still no movement from either Sigarr or Abjorn, only that blank empty staring—though if Geva wasn't mistaken, there was a distinctive growing bulge at the front of Sigarr's trousers, and perhaps a spot of increasing wetness at the front of Abjorn's.

"And I, for one," Geva flatly continued, "would be well pleased to avoid any future sightings of your bloody nose or black eyes, Abjorn, especially around the orclings—and I know Sigarr will readily oblige us in this. For example, rather than pounding you into this floor, he would likely do so into the bed, right, Sigarr?"

A very soft growl had hissed from Sigarr's throat, his glinting eyes still very intent on Abjorn. On where Abjorn was still staring back, his breaths suddenly audible through his full, parted lips, as that stain of wetness kept spreading across the front of his trousers.

Sigarr had surely seen it too, or perhaps smelled it, his nostrils flaring—and then he jerked his head sideways, toward the bed. Saying, *Go.*

And this time, Abjorn didn't pretend not to know what he meant. Instead, his gaze on Sigarr had gone almost defiant, as he swallowed, straightened his shoulders, and strode toward the bed.

But before he'd even reached it, Sigarr was there behind him, shoving him face-first down onto it. And Abjorn moaned, loud and betraying, as Sigarr found both his hands, and pinned them firmly down over his head.

"You deceitful little *wretch*," Sigarr gasped, low into Abjorn's ear. "You wished for this, all this time? From *me*?!"

Abjorn was wildly squirming beneath him, his eyes rolling back. "Ach, you fool Ash-Kai," he choked. "Can you not smell? Or follow a hint when you see one?"

Sigarr growled back and yanked at Abjorn's trousers, revealing a brief glimpse of his muscled grey backside—and then he gave it a firm, forceful slap, the sound cracking through the small room. "What hints were these?!" he hissed, as Abjorn arched and moaned beneath him. "You *always* smell thus! Whilst reeking of a new Ka-esh every other *day*!"

His hand slapped again, even harder this time, ringing in Geva's ears—and at the sound, she suddenly jerked to awareness again, angling a wide, alarmed glance up toward Rathgarr beside her. Because wait, were they just going to keep standing here, and *watching* this?!

But Rathgarr's glance back toward her was again wryly amused, his brows meaningfully rising, clearly implying that this had all been Geva's doing—and then he gave a pointed glance toward the adjoining room's door, too. Toward where Cecily was still sleeping, damn it, and Geva realized that of course he was still listening, scenting, making sure she didn't awaken. Being... a good caretaker. A good mate.

Geva smiled ruefully up toward him, her head shaking, and in return he grinned back, and drew her closer. His eyes again angling toward where Abjorn was now squirming in earnest on the bed, nearly escaping Sigarr's powerful grip—at least, until Sigarr yanked off Abjorn's belt, and then his trousers, too. And in a flurry of movement, Sigarr had wrapped the trousers' fabric around Abjorn's wrists, followed by the belt, yanking it firm and tight.

"Answer me, *kærasti*," he hissed now, with another sharp slap at Abjorn's bare arse. "What were all these *hints* you gave me? Your wounds? Your recklessness? Your constant sniping at me in my fear for you?!"

Abjorn was still moaning and squirming, even as he blatantly arched up for the next stinging slap of Sigarr's hand. "Ach, and if this vexed you so much," he gasped, "then why did you not offer *your* care instead? Why was it only snacks and pets and grumbling? I thought you did not wish for this, so ach, I sought it elsewhere!"

There was a moment's stillness from Sigarr above him, his head bowing—but then he grasped for Abjorn's thighs, yanking them up and apart, so he was kneeling spread-eagled on the bed. His upper body still pressed flat, with his bound hands out before him, while his arse was up and out toward Sigarr, his legs wide, exposing everything dangling between.

And that was another slap from Sigarr, as his other hand

reached down between, and squeezed. Grasping it all in one big clawed hand, while Abjorn thrashed and moaned beneath him. And Sigarr was moaning too, his eyes fluttering, as his free hand flicked down to his own trousers, shoving them down just far enough to release the huge, waiting grey length behind them.

"Henceforth, then," Sigarr growled, as he finally released his grip between Abjorn's legs, and stepped closer behind him, "you shall not seek it elsewhere, my devious *kœrasti*. You shall only come for *me*."

Abjorn was already nodding and moaning again, perhaps even seeking to part his legs wider, to show Sigarr what was his, to tempt him closer. And yes, Sigarr was moving closer, closer, until he'd settled himself gently into Abjorn's wide-open crease. Just waiting there, watching Abjorn spasm and shudder and preen, and then pressing himself slow and smooth inside.

"Ach," Sigarr moaned, guttural and low, as that hard grey flesh at his groin pushed in, and in, and in. "Ach. Suck me deep, my pretty little *kœrasti*. You shall welcome my good Ash-Kai prick, you shall swallow all of me, ach—"

Beneath him, Abjorn was fervently nodding, his body now shot to utter stillness, but for his dragging gasps, and the visible shudders racing up his spine. As Sigarr kept pressing in more and more, filling Abjorn with him, closer and closer, until Sigarr's hips were grinding tight against him, his claws digging into Abjorn's arse.

For a brief, dangling moment, they just held there together, locked in place, gasping and trembling—and then Sigarr drew out, and slammed inside. Making Abjorn choke and flail at the impact, his body arching up even more, and Sigarr plunged in again, and again. Driving with such vicious, furious force that it was surely painful, but the look on Abjorn's face as he reared up was all raw, angelic pleasure, his body one smooth silvery arc, meeting Sigarr again and again and again—

And then Sigarr shoved him down, crushing him against the bed, burying his face in Abjorn's exposed neck, as he clamped his hand over his mouth. And then he bit down, hard, his growl muffled and thick, as Abjorn kicked and writhed and cried out into his fingers—and then stilled all over, his eyes rolling back, as Sigarr pinned him down even harder, his hips grinding fierce and deep, one last time—

And then they shouted together, held together, as Sigarr surely poured out inside, his big body gone rigid, his muscles standing out stark against his skin. While Abjorn strained down in furious, shaky little trembles beneath him, his eyes wide and rapt with ecstasy.

But then, finally, Sigarr sagged down heavily onto Abjorn, and Geva could see him gently kissing at his neck, just the way Rathgarr had done with hers. And oh good gods, they'd indeed just stood here and watched all this, and her flushed-feeling glance up toward Rathgarr found him looking decidedly smug, his arm circling even tighter around her waist.

"I have chosen such a gifted Ash-Kai mate," he said, with complacent satisfaction. "This was good work, my clever poppet. As always."

From the bed, both Sigarr and Abjorn groaned at this—but then Sigarr pulled back from Abjorn, tugging up his own trousers with a shaky hand. And then he reached for Abjorn's bound wrists, loosening them with obvious care, and checking them over for injury before releasing them.

"Are you well, *kærasti*?" he murmured, his voice thick, as he leaned over, and pressed another gentle kiss into Abjorn's neck. "Was this too much? Do you feel any pain?"

But beneath him, Abjorn was giving a fluid, catlike stretch, and then twisting and hopping up to his feet, while also swiping for his crumpled trousers, and fishing a rag from the pocket. "Ach, no," he said brightly, as he flashed Sigarr a swift, stunning grin, his face flushed, his hand rapidly wiping at his still-bare, sticky-looking front. "I have never felt better in all my life! What do you say to a sparring-match, Sig? Or mayhap a spell of hunting? I ken I could eat a whole moose!"

Sigarr's smile back was slow, and fond, and also exasperated, and he plucked the rag from Abjorn's hand, and took over the wiping himself. "I have brought you some sweet-buns, should you like these," he said, though his voice was still a little hoarse. "And you ought to have some water, also."

"Oooh, sweet-buns," Abjorn said, with palpable glee, as he bobbed up, and pressed a furtive little kiss to Sigarr's cheek. "Thank you, Sig."

Sigarr's eyes had gone rather blank, an unmistakable blush creeping up his neck, but Abjorn had already whirled away again, pulling on his trousers. "Sorry about the bed, you two," he said over his shoulder toward Rathgarr and Geva, as he shook out his hair, his fingers visibly lingering against the fresh bite-marks on his neck. "But I should have been very happy with the floor, also, so I ken this is all *your* fault, sister."

He'd spun back around again, winking at Geva, and then clutching easily at Sigarr's big arm. "Sweet-buns, then, Sig?" he said eagerly. "And then a sparring-match? And then, mayhap"—his glance up at Sigarr's face had gone a little shy— "I ken I may need more firm handling, ach?"

Sigarr's still-creeping blush had finally reached his cheeks, but he gave an unsteady little nod. And then they strode out together, leaving Geva and Rathgarr again wryly smiling at each other, though Geva's face still felt very hot, too.

"You damned Ash-Kai and all your secrets," she said, with a shake of her head. "How many years have those two wasted dancing around each other like that?"

Rathgarr's smile softened, and he drew her even closer, his mouth pressing against her hair. "It is not... easy, to bare yourself for another thus," he murmured. "We have all long ago learnt the dangers in this, ach?"

Right. Geva's thoughts had again flicked to Rathgarr's mother, and perhaps he was thinking of it too, his hand tightening around her waist. "But... do you ken," he said, a little offhandedly, "you might ever wish... for this, from me?"

Wish for this, from him. And Geva wasn't quite following, searching his uneasy eyes. Seeing how he was purposefully glancing away, and shifting on his feet, just the same way Abjorn had...

But she had to know, damn it, and she kept searching him, now stroking her hand against his back. "How so?" she asked, very carefully. "What do you mean?"

His breaths were dragging deeper, his body stiffening beneath her touch, but she kept stroking, kept waiting. Until his throat audibly convulsed, his eyes darting a glance downward that looked almost... afraid.

"Should you wish to... have me, thus," he whispered, his voice thick. "To... bare me. Teach me... a lesson."

Geva's mouth dropped open, her thoughts suddenly whirling back to that day in the schoolroom, to that challenge that she hadn't quite forgotten, ever since. *Do you wish to teach me a lesson, my prim little schoolmarm? To punish me?*

And when Killik had said it again, earlier that very night... Rathgarr hadn't balked at the idea, had he? *You were to make me weep?* he'd asked, with that odd smile on his mouth. *And beg?*

But... really? Rathgarr really *wanted* that? *Rathgarr*?! Just the way Abjorn had?!

But as Geva kept searching his shifting eyes, his slowly reddening face, she was suddenly, powerfully sure of it. He... wanted that from her.

And he was... trusting her with this. Baring himself like this. *It is not easy. I learnt very well to keep my secrets close.*

I held the power in this, for once. And though you could have taken this from me, you never did. You made this... safe.

Oh. *Oh.* And he was still waiting, still standing here stiff all over, looking at her with that fear shifting in his eyes. As if he expected her mockery, or her contempt, or her judgement, her refusal...

But looking back up at him, at her stunning powerful mate, offering himself like this, so clearly showing his trust in her, showing her what she'd earned... there was only hunger. Craving. Anticipation.

Something new.

"I thought you'd never ask, handsome," she murmured. "Now make yourself ready for me. At once."

53

For a breath, there was only stillness. Choked, dangling stillness, in which Rathgarr stared at Geva, his body utterly unmoving, the redness darkening across his cheeks.

But then he ducked his head, and—nodded. Nodded, oh gods, as he silently lurched toward the bed, and began stripping off the wet sheets. And then—a strange, stilted affection quivered through Geva's chest—he fumbled for his pack, yanked out a clean blanket, and smoothed it out over the bed. Because of course her clever mate wouldn't travel without a set of fresh linens, would he?

"Good boy," Geva murmured, once he'd finished—and in return he instantly stilled, and whirled around to face her with wide, searching eyes. Almost as if he thought she might be mocking him, but she gave him a soft, genuine little smile, and reached to gently caress at his arm. "Thank you, love. Now, I want you to undress for me."

He again twitched all over, but then nodded, swift and jerky, as he began fumbling at his cloak, and then his tunic. Tossing them onto the nearby chair, and then loosening his belt, kicking off his boots. And when he finally dropped his trousers, he was already huge and hard and copiously dripping, jutting out hungry and betraying toward her.

Geva hissed without quite meaning to, because *gods*, he was gorgeous. Standing here with his massive, beautiful grey body entirely on display, from his long, shining black hair, to his muscled arms and powerful abdomen, to his big, hairy thighs. And most mouthwatering of all, that thick, dripping cock, stabbing straight out of him, over those huge, bulging bollocks.

"Very nice, love," Geva said, her eyes sweeping up and down, lingering, ogling as she wished. And then, in an odd burst of daring, she slowly walked around him, trailing her fingertips very lightly against his skin, feeling him shiver beneath her touch. As her eyes just kept looking, drinking him up, catching on his gorgeous hair, on the broad muscle of his back, on that firm, rounded arse.

When she came back around again, his face was even redder than before, but his full lips were parted, and the whiteness was dangling from him in a long, thick string. And gods, the *sight* of that, and Geva couldn't resist dropping her hand to catch it, feeling its slick heat sticking against her fingers... and then, before she'd quite realized it, she raised her sticky hand up toward him, brushing its wetness against his parted lips.

"Now taste it for me, love," she breathed. "Is it sweet enough, do you think? Are you being a good orc boy, and making your very best seed for me?"

And oh, the way he groaned, his eyes wildly fluttering, as he fervently sucked her nearest finger into his mouth. And then the next, and the next, all hot suction and long swirling tongue, sweet and eager against her skin.

And when she gently plucked her fingers away, raising her brows toward him, she could see him struggling to draw in air, his chest powerfully heaving. "A-ach," he finally rasped, in answer to her previous question. "It is—good. Fresh. For you."

His face was now redder than Geva had ever seen it, and she reached up to pat his hot cheek, giving him a soft, appreciative smile. "Good boy," she murmured back. "Now, why don't you lie down, and make some more for me? Show me how gorgeous you are, when you're milking out my good seed?"

His groan was again long and guttural, and he instantly lurched to the bed, dropping himself heavily down onto his back upon it. His hand already finding his swollen length, circling tightly around it, pumping up as he arched and groaned—

But Geva gently slapped his hand, snapping him to utter stillness, his eyes wide and again panicked on hers—but she was still smiling at him, so fond, as she eased onto the bed too, settling between his knees, guiding them apart. "Easy there, sweet boy," she purred at him. "No blowing your full load until I tell you. I said, I wanted a show, hmmm?"

She drew his legs a little wider apart, and oh, he wasn't resisting, just spreading those huge thighs as she wished—so she kept going, holding his watching, shimmering eyes, as she raised his knees up and wide, showing her everything, everything, between. Not just his leaking heft and swollen bollocks, but also the darkness below, the quivering clutch of heat...

"Better," she choked, as she looked, drinking it in, the sight of his huge powerful body so opened, so bared, so... vulnerable. "Now, touch. Both hands."

At that, there was a ghost of a smile on his mouth, surely recalling the familiarity of that command—but yes, he was dropping both hands, one settling more gently against his dripping length, the other curving around his heavy bollocks below.

"Better," Geva said again, with an approving caress at his trembling, upraised thigh beside her. "Soft, at first. I want you seeking. Stroking yourself. Awakening yourself for me."

His groan was hard and sustained, but he nodded, biting his lip, as he kept stroking, slow and smooth. One hand's fingers easing up and down his length, oozing out more drizzling white onto his belly, while the other massaged his bollocks below, firm and familiar. As if this really was how he did it when he was alone, how he milked and coaxed out his seed...

"Very good, love," she said, breathless, as her own swollen-feeling groin caught and clenched. "Now show me more. Show me how you work in earnest for it."

And yes, yes, he was nodding again, his eyes squeezing shut, as his big hands moved faster, harder. Sweeping further up, and further down, one long finger seeking deeper between his thighs, while another settled onto his leaking slit, nudging downwards, almost as if to slip inside. While that sticky shiny white kept spluttering out around it, spattering his hand in an ever-increasing film of dripping fluid, and oh, Geva had never seen anything so stunning, so spellbinding, in her life.

"Good boy," she gasped at him, as he kept going, as a sharp little spurt dashed up, caught across his heaving grey chest. "You're so marvellous when you behave, love. When you show me how strong and rugged and virile you are, making me all this sweet, fresh Ash-Kai seed. Milking it out of your big, loaded bollocks, squeezing it up out your good fat Ash-Kai prick—"

And oh, hell, those bollocks were pulling up, his body arching, his groan rising to nearly a shout—and just in time, Geva snatched both his hands away. Leaving him gasping and straining beneath her touch, his dripping messy cock help-lessly bobbing up again and again, but not spraying out, not yet...

"I said, not until I *tell* you, Ash-Kai," Geva hissed at him, even as she softly stroked his trembling thighs. "You would be a very devious orc indeed, if you were to blow that lovely load before I grant you leave. Now, will you be good again? Show me how well you can behave for your mistress?"

Rathgarr was fervently, frantically nodding, his tongue sweeping against his lips. "Ach," he croaked. "Aught—that you wish. Always."

Oh, hell. The rush of dark, dizzying hunger was so sharp that Geva felt faint, and she had to gulp for air, focus through her own fluttering lashes. "Good, Ash-Kai," she breathed. "Very, very good. And perhaps, as your reward"—she reached up with shaky hands, and yanked off her shift over her head—"perhaps I will allow you to touch me. To cover yourself with my scent."

Rathgarr's groan was again long and harsh, his head nodding, his eyes wide and intent on her now-bare body—but he waited, shivering, until she'd lowered down his legs, and climbed up to straddle over his waist, purposefully ignoring that straining, leaking heft behind her. And when she grasped his big, sticky hand, and brought it to the slick, swollen place between her legs, he groaned again as he stroked it, very gently, as if he was almost afraid to touch her.

But Geva was smiling at him again, and then drawing his hand away, dragging his wet fingers up his own heaving chest. "Good," she purred at him. "Just like that. Cover yourself in me, love. Make yourself *reek* of me."

And yes, yes, he was already doing it, moaning as he slipped his fingers in a little deeper against her, flaring out astonishing arcs of pleasure at the touch—and then away again, so he could swipe it up his chest, to his neck, even deep into his messy black *hair*. And then again, and again, delving deeper against her each time, the sounds slick and wet and obscene. But oh, it was good, the way he looked, the way he felt, the way he was swiping his hand across his face, surreptitiously slipping a finger between his lips...

"*Behave,*" Geva gasped at him, and before she'd followed it, caught it, she was jerking down over him, so she could fill his disobedient mouth with her breast instead. Sinking her peaked brown nipple deep between his parted lips, and he instantly moaned and sucked, his big firm hands now on Geva's arse, grinding her slick, open wetness hard against his bare abdomen. And damn, it was so good, so, so good, especially when she gently slapped his cheek, drew his blinking worshipful eyes—and then fed him the other side, watching it bulge out above his frantically sucking mouth.

And he kept grinding, rocking, kissing, covering himself with her fresh scent, and perhaps even dragging her further upwards. And gods, Geva couldn't care anymore, couldn't find the game anymore, just needed him so, so desperately it ached all over, and she willingly followed his hands, up, and up, and up. Until she was straddled over his face, his blinking eyes wide and reverent on the sight between her legs—and then he drew her downwards, and seated her on his mouth.

"Fuck!" Geva gasped, because oh, oh, she was spread wide open over him, her most secret parts pressed against his *face*, and his groan was shuddering up inside her, together with his frantically licking tongue. Kissing her, lavishing her, gorging upon her, churning up the taut chattering craving into a furious, full-on frenzy, higher and higher, his body arching, the pleasure hitching, oh, oh—

"So good," she was gasping, without thinking, the world whirling, whipping wild away. "So good, love, such a good, strong, *wonderful* Ash-Kai, Rathgarr, please, more, *please*—"

The ecstasy shot up like a blow, like a light straight from his tongue into the very core of her, and she was shaking, shouting, perhaps even sobbing, as it surged again and again, swamping her in furious swells of raging, ricocheting pleasure. While beneath her, behind her, Rathgarr was curling up harder, his own shout muffled into her heat—and something hot spattered wide across her back, across her shoulders, even up into her *hair*. But his hands were here, and her hands were there, somehow sunk into his hair, and he'd done that without even being touched, oh gods, oh *gods*.

And when Geva's shaky, shivering body finally seemed to return to itself, it was with her still sitting on an orc's face, her hands tangled in his hair, while multiple warm rivulets trickled down her back, over her arse. And while her orc—her mate—

blinked up at her with shimmering eyes, his breaths heaving hard, his face still flushed deep with red.

And suddenly Geva needed nothing more than to see him, to touch him, to hold him, please, and she scrabbled downwards, backwards. Until she was lying long atop his sticky, still-shuddering body, her hands clutched to his slick, reddened face, her eyes desperately searching his.

"Are you—" she began, but there weren't even words, here, anywhere. "Was that—"

He was blinking back at her, drawing in great, gulping breaths—and suddenly his powerful arms were here, dragging her down, crushing her tightly into his hot, sticky chest. "Ach," he rasped, on another hard, shaky breath. "Ach, my sweet. My clever, wicked, *perfect* Ash-Kai mate."

Oh. All the last lingering tension in Geva's body had seemed to collapse at once, sagging her deeper against his warm, stunning reassurance. "I... thank you, poppet," he whispered, hoarse. "This was... very kind."

There was a strange hitch in his voice at the end, and when Geva pulled up a little to look at him, he was swiftly glancing away, and biting his lip. Looking almost ashamed, suddenly, and Geva shook her head, and attempted to jab her trembling finger into his chest. "This was greedy, you mean," she croaked back. "This was me blatantly using you, love, for my own selfish entertainment."

His mouth twitched up, just a little, his eyes darting toward her, and away again. "But, I ken," he said, his throat audibly swallowing, "this was not, mayhap, what you—should wish, from your strong orc mate. This may... alter how you think of me. Your... trust in me."

What? Geva's scoff was loud and disbelieving, but then she felt her head tilting, her eyes searching his face. Seeing the genuine unease in his eyes. The... fear.

"Of course not, Rathgarr," she whispered. "Of all the secrets you've kept from me, this is absolutely not the one that would finally break my trust in you. This is"—she felt her mouth curving into a jaunty grin—"the fun one, love. The ultimate reward, for all my hard work."

Rathgarr's lips twitched a little higher, but his eyes were still uncertain, uneasy. "But... you did not even truly punish me," he whispered. "Or make me suffer or beg. You said... kind things. Sweet things. Things you knew I... wished to hear."

Oh. And searching his eyes, it occurred to Geva that maybe—maybe he'd expected her to take the opportunity to retaliate, to gain her revenge upon him, for all the wrongs he'd done to her. Because maybe... maybe he would have allowed it. Maybe he would have just looked at her with those wounded, shimmering eyes, and taken it. Like he had with all those cruel women he'd lived with, the ones who'd commanded him, and made him *beg*.

Geva felt her breaths heaving again, suddenly, her eyes blinking, her mouth pulling into a wavering little smile. "I don't want to make you suffer, Rathgarr," she replied, her voice thick. "And look, if that's—something you want, I'm sorry, but I don't think I can give it to you."

And now it was Rathgarr's eyes blinking, one of his hands slipping up, catching shaky on her face. "No, poppet," he whispered. "What you—how you did this, it was—naught I have ever tasted before, ach? To be longed for, hungered for, to be told I am good and strong and worthy"—his voice choked, his head shaking—"whilst you also tease me and challenge me and draw out my pleasure? Without one breath of anger or mockery?"

He sounded truly disbelieving now, his hand still stroking with shaky, stilted reverence at her face. "How can this be truth," he whispered, as a streak of wetness escaped from his eye, down toward the bed. "How can this be mine. I am dreaming, I ken, and I never wish to awaken."

Oh. Geva had to swallow down the rising catch in her throat, blink back the wetness behind her own eyes, and she ducked her head, and pressed a soft, reverent kiss to his mouth. To where he was already meeting her, so warm and willing, tasting so strongly of her, of him, of them.

"You can't be dreaming, love," she said, as lightly as she could, once she'd drawn away again, and bumped his nose with hers. "Because if you were, I would not have seed currently dripping *into my ear*."

She grimaced as she attempted to shake it out, and beneath her Rathgarr barked a sudden, relieved-sounding laugh, his eyes crinkling at the corners. "I ken you are painted all over, poppet," he said lightly. "Inside and out. You shall *never* stop reeking of me, after this."

He sounded very much like his usual smug self again, and Geva grinned down at him, even as she rolled her eyes. "Or, stop sticking to you, apparently," she said, with a shudder, as she peeled her upper body away from his. "Oh, good *gods*. This inn will never let us stay here *again*."

But Rathgarr was grinning back at her, with such impossible fondness in his glimmering eyes. "Rubbish, my sweet. For I have brought yet more bedding, and I ken"—he sniffed purposefully at the air, and then slapped at her arse—"Killik is creeping out in the hall. Go tell your Skai you wish for a bath, ach?"

Geva rolled her eyes again, but soon managed to unstick herself, and strode unsteadily toward the door. Toward where Killik was indeed lounging against the wall outside, and frowning irritably toward her. "Ach, ach, I heard," he snapped. "I only do this because you finally made him beg, as he ought. And because I do not wish to smell your fresh Ash-Kai *stench* all night."

With that, he spun and strode off down the hallway, as if he weren't even slightly concerned about the prospects of acquiring a bath, in a decidedly human inn. And Geva was still smiling to herself as she turned around again, finding Rathgarr now standing tall before her, streaked all over with messy white seed. While his greedy eyes raked up and down her similarly painted front, catching on her breasts, her groin, the certain chaotic mess of her hair. Which, yes—Geva sighed, even as she smiled—was unquestionably streaked with him, too.

"You are so stunning, my sweet," he whispered now, as he drew her close, and inhaled slow and deep against her hair. "The most stunning creature ever to bear my scent, ach?"

Oh. Well. Geva squeezed him back, as tightly as she could, the shivery warmth again welling up in her chest, almost too strong to bear. While Rathgarr gave a shaky exhale, his hands drawing her even tighter, his claws pricking gently against her back.

"And you must never think I have not gloried in commanding you, or bending you to my will," he murmured. "Or that I should ever wish to stop this, ach? Or"—he drew away a little, his eyes glinting dangerously on hers—"that I shall allow you to misbehave, poppet. You shall need to be very, *very* good, to again earn this right to teach me my lessons."

Oh, damn him, *praise* him, because it was a new challenge, a new game, and Geva's breath was already catching, her eyes alight on his—at least, until he abruptly spun her around, and half-carried, half-dragged her to the bed. And then propped her up on her hands and knees on it, opening her wide, just how Sigarr had done to Abjorn… and then he thrust himself all the way inside, while she yelped and flailed upon him.

"But—Rathgarr!" Geva choked between gasps, twisting around to look at where he was blatantly eyeing her arse, as he steadily plunged in and out beneath. "Killik—is coming back—with the bath!"

"Ach," Rathgarr replied coolly, raising his brow toward her. "And he shall find the pretty, brave, sign-speaking schoolmarm on her knees, being pumped full of my fat Ash-Kai prick, and my sweet Ash-Kai *stench*."

Geva attempted to make a face at him, but he only drove in faster, making her shake and moan upon his onslaught. "I ken these sneaky Skai schemes," he said darkly, his voice only slightly hitching with his thrusts. "Creeping upon *my* woman. Helping her in *my* schoolroom. Running away with her, against *my* wishes! As if it is not plain what he longs for? A sweet mother for his ward, I ken! A woman to share with *Ulfarr!*"

He actually growled at that, slamming in faster, and oh, it felt so good, and he was so enraging, so appalling, *hers*. "As if I should *ever* allow this," he hissed, between thrusts. "You are mine, woman. You shall bear *my* sons, and none shall ever touch you again, but *me!*"

And with that, he plunged in one last time, his groan rough and deep as he surged out inside—and damn him, it was at that very moment when the door banged open, and Killik strode in carrying a hot, steaming bath. But he didn't cast a single glance toward Rathgarr and Geva, not even when Rathgarr—curse the smug bastard—ground himself deeper, and gave Geva's arse a firm, satisfied slap.

"Very good, my pretty poppet," he said approvingly. "Your tight little womb is sweeter each time I plough it, ach? Each time it sucks me whole, and drinks out my—"

"Ach, shut your ever-flapping mouth, you ungrateful Ash-Kai," snapped Killik, with palpable menace. "Else *I* shall spray in your fool bath, and you shall both reek of Skai all the rest of your days!"

That effectively shut Rathgarr up, and Geva couldn't help a choked laugh, a flush-faced glance over toward Killik, while fighting to ignore the sensation of Rathgarr's half-hard cock still twitching, draining out inside her. "Thank you, Killik," she said meekly. "We're very grateful for all your help."

Killik loudly huffed, and then stalked out, again slamming the door shut behind him. While Geva laughed aloud, and Rathgarr kept viciously scowling toward the door, like the stubborn, thwarted Ash-Kai he was.

"You aren't already plotting something against him, are you?" Geva asked warily, once he'd drawn away again, resulting in yet another predictably shocking mess. "I think you need a break from all the scheming, love."

Rathgarr didn't look at all convinced, though his eyes had softened as he guided Geva's still-shaky body to the bath. "It is not *scheming*, poppet," he said, with highly dubious casualness. "Only guarding what is mine, as a good Ash-Kai should."

Geva was laughing again, and shaking her head, and then pulling him down for a long, slow kiss. Her gorgeous, greedy Ash-Kai. Her mate. Hers.

The kiss soon led to more mess in the bath, of course, but Geva didn't complain as Rathgarr washed her in it, even her hair. And then they switched places, and she washed him, telling him a tale as she combed out his hair—and then, when he didn't seem even slightly inclined to move, she ended up braiding his hair, too, putting it into multiple neat plaits, while she kept telling him tale after tale. The reckless rat. The funny fox. The porcupine who lost his shell. And then, even Kesst's tale of the skunk, but at the end, his scent instead turned sweet, and he covered the maiden all over with it, until he would be sure never to lose her again.

Once she'd finished the tale, Rathgarr gave a slow, shuddering sigh, and he turned to face her, with a rapt, flickering awe in his shining eyes. And it occurred to Geva that she'd never actually seen his face for any of her tales, because he was always curled up behind her in the dark—but gods, it was stunning, and so was his smile, slow and warm and sweet.

"You are a marvel, Geva Okoro," he whispered, so soft. "And you are *mine*. Ach?"

And maybe it was greedy, it was selfish, it was the Ash-Kai in him, always there... but maybe she was just the same, smiling back toward her beautiful, powerful mate, caught forever in her words, her clutches, her desperate longing heart.

"Yes, Rathgarr," she whispered. "Yours."

EPILOGUE

If Geva Okoro never needed to find a missing eye-mask again, it would still be too soon.

"What do you mean, you've lost it again?" she asked Erik, with as much patience as she could muster. "Haven't I already given you three new ones this week?"

Erik's little eyes blinked with wide, glimmering confusion, his head shaking. "No, Miss Gee," he said, with genuine-seeming regret. "It was four, I ken."

Geva's irritation was already rapidly crumbling beneath his adorable gaze, and she sighed, and patted his little head. "Don't worry, Erik, we'll find another one," she said, glancing help-lessly around the room—but wait, there was Cecily, smiling as she strode over toward them, a little black eye-mask in hand.

"Look what I found, Erik!" she said cheerfully, kneeling down before him. "Timo said this has your scent on it."

Erik instantly brightened and snatched the mask from Cecily's hand, flashing her a shy, worshipful smile before scam-pering off out the door. And Geva found herself smiling warmly at Cecily too, and squeezing gratefully at her shoulder.

"Thank you, sweetheart," she said. "Are you off for the wall-climbing too?"

"Yes, of course!" Cecily said, with another swift, sunny smile. "Sune has promised to teach me the proper Skai way to do it, though Timo says he is only boasting. I ken I will see for myself, ach?"

Geva heartily agreed to that, and soon Cecily had dashed off again, leaving Geva still smiling fondly behind her. It had been odd, and perhaps a bit alarming, these past six months, to see how easily Cecily had fit into life at Orc Mountain—not only with her increasingly orcish vocabulary, but with how enthusiastically she'd embraced their school, and her cozy new room, and her adorable little black kitten, born from Cat, of course.

Cecily had also firmly identified as Ash-Kai, from her very first day at the mountain, even as she spent almost every free moment running about with Timo, Trygve, and Sune. And while Geva wanted to take credit for that, she knew it was also in large part due to Rathgarr, who had proven to be a consistently excellent caretaker—to the point where Cecily had begun calling him *Pa*, even as she'd christened Geva her *heart-sister* instead.

"You don't mind, do you?" she'd uncertainly asked Geva one day, with genuine concern in her eyes. "It's only—I never knew my own Pa, but even though Mama's gone, she's still Mama, you ken?"

But Geva had only squeezed Cecily tight, and kissed the top of her head. "Whatever feels right to you, sweetheart," she'd said firmly. "And I know Rathgarr will be thrilled."

Rathgarr had indeed been thrilled, of course, and had taken to smugly speaking of his sweet, clever Ash-Kai daughter to anyone who would listen. And Geva had truly loved seeing them spending time together, playing and exploring the mountain together, and Cecily was already quite an impressive cook, thanks to multiple weekly dinners together with Rathgarr and Kesst, along with regular guidance from Alma, Gegnir, and Olga, too.

"Ach, is this all of you?" called a voice—Killik's voice—from the next room, and when Geva went over to look, he was irritably waving at the group of chattering orclings gathered around him. "Who is missing? Erik?"

There was a squeak from across the room as Erik reappeared, his eye-mask clutched in his little claws, and soon Killik and Ulfarr were herding them all out the door, Cecily included. And while Geva usually still went along on the wall-climbing trips, and all the other ongoing morning exercises, today was an important day—the first-ever Orc Mountain Educational Exhibition. The name chosen by Rosa, of course, and the goal was to show all the orclings' parents and care-takers everything they'd learned over the past six months.

And while Geva certainly wasn't objective on this front, she couldn't help but feel that the last six months had been a rather stunning success. The orclings' language skills had already noticeably improved—not only in common-tongue and Aelakesh, but also in Skai sign language—and they'd continued their clan-directed studies of scenting, hunting, sparring, tracking, gardening, swimming, music, basic medicine, and oral history. They'd also added several new classes as well, including sewing, painting, tanning, and mushroom growing, and the older orclings had even begun to delve into more complicated Ka-esh endeavours like drafting and engineering.

As the months had passed, they'd also continued to combine multiple clans' skills together, expanding upon what they'd already learned. One highlight had been a joint Grisk and Ka-esh project, scenting out old tunnels deep beneath the mountain, just like the ones Rathgarr's hoard had been hidden in. This was followed by a Skai-Grisk spying assignment, where each orcling had been matched with an adult volunteer to follow and report upon—and thanks to Killik's firm instructions to the volunteers, the orclings' reports had been filled with hilarious antics and anecdotes, up to and including the captain standing on his head on top of the mountain.

And perhaps Geva's favourite session of all had been a joint Ash-Kai, Grisk, and Ka-esh project, led by Rathgarr, Ella's mate Nattfarr, and a cheerful Ka-esh smith named Gary. And together, they'd guided the class through the process of making a small piece of jewelry—first drawing a design, and then sourcing and preparing the metal, and then finally creating their pieces together in the Ka-esh forge.

The results had been undoubtedly mixed, but the orclings had all been delighted with their work, and some of their pieces had turned out to be genuinely impressive. The three little Ka-esh had made lovely matching gold bracelets, and Trygve had made a clever little clip that hooked onto one of his fangs, turning it bright silver when he smiled. While Timo had made a beautiful braided gold cuff, which he'd promptly presented to a startled-looking Sune, whose cheeks had flushed bright pink as he'd slipped it on.

And much to Geva's astonishment, it had turned out that Rathgarr had secretly created a piece for her, too—a second wedding-ring. An elegant, shining gold band studded with tiny red stones, made to fit perfectly up against her first one, and seeming to set off the larger ruby even brighter than before.

"It is an old Ash-Kai custom, to make your mate's wedding-ring," Rathgarr had told her, with an almost shy-looking smile, as he'd held her hand up to the light, tilting it back and forth. "I could not do this for your first one, so I thought I could now make one to add to it."

Geva had thrown her arms around him, and that night they'd danced in the Ash-Kai common-room until they'd both been sweaty and desperate, tearing off each other's clothes. And then they'd made love right there on the furs in front of the fire, Geva riding Rathgarr while he'd bucked and moaned and praised her, his hands rubbing wide and possessive over her firm rounded belly.

That, of course, had been another new development, since Geva had indeed become pregnant after that memorable night at the Fitzwalds'. And while she'd perhaps expected Rathgarr to have strong feelings about their forthcoming son, she hadn't quite anticipated the level of sheer Ash-Kai obsession that had followed. With Rathgarr constantly touching and speaking to her belly, while also taking an intense interest in her eating, sleeping, and exercise habits, and demanding appointments with Efterar and Gwyn on a regular basis. And sometimes, Geva would even catch him just sitting there looking at her, with a chilly, unnerving greed glittering in his eyes.

But after spending half a year as his mate, Geva had fully accepted that Rathgarr *was* greedy, and possessive, and utterly relentless. And while he no longer had a hoard to brood over, he behaved very similarly with the people he considered his— not only Geva and their unborn son, but also Kesst, Cecily, Abjorn, and Efterar, and to a lesser degree, their entire little school. Watching over it with almost fanatical care, ensuring the students were all safe and content and accounted for, and firmly under his watchful supervision, where they belonged.

But if Geva was honest with herself, she perhaps felt the exact same way, about all the same things. And there was still something deeply, darkly satisfying about having this huge, powerful, beautiful orc so incessantly devoted to her, so voracious to claim her as his, to clutch her firmly in his greedy, ravenous grasp... and then, sometimes, when he'd decided that she'd earned it, he would kneel and beg and flaunt himself for her, leaping at her every whim, gasping for her affection and her approval. Demonstrating the depths of his trust for her, in a way she knew he never had for anyone else.

And beyond that, she and Rathgarr were still just—in accord, on so many things. On the best way to run their school. On proper bathing and braiding and grooming. On their shared love for art and music and dancing and tales. On regularly enjoying simple pleasures like good meals with family and friends. And even on their little trove-room, which still housed the best remnants of Rathgarr's hoard, including some lovely jewels, and his father's old Ash-Kai dagger—but over the past months, they'd also begun to add other prized possessions, too. Beautiful tapestries and paintings, drums and instruments, books of pictures and tales, a few of Rathgarr's childhood things that Kesst had kept for him, and multiple little gifts and trinkets from their students. And in the place of honour, a drawing Geva had commissioned all the way from her favourite artist in the capital, and it displayed Rathgarr and Kesst together, Rathgarr's big arm slung over Kesst's shoulder, both of them beaming with stunning, near-identical grins.

And speaking of Kesst—Geva frowned up from where she'd been organizing one of the tables for the exhibition—Rathgarr had gone to fetch Kesst some time ago, since Kesst had promised to help with the preparations while the students were outdoors. But neither of them had yet returned, and Geva had just begun to step toward the door when Rathgarr stalked in alone, his face pale, his mouth thin, his hands in fists. And most alarming of all, his shoulders were hunched high and stiff, in a way she hadn't seen on him in months.

"What is it, love?" Geva said, genuinely alarmed, as she rushed over to meet him, stroking her hands up his chest. "What's happened? Where's Kesst?"

Rathgarr squeezed his eyes shut, shaking his head, as a hard shudder rippled up his back. "In the sickroom," he gritted out. "On... his knees. Before... Efterar. Who, I now ken, is built like a..."

Ah. That. Geva had also unwittingly discovered the astonishing magnitude of Efterar's... *intimate proportions* several months before, so she could well follow Rathgarr's deeply felt shock on the subject. "That's very unfortunate luck, love," she murmured, wincing, as she kept firmly rubbing his chest, his shoulders, feeling him steadily soften beneath her touch. "But shouldn't you have smelled one another early enough that you didn't actually see—"

"*All* of this," Rathgarr groaned, dragging a clawed hand through his hair. "Ach. This was worse than the time I had to fetch Sigarr from the Ka-esh dungeon! And Sig was wielding *whips*, poppet!"

Geva bit back her smile, because yes, she'd indeed heard that tale too, from all sides—and most loudly of all had been from a deeply disgruntled Abjorn, who had apparently been goading Sigarr into the whips for weeks, only to have his long-awaited gratification destroyed by a highly affronted Rathgarr walking in.

But before Geva could attempt any further reassurances, Kesst stalked through the door too, his face just as pale as Rathgarr's, his spine very straight. And with a dramatic flounce, he dropped into a chair at the nearest empty table, and glared viciously down toward it.

"I think it would be best," he said crisply, "if we all forget this ever happened, and never, ever speak of it again."

Rathgarr jerked a shaky nod, and then, at Geva's prompting, he sank heavily down at the table too, pulling her tightly onto his lap. "I shall not argue this," he said thickly, as his big hands began rubbing at her belly, almost as if to draw reassurance from it. "But"—he grimaced, and darted a wincing, worried look over toward Kesst—"this is not the only reason you mated Efterar, ach? His healing power, and his overlarge...?"

Kesst flared up in his chair, fixing Rathgarr with the full force of his furious loathing. "No!" he shot back. "I mean, obviously it was a lovely bonus, yes, but Eft is a saint, and I *adore* him! Do you think I judge *you* for picking out a tall, busty, beautiful woman with a round rump and gorgeous hair?!"

Rathgarr was groaning again, rubbing at his eyes. "You ought not to notice such things," he growled. "You ought not to even *look* thus, at *my* mate!"

Kesst snorted and rolled his eyes, crossing his arms tightly over his bare chest. "Gods, you are *such* an old prude, Rath," he snapped. "But just so we're clear, yes, Eft is hung like a god, and yes, I have the deepest throat—and probably the deepest arse—in this damned mountain. And there is *nothing* you can do about it!"

Rathgarr was still shaking his head, squeezing his eyes shut, looking truly, genuinely pained—and Geva could see Kesst suddenly deflating, his throat bobbing, as his blinking eyes dropped to the table.

"It doesn't... change anything, though, right, Rath?" he asked, his voice small. "How you... see me?"

Beneath Geva, Rathgarr stiffened all over, and it was as if he'd suddenly snapped awake again, his eyes wide and alarmed on Kesst's face. "Ach, no!" he replied. "You are forever my heart-son, Kesst, and you are *perfect* as you are. There is naught in the realm that shall alter my regard or my love for you!"

Kesst was looking startled, but then unmistakably relieved, and Rathgarr exhaled, and reached across the table to briefly squeeze his hand. "I was only... surprised," he said, gruffly. "I am... sorry. I did not wish to vex you."

Kesst twitched a shrug, but he'd sagged heavily back into his chair, running both hands through his hair. "Well, don't you have a nose, Rath?" he demanded, much more in his usual tone of voice. "I mean, I know your scenting is mediocre at best, but even *you* shouldn't be clueless enough to miss something like that?!"

Rathgarr's expression abruptly darkened again, and a low growl hissed from his throat. "I was... out of sorts," he replied. "For just before this, I ran into Sken."

Sken was an elderly Ash-Kai, Geva now knew, though he'd always seemed friendly enough—but now Kesst was frowning too, and giving a distasteful little shudder. "Ugh," he replied. "That delusional old codger."

"Ach," Rathgarr said gloomily. "Just so."

Geva was definitely not following now, her eyes darting back and forth between them. "What's wrong with Sken?" she asked. "He's always seemed perfectly lovely to me."

Kesst and Rathgarr exchanged a baleful look, and then shuddered in unison this time. "Sken has the old Ash-Kai gift of farsight," Kesst replied flatly. "Or at least, he thinks he does. Grim says he's a gift from the gods, and that he's never guided him wrong! While in reality, Sken just likes wandering about making cryptic pronouncements, and watching everyone jump to attention. One time, he told me that if I wasn't careful, I'd become one of the deadliest orcs in this mountain! Or another time"—Kesst jabbed an irritated finger at Rathgarr—"he told Eft, with gravest concern, that he needed to watch out for reckless *rats* sneaking in the tunnels!"

Rathgarr blinked for an instant, his eyes very briefly darting down toward Geva, before grimacing, and shaking his head. "Ach," he said, though he didn't sound quite as certain as before. "Rubbish."

But Kesst was watching him very intently now, and perhaps kicking him under the table, too. "So?" he said, a little too offhandedly. "What did Sken tell you, then?"

Rathgarr sighed again, and dropped a furtive glance down toward where his hands had again spread wide on Geva's belly. "He said," he began heavily, "that our son shall one day become the greatest healer in the realm."

There was a moment's shocked silence, Geva included—until it was broken by Kesst's loud, incredulous laugh. "What? No. That's rubbish."

"Ach!" Rathgarr replied, with a wild-looking wave of his hand, before it clenched back to Geva's belly again. "Rubbish!"

Kesst fervently nodded, though he also shifted uncomfortably in his chair. "Did he say *why* he saw that?" he demanded. "Oh—wait. Is it because"—he again jabbed a finger toward Rathgarr—"of *your* rubbish healing? Because your healing is rubbish, Rath, it does not even *count* when you can only heal yourself and your mate! And in fact, I'm still not convinced it's not entirely a figment of your arrogant self-indulgent imagination!"

This entire point about the healing had been an ongoing source of discord between the two of them, since apparently Rathgarr's abilities hadn't manifested—or perhaps he just hadn't noticed—until well after he'd been exiled from the mountain. And since, unlike Efterar, Rathgarr was entirely incapable of healing on command, Kesst had given it all very little credence—though he was still looking distinctly unsettled, and watching very carefully as Rathgarr rubbed at his mouth.

"I ken," Rathgarr finally replied. "But Sken did not say it is because of me, ach? He said it is because my first son"—he waved sharply toward Kesst—"has stolen the eye of the realm's greatest healer, and thus forever ended his line! So the gods have seen fit to visit my *second* son with his rightful heir instead!"

There was another moment of stunned silence, in which Kesst visibly paled, and shook his head. "Good gods," he said blankly. "That can't be possible."

"Ach," Rathgarr agreed, with a wince. "No."

Another beat of silence stretched between them, and Kesst shifted in his chair again, his mouth pursed. "Do you want," he began offhandedly, "to try asking Joarr? Or maybe bringing in Nattfarr?"

Joarr and Nattfarr both also bore Seeing gifts, Geva now knew—though she'd also learned that Nattfarr's, in particular, were given a wide berth by most Ash-Kai, who strongly preferred to keep their secrets safe. And unsurprisingly, Rathgarr had barked a deep, disapproving growl, his hands spasming against Geva's waist. "No!" he replied. "*No.* And mayhap we never speak of this again also, ach?"

But by this point, Geva was feeling decidedly lost, and she

sat up a little straighter on Rathgarr's lap, frowning back and forth between them. "Forgive me, but what is the issue here, exactly?" she asked. "Efterar's skills are truly marvellous, and have likely saved *hundreds* of lives. Shouldn't we be pleased that our son might be so gifted?"

The thought of it—the actual possibility of it—had finally seemed to start sinking in, and she felt her hands sliding almost reverently against Rathgarr's on her belly. While across from them, Kesst gave a frantic flail of his hands, and then leapt up from the table, pacing back and forth.

"Yes, Eft is brilliant, sister," he snapped, "but have you not *seen* his life? He *never* stops working! If it weren't for me, he would never eat or sleep, let alone actually enjoy himself, ever! He is forever trapped in the horrible thrall of all the fool orcs in those arenas who think it's a *spectacular* idea to murder each other for fun on a daily basis!"

Rathgarr was rapidly nodding too, his mouth curling with distaste. "If the gods wish to gift us," he said, "I should much prefer true farsight, or better yet, another galdr-spinner! Why not a lovely silver-tongued galdr-spinner, to carry on *Kesst's* line?!"

He was sulking and waving at Kesst, who looked in full agreement with this, his eyes flashing, his arms folded tightly over his chest. And blinking back and forth between them, Geva felt her mouth curving into a bemused, affectionate smile, her hands spreading wider against her belly.

"But—at least our little healer would have *two* brilliant uncles to help guide him," she said. "One to teach him how to use his skills, and the other to help him set proper boundaries around them. And as he grows, maybe he could help support Efterar, too. Maybe it would be a blessing, after all."

Kesst and Rathgarr kept frowning at each other, though perhaps slightly less ferociously than before, and Geva again smiled between them, and then back down at her belly. "And should the gods allow, we would both like to have another son after this, wouldn't we, love?" she murmured, twisting up to press a light kiss to Rathgarr's cheek. "So if you really want another silver-tongued galdr-spinner that badly, perhaps you ought to start praying, hmmm?"

Rathgarr loudly harrumphed, but his expression had kept softening, his body sagging beneath Geva's—and then he twitched, and reached for his pocket. "Ach, before I forget," he said, holding out his hand toward Kesst, "this came into the Grisk hoard today, and I thought it should suit you."

It was a glittering, beautifully cut black stone, very similar to the ones Kesst so often wore, and he snatched it from Rathgarr's palm with undeniable eagerness, before inspecting it with a carefully distant coolness. "Hmmm, good catch, Rath," he said. "It would make a nice earring."

"Ach, I thought so," Rathgarr said, with satisfaction, and then a gentle slap at Geva's arse. "Now, what else must we do to ready ourselves for this Exhibition? Mayhap you shall rest here and watch, poppet, whilst we work?"

But Geva was not being thwarted that easily—luckily, her pregnancy had so far been a very straightforward one, especially with Efterar and Gwyn's regular support—and soon the three of them were bustling about, and putting the finishing touches on the room for the Exhibition. In addition to the table displays to show the orclings' work, they'd also planned a sparring demonstration, a shadow-show, a variety of tales and music, and of course, refreshments, with fresh treats from the garden—and Alma had even promised to bake the orclings' favourite cakes, too.

Geva had just finished preparing the snack table when Alma indeed strode in together with Baldr, Olga, Gegnir, Varinn, and Thrain, all of them carrying overloaded trays of cakes. At least, until Thrain stumbled sideways, and it was only Geva's quick reflexes that saved his tray of cakes, catching it just as it began to fly across the room.

"Och, sorry," Thrain said, with a false-sounding brightness, as he lurched over to help Geva re-stack the cakes on the tray. "I'm just a touch tired this morning, I suppose."

But beside them, Varinn had set down his tray, too, and he whirled around to face Thrain, his usually genial face hard and set. "You are not weary, Thrain, you are *foxed*," he snapped. "I ken you seek to hide it, but your scent *reeks* of rotten ale. And if you were wise—or ach, if you *ever* listened to me—you would not even *be* here in this schoolroom today, stinking and staggering about, where all these orclings—and their fathers—shall witness this!"

Thrain was visibly wincing, rubbing at his eyes, and then giving Geva and Rathgarr a wide, apologetic smile. "I'm only helping," he said defensively. "I'm not harming anyone. Most of all orclings, I love orclings, Varinn, you know that. Most important thing, ach?"

But Varinn had hissed a low, angry growl, and jerked a hard shake of his head. "If you truly felt thus," he snapped back, "you would not drown yourself in ale as you do! You are lucky they are kind enough to yet allow you here"—he waved furiously at Geva and Rathgarr—"for when I gain a mate and son, you shall not step foot near them thus. Or near *me*!"

Thrain's eyes had gone wide and wounded, his head shaking, his mouth twitching into an uncertain half-smile. "Och, you—you don' mean that, Varinn," he replied thickly. "I'll be your son's uncle, ach? His favourite fun uncle, with all the games and treats and sparring-matches. Ach?"

He sounded almost pleading, but Varinn growled again, shaking his head with furious purpose. "No," he hissed, "you shall not. For I shall not allow my son to spend his days with a drunkard, let alone to learn that this is the best way to have *fun*! And ach, today you only spill cakes, but mayhap next year it is a bottle, or a *weapon*!"

Thrain didn't reply to that, his mouth opening and closing, his face splotched with red, and Varinn shook his head again, his eyes flashing. "I am finished with this, Thrain," he growled. "I am finished with *you!*"

With that, he spun around and stalked out, leaving the rest of them glancing uneasily toward one another. Until Alma surreptitiously pulled Baldr after her toward the door, waving a quick, apologetic goodbye, while Olga and Gegnir hurried along behind, Gegnir's hand clasping with proprietary ease against Olga's arse.

It left Thrain standing there blinking at Geva, Kesst, and Rathgarr, his eyes very bright—until Rathgarr cleared his throat, and reached over to give him a reassuring clap on the shoulder. "Ach, I ken the struggle of this, brother," he said, with more gentleness than Geva might have expected. "I also spent years lost amidst my cups, ach? But it is not a kind mistress, and you shall be well served to face what is driving you to it, and learn to seek another way."

But Thrain's head was shaking, furtive and quick, his eyes darting between Geva and Rathgarr. "But—it's not actually *anything*," he said, or perhaps pleaded. "Not at all. I can stop anytime I please. And you—you don't mind me being here, do you? You know I'm good with orclings, I *am*."

Geva couldn't hide her helpless glance toward Rathgarr, because in truth, they had discussed this multiple times—and Rathgarr clasped Thrain's shoulder again, gave it a bracing little shake. "Ach, you are good with orclings, brother," he said firmly. "But if I were you, I should never wish them to see me foxed in their schoolroom. And I ken mayhap you ought to feel the same, ach?"

But it clearly wasn't helping, and the look on Thrain's face was undoubtedly hurt, or even betrayed—and he abruptly shoved off Rathgarr's hand, and unsteadily strode out. Leaving Rathgarr frowning after him with genuine-looking regret, while beside him Kesst shrugged, and popped a cake in his mouth.

"He had to hear it sometime," he said, once he'd finished

chewing. "I mean, *I'm* not going to let him stumble around our brilliant healer son while he's drunk off his arse and wallowing in denial, are you?"

At that, Rathgarr had blinked—perhaps at the *our son* part, or the *brilliant healer* part, or both—but then he tilted his head and shrugged, clearly conceding Kesst's point. "No, I ken not," he said, with a sigh, as he tossed a cake in his mouth, too—and then visibly brightened as he chewed. "Ach, this is good, is it not? Do you have this recipe?"

It turned out that Kesst did, but he'd already chosen the menu for their planned supper that evening, and flatly refused to change it. Leading to more good-natured bickering as they finished setting up the room together—just in time, it turned out, because the orclings had finally begun to filter back in, many of them with their parents and caretakers now in tow.

"Look, Papa!" Bram exclaimed, brandishing a sheet of his wobbly little letters at his bulky, bemused-looking father. "I can write in common-tongue, *and* Aelakesh! And do you like my stick-orc battle?"

He was proudly poking his little claw at the bottom of the page, where he'd drawn an elaborate array of stick figures with pointy ears and swords, some of them gushing copious amounts of blood. And while Geva was already wincing, Bram's father was holding the paper up closer, peering at the page. "Ach, it is me!" he said, with a toothy grin. "But wait. Is this an Ash-Kai? Why is he sending me off the page?"

Geva blanched and swiftly sidled away, over to where Erik was holding up the little gold bracelet he'd forged, and setting it into his father's waiting hand. "It is good Ka-esh forging, ach, Papa?" he said shyly. "You like?"

His father—Benjamin, Geva now knew—was blinking with genuine awe down at the little bracelet, and then pulling Erik close. "Ach, it is perfect, my son," he whispered, hoarse. "Just like you."

Erik broadly beamed at that, snuggling into his father's

chest, while Geva wiped hastily at her eyes—until she caught sight of little Isak, pulling his slim Ka-esh father over toward a smiling Abjorn. "Papa!" he shouted. "This is the Ka-esh warrior who is teaching us to fight. He is *wonderful*, ach?"

Geva blanched again, but luckily Abjorn was still well versed in Ka-esh manners, and—thanks to an ever-careful Sigarr—no longer sported any visible wounds or black eyes that could frighten off the orclings or their caretakers. And instead, he now wore a thick, gleaming gold cuff around his neck, which Geva now knew to be a distinctly Ka-esh custom, binding them to their mates. And at the sight of it, Isak's father had visibly relaxed, touching at his own cuff, too—and soon they were speaking fondly of their stubborn partners together, while an already-bored Isak raced around the room.

Once all the students had all had a chance to show off their work, Rathgarr called the room to order, and loudly welcomed his beloved heart-son Kesst to the front of the room to start the show. A strategic decision on all fronts, because Kesst's cheerful tale of dancing minnows—one he'd acquired from Geva— settled the orclings at once, while also setting the mood for the rest of the morning's entertainment.

This included a lively sparring demonstration, broken out by age, and then a scenting demonstration, which was led by a rather grim-faced Varinn, who had reappeared at the last possible moment, and then left again. And then Geva joined Othan and another Ash-Kai drummer named Bjorr to lead the orclings in a drumming circle, followed by a few dance solos— the last one from the plump little Grisk Vragi, who had turned out to be a beautiful dancer.

And after that, they returned to the tales again. Kesst again told the tale of Edom and Akva, and then the orclings all took turns telling their own tales—some they'd created themselves, some they'd gathered from their fathers or elders. And for the grand finale, Timo, Trygve, Sune, and Cecily put on a fabulous shadow-show on the wall in the firelight, their hands transformed into dragons and dangerous beasts, who sometimes cleverly switched into sign language as well.

By this point, Tengil had curled up in Geva's lap to watch, his warm little body wriggling and giggling with delight. And when it was finished, he clapped and stomped along with her, while Jule loudly whistled her approval beside them.

"That was wonderful, sister," Jule said as she stiffly rose to her feet afterwards, rubbing at the slight new swell in her belly. "You and Rathgarr have done such an incredible job with this school. I can't wait for our new son to join in, too."

Geva smiled warmly back toward Jule as she stood up too, hoisting Tengil up into her arms. "How is he doing today? Are you still feeling fatigued?"

"Some," Jule replied, with a grimace. "But Efterar says that's to be expected. And Sken insists that there's nothing to worry about, and his farsight is always impeccable, which is a great help."

Right. Geva winced, but decided to leave that one well enough alone, and soon was caught up in saying heartfelt farewells and thank-yous to all the orclings and their caretakers. They'd all seemed to thoroughly enjoy themselves, and Geva was deeply touched when two newer Ash-Kai fathers came over with their preteen sons—Falnor and Balvir—to specifically thank her and Rathgarr for offering such a valuable service, and also, for letting them know about it in the first place.

"This was a good Ash-Kai scheme," one of the fathers said, as he held out a wrinkled, familiar-looking pamphlet. "I should never have known, had I not found this in the Kentnek cross-tunnel."

It was one of the pamphlets Rathgarr had created with Rosa, but instead of being meant for humans, this one had been targeted specifically toward orcs. And along with Rosa's typical attention-grabbing headline—ORCLINGS DESERVE EDUCATION TOO!—it had included a variety of firsthand testimonials from their current students and their fathers, as well as a comprehensive list of curriculum, and a means of requesting a follow-up meeting through the Skai spy network.

And thus had begun another highly intriguing aspect of Geva's new Orc Mountain life, because shortly after their first distribution drop, Killik had stalked over during class, and handed Geva a slip of paper with a name and coordinates on it. And she'd stared blankly down toward it for a long moment, before frowning over at Rathgarr's equally confused face.

"You... don't actually expect *us* to go meet with them, in person?" she'd demanded at Killik. "But we're needed here!"

But Killik had rolled his eyes, and waved around at the rest of the adults currently helping in the classroom—at Tristan, and Varinn, and Kalfr, and Ulfarr, and Jule. "You ken we cannot handle this for a few days?" he'd flatly replied. "*You* were the one who pushed for all this *support*, ach? And who better to stand for our mountain, and yammer of all the gossip and news, and speak with ease of all your *curriculum* and *safety protocols*? Not *me*?!"

At that, he'd irritably waved at his own scarred, frowning, bare-chested form—still with those crossed shining daggers stuck in his messy hair—and then jabbed his claw between Rathgarr and Geva. At where, as always, Rathgarr had been impeccably dressed in a crisp tunic and trousers, topped by a very flattering blue waistcoat, and a tasteful smattering of jewels—his own wedding-ring, an elaborate belt buckle, an elegant cuff, and a lovely black-jewelled pendant, a recent gift from Kesst. While Geva herself had been dressed in a perfectly matching blue shift, with a light wool cape over her shoulders—at Rathgarr's insistence, in case she or their son ever felt cold—and her own beautiful jewelry that Rathgarr had chosen for the day. And of course, he'd also recently done her hair, this time into multiple beaded plaits that twisted around her head.

"Also, *he* knows the realm as well as any Skai," Killik had peevishly continued, again jabbing his claw at Rathgarr, "and most of all the places where orcs live and hide. Whilst *you*"—his accusing claw had swung toward Geva—"were raised by your mother and father to be one of these *diplomats!* You speak four tongues, woman, and what good is this to us here?!"

With that, he'd spun and stalked off, leaving Geva and Rathgarr still blinking at one another—at least, until Jule had sidled over, giving them a far-too-innocent smile. "You don't mind, do you?" she'd said lightly. "You two really are quite well suited for it, you know. And if you weren't opposed, I'm sure there are a few other meetings we could set up as well?"

It had clearly been yet another devious Ash-Kai scheme all along—no doubt direct from Grimarr himself—but neither Geva nor Rathgarr had bothered arguing it. And after now having gone on multiple diplomatic trips together—typically one or two a month, often with Cecily in tow—Geva could fully admit that it had been a brilliant plan. They both truly enjoyed meeting new people, especially orclings, and Rathgarr could be exceedingly charming when he wanted to be, and rarely lost his cool in stressful or antagonistic situations. And Geva's language skills had come in handy after all—it turned out that a small band of northern Ka-esh only spoke Kraitish, along with an incomprehensible ancient dialect of Aelakesh—and she'd discovered that her tales would often put orcs at ease, in a way that other reassurances didn't.

And it even turned out that Geva's Eziran heritage was helpful, too. Giving her a fundamental understanding of how many of these orcs felt, living as quietly as they could among a culture that wasn't their own. And in the same way that her skin and hair had often set her apart among humans, it also seemed to do the same with orcs, but resulting more in curiosity, or relief, or, sometimes, even blatant admiration.

"Ach, my sweet mate is very stunning to scent and look upon," Rathgarr would often say to that, with a rather dangerous glint in his eye, while also pulling Geva bodily closer upon him. "But if you shall not hear her words, then we shall go at once, so I can treat her as she deserves, ach?"

Thankfully, that had usually done the job, and so far Rathgarr had only ended up in one fight, which had—predictably— resulted in the offending orc lying unconscious on the floor. And while there were often still rude and mistrustful humans to deal with as well, especially on the roads, Geva had continued to find that showing themselves as a happy, united couple was a considerable help.

And best of all, their trips and meetings truly had begun to make a noticeable difference. Bringing more than a dozen new orclings—and their caretakers—to the mountain, which had in turn led to more insights into the orcs' previous homes and communities, some of which were so well-hidden that even the Skai hadn't known they existed. And in turn, that had allowed the Ka-esh to create and distribute more pamphlets, much to Rosa's ever-increasing delight.

And speaking of which, Rosa had somehow instantly popped up at the sight of her pamphlet, her little orcling Thorin clasped in her arms. "Oh, I'm so glad it was helpful!" she said, beaming beatifically back and forth between Falnor and Balvir's fathers. "Was there any other information you'd have liked to see included? Or any other places you'd have been likely to find it?"

Soon they were all embroiled in an intensive pamphlet-related discussion, and Rathgarr had swiftly made his escape, ushering Geva over toward where Cecily was helping tidy up with Timo and Sune. Although, at their approach, Cecily leapt up and whirled around, with a distinctly guilty look on her face.

"What is it, daughter?" Rathgarr asked, his voice very easy, though Geva could already feel the taut watchfulness in his big body against her. "Is aught amiss?"

"No, Pa, of course not!" Cecily replied, her voice very high-pitched, but Rathgarr clearly wasn't fooled, raising a watchful brow toward her. And beside her, Timo had gently elbowed her in the ribs, while on her other side, Sune had signed something toward her, his hands moving too swiftly for Geva to follow.

"Ach, fine," Cecily said, with a sigh, and then an almost-fearful glance between Rathgarr and Geva. "I... did something. Something... sneaky. Something... you might not like."

Geva felt her own brows rising, while Rathgarr further stiffened beside her—but she firmly rubbed at his back, and attempted a reassuring smile toward Cecily. "Well, we'd be very grateful if you'll tell us, sweetheart," she said. "That way, if you ever need help, we can do our best for you."

Timo gave Cecily another purposeful nudge, his eyes very clearly saying *I told you so*, and she reluctantly nodded, and sighed again. "I... wrote to my aunt and uncle," she whispered. "And I told them that *I* stole all their coin and jewels, right before we went on that trip to the city. And then I threw it all down the well."

Geva's mouth had fallen open, but at Sune's sharp, warning glance, she promptly snapped it shut again, while Cecily drew in another dragging breath. "Except for the servants' things," she continued unsteadily, "and my cousins' things, too. I hid all those. And when I ran away from my aunt in the city, I went back to the house, and put those things back, because I felt guilty. And then I ran away again, and found a new, safe home to live in, far away from them, for good."

Geva's disbelief was still surging, and beside her, Rathgarr had gone even stiffer than before. "But... why, sweetheart?" Geva finally said, as evenly as she could. "Why would you tell your aunt and uncle that *you* did all that, when it was actually your father? And me?"

Cecily made a face, glancing back and forth between Timo and Sune before drawing in another breath. "I did it so it will never come back for either of *you*!" she said shrilly, flapping her hand between Rathgarr and Geva. "With all our travelling now, sister, there's still a chance they could find you, and blame you for the theft—and if not, I'm sure they'll be blaming the orcs! It's a lot easier for me to blend in than it is for you, especially now that I've been eating and growing so much more! And I *want* my aunt to blame me, so she'll hate me forever, and *never* try to find me or take me back!"

Oh. Cecily had claimed to be guilty of Rathgarr's theft... for them. To protect them, at risk to herself. And so she would never be able to return to the Fitzwalds'. So she could stay with them here, safe, for always.

And without quite noticing how, Geva was clutching Cecily close, swaying her back and forth, while Rathgarr's strong arms circled tight around them both. "Oh, sweetheart," Geva said thickly. "But that's such a risk for you. And what if you change your mind about going back someday?"

"I won't," Cecily choked, into Geva's shoulder. "I hated living there. And I *want* my horrible aunt to spend the rest of her life digging for her ugly jewelry in that well, and hopefully she'll fall in while she's at it, too!"

Her voice had gone surprisingly vicious, and if Geva wasn't mistaken, that was a soft, affectionate little chuckle from Rathgarr against them. "Ach, I should long to see this also, daughter," he said, with marked approval in his voice. "The only trick is, I ken, I stole so much that your aunt shall no doubt next have the well dug. Mayhap by teams of men."

Cecily instantly yanked back from them again, her hands clapped over her mouth. "Oh noooo," she moaned. "And if they don't find anything, she'll go back to suspecting you, after all! My good Ash-Kai scheme is all a *failure!*"

Both Sune and Timo were looking deeply alarmed too, glancing urgently between Geva and Rathgarr. But Rathgarr was looking up beyond them, toward where Ulfarr was looming nearby, a ghastly scowl on his face.

"You yet have some of these jewels, then?" Ulfarr demanded at Rathgarr. "In that foolish trove-room of yours?"

Rathgarr blinked, but then nodded, a slow, satisfied grin

stealing across his mouth. "It was far too unsightly to wear," he said smugly. "Keep a trinket or two to sell as you wish, ach, brother?"

Ulfarr jerked a nod and stalked off, leaving Cecily staring in awestruck wonder after him, and then glancing excitedly toward Sune. "Does he mean—your heart-father's going to go all the way there to throw the jewels down the well for us?" she squeaked at him. "You Skai are so *thoughtful*, Sune!"

Sune's face reddened, but he was looking decidedly pleased, too, and Rathgarr reached over to give him a cheerful clap on the shoulder. "No good Ash-Kai scheme comes about without the help of a loyal Skai, ach? And"—he clapped at Timo's shoulder, too—"very oft a thoughtful Grisk, also. It was very wise of you, Timo, to guide your sister to speak to us thus, for now her clever scheme shall be saved, after all."

Timo, who had been looking rather put out, was proudly grinning again, and soon the three of them had taken off toward the corridor, happily chattering and signing together as they went. Leaving Geva and Rathgarr behind in the far quieter schoolroom, occupied now only by a few lingering Ka-esh and Ash-Kai, as well as Kalfr, who was very intently wiping off the crumb-strewn tables.

Geva's smile faded as she watched him, because of course, Kalfr's son had been one of their very first diplomatic visits together. But it had been a frustrating disappointment from start to end, and they'd been firmly sent on their way without a single short conversation, or even a glimpse of Kalfr's son. Two follow-up visits had met the exact same result, and by this point, Geva was sorely tempted to propose a proper Ash-Kai kidnapping scheme, after all.

But she knew Rathgarr had been frequently thinking of Kalfr's son, too, and she wasn't surprised when he strode over to Kalfr, and slung an arm over his slumped shoulder. "Do not lose hope yet, brother," he said firmly. "I have a new scheme hatching, ach?"

Kalfr didn't look overly comforted by this, but Geva was already feeling decidedly reassured as she and Rathgarr left the room together, his hand suggestively lingering on her arse. "A new scheme, hmmm?" she asked lightly, glancing up toward his smug, satisfied face. "I don't suppose you were planning to tell me about this anytime soon?"

"Not yet, poppet," Rathgarr replied, just as lightly, as he steered her down the corridor toward their bedroom. "An Ash-Kai always needs a few secrets."

Geva rolled her eyes at him, but didn't actually bother arguing, and once he'd led her into their room, and begun taking off their clothes, she willingly leaned into the warmth of his touch, the spread of his hungry fingers. Because yes, perhaps Rathgarr would always be his devious, enraging, secretive self... but in all the ways that mattered, he was still hers. Hers, with his generosity and his greed, his secrets and his confidences, his commands and his worship. His trust.

And hers, in the way he spread her out on their bed for him, fully bared, but for his beads and jewels. While he knelt before her clad in only his wedding-ring, his eyes shimmering bright as he bent to kiss the smooth brown swell of her waist.

"I love you, my Geva Okoro," he whispered, as he gently kissed up her belly, between her breasts, until he'd found her mouth. Meeting her so soft and sweet, his tongue curling with careful, tender reverence. "My clever schoolmarm, my pretty poppet, my fierce Ash-Kai mate. *Mine.* Ach?"

He still said it so often with the question—even now, as he parted her thighs with his, and slid himself up deep between, watching with those greedy, glinting eyes as she arched and gasped upon him. Needing to hear her say it, to know she still meant it, no matter how selfish he was, or how many secrets he kept. Needing to know that he could just be, just as he was, and still hoard her body, her heart, as his own.

But yes, he could, he would, he always, always had, because he was *hers*, and she trusted him, just as he trusted her. And

Geva revelled in the truth of it, wrapped herself around him, met his kiss with hers. Not thinking forward, or back, but just... this. Her own brightest jewel, her own hoard, here, beneath her own greedy fingers. Hers.

"Yes, Rathgarr of Clan Ash-Kai," she whispered back. "For always."

BONUS EPILOGUE

It was another delightful family dinner in the Ash-Kai common-room, full of laughter, gossip, and delicious food—and a particularly adorable orcling, gleefully giggling in his heart-father's arms.

"This cannot be sanitary," Geva halfheartedly pointed out, as she fondly watched her two-year-old son purposefully poking at Kesst's arm with his little black claws, drawing out four tiny beads of blood. "Or healthy. Or safe!"

But unsurprisingly, neither Efterar nor Rathgarr had showed the slightest concern at this—let alone Kesst—and all three of them were eagerly focused on where Reynir had giggled again, putting his tiny hand back to Kesst's arm. And where the four small wounds had been, there was now only smooth, untouched grey skin.

"Good, son!" Kesst exclaimed, with pure delight in his dancing eyes. "Now, how about this?"

He poked himself with his claw this time, deep enough to make Geva wince—but once again, Reynir's little hand spread wide over it, his brow furrowing with concentration. And when his hand drew away, there was again only smooth grey skin—though this time, it had a tiny black freckle.

"You gave me a freckle!" Kesst crowed, holding it up to the firelight, as though this was the most magnificent thing he'd ever seen in his life. "Eft, why have *you* have never given me any freckles? *Can* you even give freckles?!"

Beside him, a still-smiling Efterar was rolling his eyes, and reaching over to spread his hand against Kesst's bare shoulder—and when he pulled back, there was a mass of freckles on Kesst's skin, in the distinct shape of his big handprint. To which Kesst gave a shocked gasp, and then grinned beatifically between Reynir and Efterar.

"I *love* it," he firmly pronounced. "Now, who else would like a freckle? How about you, Papa Eft? Oooh, can we have *matching* freckles?!"

Efterar's smile had widened into a stunning, affectionate grin, and he accordingly drew Reynir close, and held out his big arm. And soon he indeed sported a matching freckle, in the exact same place as Kesst's.

"Very good, son," Efterar said, as he stroked his hand against Reynir's back, making him wriggle and squirm in delight. "I couldn't do freckles until I was six!"

Despite herself, Geva was grinning too, and angling a half-amused, half-exasperated glance toward Rathgarr beside her. But again, he was just watching Reynir across the table, and wearing a very familiar expression on his face—one of outward soft, reverent tenderness, tinged beneath with a fierce, dangerous pride.

It was a look Geva had seen him wear so often these past few years, and it was so typical of his entire attitude as a father—proud, adoring, and ferociously protective. And Geva would never forget the first time she'd seen him look like this, after Efterar had set their tiny, newborn son into her arms.

And of course, Reynir had been beautiful, from that very first moment. Big and healthy and hale, with skin a stunning shade of deep, rich grey—and he'd even sported a messy thatch of black curls atop his little head. And Rathgarr had looked at him, and looked, and looked, with that same fierce, proud reverence flashing in his eyes, and tears streaking down his cheeks.

"He is perfect, poppet," he'd croaked, as he'd settled in close beside Geva on the bed. "I always knew you should make us a stunning son, ach?"

Geva had wept, too, and cradled their perfect son, while Rathgarr had gathered them both into his big arms, holding them warm and safe. And then Kesst had sidled in, too, from where he'd been impatiently waiting just outside, and Rathgarr had waved him over, and drawn him in, too. And between Kesst's own deep, gasping sobs, he'd told a soft, wonderful tale Geva had never heard before. One of a strong, kind, and generous Ash-Kai son, who would be loved and kept safe all his long life.

By the end of it, even Efterar had been weeping too, all of them clustered together on the bed. And soon Cecily had come in, and a broadly grinning Abjorn, with Sigarr in tow—and then an excitedly running Tengil, with Jule and Grimarr after him. And as Geva had tearfully smiled around at them all, she'd felt a deep, striking peace, whispering low in her chest. She'd found her family, her purpose, her calling. Her home.

It was a certainty that had only grown over the two years since, as Geva and Rathgarr had settled into a new rhythm, one that combined parenting with teaching, travelling, and all their other priorities. And while it wasn't always an easy balance, it was greatly helped by all the support from the rest of their family, especially Reynir's two doting uncles, who had rapidly proven to be true heart-fathers themselves. To the point where Geva had happily christened them Papa Kesst and Papa Eft— names that Reynir had quickly and enthusiastically adopted, much to Kesst's ongoing satisfaction.

And of course, Rathgarr—who was just plain *Papa*—had shown himself an utterly marvellous father. And as Reynir had grown over the past two years, it had been delightful to discover the many similarities between them. Reynir was usually cheerful and charming, and openly adoring and protective of the people he cared for, especially Geva. He also loved play-fighting with his father, and hearing Geva and Kesst's tales, and enthusiastically participating in as many school activities as he could every day.

But like Rathgarr—and Geva herself, she could admit—Reynir did have a touch of a temper, too. As well as an obsessive, overprotective streak, to the point where he'd gone through a months-long phase in which he'd roundly refused to be out of Geva's sight. And most adorably amusing of all, he'd almost instantly shown a keen interest in collecting things, and had already begun to build a little hoard of his own, in the corner of their trove-room. Full of shiny rocks, and shavings from the forges, and even—much to Geva's chagrin—a wide variety of bones, claws, and teeth.

But she'd quickly come to terms with it, because truly, what else had she expected, from a son of hers and Rathgarr's? So whenever Reynir would run over, showing her some exciting new treasure he'd found, she would wonder and exclaim at it, while he shyly grinned and preened. And she would often catch Rathgarr watching her afterwards, with that same fierce, tender pride glimmering in his eyes.

And despite Rathgarr's initial dislike of the idea, he'd behaved the exact same way toward Reynir's healing, too. A skill which had shown itself very early on, when Reynir had been about six months old—he'd accidentally scraped Geva with his claw while nursing, and had then promptly healed it again, much to Geva's astonishment. But instead of being appalled at the news, as Geva had perhaps expected, Rathgarr had shown only pure, unabashed delight—he'd effusively praised Reynir, and then he'd rushed off to tell Kesst and Efterar. And ever since, he'd treated Reynir's healing with that same fierce, gleeful pride, greeting every one of his little accomplishments with unflinching support and enthusiasm.

And even now, Reynir was beaming at Rathgarr across the dinner-table, and holding up his small hand, clearly seeking his father's approval. "Freckle!" he said excitedly. "Freckle, Papa!"

Rathgarr was already grinning back, broad and bright and delighted. "Ach, this is so good, son!" he replied. "Do you ken I can have one also? And then"—he held up a sweet-bun—"you must eat some supper to fuel all this healing, ach?"

Reynir promptly scrambled over, and after another moment's intent concentration, he gifted Rathgarr with a matching freckle, too. And soon he was curled up happily in Rathgarr's arms, chomping at his sweet-bun, while Rathgarr stroked affectionately at his back, and kissed his head—which currently sported an assortment of soft, adorable little braids.

Geva smiled as she watched them together, the happiness bubbling in her chest—and then she felt her smile broadening at the sight of Cecily walking in, too. Cecily had grown a truly astonishing amount over the past three years, and these days she looked nothing like the small, lost girl Geva had once known. Instead, she was tall, athletic, and cheerful, and she confidently dressed in dramatic, elaborate outfits that she meticulously pieced together with help from her fabulously fashionable brother. Today, this included a stunning white lace dress, along with a thick leather belt, heavy black boots, and an assortment of leather cuffs and bracelets.

"There you are, sweetheart," Geva said, though she felt her head tilting at the sight of Cecily's unusually bright eyes and flushed-looking face. "Is everything all right?"

"Yes, of course!" Cecily breathlessly replied, as she slipped into the empty chair beside Geva, and gave her a quick, companionable hug before sniffing deeply at her plate. "Sorry I'm late. This looks delicious! Did you make it, brother?"

She'd flashed her smile toward Kesst, who—much to Geva's surprise—wasn't grinning back, or launching into a discussion about cooking, as he usually would have done. Instead, his brows had sharply furrowed together, and he was angling a narrow, disapproving look toward… Rathgarr?

And beside Geva, Rathgarr was looking the exact same way. A dark, disapproving frown tightening his mouth, as he pushed back his chair, and leaned around to stare at Cecily's face.

Geva's alarm was rapidly rising, and Cecily was looking disconcerted too, her fork held halfway to her mouth. But she wasn't speaking, so Geva cleared her throat, and angled a meaningful glance toward Rathgarr. "Are you feeling unwell, love?" she pointedly asked. "And yes, sweetheart, Kesst did make supper, didn't you, Kesst? It's actually an Eziran stew, and Kesst did a wonderful job with it, as usual."

But good gods, Kesst was still frowning at Cecily, his glower steadily deepening. And finally he set down his fork with a clatter, and jabbed his claw toward her.

"Sorry to pry, little sister," he said, his voice clipped, "because believe me, we *don't* want to know—but at the same time, you cannot just go around *kissing* people, and not expect us to notice! *Timo*? *Really*?!"

Oh. Ohhhhh. And beside Geva, Cecily's face instantly flushed a deep red, her eyes narrowing back toward Kesst. "Yes, really!" she snapped back. "Why not? I'm almost sixteen years old now, and we've been best friends for *years*! And Timo is lovely, and he always has been, and it's not as though we were doing anything more than—"

She grimaced, and then glanced with increasing alarm between Kesst and Rathgarr, clearly realizing how fraught certain future situations might be—and even as Geva opened her mouth to comfort her, Rathgarr huffed a sharp, disapproving growl. "Ach, you most surely shall *not* do more than this, daughter," he said flatly. "Not until you are twenty, or mayhap twenty-five! Lest you wish me to lock this male in the deepest dungeon I can find!"

Geva belatedly elbowed Rathgarr in the side, and then leaned over to put her arm around Cecily's shoulder, squeezing tight. "There will be *no locking*, sweetheart," she said, as firmly as she could. "And our biggest priority, *as always*"—she shot Rathgarr a pointed look—"is just your safety and wellbeing, all right? And if you feel this strongly about Timo, of course we're happy to hear that, aren't we?"

She again frowned between Rathgarr and Kesst, and was vaguely surprised to see both of them still frowning back, Kesst even jerking a tight, meaningful shake of his head. "Sorry, sister, but we're actually not," he said, with a grimace. "Because Timo, flighty little Grisk that he is, has been off kissing *Sune*, too!"

Beside Geva, Cecily blinked, looking genuinely astonished, and then far more uncertain than before. "No, he hasn't," she said, and then bit her lip. "Has he?"

Despite her best efforts, Geva's own anger about this was rapidly rising, too—especially at the sight of Kesst and Rathgarr both nodding, Kesst looking grim, Rathgarr with a dark, crackling fury in his eyes. While poor Cecily's eyes had gone very wide, her face pale—and without another word, she leapt up, and ran from the room.

Geva grimaced, and after a meaningful glance toward Rathgarr, she jumped up too, and headed for the door. And though there was no sign of Cecily in the corridor, Geva soon found her in her cozy little candlelit room, with her cat clutched in her lap, and tears streaking down her face.

"Oh, sweetheart," Geva said, as she dropped down to sit beside her, and squeezed her tight. "It'll be all right. Although"—she couldn't help a heavy sigh—"I know these things are already difficult enough, without adding orc noses into it, too."

Cecily gulped and nodded, rubbing at her eyes. "I—I don't want to disappoint Pa," she whispered. "He's been so good to me, sister, and I can't stand the thought of him being unhappy with me. And Timo—"

Her voice broke into another sob, her head shaking back

and forth, and Geva squeezed her even tighter, and swallowed down the rising lump in her own throat. "There is *nothing* you can do that will affect your father's love for you," she said thickly. "Or mine. As for Timo"—she made a face—"I care for him too, sweetheart, but I can't help but think he should have let you know that he—"

She stopped there, her head snapping up, because there had been a meaningful little rap against the doorframe. And when Geva went out into the corridor to look, yanking the curtain tightly shut behind her, she discovered it was none other than Timo himself. He was even taller than she was now, his shoulders far broader, and he had multiple earrings in both ears, and even his nose. But he currently also looked very much like the uncertain teenager he was, shifting awkwardly on his feet, and biting at his reddened lip.

"Ach, Miss Gee," he said, his voice hoarse. "I was hoping mayhap Cecily might—see me? I can scent—"

He'd angled an alarmed, wide-eyed look toward the closed curtain, and then rubbed at his eyes. "I should never wish to hurt her," he croaked. "I only—I did not think. It is so easy to forget she cannot scent these things, and it so oft seems as if she does, ach? And I thought—I thought her doing this with me, after Sune, that she might also—"

He kept rubbing his hand at his flushed face, his bright eyes blinking hard as they glanced down the corridor. To where— Geva couldn't help a resigned sigh—Sune was lurking in the shadows, his tall, lean body very stiff, his arms crossed over his chest.

So Geva turned back toward the room, reaching for the curtain—but suddenly it swept aside, and Cecily was standing there in the doorway, her body pulled tall, her eyes also very bright. While Timo pulled himself straight too, and again rubbed at his face, his throat audibly swallowing.

"Could we please speak of this, Cecy?" he whispered. "Mayhap with Sune, also?"

Cecily jerked a curt little nod, and waved him into the room—and then, after glancing down the corridor, she waved purposefully at Sune, too. Who very intently kept his eyes on the floor as he obliged, silently edging past Geva into the room. Where he promptly collected Cecily's cat into his arms, and then began pacing back and forth.

Geva shot a searching look toward Cecily, but she was giving a watery smile back, and then reached over for a quick, tight hug. "Thank you, sister," she said, still a little choked. "I'll meet you later, ach?"

Geva nodded and made for the door, though she pointedly pulled the curtain wide open after her, earning for her efforts three simultaneous eye-rolls from the teenagers. A response that was surprisingly comforting, to the point where Geva was almost smiling to herself as she returned to the dinner-table again. At least, until she was confronted with the sight of Kesst and Rathgarr—and gods, even Efterar and Reynir—all frowning up toward her with impatient, accusing eyes.

"So?" Kesst demanded. "What happened? *Please* tell me you followed Rath's plan, and locked that typically indiscriminate teenage Grisk disaster into an abandoned dungeon somewhere?"

"I heard that," cut in a familiar voice, and when Geva glanced over, it was a bemused-looking Baldr, who was eating together at a nearby table with Alma, Drafli, Jule, and Grimarr, his son Barden in his lap. "Grisk are not *indiscriminate*. We have *excellent* taste."

At this, Alma and Drafli exchanged distinctly satisfied glances, while Kesst loudly groaned, and threw his hands into the air. "*Disastrous*, then," he said flatly, jabbing a finger toward Baldr, "and you cannot even *try* to argue me on that one, Baldr! Now, sister"—he transferred his imperious gaze back to Geva— "did you lock Timo in a dungeon, or not?!"

Geva had been attempting to enjoy a bite of her cold supper, and belatedly swallowed it down, and shook her head.

"Sorry, brother," she said, with a wince. "But Timo came to apologize, and he seemed truly upset. And now the three of them are talking it through together, which is very mature of them, don't you think? Perhaps there's hope for the next generation yet."

None of the orcs appeared mollified by this—Kesst was angling another dark, suspicious glance toward Baldr, while Rathgarr was looking pale, and genuinely pained. Enough that even Reynir, who was still in Rathgarr's lap, was giving a concerned frown up toward him, his little hand patting at his face.

"Oh, settle down, all of you," Geva said, with a fond, exasperated half-smile between them. "Cecily is very responsible, and well aware of what we expect from her. And she's right, she *is* almost sixteen. We had to expect some teenage drama at some point, didn't we?"

But if anything, Rathgarr was looking even paler than before, enough that Geva reached to squeeze at his knee, giving it an affectionate little shake. Prompting him to twitch and look at her, his breath exhaling, his arms clutching Reynir closer against him.

"I only—" he began, grimacing. "But we have only had a few years with her, ach? To lose her to this, already—ach, when she is just the same age as when I lost *you*, son—"

He was blinking at Kesst across the table, and Geva could see Kesst's throat convulsing, and then felt him kicking at Rathgarr under the table. "Oh, don't be ridiculous, Rath," he said, though his tone didn't at all match his words. "You didn't lose me. In fact, you are never getting rid of me, all right? *Especially* now that you've given me such a brilliant little heart-son to dote on."

He'd playfully wiggled his claws toward Reynir across the table, who in turn grinned delightedly back, and squirmed down from Rathgarr's lap to run back over toward Kesst. And Geva could see Rathgarr's eyes softening as he watched, and she squeezed at his knee again, and leaned in closer against him.

"And you won't lose Cecily, either," she said firmly. "She adores you, love, just like we all do. Just like your next son will, too."

It was a blatant Ash-Kai attempt at distraction, she well knew, but she hadn't quite anticipated its immediate effect on the table. Kesst had let out a high-pitched little squeal, Efterar was mightily frowning over the table toward her midsection, and Rathgarr had gone very still beneath her touch, his eyes glinting strange and heavy on hers.

"Look, I didn't mean—" Geva flapped her hand at her suddenly hot face, and gave them all an apologetic smile. "I didn't mean I'm pregnant right *now*. I just mean—we would like to, wouldn't we, love? Soon?"

Rathgarr was still just looking at her like that, and yes, that was his tongue, brushing brief against his lips. And it belatedly occurred to Geva that they hadn't actually discussed this lately, perhaps because she'd thought it had already been settled— but looking back at Rathgarr, she realized that clearly he'd wanted to bring it up, but hadn't. That he hadn't wanted her to feel pressured or rushed, perhaps. And that he'd been showing himself a kind, generous mate, again—even while keeping this secret from her, like the devious Ash-Kai he was.

"Well, *when*, then?" Kesst demanded, from across the table. "I mean, you cannot just throw around incendiary statements like that, sister! And have you talked to Eft about it yet?!"

He'd angled a wild-eyed glance toward Efterar beside him, and Efterar shook his head, and slid his big arm around Kesst's shoulder. "No, Sweet-Fang," he said, though his eyes were still intent on Geva. "But I would be very happy to help, sister, whenever you feel ready. But"—his gaze had dropped to her midsection again—"if you wanted your pregnancy protection removed, this... *would* be an excellent time to conceive."

Oh. Well. And damn it, Geva had been the one to start this,

and all three of them were still staring expectantly toward her, Rathgarr still with that bare, blatant craving in his eyes. That... longing.

"Oh, fine, then," she snapped, as she shoved up out of her chair, and lurched over to stand in front of Efterar. "Will you be so kind as to sort it out, then, brother?"

Kesst excitedly squealed again, and Efterar was already snapping up his hand over Geva's belly, his fingers spreading wide. While Rathgarr just kept looking at her like that, so hungry and intent that Geva felt her face flushing, her throat swallowing as she held his eyes.

"As long as—you're sure, love," she said thickly. "Are you?"

But he was rapidly nodding, his breath exhaling hard, his tongue again sweeping his lips. "Ach, my brave, stunning poppet," he breathed. "I am sure."

Efterar's hand had already dropped again, and he gave Geva an approving little nod. While beside him, Kesst had begun gleefully cackling to himself, rocking back and forth with Reynir, while also frantically waving Geva—and Rathgarr—toward the door. "Well, what are you waiting for, then?" he demanded. "Off with you. And make it quick, and report back!"

Geva groaned and rolled her eyes at him, but couldn't seem to find the will to argue—especially once Rathgarr slipped over to stand behind her, his hand curling around her waist, his breaths thick on her neck. And without another look at Kesst or Efterar, Geva grasped his hand, and dragged him out of the room behind her.

But he didn't speak again, not even when they were back in their own bedroom again, with the wooden door they'd installed firmly closed behind them. And when Geva drew his big body close, and smiled up at his face, he was looking almost dazed, his lips parted, his eyes blinking again and again on hers.

"You are... sure, poppet," he whispered. "This is not only some scheme to please me, or soothe me, or..."

Geva blinked back toward him, as a sudden, dizzying surge of emotion churned in her chest, drowning out all the rest. Rathgarr was so rarely suspicious or mistrustful like this anymore—at least, not outwardly—but it still did slip through, now and then. And damn it, here it was now, about—this? Because gods, perhaps he'd begun to convince himself that Geva didn't want a second son after all. And *wait*, was that why he hadn't brought it up recently, either? Because he'd been doing that damned Ash-Kai self-protecting rigmarole, where he couldn't bear the thought of being hurt over this?

And for an instant, Geva longed for nothing more than to leap back in time, and lock his cursed *mother* into a dungeon, and leave her there to rot forever. Along with every other woman who had used Rathgarr, and hurt him, and made him think he wasn't worth this.

But he was hers now. Hers. And he needed her help, her reassurance, and he would damn well get it.

"You *dare* to question your bondmate on this, love?" Geva asked coolly, raising her brows toward him. "Do you not know what happens to devious, suspicious Ash-Kai boys like you?"

Rathgarr's breath caught, and his big body before her had snapped to utter, perfect stillness. Waiting for this, wanting this, and Geva felt her eyes softening, her mouth pulling up into a slow, hungry smile.

"I'm afraid you need to be taught an important lesson, pretty boy," she purred. "Clothes off. Now."

Rathgarr's body jerked all over, his eyes very wide on hers—but then he fervently nodded, and fumbled to obey. Yanking off his tunic, and then his belt and his trousers. Showing Geva the marvellous, mouthwatering sight of his huge bared body... and that gorgeous fat cock, already fully swollen, jutting out hungry and betraying toward her.

Geva's breath stilled at the sight—gods, it was stunning, *he* was stunning, and he was going to use that to put a *son* inside her—but she made her eyes lift up again, to where he was clutching at the black-jewelled pendant around his neck, his brows rising in a silent question.

"No, leave that, love," she said lightly. "I want to see my beautiful Ash-Kai in all his beautiful jewels, hmmm?"

It wasn't even slightly an exaggeration, because damn, Rathgarr looked so good like this. With his big, powerful body fully aroused and on display, his muscles rigid, his lips plump and parted, his eyes dazed with hunger. And against it all, accenting it all, were all those tasteful touches of gold. The pendant around his neck, the cuff around his big bicep, the wedding-ring. And also—for the past year or so—the handful of small, shiny braids embedded throughout his own hair, all of them studded with beautiful gold beads that flickered and shone every time he moved. Beads that perfectly matched Geva's, and now Reynir's, too.

"Gorgeous, love," Geva murmured, as she stroked an appreciative hand against one of those smooth braids, and then down his chest, his front. Until she found that hard, prodding pole at his groin, and gently squeezed her fingers around it. Earning an instant, shuddering gasp from him in return, along with a flutter of his hazy eyes, and a highly satisfying little splatter of wetness against her skin.

"But I'm afraid you'll need to do a little more for me, handsome," Geva continued, as she reached toward the nearby wardrobe, and drew out the thick gold cuff tucked inside. "I want you fully on display for me while you learn your lesson, hmmm?"

Rathgarr gasped again, but fervently nodded, and snatched the cuff from Geva's hand. And then, as she watched, he slid it down over his pulsing, leaking length, and then—with a heated hiss—he drew his full bollocks through, too. Settling the thick gold ring firmly against the skin of his groin, and showing off the mouthwatering sight of his bulging cock and bollocks, now beautifully, brazenly encircled in bright, gleaming gold.

"Very nice, sweet boy," Geva purred, as her greedy hands dropped to stroke at him, to revel in the way he whimpered and trembled at her touch, as more thick streaks of white spattered across her hands. "Now, only one more thing, hmmm?"

Rathgarr's body again jerked against her, his eyes flashing, but he kept standing there, waiting, as she reached for the wardrobe again. This time coming back with a small, narrow gold item, shaped rather like a long tapered finger, with a large jewelled bauble at one end.

It had been one of the items Rathgarr had kept from his father's hoard, though he'd hidden it at the back of a shelf, well out of sight. But when Geva had noticed it, and asked him about it, she hadn't missed how his face had flushed, his eyes angling purposefully away.

"It is... an Ash-Kai pleasure-jewel," he'd told her. "Another way for an Ash-Kai to adorn himself, for his mate."

It had turned out to be utterly marvellous, most of all because Rathgarr had never worn one before—and Geva would never forget how he'd trembled and begged that first time, and then sprayed out across the room, at only her heated command. And gods, she felt her breath catch at even the way he was looking at it now, with mingled eagerness and apprehension and craving in his eyes.

"That's right, handsome," Geva told him, smiling sweetly as she smeared her hand with his steadily spurting wetness, and generously coated the long, slim gold finger with it. "You're going to be so pretty with this inside you, aren't you?"

Rathgarr jerked a nod, his cheeks flushed deep with red, and Geva gave him another approving smile, a gentle grip of her hand to his arse. "Good boy," she murmured. "Now, bend over for me, and open wide. Hands on the bed."

He'd moaned again, thick and hoarse, but he swiftly spun around, and obliged. Showing Geva the breathtaking sight of his huge, trembling, bent-double body, his firm, rounded bare arse fully exposed for her viewing, and her use.

But Geva wanted even more, damn it, and she gave that arse a gentle slap, making him shudder and shake all over. "I said, open, handsome," she hissed, and in return he frantically nodded, and spread his legs wider, arching himself out more. Showing her absolutely everything that was hers, oh gods, and Geva greedily stroked him as she brought up the slick, dripping gold tip, and began gently easing it inside.

"So good, pretty boy," she breathed, as he kept trembling and gasping beneath her touch, while that gold rod sank deeper and deeper inside. "Such a good Ash-Kai, dressing up so fine for your mistress, hmmm? Wearing all your best jewels for me?"

Rathgarr's moan was almost like a cry this time, because yes, it was all the way in now, and Geva's hungry eyes couldn't stop looking away. Her own huge, dangerous mate, bared and bent over for her, now with a glittering gold jewel embedded deep between his arse-cheeks. And even when she drew him up to standing again, she could still just see it tucked in there, glinting and teasing with every twitch of his trembling body.

And oh, yes, he was trembling all over now, his cheeks bright red, his lips parted, his huge, gold-ringed cock visibly bobbing, and oozing out more of that silken decadent seed. Enough that it was swinging and swaying as it dangled from him, nearly reaching the floor, and Geva felt her tongue brushing her lips as she looked, and looked, and looked. Her beautiful, powerful mate, the father of her son, the beloved mentor and teacher to the orcs who would create and shape the future. The gorgeous, gifted crown jewel of the Ash-Kai, here, dressed for her, displayed for her, *hers*.

"Look at you, Ash-Kai," she breathed at him. "Look how strong and stunning you are. Look how perfect you are."

Rathgarr's chest powerfully heaved, his swollen cock throbbing out another generous spurt of seed, and Geva couldn't help reaching a shaky hand to catch some of that slick sweet-ness, bringing it to her mouth. "And how sweet you taste," she continued, gasping as she sucked in more, more. "How much good Ash-Kai seed you're making for me, out of this big, fat orc-prick of yours. You're so virile, love. So rugged. So strong."

Rathgarr's heavy breaths had deepened, his eyes feverishly glittering, and Geva nodded at him, licked at her lips. "And wearing all this gold, even *inside* you," she added, her voice catching. "Flaunting all your wealth and riches for me. Showing me just a taste of your overflowing trove-room, and proving your high standing among your clan. Reassuring me that you can keep and care for me, and for our sons."

Rathgarr was nodding back now, still with that fevered intensity in his glittering eyes, enough that Geva had to close her own eyes for an instant, draw in breath. And then, without quite meaning to, she was fumbling for her own shift, yanking it off, hurling it aside. Leaving her fully bared for him, too, but for her own jewels, her beads, her wedding-rings.

Rathgarr's growl hitched deeper, his eyes now sweeping up and down her bared body, but he still didn't move, and Geva gave a wavering smile at that, too. "And even amidst all your strength," she said, "you keep showing me that you know how to control yourself. You know how to behave with those who are smaller or weaker than you. You know how to show care, and respect, and kindness. You're not too proud to humble yourself, for someone else's gain. You keep showing me"—her voice was truly wavering now—"what a good mate you are. What a good teacher and mentor you are. What a *damned* good father you are."

Rathgarr's eyes had squeezed shut, his throat bobbing, but Geva couldn't stop now, couldn't. "You're the best father, Rath-garr," she croaked. "You're the best orc. The best Ash-Kai. The brightest, greatest jewel of your entire clan."

Something choked in his breath, his head shaking, but Geva put her hands to his heaving chest, waited until his eyes opened, met hers again. "You are, Rathgarr of Clan Ash-Kai," she insisted. "And you've already made one perfect, brilliant son, who's going to change our world—so now, you're going to give me another one."

Rathgarr moaned, his eyes furiously fluttering, and Geva reached down, gave her favourite jewels a gentle, proprietary squeeze. "You're going to use these fat Ash-Kai bollocks to make your very best seed for me," she breathed. "And you're going to use this good, fat Ash-Kai prick to fuck me. You're going to fuck me until I scream your name, and my empty, hungry womb milks out every last *drop* of this priceless, *perfect* Ash-Kai seed."

Rathgarr's moan was heavy and sustained now, a strong spurt of seed splattering against Geva's bare belly, and she nodded as she rubbed it in, and held his eyes. "Yes," she whispered. "It's perfect. You're perfect, Rathgarr of Clan Ash-Kai. And I want your son. I need your son. He's *mine*."

Her voice seemed to shudder out between them, greedy, vicious, victorious. While before her, Rathgarr was nearly vibrating with tension, every single muscle standing out stark beneath his skin, his claws out, his eyes flashing and flaring on hers—

And then—he tackled her. Hurling her back onto the bed with raw, astonishing power, hard enough that her teeth chattered—but oh, he was already here, catching her with gentle, purposeful hands. Hands that set her down, spread her out, yanked her legs wide apart. Opening her for him, exposing her, so he could—

Geva screamed as he slammed inside, sinking himself to the hilt in one fierce, furious plunge. And then he stayed there, arched and grinding into her, stabbing her full of hot ravenous flesh, while she shouted and writhed upon him, her hands wildly clutching him tighter, needing more, more, more...

"Yes," she gasped, as her fingernails dragged down his huge, powerful back. "Yes. Fuck me, Rathgarr. Fill my empty womb. Put your strong Ash-Kai son inside me. Please. *Please.*"

And gods, how he growled, the sound almost a roar in her ear, as he drew out, long and slow—and then plunged in again, filling Geva to the root, while she again kicked and screamed upon him. And oh, he felt so big like this, bigger than he'd perhaps ever felt before, with both his jewels helping to swell him, and drive him—and he was already picking up speed, slamming in faster and faster, fucking her with furious, relentless purpose. Until there was nothing left but raw, shattering sensation, and the pounding, pummelling Ash-Kai cock, ploughing deep between her legs. Her Ash-Kai cock, her Ash-Kai orc, and she was still pleading, dragging him closer, please...

"Yes, Rathgarr," she gasped. "So good. So perfect. Give me your seed. Give me your son. Oh gods, Rathgarr, please, Rathgarr, please!"

And yes, yes, his roar deepening, shuddering all through him, into the very core of her—and then he obeyed. That huge, invading pole driving in one last time, straining, holding deep—and then surging out inside her. Pumping again and again as he roared, as he emptied out those swollen bollocks in great, juddering spasms, pouring her full of his seed, and his son.

Geva couldn't speak once he'd finished, and perhaps, neither could he—but she shivered all over at the feel of him nosing aside her hair, and putting his teeth to her neck. And then biting down on a sharp, desperate little cry, his breath hitching as he began rhythmically, hungrily swallowing.

But it didn't hurt—orc-bites rarely did, Geva had learned, even without Rathgarr's healing power—and she shuddered and gasped at the contrast of his sharp, vicious teeth with his gentle lips and tongue. And with how his cock was still shuddering and spasming inside her, squeezing out every last drop—and perhaps even swelling fuller again, in another gift from those jewels. His hips already grinding, circling, dragging up more...

So Geva praised him and caressed him, running her hands up and down his sweaty back as she arched and moaned upon him. Telling him what a good Ash-Kai he was, how strong and handsome he was, how generous he was, to be wearing his jewels for her, giving her so much of his good seed. And when her own pleasure arched and flared, sucking him in deeper, she gasped and begged and thanked him, told him how good he felt, how much she would love to have another good load from him, how deeply she longed for his strong fresh scent...

He almost whimpered into her neck as he did it, flooding into her with even more hot, dizzying sweetness—and then they did it again, and again, and again. Feeling more intense and unreal each time, until their previously pristine bed was a sticky, squelching mess, and both of them were painted all over in red and white. And a steady stream of white was oozing from between Geva's legs, and perhaps from both her full breasts— and she could feel the fresh bite-marks on both sides of her neck, down her shoulder, and on one of those leaking breasts, too.

And as Rathgarr finally drew up, his eyes just as glassy and dazed as Geva felt, she could only seem to touch at him, and marvel at him, and adore him. Drinking up the sight of her stunning, exquisite Ash-Kai, utterly debauched and undone and empty, for her. Hers.

"So good, love," she finally breathed, at his hazy half-lidded eyes. "Such a good Ash-Kai."

The awareness shifted a little closer in those eyes, and he huffed a choked laugh, shook his head. "That is you, poppet," he rasped. "All you. *Ach.*"

Geva's eyes were already prickling, her head shaking, but Rathgarr stopped her with a soft, gentle kiss to her lips. "I love you so, my sweet," he whispered. "And I thank you, for this lesson. This... gift."

Geva attempted a shrug, and a dismissive wave of her trembling hand—and at that, Rathgarr's awareness seemed to jerk even closer, his hand snatching up to catch hers, squeezing it tight. "Ach, poppet," he breathed, with a wince. "Look at you. You must eat, and drink, and bathe. Come, and I shall tend to you, ach?"

Geva didn't try to argue, though she definitely did need help standing up again, finding her balance on her shaky feet. And thankfully, Rathgarr seemed far more capable than she felt, and he cleaned off the worst of the mess before throwing on both of their robes, and escorting Geva to the Skai bath.

The cold water certainly helped to snap her to full wakefulness again, and so did Rathgarr's deft hands as they washed her, wiping all the sticky fluids away. And then he thoroughly washed and detangled her hair, until he was gently carding his claws through its full length, drawing it all the way to her arse.

And then, once he'd turned her around again, he bent his head to those bite-marks he'd made, kissing and caressing with his tongue again and again. Until there wasn't even a twinge or a sting left behind, only the very faint dark marks from his teeth.

But Geva didn't mind—in truth, there was something strangely powerful in having her mate's marks on her skin, in bearing that tangible proof of his hunger and his affection. And Rathgarr liked it too, she knew, greedy Ash-Kai that he was, and she felt herself smiling at the sight of him studying the marks he'd made, running his fingers over them with palpable reverence.

"You are sure—" he began, once he'd glanced up at her eyes—but Geva was already pressing her fingers to his mouth, and nodding her head.

"Very sure, Rathgarr," she whispered. "*Mine.*"

The gratefulness flashed across his eyes, together with the appreciation, because yes, he understood that, because he was just the same. And suddenly they were both grinning at each other, and Geva couldn't deny a sudden surge of excitement, rising in her belly. They'd made a son. Maybe. Maybe?

"Do you want to go ask Efterar?" she asked him, with too much eagerness in her voice. "Just to see?"

"Ach, yes," he breathed, his own eyes dancing, as he swiftly drew her out of the water, and dried her off. "But I ken I scent... mayhap..."

Geva's eyes widened, but Rathgarr didn't continue, only handing over her robe, and pulling his on, too. And then leading her toward the door again—to where, it turned out, Ulfarr was just striding in. His huge form stilling at the sight of Geva and Rathgarr, his head tilting as he inhaled—and without warning, he grasped for Rathgarr, and yanked him close.

"I see your great gain, brother," he said, his voice choked, as he clapped Rathgarr on the back. "Our best wishes for another hale, healthy son, ach?"

Geva's heart leapt in her chest, the grin widening on her mouth—and Rathgarr was laughing, and giving Ulfarr a delighted little shake. "I thank you, brother," he said fervently. "Mayhap some sparring later, ach?"

With that, he yanked a still-grinning Geva out into the corridor—to where, it turned out, there were already more people waiting. A frowning, impatient Kesst, clutching at an amused-looking Efterar, who was holding a wide-eyed Reynir in his arms. And beside them there was Cecily, and Timo and Sune, too—and Cecily was purposefully elbowing at Timo, who was inhaling deeply, his eyes fluttering closed. But then they snapped open again, and he flashed Geva a broad, stunning grin.

"Ach, you are having a son, Miss Gee," he said brightly. "We cannot wait to meet him, ach?"

Oh. Well. And suddenly there were tears streaking down Geva's cheeks, and she was clutching at Rathgarr, just as he was clutching at her, squeezing her tight and safe into his arms.

"Thank you, poppet," he whispered, hot and close into her ear. "Ach. Thank you."

Geva hugged him tighter, sniffling into his chest, but she was still laughing, too—and then she somehow found that she was hugging Cecily, too, and Reynir and Kesst, all of them rocking together in the middle of the corridor.

"I get to name this one, you know," Kesst was saying, his voice thick. "And it really ought to be a K name, after his heart-father. Right?"

"Ach, I should endorse this, my son," Rathgarr said back, his voice just as thick, his huge arms squeezing them all tighter. "But only if my sweet mate agrees also."

But of course Geva agreed, and she gave Kesst a watery smile over her shoulder. "We'll come up with a good one together," she said, between happy little sniffs. "And Cecily too, right, sweetheart?"

"Ach, yes," Cecily said, though her voice wavered too—and then sharpened into a high-pitched little yelp. Which was, it turned out, because Kesst had poked at her with his claw, and when Geva drew away to look, he was frowning toward her, and then toward Sune. Who was silently backing away toward the opposite wall, his eyes very wary on Kesst's face.

"Look here, you three," Kesst snapped. "Believe me, we do *not* want to know the details of your teenage love lives—but you are making this very difficult! Just earlier tonight, Cecily was weeping over *you*"—his accusing claw jabbed toward Timo—"and now she scents of *Skai*?! What the hell, little sister!"

Cecily's face had flushed a bright pink, and she defiantly tossed her hair over her shoulder—while behind her, Sune continued silently easing away into the shadows. And finally it was Timo who cleared his throat and stepped forward, his eyes flicking purposefully between Geva, Kesst, and Rathgarr.

"We three spoke of this at length," he said. "And as we all care for one another thus, we wished to make this—even, between us. But we should not wish this to bring you fear or unease, or to bring risk upon Cecy. So should you agree, Sune and I should be happy to swear a vow upon this, to safeguard Cecy's freedom and safety, for as long as she might wish."

Behind him, Cecily didn't look slightly surprised by this—if anything, she looked even more defiant than before—while beside Geva, Kesst was loudly spluttering, and throwing up his hands. "You want to swear a *vow* to her?!" he demanded, with a wincing curl of his lip. "And you've dragged your Skai into it, too?! Gods, you Grisk. *Disastrous*, I tell you. My poor *teeth*."

With that, he spun and stalked off, while Efterar gave a wry smile, and then turned to follow. "Come to the sickroom tomorrow, sister?" he said over his shoulder toward Geva. "And rest well tonight, all right?"

Geva smiled and called back a thank-you, and then glanced up at where Rathgarr—who now had Reynir in his arms—was rubbing purposefully at his eyes. "Ach, we thank you for your thoughtful offer upon this, Timo," he said, with far more steadiness in his voice than Geva would have expected. "Mayhap we can speak of this more tomorrow. I should wish to hear more from our daughter first."

Cecily rapidly nodded at this, her eyes gone bright, and she lurched back toward Rathgarr again, flinging her arm around his waist. "Thank you, Pa," she whispered. "I love you."

Rathgarr whispered it back as he squeezed her tight, patting her blonde head with his big hand. And when Cecily drew away, she was excitedly grinning again, and then promptly dashing away with Timo and Sune down the corridor.

It left Geva alone with Rathgarr and Reynir again, Rathgarr's eyes looking both fond and aggrieved, while Reynir gave a large, loud yawn. And Geva couldn't seem to stop smiling between them both, leaning in for another warm, reassuring hug.

"You ought to rest now, poppet," Rathgarr murmured,

against her hair. "Mayhap you can settle in our room, whilst I bring you the rest of your supper?"

Geva certainly wasn't about to argue, and a short time later, she found herself sitting on their bed, sharing her delicious bowl of re-heated stew with Reynir, while Rathgarr carefully braided her hair. And once she'd finished eating, they all curled up in bed together, with Reynir nursing in Geva's arms, and Rathgarr tucked into his usual place behind her.

"How about a tale, then?" Geva asked them, stroking gently at Reynir's soft, smooth little braids. "About our father Reykur, perhaps?"

Rathgarr had gone briefly still against her, but then he nodded, and kissed at Geva's hair. So she willingly launched into the tale of the proud, powerful Ash-Kai warrior, who not only gained one of the grandest hoards in the realm, but single-handedly raised his Ash-Kai son with deep care, affection, and kindness. Knowing that his son would pass on his great gifts to those who came after him, and most of all to his own sons, carrying on his line and his name.

It had become Rathgarr's favourite tale over the past few years, and Kesst had begun to tell it too, especially to a wide-eyed, worshipful Reynir. And in Kesst's clever, capable hands, the tale had grown and expanded—so Geva continued on with his part of the tale, too. Telling of what a good, generous father Rathgarr became, and how he cared for his first son with unflinching devotion, even at great cost and danger to himself. And how despite great odds, Rathgarr and his first son defeated all their foes, and helped to create a new world of healing and light. A world where they could all welcome a second gifted Ash-Kai son together, and keep him happy and safe from all they'd borne, just as Reykur had wished.

"And now, we'll welcome our third Ash-Kai son," Geva's voice continued, her voice quiet and reverent in the darkness. "And he'll become part of our tale, too. And someday, he'll make it his own, and tell it to his own sons after him."

Her voice stopped there, but the words seemed to keep hanging, hovering, all on their own. Until the spell was broken by the sound of Rathgarr's heavy exhale, his mouth again pressing to Geva's braids.

"And in this tale, he shall forever praise his mother," he murmured. "His stunning, sun goddess mother, with her silver tongue and her golden heart. For without her great gifts, we would never have found one another, or made this tale our truth."

And for an instant, it was as though his words hung there too, weaving and shimmering with hers, with Kesst's, with the tales and times to come. Like the old Ash-Kai magic was spinning and singing on its own, catching them here in its spell. Holding Geva safe and whole, with her son in her arms, and peace in her heart.

"Now sleep, my sweet poppet," Rathgarr breathed, so soft, so safe. "And my sweet sons, also."

His hand had slipped down from Reynir's back, and spread wide against Geva's belly. So with one last, happy little sigh, Geva curled closer into the warm, whispering wonder of it, and slipped away into sleep.

THANKS FOR READING
AND GET A FREE BONUS STORY!

Thank you so much for joining me for Geva and Rathgarr's story! I really wanted to write a tangled, tricky tale worthy of our clever Ash-Kai clan, and I hope it was a fun twisty time for you!

If you've read my other Orc Sworn books, you'll know that the Ash-Kai are a proud, passionate bunch, with an unfortunate tendency toward villainy. So I loved getting a chance to explore the clan's more creative, nurturing side in this book, and to show how they can be fantastic leaders and community builders, too. (Even if they do still keep a few secrets now and then!) I especially loved writing about Geva's gift of story-telling—many of her tales were inspired by real-life Igbo folktales, and I highly recommend checking them out!

I also loved finally giving Kesst his full-on happily ever after in this book! It's been a long time coming for our fabulous galdr-spinner, and he will thoroughly enjoy the rest of his very long life—running his sickroom, helping to raise his gifted heart-sons, and worshipping his generous, well-proportioned mate. :)

As for what's next! I'm currently working on Varinn and Thrain's story, and hope to release that next year... those Grisk disaster boys will need a LOT of sorting out from a special woman, ha. But I also think we have plenty of unfinished business with Ulfarr (and Killik...) and obviously with Kalfr too! If you have thoughts, I'd love to hear them at my Facebook group, or over on my Discord server.

AND! If you'd like to spend a little more time with these orcs, I've written a bonus story just for my mailing list subscribers at finleyfenn.com. I'd love to stay in touch with you!

ACKNOWLEDGMENTS

As always, I'm just so deeply grateful to readers like you for supporting me and my books. I've been continually awed and humbled by your generosity, and by the incredible community that's grown around these books. Thank you!

I also want to thank my advance reviewers, and the awesome team of beta and sensitivity readers who supported this book: Amy F., Ari, Carmilla Quinn, Christina Ayala, Cookie, Erin, Jane Mwaniki, Jennifer N., Jen R., Judi S., Kahaula, Lauren Maunchley, Lexi K. Jordan, Rowan Phillips, Serena, Stacy, and Twilla Love. I'm especially grateful to my sensitivity readers and cultural advisors for taking the time to share their insights, experiences, and encouragement with me—I've learned so much from all of you, and your guidance on this book was just SUCH a gift.

I'm also extremely grateful to all my fellow authors who've helped me on this journey. In particular, I want to mention Goddess Ruby Dixon (whose kindness and generosity continues to boggle my mind!), and the fabulous Eris Adderly/Octavia Hyde, who provided in-depth editing support on this book. Ruby and Eris remain two of my all-time favourite romance authors, and I highly encourage you to check out their brilliant books!

I also want to specifically mention just a few of the many, many folks who have gone above and beyond to support my books over the past year. My deepest thanks to the truly phenomenal MK, who keeps everything running while I'm off obsessing over orcs; to Elizabeth, for the stunning artwork and

Discord expertise; to our Discord Skaibrarian Amy, with her wonderful trailers and always-on-point reading recs; to Katie (aka Romantically Inclined Reviews) for so delightfully sharing all the orc love; to Coco for the fantastic fanart and character designs; to Morning Dove for all the Grisk loveliness and beautiful tales; and to Erin for her art, enthusiasm, and fearless leadership of the Skai Mafia PR Team!

I'm also ridiculously grateful to all my friends on my Discord server and Facebook group—you've all brought so much fun, laughter, and inspiration into my life. From the Good Orc Seed Bakery, to Tryggr's silver fox Pa (coming soon!), to the Tales from the Orc Den podcast, to Geva's tale of a sexy shifter skunk. :)

And finally, as always, I'm so grateful to my own stubborn, sexy, supportive mate (whose gorgeous hair I even get to braid sometimes!). You are a saint, love, and I utterly adore you.

ALSO BY FINLEY FENN

THE LADY AND THE ORC

He's the most feared monster in the realm. And she's what he needs to win his war...

In a world of warring orcs and men, Lady Norr is condemned to a childless marriage, a cruel lord husband, and a life of genteel poverty—until the day her home is ransacked by a horde. And leading the charge is their hulking, deadly orc captain: the infamous Grimarr.

And Grimarr has a wicked plan for Lady Norr, and for ending this war once and for all. She's going to become his captive—and the perfect snare for Lord Norr.

There's no possible escape, and soon Lady Norr is dragged off toward Orc Mountain in the powerful arms of her greatest enemy. A ruthless, commanding warlord, with a velvet voice and mouthwatering scent, who awakens every forbidden hunger she never knew she had...

But Grimarr refuses to accept half measures—in war, or in pleasure. And before he'll conquer Lady Norr's deepest, darkest desires, she needs to surrender *everything*.

Her allegiance.

Her wedding-ring.

Her future...

And with her husband's forces giving chase, Lady Norr can't afford to play such a dangerous game—or can she? **Even if this deadly orc's plans might be the only way to save them all?**

ALSO BY FINLEY FENN

THE LIBRARIAN AND THE ORC

He's a fierce, ferocious, death-dealing beast. And he's reading a book in her library...

In a world of recently warring orcs and men, Rosa Rolfe leads a quiet, scholarly life as an impoverished librarian—until the day she finds an *orc*. In her library. Reading a *book*.

He's rude, aggressive, and deeply terrifying, with his huge muscled form, sharp black claws, and cold, dismissive commands. But he doesn't *seem* truly dangerous... at least, until night falls. **And he makes Rosa a shocking, scandalous offer...**

Her books, for her surrender.

Her ecstasy.

Her enlightenment...

Rosa's no fool, and she knows she can't possibly risk her precious library for this brazen, belligerent orc. Even if he *is* surprisingly well-read. Even if he smells like sweet, heated honey. Even if he makes Rosa's heart race with fear, and ignites all her deepest, darkest cravings at once...

But surrender demands a dangerous, devastating price. A bond that can't easily be broken. And a breakneck journey to the fearsome, forbidding Orc Mountain, where a curious, clever librarian might be just what's needed to stop another war...

THE DUCHESS AND THE ORC

He's a massive, mocking, murderous monster. And there's only one thing he wants from her...

In a world of recently warring orcs and men, Maria is desperate for escape. She's trapped in an opulent prison, tainted by rumours of madness, and wed to a cold, vindictive duke who hungers only for war.

But with no family, no funds, and no hope, there's nowhere left to run—except for the one place even a duke can't reach. The place where women almost always meet their doom...

Orc Mountain.

It's a grim, deadly fortress, filled with fierce, bloodthirsty beasts—**and the first orc Maria meets is the most terrifying of them all.** A huge, hostile, hideous brute, hardened by hatred and war, who instantly accuses her of foul trickery, and threatens her with death—

But this orc also wants something. Something that kindles deep in his gleaming black eyes, in his rough, rugged scent, in the velvet heat of his voice. Something that just might grant Maria his safety... but only if she grants him *everything* in return.

Her defeat.

Her dignity.

Her devotion...

And surely, a duchess wouldn't dare make such a shameful deal with the devil—or would she? Especially when surrender might spark yet more war... **or bring the mighty Orc Mountain to its knees?**

ALSO BY FINLEY FENN

THE MIDWIFE AND THE ORC

Orc Mountain needs a midwife. And this devious, deadly orc is determined to find one...

In a world of recently warring orcs and men, Gwyn Garrett is a lord's daughter on a mission—to escape her lord father, dump her cheating betrothed, and pursue her true calling as a plant-obsessed midwife.

Until the night her brand-new house is invaded by an *orc*. A tall, taunting, treacherous monster, with sharp teeth, vicious claws, and gleaming black eyes. And worst of all, a blatant, brutal mission of his own...

He's come to court her.

Claim her.

Compromise her.

But Gwyn is far too clever to fall for this sneaky orc's schemes—right? Even if he moves like a graceful god, if his voice is sweet syrup in her ears. If his low, mocking laugh sparks something hot and reckless, deep in her soul...

It's hunger, it's *home*, it's everything Gwyn never knew she needed—but in its wake, there's only devastation. Defeat. And the realization that she's forever linked with this horrible orc, and his horrible plans...

And with the war. The fates of hundreds of women like her. And the truth that **Orc Mountain desperately needs her, and maybe this proud, lonely orc does too...**

ALSO BY FINLEY FENN

THE MAID AND THE ORCS

She's fallen for an angel... but he's mated to a monster.

In a realm of orcs and powerful men, housemaid Alma Andersson is drowning—in grief, debt, and drudgery. And when her awful employer makes his darkest demand yet, she flees for the forest, and tumbles toward her doom...

Until she's snatched to safety by a **huge, vicious green beast.**

An *orc*.

He's utterly terrifying, with his towering bulk, sharp teeth, and deadly black claws—but his touch is gentle, and his eyes are kind. And his scent is a deep, decadent sweetness, sparking a furious flame between them...

But it's only more disaster, because **Alma's shy, soft-hearted rescuer is already mated... to another *orc*.** A tall, silent, snarling monster named Drafli, who loathes Alma on sight, and clearly longs for her death.

Yet Drafli will do anything for his sweet mate, even if it means tolerating a weak, worthless human. So he makes Alma a cold, calculated offer: **he'll share his mate with her... but only on his terms.**

He wants her silence.

Her surrender.

Her servitude.

And with Alma's fate firmly in Drafli's ruthless hands, how can she face her own dark desires—or all the secrets hidden behind Orc Mountain's walls? **Can a lost, lonely housemaid come between two orcs... without being crushed?**

ALSO BY FINLEY FENN

THE SINS OF THE ORC

He's fallen too far to save... but his enemy is going to try.

In a world of warring orcs and men, Kesst of Clan Ash-Kai is a pawn. A pretty, pliant plaything, bound to the cruelest orcs in the realm.

Until the new healer storms in.

He's huge, hostile, and hideous, with a powerful scarred body and terrifying ancient magic. And it only takes one disastrous meeting before he and Kesst are bitter enemies, and Kesst vows to see the vile brute destroyed...

And then **a sudden, deadly attack** hurls his helpless body straight at the healer's feet.

Kesst fully expects to be mocked, belittled, abandoned to his doom— **but instead, his new enemy picks him up.**

Soothes his wounds.

And carries him home...

Soon Kesst is trapped in a tiny sickroom beneath Orc Mountain, caught in the thrall of the healer's impossible magic. In the surprising gentleness of his touch. In the strength of his stubborn, seductive safety...

But with his horrid handlers close on their scent, Kesst can't possibly be falling for his forbidden foe... can he? **Can a healer save him from his sins... or destroy him?**

ABOUT THE AUTHOR

Finley Fenn has been writing about people falling in love for as long as she can remember. She creates steamy fantasy romance tales with cranky-but-sexy men and monsters, loads of angst and drama, a dash of mystery and action, and wholehearted happily ever afters.

When she's not obsessing over her stories, Finley reads everything she can get her hands on, and drools over delicious orc artwork (find her latest faves on Facebook at Finley Fenn Readers' Den). She lives in Canada with her beloved family, including her very own grumpy, gorgeous orc husband.

To get free bonus content, character illustrations, and news about upcoming books, sign up at www.finleyfenn.com.

www.ingramcontent.com/pod-product-compliance
Lightning Source LLC
Chambersburg PA
CBHW050841210726
48290CB00004B/1026